Luise Mühlbach, F. Jordan

Louisa of Prussia and Her Times

An historical novel

Luise Mühlbach, F. Jordan

Louisa of Prussia and Her Times
An historical novel

ISBN/EAN: 9783337299057

Printed in Europe, USA, Canada, Australia, Japan

Cover: Foto ©Andreas Hilbeck / pixelio.de

More available books at **www.hansebooks.com**

NAPOLEON AND COUNT COBENZL

P. 79

ND HER TIMES.

AN HISTORICAL NOVEL.

BY

L. MÜHLBACH

AUTHOR OF "JOSEPH II. AND HIS COURT," "FREDERICK THE GREAT AND HIS FAMILY,"
"BERLIN AND SANS-SOUCI," "HENRY VIII. AND HIS COURT," ETC., ETC.

TRANSLATED FROM THE GERMAN, BY

F. JORDAN.

COMPLETE IN ONE VOLUME.

With Illustrations.

NEW YORK:
D. APPLETON AND COMPANY,
443 & 445 BROADWAY.
1867.

CONTENTS.

CAMPO FORMIO.

CHAPTER I.

DREADFUL TIDINGS.

THE population of Vienna was paralyzed with terror; a heavy gloom weighed down all minds, and the strength of the stoutest hearts seemed broken. Couriers had arrived to-day from the camp of the army, and brought the dreadful tidings of an overwhelming defeat of the Austrian forces. Bonaparte, the young general of the French Republic, who, in the course of one year (1796), had won as many battles and as much glory as many a great and illustrious warrior during the whole course of an eventful life—Bonaparte had crossed the Italian Alps with the serried columns of his army, and the most trusted military leaders of Austria were fleeing before him in dismay. The hero of Lodi and Arcole had won new victories, and these victories constantly diminished the distance between his army and the menaced capital of Austria.

Archduke Charles had been defeated by Massena, and driven back to Villach; Bernadotte had reached Laybach; the citadels of Goritz, Triest, and Laybach had surrendered; Klagenfurth, after a most desperate struggle, had been forced to open its gates to the conquerors; Loudon, with his brave troops, had been dispersed in the Tyrol; Botzen had opened its gates to General Joubert, who, after a brief sojourn, left that city in order to join Bonaparte, who, in his victorious career, was advancing resistlessly toward Vienna.

Such were tidings which the couriers had brought, and these tidings were well calculated to produce a panic in the Austrian capital. While the court and the nobility were concealing their grief and their sorrows in the interior of their palaces, the populace rushed into the streets, anxiously inquiring for later intelligence, and still hopeful that God in His mercy might perhaps send down some ray of light that would dispel this gloom of anguish and despair.

But a pall covered Vienna, and everybody looked sad and dejected. Suddenly some new movement of terror seemed to pervade the crowd that had gathered on the Kohlmarkt.* As if a storm were raising up the waves of this black sea of human figures, the dense mass commenced to undulate to and fro, and a wail of distress arose, growing louder and louder, until it finally broke out into the terrible cry: "The emperor has deserted us! the emperor and the empress have fled from Vienna!"

While the masses were bewailing this new misfortune with the manifestations of despair, while they assembled in small groups to comment vociferously on this last and most dreadful event of the day, all of a sudden Hungarian hussars galloped up and commanded the people, in the most peremptory manner, to stand aside and to open a passage for the wagons which were about to enter the market from one of the adjoining streets.

The people, intimidated by the flashing swords and harsh words of the soldiers, fell back and gazed with an expression of anxious suspense upon the strange procession which now made its appearance.

This procession consisted of twelve wagons, apparently not destined to receive living men, but

---

* Cabbage-Market.

the remains of the dead. The broad and heavy wheels were not surmounted by ordinary carriage-boxes, but by immense iron trunks, large enough to enclose a coffin or a corpse; and these trunks were covered with heavy blankets, the four corners of which contained the imperial crown of Austria in beautiful embroidery. Every one of these strange wagons was drawn by six horses, mounted by jockeys in the imperial livery, while the hussars of the emperor's Hungarian body-guard rode in serried ranks on both sides.

The horses drew these mysterious wagons slowly and heavily through the streets; the wheels rolled with a dull, thundering noise over the uneven pavement; and this noise resounded in the ears and hearts of the pale and terrified spectators like the premonitory signs of some new thunder-storm.

What was concealed in these mysterious wagons? What was taken away from Vienna in so careful a manner and guarded so closely? Everybody was asking these questions, but only in the depth of his own heart, for nobody dared to interrupt the painful and anxious silence by a loud word or an inquisitive phrase. Every one seemed to be fascinated by the forbidding glances of the hussars, and stunned by the dull rumbling of the wheels.

But, when finally the last wagon had disappeared in the next street, when the last horseman of the hussar escort had left the place, the eyes of the anxious spectators turned once more toward the speakers who had previously addressed them, and told them of the misfortunes of Austria, and of the brilliant victories of the youthful French General Bonaparte.

"What do those wagons contain?" shouted the crowd. "We want to know it, and we must know it!"

"If you must know it, why did you not ask the soldiers themselves?" shouted a sneering voice in the crowd.

"Yes, yes," said another voice, "why did you not approach the wagons and knock at the trunks?—may be the devil would have jumped out and shown you his pretty face!"

The people paid no attention to these sneering remarks. The painful uncertainty, the anxious excitement continued unabated, and everybody made surmises concerning the contents of the wagons.

"The trunks contain perhaps the coffins of the imperial ancestors, which have been removed from the *Kapuzinergruft*, in order to save them from the French," said an honest tailor to his neighbor, and this romantic idea rolled immediately, like an avalanche, through the vast crowd.

"They are removing the remains of the old em-

perors from Vienna!" wailed the crowd. "Even the tombs are no longer safe! They are saving the corpses of the emperors, but they are forsaking us—the living! They abandon us to the tender mercies of the enemy! All who have not got the money to escape are lost! The French will come and kill us all!"

"We will not permit it!" shouted a stentorian voice. "We want to keep the remains of Maria Theresa and of the great Emperor Joseph here in Vienna. As long as they lived they loved the people of the capital, and they will protect us in death. Come, brethren, come; let us follow the wagons—let us stop them and take the bodies back to the *Kapuzinergruft*." *

"Yes, let us follow the wagons and stop them" yelled the crowd, which now, when it could no longer see the flashing and threatening weapons of the soldiers, felt exceedingly brave.

Suddenly, however, these furious shouts and yells were interrupted by a powerful voice which ordered the people to desist, and they beheld a man who, with cat-like agility, climbed up an iron lamp-post in the centre of the square.

"Stop, stop!" roared this man, extending his arms over the crowd as if a new Moses wanted to allay the fury of the sea and make it stand still.

The crowd instantly obeyed this powerful voice, and all these indignant, anxious, terrified faces now turned toward the man who stood above them on top of the lamp.

"Don't make fools of yourselves," he—"don't give these Hungarians—who would be only too glad to quench their present German blood—a chance to break your head. Have you any arms to compel them to show you the wagons and their contents? And even if you were armed, the soldiers would overpower you, for most of you would run away as soon as a fight broke out, and the balance of you would be taken to the ca_-boose. I will do you the favor, however, to tell you all about those wagons. Do you want to know it?"

"Yes, yes, we do!" shouted the crowd, emphatically. "Be quiet over there!—Stop your noise!—Do not cry so loud!—Hush!—Let us hear what is in the wagons.—Silence, silence!"

Profound silence ensued—everybody held his breath and listened.

"Well, then, listen to me. These wagons do not contain the remains of the former emperors, but the gold and the jewels of the present emperor. It is the state treasure which those hussars are es-

* Vaults of the Capuchins.

corting from Vienna to Presburg, because the government deems it no longer safe here. Just think of what we have come to now-a-days! Our imperial family, and even the state treasure, must flee from Vienna! And whose fault is it that we have to suffer all this? Who has brought these French down upon us? Who is inundating all Austria with war and its calamities? Shall I tell you who is doing it?"

"Yes, tell us, tell us!" shouted the crowd. "Woe unto him who has plunged Austria into war and distress, and caused the flight of the emperor and the removal of the treasure from Vienna!"

The speaker waited until the angry waves of the people's wrath had subsided again, and then said in the clear, ringing tones of his powerful voice: "It is the fault of our prime minister, Baron von Thugut. He don't want us to make peace with the French. He would rather ruin us all than to make peace with the French Republic."

"But we don't want to be ruined!" shouted the crowd—"we don't want to be led to the shambles like sheep. No, no; we want peace—peace with France. Prime Minister Thugut shall give us peace with France!"

"You had better go and inform the proud minister himself of what you want," said the speaker with a sneer. "First compel him to do what the emperor and even our brave Archduke Charles wanted to be done—compel the omnipotent minister to make peace."

"We will go and ask him to give us peace," said several voices in the crowd.

"Yes, yes, we will do that!" shouted others. "Come, come; let us all go to the minister's house and ask him to give us back the emperor and the state treasure, and to make peace with Bonaparte."

The speaker now descended hurriedly from the lamp-post. His tall, herculean figure, however, towered above the crowd even after his feet had touched the pavement.

"Come," said he to the bystanders in a loud and decided tone, "I will take you to the minister's house, for I know where he lives, and we will shout and raise such a storm there until the proud gentleman condescends to comply with our wishes."

He led the way rapidly, and the crowd, always easily guided and pliable, followed its improvised leader with loud acclamations. Only one idea, only one wish, animated all these men: they wanted peace with France, lest Bonaparte might come to Vienna and lay their beautiful capital in ashes in the same manner in which he had treated so many Italian cities.

Their leader walked proudly at the head of the irregular procession, and as the crowd continued to shout and yell, "Peace with France!" he muttered, "I think I have accomplished a good deal to-day. The archduke will be satisfied with what I have done, and we may compel the minister after all to make peace with France."

CHAPTER II.

MINISTER VON THUGUT.

THE prime minister, Baron von Thugut, was in his cabinet, in eager consultation with the new police minister, Count von Saurau, who had given him an account of the safe removal of the imperial state treasure which, like the emperor and the empress, had set out for Hungary.

"All right! all right!" said Thugut, with a sinister chuckle. "In Hungary both will be safe enough, for I think I have intimidated the Hungarians so much that they will remain very quiet and very humble."

"Your excellency refers to the conspiracy which we discovered there two years ago," said Count Saurau, smiling, "and which the accursed traitors expiated on the gallows!"

"*De mortuis nil nisi bene!*" exclaimed Thugut. "We are under many obligations to these excellent traitors, for they have enabled us to render the Hungarians submissive, just as the traitors who conspired here at Vienna two years ago enabled us to do the same thing to the population of the capital. A conspiracy discovered by the authorities is always a good thing, because it furnishes us with an opportunity to make an example, to tell the nation through the bloody heads of the conspirators: 'Thus, thus, all will be treated who dare to plot against the government and against their masters!' The Viennese have grown very humble and obedient since the day they saw Hebenstreit, the commander of the garrison, on the scaffold, and Baron Riedel, the tutor of the imperial children, at the pillory. And the Hungarians, too, have learned to bow their heads ever since the five noble conspirators were beheaded on the *Generalwiese*, in front of the citadel of Ofen. Believe me, count, that day has contributed more to the submissiveness of Hungary than all the favors and privileges which the Emperors of Austria have bestowed upon the Magyars. Nations are always frivolous and impudent children: he who tries to educate them tenderly is sure to spoil them; but raise them in fear and trembling, and they will become quiet and obedient men. And for that reason, I tell you once more, don't call those men, now that they are dead, accursed traitors, for they have been very useful to us; they have been the instrument with which we have chastised the whole overbearing people of Austria and Hungary, and those were blessed days for us when we mowed down the high-born traitors of both countries. The sword of our justice performed a noble work on that day, for it struck down a savant and a poet, a count and a distinguished prelate. Oh, what a pity that there was no prince among them!"

"Well, a prince might have been found likewise," said Count Saurau, "and perhaps he may get into our meshes on some other occasion. Your excellency is an adroit hunter."

"And you are an excellent pointer for me. You scent such things on the spot," Count Thugut exclaimed, and broke out into a loud burst of laughter.

Count Saurau laughed also, and took good care not to betray how cruelly the joke had wounded his aristocratic pride. The Austrian aristocracy was accustomed to such insults at the hands of the powerful and proud prime minister, and everybody knew that Thugut, the son of a poor ship-builder, in the midst of his greatness, liked to recall his modest descent, and to humble the nobility through the agency of the ship-builder's son.

"Your excellency will permit me to render myself at once worthy of the praise you have kindly bestowed upon me," said the police minister, after a short pause. "I believe we have discovered another conspiracy here. True, it is only an embryo as yet, but it may grow into something if we give it the necessary time."

"What is it, Saurau?" said Thugut, joyfully—"tell me at once what it is! A conspiracy—a good, sound conspiracy?"

"Yes, a most malignant and important conspiracy! A conspiracy against your excellency's life!"

"Bah!—is that all?" said Thugut carelessly, and with evident disappointment. "I was in hopes that by this time you would hand over to me some high-born aristocrats who had held secret intercourse with that execrable French Republic. It would have been a splendid example for all those hare-brained fools who are so fond of repeating the three talismanic words of the republican regicides, and who are crazy with delight when talking of liberté, égalité, fraternité. I would have liked to chastise a few of these madmen, in order to put a stop to the prevailing republican enthusiasm. But instead of that, you talk to me of a conspiracy only aimed at myself!" ·

"Only at yourself!" repeated the count, with great indignation. "As if it were not the most dreadful calamity for Austria if she should be deprived of your services. You know that we are standing on the verge of a precipice; in the interior, the liberal and seditious desires which the senseless reforms of the Emperor Joseph have stirred up, are still prevalent, and the people only submit with reluctance and with spiteful feelings to the reforms which your excellency has inaugurated with a view to the best interests of Austria. Abroad, on the other hand, the blood-stained French Republic incites the malcontents to imitate its own infamies; they would like to see the victorious banners of General Bonaparte here in order to have his assistance in establishing a republican government in Austria."

"It is true," said Thugut, "the Austrian empire, at the present time, is exposed to great dangers from within and without; the reins must be held very firmly in order to conduct the ship of state safely through the breakers, and I believe I am the man to do it. You see, count, I do not underrate my own importance. I know only too well that Austria needs me. Still, the plots and conspiracies that are merely directed against myself, make me laugh. For let me tell you, my dear little count, I really fancy that my person has nothing to fear either from daggers, or from pistols, or from poisoned cups. Do you believe in a Providence, count? Ah!—you look surprised, and wonder how such a question could fall from infidel lips like mine. Yes, yes, I am an infidel, and I honestly confess that the heaven of Mohammed, where you are smoking your chibouk, seated on cushions of clouds, while houris, radiant with beauty, are tickling the soles of your feet with rosy fingers, appears to me by far more desirable than the Christian heaven where you are to stand in eternal idleness before the throne of God Almighty, singing hymns, and praising His greatness. Ah! during the happy days of my sojourn at Constantinople, I have had a slight foretaste of the heaven of Mohammed; and again, in the tedious days of Maria Theresa, I have had a foretaste of the heaven of Christianity!"

"And which Providence did your excellency refer to?" asked Saurau. "I pray your excellency to tell me, because your faith is to be the model of mine."

"I believe in a Providence that never does anything in vain, and never creates great men in order to let them be crushed, like flies, by miserable monkeys. That is the reason why I am not afraid of any conspiracy against myself. Providence has created me to be useful to Austria, and to be her bulwark against the surging waves of the revolution, and against the victorious legions of General Bonaparte. I am an instrument of Providence, and therefore it will protect me as long as it needs me. But if, some day, it should need me no longer, if it intended then that I should fall, all my precautions would be fruitless, and all your spies, my dear count, would be unable to stay the hand of the assassin."

"You want me to understand, then, that no steps whatever, are to be taken against the criminals conspiring against your excellency's life?"

"By no means, count—indeed, that would be an exaggeration of fatalism. I rely greatly on your sagacity and on the vigilance of your servants, count. Let them watch the stupid populace—see to it that faux frères always attend the meetings of my enemies, and whenever they inform you of conspiracies against myself, why, the malefactors shall be spirited away without any superfluous noise. Thank God, we have fortresses and state prisons, with walls too thick for shrieks or groans to penetrate, and that no one is able to break through. The public should learn as little as possible of the fate of these criminals. The public punishment of an assassin who failed to strike me, only instigates ten others to try if they cannot hit me better. But the noiseless disappearance of a culprit fills their cowardly souls with horror and dismay, and the ten men shrink back from the intended deed, merely because they do not know in what manner their eleventh accomplice has expiated his crime. The disappearance of prisoners, the oubliettes, are just what is needed. You must quietly remove your enemies and adversaries—it must seem as if some hidden abyss had ingulfed them; everybody, then, will think this abyss might open one day before his own feet, and he grows cautious, uneasy, and timid. Solely by the wisdom of secret punishments, and through the terror inspired by its mysterious tribunals, Venice has been able to prolong her existence for so many centuries. Because the spies of the Three were believed to be ubiquitous—and because everybody was afraid of the two lions on the Piazzetta, the Venetians obeyed these invisible rulers whom they did not know, and whose avenging hand was constantly hanging over them."

"Now, however, it seems that a visible hand, a hand of iron, is going to strike away the invisible hands of the Three," said Count Saurau, quickly. "Bonaparte seems to desire to force Venice, too, into the pale of his Italian republics. The city is full of French emissaries, who, by means of their eloquent and insidious appeals,

try to bring about a rising of the Venetians against their rulers, in order—but hark!" said the count, suddenly interrupting himself. "What is that? Don't you hear the clamor in the street, right under our window?"

He paused, and, like the minister, turned his eyes and ears toward the window. A confused noise, loud shouts and yells, resounded below.

The two ministers, without uttering a word, arose from their arm-chairs and hurried to one of the windows, which looked upon the wide street extending from the Kohlmarkt to the minister's palace. A vast mass of heads, broad shoulders, and uplifted arms, was visible there, and the angry roar of the excited populace was approaching already the immediate neighborhood of the palace.

"It seems, indeed, as if these honorable representatives of the people, intended to pay me a visit," said Thugut, with great composure. "Just listen how the fellows are roaring my name, as if it were the refrain of some rollicking beer-song!"

"Why, it is a regular riot!" exclaimed the police minister, angrily. "Your excellency will permit me to withdraw—"

He left the window hastily, and took his hat, but Thugut's vigorous hand kept him back.

"Where are you going, count?" said he, smiling.

"To the governor of Vienna," said Saurau. "I want to ask him why he permits this nonsense, and order him to disperse the rabble in the most summary manner!"

"Pray, stay here," said Thugut, quietly. "The governor of Vienna is a man of great sagacity, who knows perfectly well how we have to treat the people. Why, it would be an unparalleled tyranny if the poor people were not even allowed to give the prime minister their good advice, and tell him what they think of the state of affairs. Just give them this permission, and they will believe they have performed a most heroic deed, and it will seem to them as if they could boast of great liberty. True political wisdom, my dear little count, commands us to give the people a semblance of liberty; we thereby succeed in dazzling their eyes so well that they do not perceive that they have no real liberty whatever."

The clamor and noise in the street below had increased in fury. The people, whose dense masses now entirely obstructed the street, impetuously moved up to the portal of the ministerial palace, the front door of which had been locked and barred already by the cautious porter. Vigorous fists hammered violently against the door, and as an accompaniment to this terrible music of their leaders, the people howled and yelled their furious refrain: "We want to see the minister! He shall give us peace! peace! peace!"

"Ah! I know what it means!" exclaimed Count Saurau, gnashing his teeth. "Your enemies have instigated these scoundrels. The party that would like to overthrow you and me, that wants to make peace with France at any price, and to keep Belgium united with Austria—this party has hired the villans below to get up a riot. They want to compel your excellency either to resign or to comply with the wishes of the people, and make peace with the French Republic."

Thugut laughed. "Compel *me!*" said he, laconically.

At that moment the mob yelled louder than ever, and the shout—"Peace! we want peace!" shook the windows.

Simultaneously the furious blows against the front door redoubled in violence.

"Assuredly, I cannot stand this any longer!" exclaimed the police minister, perfectly beside himself. "I ought not to listen quietly to this outrage."

"No," said Thugut, very quietly, "we won't listen to it any longer. This is my breakfast-hour, and I invite you to be my guest. Come, let us go to the dining-room."

He took the count's arm, and proceeded with him to the adjoining room. Breakfast for eight persons was served in this room, for Baron Thugut was in the habit of keeping every day open table for seven uninvited guests, and his intimate acquaintances, as well as his special favorites, never failed to call on the minister at least once a week during his well-known breakfast and dinner hours.

To-day, however, the minister's rapid and inquisitive glances did not discover a single guest. Nobody was in the room except the eight footmen who stood behind the chairs. Well aware of their master's stern and indomitable spirit, they occupied their usual places, but their faces were very pale, and their eyes turned with an expression of extreme anxiety toward the windows which, just then, trembled again under the heavy, thundering blows levelled at the front door.

"Cowards!" muttered Thugut, while walking to his chair at the upper end of the table and beckoning Count Saurau to take a seat at his side.

At this moment, however, the door was hastily opened, and the steward, pale and with distorted features, rushed into the room.

CHAPTER III.

THE INTERVIEW.

"Excuse me, your excellency," said he, "but this time they are assuredly in earnest. The people are storming the front door—the hinges are beginning to give way, and in fifteen minutes, at the latest, the scoundrels will have forced an entrance!"

"You had no business to close the door," said the minister. "Who ordered you to do so? Who ordered you to barricade the house, as if it were a fortress—as if we had a bad conscience and were afraid of the people?"

The steward looked aghast, and did not know what to reply.

"Go down-stairs at once," continued the minister; "order the porter to open the door, and admit everybody. Show the people up-stairs; and you rascals who are standing there with pale faces and trembling knees, open the two folding-doors so that they can get in without hurting each other. Now do what I have told you."

The steward bowed with a sigh expressive of the agony he felt, and hurriedly left the room.

The footmen, meanwhile, hastened to open the folding-doors of the dining-room, as well as those of the antechamber. The two gentlemen at the table obtaining thereby a full view of the landing of the large staircase, directly in front of the open door of the first room.

"And now, Germain," said Thugut to the footman behind his chair, "now let us have our breakfast. Be wise, my dear count, and follow my example; take some of this sherbet. It cools the blood, and, at the same time, is quite invigorating. Drink, dear count, drink! Ah! just see, my cook has prepared for us to-day a genuine Turkish meal, for there is a turkey boiled with rice and *paprica*. The chief cook of the grand vizier himself furnished me the receipt for this exquisite dish, and I may venture to assert that you might look for it everywhere in Vienna without finding it so well prepared as at my table."

Heavy footsteps and confused voices were now heard on the staircase.

"They are coming—they really dare to enter here!" said Count Saurau, trembling with anger. "Pardon me, your excellency; I admire your heroic equanimity, but I am unable to imitate it. It is an utter impossibility for me to sit here calmly and passively, while a gang of criminals is bold enough to break into your house!"

"I beg your pardon, count; these people did not break into my house, but I voluntarily opened the door to admit them," said Baron Thugut, coolly. "And as far as your official position is concerned, I pray you to forget it for half an hour, and remember only that I have the honor of seeing you—a rare guest—at my table. Let me beg you to take some of that fowl; it is really delicious!"

Count Saurau, heaving a loud sigh, took a piece of the fowl which Germain presented to him, and laid it on the silver plate that stood before him. But just as he was going to taste the first morsel, he hesitated, and looked steadily through the open doors. Several heads with shaggy hair and flashing eyes emerged above the railing of the staircase; many others followed—now the entire figures became visible, and in the next moment, from twenty to thirty wild-looking men reached the landing, behind whom, on the staircase, a dense mass of other heads rose to the surface.

But the loud shouts, the fierce swearing and yelling, had ceased; the awe with which the intruders were filled by the aristocratic appearance of every thing they beheld, had hushed their voices, and even the intrepid orator, who previously, on the *Kohlmarkt*, had excited the people to commit acts of violence, and brought them to the minister's house—even he stood now hesitating and undecided, at the door of the dining-room, casting glances full of savage hatred and rage into the interior.

Thugut took apparently no notice whatever of what was going on; his breakfast entirely absorbed him, and he devoted his whole attention to a large piece of the turkey, which he seemed to relish greatly.

Count Saurau merely feigned to eat, and looked steadfastly at his plate, as he did not want the rioters to read in his eyes the furious wrath that filled his breast.

The men of the people did not seem to feel quite at ease on beholding this strange and unexpected scene, which all of a sudden commenced to cool their zeal and heroism, like a wet blanket. They had triumphantly penetrated into the palace, shouting vociferously, and quite sure that the minister would appear before them trembling and begging for mercy; and now, to their utter amazement, they beheld him sitting very calmly at the breakfast-table!

There was something greatly embarrassing for the poor men in this position. They suddenly grew quite sober, and even intimidated, and many of those who had ascended the staircase so boisterously and triumphantly, now deemed it prudent to withdraw as quietly as possible. The number of the heads that had appeared above the balusters

was constantly decreasing, and only about twenty of the most resolute and intrepid remained at the door of the anteroom.

At length, the speaker who had addressed them on the *Kohlmarkt*, conscious of his pledges and of the reward promised to him, overcame his momentary bashfulness and stepped boldly into the anteroom, where the others, encouraged by his example, followed him at once.

Baron Thugut now raised his eyes with an air of great indifference from his plate and glanced at the men who with noisy steps approached through the anteroom. Then turning to the footman behind him, he said, in a loud voice:

"Germain, go and ask these gentlemen if they want to see me? Ask them likewise whom you will have the honor to announce to your master?"

The men, overhearing these words, grew still more confused when the servant in his gorgeous livery stepped up to them, and, with a most condescending smile, informed them of the errand his master had given to him.

But now it was out of the question to withdraw, as there was nothing left to them but to arm themselves with whatever pluck and boldness they had at their command in order to carry out the *rôle* they had undertaken to play in the most becoming manner.

"Yes," said the speaker of the *Kohlmarkt*, loudly and resolutely, "we want to see the minister; and as for our names, I am Mr. Wenzel, of the tailors' guild; my neighbor here is Mr. Kahlbaum, also a tailor; and others may mention their own names, so that this polite gentleman may announce them to his excellency."

But none of the other men complied with this request; on the contrary, all looked timidly aside, a misgiving dawning in their minds that such a loud announcement of their names might not be altogether without danger for them.

Germain did not wait for the final conclusion, but hastily returned to his master, in order to inform him of what he had heard.

"Mr. Wenzel, of the tailors' guild, Mr. Tailor Kahlbaum, and the other gentlemen, whatever their names may be, are welcome," said the minister, aloud, but without interrupting his meal for a single moment.

The men thereupon advanced to the door of the dining-room. But here a proud and imperious glance from the minister caused them suddenly to halt.

"I believe you have breakfasted already?" asked Thugut.

"Yes, we have breakfasted already," replied Mr. Wenzel, in a surly voice.

"Well, unluckily, I have not, and so I request you to let me finish my breakfast first," said Thugut, attacking once more the wing of the turkey on his plate.

A long pause ensued. The men stood in the most painful embarrassment at the door, where the minister's stern glance had arrested them, and a most unpleasant apprehension of what might be the result of this scene began to take hold of their minds. Flashing sword-blades and muskets aimed at their breasts would not have frightened them so much as the aspect of the calm, proud, and forbidding figure of the minister, and the utter indifference, the feeling of perfect security with which he took his breakfast in full view of a seditious mob filled the rioters with serious apprehensions for the safety of their own persons.

"I am sure a good many soldiers and policemen are hidden about the palace," thought Mr. Wenzel, "and that is the reason why he permitted us to enter, and why he is now so calm and unconcerned; for as soon as we get into the dining-room, these fine-looking footmen will lock the door behind, and the soldiers will rush out of that other door and arrest us."

These pleasant reflections were interrupted by another terrible glance from the minister, which caused poor Mr. Wenzel to tremble violently.

"Now, gentlemen, if you please, come in; I have finished my breakfast," said Thugut, with perfect coolness. "I am quite ready and anxious to hear what you wish to say to me. So, come in, come in!"

The men who stood behind Mr. Wenzel moved forward, but the tall, herculean figure of the member of the tailors' guild resisted them and compelled them to stand still.

"No, I beg your excellency's pardon," said Mr. Wenzel, fully determined not to cross the fatal threshold of the dining-room, "it would not become poor men like us to enter your excellency's dining-room. Our place is in the anteroom—there we will wait until your excellency will condescend to listen to us."

This humble language, this tremulous voice, that did not tally at all with the air of a lion-hearted and out-spoken popular leader, which Mr. Wenzel had assumed in the street, struck terror and consternation into the souls of the men who had so easily followed him into the palace.

The minister rose; his broad-shouldered figure loomed up proudly, a sarcastic smile played on his angular and well-marked features; his shaggy white eyebrows convulsively contracted up to this moment—the only outward symptom of anger which Thugut, even under the most provoking circumstances, ever exhibited—relaxed and became calm and serene again, as he approached the men with slow and measured steps.

"Well, tell me now what you have come for? What can I do for you?" asked Thugut, in the full consciousness of his power.

"We want to implore your excellency to give us peace. The poor people—"

"Peace with whom?" calmly asked the minister.

"Peace with France, your excellency—peace with General Bonaparte, who is said to be a magician, bewitching everybody, and capable of conquering all countries by a glance, by a motion of his hands, whenever he wishes to do so. If we do not make peace, he will conquer Austria too, come to Vienna, and proclaim himself emperor; whereupon he will dismiss our own wise and good ministers, and give us French masters. But we would like to keep our emperor and our excellent ministers, who take care of us so paternally. And that is the only reason why we have come here—just to implore your excellency to have mercy with the poor people and make peace, so that the emperor may return to Vienna, and bring his state treasury back to the capital. Yes, men, that is all we wanted, is it not? We just wanted to pray your excellency to give us peace!"

"Yes, your excellency," shouted the men, "have mercy with us, and give us peace!"

"Well, for angels of peace, you have penetrated rather rudely into my house," said the minister, sternly. "You got up a riot in order to obtain peace."

"It was merely our anxiety that made us so hasty and impetuous," said Mr. Wenzel, deprecatingly. "We ask your excellency's pardon if we have frightened you."

"Frightened me!" echoed Thugut, in a tone of unmeasured contempt. "As if you were the men to frighten me! I knew that you would come, and I knew, too, who had bribed you to do it. Yes, yes, I know they have paid you well, Mr. Wenzel, to get up a riot—they have given you shining ducats for leading a mob into my house. But will their ducats be able to get you out of it again?"

Mr. Wenzel turned very pale; he uttered a shriek and staggered back a few paces.

"Your excellency knew—" he said.

"Yes, I knew," continued Thugut, sternly, "that men who have no regard for the honor and dignity of their country—men who are stupid enough to believe that it would be better to submit voluntarily to the dominion of the French Republic, instead of resisting the demands of the regicides manfully and unyieldingly—that these men have hired you to open your big mouth, and howl about things which you do not understand, and which do not concern you at all."

At this moment, shrieks of terror and loud supplications, mingled with violent and threatening voices, and words of military command were heard outside.

The men turned anxiously around, and beheld with dismay that the staircase, which only a few minutes ago was crowded with people, was now entirely deserted.

Suddenly, however, two men appeared on the landing, who were little calculated to allay the apprehensions of the rioters, for they wore the uniform of that dreaded and inexorable police who, under Thugut's administration, had inaugurated a perfect reign of terror in Vienna.

The two officers approached the door of the anteroom, where they were met by Germain, the footman, who conversed with them in a whisper. Germain then hastened back to the door of the dining-room and walked in, scarcely deigning to cast a contemptuous glance on the dismayed rioters.

"Well, what is it?" asked Thugut.

"Your excellency, the chief of police sends word that his men are posted at all the doors of the palace, and will prevent anybody from getting out. He has cleared the streets, besides, and dispersed the rioters. The chief of police, who is in the hall below, where he is engaged in taking down the names of the criminals who are yet in the house, asks for your excellency's further orders."

"Ah, he does not suspect that his own chief, the minister of police is present," said Thugut, turning with a smile to Count Saurau, who, being condemned to witness this scene in the capacity of an idle and passive spectator, had withdrawn into a bay-window, where he had quietly listened to the whole proceedings.

"My dear count, will you permit the chief of police to come here and report to yourself?" asked Thugut.

"I pray you to give him this permission," replied the count, approaching his colleague.

Germain hastened back to the policemen in the anteroom.

"And what are we—?" asked Mr. Wenzel, timidly.

"You will wait!" thundered the minister. "Withdraw into yonder corner! may be the chief of police will not see you there."

They withdrew tremblingly into one of the corners of the anteroom, and did not even dare to whisper to each other, but the glances they exchanged betrayed the anguish of their hearts.

The two ministers, meanwhile, had likewise gone into the anteroom, and, while waiting for the arrival of the chief of police, conversed in a whisper.

In the course of a few minutes, the broad-shouldered and erect figure of the chief of the Viennese police appeared in the official uniform so well known to the people of the capital, who, for good reasons, were in the utmost dread of the terrible functionary. When the rioters beheld him, they turned even paler than before; now they thought that every thing was lost, and gave way to the most gloomy forebodings.

Count Saurau beckoned the chief to enter; the latter had a paper in his right hand.

"Your report," said the count, rather harshly. "How was it possible that this riot could occur? Was nobody there to disperse the seditious scoundrels before they made the attack on his excellency's palace?"

The chief of police was silent, and only glanced anxiously at Baron Thugut. The latter smiled, and turned to the count:

"I beg you, my dear count, don't be angry with our worthy chief of police. I am satisfied he has done his whole duty."

"The whole house is surrounded," hastily added the chief. "Nobody can get out, and I have taken down the names of all the criminals."

"Except these here," said Thugut, pointing at Mr. Wenzel and his unfortunate companions, who vainly tried to hide themselves in their corner. "But that is unnecessary, inasmuch as they have given us their names already, and informed us of their wishes. Then, sir, the whole honorable meeting of the people is caught in my house as in a mouse-trap?"

"Yes, we have got them all," said the chief. "Now, I would like to know of his excellency, the minister of police, what is to be done with them."

"I beg you, my dear count," said Thugut, turning to Count Saurau, "let me have my way in this matter, and treat these men in a spirit of hospitality. I have opened them the doors of my palace and admitted them into my presence, and it would be ungenerous not to let them depart again. Do not read the list of the names which the chief holds in his hand, but permit him to give it to me, and order him to withdraw his men from my house, and let the prisoners retire without molestation, and with all the honors of war."

"Your will shall be done, of course, your excellency," said the count, bowing respectfully. "Deliver your list to the prime minister, and go downstairs to carry out the wishes of his excellency."

The chief delivered the list of t

rioters, and left the room, after saluting the two dignitaries in the most respectful manner.

"And we—? may we go likewise, your excellency?" asked Mr. Wenzel, timidly.

"Yes, you may go," said Thugut. "But only on one condition. Mr. Wenzel, you must first recite to me the song which the honorable people were howling when you came here."

"Ah, your excellency, I only know a single verse by heart!"

"Well, then, let us have that verse. Out with it! I tell you, you will not leave this room until you have recited it. Never fear, however; for whatever it may be, I pledge you my word that no harm shall befall you."

"Very well," said Mr. Wenzel, desperately. "I believe the verse reads as follows:

"'Triumph! triumph! es siegt die gute Sache!
Die Türkenknechte flieh'n!
Laut tönt der Donner der gerechten Sache,
Nach Wien und nach Berlin.'" *

"Indeed, it is a very fine song," said Thugut, "and can you tell me who has taught you this song?"

"No, your excellency, I could not do it. Nobody knows it besides. It was printed on a small handbill, and circulated all over the city. A copy was thrown into every house, and the workingmen, when setting out early one morning, found it in the streets."

"And did you not assist a little in circulating this excellent song, my dear Mr. Wenzel?"

"I? God and the Holy Virgin forbid!" exclaimed Mr. Wenzel, in dismay. "I have merely sung it, like all the rest of us, and sung it to the tune which I heard from the others."

"Well, well, you did right, for the melody is really pleasing. Such songs generally have the peculiarity that not a single word of them is true; people call that poetry. Now, you may go, my poetical Mr. Wenzel, and you others, whom the people sent with this pacific mission to me. Tell your constituents that I will this time comply mercifully with their wishes, and give them peace, that is, I will let them go, and not send them to the calaboose, as they have abundantly deserved. But if you try this game again, and get up another riot, and sing that fine song once more, you may

* "Triumph! triumph! the good cause conquers!
The despots' minions flee!
The thunders of the just cause
Reach Vienna and Berlin!"

This hymn was universally sung at that time (1797) in all the German states, not merely by the popular classes, but likewise in the exclusive circles of the aristocracy. It is found in a good many memoirs of that period.

rest assured that you will be taken to jail and taught there a most unpleasant lesson. Begone now!"

He turned his back on the trembling citizens, and took no notice of the respectful bows with which they took leave of him, whereupon they retired with soft but hasty steps, like mice escaping from the presence of the dreaded lion.

"And now, my dear count, as we have finished our breakfast, let us return to my cabinet, for I believe we have to settle some additional matters."

CHAPTER IV.

THE TWO MINISTERS.

Baron Thugut took the count's arm and led him back to his cabinet.

"I read a question in your eyes," he said, smiling; "may I know what it is?"

"Why, yes, your excellency," replied Count Saurau.

"Let me ask you, then, what all this means? Why did you excuse the chief of police, who evidently had not done his duty and been guilty of a lack of vigilance? And why did you let these rascals go, instead of having them whipped to death?"

"You were away from Vienna, count? You were absent from the capital because you accompanied their majesties on their trip to Presburg, and have returned only an hour ago. Am I right?"

"Perfectly right, your excellency."

"Then you could not be aware of what has happened meanwhile here in Vienna, and the chief of police could not have informed you of the particulars. Well, then, he came to me and told me that an insurrection had been planned against the two emperors—(I believe you know that the people does us the honor of calling us the two emperors of Vienna), and that the faction hostile to us was going to make an attempt to overthrow us. A great deal of money had been distributed among the populace. Prince Carl von Schwarzenberg himself had dropped some indiscreet remarks. In short, the faction which hates me because I do not deem seditious Belgium a priceless jewel of the crown of Austria, and do not advise the emperor to keep that remote province at any price—the faction which detests both of us because we do not join its enthusiastic hymns in honor of the French Republic and the republican General Bonaparte—this faction has hired the miserable rabble to represent the people, to break my windows, and frighten me sufficiently to make me ready and willing to adopt its insane policy. The chief of police came to see me yesterday. He gave me an account of the whole affair, and declared himself fully prepared to protect my palace, and to nip the riot in the bud. I begged him not to do any thing of the kind, but to look on passively and attentively, and only come to my palace after the mob had entered it. I was very anxious for once to find out something definite about the strength, courage, and importance of the opposing faction. It is always desirable to know one's adversaries, and to learn as accurately as possible what they are capable of. Besides, it was a splendid opportunity for the police to discover the sneaking demagogues and ringleaders of the mob, and to take down their names for the purpose of punishing them by and by, as we Europeans unfortunately cannot imitate the example of that blessed Queen of Egypt, who took a thousand conspirators by the tails, and, holding them in her left hand, cut off their thousand seditious heads with one stroke of the sword in her right hand. Unfortunately, we have to act by far more cautiously."

"But why did you dismiss all the rioters this time without giving them into custody?" asked the count, moodily.

"Why, we have them all by the tails, anyhow," laughed Thugut, "for have not we got the list of the names here? Ah, my dear little count, perhaps you thought I would have gone in my generosity so far as to tear this list, throw the pieces away, and avert my head, like the pious bishop who found a murderer under his bed, permitted him to escape, and averted his head in order not to see the fugitive's face and maybe recognize him on some future occasion? I like to know the faces of my enemies, and to find out their names, and, depend upon it, I shall never, never forget the names I read on this list."

"But for the time being, these scoundrels, having escaped with impunity, will go home in triumph, and repeat the same game as soon as another occasion offers."

"Ah, I see you do not know the people at all! Believe me, we could not have frightened them worse than by letting them go. They are perfectly conscious of their guilt. The very idea of not having received any punishment at our hands fills them with misgivings, and they tremble every moment in the expectation that they will have to suffer yet for their crime. Remorse and fear are tormenting them, and they are the best instruments to rule a people with. My God, what should

be done with a nation consisting of none but pure and virtuous men? It would be perfectly unassailable, while its vices and foibles are the very things by which we control it. Therefore, do not blame the people on account of its vices. I love it for the sake of them, for it is through them that I succeed in subjecting it to my will. The idea of acting upon men by appealing to their virtues, is simply preposterous. You must rely on their faults and crimes, and, owing to the latter, all these fellows whom we dismissed to-day without punishment have become our property. The discharged and unpunished criminal is a sbirro—the police has only to hand him a dagger, and tell him, 'Strike there!' and he will strike."

"Your excellency believes, then, that even the ringleaders should not be punished?"

"By no means. Of course some of them should be chastised, in order to increase the terror of the others. But for God's sake, no public trials—no public penalties! Wenzel should be secretly arrested and disposed of. Let him disappear—he and the other ringleaders who were bold enough to come up here. Let us immure them in some strong, thick-walled prison, and while the other rioters are vainly tormenting their heavy skulls by trying to guess what has become of their leaders, we shall render the latter so pliable and tame by all kinds of tortures and threats of capital punishment, that when we finally set them free again, they will actually believe they are in our debt, and in their gratitude become willing tools in our hands to be used as we may deem best."

"By the eternal, you are a great statesman, a sagacious ruler!" exclaimed Count Saurau, with the gushing enthusiasm of sincere admiration. "Men grow wise by listening to you, and happy and powerful by obeying you! I am entirely devoted to you—full of affection and veneration—and do not want to be any thing but your attentive and grateful pupil."

"Be my friend," said Thugut. "Let us pursue our career hand in hand—let us always keep our common goal in view, and shrink back from no step in order to reach it."

"Tell me what I am to do. I shall follow you as readily as the blind man follows his guide."

"Well, if you desire it, my friend, we will consider a little how we have to steer the ship of state during the next months in order to get her safely through the breakers that are threatening her on all sides. During the few days of your absence from the capital, various events have occurred, materially altering the general state of affairs. When you departed, I advised the emperor not to make peace with France under any circumstances. We counted at that time on the regiments of grenadiers whom we had sent to the seat of war, and who, under the command of Archduke Charles, were to defend the defiles of Neumarkt against the advancing columns of the French army. We knew, besides, that the French troops were worn out, exhausted, and anxious for peace, or that General Bonaparte would not have addressed that letter to the Archduke Charles, in which he requested the latter to induce the Emperor of Austria to conclude peace with France. In accordance with our advice, the archduke had to give Bonaparte an evasive answer, informing him that, in case of further negotiations, he would have to send to Vienna for fresh instructions."

"But, your excellency, you were firmly determined not to make peace with France!"

"So I was, and even now I have not changed my mind; but we are frequently compelled to disguise our real intentions, and events have occurred, which, for the present, render peace desirable. You need not be frightened, my dear count—I merely say, for the present. In my heart I shall never make peace with France, and my purpose remains as fixed as ever—to revenge Austria one day for the humiliations we have suffered at her hands. Never forget that, my friend; and now listen to me. Late dispatches have arrived. Massena, after a bloody struggle with our troops, has taken Friesach, and advanced on the next day to attack the fresh regiments of our grenadiers in the gorges of Neumarkt. Archduke Charles had placed himself at the head of these regiments, firing the courage of the soldiers by his own heroic example. But he was confronted by the united French forces from Italy and Germany, and in the evening of that disastrous day the archduke and his grenadiers were compelled to evacuate Neumarkt, which was occupied by the victorious French. The archduke now asked the French general for a cessation of hostilities during twenty-four hours in order to gain time, for he was in hopes that this respite would enable him to bring up the corps of General von Kerpen, and then, with his united forces, drive the enemy back again. But this little General Bonaparte seems to possess a great deal of sagacity, for he rejected the request, and sent a detached column against Von Kerpen's corps, which separated the latter still farther from our main army. Bonaparte himself advanced with his forces as far as Fudenberg and Leoben. In order to save Vienna, there was but one course left to the archduke: he had to make proposals of peace."

"Did he really do so?" asked Count Sauran, breathlessly.

"He did. He sent two of our friends—Count Meerveldt, and the Marquis de Gallo—to Bonaparte's headquarters at Leoben, for the purpose of opening negotiations with him."

"Did your excellency authorize the archduke to do so?" asked the count.

"No, I did not, and I might disavow it now if it suited me, but it does not—it would not promote our interests—and I know but one policy, the policy of interest. We should always adopt those measures which afford us a reasonable prospect of gain, and discard those which may involve us in loss. Power alone is infallible, eternal, and divine, and power has now decided in favor of France. Therefore we must yield, and don the garb of peace until we secure once more sufficient power to renew hostilities. We must make peace! Our aim, however, should be to render this peace as advantageous to Austria as possible—"

"You mean at the expense of France?"

"Bah!—at the expense of Germany, my dear little count. Germany is to compensate us for the losses which peace may inflict. If we lose any territory in Italy, why, we shall make it up in Germany, that is all."

"But in that case, there will be another terrible hue and cry about the infringement of the rights of the holy German empire," said Count Sauran, smiling; "Prussia will have a new opportunity of playing the defender of the German fatherland."

"My dear count, never mind the bombastic nonsense in which Prussia is going to indulge—we shall take good care that nothing comes of it. Prussia has no longer a Frederick the Great at her head, but the fat Frederick William the Second—"

"But his life," said the count, interrupting him, "I know for certain, will last but a few days, at best for a few weeks; for his disease, dropsy of the chest, you know, does not even respect kings."

"And when Prussia has lost her present fat king, she will have another, Frederick William—a young man twenty-seven years of age, voilà tout! He is just as old as General Bonaparte, and was born in the same year as this general whose glory already fills the whole world; but of the young heir of the Prussian throne the world has heard nothing as yet, except that he has a most beautiful wife. He is not dangerous, therefore, and I hope and believe that Austria never will lack the power to humiliate and check this Prussian kingdom—this revolutionary element in the heart of the German empire. The danger, however, that threatens us now, does not come from Prussia, but from France, and especially from this General Bonaparte, who, by his glory and his wonderful battles, excites the wildest enthusiasm for the cause of the revolution, and delights the stupid masses so much that they hail him as a new messiah of liberty. Liberty, detestable word! that, like the fatal bite of the tarantula, renders men furious, and causes them to rave about in frantic dances until death strikes them down."

"This word is the talismanic charm with which Bonaparte has conquered all Italy, and transformed the Italians into insurgents and rebels against their legitimate sovereigns," said Count Sauran, mournfully.

"All Italy? Not yet, my friend. A portion of it still stands firm. The lion of St. Mark has not yet fallen."

"But he will fall. His feet are tottering already."

"Well, then, we must try to make him fall in a manner which will entitle us to a portion of the spoils. And now, my dear little count, we have reached the point which claims our immediate attention. The preliminaries of the peace have been concluded at Leoben, and until peace itself is established, we should pursue such a policy that the peace, instead of involving Austria in serious losses, will give her a chance to increase her strength and enlarge her territory. We must keep our eyes on Bavaria—for Bavaria will and must be ours as soon as a favorable opportunity offers. If France should object and refuse to let us seize our prey, why, we will be sure to revive the old quarrel about Belgium, which will render her willing and tame enough."

"But what shall we do if Prussia should support the objections of France? Shall we satisfy her, too, by giving her a piece of Germany?"

"On the contrary, we shall try to take as much as possible from her; we shall try to humiliate and isolate her, in order to deprive her of the power of injuring us. We shall endeavor so to arrange the peace we are going to conclude with France as to benefit Austria, and injure Prussia as much as we can. In the north, we shall increase our territory by the acquisition of Bavaria; in the south, by the annexation of Venice."

"By the annexation of Venice!" ejaculated Count Sauran, greatly astonished at what he had had heard. "But did you not just tell me that Venice still stood firm?"

"We must bring about her fall, my dear count; that is our great task just now; for, I repeat, Venice is to compensate us on our southern frontier for our losses elsewhere. Of course, we

ought to receive some substantial equivalent for ceding Belgium to France, and if it cannot be Bavaria, then let it be Venice."

"Nevertheless, I do not comprehend—"

"My dear count, if my schemes were so easily fathomed, they could not be very profound. Everybody may guess the game I am playing now; but the cards I have got in my hand must remain a secret until I have played them out, or I would run the risk of losing every thing. But this time I will let you peep into my cards, and you shall help me win the game. Venice is the stake we are playing for, my dear count, and we want to annex her to Austria. How is that to be brought about?"

"I confess, your excellency, that my limited understanding is unable to answer that question, and that I cannot conceive how a sovereign and independent state is to become an Austrian province in the absence of any claims to its territory, except by an act of open violence."

"Not exactly, my dear count. Suppose we set a mouse-trap for Venice, and catch her, like a mouse, in it? Listen to me! We must encourage Venice to determine upon open resistance against the victor of Lodi, and make war upon France."

"Ah, your excellency, I am afraid the timid signoria will not be bold enough for that, after hearing of our late defeats, and of the new victories of the French."

"Precisely. It is of the highest importance, therefore, that the signoria should hear nothing of it, but believe exactly the reverse, viz., that our troops are victorious; and this task, my friend, devolves upon you. Pray dispatch, at once, some reliable agents to Venice, and to other parts of the Venetian territory. Inform the signoria that the French have been defeated in the Tyrol and in Styria, and was now in the most precarious position. Through some other confidential messenger send word to Count Adam Neipperg, who, with some of our regiments occupies the southern Tyrol in close proximity to the Venetian frontier, that Venetia is ready to rise, and needs his assistance, and order him to advance as far as Verona. The Venetians will look upon this a France as a confirmation of the news of our victories. The wise little mice will only smell the bait, and, in their joy, not see the trap we have set for them. They will rush into it, and we shall catch them. For a rising in Venice will be called nowadays a rebellion against France, and France will hasten to punish so terrible a crime. The Venetian Republic will be destroyed by the French Republic, and then we shall ask

France to cede us Venice as a compensation for
the loss of Belgium."

"By the Eternal! it is a splendid—a grand
scheme!" exclaimed Count Saurau—"a scheme
worthy of being planned by some great statesman.
In this manner we shall conquer a new province
without firing a gun, or spilling a drop of blood."

"No. Some blood will be shed," said Thugut,
quietly. "But it will not be Austrian blood—it
will be the blood of the Venetian insurgents whom
we instigate to rise in arms. This bloodshed will
glue them firmly to us, for no cement is more
tenacious than blood. And now, my dear count,
as you know and approve of my plans, I pray
you to carry them out as rapidly as possible.
Dispatch your agents without delay to Venice and
to the Tyrol. We have no time to lose, for the
preliminaries of Leoben only extend to the eighteenth of April, and until then Venice must
have become a ripe fruit, which, in the absence
of hands to pluck it, will spontaneously fall to the
ground."

"In the course of an hour, your excellency, I
shall have executed your orders, and my most
skilful spies and agents will be on their road."

"Whom are you going to send to the Venetian
signoria?"

"The best confidential agent I have—Anthony
Schulmeister."

"Oh, I know him; he has often served me, and
is very adroit, indeed. But do not forget to pay
him well in order to be sure of his fidelity, for
fortunately he has a failing which renders it easy
for us to control him. He is exceedingly covetous, and has a pretty wife who spends a great deal
of money. Pay him well, therefore, and he will
do us good service. And now, farewell, my dear
count. I believe we understand each other perfectly, and know what we have to do."

"I have found out once more that the Austrian
ship of state is in the hands of a man who knows
how to steer and guide her, as no other ruler
does," said Count Saurau, who rose and took his
hat.

"I have inherited this talent, perhaps, my dear
count. My father, the ship-builder, taught me all
about the management of ships. Addio, caro
amico mio."

They cordially shook hands, and Count Saurau,
with a face radiant with admiration and affection,
withdrew from the cabinet of the prime minister.
A smile still played on his features when the footman in the anteroom assisted him in putting on
his cloak, whereupon he rapidly descended the
magnificent marble staircase which an hour ago
had been desecrated by the broad and clumsy feet

of the populace. But when the door of his carriage had closed behind him, and no prying eyes,
no listening ears were watching him any longer,
his smile disappeared as if by magic, and savage
imprecations burst from his lips.

"Intolerable arrogance! Revolting insolence!"
said he, angrily. "He thinks he can play the
despot, and treat all of us—even myself—worse
than slaves. He dares to call me 'his little count!'
His little count! Ah, I shall prove to this ship-
builder's son one day that little Count Saurau is,
after all, a greater man than our overbearing and
conceited prime minister. But patience, patience!
My day will come. And on that day I shall hurl
little Thugut from his eminent position!"

CHAPTER V.

THE HOUSE IN THE GUMPENDORFER SUBURB.

VIENNA was really terribly frightened by the
near approach of the French army, and the conviction of their dangerous position had excited the
people so fearfully that the Viennese, generally noted for their peaceful and submissive disposition,
had committed an open riot—for the sole purpose,
however, of compelling the all-powerful prime minister to make peace with France. Archduke
Charles had been defeated—the emperor had fled
to Hungary.

None of all these disastrous tidings had disturbed the inmates of a small house on the out-
skirts of the Gumpendorfer suburb, in close proximity to the Mariahilf line. This little house was
a perfect image of peace and tranquillity. It stood
in the centre of a small garden which showed the
first tender blossoms of returning spring on its
neatly arranged beds. Dense shrubbery covered
the white walls of the house with evergreen verdure. Curtains as white and dazzling as fresh
snow, and, between them, flower-pots filled with
luxuriant plants, might be seen behind the glittering window-panes. Although there was nothing
very peculiar about the house, which had but two
stories, yet nobody passed by without looking up
to the windows with a reverential and inquisitive
air, and he who only thought he could discover
behind the panes the fugitive shadow of a human
being, made at once a deep and respectful bow,
and a proud and happy smile overspread his features.

And still, we repeat, there was nothing very
peculiar about the house. Its outside was plain
and modest, and the inside was equally so. The

most profound silence prevailed in the small hall, the floor of which had been sprinkled with fresh white sand. A large spotted cat—a truly beautiful animal—lay not far from the front door on a soft, white cushion, and played gracefully and gently with the ball of white yarn that had just fallen from the woman sitting at the window while she was eagerly engaged in knitting. This woman, in her plain and unassuming dress, seemed to be a servant of the house, but at all events a servant in whom entire confidence was reposed, as was indicated by the large bunch of keys, such as the lady of the house or a trusted housekeeper will carry, which hung at her side. An expression of serene calmness rendered her venerable features quite attractive, and a graceful smile played on her thin and bloodless lips as she now dropped her knitting upon her lap, and, with her body bent forward, commenced watching the merry play of the cat on the cushion. Suddenly the silence was interrupted by a loud and shrill scream, and a very strange-sounding voice uttered a few incoherent words in English.

At the same time a door was opened hastily, and another woman appeared—just as old, just as kind-looking, and with as mild and serene features as the one we have just described. Her more refined appearance, however, her handsome dress, her beautiful cap, her well-powdered toupet, and the massive gold chain encircling her neck, indicated that she was no servant, but the lady of the house.

However, peculiarly pleasant relations seemed to prevail between the mistress and the servant, for the appearance of the lady did not cause the latter to interrupt her merry play with the cat; and the mistress, on her part, evidently did not consider it strange or disrespectful, but quietly approached her servant.

"Catharine," she said, "just listen how that abominable bird, Paperl, screams again to-day. I am sure the noise will disturb the doctor, who is at work already."

"Yes, Paperl is an intolerable nuisance," sighed Catharine. "I cannot comprehend why the Kapellmeister—I was going to say the doctor—likes the bird so well, and why he has brought it along from England. Yes, if Paperl could sing, in that case it would not be strange if the Ka—, I mean the doctor, had grown fond of the bird. But no, Paperl merely jabbers a few broken words which no good Christian is able to understand."

"He who speaks English can understand it well enough, Catharine," said the lady, "for the bird talks English, and in that respect Paperl knows more than either of us."

"But Paperl cannot talk German, and I think that our language, especially our dear Viennese dialect, sounds by far better than that horrid English. I don't know why the doctor likes the abominable noise, and why he suffers the bird to disturb his quiet by these outrageous screams."

"I know it well enough, Catharine," said the doctor's wife, with a gentle smile. "The parrot reminds my husband of his voyage to England, and of all the glory and honor that were showered upon him there."

"Well, as far as that is concerned, I should think it was entirely unnecessary for my master to make a trip to England," exclaimed Catharine. "He has not returned a more famous man than he was already when he went away. The English were unable to add to his glory, for he was already the most celebrated man in the whole world when he went there, and if that had not been the case, they would not have invited him to come and perform his beautiful music before them, for then they would not have known that he is such a splendid musician."

"But they were delighted to see him, Catharine, and I tell you they have perfectly overwhelmed him with honors. Every day they gave him festivals, and even the king and queen urged him frequently to take up his abode in England. The queen promised him splendid apartments in Windsor Castle, and a large salary, and in return my husband was to do nothing but to perform every day for an hour or so before her majesty, or sing with her. Nevertheless, he had the courage to refuse the brilliant offers of the king and queen, and do you know, Catharine, why he rejected them?"

Catharine knew it well enough; she had frequently heard the story from her mistress during the two years since the doctor had returned from England, but she was aware that the lady liked to repeat it, and she liked it very much, too, to hear people talk about her beloved master's fame and glory, having faithfully served him for more than twenty years. Hence she said, with a kind-hearted smile:

"No, indeed, I don't know it, and I cannot comprehend why the doctor said no to the king and queen of England."

"He did so for my sake, Catharine!" said the lady, and an expression of joyful pride shed a lustre of beauty and tenderness over her kind old face. "Yes, I tell you, it was solely for my sake that my husband came home again. 'Remain with us!' said the king to him. 'You shall have every thing the queen has offered you. You shall live at Windsor, and sing once a day with the queen. Of you, my dear doctor, I shall not be jealous, for you are an excellent and honest German gentleman.' And when the king had told him that, my husband bowed respectfully, and replied : 'Your majesty, it is my highest pride to maintain this reputation. But just because I am an honest German, I must tell you that I cannot stay here—I cannot leave my country and my wife forever!'

"'Oh, as far as that is concerned,' exclaimed the king, 'we shall send for your wife. She shall live with you at Windsor.' But my husband laughed and said : 'She will never come, your majesty. She would not cross the Danube in a skiff, much less make a trip beyond the sea. And, therefore, there is nothing left to me but to return myself to my little wife'. And he did so, and left the king, and the queen, and all the noble lords and ladies, and came back to Vienna, and to his little wife. Say, Catharine, was not that well done of him ?"

"Of course it was," said Catharine ; "the fact was, our good doctor loved his wife better than the queen, and all the high-born people who treated him so well in England. And, besides, he knew that people hereabouts treat him with as much deference as over there, and that if he only desired it, he could hold daily intercourse with the emperor, the princes, and the highest dignitaries in the country. But he does not care for it. The fact is, our master is by far too modest ; he is always so quiet and unassuming, that nobody, unless they knew him, would believe for a single moment that he is so far-famed a man ; and then he dresses so plainly, while he might deck himself with all the diamond rings and breast-pins, the splendid watches and chains, which the various sovereigns have given to him. But all these fine things he keeps shut up in his desk, and constantly wears the same old silver watch which he has had already God knows how long !"

"Why, Catharine, that was the wedding-present I gave him," said the good wife, proudly ; "and just for that reason my husband wears it all the time, although he has watches by far more beautiful and valuable. At the time I gave him that watch, both of us were very poor. He was a young music-teacher, and I was a hair-dresser's daughter. He lived in a small room in my father's house, and as he often could not pay the rent, he gave me every day a lesson on the piano. But in those lessons, I did not only learn music—I learned to love him, too. He asked me to become his wife, and on our wedding-day, I gave him the silver watch, and that is just the reason why he wears it all the time, although he has by far better ones. His wife's present is more precious

to him than what kings and emperors have given to him."

"But he might wear at least a nice gold chain to it," said Catharine. "Why, I am sure he has no less than a dozen of them. But he never wears one of them, not even the other day when the Princess Esterhazy called for him with her carriage to drive with him to the emperor. The doctor wore on that occasion only a plain blue ribbon, on which his own name was embroidered in silver."

"Well, there is a story to that ribbon," said the mistress, thoughtfully. "My husband brought it likewise from London, and he got it there on one of his proudest days. I did not know the story myself, for you are aware my husband is always so modest, and never talks about his great triumphs in London, and I would not have learned any thing about the ribbon if he had not worn it the other day when he accompanied the princess to the emperor. Ah, Catharine, it is a very beautiful and touching story !"

Catharine did not know this story at all ; hence she asked her mistress with more than usual animation to tell her all about the ribbon.

The doctor's wife assented readily. She sat down on a chair at Catharine's side, and looked with a pleasant smile at the cat who had come up to her, and, purring comfortably, lay down on the hem of her dress.

"Yes," said she, "the story of that ribbon is quite touching, and I do not know really, Catharine, but I will have to shed a few tears while telling it. It was in London, when my husband had just returned from Oxford, where the university had conferred upon him the title of Doctor of—"

"Yes, yes, I know," grumbled Catharine, "that is the reason why we now have to call him doctor, which does not sound near as imposing and distinguished as our master's former title of Kapellmeister."

"But then it is a very high honor to obtain the title of doctor of music in England, Catharine. The great composer Handel lived thirty years in England without receiving it, and my husband had not been there but a few months when they conferred the title upon him. Well, then, on the day after his return from Oxford, he was invited to the house of a gentleman of high rank and great wealth, who gave him a brilliant party. A large number of ladies and gentlemen were present, and when my husband appeared among them they rose and bowed as respectfully as though he were a king. When the doctor had returned the compliment, he perceived that every lady in the room wore in her hair a ribbon of blue silk, on which his name had been embroidered in silver. His host wore the same name in silver beads on his coat-facings, so that he looked precisely as if he were my husband's servant, and dressed in his livery. Oh, it was a splendid festival which Mr. Shaw—that was the gentleman's name—gave him on that day. At length Mr. Shaw asked the doctor to give him a souvenir, whereupon he presented him with a snuff-box he had purchased in the course of the day for a few shillings; and when my husband requested the lady of the house, whom he pronounces the most beautiful woman on earth, to give him likewise a souvenir; Mrs. Shaw thereupon took the ribbon from her head and handed it to him; and my husband pressed it to his lips, and assured her he would always wear that ribbon on the most solemn occasions. You see, Catharine, he keeps his promise religiously, for he wore the ribbon the other day when he was called to the imperial palace. But my story is not finished yet. Your master called a few days after that party on Mr. Shaw, when the latter showed him the snuff-box he had received from my husband. It was enclosed in a handsome silver case, a beautiful lyre was engraved on the lid, with an inscription stating that my great and illustrious husband had given him the box.* How do you like my story, Catharine?"

"Oh, it is beautiful," said the old servant, thoughtfully; "only, what you said about that beautiful Mrs. Shaw did not exactly please me. I am sure the doctor got the parrot also from her, and for that reason likes the bird so well, although it screeches so horribly, and doubtless disturbs him often in his studies."

"Yes, he got the bird from Mrs. Shaw," replied her mistress, with a smile. "She taught Paperl to whistle three airs from my husband's finest quartets, singing and whistling the music to the bird every day during three or four weeks for several hours, until Paperl could imitate them; and when my husband took leave of her, she gave him the parrot."

"But the bird never whistles the tunes any more. I have only heard Paperl do it once, and that was on the day after the doctor's return from England."

"I know the reason why. The bird hears here every day so much music, and so many new melodies which the doctor plays on his piano, that its head has grown quite confused, and poor Paperl has forgotten its tunes."

"It has not forgotten its English words, though," murmured Catharine. "What may be the mean-

ing of these words which the bird is screaming all the time?"

"That beautiful Mrs. Shaw taught Paperl to pronounce them, Catharine. I do not know their precise meaning, but they commence as follows: 'Forget me not, forget me not—' Good Heaven the bird has commenced screaming again. I am sure it has not had any sugar to-day. Where is Conrad? He ought to attend to the bird."

"He has gone down town. The doctor has given him several errands."

"Good Heaven! the screams are almost intolerable. Go, Catharine, and give poor Paperl a piece of sugar."

"I dare not, madame; it always snaps at me with its abominable beak, and if the chain did not prevent it from attacking me, it would scratch out my eyes."

"I am afraid of it, too," said the lady, anxiously; "nevertheless we cannot permit the bird to go on in this manner. Just listen to it—it is yelling as though it were going to be roasted. It will disturb my husband, and you know the doctor is composing a new piece. Come, Catharine, we must quiet the bird. I will give him the sugar."

"And I shall take my knitting-needles along, and if it should try to bite, I will hit it on the beak. Let us go now, madame."

And the two women walked boldly across the anteroom, toward the door of the small parlor, in order to commence the campaign against the parrot. The cat followed them gravely and solemnly, and with an air as though it had taken the liveliest interest in the conversation, and thought it might greatly assist them in pacifying the screaming bird.

CHAPTER VI.

JOSEPH HAYDN.

WHILE the parrot's screams had rendered the mistress and her maid so uneasy, the most profound stillness and quiet reigned in the upper rooms of the little house. Not a sound interrupted the silence of this small, elegantly-furnished sitting-room. Even the sun apparently dared only to send a few stealthy beams through the windows, and the wind seemed to hold its breath in order not to shake the panes of the small chamber adjoining, venerated by all the inmates of the house as a sacred temple of art.

In this small chamber, in this temple of art, a gentleman, apparently engaged in reading, was seated at a table covered with papers and music-

---

* The inscription was: "Ex dono celeberrimi Josephi Haydn."

books, close to an open piano. He was no longer young; on the contrary, beholding only the thin white hair hanging down on his expansive and wrinkled forehead, and his stooping form, it became evident that he was an old man, nearly seventy years of age. But as soon as he raised his eyes from the paper, as soon as he turned them toward heaven with an air of blissful enthusiasm, the fire of eternal youth and radiant joyousness burst forth from those eyes; and whatever the white hair, the wrinkled forehead, the furrowed cheeks and the stooping form might tell of the long years of his life, those eyes were full of youthful ardor and strength—only the body of this white-haired man was old; in his soul he had remained young—a youth of fervid imagination, procreative power, and nervous activity.

This venerable man with the soul, the heart, and the eyes of a youth, was Joseph Haydn, the great composer, whose glory, even at that time, filled the whole world, although he had not yet written his greatest masterpieces—the "Creation" and the "Seasons."

He was working to-day at the "Creation."[*] The poem, which had been sent to him from England, and which his worthy friend Von Swieten had translated into German, lay before him. He had read it again and again, and gradually it seemed as if the words were transformed into music; gradually he heard whispering—low at first, then louder, and more sublime and majestic—the jubilant choirs of heaven and earth, that were to resound in his "Creation."

As yet he had not written a single note; he had only read the poem, and composed in reading, and inwardly weighed and tried the sublime melodies which, when reduced to time and measure, and combined into an harmonious whole, were to form the new immortal work of his genius. While thus reading and composing, the aged musician was transformed more and more into a youth, and the glowing enthusiasm which burst forth from his eyes became every moment more radiant, surrounding his massive forehead with a halo of inspiration, and shedding the purple lustre of ecstatic joy upon his furrowed cheeks.

"Yes, yes, it will do. I shall succeed!" he exclaimed suddenly, in a loud and full voice. "God will give me the strength to complete this work; but it must be commenced with Him—strength and inspiration come from Him alone!"

And Joseph Haydn, perhaps not quite conscious of what he was doing, knelt down and with folded hands, and beaming eyes lifted up to heaven, he

prayed: "O, Lord God, give me Thy blessing and Thy strength, that I may gloriously and successfully carry out this work, which praiseth Thee and Thy creation. Breathe Thy Holy Spirit into the words which Thou speakest in my work. Speak through me to Thy creatures, and let my music be Thy language!"

He paused, but remaining on his knees, continued to look up to heaven. Then he rose slowly, and like a seer or a somnambulist, with eyes opened but seeing nothing, he went to his piano without knowing what he was doing. He sat down on the stool, and did not know it; his hands touched the keys and drew magnificent chords from them, and he did not hear them. He only heard the thousands of seraphic voices which in his breast chanted sublime anthems; he only heard the praise of his own winged soul which, in divine ecstasy, soared far into the realm of eternal harmonies.

Louder and louder rolled the music he drew from the keys; now it burst forth into a tremendous jubilee, then again it died away in melancholy complaints and gentle whispers, and again it broke out into a swelling, thundering anthem.

At length Haydn concluded with a sonorous and brilliant passage, and then with youthful agility jumped up from his seat.

"That was the prelude," he said, aloud, "and now we will go to work."

He hastily threw the white and comfortable dressing-gown from his shoulders and rapidly walked toward the looking-glass which hung over the bureau. Every thing was ready for his toilet, the footman having carefully arranged the whole. He put the cravat with lace trimmings around his neck and arranged the tie before the looking-glass in the most artistic manner; then he slipped into the long waistcoat of silver-lined velvet, and finally put on the long-tailed brown coat with bright metal buttons. He was just going to put the heavy silver watch, which his wife had given him on their wedding-day, into his vest-pocket, when his eye fell upon the blue ribbon embroidered with silver, which, ever since his visit to the imperial palace, had lain on the bureau.

"I will wear it on this holiday of mine," said Haydn, with great warmth, "for I think the day on which a new work is begun is a holiday, and we ought to wear our choicest ornaments to celebrate it."

He attached the ribbon to his watch, threw it over his neck, and slipped the watch into his vest-pocket.

"If that beautiful Mrs. Shaw could see me now," he whispered, almost inaudibly, "how her

[*] Haydn commenced the "Creation" in 1797, and finished it in April, 1798.

magnificent eyes would sparkle, and what a heavenly smile would animate her angelic features! Yes, yes, I will remember her smile—it shall find an echo in the jubilant accords of my *Creation*. But let us begin—let us begin!"

He rapidly walked toward his desk, but stopped suddenly. "Hold on!" said he; "I really forgot the most important thing—my ring. While looking at the precious ribbon of my beautiful English friend, I did not think of the ring of my great king—and still it is the talisman without which I cannot work at all."

Returning once more to the bureau, he opened a small case and took from it a ring which he put on his finger. He contemplated the large and brilliant diamonds of the ring with undisguised admiration.

"Yes," he exclaimed—"yes, thou art my talisman, and when I look at thee, it seems to me as if I saw the eyes of the great king beaming down upon me, and pouring courage and enthusiasm into my heart. That is the reason, too, why I cannot work unless I have the ring on my finger.* But now I am ready and adorned like a bridegroom who is going to his young bride. Yes, yes, it is just so with me. I am going to my bride—to St. Cecilia!"

When he now returned to his desk, his features assumed a grave and solemn expression. He sat down once more at the piano and played an anthem, then he resumed his seat at the desk, took a sheet of music-paper and commenced writing. He wielded his pen with the utmost rapidity, and covered page after page with the queer little dots and dashes which we call notes.

And Haydn's eyes flashed and his cheeks glowed, and a heavenly smile played on his lips while he was writing. But all of a sudden his pen stopped, and a slight cloud settled on his brow. Some passage, may be a modulation, had displeased him, in what he had just composed, for he glanced over the last few lines and shook his head. He looked down sadly and dropped the pen.

"Help me, O Lord God—help me!" he exclaimed, and hastily seized the rosary which always lay on his desk. "Help me!" he muttered once more, and, while hurriedly pacing the room, he slipped the beads of the rosary through his fingers and whispered an *Ave Maria*.

His prayer seemed to have the desired effect,

for the cloud disappeared from his forehead, and his eyes beamed again with the fervor of inspiration. He resumed his seat and wrote on with renewed energy. A holy peace now settled on his serene features, and reigned around him in the silent little cabinet.

But all at once this peaceful stillness was interrupted by a loud noise resounding from below. Vociferous lamentations were heard, and heavy footsteps ascended the staircase.

Haydn, however, did not hear any thing—his genius was soaring far away in the realm of inspiration, and divine harmonies still enchanted his ears.

But now the door of the small parlor was opened violently, and his wife, with a face deadly pale and depicting the liveliest anxiety, rushed into the room. Catharine and Conrad, the aged footman, appeared behind her, while the cat slipped in with her mistress, and the parrot ejaculated the most frantic and piercing screams.

Haydn started in dismay from his seat and stared at his wife without being able to utter a single word. It was something unheard of for him to be disturbed by his wife during his working hours, hence he very naturally concluded that something unusual, something really terrible must have occurred, and the frightened looks of his wife, the pale faces of his servants, plainly told him that he was not mistaken.

"Oh, husband—poor, dear husband!" wailed his wife, "pack up your papers, the time for working and composing is past. Conrad has brought the most dreadful tidings from the city. We are all lost!—Vienna is lost! Oh, dear, dear! it is awful, and I tell you I am almost frightened out of my senses!"

And the old lady, trembling like an aspen-leaf, threw herself into an arm-chair.

"What in Heaven's name is the matter?" asked Haydn—"what is it that has frightened you thus? Conrad, tell me what is the news?"

"Oh, my dear master," wailed Conrad, approaching the doctor with folded hands and shaking knees, "it is all up with us! Austria is lost —Vienna is lost—and consequently we are lost, too! Late dispatches have arrived from the army. Ah! what do I say?—army? We have no longer an army—our forces are entirely dispersed—Archduke Charles has lost another battle—old Wurmser has been driven back—and General Bonaparte is advancing upon Vienna."

"These are sad tidings, indeed," said Haydn, shrugging his shoulders, "still they are no reason why we should despair. If the archduke has lost a battle—why, all generals have lost battles—"

---

* Haydn had dedicated six quartets to Frederick the Great, who acknowledged the compliment by sending him a most valuable diamond ring. Haydn wore this ring whenever he composed a new work, and it seemed to him as though inspiration failed him unless he wore the ring. He stated this on many occasions.

"Bonaparte never lost one," replied Conrad, with a profound sigh, "he wins every battle, and devours all countries he wants to conquer."

"We must pack up our things, Joseph," said Mrs. Haydn—"we must bury our money, our plate, and especially your jewels and trinkets, so that those French robbers and cannibals will not find them. Come, husband, let us go to work quickly, before they come and take every thing from us."

"Hush, wife, hush!" said Haydn, mildly, and a gentle smile overspread his features. "Never fear about our few trifles, and do not think that the French just want to come to Vienna for what few gold snuff-boxes and rings I have got. If they were anxious for gold and jewels, coming as they do as enemies, they might simply open the imperial treasury and take there all they want."

"Yes, but they would not find any thing," said Conrad. "The treasury is empty, doctor, entirely empty. Every thing is gone; there is not a single crown, not a single precious stone left in the treasury."

"Well, and where is the whole treasure then, you fool?" asked Haydn, with a smile.

"They have taken it to Presburg, master. I saw the wagons myself—soldiers rode in front of them, soldiers behind them. All streets, all places were crowded with people, and a riot broke out, and oh! such lamentations, such wails!—and finally the people became desperate, and roared and yelled that the government should make peace, and prevent the French from coming to Vienna and bombarding the city; and in their desperation they grew quite bold and brave, and thousands of them marched to the house of Minister Thugut, whom they call the real emperor of Vienna, and tried to compel him to make peace."

"Sad, sad tidings, indeed!" sighed Haydn, shaking his head. "Worse than I thought! The people riotous and rebellious—the army defeated—and the enemy marching upon Vienna. But don't despair—courage, courage, children; let us put our trust in God and our excellent emperor. Those two will never forsake us—they will guard and protect Vienna, and never suffer a single stone to be taken from its walls."

"Ah, husband, don't count any longer upon the emperor," said his wife. "For that is the worst part of the news, and shows that every thing is lost: the emperor has left Vienna."

"What!" exclaimed Haydn, and his face grew flushed with anger. "What, they dare to slander the emperor so infamously as that! They dare to assert that the emperor has forsaken his Viennese when they are in danger? No, no, the emperor is an honest man and a faithful prince; he will share good and evil days alike with his people. A good shepherd does not leave his flock, a good prince does not leave his people".

"But the emperor has forsaken us," said Conrad; "it is but too true, master. All Vienna knows it, and all Vienna mourns over it. The emperor is gone, and so are the empress and the imperial children. All are gone and off for Presburg."

"Gone! the emperor gone!" muttered Haydn, mournfully, and a deadly paleness suddenly covered his cheeks. "Oh, poor Austria! poor people! Thy emperor has forsaken thee—he has fled from thee!"

He sadly inclined his head, and profound sighs escaped from his breast.

"Do you see now, husband, that I was right?" asked his wife. "Is it not true that it is high time for us to think of our property, and to pack up and bury our valuables?"

"No!" exclaimed Haydn, raising his head again; "this is no time to think of ourselves, and of taking care of our miserable property. The emperor has left—that means, the emperor is in danger; and therefore, as his faithful subjects, we should pray for him, and all our thoughts and wishes should only be devoted to his welfare. In the hour of danger we should not be faint-hearted, and bow our heads, but lift them up to God, and hope and trust in Him! Why do the people of Vienna lament and despair? They should sing and pray, so that the Lord God above may hear their voices—they should sing and pray, and I will teach them how!"

And with proud steps Haydn went to the piano, and his hands began to play gently, at first, a simple and choral-like air; but soon the melody grew stronger and more impressive. Haydn's face became radiant; instinctively opening his lips, he sang in an enthusiastic and ringing voice words which he had never known before—words which, with the melody, had spontaneously gushed from his soul. What his lips sang was a prayer, and, at the same time, a hymn of victory—full of innocent and child-like piety:

> "Gott erhalte Franz den Kaiser,
> Unsern guten Kaiser Franz,
> Lange lebe Franz der Kaiser
> In des Glückes hellem Glanz!
> Ihm erblühen Lorbeerreiser,
> Wo er geht, zum Ehrenkranz!
> Gott erhalte Franz den Kaiser,
> Unsern guten Kaiser Franz!" *

Profound silence prevailed while Haydn was

---

* The celebrated Austrian hymn, "God save the Emperor Francis."

singing, and when he concluded with a firm and ringing accord and turned around, he saw that his wife, overcome with emotion, with folded hands and eyes lifted up to heaven, had sunk down on her knees, and that old Catharine and Conrad were kneeling behind her, while the cat stood between them listening to the music as it were, and even the parrot below seemed to listen to the new hymn, for its screams had ceased.

A smile of delight played on Haydn's lips and rendered his face again young and beautiful. "Now, sing with me, all three of you," he said. "Sing loudly and firmly, that God may hear us. I will commence again at the beginning, and you shall accompany me."

He touched the keys vigorously, and sang once more, "God save the Emperor Francis!" and carried away by the melody so simple and yet so beautiful, the two women and the old footman sang with him the tender and artless words.

"And now," said Haydn, eagerly, "now, I will write down the melody on the spot, and then you shall run with it to Councillor von Swieten. He must add a few verses to it. And then we will have it copied as often as possible—we will circulate it in the streets, and sing it in all public places, and if the French really should come to Vienna, the whole people shall receive them with the jubilant hymn, 'God save the Emperor Francis!' And God will hear our song, and He will be touched by our love, and He will lead him back to us, our good Emperor Francis."

He sat down at his desk, and in youthful haste wrote down the music. "So," he said then, "take it, Conrad, take it to Herr von Swieten; tell him it is my imperial hymn. Oh, I believe it will be useful to the emperor, and therefore I swear that I will play it every day as long as I live. My first prayer always shall be for the emperor." And now run, Conrad, and ask Herr von Swieten to finish the poem quickly, and you, women, leave me. I feel the ideas burning in my head, and the melodies gushing from my heart. The hymn

---

* Haydn kept his word, and from that time played the hymn every day. It was even the last piece of music he performed before his death. On the 26th of May, 1809, he played the hymn three times in succession. From the piano he had to be carried to his bed, which he never left again. When Iffland paid him a visit in 1807, Haydn played the hymn for him. He then remained a few moments before the instrument—placed his hands on it, and said, in the tone of a venerable patriarch: "I play this hymn every morning, and in times of adversity have often derived consolation and courage from it. I cannot help it—I must play it at least once a day. I feel greatly at ease whenever I do so, and even a good while afterward."—"Iffland's Theatrical Almanac for 1855," p. 181.

---

has inspired me with genuine enthusiasm; and now, with God and my emperor, I will commence my *Creation!* But you, you must not despair—and whenever you feel dejected, sing my imperial hymn, and pour consolation and courage into your hearts—into the hearts of all Austrians who will sing it. For not only for you, but for Austria, I have sung my hymn, and it shall belong to the whole Austrian people!"

CHAPTER VII.

GENERAL BONAPARTE.

At length peace was to be concluded. For several weeks had the three Austrian plenipotentiaries been at Udine; the Austrian court having sent with Count Meerveldt and Count Louis Cobenzl the Marquis de Gallo, who, although Neapolitan ambassador at Vienna, and therefore not in the imperial service, acted as their adviser.

General Bonaparte was at Passeriano: he alone had been authorized by the great French Republic to conclude peace with Austria, or to renew the war, just as he saw fit.

The eyes of France and Germany, nay of all Europe, were riveted upon this small point on the border of Germany and Italy, for there the immediate future of Europe was to be decided; there the dice were to fall which were to bring peace or war to the world.

Austria wanted peace; it was a necessity for her, because she did not feel strong enough for war, and was afraid of the dangers and losses of continued defeats. But she did not want peace, *coûte qui coûte;* she wanted to derive substantial advantages from it—she intended to aggrandize herself at the expense of Italy, at the expense of Prussia—and, if need be, at the expense of Germany.

But what did France want, or rather, what did General Bonaparte want? None but himself knew. None could read his thoughts in his marble countenance. None could decipher his future actions from his laconic utterances. None could tell what Bonaparte intended to do, and what aim his ambition had in view.

The negotiations with Austria had been going on for months. For several weeks the Austrian plenipotentiaries and General Bonaparte had had daily interviews of many hours' duration, which alternately took place at Udine and at Passeriano, but the work of pacification would not come to a satisfactory conclusion. Austria demanded too much, and France would not yield enough. These conferences had frequently assumed a very stormy character, and often, during the debates, Bonaparte's voice had resounded in thundering tones, and flashes of anger had burst forth from his eyes. But the Austrian plenipotentiaries had not been struck by them. The flashes from the great chieftain's eyes had recoiled powerlessly from their imperturbable smile. When his voice thundered at them, they had lowered their heads only to raise them slowly again as soon as the general was silent.

To-day, on the thirteenth of October, another interview was to take place, at the hotel of Count Cobenzl, and perhaps that was the reason why General Bonaparte had risen at an unusually early hour in the morning. He had just finished his toilet; the four valets who had assisted him had just concluded their task. As usual, Bonaparte had suffered them to dress and wash him like a child.* With a silent gesture he now ordered the servants to withdraw, and called out, "Bourrienne!"

The door was opened at once, and a tall young man, in the citizen's dress of that period, stepped in. Bonaparte, greeting his youthful secretary with a slight nod of his head, pointed with his hand at the desk.

Bourrienne walked noiselessly to the desk, sat down, took a pen and some blank paper, and waited for what the general would have to dictate.

But Bonaparte was silent. With his hands folded on his back, he commenced rapidly walking up and down. Bourrienne, holding the pen in his hand and momentarily ready to write, enjoyed this pause, this absorbed pondering of the general, with genuine delight; for it afforded him leisure to contemplate Bonaparte, to study his whole appearance, and to engrave every feature, every gesture of the conqueror of Italy upon his mind.

Bourrienne was an old friend of Bonaparte; they had been together at the military academy; they had met afterward at Paris—and poor young Lieutenant Bonaparte had often been glad enough to accept a dinner at the hands of his wealthier friend.

Only a few years had elapsed since that time, and now Lieutenant Bonaparte had become already an illustrious general; while Bourrienne, whom the Terrorists had proscribed, thankfully accepted the protection of his old comrade, and

now filled the position of private secretary under him.

He had been with him in this capacity only two days—for two days he had seen Bonaparte every hour, and yet he contemplated with ever new surprise this wonderful countenance, in which he vainly tried to recognize the features of the friend of his youth. True, the same outlines and contours were still there, but the whole face was an entirely different one. No traces of the carelessness, of the harmless hilarity of former days, were left in these features. His complexion was pale almost to sickliness; his figure, which did not rise above the middle height, was slender and bony. Upon looking at him, you seemed at first to behold a young man entirely devoid of strength, and hopelessly doomed to an early death. But the longer you examined him, the more his features seemed to breathe vitality and spirit, and the firmer grew the conviction that this was an exceptional being—a rare and strange phenomenon. Once accustomed to his apparent pale and sickly homeliness, the beholder soon saw it transformed into a fascinating beauty such as we admire on the antique Roman cameos and old imperial coins. His classical and regular profile seemed to be modelled after these antique coins; his forehead, framed in on both sides with fine chestnut hair, was high and statuesque. His eyes were blue, but brimful of the most wonderful expression and sparkling with fire, a faithful mirror of his fiery soul, now exceedingly mild and gentle, and then again stern and even harsh. His mouth was classically beautiful—the finely-shaped lips, narrow and slightly compressed, especially when in anger; when he laughed, he displayed two rows of teeth, not faultlessly fine, but of pearly white. Every lineament, every single feature of his face was as regular as if modelled by a sculptor; nevertheless there was something ugly and repulsive in the whole, and in order to be able to admire it, it was necessary first to get accustomed to this most extraordinary being. Only the feet and the small white hands were so surpassingly beautiful that they enlisted at once the liveliest admiration, and this was perhaps the reason why General Bonaparte, who otherwise observed the greatest simplicity in his toilet, had adorned his hands with several splendid diamond rings.*

Bourrienne was still absorbed in contemplating the friend of his youth, when the latter suddenly stood still before him and looked at him with a pleasant smile.

"Why do you stare at me in this manner,

---

* "Mémoires de Constant, premier valet de chambre de l'Empereur Napoléon," vol. i., p. 190.

* Mémoires de Constant, vol. i., p. 52.

Bourrienne?" he asked in his abrupt and hasty tone.

"General, I only contemplate the laurels which your glorious victories have woven around your brow, since I saw you the last time," said Bourrienne.

"Ah, and you find me a little changed since you saw me the last time," replied Bonaparte, quickly. "It is true, the years of our separation have produced a great many changes, and I was glad that you had the good taste to perceive this, and upon meeting me under the present circumstances, to observe a becoming and delicate reserve. I am under obligations to you for it, and from to-day you shall be chief of my cabinet, my first private secretary." *

Bourrienne rose to thank the young general by bowing respectfully, but Bonaparte took no further notice of him, and walked again rapidly up and down. The smile had already vanished from his face, which had resumed its immovable and impenetrable expression.

Bourrienne quietly sat down again and waited; but now he dared no longer look at Bonaparte, the general having noticed it before.

After a lengthy pause, Bonaparte stood still close to the desk. "Have you read the dispatches which the Directory sent me yesterday through their spy, M. Botot?" asked the general, abruptly.

"I have, general!"

"They are unreasonable fools," exclaimed Bonaparte, angrily, "they want to direct our war from their comfortable sofas in the Luxembourg, and believe their ink-stained hands could hold the general's *bâton* as well as the pen. They want to dictate to us a new war from Paris, without knowing whether we are able to bear it or not. They ask us to conclude peace with Austria without ceding Venice to her as compensation for Belgium. Yes, Talleyrand is senseless enough to ask me to revolutionize the whole of Italy once more, so that the Italians may expel their princes, and that liberty may prevail throughout the entire peninsula. In order to give them liberty, they want me to carry first war and revolution into their midst. These big-mouthed and ignorant Parisians do not know that Italy will not belong to us in reality until after the restoration of peace, and that the Directory, even at the first dawn of peace, will rule her from the mountains of Switzerland to the capes of Calabria. Then, and only then, the Directory will be able to alter the various governments of Italy, and for this very reason we have to attach Austria to our cause by a treaty of peace. As soon as she has signed it, she will no longer molest us: first, because she is our ally; and principally because she will apprehend that we might take back from her what we generously gave, in order to win her over to our side. The war party at Vienna, however, will not submit without hoping for some counter-revolution—a dream which the *émigrés* and the diplomacy of Pillnitz still cherishes with the utmost tenacity. * And these unreasonable gentlemen of the Directory want war and revolution, and they dare to accuse me of selfish motives. Ah, I am yearning for repose, for retirement—I feel exhausted and disgusted, and shall for the third time send in my resignation, which the Directory twice refused to accept."

He had said all this in a subdued and rapid voice, apparently only talking to himself—the only man worthy of learning the most secret thoughts of his soul—and still with proud disdain toward him who could overhear every word he said. He felt as though he were alone, and he only spoke and consulted with himself, notwithstanding the secretary's presence.

Another long pause ensued, Bonaparte pacing the room once more with rapid steps. Violent and impassioned feelings seemed to agitate his breast; for his eyes became more lustrous, his cheeks were suffused with an almost imperceptible blush, and he breathed heavily; as if oppressed by the closeness of the room, and in want of fresh air, for he stepped up to the window and opened it violently.

An expression of amazement escaped from his lips, for the landscape, which yesterday was clad in the gorgeous hues of autumn, now offered an entirely different aspect. Hoar-frost, dense and glittering, covered the trees and the verdure of the meadows; and the Noric Alps, which crowned the horizon with a majestic wreath, had adorned themselves during the night with sparkling robes of snow and brilliant diadems of ice.

Bonaparte looked at the unexpected spectacle long and thoughtfully. "What a country!" He then whispered, "Snow and ice in the first part of October! Very well! we must make peace!" †

He closed the window and returned to the desk.

"Give me the army register," he said to Bourrienne, and took a seat at his side.

Bourrienne laid the books and papers in succession before him, and Bonaparte read and examined them with close attention.

---

* Mémoires de Monsieur de Bourrienne, vol. i., p. 33.

* Bonaparte's own words. See "Mémoires d'un Homme d'État, vol. iv., p. 37».

† Bonaparte's own words. Bourrienne, vol. i., p. 313.

"Yes," he then said, after a long pause, "it is true I have an army of nearly eighty thousand men; I have to feed and pay them, but, on the battle-field, I could not count on more than sixty thousand men. I should win the battle, but lose again twenty thousand men in killed, wounded, and prisoners. How, then, should I be able to resist the united Austrian forces, which would hasten to the assistance of Vienna? It would take the armies on the Rhine more than a month to come up in supporting distance, and in the course of two weeks the snow will have blocked up all roads and mountain-passes. I am determined, therefore, to make peace. Venice must pay for the war, and the frontier of the Rhine. The Directory and the learned lawyers may say what they please.* Write, Bourrienne, I will now dictate my reply."

Bourrienne took his pen; Bonaparte arose from his seat, and folding his arms on his breast, he resumed his promenade across the room, dictating slowly and clearly, so that every word dropped from his lips like a pearl, until gradually the course of his speech grew more rapid and rolled along in an unbroken, fiery, and brilliant torrent.

"We shall sign the treaty of peace to-day," he dictated, in his imperious tone, "or break off the negotiations altogether. Peace will be advantageous to us—war with Austria will injure us; but war with England opens an extensive, highly important and brilliant field of action to our arms."

And now he explained to the Directory the advantages of a treaty of peace with Austria, and of a war with England, with logical acuteness and precision. His words were no less pointed and sharp than the edge of his sword, and as brief, stern, and cold as the utterances of a Cato.

He then paused for a moment, not in order to collect his thoughts, but only to give his secretary a few seconds' rest, and to get a breathing-spell for himself.

"Let us go on now," he said, after a short interval, and dictated in an enthusiastic voice, and with flaming eyes: "If I have been mistaken in my calculations, my heart is pure, and my intentions are well meaning. I have not listened to the promptings of glory, of vanity and ambition; I have only regarded the welfare of the country and government. If they should not approve of my actions and views, nothing is left to me but to step back into the crowd, put on the wooden shoes of Cincinnatus, and give an example of respect for the government, and of aversion to mili-

tary rule, which has destroyed so many republics, and annihilated so many states." *

"Are you through?" asked Bonaparte, drawing a long breath.

"Yes, general, I am."

"Then take another sheet, my friend. We are going to write now to the sly fox who generally perceives every hole where he may slip in, and who has such an excellent nose that he scents every danger and every advantage from afar. But this time he has lost the trail and is entirely mistaken. I will, therefore, show him the way. 'To Citizen Talleyrand, Minister of Foreign Affairs.' Did you write the address?"

"Yes, general."

"Well, go on."

And without stopping a single time, and even without hesitating, Bonaparte dictated the following letter:

"In three or four hours, citizen minister, every thing will be decided—peace or war. I confess that I shall do every thing to make peace, in consequence of the advanced season and the slim prospect of achieving important successes.

"You know very little about the nations of the peninsula; they do not deserve that forty thousand French soldiers should be killed for their sake. I see from your letter that you always argue from unfounded premises. You fancy that liberty would make a great impression upon a lazy, superstitious, cowardly, and degraded people.

"You ask me to do miracles, and I cannot perform them. Ever since I came to Italy, the nation's desire for liberty and equality was not my ally, or at best it was but a very feeble one. Whatever is merely good to be mentioned in proclamations and printed speeches is worth no more than a novel.

"Hoping that the negotiations will have a favorable issue, I do not enter upon further details to enlighten you about many matters which apparently have been misunderstood. Only by prudence, sagacity, and determination we are able to realize great objects and surmount all obstacles; otherwise all our efforts will prove unavailing. Frequently there is but a single step from victory to ruin. In highly critical times, I have always noticed that a mere nothing decided the most important events.

"It is characteristic of our nation to be too rash and fiery in prosperity. If we adopt a sagacious policy, which is nothing but the result of the calculation of combination and chances as a base for our operations, we shall long remain the greatest nation and most powerful state in Europe—nay, more, we shall hold the balance of power, we shall make it incline wherever we desire, and if it were the will of Providence, it would be no impossibility to achieve in the course of a few years those great results which a glowing and excited imagination perhaps foresees, but which only a man of extraordinary coolness, perseverance, and prudence is able to accomplish if—" *

Bonaparte paused suddenly as if he had been about to betray a profound secret, and stopped exactly when it was not yet too late to keep it buried within his own breast.

"It is enough," he then said, "erase the last word and close the letter. What makes you look at me so strangely, Bourrienne?"

"I beg your pardon, general, I had a vision. It seemed to me as if an oriflamme were burning on your head, and I believe if all nations and all men could behold you as I saw you just now, they would believe once more in the fables of pagan mythology, and feel satisfied that Jove the Thunderer had deigned to descend once more into our human world."

Bonaparte smiled, and this smile lighted up his face, previously so stern and rigid.

"You are a flatterer and a courtier," he said, playfully pinching Bourrienne's ear so violently that the latter was scarcely able to conceal a shriek of pain under a smile. "Yes, indeed, you are a regular courtier, and the republic has done well to banish you, for flattery is something very aristocratic, and injurious to our stiff republican dignity. And what an idea, to compare me to Jove appearing on earth! Don't you know, then, you learned scholar and flatterer, that Jove, whenever he descended from Olympus, was in pursuit of a very worldly and entirely ungodly adventure? It would only remain for you to inform my Josephine that I was about to transform myself into an ox for the sake of some beautiful Europa, or drop down in the shape of a golden rain to gain the love of a Danae."

"General, the sagacious and spirited Josephine would believe the former to be impossible, for even if you should succeed in performing all the miracles of the world, you could never transform yourself into an ox."

"What! you compared me a minute ago with Jove, and now you doubt already whether I could accomplish what Jove has done!" exclaimed Bonaparte, laughing. "Ah, flatterer, you see I have caught you in your own meshes. But would my Josephine believe, then, that I could transform

myself into a golden rain for the purpose of winning a Danae, you arrant rogue?"

"Yes, general, but she always would take good care to be that Danae herself."

"Yes, indeed, you are right," replied Bonaparte, laughing even louder than before. "Josephine likes golden rains, and should they be ever so violent, she would not complain; for if they should immerse her up to the neck, in the course of a few hours she would have got rid of the whole valuable flood."

"Your wife is as liberal and generous as a princess, and that is the reason why she spends so much money. She scatters her charities with liberal hands."

"Yes, Josephine has a noble and magnanimous heart," exclaimed Napoleon, and his large blue eyes assumed a mild and tender expression. "She is a woman just as I like women—so gentle and good, so childlike and playful, so tender and affectionate, so passionate and odd! And at the same time so dignified and refined in her manners. Ah, you ought to have seen her at Milan receiving the princes and *noblesse* in her drawing-room. I assure you, my friend, the wife of little General Bonaparte looked and bore herself precisely like a queen holding a levee, and she was treated and honored as though she were one. Ah, you ought to have seen it!"

"I *did* see it, general. I was at Milan before coming here."

"Ah, yes, that is true. I had forgotten it. You lucky fellow, you saw my wife more recently than I did myself. Josephine is beautiful, is she not? No young girl can boast of more freshness, more grace, innocence, and loveliness. Whenever I am with her, I feel as contented, as happy and tranquil as a man who, on a very warm day, is reposing in the shade of a splendid myrtle-tree, and whenever I am far from her—"

Bonaparte paused, and a slight blush stole over his face. The young lover of twenty-eight had triumphed for a moment over the stern, calculating general, and the general was ashamed of it.

"This is no time to think of such things," he said, almost indignantly. "Seal the letters now, and dispatch a messenger to Paris. Ah, Paris! Would to God I were again there in my little house in the *Rue Chantereine*, alone and happy with Josephine! But in order to get there, I must first make peace here—peace with Austria, with the Emperor of Germany. Ah, I am afraid Germany will not be much elated by this treaty of peace which her emperor is going to conclude, and by which she may lose some of her most splendid fortresses on the Rhine."

---

* "Mémoires d'un Homme d'État," vol. iv., p. 551.

"And the Republic of Venice, general?"

"The Republic of Venice is about to disappear," exclaimed Bonaparte, frowning. "Venice has rendered herself unworthy of the name of a republic—she is about to disappear."

"General, the delegates of the republic were all day yesterday in your anteroom, vainly waiting for an audience."

"They will have to wait to-day likewise until I return from the conference which is to decide about war or peace. In either case, woe unto the Venetians! Tell them, Bourrienne, to wait until I return. And now, my carriage. I cannot let the Austrian plenipotentiaries wait any longer for my ultimatum."

CHAPTER VIII.

THE TREATY OF CAMPO FORMIO.

THE Austrian plenipotentiaries were at the large Alberga of Udine, waiting for General Bonaparte. Every thing was prepared for his reception; the table was set, and the cooks were only looking for the arrival of the French chieftain in order to serve up the magnificent *déjeuner* with which to-day's conference was to begin.

Count Louis Cobenzl and the Marquis de Gallo were in the dining-room, standing at the window and looking at the scenery.

"It is cold to-day," said Count Cobenzl, after a pause in the conversation. "For my part, I like cold weather, for it reminds me of the most memorable years of my life—of my sojourn at the court of the Russian Semiramis. But you, marquis, are probably reminded by this frosty weather even more sensibly of your beautiful Naples and the glowing sun of the south. The chilly air must make you homesick."

"That disease is unknown to me, count," said the marquis. "I am at home wherever I can serve my king and my country."

"But to-day, my dear marquis, you have to serve a foreign prince."

"Austria is the native country of my noble Queen Caroline," said the marquis, gravely, "and the empress is my king's daughter. The Austrian court, therefore, may command my whole power and ability."

"I am afraid that we are going to have hard work to-day, marquis," remarked Count Cobenzl, gloomily. "This French general is really a *sans-culotte* of the worst kind. He is entirely devoid of *noblesse, bon ton*, and refinement."

"My dear count, for my part I take this Bona-parte to be a very long-headed man, and I am sure we must be greatly on our guard to be able to wrest a few concessions from him."

"Do you really believe that, marquis?" asked the count, with an incredulous smile. "You did not see, then, how his marble face lighted up when I handed him the other day that autograph letter from his majesty the emperor? You did not see how he blushed with pleasure while reading it? Oh, I noticed it, and, at that moment, I said to myself: 'This republican bear is not insensible to the favors and affability of the great.' Flattery is a dish which he likes to eat; we will, therefore, feed him with it, and he will be ours, and do whatever we may want without even noticing it. The great Empress Catharine used to say: 'Bears are best tamed by sweetmeats, and republicans by titles and decorations.' Just see, marquis, how I am going to honor him! I let him drink his chocolate to-day from my most precious relic—from this cup here, which the great empress gave to me, and which you see contains the czarina's portrait. Ah, it was at the last festival at the *Ermitage* that she handed me the cup with chocolate, and, in order to give it its real value, she touched the rim of the cup with her own sublime lips, sipped of the chocolate, and then permitted me to drink where she had drunk. This cup, therefore, is one of my most cherished reminiscences of St. Petersburg, and little General Bonaparte may be very proud to be permitted to drink from Catharine's cup. Yes, yes, we will give sweetmeats to the bear, but afterward he must dance just as we please. We will not yield, but *he* must yield to us. Our demands ought to be as exorbitant as possible!"

"By straining a cord too much, you generally break it," said the Italian, thoughtfully. "General Bonaparte, I am afraid, will not consent to any thing derogatory to the honor and dignity of France. Besides, there is another bad feature about him—he is incorruptible, and even the titles and decorations of the Empress Catharine would not have tamed this republican. Let us proceed cautiously and prudently, count. Let us demand much, but yield in time, and be content with something less in order not to lose every thing."

"Austria can only consent to a peace which extends her boundaries, and enlarges her territory," exclaimed Cobenzl, hastily.

"You are right, certainly," replied the Marquis de Gallo, slowly; "but Austria cannot intend to aggrandize herself at the expense of France. What is that so-called Germany good for? Let Austria take from her whatever she wants—a piece of Bavaria, a piece of Prussia—I would not care if she even gave to France a piece of Germany, for instance the frontier of the Rhine. In the name of Heaven, I should think that the so-called German empire is decayed enough to permit us to break off a few of its pieces."

"You are very unmerciful toward the poor German empire," said Count Cobenzl, with a smile, "for you are no German, and owing to that, it seems you are much better qualified to act as Austrian plenipotentiary in this matter. Nevertheless it is odd and funny enough that in these negotiations in which the welfare of Germany is principally at stake, the Emperor of Germany should be represented by an Italian, and the French Republic by a Corsican!"

"You omit yourself, my dear count," said the marquis, politely. "You are the real representative of the German emperor, and I perceive that the emperor could not have intrusted the interests of Germany to better hands. But as you have permitted me to act as your adviser, I would beg you to remember that the welfare of Austria should precede the welfare of Germany. And—but listen! a carriage is approaching."

"It is General Bonaparte," said Count Cobenzl, hastening to the window. "Just see the splendid carriage in which he is coming. Six horses—four footmen on the box, and a whole squadron of lancers escorting him! And you believe this republican to be insensible to flattery? Ah, ha! we will give sweatmeats to the bear! Let us go and receive him."

He took the arm of the marquis, and both hastened to receive the general, whose carriage had just stopped at the door.

The Austrian plenipotentiaries met Bonaparte in the middle of the staircase and escorted him to the dining-room, where the *déjeuner* was waiting for him.

But Bonaparte declined the *déjeuner*, in spite of the repeated and most pressing requests of Count Cobenzl.

"At least take a cup of chocolate to warm yourself," urged the count. "Drink it out of this cup, general, and if it were only in order to increase its value in my eyes. The Empress Catharine gave it to me, and drank from it; and if you now use this cup likewise, I might boast of possessing a cup from which the greatest man and the greatest woman of this century have drunk!"

"I shall not drink, count!" replied Bonaparte, bluntly. "I will have nothing in common with this imperial Messalina, who, by her dissolute life, equally disgraced the dignity of the crown and

of womanhood. You see I am a strong-headed republican, who only understands to talk of business. Let us, therefore, attend to that at once."

Without waiting for an invitation, he sat down on the divan close to the breakfast-table, and, with a rapid gesture, motioned the two gentlemen to take seats at his side.

"I informed you of my ultimatum the day before yesterday," said Bonaparte, coldly; "have you taken it into consideration, and are you going to accept it?"

This blunt and hasty question, so directly at the point, disconcerted the two diplomatists.

"We will weigh and consider with you what can be done," said Count Cobenzl, timidly. "France asks too much and offers too little. Austria is ready to cede Belgium to France, and give up Lombardy, but in return she demands the whole territory of Venice, Mantua included."

"Mantua must remain with the new Cisalpine Republic!" exclaimed Bonaparte, vehemently. "That is one of the stipulations of my ultimatum, and you seem to have forgotten it, count. And you say nothing about the frontier of the Rhine, and of the fortress of Mentz, both of which I have claimed for France."

"But, general, the Rhine does not belong to Austria, and Mentz is garrisoned by German troops. We cannot give away what does not belong to us."

"Do not I give Venice to you?" exclaimed Bonaparte—"Venice, which, even at the present hour, is a sovereign state, and whose delegates are at my headquarters, waiting for my reply! The Emperor of Germany has certainly the right to give away a German fortress if he choose."

"Well, Austria is not indisposed to cede the frontier of the Rhine to France," remarked the Marquis de Gallo. "Austria is quite willing and ready to form a close alliance with France, in order to resist the ambitious schemes of Prussia."

"If Austria should acquire new territory in consequence of an understanding with France, she must be sure that no such right of aggrandizement should be granted to Prussia," said Count Cobenzl, hastily.

"France and Austria might pledge themselves in a secret treaty not to permit any further aggrandizement of Prussia, but to give back to her simply her former possessions on the Rhine," said De Gallo.

"No digressions, if you please!" exclaimed Bonaparte, impatiently. "Let us speak of my ultimatum. In the name of France, I have offered you peace, provided the territories on the left bank of the Rhine with their stipulated boundaries, including Mentz, be ceded to France, and provided, further, that the Adige form the boundary-line between Austria and the Cisalpine Republic, Mantua to belong to the latter. You cede Belgium to France, but, in return, we give you the continental possessions of Venice; only Corfu and the Ionian Islands are to fall to the share of France, and the Adige is to form the frontier of Venetian Austria."

"I told you already, general," said Count Cobenzl, with his most winning smile, "we cannot accept the last condition. We must have Mantua, likewise; in return, we give you Mentz; and not the Adige, but the Adda, must be our frontier."

"Ah! I see—new difficulties, new subterfuges!" exclaimed Bonaparte, and his eyes darted a flash of anger at the diplomatist.

This angry glance, however, was parried by the polite smile of the count, "I took the liberty of informing you likewise of our ultimatum, general," he said, gently, "and I am sorry to be compelled to declare that I shall have to leave this place unless our terms be acceded to. But in that case, I shall hold you responsible for the blood of the thousands which may be shed in consequence."

Bonaparte jumped up, with flaming eyes, and lips quivering with rage.

"You dare to threaten me!" he shouted, angrily. "You resort to subterfuge after subterfuge. Then you are determined to have war? Very well, you shall have it."

He extended his arm hastily and seized the precious cup which the Empress Catharine had given to Count Cobenzl, and, with an impetuous motion hurled it to the ground where it broke to pieces with a loud crash.

"See there!" he shouted in a thundering voice. "Your Austrian monarchy shall be shattered like this cup within less than three months. I promise you that."

Without deigning to cast another glance upon the two gentlemen, he hurried with rapid steps to the door, and left the room.

Pale with anger and dismay, Count Cobenzl stared at the débris of the precious cup, which so long had been the pride and joy of his heart.

"He is leaving," muttered the Marquis de Gallo. "Shall we let him go, count?"

"How is that bear to be kept here?" asked the count, sighing, and shrugging his shoulders.

At this moment Bonaparte's powerful voice was heard in the anteroom, calling out:

"An orderly—quick!"

"He calls out of the window," whispered the marquis. "Let us hear what he has got to say."

The two plenipotentiaries slipped on tiptoe to the window, cautiously peeping from behind the curtains. They saw a French lancer galloping up below, and stopping and saluting under the window of the adjoining room.

Again they heard Bonaparte's thundering voice "Ride over to the headquarters of Archduke Charles," shouted Bonaparte. "Tell him on my behalf that the armistice is at an end, and that hostilities will recommence from the present hour. That is all. Depart!"

Then they heard him close the window with a crash, and walk with loud steps through the anteroom.

The two plenipotentiaries looked at each other in dismay. "Count," whispered the marquis, "listen! he leaves and has threatened to shatter Austria. He is the man to fulfil his threat. My God, must we suffer him to depart in anger? Have you been authorized to do that?"

"Will you try to command the storm to stand still?" asked Count Cobenzl.

"Yes, I will try, for we must not break off the negotiations in this way and recommence hostilities. We must conciliate this terrible warrior!"

He rushed out of the room, and hastened through the anteroom and down-stairs to the front door.

Bonaparte had already entered his carriage; his escort had formed in line, the driver had seized the reins and whip in order to give the impatient horses the signal to start.

At this moment, the pale and humble face of the Marquis de Gallo appeared at the carriage door. Bonaparte did not seem to see him. Leaning back into the cushions, he gloomily looked up to heaven.

"General," said the marquis, imploringly, "I beseech you not to depart!"

"Marquis," replied Bonaparte, shrugging his shoulders, "it does not become me to remain peaceably among my enemies. War has been declared, for you have not accepted my ultimatum."

"But, general, I take the liberty to inform you that the Austrian plenipotentiaries have resolved to accept your ultimatum."

Bonaparte's marble countenance did not betray the slightest emotion of surprise and joy; his large eyes only cast a piercing glance upon the marquis.

"You accept it without subterfuge or reserve?" he asked, slowly.

"Yes, general, precisely as you have stated it. We are ready to sign the treaty of peace, and accept the ultimatum. Just be kind enough to alight once more, and continue the conference with us."

"No, sir," said Bonaparte, "*nulla vestigia retrorsam!* Being already in my carriage, I shall not return to you. Besides, the delegates of the Venetian Republic are waiting for me at Passeriano, and I believe it is time for me to inform them too of my ultimatum. At the end of three hours, I ask you, marquis, and Count Cobenzl to proceed to my headquarters at Passeriano. There we will take the various stipulations of the treaty into consideration, and agree upon the public and secret articles."

"But you forget, general, that your orderly is already on the way to the Austrian headquarters in order to announce the reopening of hostilities."

"That is true," said Napoleon, quietly. "Here, two orderlies. Follow the first orderly, and command him to return. You see, marquis, I believe in the sincerity of your assurances. In three hours, then, I shall expect you at Passeriano for the purpose of settling the details of the treaty. We shall sign it, however, on neutral ground. Do you see that tall building on the horizon?"

"Yes, general, it is the decayed old castle of Campo Formio."

"Well, in that castle, the treaty shall be signed. In three hours, then. Until then, farewell."

He nodded carelessly to the marquis, who, as humble as a vassal, at the feet of the throne, stood at the carriage door, constantly bowing deeply, and waving his plumed hat.

"Forward!" shouted Bonaparte, and the carriage, followed by a brilliant suite, rolled away. Bonaparte, carelessly leaning into the corner, muttered, with a stealthy smile: "It was a *coup de théâtre*, and it had evidently great success. They had to accept peace at my hands as a favor. Ah, if they had guessed how much I needed it myself! But these men are obtuse; they cannot see anything. They have no aim; they only live from minute to minute, and whenever they find a pre-

cipice on their route, they stumble over it, and are lost beyond redemption. My God, how scarce real men are! There are eighteen millions in Italy, and I have scarcely found two men among them. I want to save these two men, but the rest may fulfil their destiny. The Republic of Venice shall disappear from the earth—this cruel and bloodthirsty government shall be annihilated. We shall throw it as a prey to hungry Austria; but when the latter has devoured her, and stretched herself in the lazy languor of digestion, then it will be time for us to stir up Austria. Until then, peace with Austria—peace!"

Three hours later the treaty between Austria and France was signed at the old castle of Campo Formio. France, by this treaty, acquired Belgium, the left bank of the Rhine, and the fortress of Mentz. Austria acquired the Venetian territory. But to these acquisitions, which were published, secret articles were added. In these secret articles, France promised, in case Prussia should demand an enlargement of her dominions, like Austria, not to consent to it.

The Emperor of Austria, on his part, pledged himself to withdraw his troops, even before the conclusion of the treaty with the German empire, to be agreed upon at Rastadt, from all the fortresses on the Rhine—in other words, to surrender the German empire entirely to its French neighbors.

Austria had enlarged her territory, but, for this aggrandizement, Germany was to pay with her blood, and finally with her life. Austria had made peace with France at Campo Formio, and it was stipulated in the treaty that the German empire likewise should conclude peace with France. For this purpose, a congress was to meet at Rastadt; all German princes were to send their ambassadors to that fortress, in order to settle, jointly, with three representatives of the French Republic, the fate of the empire.

THE YOUNG QUEEN OF PRUSSIA.

CHAPTER IX.

QUEEN LOUISA.

THE most noble Countess von Voss, mistress of ceremonies at the court of Prussia, was pacing the anteroom of Queen Louisa in the most excited manner. She wore the regular court dress—a long black robe and a large cap of black crape. In her white hands, half covered with black silk gloves, she held a gorgeous fan, which she now impatiently opened and closed, and then again slowly moved up and down like a musical leader's *baton.*

If anybody had been present to observe her, the noble mistress of ceremonies would not have permitted herself such open manifestations of her impatience. Fortunately, however, she was quite alone, and under these circumstances even a mistress of ceremonies at the royal court might feel at liberty to violate the rules of that etiquette which on all other occasions was the noble lady's most sacred gospel.

Etiquette, however, was just now the motive of her intense excitement, and in its interest she was going to fight a battle on that very spot in Queen Louisa's anteroom.

"Now or never!" she murmured. "What I was at liberty to overlook as long as Frederick William and Louisa were merely 'their royal highnesses, the crown prince and crown princess,' I cannot permit any longer now that they have ascended the royal throne. Hence I am determined to speak to the young king on this first day of his reign[*] in as emphatic and sincere a manner as is required by a faithful discharge of my responsible duties."

Just at that moment the large folding doors were opened, and a tall and slender young man in a dashing uniform entered the room. It was

[*] November 17, 1797.

young King Frederick William III., on his return from the interior palace-yard where he had received the oath of allegiance at the hands of the generals of the monarchy.

The noble and youthful countenance of this king of twenty-seven years was grave and stern, but from his large blue eyes the kindness and gentleness of his excellent heart was beaming, and his handsome and good-natured features breathed a wonderful spirit of serenity and sympathy.

He crossed the room with rapid and noiseless steps, and, politely bowing to the mistress of ceremonies, approached the opposite door.

But the mistress of ceremonies, evidently anxious to prevent him from opening that door, placed herself in front of it and gravely said to him:

"Your majesty, it is impossible. I cannot permit etiquette to be violated in this manner, and I must beg your majesty to inform me most graciously of what you are going to do in these rooms?"

"Well," said the king, with a pleasant smile, "I am going to do to-day what I am in the habit of doing every day at this hour—I am going to pay a visit to my wife."

"To your *wife!*" exclaimed the mistress of ceremonies, in dismay. "But, your majesty, a king has no *wife!*"

"Ah! in that case a king would be a very wretched being," said the king, smiling, "and, for my part, I would sooner give up my crown than my beloved wife."

"Good Heaven, your majesty, you may certainly have a wife, but let me implore you not to apply that vulgar name to her majesty in the presence of other people. It is contrary to etiquette and injurious to the respect due to royalty."

"My dear countess," said the young king, gravely, "I believe, on the contrary, that it will only increase the respect which people will feel for us, if her majesty remains a woman in the noblest and truest meaning of the word, and my wife—I beg your pardon, I was going to say the queen—is such a woman. And now, my dear countess, permit me to go to her."

"No," exclaimed the mistress of ceremonies, resolutely. "Your majesty must first condescend to listen to me. For an hour already I have been waiting here for your majesty's arrival, and you must now graciously permit me to speak to you as frankly and sincerely as is required by my duty and official position."

"Well, I will listen to you, my dear countess," said the king, with an inaudible sigh.

"Your majesty," said the mistress of ceremonies, "I consider it my duty to beseech your majesty on this memorable day to confer upon me the power of enforcing the privileges of my office with more severity and firmness."

"And to submit myself to your sceptre. That is what you want me to do, I suppose, dear countess?" asked the king, smiling.

"Sire, at all events it is impossible to keep up the dignity and majesty of royalty if the king and queen themselves openly defy the laws of etiquette."

"Ah!" exclaimed the king, sharply, "not a word against the queen, if you please, my dear mistress of ceremonies! You may accuse me just as much as you please, but pray let me hear no more complaints about my Louisa! Well, then, tell me now what new derelictions I have been guilty of."

"Sire," said the countess, who did not fail to notice the almost imperceptible smile playing on the king's lips—"sire, I perceive that your majesty is laughing at me; nevertheless, I deem it incumbent on me to raise my warning voice. Etiquette is something sublime and holy—it is the sacred wall separating the sovereign from his people. If that ill-starred queen, Marie Antoinette, had not torn down this wall, she would probably have met with a less lamentable end."

"Ah! countess, you really go too far; you even threaten me with the guillotine," exclaimed the king, good-naturedly. "Indeed, I am afraid I must have committed a great crime against etiquette. Tell me, therefore, where you wish to see a change, and I pledge you my word I shall grant your request if it be in my power to do so."

"Sire," begged the mistress of ceremonies, in a low and impressive voice, "let me implore you to be in your palace less of a father and husband, and more of a king, at least in the presence of others. It frequently occurs that your majesty, before other people, addresses the queen quite un-

ceremoniously with 'thou,' nay, your majesty even in speaking of her majesty to strangers or servants, often briefly calls the queen 'my wife.' Sire, all that might be overlooked in the modest family circle and house of a crown prince, but it cannot be excused in the palace of a king."

"Then," asked the king, smiling, "this house of mine has been transformed into a palace since yesterday?"

"Assuredly, sire, you do not mean to say that you will remain in this humble house after your accession to the throne?" exclaimed the mistress of ceremonies, in dismay.

"Now tell me sincerely, my dear countess, cannot we remain in this house?"

"I assure your majesty it is altogether out of the question. How would it be possible to keep up the court of a king and queen in so small a house with becoming dignity? The queen's household has to be largely increased; hereafter we must have four ladies of honor, four ladies of the bedchamber, and other servants in the same proportion. According to the rules of etiquette, Sire, you must likewise enlarge your own household. A king must have two adjutant-generals, four chamberlains, four gentlemen of the bedchamber, and—"

"Hold on," exclaimed the king, smiling, "my household fortunately does not belong to the department of the mistress of ceremonies, and therefore we need not allude to it. As to your other propositions and wishes, I shall take them into consideration, for I hope you are through now."

"No, your majesty, I am not. I have to mention a good many other things, and I must do so to-day—my duty requires it," said the mistress of ceremonies, in a dignified manner.

The king cast a wistful glance toward the door.

"Well, if your duty requires it, you may proceed," he said, with a loud sigh.

"I must beseech your majesty to assist me in the discharge of my onerous duties. If the king and queen themselves will submit to the rigorous and just requirements of etiquette, I shall be able to compel the whole court likewise strictly to adhere to those salutary rules. Nowadays, however, a spirit of innovation and disinclination to observe the old-established ceremonies and customs, which deeply afflicts me, and which I cannot but deem highly pernicious, is gaining ground everywhere. It has even now infected the ladies and gentlemen of the court. And having often heard your majesty, in conversation with her majesty the queen, contrary to etiquette, use the vulgar German language instead of the

French tongue, which is the language of the courts throughout Germany, they believe they have a perfect right to speak German whenever they please. Yes, it has become a regular custom among them to salute each other at breakfast with a German ' *Guten morgen !*' * That is an innovation which should not be permitted to anybody, without first obtaining the consent of her majesty's mistress of ceremonies and your majesty's master of ceremonies."

"I beg your pardon," said the king, gravely, "as to this point, I altogether differ from you. No etiquette should forbid German gentlemen or German ladies to converse in their mother tongue, and it is unnatural and mere affectation to issue such orders. In order to become fully conscious of their national dignity, they should especially value and love their own language, and no longer deign to use in its place the tongue of a people who have shed the blood of their king and queen, and whose deplorable example now causes all thrones to tremble. Would to God that the custom of using the German language would become more and more prevalent at my court, for it behooves Germans to feel and think and speak like Germans; and that will also be the most reliable bulwark against the bloody waves of the French Republic, in case it should desire to invade Germany. Now you know my views, my dear mistress of ceremonies, and if your book of ceremonies prescribes that all court officers should converse in French, I request you to expunge that article and to insert in its place the following: ' Prussia, being a German state, of course everybody is at liberty to speak German.' This will also be the rule at court, except in the presence of persons not familiar with the German language. Pray don't forget that, my dear countess, and now, being so implacable a guardian of that door, and of the laws of etiquette, I request you to go to her majesty the queen, and ask her if I may have the honor of waiting upon her majesty. I should like to present my respects to her majesty; and I trust she will graciously grant my request." †

The mistress of ceremonies bowed deeply, her face radiant with joy, and then rapidly entered the adjoining room.

The king looked after her for a moment, with a peculiar smile.

"She has to pass through six large rooms before reaching Louisa's boudoir," he murmured; " this door, however, directly leads to her through the small hall and the other anteroom. That is the shortest road to her, and I shall take it."

Without hesitating any longer, the king hastily opened the small side door, slipped through the silent hall and across the small anteroom, and knocked at the large and heavily-curtained door.

A sweet female voice exclaimed, "Come in!" and the king immediately opened the door. A lady in deep mourning came to meet him, extending her hands toward him.

"Oh, my heart told me that it was you, my dearest!" she exclaimed, and her glorious blue eyes gazed upon him with an indescribable expression of impassioned tenderness.

The king looked at her with a dreamy smile, quite absorbed in her aspect. And indeed it was a charming and beautiful sight presented by this young queen of twenty years.

Her blue eyes were beaming in the full fire of youth, enthusiasm, and happiness; a sweet smile was always playing on her finely-formed mouth, with the ripe cherry lips. On both sides of her slightly-blushing cheeks her splendid auburn hair was flowing down in waving ringlets; her noble and pure forehead arose above a nose of classical regularity, and her figure, so proud and yet so charming, so luxuriant and yet so chaste, full of true royal dignity and winning womanly grace, was in complete harmony with her lovely and youthful features.

"Well?" asked the queen, smiling. "Not a word of welcome from you, my beloved husband?"

"I only say to you, God bless you on your new path, and may He preserve you to me as long as I live!" replied the king, deeply moved, and embracing his queen with gushing tenderness.

She encircled his neck with her soft, white arms, and leaned her head with a happy smile upon his shoulder. Thus they reposed in each other's arms, silent in their unutterable delight, solemnly moved in the profound consciousness of their eternal and imperishable love.

Suddenly they were interrupted in their blissful dream by a low cry, and when they quickly turned around in a somewhat startled manner, they beheld the Countess von Voss, mistress of ceremonies, standing in the open door, and gloomily gazing upon them.

The king could not help laughing.

"Do you see now, my dear countess?" he said. "My wife and I see each other without any previous interruption as often as we want to do so, and that is precisely as it ought to be in a Chris-

---

* Vide Ludwig Haüsser's "History of Germany," vol. II.

† The king's own words.—Vide "Characterzüge und Historische Fragmente aus dem Leben des Königs von Preussen, Friedrich Wilhelm III. Gesammelt und herausgegeben von R. Fr. Eylert, Bishop, u.s.w. Th. II., p. 21.

tian family. But you are a charming mistress of ceremonies, and hereafter we will call you *Dame d'Etiquette.** Moreover, I will comply with your wishes as much as I can."

He kindly nodded to her, and the mistress of ceremonies, well aware of the meaning of this nod, withdrew with a sigh, closing the door as she went out.

The queen looked up to her husband with a smile.

"Was it again some quarrel about etiquette?" she asked.

"Yes, and a quarrel of the worst kind," replied the king, quickly. "The mistress of ceremonies demands that I should always be announced to you before entering your room, Louisa."

"Oh, you are always announced here," she exclaimed, tenderly; "my heart always indicates your approach—and that herald is altogether sufficient, and it pleases me much better than the stern countenance of our worthy mistress of ceremonies."

"It is the herald of my happiness," said the king, fervently, laying his arm upon his wife's shoulder, and gently drawing her to his heart.

"Do you know what I am thinking of just now?" asked the queen, after a short pause. "I believe the mistress of ceremonies will get up a large number of new rules, and lecture me considerably about the duties of a queen in regard to the laws of etiquette."

"I believe you are right," said the king, smiling.

"But I don't believe *she* is right!" exclaimed the queen, and, closely nestling in her husband's arms, she added: "Tell me, my lord and king, inasmuch as this is the first time that you come to me as a king, have I not the right to ask a few favors of you, and to pray you to grant my requests?"

"Yes, you have that right, my charming queen," said the king, merrily; "and I pledge you my word that your wishes shall be fulfilled, whatever they may be."

"Well, then," said the queen, joyfully, "there are four wishes that I should like you to grant. Come, sit down here by my side, on this small sofa, put your arm around my waist, and, that I may feel that I am resting under your protection, let me lean my head upon your shoulder, like the ivy supporting itself on the trunk of the strong oak. And now listen to my wishes. In the first place, I want you to allow me to be a wife and mother in my own house, without any restraint

whatever, and to fulfil my sacred duties as such without fear and without regard to etiquette. Do you grant this wish?"

"Most cordially and joyfully, in spite of all mistresses of ceremonies!" replied the king.

The queen nodded gently and smiled. "Secondly," she continued, "I beg you, my beloved husband, on your own part, not to permit etiquette to do violence to your feelings toward me, and always to call me, even in the presence of others, your 'wife,' and not 'her majesty the queen.' Will you grant that, too, my dearest friend?"

The king bent over her and kissed her beautiful hair.

"Louisa," he whispered, "you know how to read my heart, and, generous as you always are, you pray me to grant what is only my own dearest wish. Yes, Louisa, we will always call each other by those most honorable of our titles, 'husband and wife.' And now, your third wish, my dear wife?"

"Ah, I have some fears about this third wish of mine," sighed the queen, looking up to her husband with a sweet smile. "I am afraid you cannot grant it, and the mistress of ceremonies, perhaps, was right when she told me etiquette would prevent you from complying with it."

"Ah, the worthy mistress of ceremonies has lectured you also to-day already?" asked the king, laughing.

The queen nodded. "She has communicated to me several important sections from the 'book of ceremonies,'" she sighed. "But all that shall not deter me from mentioning my third wish to you. I ask you, my Frederick, to request the king to permit my husband to live as plainly and modestly as heretofore. Let the king give his state festivals in the large royal palace of his ancestors—let him receive in those vast and gorgeous halls the homage of his subjects, and the visits of foreign princes, and let the queen assist him on such occasions. But these duties of royalty once attended to, may we not be permitted, like all others, to go home, and in the midst of our dear little family circle repose after the fatiguing pomp and splendor of the festivities? Let us not give up our beloved home for the large royal palace! Do not ask me to leave a house in which I have passed the happiest and finest days of my life. See, here in these dear old rooms of mine, every thing reminds me of you, and whenever I am walking through them, the whole secret history of our love and happiness stands again before my eyes. Here, in this room, we saw each other for the first time after my arrival in Berlin, alone and

---

* The king's own words.—Vide Eylert, part ii., p. 93.

3

without witnesses. Here you imprinted the first kiss upon your wife's lips, and, like a heavenly smile, it penetrated deep into my soul, and it has remained in my heart like a little guardian angel of our love. Since that day, even in the fullest tide of happiness, I always feel so devout and grateful to God; and whenever you kiss me, the little angel in my heart is praying for you, and whenever I am praying, he kisses you."

"Oh, Louisa, you are my angel—my guardian angel!" exclaimed the king, enthusiastically.

The queen apparently did not notice this interruption—she was entirely absorbed in her recollections. "On this sofa here," she said, "we were often seated in fervent embrace like to-day, and when every thing around us was silent, our hearts spoke only the louder to each other, and often have I heard here from your lips the most sublime and sacred revelations of your noble, pure, and manly soul. In my adjoining cabinet, you were once standing at the window, gloomy and downcast; a cloud was covering your brow, and I knew you had heard again sorrowful tidings in your father's palace. But no complaint ever dropped from your lips, for you always were a good and dutiful son, and even to me you never alluded to your father's failings. I knew what you were suffering, but I knew also that at that hour I had the power to dispel all the clouds from your brow, and to make your eyes radiant with joy and happiness. Softly approaching you, I laid my arm around your neck, and my head on your breast, and thereupon I whispered three words which only God and my husband's ears were to hear. And you heard them, and you uttered a loud cry of joy, and before I knew how it happened, I saw you on your knees before me, kissing my feet and the hem of my garment, and applying a name to me that sounded like heavenly music, and made my heart overflow with ecstasy and suffused my cheeks with a deep blush. And I don't know again how it happened, but I felt that I was kneeling by your side, and we were lifting up our folded hands to heaven, thanking God for the great bliss He had vouchsafed to us, and praying Him to bless our child, unknown to us as yet, but already so dearly beloved. Oh, and last, my own Frederick, do you remember that other hour in my bedroom? You were sitting at my bedside, with folded hands, praying, and yet, during your prayer, gazing upon me, while I was writhing with pain, and yet so supremely happy in my agony, for I knew that Nature at that hour was about to consecrate me for my most exalted and sacred vocation, and that God would bless our love with a visible pledge of our happiness. The mo-

mentous hour was at hand—a film covered my eyes, and I could only see the Holy Virgin surrounded by angels, on Guido Reni's splendid painting, opposite my bed. Suddenly a dazzling flash seemed to penetrate the darkness surrounding me, and through the silence of the room there resounded a voice that I had never heard before—the voice of my child. And at the sound of that voice I saw the angels descending from the painting and approaching my bedside in order to kiss me, and the Mother of God bent over me with a heavenly smile, exclaiming: 'Blessed is the wife who is a mother!' My consciousness left me—I believe my ineffable happiness made me faint."

"Yes, you fainted, beloved wife," said the king, gently nodding to her; "but the swoon had not dispelled the smile from your lips, nor the expression of rapturous joy from your features. You lay there as if overwhelmed with joy and fascinated by your ecstatic bliss. Knowing that you were inexpressibly happy, I felt no fear whatever—"

"Well, I awoke soon again," added the queen, joyfully. "I had no time to spare for a long swoon, for a question was burning in my heart. I turned my eyes toward you—you were standing in the middle of the room, holding the babe that, in its new little lace dress, had just been laid into your arms. My heart now commenced beating in my breast like a hammer. I looked at you, but my lips were not strong enough to utter the question. However, you understood me well enough, and drawing close to my bedside, and kneeling down and laying the babe into my arms, you said, in a voice which I shall never forget, 'Louisa, give your blessing to your son!' Ah, at that moment it seemed as if my ecstasy would rend my breast. I had to utter a loud scream, or I should have died from joy. 'A son!' I cried, 'I have given birth to a son!' And I drew my arms around you and the babe, and we wept tears—oh, such tears—"

She paused, overwhelmed with emotion, and burst into tears.

"Ah!" she whispered, deprecatingly, "I am very foolish—you will laugh at me."

But the king did not laugh, for his eyes also were moist; only he was ashamed of his tears and kept them back in his eyes. A pause ensued, and the queen laid her head upon the shoulder of her husband, who had drawn his arm around her waist. All at once she raised her head, and fixing her large and radiant eyes upon the deeply-moved face of the king, she asked:

"My Frederick, can we leave a house in which I bore you a son and crown prince? Will we give up our most sacred recollections for the sake of a large and gorgeous royal palace?"

"No, we will not," said the king, pressing his wife closer to his heart. "No, we will remain in this house of ours—we will not leave it. Our happiness has grown and prospered here, and here it shall bloom and bear fruit. Your wish shall be fulfilled; we will continue living here as man and wife, and if the king and queen have to give festivals and to receive numerous guests, then they will go over to the palace to comply with their royal duties, but in the evening they will return to their happy home."

"Oh, my friend, my beloved friend, how shall I thank you?" exclaimed the queen, encircling his neck with her arms, and imprinting a glowing kiss upon his lips.

"But now, dear wife, let me know your fourth wish," said the king, holding her in his arms. "I hope your last wish is a real one, and not merely calculated to render me happy, but one that also concerns yourself?"

"Oh, my fourth wish only concerns myself," said the queen, with an arch smile. "I can confide it to you, to you alone, and you must promise to keep it secret, and not to say a word about it to the mistress of ceremonies."

"I promise it most readily, dear Louisa."

"Well," said the queen, placing her husband's hand upon her heart, and gently stroking it with her fingers. "I believe during the coming winter we shall often have to be king and queen. Festivals will be given to us, and we shall have to give others in return; the country will do homage to the new sovereign, and the nobility will solemnly take the oath of allegiance to him. Hence there will be a great deal of royal pomp, but very little enjoyment for us during the winter. Well, I will not complain, but endeavor, to the best of my ability, to do honor to my exalted position by your side. In return, however, my beloved lord and friend—in return, next summer, when the roses are blooming, you must give me a day —a day that is to belong exclusively to myself; and on that day we will forget the cares of royalty, and only remember that we are a pair of happy young lovers. Of course, we shall not spend that day in Berlin, nor in Parez either; but like two merry birds, we will fly far, far away to my home in Mecklenburg, to the paradise of my early years—to the castle of Hohenzieritz; and no one shall know any thing about it. Without being previously announced, we will arrive there, and in the solitude of the old house and garden we will perform a charming little idyl. On that day you only belong to me, and to nobody else. On that day I am your wife and sweetheart and nothing else, and I shall provide amusement and food for you. Yes, dearest Frederick, I shall prepare your meals all alone, and set the table and carve for you. Oh, dear dear friend; give me such a day, such an idyl of happiness!"

"I give it to you and to myself, most joyfully; and let me confess, Louisa, I wish the winter were over already, and the morning of that beautiful day were dawning."

"Thanks—thousand thanks!" exclaimed the queen, enthusiastically. "Let the stiff and ceremonious days come now, and the sneaking, fawning courtiers and the incense of flattery. Through all the mist I shall constantly inhale the sweet fragrance of the roses of the future, and on the stiff gala-days I shall think of the idyl of that day that will dawn next summer and compensate me for all the annoyances and fatigues of court life."

The king placed his right hand on her head, as if to bless her, and with his left lifted up her face that was reposing on his breast. "And you really think, you charming, happy angel, that I do not understand you?" he asked, in a low voice. "Do you think I do not feel and know that you want to offer me this consolation and to comfort me by the hope of such a blissful day for the intervening time of care, fatigue, and restlessness? Oh, my dear Louisa, you need no such consolation, for God has intended you for a queen, and even the burdens and cares of your position will only surround you like enchanting genii. You know at all times how to find the right word and the right deed, and the Graces have showered upon you the most winning charms to fascinate all hearts, in whatever you may be doing. On the other hand, I am awkward and ill at ease; I know it only too well; my unhappy childhood, grief and cares of all kinds, have rendered my heart reserved and bashful. Perhaps I am not always lacking right ideas, but I fail only too often to find the right word for what I think and feel. Hereafter, my dear Louisa, frequent occasions will arise when you will have to speak for both of us. By means of your irresistible smile and genial conversation you will have to win the hearts of people, while I shall be content if I can only win their heads."

"Shall I be able to win their hearts?" asked the queen, musingly. "Oh, assist me, my dearest friend. Tell me what I have to do in order to be beloved by my people."

"Remain what you are, Louisa," said the king, gravely—"always remain as charming, graceful, and pure as I beheld you on the most glorious two days of my life, and as my inward eye always will behold you. Oh, I also have some charming recollections, and although I cannot narrate them in words as fascinating and glowing as yours, yet they are engraved no less vividly on my mind, and, like beautiful genii, accompany me everywhere. Only before others they are bashful and reticent like myself."

"Let me hear them, Frederick," begged the queen, tenderly leaning her beautiful head on her husband's shoulder. "Let us devote another hour to the recollections of the past."

"Yes, let another hour be devoted to the memories of past times," exclaimed the king, "for can there be any thing more attractive for me than to think of you and of that glorious hour when I saw you first? Shall I tell you all about it, Louisa?"

"Oh, do so, my beloved friend. Your words will sound to me like some beautiful piece of music that one likes better and understands better the more it is heard. Speak, then, Frederick, speak."

CHAPTER X.

THE KING'S RECOLLECTIONS.

"WELL," said the king, "whenever I look back into the past, every thing seems to me covered with a gray mist, through which only two stars and two lights are twinkling. The stars are your eyes, and the lights are the two days I alluded to before—the day on which I saw you for the first time, and the day on which you arrived in Berlin. Oh, Louisa, never shall I forget that first day! I call it the first day, because it was the first day of my real life. It was at Frankfort-on-the-Main, during the campaign on the Rhine. My father, the king, accompanied by myself, returned the visit that the Duke of Mecklenburg, your excellent father, had paid on the previous day. We met in a small and unpretending villa, situated in the midst of a large garden. The two sovereigns conversed long and seriously, and I was listening to them in silence. This silence was, perhaps, disagreeable to my father the king."

"'What do you think, your highness?' he suddenly asked your father. 'While we are talking about the military operations, will we not permit the young gentleman there to wait upon the ladies? As soon as we are through, I shall ask you to grant me the same privilege.'

"The duke readily assented, and calling the footman waiting in the anteroom, he ordered him to go with me to the ladies and to announce my visit to them. Being in the neighborhood of the seat of war, you know, little attention was paid to ceremonies. I followed the footman, who told me the ladies were in the garden, whither he conducted me. We walked through a long avenue and a number of side-paths. The footman, going before me, looked around in every direction without being able to discover the whereabouts of the ladies. Finally, at a bend in the avenue, we beheld a bower in the distance, and something white fluttering in it.

"'Ah, there is Princess Louisa,' said the footman, turning to me, and he then rapidly walked toward her. I followed him slowly and listlessly, and when he came back and told me Princess Louisa was ready to receive me, I was perhaps yet twenty yards from the rose-bower. I saw there a young lady rising from her seat, and accelerated my steps. Suddenly my heart commenced pulsating as it never had done before, and it seemed to me as if a door were bursting open in my heart and making it free, and as if a thousand voices in my soul were singing and shouting, 'There she is! There is the lady of your heart!' The closer I approached, the slower grew my steps, and I saw you standing in the entrance of the bower in a white dress, loosely covering your noble and charming figure, a gentle smile playing on your pure, sweet face, golden ringlets flowing down both sides of your rosy cheeks, and your head wreathed with the full and fragrant roses which seemed to bend down upon you from the bower in order to kiss and adorn you, your round white arms only half covered with clear lace sleeves, and a full-blown rose in your right hand which you had raised to your waist. And seeing you thus before me, I believed I had been removed from earth, and it seemed to me I beheld an angel of innocence and beauty, through whose voice Heaven wished to greet me." At last I stood close before you, and in my fascination I entirely forgot to salute you. I only looked at you. I only heard those jubilant voices in my heart, singing, 'There is your wife—the wife you will love now and forever!' It was no maudlin sentimentality, but a clear and well-defined consciousness which, like an inspiration, suddenly moistened my eyes with tears of joy.† Oh, Louisa, why am I no painter to perpetuate that sublime moment in a beautiful and glorious picture? But what I cannot do, shall be tried by others. A true artist shall render and eternize that moment for me,‡ so that

* Goethe saw the young princess at the same time, and speaks of her "divine beauty."

† The king's own words, vide Bishop Eylert's work, vol. ii., p. 22.

‡ This painting was afterward executed, and may now be seen at the royal palace of Berlin. The whole account of the first meeting of the two lovers is based upon the communication the king made himself to Bishop Eylert.

one day when we are gone, our son may look up to the painting and say: 'Such was my mother when my father first saw her. He believed he beheld an angel, and he was not mistaken, for she was the guardian angel of his whole life.'"

"Oh! you make me blush—you make me too happy, too happy!" exclaimed the queen, closing her husband's lips with a burning kiss. "Don't praise me too much, lest I should become proud and overbearing."

The king gently shook his head. "Only the stupid, the guilty, and the base are proud and overbearing," he said. "But, whoever has seen you, Louisa, on the day of your first arrival in Berlin, will never forget your sweet image in its radiance of grace, modesty, and loveliness. It was on a Sunday, a splendid clear day in winter, the day before Christmas, which was to become the greatest holiday of my life. A vast crowd had gathered in front of the Arsenal *Unter den Linden*. Every one was anxious to see you. At the entrance of the *Linden*, not far from the Opera-Place, a splendid triumphal arch had been erected, and here a committee of the citizens and a number of little girls were to welcome you to Berlin. In accordance with the rules of court etiquette, I was to await your arrival at the palace. But my eagerness to see you would not suffer me to remain there. Closely muffled in my military cloak, my cap drawn down over my face, in order not to be recognized by anybody, I had gone out among the crowd and, assisted by a trusty servant, obtained a place behind one of the pillars of the triumphal arch. Suddenly tremendous cheers burst forth from a hundred thousand throats, thousands of arms were waving white handkerchiefs from the windows and roofs of the houses, the bells were rung, the cannon commenced thundering, for you had just crossed the Brandenburger Gate. Alighting from your carriage, you walked up the *Linden* with your suite, the wildest enthusiasm greeting every step you made, and finally you entered the triumphal arch, not suspecting how near I was to you, and how fervently my heart was yearning for you. A number of little girls in white, with myrtle-branches in their hands, met you there; and one of them, bearing a myrtle-wreath on an embroidered cushion, presented it to you and recited a simple and touching poem. Oh, I see even now, how your eyes were glowing, how a profound emotion lighted up your features, and how, overpowered by your feelings, you bent down to the little girl, clasped her in your arms and kissed her eyes and lips. But behind you there stood the mistress of ceremonies, Countess von Voss, pale with indignation, and

trembling with horror at this unparalleled occurrence. She hastily tried to draw you back, and in her amazement she cried almost aloud, 'Good Heaven! how could your royal highness do that just now? It was contrary to good-breeding and etiquette!' Those were harsh and inconsiderate words, but in your happy mood you did not feel hurt, but quietly and cheerfully turned around to her and asked innocently and honestly: 'What! cannot I do so any more?' * Oh, Louisa, at that moment, and in consequence of your charming question, my eyes grew moist, and I could hardly refrain from rushing out of the crowd and pressing you to my heart, and kissing your eyes and lips as innocently and chastely as you had kissed those of the little girl.

"See," said the king, drawing a deep breath, and pausing for a minute, "those are the two great days of my life, and as you ask me now, what you ought to do in order to win the love of your people, I reply to you once more: Remain what you are, so that these beautiful pictures of you, which are engraved upon my heart, may always resemble you, and you will be sure to win all hearts. Oh, my Louisa, your task is an easy one, you only have to be true to yourself, you only have to follow your faithful companions the Graces, and success will never fail you. My task, however, is difficult, and I shall have to struggle, not only with the evil designs, the malice, and stupidity of others, but with my own inexperience, my want of knowledge, and a certain irresolution, resulting, however, merely from a correct appreciation of what I am lacking."

The queen with a rapid gesture placed her hand upon the king's shoulder.

"You must be more self-reliant, for you may safely trust yourself," she said, gravely. "Who could be satisfied with himself, if you were to despair? What sovereign could have the courage to grasp the sceptre, if your hands should shrink back from it?—your hands, as free from guilt and firm and strong as those of a true man should be! I know nothing about politics, and shall never dare to meddle with public affairs and to advise you in regard to them; but I know and feel that you will always be guided by what you believe to be the best interests of your people, and that you never will deviate from that course. The spirit of the Great Frederick is looking upon you; he will guide and bless you!"

The king seemed greatly surprised by these words.

"Do you divine my thoughts, Louisa?" he

---

* Eylert, vol. ii., p. 79.

asked. "Do you know my soul has been with him all the morning—that I thus conversed with him and repeated to myself every thing he said to me one day in a great and solemn hour. Oh, it was indeed a sacred hour, and never have I spoken of it to anybody, for every word would have looked to me like a desecration. But you, my noble wife, you can only consecrate and sanctify the advice I received in that momentous hour; and as I am telling you to-day about my most glorious reminiscences, you shall hear also what Frederick the Great once said to me."

The queen nodded approvingly, raising her head from his shoulder and folding her hands on her lap as if she were going to pray.

The king paused for a moment, and seemed to reflect.

"In 1785," he then said, "on a fine, warm summer day, I met the king in the garden at Sans-Souci. I was a youth of fifteen years at that time, strolling carelessly through the shrubbery and humming a song, when I suddenly beheld the king, who was seated on the bench under the large beech-tree, at no great distance from the Japanese palace. He was alone; two greyhounds were lying at his feet, in his hands he held his old cane, and his head reposed gently on the trunk of the beech-tree. A last beam of the setting sun was playing on his face, and rendered his glorious eyes even more radiant. I stood before him in reverential awe, and he gazed upon me with a kindly smile. Then he commenced examining me about my studies, and finally he drew a volume of La Fontaine's 'Fables' from his pocket, opened the book and asked me to translate the fable on the page he showed me. I did so—but when he afterward was going to praise me for the skill with which I had rendered it, I told him it was but yesterday that I had translated the same fable under the supervision of my teacher. A gentle smile immediately lighted up his face, and tenderly patting my cheeks, he said to me, in his sonorous, soft voice: 'That is right, my dear Fritz, always be honest and upright. Never try to seem what you are not—always be more than what you seem!' I never forgot that exhortation, and I have always abhorred falsehood and hypocrisy."

The queen gently laid her hand upon his heart. "Your eye is honest," she said, "and so is your heart. My Frederick is too proud and brave to utter a lie. And what did you say to your great ancestor?"

"I? He spoke to me—I stood before him and listened. He admonished me to be industrious, never to believe that I had learned enough; never to stand still, but always to struggle on. After that

he arose and, conversing with me all the time, slowly walked down the avenue leading to the garden gate. All at once he paused, and leaning upon his cane, his piercing eyes looked at me so long and searchingly, that his glance deeply entered into my heart. 'Well, Fritz,' he said, 'try to become a good man, a good man par excellence Great things are in store for you. I am at the end of my career, and my task is about accomplished. I am afraid that things will go pell-mell when I am dead. A portentous fermentation is going on everywhere, and the sovereigns, especially the King of France, instead of calming it and extirpating the causes that have produced it, unfortunately are deluded enough to fan the flame. The masses below commence moving already, and when the explosion finally takes place, the devil will be to pay. I am afraid your own position one day will be a most difficult one. Arm yourself, therefore, for the strife!—be firm!—think of me! Watch over our honor and our glory! Beware of injustice, but do not permit any one to treat you unjustly!' He paused again, and slowly walked on. While deeply moved and conscious of the importance of the interview, I inwardly repeated every word he had said, in order to remember them as long as I lived. We had now reached the obelisk, near the gate of Sans-Souci. The king here gave me his left hand, and with his uplifted right hand he pointed at the obelisk. 'Look at it,' he said, loudly and solemnly; 'the obelisk is tall and slender, and yet it stands firm amid the most furious storms. It says to you: *Ma force est ma droiture*. The culmination, the highest point overlooks and crowns the whole; it does not support it, however, but is supported by the whole mass underlying it, especially by the invisible foundation, deeply imbedded in the earth. This supporting foundation is the people in its unity. Always be on the side of the people, so that they will love and trust you, as they alone can render you strong and happy.' He cast another searching glance upon me, and gave me his hand. When I bent over it in order to kiss it, he imprinted a kiss on my forehead. 'Don't forget this hour,' he said kindly, nodding to me. He turned around, and accompanied by his greyhounds, slowly walked up the avenue again.* I never forgot that hour, and shall remember it as long as I live."

"And the spirit of the great Frederick will be with you and remain with you," said the queen, deeply moved.

"Would to God it were so!" sighed the king. "I know that I am weak and inexperienced; I

<hr>

* The king's own account to Bishop Eylert, in the latter's work, vol. i., p. 455.

stand in need of wise and experienced advisers; I—"

A rap at the door interrupted the king, and on his exclaiming, "Come in!" the door was opened and the court marshal appeared on the threshold.

"I humbly beg your majesty's pardon for venturing to disturb you," he said, bowing reverentially; "but I must request your majesty to decide a most important domestic matter—a matter that brooks no delay."

"Well, what is it?" said the king, rising and walking over to the marshal.

"Your majesty, it is about the bill of fare for the royal table, and I beseech your majesty to read and approve the following paper I have drawn up in regard to it."

With an obsequious bow, he presented a paper to the king, who read it slowly and attentively.

"What!" he suddenly asked, sharply, "two courses more than formerly?"

"Your majesty," replied the marshal, humbly, "it is for the table of a *king!*"

"And you believe that my stomach has grown larger since I am a king?" asked Frederick William. "No, sir, the meals shall remain the same as heretofore,* unless," he said, politely turning to the queen, "unless *you* desire a change, my dear?"

The queen archly shook her head. "No," she said, with a charming smile; "neither has my stomach grown larger since yesterday."

"There will be no change, then," said the king, dismissing the marshal.

"Just see," he said to the queen, when the courtier had disappeared, "what efforts they make in order to bring about a change in our simple and unassuming ways of living; they flatter us wherever they can, and even try to do so by means of our meals."

"As for ourselves, however, dearest, we will remember the words of your great uncle," said the queen, "and when they overwhelm us on all sides with their vain and ridiculous demands, we will remain firm and true to ourselves."

"Yes, Louisa," said the king, gravely, "and whatever our new life may have in store for us, we will remain the same as before."

Another rap at the door was heard, and a royal footman entered.

"Lieutenant-Colonel von Köckeritz, your majesty, requests an audience."

"Ah, yes, it is time," said the king, looking at the clock on the mantel-piece. "I sent him word to call on me at this hour. Farewell, Louisa, I must not let him wait."

He bowed to his wife, whose hand he tenderly pressed to his lips, and turned to the door.

The footman who had meantime stood at the door as straight as an arrow, waiting for the king's reply, now hastened to open both folding-doors.

"What!" asked the king, with a deprecating smile, "have I suddenly grown so much stouter that I can no longer pass out through one door?" *

The queen's eyes followed her husband's tall and commanding figure with a proud smile, and then raising her beautiful, radiant eyes with an indescribable expression to heaven, she whispered: "Oh, what a man! my husband!" †

CHAPTER XI.

THE YOUNG KING.

The king rapidly walked through the rooms and across the hall, separating his own rooms and apartments from those of the queen. He had scarcely entered his cabinet, when he opened the door of the anteroom, and exclaimed:

"Pray, come in, my dear Köckeritz."

A corpulent little gentleman, about fifty years of age, with a kind, good-natured face, small, vivacious eyes, denoting an excellent heart, but little ability, and large, broad lips, which never perhaps had uttered profound truths, but assuredly many pleasant jests, immediately appeared on the threshold.

While he was bowing respectfully, the king extended his hand to him.

"You have received my letter, my friend?" he asked.

"Yes, your majesty. I received it yesterday, and I have been studying it all night."

"And what are you going to reply to me?" asked the king, quickly. "Are you ready to accept the position I have tendered to you? Will you become my conscientious and impartial adviser—my true and devoted friend?"

"Your majesty," said the lieutenant-colonel, sighing, "I am afraid your majesty has too good an opinion of my abilities. When I read your truly sublime letter, my heart shuddered, and I said to myself, 'The king is mistaken about you. To fill the position he is offering to you, he needs a man of the highest ability and wisdom. The

---

* Vide Eylert, vol. i., p. 18.

* Vide Eylert, vol. i., p. 19.

† "O, welch ein Mann! mein Mann!"—Eylert, vol. ii., p. 157.

king has confounded your heart with your head.' Yes, your majesty, my heart is in the right place; it is brave, bold, and faithful, but my head lacks wisdom and knowledge. I am not a learned man, your majesty."

"But you are a man of good common-sense and excellent judgment, and that is worth more to me than profound learning," exclaimed the king. "I have observed you for years, and these extended observations have confirmed my conviction more and more that I was possessing in you a man who would be able one day to render me the most important services by his straightforwardness, his unerring judgment, his firm character, and well-tried honesty. I have a perfect right to trust you implicitly. I am a young man, as yet too ignorant of the world to rely exclusively upon myself, and not to fear lest dishonest men, in spite of the most earnest precautions, should deceive me. Hence every well-meant advice must be exceedingly welcome to me, and such advice I can expect at your hands, I pray you, sir, remain my friend, do not change your bearing toward me, become my adviser.* Köckeritz, will you reject my request?"

"No," exclaimed Herr von Köckeritz; "if that is all your majesty asks of me, I can promise it and fulfil my promise. Your majesty shall always find me to be a faithful, devoted, and honest servant."

"I ask more than that," said the king, gently. "Not only a faithful servant, but a devoted _friend_—a friend who will call my attention to my short-comings and errors. Assist me with your knowledge of men and human nature. For nobody is more liable to make mistakes in judging of men than a prince, and it cannot be otherwise. To a prince no one shows himself in his true character. Every one tries to fathom the weaknesses and inclinations of rulers—and then assumes such a mask as seems best calculated to accomplish his purposes. Hence, I expect you to look around quietly, without betraying your intentions, for honest and sagacious men, and to find out what positions they are able to fill in the most creditable manner." †

"I shall take pains, your majesty, to discover such men," said Herr von Köckeritz, gravely. "It seems to me, however, sire, that fortunately you have got many able and excellent men close at hand, and for that reason need not look very far for other assistants."

"To whom do you allude?" exclaimed the king, sharply, and with a slight frown.

* Vide "A letter to Lieutenant-Colonel von Köckeritz, by Frederick William III."

† Ibid.

Herr von Köckeritz cast a rapid glance upon the king's countenance and seemed to have read his thoughts upon his clouded brow.

"Your majesty," he said, gravely and slowly, "I do not mean to say any thing against Wöllner, the minister, and his two counsellors, Hermes and Hiller, nor against Lieutenant-General von Bischofswerder."

The frown had already disappeared from the king's brow. Stepping up to his desk, he seized a piece of paper there, which he handed to his friend.

"Just read that paper, and tell me what to do about it."

"Ah, Lieutenant-General von Bischofswerder has sent in his resignation!" exclaimed Herr von Köckeritz, when he had read the paper. "Well, I must confess that the general has a very fine nose, and that he acted most prudently."

"You believe, then, I would have dismissed him anyhow?"

"Yes, I believe so, your majesty."

"And you are right, Köckeritz. This gloomy and bigoted man has done a great deal of mischief in Prussia, and the genius of our country had veiled his head and fled before the spirits which Bischofswerder had called up. Oh, my friend, we have passed through a gloomy, disastrous period, and seen many evil spirits here, and been tormented by them. But not another word about it! It does not behoove me to judge the past, for it does not belong to me. Only the future is mine; and God grant when it has, in turn, become the past, that it may not judge me! Lieutenant-General von Bischofswerder was the friend and confidant of my lamented father, the king, and in that capacity I must and will honor him. I shall accept his resignation, but grant him an ample pension."

"That resolution is highly honorable to your majesty's heart," exclaimed Herr von Köckeritz, feelingly.

"As to Minister Wöllner," said the king, frowning, "in respectful remembrance of my lamented father's partiality for him, I shall not at once dismiss him, but leave it to himself to send in his resignation. Let him see if he will be able to reconcile himself to the new era, for a new era, I hope, is to dawn for Prussia—an era of toleration, enlightenment and true piety, that does not seek satisfaction in mere lip-service and church-going, but in good and pious deeds. Religion is not an offspring of the church, but the reverse is true; the church is an offspring of religion, and the church therefore, ought to be subordinate to religion, and never try to place itself above it.

Henceforth there shall be no more compulsion in matters of faith, and all fanatical persecutions shall cease. I honor religion myself; I devoutly follow its blessed precepts, and under no circumstances would I be the ruler of a people devoid of religion. But I know that religion always must remain a matter of the heart and of personal conviction, and if it is to promote virtue and righteousness, it must not, by a mere methodical constraint, be degraded to an empty and thoughtless ritualism. Hereafter Lutheran principles shall be strictly adhered to in religious affairs, for they are entirely in harmony with the spirit and Founder of our religion. No compulsory laws are necessary to maintain true religion in the country and to increase its salutary influence upon the happiness and morality of all classes of the people.* These, I am afraid, are principles which Minister Wöllner cannot adopt; and if he is an honest man, he will consequently send in his resignation. If he should not do so in the course of a few weeks, of course I shall dismiss him. You see, Köckeritz, I am speaking to you frankly and unreservedly, as if you were a true friend of mine, and I am treating you already as my adviser. Now tell me who are the men of whom you wished to speak, and whom you believe to be able and reliable."

The face of Herr von Köckeritz assumed an embarrassed and anxious air, but the king was waiting for an answer, and therefore he could not withhold it any longer.

"Well, your majesty," he said, somewhat hesitatingly, "I alluded to the minister of foreign affairs, Herr von Haugwitz, whom I believe to be an honest man, while I am equally satisfied that his first assistant, Lombard, is a man of excellent business qualifications and great ability."

The king nodded his assent. "I am entirely of your opinion," he said; "Minister von Haugwitz is not only an honest man, but an able-minded and skilful diplomatist, and an experienced statesman. I stand in need of his experience and knowledge, and as I moreover believe him to be a good patriot, he may remain at the head of his department."

A gleam of joy burst from the eyes of Herr von Köckeritz, but he quickly lowered them, in order not to betray his feelings.

"As to Lombard," said the king, "you are likewise right; he is an excellent and most able man, though a little tinctured with Jacobinism. His French blood infects him with all sorts of democratic notions. I wish he would get rid of

them, and I shall assist him in doing so, in case he should prove to be the man I take him for. His position is too exalted and important that I should not deem it desirable to see him occupy a place in society in accordance with the old established rules. I want him to apply for letters of nobility. I shall grant the application at once. Please, tell him so."

Herr von Köckeritz bowed silently.

"Is there anybody else whom you wish to recommend to me?" asked the king with an inquiring glance.

"Your majesty," said Köckeritz, "I do not know of anybody else. But I am sure your majesty will always find the right man for the right place. Even in my case, I trust, your majesty has done so, for if it is of importance for you to have a faithful and devoted servant close to your person, who values nothing in the world so greatly, who loves nothing so fervently, and adores nothing so much as his young king, then I am the right man, and in this regard I do not acknowledge any superior. And further, if it be of importance that your majesty should at all times hear the truth, then I am the right man again, for I hate falsehood, and how should I, therefore, ever be false toward your majesty, inasmuch as I love your majesty?"

"I believe you, I believe you," exclaimed the king, taking the lieutenant-colonel by the hand. "You love me and are an honest man; I shall, therefore, always hear the truth from you. But you shall inform yourself also of the state of public opinion concerning myself and my government, weigh the judgment passed on me and my counsellors, and if you believe it to be correct, then discuss it with men whom you know to be impartial and able to speak understandingly of the matter. Having thus ascertained public opinion and familiarized yourself with every thing, I expect you to lay the matter before me and tell me your opinion firmly and unreservedly. I shall never question your good intentions, but always endeavor to profit by your advice. And I shall now directly give you a trial. What do you think of the congress which met a few weeks ago at Rastadt, and at which the German empire is to negotiate a treaty of peace with France?"

"Your majesty, I believe it will be good for all of us to live at peace with France," exclaimed Herr von Köckeritz, earnestly. "If Prussia should quarrel with France, it would only afford Austria an opportunity to carry out its long-standing designs upon Bavaria, while Prussia would be occupied elsewhere; and in order not to be hindered by Prussia in doing so, Austria, who

* Vide "Menzel's Twenty Years of Prussian History," p. 534.

now has just concluded so favorable a treaty of peace with France at Campo Formio, would become the ally of France and thus strengthen her old hostility toward Prussia. A war between Austria and Prussia would be the unavoidable consequence; the whole of Germany would dissolve itself into parties favorable or hostile to us, and this state of affairs would give France an opportunity and a pretext to carry out her own predatory designs against Germany; and, while we would be fighting battles perhaps in Silesia and Bavaria, to seize the left bank of the Rhine."

"I am entirely of your opinion," exclaimed the king. "I am very glad to find my views in complete harmony with yours."

It is true Lieutenant-Colonel von Köckeritz was well aware of this, for all he had said just now was nothing but a repetition of what the king, while yet a crown prince, had often told him in their confidential conversations. But of this he took good care not to remind the king, and merely bowed with a grateful smile.

"Yes," added the king, "like you, I believe prudence and sound policy command us to remain at peace with France, and to form a closer alliance with this power. That is the only way for us to prevent Austria from realizing her schemes of aggrandizement. Austria, not France, is dangerous to us; the latter is our natural ally, and the former our natural adversary. Every step forward made by Austria in Germany, forces Prussia a step backward. Let Austria enlarge her territory in the south, toward Italy, but never shall I permit her to extend her northern and western frontiers farther into Germany. The peace of Campo Formio has given Venice to the Austrians but they never shall acquire Bavaria. It is Prussia's special task to induce France not to permit it, and, precisely for that reason, we must form a closer alliance with France. That, my dear Köckeritz, is *my* view of the political course that we should pursue in future. Peace abroad and peace at home! No violent commotions and convulsions, no rash innovations and changes. New institutions should gradually and by their own inherent force grow from the existing ones, for only in that case we may be sure that they really have taken root. I shall not head the world in the capacity of a creative and original reformer, but I shall always take pains to adopt such reforms as have proven valuable, and gradually to transform and improve such institutions as at present may be defective and objectionable. And in all these endeavors, my dear Köckeritz, you shall be my adviser and assistant. Will you promise me your aid?"

He looked earnestly and anxiously at the lieutenant-colonel and gave him his hand.

"I promise it to your majesty," exclaimed Herr von Köckeritz, gravely, and grasping the king's hand.

"Well," said the king, "with this solemn pledge you may enter upon your official position, and I am satisfied that my choice has been a judicious one. Remain what you are, sir, an upright, honest man! As far as I am concerned, you may always be sure of my heart-felt gratitude; on the other hand, however, you should remember that you not only oblige me personally, but that I request you, as it were, in the name of the state, to labor for the latter. At some future time you will gain the sweet conviction and satisfaction that you have done not a little for the welfare of the commonwealth and thereby earned the thankfulness of every well-meaning patriot. I am sure there cannot be a sweeter reward for a man of true honor and ambition like yourself." [*]

CHAPTER XII.

FREDERICK GENTZ.

It was yet early in the morning; the blinds of all the windows in the *Taubenstrasse* were as yet firmly closed, and only in a single house an active, bustling life prevailed. At its door there stood a heavy travelling-coach which a footman was busily engaged in loading with a large number of trunks, boxes, and packages. In the rooms of the first story people were very active; industrious hands were assiduously occupied with packing up things generally; straw was wrapped around the furniture, and then covered with linen bags. The looking-glasses and paintings were taken from the walls and laid into wooden boxes, the curtains were removed from the windows, and every thing indicated that the inmates of the house were not only about to set out on a journey, but entirely to give up their former mode of living.

Such was really the case, and while the servants filled the anterooms and the halls with the noise of their preparations, those for whom all this bustle and activity took place were in their parlor, in a grave and gloomy mood.

There were two of them—a lady, scarcely twenty-four years of age, and a gentleman, about twelve years older. She was a delicate and lovely woman, with a pale, sad face, while he was a vig-

[*] Vide the king's letter to Lieutenant-Colonel von Köckeritz.

orous, stout man with full, round features, and large vivacious eyes which at present tried to look grave and afflicted without being able to do so; she wore a travelling-dress, while his was an elegant morning costume.

Both of them had been silent for awhile, standing at the window, or rather at different windows, and witnessing the removal of the trunks and packages to the travelling-coach. Finally, the lady, with a deep sigh, turned from the window and approached the gentleman who had likewise stepped back into the room.

"I believe the trunks are all in the carriage, and I can set out now, Frederick," she said, in a low and tremulous voice.

He nodded, and extended his hand toward her. "And you are not angry with me, Julia?" he asked.

She did not take his hand, but only looked up to him with eyes full of eloquent grief. "I am not angry," she said. "I pray to God that He may forgive you."

"And will you forgive me, too, Julia? For I know I have sinned grievously against you. I have made you shed many tears—I have rendered you wretched and miserable for two years, and these two years will cast a gray shadow over your whole future. When you first entered this room, you were an innocent young girl with rosy cheeks and radiant eyes, and now, as you leave it forever, you are a poor, pale woman with a broken heart and dimmed eyes."

"A *divorced* wife, that is all," she whispered, almost inaudibly. "I came here with a heart overflowing with happiness—I leave you now with a heart full of wretchedness. I came here with the joyous resolution and fixed purpose to render you a happy husband, and I leave you now with the painful consciousness that I have not bestowed upon you that happiness which I sought so earnestly to obtain for myself. Ah, it is very sad and bitter to be under the necessity of accepting this as the only result of two long years!"

"Yes, it is very sad," he said, sighing. "But after all, it is no fault of ours. There was a dissonance in our married life from the start, and for that reason there never could be any genuine harmony between us. This dissonance—well, at the present hour I may confess it to you, too—this dissonance simply was the fact that I *never* loved you!"

A convulsive twitching contracted the pale lips of the poor lady. "You were a great hypocrite, then," she whispered, "for your words, your solemn vows never made me suspect it."

"Yes, I was a hypocrite, a wretch, a coward!"

he exclaimed, impetuously. "They overwhelmed me with exhortations, supplications, and representations. They knew so well to flatter me with the idea that the beautiful, wealthy, and much-courted heiress, Julia Gilly, had fallen in love with me, the poor, unknown Frederick Gentz, the humble military counsellor. They knew so well to depict to me the triumph I would obtain by marrying you, to the great chagrin of all your other suitors. Flattery intoxicates me, and a success, a triumph over others, fills me with the wildest delight. My father spoke of my debts, my creditors threatened me with suits and imprisonment—"

"And thus," she interrupted him—"thus you sacrificed me to your vanity and to your debts—you falsely vowed a love to me which you never felt, and accepted my hand. My father paid your debts, you solemnly promised to all of us not to incur any new ones, but you utterly broke your pledges. Instead of squandering hundreds as heretofore, you henceforth lavished thousands, until my whole maternal property was gone—until my father, in a towering passion, turned his back upon us and swore never to see us again. The creditors, the debts, the embarrassments, reappeared, and as I had no money left with which to extricate you from your difficulties, you thought you owed me no further respect and were not under the necessity of remembering that I was your wife. You had a number of love-affairs, as I knew very well, but was silent. Love-letters arrived for you, not from one woman with whom you had fallen in love, but from God knows how many. I was aware of it and was silent. And when you were finally shameless enough to let the whole city witness your passion for an actress—when all Berlin spoke contemptuously of this flame of yours and of the follies you committed in consequence—then I could be silent no longer, and my honor and dignity commanded me to apply for a divorce."

"And every one must acknowledge that you were perfectly right. As a friend I could not have given you myself any other advice, for I shall not and cannot alter my nature. I am unable to accustom myself to a quiet and happy family life—domestic felicity is repulsive to me, and a feeling of restraint makes me rear and plunge like the noble charger feeling his bit and bridle for the first time. I can bear no chains, Julia, not even those of an excellent and affectionate wife such as you have been to me."

"You can bear no chains," she said, bitterly, "and yet you are always in chains—in the chains of your debts, your love-affairs, and your frivolity. Oh, listen to me—heed my words for once. They are as solemn as though they were uttered on a death-bed, for we shall never see each other again. Fancy a mother were speaking to you—a mother tenderly loving you. For I confess to you that I still love you, Gentz—my heart cannot yet break loose from you, and even now that I have to abandon you, I feel that I shall forever remain tenderly attached to you. Oh, true love is ever hopeful, and that was the reason why I remained in your house, although my father had applied for a divorce. I was always in hopes that your heart would return to me—oh, I did not suspect that you had never loved me!—and thus I hoped in vain, and must go now, for our divorce will be proclaimed to-day, and honor forbids me to remain here any longer. But now that I am going, listen once more to the warning voice of a friend. Frederick Gentz, turn back! Pursue no longer the slippery path of frivolity and voluptuousness. Break loose from the meshes of pleasures and sensuality. God has given you a noble mind, a powerful intellect—make good use of your surpassing abilities. Become as great and illustrious as Providence has intended you if you but be true to yourself. See, I believe in you, and although you only seem to live for pleasure and enjoyment, I know you are destined to accomplish great things, provided you strive to do so. Oh, let me beseech you to change your course, and to emerge from this whirlpool of dissipation and profligacy. Close your ears to the alluring songs of the sirens, and listen to the sublime voices resounding in your breast and calling you to the path of glory and honor. Follow them, Frederick Gentz—be a man, do not drift any longer aimlessly in an open boat, but step on a proud and glorious ship, grasp the helm and steer it out upon the ocean. You are the man to pilot the ship, and the ocean will obey you, and you will get into port loaded with riches, glory, and honor. Only make an effort. Remember my words, and now, Frederick Gentz, in order to live happily, never remember me!"

She turned round and hastily left the room. He stood immovable for several minutes, dreamily gazing after her, while her words were still resounding in his ears like an inspired prophecy. But when he heard the carriage roll away on the street, he started, passed his hand across his quivering face and whispered: "I have deeply wronged her; may God forgive me!"

Suddenly, however, he drew himself up to his full height, and a gleam of intense joy burst forth from his eyes. "I am free!" he exclaimed, loudly and in a tone of exultation. "Yes, I am free! My life and the world belong to me again. All women are mine again, Cupid and all the gods of love will boldly flit toward me, for they need not conceal themselves any longer from the face of a husband strolling on forbidden grounds, nor from the spying eyes of a jealous wife. Life is mine again, and I will enjoy it; yes I enjoy it. I will enjoy it like fragrant wine pressed to our lips in a golden goblet, sparkling with diamonds. Ah, how they are hammering and battering in the anteroom! Every stroke of theirs is a note of the glorious song of my liberty. The furniture of my household is gone; the pictures and looking-glasses are all gone—gone. The past and every thing reminding me thereof shall disappear from these rooms. I will have new furniture—furniture of gold and velvet, large Venetian mirrors, and splendid paintings. Oh, my rooms shall look as glorious and magnificent as those of a prince, and all Berlin shall speak of the splendor and luxury of Frederick Gentz. And to whom shall I be indebted for it? Not to my wife's dower, but to myself—to myself alone, to my talents, to my genius! Oh, in regard to this at least, poor Julia shall not have been mistaken. I shall gain fame, and glory, and honors; my name shall become a household word throughout Europe; it shall reecho in every cabinet; every minister shall have recourse to me, and—hark! What's that?" he suddenly interrupted himself. "I really believe they are quarrelling in the anteroom."

Indeed, a violent altercation was heard outside. Suddenly the door was pushed open, and a vigorous, broad-shouldered man, with a flushed and angry face, appeared on the threshold.

"Well," he exclaimed, with a bitter sneer, turning to the footman who stood behind him, "was I not right when I told you that Mr. Counsellor Gentz was at home? You would not announce me, because your master had ordered you not to admit any visitors of my class. But I want to be admitted. I will not permit myself to be shown out of the anteroom like a fool, while the counsellor here is snugly sitting on his sofa laughing at me."

"You see, my dear Mr. Werner, I am neither sitting on my sofa nor laughing at you," said Gentz, slowly approaching his angry visitor. "And now let me ask you what you want of me."

"What I want of you?" replied the stranger, with a sneer. "Sir, you know very well what I want of you. I want my money! I want the five hundred dollars you have been owing me for the last twelve months. I trusted your word and your name; I furnished you my best wines—my choicest champagne and the most exquisite delicacies for your dinner parties. You have treated your friends; that was all right enough, but it should have been done at your expense, and not at mine. For that reason I am here, and you *must* pay me. For the hundredth and last time, I demand my money!"

"And if I now tell you for the hundredth, but not the last time, that I have not got any money?"

"Then I shall go to the war department and attach your salary."

"Ah, my dear friend, there you would be altogether too late," exclaimed Gentz, laughing. "My honorable landlord has outstripped you as far as that is concerned; he has attached my salary for a whole year, and I believe it is even insufficient to cover what I owe him."

"But in the d—l's name, sir, you must find some other means of satisfying my claim, for I tell you I shall not leave this room without getting my money."

"My dear Mr. Werner, pray do not shout so dreadfully," said Gentz, anxiously; "my ears are very sensitive, and such shouting terrifies me as much as a thunderstorm. I am quite willing to pay you, only point out to me a way to do it!"

"Borrow money of other people and then pay me!"

"My dear sir, that is a way I have exhausted long ago. There is no one willing to advance me money either on interest or on my word of honor."

"But how in the d—l's name are you going to pay me then, sir?"

"That is exactly what I don't know yet, but after a while I shall know, and that time will come very soon. For I tell you, sir, these days of humiliations and debts will soon cease for me. I shall occupy an exalted and brilliant position; the young king will give it to me, and—"

"Fiddlesticks!" exclaimed Werner, interrupting him; "do not feed me with such empty hopes after I have fed you with delicacies and quenched your thirst with my champagne."

"My dear sir, I have not partaken all alone of your good cheer; my friends have helped me, and now you ask me alone to pay the whole bill. That is contrary to natural law and to political economy."

"Mr. Counsellor, are you mocking me with your political economy? What do you know about economy?"

"Ah, I am quite familiar with it, and my book on English finances has brought me fame and honor."

"It would have been better for you, Mr. Counsellor, if you had attended to your own finances. All Berlin knows in what condition they are."

"Nevertheless, there were always excellent men putting a noble trust in me, and believing that I would repay the money I borrowed of them. You are one of those excellent men, Mr. Werner, and I shall never forget it. Have a little patience, and I will pay you principal and interest."

"I cannot wait, Mr. Counsellor. I am in the greatest embarrassment myself; I have to redeem large notes in the course of a few days, and unless I can do so I am lost, my whole family is ruined, and my reputation gone; then I must declare myself insolvent, and suffer people to call me an impostor and villain, who incurs debts without knowing wherewith to pay them. Sir, I shall never suffer this, and therefore I must have my money, and I will not leave this room until you have paid my claim in full."

"In that case, my dear sir, I am afraid you will have to remain here and suffer the same distressing fate as Lot's unfortunate wife—"

"Sir, pray be serious, for my business here is of a very serious character. Five hundred dollars is no trifle; a man may squander them in a few days, but they may cause him also to commit suicide. Pay me, sir, pay me; I want my money!"

"For God's sake, do not shout in this manner. I told you once already that I cannot stand it. I know very well that five hundred dollars is a serious matter, and that you must have your money. I will make an effort, nay, I will do my utmost to get it for you; but you must be quiet. I pledge you my word that I will exert myself to the best of my power in order to obtain that amount for you, but in return you must promise me to go home quietly and peaceably, and to wait there until I bring you the money."

"What are you going to do? How are you going to get the money? You told me just now you were unable to borrow any thing."

"But somebody may give me those miserable five hundred dollars, and it seems to me that would do just as well."

"Oh, you are laughing at me."

"By no means, sir. Just be still and let me write a letter. I will afterward show you the address, and thereby let you know from whom I am expecting assistance."

He walked rapidly to his desk, penned a few lines, and placed the paper in a large envelope, which he sealed and directed.

"Read the address," he said, showing the letter to Mr. Werner.

"To his excellency the minister of the treasury, Count von Schulenburg-Kehnert, general of artillery," read Werner, with a hesitating tongue, and casting astonished and inquisitive glances upon Gentz. "And this is the distinguished gentleman to whom you apply for the money, Mr. Counsellor?"

"Yes, my friend; and you must confess that a minister of finance is the best man to apply to for money. I have written to his excellency that I stand in urgent need of five hundred dollars to-day, and I request him to extricate me from my embarrassment. I ask him to appoint an hour during the forenoon when I may call upon him and get the money."

"And you really believe that he will give you the money?"

"My dear sir, I am perfectly sure of it, and in order to satisfy you likewise, I will make a proposition. Accompany my footman to the minister's house, carry the letter to him yourself, and hear his reply. You may then repeat this reply to my footman, go home in good spirits, and wait there until I bring you the money."

"And if you should fail to come?" asked Werner.

"Then that last remedy you alluded to, suicide, always remains to you. Now go, my dear sir. John! John!"

The footman opened the door with a rapidity indicating that his ears probably had not been very far from the keyhole.

"John," said Gentz, "accompany this gentleman to the house of Minister Schulenburg-Kehnert, and wait at the door for the reply he will repeat to you. And now, Mr. Werner, good-by; you see I have done all I can, and I hope you will remember that in future, and not make so much noise for the sake of a few miserable dollars. Good gracious, if I did not owe any one more than you, my creditors might thank their stars—"

"Poor creditors!" sighed Mr. Werner, saluting Gentz, and left the room with the footman, holding the letter like a trophy in his hand.

CHAPTER XIII.

THE INTERVIEW WITH THE MINISTER OF FINANCE.

"WELL, I am really anxious to know whether the minister will give me the money," murmured Gentz; "his reply will indicate to me, if the letter to the king I intrusted yesterday to Menken, has made a favorable impression, and if I may hope at length for promotion and other favors. My God, I am pining away in my present miserable and subordinate position! I am able to accomplish greater things. I am worth more than all these generals, ministers, and ambassadors, who are so proud and overbearing, and dare to look down upon me as though I were their inferior. Ah! I shall not stoop so low as to knuckle to them and flatter them. I don't want to be lifted up by them, but I will be their equal. I feel that I am the peer of the foremost and highest of all these so-called statesmen. I do not need *them*, but *they* need me. Ah, my God! somebody knocks at the door again, and John is not at home. Good Heaven, if it should be another of those noisy, impertinent creditors! I am indebted to Julia for all these vexations. Because her things are being sent away, every door in the house is open, and every one can easily penetrate into my room. Yes, yes, I am coming. I am already opening the door."

He hastened to the door and unlocked it. This time, however, no creditor was waiting outside, but a royal footman, who respectfully bowed to the military counsellor.

"His royal highness Prince Louis Ferdinand," he said, "requests Mr. Counsellor Gentz to dine with him to-morrow."

Gentz nodded haughtily. "I shall come," he said briefly, and then looked inquiringly at his own footman who had just entered the other room.

"Well, John, what did the minister reply?"

"His excellency requests Mr. Counsellor Gentz to call on him in the course of an hour."

"All right!" said Gentz, and an expression of heart-felt satisfaction overspread his features. He closed the door, and stepped back into his study, and, folding his hands on his back, commenced pacing the room.

"He is going to receive me in the course of an hour," he murmured. "I may conclude, therefore that the king was pleased with my letter, and that I am at last to enter upon a new career. Ah, now my head is light, and my heart is free; now I will go to work."

He sat down at his desk and commenced writing rapidly. His features assumed a grave expression, and proud and sublime thoughts beamed on his expansive forehead.

He was so absorbed in his task that he entirely forgot the audience the minister had granted to him, and his footman had to come in and remind him that the hour for calling upon his excellency was at hand.

"Ah! to be interrupted in my work for such a miserable trifle," said Gentz, indignantly laying down his pen and rising. "Well, then, if it must be, give me my dress-coat, John, and I will go to his excellency."

A quarter of an hour later Counsellor Frederick Gentz entered the anteroom of Count Schulenburg-Kehnert, minister of finance. "Announce my arrival to his excellency," he said to the footman in waiting, with a condescending nod, and then quickly followed him to the door of the minister's study.

"Permit me to announce you to his excellency," said the footman, and slipped behind the *portière*. He returned in a few minutes.

"His excellency requests Mr. Gentz to wait a little while. His excellency has to attend to a few dispatches yet, but will very soon be ready to admit Mr. Gentz."

"Very well, I shall wait," said Gentz, with a slight frown, and he approached the splendidly bound books which were piled up in gilt cases on the walls of the room. The most magnificent and precious works of ancient and modern literature, the rarest editions, the most superb illustrated books were united in this library, and Gentz noticed it with ill-concealed wrath.

"These men can have all these treasures, nay, they have got them, and value them so little as to keep them in their anterooms," he murmured, in a surly tone, forgetting altogether that the footman was present and could overhear every word he said. He had really heard his remark, and replied to it, approaching Gentz:

"I beg your pardon, Mr. Counsellor, his excellency does not undervalue these treasures, but appreciates them highly, and is always glad enough when the bookbinder delivers new volumes in gorgeous bindings. For this very reason his excellency has ordered the library to be placed in this anteroom, so that it also may gladden the hearts of other people, and those gentlemen who have to wait here may have something wherewith to while away their time."

"They are permitted, then, to take the books down and read them?" asked Gentz.

The footman looked somewhat embarrassed. "I believe," he said, timidly, "that would not be altogether agreeable to his excellency, for you see, Mr. Counsellor, all of these beautiful books are gilt-edged, and gilt edges suffer greatly if the books are read. You cannot even open the books without injuring them slightly."

"And the gilt edges on this row of the books before me are as good as new, and perfectly uninjured," said Gentz, gravely.

"Well, that is easily explained. They have not been disturbed since the bookbinder brought them here," exclaimed the footman, solemnly. "No one would dare to handle them."

"Does not his excellency read these books?"

"God forbid! His excellency likes books, but he has not got time to read much. But whenever his excellency passes through this anteroom, he pauses before his bookcases, and looks at them, and, with his own hands, frequently wipes off the dust from the gilt edges of the books."

"Indeed, that is a most honorable occupation for a minister of finance," said Gentz, emphatically. "It is always a great consolation to know that a minister of finance wipes off the dust from the gold. I should be very happy if his excellency should consent to do that also for me as often as possible. But does it not seem to you, my dear fellow, that it takes his excellency a good while to finish those dispatches? It is nearly half an hour since I have been waiting here."

"I am sure his excellency will soon ring the bell."

"Ring the bell?" asked Gentz, uneasily, "for whom?"

"Why, for myself, in order to notify me to admit you, Mr. Counsellor."

"Ah, for you?" said Gentz, drawing a deep breath, and turning once more to the books in order to while away the time by reading at least the titles, as he was not permitted to take down and open one of the magnificent volumes.

Time passed on in this manner, and Gentz was walking up and down near the bookcases, studying the titles, and waiting. The footman had withdrawn into the most remote window, and was waiting likewise.

Suddenly the large clock commenced striking solemnly and slowly, and announced to Gentz that he had been a whole hour in his excellency's anteroom. And his excellency had not yet rung the bell.

At this moment Gentz turned toward the footman with a gesture of indignation and impatience.

"I am satisfied that his excellency has entirely forgotten that I am waiting here in the anteroom," he said, angrily. "The dispatches must be quite lengthy, for I have been here now for an hour already. Hence I must beg you to inform the minister that I cannot wait any longer, for I am quite busy too, and have to return to my study. Please say that to his excellency."

"But can I dare to disturb his excellency?" asked the footman, anxiously. "He has not rung the bell, sir."

"Well, you must be kind enough to disturb him and tell him I must leave unless he can admit me at once," exclaimed Gentz, energetically. "Go, sir, go!"

The footman sighed deeply. "Well, I will do

so at your risk, Mr. Counsellor," he said, in a low voice, stepping behind the *portière*. He soon returned, a malicious smile playing on his lips.

"His excellency regrets that you cannot wait any longer, Mr. Counsellor," he said. "His excellency being so busy that he cannot be disturbed, he requests you to call again to-morrow at the same hour."

"So his excellency dismisses me after detaining me here in the anteroom for more than an hour?" asked Gentz, incredulously.

"His excellency is overwhelmed with unexpected business," said the footman, with a shrug of his shoulders. "His excellency therefore requests you, Mr. Counsellor, to call again to-morrow."

Gentz cast upon the footman a glance which would have shivered him like a thunderbolt if he had not been a man of stone. But being a man of stone, the thunderbolt harmlessly glanced off from him. With a peculiar smile, he assisted the enraged counsellor in putting on his cloak, handed him his hat with a polite bow, and then hastened to the door in order to open it to him.

At this moment the minister in his study rang the bell loudly and violently. The footman quickly opened the door leading to the hall, and, with a polite gesture, invited Gentz to step out. The latter, however, did not stir. He had hastily placed his hat on his head and was now putting on his gloves with as grave an air as if they were gauntlets with which he was going to arm himself for the purpose of stepping out into the arena.

The minister's bell resounded even louder and more violently than before.

"I beg your pardon, Mr. Counsellor," the footman exclaimed, impatiently, "his excellency is calling me. Be kind enough to close the door when you leave. I must go to his excellency."

He hurriedly crossed the room and hastened into the minister's study.

Gentz now put on his gloves and approached the door. He bent one more glance full of anger upon the anteroom, and finally fixed his eyes upon the glittering books in the cases on the wall. An expression of malicious joy suddenly overspread his features. He drew back from the door, and hurriedly crossing the room, he approached the books. Without any hesitation whatever, he took down one of the largest and most richly ornamented volumes, concealed the book under his cloak, hastened back to the door, and left the house of the minister of finance with a haughty and defiant air.

Without nodding or greeting any one, he hastened through the streets back to his own house.

At the door of the latter there stood two huge furniture-wagons, half filled with the sofas, armchairs, tables, and looking-glasses which heretofore had adorned his rooms, and which he was now going to lose with his wife.

The servants had not finished removing the furniture, and he had to pause in the hall in order to let them pass with the large silken sofa which had been the chief ornament of his own parlor. This greatly increased his anger; with furious gestures he rapidly ascended the staircase and went to his rooms. Every door was open—the apartments which he crossed with ringing steps, were empty and deserted, and finally he reached the door of his study, where his footman had posted himself like a faithful sentinel. Gentz silently beckoned him to open it, and entered. But when the servant was going to follow him, he silently but imperiously kept him back, and slammed the door in his face.

Now at last he was alone; now no one could see and watch him any longer; now he could utter the cry of rage that was filling his breast and almost depriving him of the power of speech; and after uttering this cry, he could appease his wrath still in some other way.

He threw his cloak and hat upon a chair, seized the splendidly bound and richly gilt volume from the minister's library with both hands and hurled it upon the floor.

"Lie there, toy of a proud minister!" he exclaimed furiously. "I will treat you as I would like to treat him. I will abuse you as I would like to abuse him. There! take this! and this! and that!"

And he stamped with his heels upon the magnificent work, clinching his fists and swearing fearfully.*

A loud and merry laugh was heard behind him, and upon turning round he beheld in the door one of his friends, who was looking at him with a radiant face.

"Herr von Gualtieri, you laugh, and I am furious," exclaimed Gentz, stamping again upon the costly volume.

"But why, for God's sake, are you furious?" asked Herr von Gualtieri. "Why do you perpetrate such vandalism upon that magnificent volume under your feet?"

"Why? Well, I will tell you. I was to-day at the house of Count Schulenburg-Kehnert; he had sent me word to call on him at ten o'clock, and when I was there, he made me stand for an hour in his anteroom like his gorgeous, gilt-edged

---

* Vide "Gallerie von Bildnissen aus Rahel's Umgang," edited by Varnhagen von Ense, vol. ii., p. 168.

books, which his footman told me he never opens because he is afraid of injuring their gilt edges."

"And did he admit you after you had been in the anteroom for an hour?"

"No. When I had been there for an hour, he sent me word through his footman that he was too busy to receive me, and that I had better call again to-morrow. Bah! He wanted to treat me like those books of his, which he never opens; he did not want to open me either—me, a man who has got more mind, more knowledge, and information than all his books together. He made me wait in his anteroom for a whole hour, and then dismissed me!"

"And you allowed yourself to be dismissed?"

"Yes, sir, I did; but I took one of his splendid gilt-edged volumes along, in order to stamp on it and maltreat it, as I would like to maltreat him. Thus! and thus! To crush it under my heels. It does me good. It relieves me. At this moment this is the only revenge I can take against the miserable fellow." *

Herr von Gualtieri laughed uproariously. "Ah! that is an entirely novel *jus gentium*," he exclaimed; "an exceedingly funny *jus gentium*. My friend, let me embrace you; you are a glorious fellow!"

With open arms he approached Gentz and pressed him tenderly, laughing all the while, to his heart.

Gentz was unable to withstand this kindness and this laughter, and suddenly forgetting his anger, he boisterously joined his friend's mirth.

"You like my revenge?" he asked.

"Ah! it is admirable; it is the revenge of a genuine Corsican!" said Gualtieri, gravely.

"Of a Corsican?" asked Gentz, shrinking back. "That is an ugly comparison, sir. I do not want to have any thing in common with that Corsican, General Bonaparte. I tell you I am afraid that man will some day prove a terrible scourge for us."

"And I adore him!" exclaimed Gualtieri. "He is the resuscitated Alexander of Macedon, the conqueror of the world, the master of the world. He alone has stemmed the tide of revolution in France. To him alone the French are indebted for the restoration of order and tranquillity in their country. The thirteenth of Vendémiaire is as heroic a deed, as great a victory, as the battles of Lodi and Arcole."

"That may be," said Gentz, morosely. "I am no soldier, and do not like battles and warfare.

And what do we Germans care for the Corsican? Have we not got enough to do at home? Germany, however, is so happy and contented that, like the Pharisee, she may look upon republican France and exclaim: 'I thank thee, my God, that I am not like this man.'"

"You are right," replied Gualtieri. "We also stand in need of a revolution. In Germany, too, a guillotine must be erected—heads must fall, and death must hold its bloody harvest."

"Hush, my friend, hush!" said Gentz, drawing back in dismay. "Did you merely come to me for the purpose of speaking of such dreadful matters, while you are well aware that I don't like to hear anybody allude to bloodshed, murders, and similar horrors?"

"I merely wanted to try you a little in order to see whether you are still the same dear old childish coward," exclaimed Gualtieri, laughing. "The same great child with the strong, manly soul, and the gentle, weak, and easily moved child's heart. Now, let me know quickly what you wanted of the minister of finance, and I shall reward you then by telling you some good news. Well, then, what did you want of Schulenburg?"

"I had asked him to lend me five hundred dollars, and to appoint an hour when I might call for the money. He named ten o'clock, and I went to his house, merely to leave it an hour after in a towering passion and with empty hands. Oh, it is infamous, it is dreadful! It is—"

At that moment the door opened, and the footman entered.

"From his excellency, General von Schulenburg-Kehnert," he said, delivering to Gentz a small sealed package and a letter. "The servant who brought it has left, as he said no reply was required."

Gentz beckoned his servant to withdraw, and he then hastily opened the package.

"Twelve fifty-dollar bills!" he exclaimed, triumphantly. "One hundred dollars more than I had asked for! That is very kind, indeed."

"May be he does not give it to you, but merely lends it to you," said Gualtieri, smiling.

"Lend it to me!" exclaimed Gentz, scornfully. "People don't lend any money to me, because they know that I am unable to pay it back; people reward me, sir; they show their gratitude toward me in a substantial manner, but they are not so mean as to lend me what I ask for."

"Does the minister tell you so in his letter?" asked Gualtieri, dryly.

"Ah! that is true. I have not yet read the letter," said Gentz, breaking the seal. While he was reading it, a slight blush suffused his cheeks, and an expression of shame overspread his features.

---

* Gentz's own words.—Vide "Rahel's Umgang," vol. ii., p. 168.

4

"Here, read it," he murmured, handing the letter to his friend.

Gualtieri took it and read as follows:

"MY DEAR COUNSELLOR,—You wished to see me, and I begged you to call at ten o'clock, although I was overwhelmed with business and hardly had any time to spare. Precisely at ten o'clock I was ready to receive you, for in all matters of business I am a very punctual man. However, after vainly waiting for you for half an hour, I resumed my work. I had to examine some very complicated accounts, and could not allow myself to be interrupted after once taking them up. Hence I had to ask you to wait, and when, after waiting for half an hour, *like myself*, you grew impatient and would not stay any longer, I sent you word to call again to-morrow. Now, that I have concluded my pressing business, however, I hasten to comply with your request. You asked me for five hundred dollars; here they are. Knowing, however, how precious your time is, and that you had to wait for half an hour through my fault, I take the liberty of adding one hundred dollars for the time you have lost to-day. Farewell, sir, and let me conclude with expressing the hope that you will soon again delight the world and myself with one of your excellent works."

CHAPTER XIV.

THE MEMORIAL TO FREDERICK WILLIAM III.

"I BELIEVE," said Gualtieri, returning the letter to Gentz, "I believe the minister wanted to teach you a lesson. He made you wait in order to teach you the necessity of being punctual."

"And I shall not forget the lesson."

"You will be punctual hereafter?"

"On the contrary. This time I was half an hour behind time, and he paid me one hundred dollars for it. Hereafter I shall be an hour too late; he will make me wait an hour and pay me two hundred dollars for it. I believe that is sound arithmetic. Don't look at me so scornfully, Gualtieri; this state of affairs will not last for any length of time; there will be a time at no distant period when no minister will dare to make me wait in his anteroom, nor to pay me such petty, miserable sums. The ministers then will wait in my anteroom, and will be only too happy if I accept the thousands which they will offer to me. I have formed the fixed resolution to obtain a brilliant position and to coin wealth out of my mind."

"And I am sure you will succeed in accomplishing your purpose," said Gualtieri. "Yes, I am satisfied a brilliant future is in store for you. You are a genius such as Germany has not seen heretofore, for you are a political genius, and you may just as well confess that Germany greatly lacks politicians who are able to wield their pen like a pointed two-edged sword, to strike fatal blows in all directions and obtain victories. Germany has already fixed her eyes upon you, and even in England your name is held in great esteem since you published your excellent translation of Burke's work on the French Revolution. The political pamphlets you have issued since that time, and the excellent political magazine you have established, have met with the warmest approval, and the public hopes and expects that you will render great and important services to the country. Go on in this manner, my friend; boldly pursue the path you have entered, and it will become for you a path of glory, honor, and wealth."

Gentz looked at him almost angrily.

"I hope," he said, "you will not believe me to be an avaricious and covetous man. I value money merely because it is an instrument wherewith to procure enjoyment, and because, without it, we are the slaves of misery, privations, and distress. Money renders us free, and now that people would like to set up freedom as the religion of all nations, every one ought to try to make as much money as possible, that alone rendering him really free. The accursed French Revolution, which has dragged all principles, all laws and old established institutions under the guillotine, was under the necessity of leaving one power unharmed—the power of money. The aristocracy, the clergy, nay, even royalty had to bleed under the guillotine, but money never lost its power, its influence, and its importance. Money speaks a universal language, and the *sans-culotte* and Hottentot understand it as well as the king, the minister, and the most beautiful woman. Money never needs an interpreter; it speaks for itself. See, my friend, that is the reason why I love money and try to make as much as possible, not in order to amass it, but because with it I can buy the world, love, honor, enjoyment, and happiness. But not being one of those who find money in their cradles, I must endeavor to acquire it and avail myself of the capital God has given me in my brains. And that I shall and will do, sir, but I pledge you my word, never in a base and unworthy manner. I shall probably make people *pay* very large sums of money for my services, but never shall I *sell* myself; all the millions of the world could not induce me to write *against my principles*, but all the millions of the world I shall demand, when they ask me to write *for my principles !* See, my friend, that is my programme, and you may be sure that I shall live up to it. I am an aristocrat by nature and conviction; hence I hate the French Revolution which intended to overthrow every aristocracy, not only that of pedigree, but also that of the mind, and therefore I have sworn to oppose it as an indefatigable and indomitable champion, and to strike it as many blows with my pen and tongue as I can. Hence I shall never join the hymns of praise which the Germans, always too complaisant, are now singing to the little Corsican, General Bonaparte. Whatever you may say about his heroism and genius, I believe him to be an enemy of Germany, and am, therefore, on my guard."

"So you do not admire his victories, the incomparable plans of his battles, which he conceives with the coolness of a wise and experienced chieftain, and carries out with the bravery and intrepidity of a hero of antiquity ? "

" I admire all that, but at the same time it makes me shudder when I think that it might some day come into the head of this man who conquers every thing, to invade and conquer Germany also. I believe, indeed, he would succeed in subjugating her, for I am afraid we have no man of equal ability on our side who could take the field against him. Ah, my friend, why does not one of our German princes resemble this French general, this hero of twenty-seven years ? Just think of it, he is no older than our young king; both were born in the same year."

"You must not count his years," exclaimed Gualtieri, "count his great days, his great battles. The enthusiasm of all Europe hails his coming, for he fights at the head of his legions for the noblest boons of mankind—for freedom, honor, and justice. No wonder, therefore, that he is victorious everywhere ; the enslaved nations everywhere are in hopes that he will break their fetters and give them liberty."

" He is a scourge God has sent to the German princes so that they may grow wiser and better. He wishes to compel them to respect the claims of their subjects to freedom and independence, that being the only way for them to erect a bulwark against this usurper who fights his battles not only with the sword, but also with ideas. Oh, I wish our German sovereigns would comprehend all this, and that all those who have a tongue to speak, would shout it into their ears and arouse them from their proud security and infatuation."

" W   are not you a tongue to speak, and yet you   silent ? " asked Gualtieri, smiling.

"No,   e not been silent," exclaimed Gentz,

enthusiastically. " I have done my duty as a man and citizen, and told the whole truth to the king."

"That means—"

"That means that I have written to the king, not with the fawning slavishness of a subject, but as a man who has seen much, reflected much, and experienced much, and who speaks to a younger man, called upon to act an important part, and holding the happiness of millions of men in his hands. It would be a crime against God and humanity, if we knew the truth and should not tell it to such a man. Because I believe I know the truth, I have spoken to the king, not in a letter which he may read to-day and throw to-morrow into his paper-basket, but in a printed memorial, which I shall circulate in thousands of copies as soon as I have heard that it is in the hands of the king."

" And you believe the king will accept this printed memorial of yours ? "

" My friend, Counsellor Menken, has undertaken to deliver it to the king."

" In that case he will accept it, for he thinks very highly of Menken. But what did you tell the king in this memorial ? "

" I gave him sound advice about government affairs."

" Advice ! my friend, kings do not like to listen to advice, especially when it is given to them spontaneously. Did you confine yourself to general suggestions ? You see I am very anxious to learn more about your bold enterprise. Just read the memorial to me, friend Gentz ! "

" Ah, that would be a gigantic task for you to hear it, and for myself to read it, the memorial being quite lengthy. I ask the king therein in impressive and fervent words—oh, I wept myself when I penned them—to make his people happy and prosperous. I directed his attention to the various branches of our administration; first, to military affairs—"

" And you advise him to make war ? " asked Gualtieri, hastily.

" No, I advise him always to be armed and prepared, but to maintain peace as long as it is compatible with his honor. Next I allude to the condition of our judicial and financial affairs. I beseech him to abstain from interference with the administration of justice, to insist upon a constant equilibrium being maintained between the expenses and revenues of the state, so as not to overburden his subjects with taxes, and not to curtail the development of commerce and industry by vexatious monopolies. Finally, I ask him to devote some attention to intellectual affairs and to the press."

"Oh, I expected that," said Gualtieri, smiling, "and I should not be surprised at all if you had been bold enough to ask the timid and diffident young king to grant freedom of the press to his people."

"Yes, that is what I ask him to do," said Gentz, enthusiastically. "You want me to read the whole memorial to you. Let me read at least what I have said about the freedom of the press. Will you listen to it?"

"Oh, I am most anxious to hear it," said Gualtieri, sitting down on the sofa.

Gentz took several sheets of paper from his desk, sat down opposite his friend and commenced reading in a loud and enthusiastic voice:

"Of all things repugnant to fetters, none can bear them as little as human thought. The oppression weighing down the latter is not merely injurious because it impedes what is good, but also because it promotes what is bad. Compulsion in matters of faith may be passed over in silence. It belongs to those antiquated evils on which now that there is greater danger of an utter prostration of religious ideas than of their fanatical abuse, only narrow-minded babblers are declaiming. Not so, however, with regard to freedom of the press. Misled by unfounded apprehensions, arising from the events of the times, even sagacious men might favor a system which, viewed in its true light, is more injurious to the interests of the government than it ever can be to the rights of the citizens, even in its most deplorable abuses.

"What, even aside from all other considerations, peremptorily and absolutely condemns any law muzzling the press, is the important fact that it is impossible to enforce it. Unless there be a regular inquisition watching over the execution of such a law, it is now-a-days utterly impossible to carry it out. The facilities for bringing ideas before the public are so great, as to render any measure destined to curtail this publicity a mere matter of derision. But if these laws prove ineffectual they may yet exasperate the people, and that is precisely their most dangerous feature; they exasperate without deterring. They instigate those against whom they are directed to offer a resistance which frequently not only remains successful, but moreover becomes glorious and honorable. The most wretched productions, whose real value would not secure a life of two hours, obtain general circulation because it seems to have required some degree of courage to write them. The most insignificant scribblers will be looked upon as men of mind, and the most venal writers suddenly become 'martyrs of truth.' A thousand noxious insects, whom a sunbeam of truth and real sagacity would have dispersed, favored by the darkness created for them with deplorable short-sightedness, insinuate themselves into the unarmed minds of the people, and instil their poison to the last drop, as though it were a forbidden delicacy of the most exquisite character. The only antidote, the productions of better writers, loses its strength because the uninformed only too easily mistake the advocates of salutary restrictions for the defenders of such as are manifestly unjust and oppressive.

"Let freedom of the press, therefore, be the immovable principle of your government, not as though the state or mankind, in this age so prolific in books, were interested in the publication of a thousand works more or less, but because your majesty is too great to maintain an unsuccessful, and therefore disastrous struggle, with petty adversaries. Every one should be held responsible, strictly responsible for unlawful acts and writings assuming such a character, but mere opinion should meet with no other adversary than its opposite, and if it be erroneous, with the truth. Never will such a system prove dangerous to a well-regulated state, and never has it injured such a one. Where it apparently became pernicious, destruction had preceded it already, and mortification and putrefaction had set in." *

"Well?" asked Gentz, with glowing cheeks and flashing eyes, when he had ceased reading, "what do you think of my exposition of the freedom of the press? Is it not clear, convincing, and unanswerable? Will not the king see that my words contain the truth, and hence follow them?"

Gualtieri looked at his friend with an air of compassionate tenderness.

"Oh, you are a full-grown child," he said; "you still believe in the possibility of realizing Utopian dreams, and your faith is so honest, so manly! You want to force a scourge upon a timid young king, who most ardently desires to maintain peace, and to remain unnoticed, and tell him, 'With this scourge drive out the evil spirits and expel the lies, so as to cause daylight to dawn, and darkness to disappear!'—as though that daylight would not be sure to lay bare all the injuries and ulcers of which our own poor Prussia is suffering, and for which she greatly needs darkness and silence."

"What! you think the king will take no notice of my demands?"

"I believe," said Gualtieri, shrugging his shoul-

* Memorial respectfully presented to his majesty Frederick William III., on his accession to the throne, November 16, 1797, by Frederick Gentz.

ders, "that you are a highly-gifted visionary, and that the king is a tolerably intelligent and tolerably sober young gentleman, who, whenever he wants to skate, does not allow himself to be dazzled and enticed by the smooth and glittering surface, but first repeatedly examines the ice in order to find out whether it is firm enough to bear him. And now good-by, my poor friend. I came here to congratulate you for having regained your liberty, and for belonging again to the noble and only happy order of bachelors; but instead of hearing you rejoice, I find in you a philanthropic fanatic, and an enthusiastic advocate of a free press."

"But that does not prevent you from wishing me joy at my return to a bachelor's life," exclaimed Gentz, laughing. "Yes, my friend, I am free; life is mine again, and now let the flames of pleasure close again over my head—let enjoyment surround me again in fiery torrents, that I shall exultingly plunge into the whirlpool and feel as happy as a god! We must celebrate the day of my regeneration in a becoming manner; we must celebrate it with foaming champagne, *pâtés de foie gras*, and oysters; and if we want to devote a last tear to the memory of my wife, why, we shall drink a glass of *Lacrymae Christi* in her honor. You must come and see me to-night, Gualtieri. I shall invite a few other friends, and if you will afford us a rare pleasure, you will read to us some of La Fontaine's Fables, which no one understands to recite so well as you."

"I shall do so," said Gualtieri, extending his hand to Gentz. "I shall read to you one of La Fontaine's Fables, the first two lines of which eloquently express the whole history of your past."

"Let me hear those two lines."

Gualtieri covered his head, and standing in the door he had opened, he said with a deep pathos and in a profoundly melancholy voice:

"Deux coqs vivaient en paix; une poule survint,
Et voilà la guerre allumée"—

and nodding a last adieu, he disappeared.

Gentz laughed. "Indeed, he is right," he exclaimed; "that is the end of wedded life. But, thank God, mine is over, and, I swear by all my hopes, never will I be such a fool as to marry again! I shall remain a bachelor as long as I live; for he who belongs to no woman owns all women. It is time, however, to think of to-night's banquet. But in order to give a banquet, I must first procure new furniture for my rooms, and this time I won't have any but beautiful and costly furniture. And how shall I get it? Ah, *parbleu*, I forgot the six hundred dollars I received from the minister. I shall buy furniture for that sum

No, that would be very foolish, inasmuch as I greatly need it for other purposes. The furniture dealers, I have no doubt, will willingly trust me, for I never yet purchased any thing of them. Unfortunately, I cannot say so much in regard to him who is to furnish me the wines and delicacies for the supper, and I have only one hundred dollars in my pocket. The other five hundred dollars I must send to that bloodsucker, that heartless creditor Werner. But must I do so? Ah! really, I believe it would be rank folly. The fellow would think he had frightened me, and as soon as I should owe him another bill, he would again besiege my door, and raise a fresh disturbance here. No; I will show him that I am not afraid of him, and that his impudent conduct deserves punishment. Oh, John! John!"

The door was opened immediately, and the footman entered.

"John," said Gentz, gravely, "go at once to Mr. Werner. Tell him some friends are coming to see me to-night. I therefore want him to send me this evening twenty-four bottles of champagne, three large *pâtés de foie gras*, two hundred oysters, and whatever is necessary for a supper. If he should fill my order promptly and carefully, he can send me to-morrow a receipt for two hundred dollars, and I will pay him the money. But if a single oyster should be bad, if a single bottle of champagne should prove of poor quality, or if he should dare to decline furnishing me with the supper, he will not get a single *groschen*. Go and tell him that, and be back as soon as possible."

"Meantime, I will write a few invitations," said Gentz, as soon as he was alone. "But I shall invite none but unmarried men. In the first place, the Austrian minister, Prince von Reuss. This gentleman contents himself with one mistress, and as he fortunately does not suspect that the beautiful Marianne Meier is at the same time my mistress, he is a great friend of mine. Yes, if he knew that—ah!" he interrupted himself, laughing, "that would be another illustration of La Fontaine's fable of the two cocks and the hen. Well, I will now write the invitations."

He had just finished the last note when the door opened, and John entered, perfectly out of breath.

"Well, did you see Mr. Werner?" asked Gentz, folding the last note.

"Yes, sir. Mr. Werner sends word that he will furnish the supper promptly and satisfactorily, and will deliver here to-night twenty-four bottles of his best champagne, three large *pâtés de foie gras*, two hundred oysters, etc., but only on one condition."

"What! the fellow actually dares to impose conditions?" exclaimed Gentz, indignantly. "What is it he asks?"

"He asks you, sir, when he has delivered everything you have ordered, and before going to supper, to be kind enough to step out for a moment into the anteroom, where Mr. Werner will wait for you in order to receive there his two hundred dollars. I am to notify him if you accept this condition, and if so, he will furnish the supper."

"Ah, that is driving me to the wall," exclaimed Gentz, laughing. "Well, go back to the shrewd fellow and tell him that I accept his conditions. He is to await me in the anteroom, and as he would, of course, make a tremendous noise in case I should disappoint him, he may be sure that I shall come. So go to him, John."

"As for myself," said Gentz, putting on his cloak, "I shall go and purchase several thousand dollars' worth of furniture; my rooms shall hereafter be as gorgeous as those of a prince. By the by, I believe I have been too generous. If I had offered Werner one hundred dollars, he would have contented himself with that sum."

CHAPTER XV.

THE WEDDING.

AT the house of the wealthy banker Itzig a rare festival took place to-day, a festival which all Berlin had been talking of for the last few days, and which had formed the topic of conversation, no less among the people on the streets, than among the aristocratic classes in their palatial mansions. To-day the wedding of three of his beautiful young daughters was to take place, and the rich, ostentatious, and generous gentleman had left nothing undone in order to celebrate this gala-day in as brilliant and imposing a manner as possible. All the manufacturers of Berlin had been employed for months to get up the *trousseaux* of his daughters, for he had declared that they should wear exclusively the productions of German industry, and that not a single piece of their new household goods should be of French manufacture. Hence, all the gorgeous brocades, velvets, and laces for their dresses and furniture had been woven in Berlin manufactories; the most magnificent linen had been ordered from Silesia, and a host of milliners and seamstresses had got up everything required for the wardrobe of the young ladies, in the most skilful and artistic manner. Even the plate and costly jewelry had been manufactured by Berlin jewellers, and the rich and ex-

quisitely painted china had been purchased at the royal *Porzellanfabrik*. These three *trousseaux*, so beautiful and expensive, had been, as it were, a triumph of home art and home industry, and for this reason they excited general attention. Herr Itzig had finally, though very reluctantly, yielded to the urgent entreaties of his friends and admitted the public to the rooms and halls of his house in which the *trousseaux* of his daughters were displayed. However, in order not to lay himself open to the charge of boastful ostentation, he had tried to impart a useful and charitable character to this exhibition. He had fixed a tablet over the entrance to those rooms, bearing the inscription of "Exhibition of Productions of Home Industry;" in addition, every visitor had to buy a ticket of admission for a few *groschen*, the proceeds to be distributed among the poor.

Every one hastened to the banker's house in order to admire the "productions of home industry." Even the queen had come with one of her ladies of honor to inspect the gorgeous display, and while admiring the magnificence of the silks and velvets and the artistic setting of the diamonds, she had exclaimed joyfully: "How glad I am to see that Germany is really able to do entirely without France, and to satisfy all her wants from her own resources!"

The queen had uttered these words perhaps on the spur of the moment, but the public imparted to them a peculiar meaning and tendency; and the newspapers, the organs of public opinion, never tired of praising the royal words, and of admonishing the inhabitants of Berlin to visit the patriotic exhibition at the banker's house. Curiosity, moreover, stimulated the zeal of the ladies, while political feeling caused the male part of the population to appear at the exhibition. But when it became known that the French embassy had taken umbrage at the zeal manifested by the people of Berlin, and that the French minister had even dared at the royal table to complain loudly and bitterly of the words uttered by the queen in Herr Itzig's house, the indignation became general, and the visits to the exhibition assumed the character of a national demonstration against the overbearing French. Hosts of spectators now hastened to Herr Itzig's house, and gay, mischievous young men took pleasure in stationing themselves in groups in the street on which the French minister was living, right in front of the house, in order to converse loudly in the French language about the rare attractions of the banker's exhibition, and to praise the noble patriot who disdained to buy abroad what he could get at home just as well, if not better.

The success of his exhibition, however, far exceeded the wishes of the banker, and he was glad when the days during which the exhibition was to continue were at an end, so that he could exclude the inquisitive visitors from his house.

But to-day the house was to be opened to the invited guests, for to-day, as we stated before, Herr Itzig was going to celebrate simultaneously the wedding of three of his beautiful daughters, and the whole place was astir with preparations for a becoming observance of the gala-day.

While the footmen and other servants, under the direction of skilful artists, were engaged in gorgeously decorating the parlors and halls; while a hundred busy hands in the kitchen and cellar were preparing a sumptuous repast; while Herr Itzig and wife were giving the last directions for the details of the festival, the three brides were chatting confidentially in their own room. All of them were quite young yet, the eldest sister having scarcely completed her twenty-first year. They were very beautiful, and theirs was the striking and energetic beauty peculiar to the women of the Orient—that beauty of flaming black eyes, glossy black hair, a glowing olive complexion, and slender but well-developed forms. They wore a full bridal costume; their bare, beautifully rounded arms and necks were gorgeously adorned with diamonds and other precious stones; their tall and vigorous figures were clad in white silk dresses, trimmed with superb laces. He who would have seen them thus in the full charm of beauty, grace, and youth, in their magnificent costumes, and with delicate myrtle-crowns on their heads, would have believed he beheld three favorite daughters of Fate, who had never known care and grief, and upon whose heads happiness had poured down an uninterrupted sunshine.

Perhaps it was so; perhaps it was only the beautiful myrtle-crowns that cast a shadow over the faces of the three brides, and not their secret thoughts—their silent wishes.

They had eagerly conversed for a while, but now, however, they paused and seemed deeply absorbed. Finally, one of them slowly raised her glowing black eyes and cast a piercing glance upon her sisters. They felt the magic influence of this glance, and raised their eyes at the same time.

"Why do you look at us so intently, Fanny?" they asked.

"I want to see if I can read truth on your brow," said Fanny; "or if the diamonds and the myrtle-crowns conceal every thing. Girls, suppose we take off for a moment the shining but lying masks with which we adorn ourselves in the eyes of the world, and show to each other our true and natural character? We have always lied to each other. We said mutually to each other: 'I am happy. I am not jealous of you, for I am just as happy as you.' Suppose we now open our lips really and tell the truth about our hearts? Would not it be novel and original? Would it not be an excellent way of whiling away these few minutes until our betrothed come and lead us to the altar? See, this is the last time that we shall be thus together—the last time that we bear the name of our father; let us, therefore, for once tell each other our true sentiments. Shall we do so?"

"Yes," exclaimed the two sisters. "But about what do you want us to tell you the truth?"

"About our hearts," replied Fanny, gravely. "Esther, you are the eldest of us three. You must commence. Tell us, therefore, if you love your betrothed, Herr Ephraim?"

Esther looked at her in amazement. "If I love him?" she asked. "Good Heaven! how should I happen to love him? I scarcely know him. Father selected him for me; it is a brilliant match; I shall remain in Berlin; I shall give splendid parties and by my magnificent style of living greatly annoy those ladies of the so-called *haute volée*, who have sometimes dared to turn up their noses at the 'Jewesses.' Whether I shall be able to love Ephraim, I do not know; but we shall live in brilliant style, and as we shall give magnificent dinner-parties, we shall never lack guests from the most refined classes of society. Such are the prospects of my future, and although I cannot say that I am content with them, yet I know that others will deem my position a most enviable one, and that is at least something."

"The first confession!" said Fanny, smiling. "Now it is your turn, Lydia. Tell us, therefore, do you love Baron von Eskeles, your future husband?"

Lydia looked at her silently and sadly. "Do not ask me," she said, "for you and Esther know very well that I do not love him. I once had a splendid dream. I beheld myself an adored wife by the side of a young man whom I loved and who loved me passionately. He was an artist, and when he was sitting at his easel, he felt that he was rich and happy, even without money, for he had his genius and his art. When I was looking at his paintings, and at the handsome and inspired artist himself, it seemed to me there was but one road to happiness on earth: to belong to that man, to love him, to serve him, and, if it must be, to suffer and starve with him. It was a dream, and father aroused me from it by telling me that

I was to marry Baron von Eskeles, that he had already made an agreement with the baron's father, and that the wedding would take place in two weeks."

"Poor Lydia!" murmured the sisters.

A pause ensued. "Well," asked Esther, "and you, Fanny? You examine us and say nothing about yourself. What about your heart, my child? Do you love your betrothed, Baron von Arnstein, the partner of Eskeles, your future brother-in-law? You are silent? Have you nothing to say to us?"

"I have to say to you that we are all to be pitied and very unhappy," said Fanny, passionately. "Yes, to be pitied and very unhappy, notwithstanding our wealth, our diamonds, and our brilliant future! We have been sold like goods; no one has cared about the hearts which these goods happen to have, but every one merely took into consideration how much profit he would derive from them. Oh, my sisters, we rich Jewesses are treated just in the same manner as the poor princesses; we are sold to the highest bidder. And we have not got the necessary firmness, energy, and independence to emancipate ourselves from this degrading traffic in flesh and blood. We bow our heads and obey, and, in the place of love and happiness, we fill our hearts with pride and ostentation, and yet we are starving and pining away in the midst of our riches."

"Yes," sighed Lydia, "and we dare not even complain! Doomed to eternal falsehood, we must feign a happiness we do not experience, and a love we do not feel."

"I shall not do so!" exclaimed Fanny, proudly. "It is enough for me to submit to compulsion, and to bow my head; but never shall I stoop so low as to lie."

"What! you are going to tell your husband that you do not love him?" asked the sisters.

"I shall not say that to my *husband*, but to my *betrothed* as soon as he makes his appearance."

"But suppose he does not want to marry a girl who does not love him?"

"Then he is the one who breaks off the match, not I, and father cannot blame me for it. But do you not hear footsteps in the hall? It is my betrothed. I begged him to be here a quarter of an hour previous to the commencement of the ceremony, because I desired to speak to him about a very serious matter. He is coming. Now pray go to the parlor, and wait for me there. I shall rejoin you, perhaps alone, and in that case I shall be free; perhaps, however, Arnstein will accompany me, and in that eventuality he will have accepted the future as I am going to offer it to him. Farewell, sisters; may God protect us all!"

"May God protect *you!*" said Lydia, tenderly embracing her sister. "You have a courageous and strong soul, and I wish mine were like yours."

"Would that save you, Lydia?" asked Fanny, sharply. "Courage and energy are of no avail in our case; in spite of our resistance, we should have to submit and to suffer. He is coming."

She pushed her sisters gently toward the parlor door, and then went to meet her betrothed, who had just entered.

"Mr. Arnstein," said Fanny, giving him her hand, "I thank you for complying so promptly with my request."

"A business man is always prompt," said the young baron, with a polite bow.

"Ah, and you treat this interview with me likewise as a business affair?"

"Yes, but as a business affair of the rarest and most exquisite character. A conference with a charming young lady is worth more than a conference with the wealthiest business friend, even if the interview with the latter should yield a profit of one hundred per cent."

"Ah, I believe you want to flatter me," said Fanny, closely scanning the small and slender figure and the pale face of the baron.

He bowed with a gentle smile, but did not raise his eyes toward her. Fanny could not help perceiving that his brow was slightly clouded.

"Baron," she said, "I have begged you to come and see me, because I do not want to go to the altar with a lie on my soul. I will not deceive God and yourself, and therefore I now tell you, frankly and sincerely, I do not love you, baron; only my father's will gives my hand to you!"

There was no perceptible change in the young baron's face. He seemed neither surprised nor offended.

"Do you love another man?" he asked quietly.

"No, I love no one!" exclaimed Fanny.

"Ah, then, you are fortunate indeed," he said, gloomily. "It is by far easier to marry with a cold heart, than to do so with a broken one; for the cold heart may grow warm, but the broken one never."

Fanny's eyes were fixed steadfastly on his features.

"Mr. Arnstein," she exclaimed, impetuously, "you do not love me either!"

He forced himself to smile. "Who could see you—you, the proud, glorious beauty—without falling in love with you?" he exclaimed, emphatically.

"Pray, no empty flatteries," said Fanny, impatiently. "Oh, tell me the truth! I am sure you do not love me!"

"I saw you too late," he said, mournfully ; "if I had known you sooner, I should have loved you passionately."

"But now I am too late—and have you already loved another?" she asked, hastily.

"Yes, I love another," he said, gravely and solemnly. "As you ask me, I ought to tell you the truth. I love another."

"Nevertheless, you want to marry me?" she exclaimed, angrily.

"And you?" he asked, gently. "Do you love me?"

"But I told you already my heart is free. I love no one, while you—why don't you marry her whom you love?"

"Because I cannot marry her."

"Why cannot you marry her?"

"Because my father is opposed to it. He is the chief of our house and family. He commands, and we obey. He is opposed to it because the young lady whom I love is poor. She would not increase the capital of our firm."

"Oh, eternally, eternally that cold mammon, that idol to whom our hearts are sacrificed so ruthlessly!" exclaimed Fanny, indignantly. "For money we sell our youth, our happiness, and our love."

"I have not sold my love. I have sacrificed it," said Baron Arnstein, gravely ; "I have sacrificed it to the interests of our firm. But in seeing you so charming and sublime in your loveliness and glowing indignation, I am fully satisfied already that I am no longer to be pitied, for I shall have the most beautiful and generous wife in all Vienna."

"Then you really want to marry me? You will not break off the match, although your heart belongs to another woman, and although you know that I do not love you?"

"My beautiful betrothed, let us not deceive each other," he said, smiling ; "it is not a marriage, but a partnership we are going to conclude in obedience to the wishes of our fathers. In agreeing upon this partnership only our fortunes, but not our hearts, were thought of. The houses of Itzig, Arnstein, and Eskeles will flourish more than ever; whether the individuals belonging to these houses will wither is of no importance. Let us therefore submit to our fate, my dear, for we cannot escape from it. Would it be conducive to your happiness if I should break off the match? Your father would probably select another husband for you, perhaps in Poland or in Russia, and you would be buried with all the treasures of your beauty and accomplishments in some obscure corner of the world, while I shall take you to Vienna,

to the great theatre of the world—upon a stage where you will at least not lack triumphs and homage. And I? Why should I be such a stupid fool as to give you up—you who bring to me much more than I deserve—your beauty, your accomplishments, and your generous heart? Ah, I shall be the target of general envy, for there is no lady in Vienna worthy of being compared with you. As I cannot possess her whom I love, I may thank God that my father has selected you for me. You alone are to be pitied, Fanny, for I cannot offer you any compensation for the sacrifices you are about to make in my favor. I am unworthy of you; you are my superior in beauty, intellect, and education. I am a business man, that is all. But in return I have at least something to give—wealth, splendor, and a name that has a good sound, even at the imperial court. Let me, then, advise you as a friend to accept my hand—it is the hand of a friend who, during his whole life, will honestly strive to compensate you for not being able to give his love to you and to secure your happiness."

He feelingly extended his hand to her, and the young lady slowly laid hers upon it.

"Be it so!" she said, solemnly ; "I accept your hand and am ready to follow you. We shall not be a pair of happy lovers, but two good and sincere friends."

"That is all I ask," said Arnstein, gently. "Never shall I molest you with pretensions and demands that might offend your delicacy and be repugnant to your heart ; never shall I ask more of you than what I hope I shall be able to deserve —your esteem and your confidence. Never shall I entertain the infatuated pretensions of a husband demanding from his wife an affection and fidelity he is himself unable to offer her. In the eyes of the world we shall be man and wife, but in the interior of your house you will find liberty and independence. There you will be able to gratify all your whims and wishes ; there every one will bow to you and obey you. First of all, I shall do so myself. You shall be the pride, the glory and joy of my house, and secure to it a brilliant position in society. We shall live in princely style, and you shall rule as a queen in my house. Will that satisfy you? Do you accept my proposition?"

"Yes, I accept it," exclaimed Fanny, with radiant eyes, "and I assure you no other house in Vienna shall equal ours. We will make it a centre of the best society, and in the midst of this circle which is to embrace the most eminent representatives of beauty, intellect, and distinction, we will forget that we are united without happiness and without love."

"But there will be a day when your heart will love," said Arnstein. "Swear to me that you will not curse me on that day because I shall then stand between you and your love. Swear to me that you will always regard me as your friend, that you will have confidence in me, and tell me when that unhappy and yet so happy hour will strike, when your heart begins to speak."

"I swear it to you!" said Fanny, gravely. "We will always be sincere toward each other. Thus we shall always be able to avert wretchedness, although it may not be in our power to secure happiness. And now, my friend, come, give me your arm and accompany me to the parlor where they are already waiting for us. Now, I shall no longer weep and mourn over this day, for it has given to me a friend, a brother!"

She took his arm and went with him to the parlor. A gentle smile was playing on her lips when the door was opened and they entered. With an air of quiet content she looked at her sisters, who were standing by the side of their betrothed, and had been waiting for her with trembling impatience.

"There is no hope left," murmured Lydia; "she accepts her fate, too, and submits."

"She follows my example," thought Esther; "she consoles herself with her wealth and brilliant position in society. Indeed, there is no better consolation than that."

At that moment the door opened, and the rabbi in his black robe, a skull-cap on his head, appeared on the threshold, followed by the precentor and sexton. Solemn silence ensued, and all heads were lowered in prayer while the rabbi was crossing the room in order to salute the parents of the brides.

CHAPTER XVI.

MARIANNE MEIER.

At that moment of silent devotion, no one took any notice of a lady who crossed the threshold a few seconds after the rabbi had entered. She was a tall, superb creature of wonderful beauty. Her black hair, her glowing eyes, her finely-curved nose, the whole shape of her face imparted to her some resemblance to Fanny Itzig, the banker's beautiful daughter, and indicated that she belonged likewise to the people who, scattered over the whole world, have with unshaken fidelity and constancy preserved everywhere their type and habits. And yet, upon examining the charming stranger somewhat more closely, it became

evident that she bore no resemblance either to Fanny or to her sisters. Hers was a strange and peculiar style of beauty, irresistibly attractive and chilling at the same time—a tall, queenly figure, wrapped in a purple velvet dress, fastened under her bosom by a golden sash. Her shoulders, dazzling white, and of a truly classical shape, were bare; her short ermine mantilla had slipped from them and hung gracefully on her beautiful, well-rounded arms, on which magnificent diamond bracelets were glittering. Her black hair fell down in long, luxuriant ringlets on both sides of her transparent, pale cheeks, and was fastened in a knot by means of several large diamond pins. A diamond of the most precious brilliants crowned her high and thoughtful forehead.

She looked as proud and glorious as a queen, and there was something haughty, imperious, and cold in the glance with which she now slowly and searchingly surveyed the large room.

"Tell me," whispered Baron Arnstein, bending over Fanny Itzig, "who is the beautiful lady now standing near the door?"

"Oh!" exclaimed Fanny, joyfully, "she has come after all. We scarcely dared to hope for her arrival. It is Marianne Meier."

"What! Marianne Meier?" asked Baron Arnstein. "The celebrated beauty whom Goethe has loved—for whom the Swedish ambassador at Berlin, Baron Bernstein, has entertained so glowing a passion, and suffered so much—and who is now the mistress of the Austrian minister, the Prince von Reuss?"

"Hush, for Heaven's sake, hush!" whispered Fanny. "She is coming toward us."

And Fanny went to meet the beautiful lady. Marianne gently inclined her head and kissed Fanny with the dignified bearing of a queen.

"I have come to congratulate you and your sisters," she said, in a sonorous, magnificent alto voice. "I wanted to see how beautiful you looked, and whether your betrothed was worthy of possessing you or not."

Fanny turned round to beckon Baron Arnstein to join them, but he had just left with the rabbi and the other officers of the synagogue.

The ladies were now alone, for the ceremony was about to begin. And now the women entered, whose duty it was to raise loud lamentations and weep over the fate of the brides who were about to leave the parental roof and to follow their husbands. They spread costly carpets at the feet of the brides, who were sitting on arm-chairs among the assembled ladies, and strewing flowers on these carpets, they muttered, sobbing and weeping, ancient Hebrew hymns. The mother stood behind them with trembling lips; and, raising her tearful eyes toward heaven. The door was opened, and the sexton in a long robe, his white beard flowing down on his breast, appeared, carrying in his hand a white cushion with three splendid lace veils. He was followed by Mr. Itzig, the father of the three brides. Taking the veils from the cushion, and muttering prayers all the while, he laid them on the heads of his daughters so that their faces and bodies seemed to be surrounded by a thin and airy mist. And the mourning-women sobbed, and two tears rolled over the pale cheeks of the deeply-moved mother. The two men withdrew silently, and the ladies were alone again.

But now, in the distance, the heart-stirring sounds of a choir of sweet, sonorous children's voices were heard. How charming did these voices re-echo through the room! They seemed to call the brides, and, as if fascinated by the inspiring melody, they slowly rose from their seats. Their mother approached the eldest sister and offered her hand to her. Two of the eldest ladies took the hands of the younger sisters. The other ladies and the mourning-women formed in pairs behind them, and then the procession commenced moving in the direction of the inviting notes of the anthem. Thus they crossed the rooms—nearer and nearer came the music—and finally, on passing through the last door, the ladies stepped into a long hall, beautifully decorated with flowers and covered with a glass roof through which appeared the deep, transparent azure of the wintry sky. In the centre of this hall there arose a purple canopy with golden tassels. The rabbi, praying and with uplifted hands, was standing under it with the three bridegrooms. The choir of the singers, hidden behind flowers and orange-trees, grew louder and louder, and to this jubilant music the ladies conducted the brides to the canopy, and the ceremony commenced.

When it was concluded, when the veils were removed from the heads of the brides so that they could now look freely into the world, the whole party returned to the parlor, and brides and bridegrooms received the congratulations of their friends.

Fanny and Marianne Meier were chatting in a bay-window at some distance from the rest of the company. They were standing there, arm in arm —Fanny in her white bridal costume, like a radiant lily, and Marianne in her purple dress, resembling the peerless queen of flowers.

" You are going to leave Berlin to-day with your husband ? " asked Marianne.

" We leave in an hour," said Fanny, sighing.

Marianne had heard this sigh. " Do you love your husband ? " she asked, hastily.

" I have seen him only twice," whispered Fanny.

A sarcastic smile played on Marianne's lips. "Then they have simply sold you to him like a slave-girl to a wealthy planter," she said. " It was a mere bargain and sale, and still you boast of it, and pass your disgusting trade in human hearts for virtue, and believe you have a right to look proudly and contemptuously down upon those who refuse to be sold like goods, and who prefer to give away their love to being desecrated without love."

" I do not boast of having married without love," said Fanny, gently. " Oh, I should willingly give up wealth and splendor—I should be quite ready to live in poverty and obscurity with a man whom I loved."

" But first the old rabbi would have to consecrate your union with such a man, I suppose ?— otherwise you would not follow him, notwithstanding your love ? " asked Marianne.

" Yes, Marianne, that would be indispensable," said Fanny, gravely, firmly fixing her large eyes upon her friend. " No woman should defy the moral laws of the world, or if she does, she will always suffer for it. If I loved and could not possess the man of my choice, if I could not belong to him as his wedded wife, I should give him up. The grief would kill me, perhaps, but I should die with the consolation of having remained faithful to virtue—"

" And of having proved false to love," exclaimed Marianne, scornfully. " Phrases ! Nothing but phrases learned by heart, my child, but the world boasts of such phrases, and calls such sentiments moral ! Oh, hush ! hush ! I know what you are going to say, and how you wish to admonish me. I heard very well how contemptuously your husband called me the mistress of the Prince von Reuss. Don't excuse him, and don't deny it, for I have heard it. I might reply to it what Madame de Balbi said the other day upon being upbraided with being the mistress of the Royal Prince d'Artois: ' Le sang des princes ne souille pas !' But I do not want to excuse myself; on the contrary, all of you shall some day apologize to me. For I tell you, Fanny, I am pursuing my own path and have a peculiar aim steadfastly in view. Oh, it is a great, a glorious aim. I want to see the whole world at my feet; all those ridiculous prejudices of birth, rank, and virtue shall bow to the Jewess, and the Jewess shall become the peer of the most distinguished representatives of society. See, Fanny, that is my plan and my aim, and it is yours too; we are only pursuing it in different ways—*you*, by the side of a man whose wife you are, and to whom you have pledged at the altar love and fidelity *without* feeling them; *I*, by the side of a man whose friend I am—to whom, it is true, I have not pledged at the altar love and fidelity, but whom I shall faithfully love *because* I have given my heart to him. Let God decide whose is the true morality. The world is on your side and condemns me, but some day I shall hurl back into its teeth all its contempt and scorn, and I shall compel it to bow most humbly to me."

"And whosoever sees you in your proud, radiant beauty, must feel that you will succeed in accomplishing what you are going to undertake," said Fanny, bending an admiring glance on the glorious creature by her side.

Marianne nodded gratefully. "Let us pursue our aim," she said, "for it is one and the same. Both of us have a mission to fulfil, Fanny; we have to avenge the Jewess upon the pride of the Christian women; we have to prove to them that we are their equals in every respect, that we are perhaps better, more accomplished, and talented than all of those haughty Christian women. How often did they neglect and insult us in society! How often did they offensively try to eclipse us! How often did they vex us by their scorn and insolent bearing! We will pay it all back to them; we will scourge them with the scourges with which they have scourged us, and compel them to bow to us!"

"They shall at least consider and treat us as their equals," said Fanny, gravely. "I am not longing for revenge, but I want to hold my place in society, and to prove to them that I am just as well-bred and aristocratic a lady, and have an equal, nay, a better right to call myself a representative of true nobility; for ours is a more ancient nobility than that of all these Christian aristocrats, and we can count our ancestors farther back into the most remote ages than they—our fathers, the proud Levites, having been high-priests in Solomon's temple, and the people having treated them as noblemen even at that time. We will remind the Christian ladies of this whenever they talk to us about their own ancestors, who, at best, only date back to the middle ages or to Charlemagne."

"That is right. I like to hear you talk in this strain," exclaimed Marianne, joyfully. "I see you will represent us in Vienna in a noble and proud manner, and be an honor to the Jews of Berlin. Oh, I am so glad, Fanny, and I shall always love you for it. And do not forget me either. If

it pleases God, I shall some day come to Vienna, and play there a brilliant part. However, we shall never be rivals, but always friends. Will you promise it?"

"I promise it," said Fanny, giving her soft white hand to her friend. Marianne pressed it warmly.

"I accept your promise and shall remind you of it some day," she said. "But now farewell, Fanny, for I see your young husband yonder, who would like to speak to you, and yet does not come to us for fear of coming in contact with the mistress of the Prince von Reuss. God bless and protect his virtue, that stands in such nervous fear of being infected! Farewell; don't forget our oath, and remember me."

She tenderly embraced her friend and imprinted a glowing kiss upon her forehead, and then quickly turning around, walked across the room. All eyes followed the tall, proud lady with admiring glances, and some whispered, "How beautiful she is! How proud, how glorious!" She took no notice, however; she had so often received the homage of these whispers, that they could no longer gladden her heart. Without saluting any one, her head proudly erect, she crossed the room, drawing her ermine mantilla closely around her shoulders, and deeming every thing around her unworthy of notice.

In the anteroom a footman in gorgeous livery was waiting for her. He hastened down-stairs before her, opened the street door, and rushed out in order to find his mistress's carriage among the vast number of coaches encumbering both sides of the street, and then bring it to the door.

Marianne stood waiting in the door, stared at by the inquisitive eyes of the large crowd that had gathered in front of the house to see the guests of the wealthy banker Itzig upon their departure from the wedding.

Marianne paid no attention whatever to these bystanders. Her large black eyes swept over all these faces before her with an air of utter indifference; she took no interest in any one of them, and their impertinent glances made apparently no impression upon her.

But the crowd took umbrage at her queenly indifference.

"Just see," the bystanders whispered here and there, "just see the proud Jewess! How she stares at us, as if we were nothing but thin air! What splendid diamonds she has got! Wonder if she is indebted for them to her father's usury?"

On hearing this question, that was uttered by an old woman in rags, the whole crowd laughed uproariously. Marianne even then took no notice. She only thought that her carriage was a good while coming up, and the supposed slowness of her footman was the sole cause of the frown which now commenced clouding her brow. When the crowd ceased laughing, a woman, a Jewess, in a dirty and ragged dress, stepped forth and placed herself close to Marianne.

"You think she is indebted to her father for those diamonds!" she yelled. "No, I know better, and can tell you all about it. Her father was a good friend of mine, and frequently traded with me when he was still a poor, peddling Jew. He afterward made a great deal of money, while I grew very poor; but he never bought her those diamonds. Just listen to me, and I will tell you what sort of a woman she is who now looks down on us with such a haughty air. She is the Jewess Marianne Meier, the mistress of the old Prince von Reuss!"

"Ah, a mistress!" shouted the crowd, sneeringly. "And she is looking at us as though she were a queen. She wears diamonds in her hair, and wants to hide her shame by dressing in purple velvet. She—"

At that moment the carriage rolled up to the door; the footman obsequiously opened the coach door and hastened to push back the crowd in order to enable Marianne to walk over the carpet spread out on the sidewalk to her carriage.

"We won't be driven back!" roared the crowd; "we want to see the beautiful mistress—we want to see her close by."

And laughing, shouting, and jeering, the bystanders crowded closely around Marianne. She walked past them, proud and erect, and did not seem to hear the insulting remarks that were being levelled at her. Only her cheeks had turned even paler than before, and her lips were quivering a little.

Now she had reached her carriage and entered. The footman closed the door, but the mob still crowded around the carriage, and looked through the glass windows, shouting, "Look at her! look at her! What a splendid mistress she is! Hurrah for her! Long live the mistress!"

The coachman whipped the horses, and the carriage commenced moving, but it could make but little headway, the jeering crowd rolling along with it like a huge black wave, and trying to keep it back at every step.

Marianne sat proudly erect in her carriage, staring at the mob with flaming and disdainful eyes. Not a tear moistened her eyes; not a word, not a cry issued from her firmly-compressed lips. Even when her carriage, turning around the cor-

ner, gained at last a free field and sped away with thundering noise, there was no change whatever in her attitude, or in the expression of her countenance. She soon reached the embassy buildings. The carriage stopped in front of the vestibule, and the footman opened the coach door. Marianne alighted and walked slowly and proudly to the staircase. The footman hastened after her, and when she had just reached the first landing-place he stood behind her and whispered:

"I beg your pardon, madame; I was really entirely innocent. Your carriage being the last to arrive, it had to take the hindmost place; that was the reason why it took us so long to get it to the door. I beg your pardon, madame."

Marianne only turned to him for a moment, bending a single contemptuous glance upon him, and then, without uttering a word, continued ascending the staircase.

The footman paused and looked after the proud lady, whispering with a sigh—

"She will discharge me—she never forgives!"

Marianne had now reached the upper story, and walked down the corridor as slowly and as proudly as ever. Her valet stood at the door, receiving her with a profound bow, while opening the folding door. She crossed gravely and silently the long suite of rooms now opening before her, and finally entered her dressing-room. Her two lady's maids were waiting for her here in order to assist her in putting on a more comfortable dress.

When they approached their mistress, she made an imperious, repelling gesture.

"Begone!" she said, "begone!"

That was all she said, but it sounded like a scream of rage and pain, and the lady's maids hastened to obey, or rather to escape. When the door had closed behind them, Marianne rushed toward it and locked it, and drew the heavy curtain over it.

Now she was alone—now nobody could see her, nobody could hear her. With a wild cry she raised her beautiful arms, tore the splendid diadem of brilliants from her hair, and hurled it upon the floor. She then with trembling hands loosened the golden sash from her tapering waist, and the diamond pins from her hair, and threw all these precious trinkets disdainfully upon the floor. And now with her small feet, with her embroidered silken shoes, she furiously stamped on them with flaming eyes, and in her paroxysm of anger slightly opening her lips, so as to show her two rows of peerless teeth which she held firmly pressed together.

Her fine hair, no longer fastened by the diamond pins, had fallen down, and was now floating around her form like a black veil, and closely covered her purple dress. Thus she looked like a goddess of vengeance, so beautiful, so proud, so glorious and terrible—her small hands raised toward heaven, and her feet crushing the jewelry.

"Insulted, scorned!" she murmured. "The meanest woman on the street believes she has a right to despise me—me, the celebrated Marianne Meier—me, at whose feet counts and princes have sighed in vain! And who am I, then, that they should dare to despise me?"

She asked this question with a defiant, burning glance toward heaven, but all at once she commenced trembling, and hung her head humbly and mournfully.

"I am a disgraced woman," she whispered. "Diamonds and velvet do not hide my shame. I am the prince's mistress. That's all!

"But it shall be so no longer!" she exclaimed, suddenly. "I will put a stop to it. I *must* put a stop to it! This hour has decided my destiny and broken my stubbornness. I thought I could defy the world in *my* way. I believed I could laugh at its prejudices; but the world is stronger than I, and therefore I have to submit, and shall hereafter defy it in its own way. And I shall do so most assuredly. I shall do so on the spot."

Without reflecting any further, she left her chamber and hastened once more through the rooms. Her hair now was waving wildly around her shoulders, and her purple dress, no longer held together by the golden sash, was floating loosely around her form.

She took no notice whatever of her *dishabille;* only one idea, only one purpose filled her heart.

In breathless haste she hurried on, and now quickly opened a last door, through which she entered a room furnished in the most sumptuous and comfortable manner.

At her appearance, so sudden, and evidently unexpected, the elderly gentleman, who had reposed on the silken sofa, arose and turned around with a gesture of displeasure.

On recognizing Marianne, however, a smile overspread his features, and he went to meet her with a pleasant greeting.

"Back already, dearest?" he said, extending his hand toward her.

"Yes, your highness—I am back already," she said drily and coldly.

The gentleman upon whose features the traces of a life of dissipation were plainly visible, fixed his eyes with an anxious air upon the beautiful lady. He only now noticed her angry mien and the strange *dishabille* in which she appeared before him.

"Good Heaven, Marianne!" he asked, sharply, "what is the cause of your agitation, of your coldness toward me? What has happened to you?"

"What has happened to me? The most infamous insults have been heaped upon my head!" she exclaimed with quivering lips, an angry blush suffusing her cheeks. "For a quarter of an hour, nay, for an eternity, I was the target of the jeers, the contempt, and the scorn of the rabble that publicly abused me in the most disgraceful manner!"

"Tell me," exclaimed the old gentleman, "what has occurred, and whose fault it was!"

"Whose fault it was?" she asked, bending a piercing glance upon him. "Yours, my prince; you alone are to blame for my terrible disgrace and humiliation. For your sake the rabble has reviled me, called me your mistress, and laughed at my diamonds; calling them the reward of my shame! Oh, how many insults, how many mortifications have I not already suffered for your sake—with how many bloody tears have I not cursed this love which attaches me to you, and which I was nevertheless unable to tear from my heart, for it is stronger than myself. But now the cup of bitterness is full to overflowing. My pride cannot bear so much contumely and scorn. Farewell, my prince, my beloved! I must leave you. I cannot stay with you any longer. Shame would kill me. Farewell! Hereafter, no one shall dare to call me a mistress."

With a last glowing farewell, she turned to the door, but the prince kept her back. "Marianne," he asked, tenderly, "do you not know that I love you, and that I cannot live without you?"

She looked at him with a fascinating smile. "And I?" she asked, "far from you, shall die of a broken heart; with you, I shall die of shame. I prefer the former. Farewell! No one shall ever dare again to call me by that name." And her hand touched already the door-knob.

The prince encircled her waist with his arms and drew her back.

"I shall not let you go," he said, ardently. "You are mine, and shall remain so! Oh, why are you so proud and so cold? Why will you not sacrifice your faith to our love? Why do you insist upon remaining a Jewess?"

"Your highness," she said, leaning her head on his shoulder, "why do you want me to become a Christian?"

"Why?" he exclaimed. "Because my religion and the laws of my country prevent me from marrying a Jewess."

"And if I should sacrifice to you the last that

nas remained to me?" she whispered—"my conscience and my religion."

"Marianne," he exclaimed, solemnly, "I repeat to you what I have told you so often already: 'Become a Christian in order to become my wife.'"

She encircled his neck impetuously with her arms and clung to him with a passionate outburst of tenderness. "I will become a Christian!" she whispered.

CHAPTER XVII.

LOVE AND POLITICS.

"At last! at last!" exclaimed Gentz, in a tone of fervid tenderness, approaching Marianne, who went to meet him with a winning smile. "Do you know, dearest, that you have driven me to despair for a whole week? Not a word, not a message from you! Whenever I came to see you, I was turned away. Always the same terrible reply, 'Madame is not at home,' while I felt your nearness in every nerve and vein of mine, and while my throbbing heart was under the magic influence of your presence. And then to be turned away! No reply whatever to my letters, to my ardent prayers to see you only for a quarter of an hour."

"Oh, you ungrateful man!" she said, smiling, "did I not send for you to-day? Did I not give you this rendezvous quite voluntarily?"

"You knew very well that I should have died if your heart had not softened at last. Oh, heavenly Marianne, what follies despair made me commit already! In order to forget you, I plunged into all sorts of pleasures, I commenced new works, I entered upon fresh love-affairs. But it was all in vain. Amidst those pleasures I was sad; during my working hours my mind was wandering, and in order to impart a semblance of truth and tenderness to my protestations of love, I had to close my eyes and imagine you were the lady whom I was addressing."

"And then you were successful?" asked Marianne, smiling.

"Yes, then I was successful," he said, gravely; "but my new lady-love, the beloved of my distraction and despair, did not suspect that I only embraced her so tenderly because I kissed in her the beloved of my heart and of my enthusiasm."

"And who was the lady whom you call the beloved of your distraction and despair?" asked Marianne.

"Ah, Marianne, you ask me to betray a woman?"

"No, no; I am glad to perceive that you are a discreet cavalier. You shall betray no woman. I will tell you her name. The beloved of your distraction and despair was the most beautiful and charming lady in Berlin—it was the actress Christel Enghaus. Let me compliment you, my friend, on having triumphed with that belle over all those sentimental, lovesick princes, counts, and barons. Indeed, you have improved your week of 'distraction and despair' in the most admirable manner."

"Still, Marianne, I repeat to you, she was merely my sweetheart for the time being, and I merely plunged into this adventure in order to forget you."

"Then you love me really?" asked Marianne.

"Marianne, I adore you! You know it. Oh, now I may tell you so. Heretofore you repelled me and would not listen to my protestations of love because I was a married man. Now, however, I have got rid of my ignominious fetters, Marianne; now I am no longer a married man. I am free, and all the women in the world are at liberty to love me. I am as free as a bird in the air!"

"And like a bird you want to flit from one heart to another?"

"No, most beautiful, most glorious Marianne; your heart shall be the cage in which I shall imprison myself."

"Beware, my friend. What would you say if there was no door in this cage through which you might escape?"

"Oh, if it had a door, I should curse it."

"Then you love me so boundlessly as to be ready to sacrifice to me the liberty you have scarcely regained?"

"Can you doubt it, Marianne?" asked Gentz, tenderly pressing her beautiful hands to his lips.

"Are you in earnest, my friend?" she said, smiling. "So you offer your hand to me? You want to marry me?"

Gentz started back, and looked at her with a surprised and frightened air. Marianne laughed merrily.

"Ah!" she said, "your face is the most wonderful illustration of Goethe's poem. You know it, don't you?" And she recited with ludicrous pathos the following two lines:

"'Heirathen, Kind, ist wunderlich Wort,
Hör'ich's, möcht' ich gleich wieder fort.'

"Good Heaven, what a profound knowledge of human nature our great Goethe has got, and how proud I am to be allowed to call him a friend of mine—*Heirathen, Kind, ist wunderlich Wort.*"

"Marianne, you are cruel and unjust, you—"

"And you know the next two lines of the

poem?" she interrupted him. "The maiden replied to him:

> "' Heirathen wir eben,
> Das Ubrige wird sich geben.'"

"You mock me," exclaimed Gentz, smiling, "and yet you know the maiden's assurance would not prove true in our case, and that there is something rendering such a happiness, the prospect of calling you my wife, an utter impossibility. Unfortunately, you are no Christian, Marianne. Hence I cannot marry you." *

"And if I were a Christian?" she asked in a sweet, enchanting voice.

He fixed his eyes with a searching glance upon her smiling, charming face.

"What!" he asked, in evident embarrassment. "If you were a Christian? What do you mean, Marianne?"

"I mean, Frederick, that I have given the highest proof of my love to the man who loves me so ardently, constantly, and faithfully. For his sake I have become a Christian. Yesterday I was baptized. Now, my friend, I ask you once more, I ask you as a Christian woman: Gentz, will you marry me? Answer me honestly and frankly, my friend! Remember that it is 'the beloved of your heart and of your enthusiasm,' as you called me yourself a few moments ago, who now stands before you and asks for a reply. Remember that this moment will be decisive for our future—speedily, nay, immediately decisive. For you see I have removed all obstacles. I have become a Christian, and I tell you I am ready to become your wife in the course of the present hour. Once more, then, Gentz, will you marry me?"

He had risen and paced the room in great excitement. Marianne followed him with a lurking glance and a scornful smile, but when he now stepped back to her, she quickly assumed her serious air.

"Marianne," he said, firmly, "you want to know the truth, and I love you too tenderly to conceal it from you. I will not, must not, cannot marry you. I will not, because I am unable to bear once more the fetters of wedded life. I must not, because I should make you unhappy and wretched. I cannot, while, doing so, I should act perfidiously toward a friend of mine, for you know very well that the Prince von Reuss is my intimate friend."

"And I am his mistress. You wished to intimate that to me by your last words, I suppose?"

"I wished to intimate that he loves you boundlessly, and he is a generous, magnanimous man,

Marriages between Christians and Jews were prohibited in the German states at that period.

whose heart would break if any one should take you from him."

"For the last time, then: you will not marry me?"

"Marianne, I love you too tenderly—I cannot marry you!"

Marianne burst into a fit of laughter. "A strange reason for rejecting my hand, indeed!" she said. "It is so original that in itself it might almost induce me to forgive your refusal. And yet I had counted so firmly and surely upon your love and consent that I had made already the necessary arrangements in order that our wedding might take place to-day. Just look at me, Gentz. Do you not see that I wear a bridal-dress?"

"Your beauty is always a splendid bridal-dress for you, Marianne."

"Well said! But do you not see a myrtle-wreath, my bridal-wreath, on the table there? *Honi soit qui mal y pense!* The priest is already waiting for the bride and bridegroom in the small chapel, the candles on the altar are lighted, every thing is ready for the ceremony. Well, we must not make the priest wait any longer. So you decline being the bridegroom at the ceremony? Well, attend it, then, as a witness. Will you do so? Will you assist me as a faithful friend, sign my marriage-contract, and keep my secret!"

"I am ready to give you any proof of my love and friendship," said Gentz, gravely.

"Well, I counted on you," exclaimed Marianne, smiling, "and, to tell you the truth, I counted on your refusal to marry me. Come, give me your arm. I will show you the small chapel which the Prince von Reuss has caused to be fitted up here in the building of the Austrian embassy. The servants will see nothing strange in our going there, and I hope, moreover, that we shall meet with no one on our way thither. At the chapel we shall perhaps find Prince Henry—that will be a mere accident, which will surprise no one. Come, assist me in putting on this long black mantilla which will entirely conceal my white silk dress. The myrtle-wreath I shall take under my arm so that no one will see it. And now, come!"

"Yes, let us go," said Gentz, offering his arm to her. "I see very well that there is a mystification in store for me, but I shall follow you wherever you will take me, to the devil or—"

"Or to church," she said, smiling. "But hush now, so that no one may hear us."

They walked silently through the rooms, then down a long corridor, and after descending a narrow secret staircase, they entered a small apartment where three gentlemen were waiting for them. One of them was a Catholic priest in his vestments, the second the Prince von Reuss, Henry XIII., and the third the first *attaché* of the Austrian embassy.

The prince approached Marianne, and after taking her hand he saluted Gentz in the most cordial manner.

"Every thing is ready," he said; "come, Marianne, let me place the wreath on your head."

Marianne took off her mantilla, and, handing the myrtle-wreath to the prince, she bowed her head, and almost knelt down before him. He took the wreath and fastened it in her hair, whereupon he beckoned the *attaché* to hand to him the large casket standing on the table. This casket contained a small prince's coronet of exquisite workmanship and sparkling with the most precious diamonds.

The prince fastened this coronet over Marianne's wreath, and the diamonds glistened now like stars over the delicate myrtle-leaves.

"Arise, Marianne," he then said, loudly. "I have fastened the coronet of your new dignity in your hair; let us now go to the altar."

Marianne arose. A strange radiance of triumphant joy beamed in her face; a deep flush suffused her cheeks, generally so pale and transparent; a blissful smile played on her lips. With a proud and sublime glance at Gentz, who was staring at her, speechless and amazed, she took the prince's arm.

The priest led the way, and from the small room they now entered the chapel of the embassy. On the altar, over which one of Van Dyck's splendid paintings was hanging, large wax-tapers were burning in costly silver chandeliers. On the carpet in front of the altar two small *prie-dieus* for Marianne and the prince were placed, and two armchairs for the witnesses stood behind them. Opposite the altar, on the other side of the chapel, a sort of choir or balcony with an organ had been fitted up.

But no one was there to play on that organ. All the other chairs and benches were vacant; the ceremony was to be performed secretly and quietly.

Gentz saw and observed every thing as though it were a vision, he could not yet make up his mind that it was a reality; he was confused and almost dismayed, and did not know whether it was owing to his surprise at what was going on, or to his vexation at being so badly duped by Marianne. He believed he was dreaming when he saw Marianne and the prince kneeling on the *prie-dieus*, Marianne Meier, the Jewess, at the right hand of the high-born nobleman, at the place of honor, only to be occupied by legitimate brides of equal

rank; and when he heard the priest, who stood in front of the altar, pronounce solemn words of exhortation and benediction, and finally ask the kneeling bride and bridegroom to vow eternal love and fidelity to each other. Both uttered the solemn "Yes" at the same time, the prince quietly and gravely, Marianne hastily and in a joyful voice. The priest thereupon gave them the benediction, and the ceremony was over. The whole party then returned to the anteroom serving as a sacristy. They silently received the congratulations of the priest and the witnesses. The *attaché* then took a paper from his memorandum-book; it contained the minutes of the ceremony, which he had drawn up already in advance. Marianne and the prince signed it; the witnesses and the priest did the same, the latter adding the church seal to his signature. It was now a perfectly valid certificate of their legitimate marriage, which the prince handed to Marianne, and for which she thanked him with a tender smile.

"You are now my legitimate wife," said the Prince von Reuss, gravely; "I wish to give you this proof of my love and esteem, and I return my thanks to these gentlemen for having witnessed the ceremony; you might some day stand in need of their testimony. For the time being, however, I have cogent reasons for keeping our marriage secret, and you have promised not to divulge it."

"And I renew my promise at this sacred place and in the presence of the priest and our witnesses, my dear husband," said Marianne. "No one shall hear from me a word or even an intimation of what has occurred here. Before the world I shall be obediently and patiently nothing but your mistress until you deem it prudent to acknowledge that I am your wife."

"I shall do so at no distant day," said the prince. "And you, gentlemen, will you promise also, will you pledge me your word of honor that you will faithfully keep our secret?"

"We promise it upon our honor!" exclaimed the two gentlemen.

The prince bowed his thanks. "Let us now leave the chapel separately, just as we have come," he said: "if we should withdraw together, it would excite the attention and curiosity of the servants, some of whom might meet us in the hall. Come, baron, you will accompany me." He took the *attaché's* arm, and left the small sacristy with him.

"And you will accompany me," said Marianne, kindly nodding to Gentz.

"And I shall stay here for the purpose of praying for the bride and bridegroom," muttered the priest, returning to the altar.

Marianne now hastily took the coronet and myrtle-wreath from her hair and concealed both under the black mantilla which Gentz gallantly laid around her shoulders.

They silently reascended the narrow staircase and returned through the corridor to Marianne's rooms. Upon reaching her boudoir, Marianne doffed her mantilla with an indescribable air of triumphant joy, and laid the coronet and myrtle-wreath on the table. "Well," she asked in her sonorous, impressive voice, "what do you say now, my tender Gentz?"

He had taken his hat, and replied with a deep bow: "I have to say that I bow to your sagacity and talents. That was a master-stroke of yours, dearest."

"Was it not?" she asked, triumphantly. "The Jewess, hitherto despised and ostracized by society, has suddenly become a legitimate princess; she has now the power to avenge all sneers, all derision, all contempt she has had to undergo. Oh, how sweet this revenge will be—how I shall humble all those haughty ladies who dared to despise me, and who will be obliged henceforth to yield the place of honor to me!"

"And will you revenge yourself upon me too, Marianne?" asked Gentz, humbly—"upon me who dared reject your hand? But no, you must always be grateful to me for that refusal of mine. Just imagine I had compelled you to stick to your offer: instead of being a princess, you would now be the unhappy wife of the poor military counsellor, Frederick Gentz."

Marianne laughed. "You are right," she said, "I am grateful to you for it. But, my friend, you must not and shall not remain the poor military counsellor Gentz."

"God knows that that is not my intention either," exclaimed Gentz, laughing. "God has placed a capital in my head, and you may be sure that I shall know how to invest it at a good rate of interest."

"But here you will obtain no such interest," said Marianne, eagerly, "let us speak sensibly about that matter. We have paid our tribute to love and friendship; let us now talk about politics. I am authorized—and she who addresses you now is no longer Marianne Meier, but the wife of the Austrian ambassador—I am authorized to make an important offer to you. Come, my friend, sit down in the arm-chair here, and let us hold a diplomatic conference."

"Yes, let us do so," said Gentz, smiling, and taking the seat she had indicated to him.

"Friend Gentz, what are your hopes for the future?"

"A ponderous question, but I shall try to answer it as briefly as possible. I am in hopes of earning fame, honor, rank, influence, and a brilliant position by my talents."

"And you believe you can obtain all that here in Prussia?"

"I hope so," said Gentz, hesitatingly.

"You have addressed a memorial to the young king; you have urged him to give to his subjects prosperity, happiness, honor, and freedom of the press. How long is it since you sent that memorial to him?"

"Four weeks to-day."

"Four weeks, and they have not yet rewarded you for your glorious memorial, although the whole Prussian nation hailed it with the most rapturous applause? They have not yet thought of appointing you to a position worthy of your talents? You have not yet been invited to court?"

"Yes, I was invited to court. The queen wished to become acquainted with me. Gualtieri presented me to her, and her majesty said very many kind and flattering things to me." *

"Words, empty words, my friend! Their actions are more eloquent. The king has not sent for you, the king has not thanked you. The king does not want your advice, and as if to show to yourself, and to all those who have received your letter so enthusiastically, that he intends to pursue his own path and not to listen to such advice, the king, within the last few days, has addressed a decree to the criminal court, peremptorily ordering the prosecuting attorneys to proceed rigorously against the publishers of writings not submitted to or rejected by the censors." †

"That cannot be true—that is impossible!" exclaimed Gentz, starting up.

"I pardon your impetuosity in consideration of your just indignation," said Marianne, smiling. "That I told you the truth, however, you will see in to-morrow's *Gazette*, which will contain the royal decree I alluded to. Oh, you know very well the Austrian ambassador has good friends everywhere, who furnish him the latest news, and keep him informed of all such things. You need not hope, therefore, that the young king will make any use of your talents or grant you any favors. Your splendid memorial has offended him instead of winning him; he thought it was altogether too bold. Frederick William the Third is not partial to bold, eccentric acts; he instinctively shrinks back from all violent reforms. The present King of Prussia will not meddle with the great affairs

---

* Varnhagen, "Gallerie von Bildnissen," etc., vol. II.
† F. Foerster, "Modern History of Prussia," vol. I., p. 493.

of the world; the King of Prussia wishes to remain neutral amidst the struggle of contending parties. Instead of thinking of war and politics, he devotes his principal attention to the church service and examination of the applicants for holy orders, and yet he is not even courageous enough formally to abolish Wöllner's bigoted edict, and thus to make at least one decisive step forward. Believe me, lukewarmness and timidity will characterize every act of his administration. So you had better go to Austria."

."And what shall I do in Austria?" asked Gentz, thoughtfully,

"What shall you do there?" exclaimed Marianne, passionately. "You shall serve the fatherland—you shall serve Germany, for Germany is in Austria just as well as in Prussia. Oh, believe me, my friend, only in Austria will you find men strong and bold enough to brave the intolerable despotism of the French. And the leading men there will welcome you most cordially; an appropriate sphere will be allotted to your genius, and the position to which you will be appointed will amply satisfy the aspirations of your ambition. I am officially authorized to make this offer to you, for Austria is well aware that, in the future, she stands in need of men of first-class ability, and she therefore desires to secure your services, which she will reward in a princely manner. Come, my friend, I shall set out to-day with the prince on a journey to Austria. Accompany us—become one of ours!"

"Ours! Are you, then, no longer a daughter of Prussia?"

"I have become a thorough and enthusiastic Austrian, for I worship energy and determination, and these qualities I find only in Austria, in the distinguished man who is holding the helm of her ship of state, Baron Thugut. Come with us; Thugut is anxious to have you about his person; accompany us to him."

"And what are you going to do in Vienna?" asked Gentz, evasively. "Is it a mere pleasure-trip?"

"If another man should put that question to me, I should reply in the affirmative, but to you I am going to prove by my entire sincerity that I really believe you to be a devoted friend of mine. No, it is no pleasure-trip. I accompany the prince to Vienna because he wants to get there instructions from Baron Thugut and learn what is to be done at Rastadt."

"Ah, at Rastadt—at the peace congress," exclaimed Gentz. "The emperor has requested the states of the empire to send plenipotentiaries to Rastadt to negotiate there with France a just and equitable peace. Prussia has already sent there her plenipotentiaries, Count Goertz and Baron Dohm. Oh, I should have liked to accompany them and participate in performing the glorious task to be accomplished there. That congress at Rastadt is the last hope of Germany; if it should fail, all prospects of a regeneration of the empire are gone. That congress will at last give to the nation all it needs; an efficient organization of the empire, a well-regulated administration of justice, protection of German manufactures against British arrogance, and last, but not least, freedom of the press, for which the Germans have been yearning for so many years."

Marianne burst into a loud fit of laughter. "Oh, you enthusiastic visionary!" she said, "but let us speak softly, for even the walls must not hear what I am now going to tell you."

She bent over the table, drawing nearer to Gentz, and fixing her large, flaming eyes upon him, she asked in a whisper, "I suppose you love Germany? You would not like to see her devoured by France as Italy was devoured by her? You would not like either to see her go to decay and crumble to pieces from inherent weakness?"

"Oh, I love Germany!" said Gentz, enthusiastically. "All my wishes, all my hopes belong to her. Would to God I could say some day, all my talents, my energy, my perseverance are devoted to my fatherland—to Germany!"

"Well, if you really desire to be useful to Germany," whispered Marianne, "hasten to Rastadt. If Germany is to be saved at all, it must be done at once. You know the stipulations of the treaty of Campo Formio, I suppose?"

"I only know what every one knows about them."

"But you do not know the secret article. I will tell you all about it. Listen to me. The secret article accepted by the emperor reads as follows: 'The emperor pledges himself to withdraw his troops from Mentz, Ehrenbreitstein, Mannheim, Königstein, and from the German empire in general, twenty days after the ratification of the peace, which has to take place in the course of two months'" *

"But he thereby delivers the empire to the tender mercies of the enemy," exclaimed Gentz, in dismay. "Oh, that cannot be! No German could grant and sign such terms without sinking into the earth from shame. That would be contrary to every impulse of patriotism—"

"Nevertheless, that article has been signed and will be carried out to the letter. Make haste,

* Schlosser's "History of the Eighteenth Century," vol. v., p. 43.

therefore, Germany is calling you; assist her, you have got the strength. Oh, give it to her! Become an Austrian just as Brutus became a servant of the kings; become an Austrian in order to save Germany!"

"Ah, you want to entice me, Delilah!" exclaimed Gentz. "You want to show me a beautiful goal in order to make me walk the tortuous paths which *may* lead thither! No, Delilah, it is in vain! I shall stay here; I shall not go to Austria, for Austria is the state that is going to betray Germany. Prussia may be able to save her; she stands perhaps in need of my arm, my pen, and my tongue for that purpose. I am a German, but first of all I am a Prussian, and every good patriot ought first to serve his immediate country, and wait until she calls him. I still hope that the king will prove the right man for his responsible position; I still expect that he will succeed in rendering Prussia great and Germany free. I must, therefore, remain a Prussian as yet and be ready to serve my country."

"Poor enthusiast! You will regret some day having lost your time by indulging in visionary hopes."

"Well, I will promise, whenever that day comes, whenever Prussia declares that she does not want my services, then I will come to you—then you shall enlist me for Austria, and perhaps I may then still be able to do something for Germany. But until then, leave me here. I swear to you, not a word of what you have just told me here shall be betrayed by my lips; but I cannot serve him who has betrayed Germany."

"You cannot be induced, then, to accept my offer? You want to stay here? You refuse to accompany me to Vienna, to Rastadt, in order to save what may yet be saved for Germany?"

"If I had an army under my command," exclaimed Gentz, with flaming eyes, "if I were the King of Prussia, then I should assuredly go to Rastadt, but I should go thither for the purpose of dispersing all those hypocrites, cowards, and scribblers who call themselves statesmen, and of driving those French republicans who put on such disgusting airs, and try to make us believe they had a perfect right to meddle with the domestic affairs of Germany—beyond the Rhine! I should go thither for the purpose of garrisoning the fortresses of the Rhine—which the Emperor of Germany is going to surrender to the tender mercies of the enemy—with my troops, and of defending them against all foes from without or from within. That would be my policy if I were King of Prussia. But being merely the poor military counsellor, Frederick Gentz, and having nothing but some ability and a sharp pen, I shall stay here and wait to see whether or not Prussia will make use of my ability and of my pen. God save Germany and protect her from her physicians who are concocting a fatal draught for her at Rastadt! God save Germany!"

CHAPTER XVIII.

CITOYENNE JOSEPHINE BONAPARTE.

A JOYFUL commotion reigned on the eighth of November, 1797, in the streets and public places of the German fortress of Rastadt. The whole population of the lower classes had gathered in the streets, while the more aristocratic inhabitants appeared at the open windows of their houses in eager expectation of the remarkable event for which not only the people of the whole city, but also the foreign ambassadors, a large number of whom had arrived at Rastadt, were looking with the liveliest symptoms of impatience.

And, indeed, a rare spectacle was in store for them. It was the arrival of General Bonaparte and his wife Josephine that all were waiting for this morning. They were not to arrive together, however, but both were to reach the city by a different route. Josephine, who was expected to arrive first, was coming from Milan by the shortest and most direct route; while Bonaparte had undertaken a more extended journey from Campo Formio through Italy and Switzerland. It was well known already that he had been received everywhere with the most unbounded enthusiasm, and that all nations had hailed him as the Messiah of liberty. There had not been a single city that had not received him with splendid festivities, and honors had been paid to him as though he were not only a triumphant victor, but an exalted ruler, to whom every one was willing to submit. Even free Switzerland had formed no exception. At Geneva the daughters of the first and most distinguished families, clad in the French colors, had presented to him in the name of the city a laurel-wreath. At Berne, his carriage had passed through two lines of handsomely decorated coaches, filled with beautiful and richly adorned ladies,

who had hailed him with the jubilant shout of " Long live the pacificator !"

In the same manner the highest honors had been paid to his wife Josephine, who had been treated everywhere with the deference due to a sovereign princess. The news of these splendid receptions had reached Rastadt already; and it was but natural that the authorities and citizens of the fortress did not wish to be outdone, and that they had made extensive arrangements for welcoming the conqueror of Italy in a becoming manner.

A magnificent triumphal arch had been erected in front of the gate through which General Bonaparte was to enter the city, and under it the city fathers, clad in their official robes, were waiting for the victorious hero, in order to conduct him to the house that had been selected for him. In front of this house, situated on the large market-place, a number of young and pretty girls, dressed in white, and carrying baskets with flowers and fruits which they were to lay at the feet of the general's beautiful wife, had assembled. At the gate through which Josephine was to arrive, a brilliant cavalcade of horsemen had gathered for the purpose of welcoming the lady of the great French chieftain, and of escorting her as a guard of honor.

Among these cavaliers there were most of the ambassadors from the different parts of Germany, who had met here at Rastadt in order to accomplish the great work of peace. Every sovereign German prince, every elector and independent count had sent his delegates to the southwestern fortress for the purpose of negotiating with the French plenipotentiaries concerning the future destinies of Germany. Even Sweden had sent a representative, who had not appeared so much, however, in order to take care of the interests of Swedish Pomerania, as to play the part of a mediator and reconciler.

All these ambassadors had been allowed to

enter Rastadt quietly and entirely unnoticed. The *German* city had failed to pay any public honors to these distinguished *German* noblemen; but every one hastened to exhibit the greatest deference to the French general—and even the ambassadors deemed it prudent to participate in these demonstrations: only they tried to display, even on this occasion, their accustomed diplomacy, and instead of receiving the victorious chieftain in the capacity of humble vassals, they preferred to present their respects as gallant cavaliers to his beautiful wife and to escort her into the city.

The German ambassadors, therefore, were waiting for Mme. General Bonaparte on their magnificent prancing steeds in front of the gate through which she was to pass. Even old Count Metternich, the delegate of the Emperor of Austria and ruler of the empire, notwithstanding the stiffness of his limbs, had mounted his horse; by his side the other two ambassadors of Austria were halting—Count Lehrbach, the Austrian member of the imperial commission, and Count Louis Cobenzl, who was acting as a delegate for Bohemia and Hungary. Behind old Count Metternich, on a splendid and most fiery charger, a young cavalier of tall figure and rare manly beauty might be seen; it was young Count Clemens Metternich, who was to represent the corporation of the Counts of Westphalia, and to begin his official diplomatic career here at Rastadt under the eye of his aged father. By his side the imposing and grave ambassadors of Prussia made their appearance—Count Goertz, who at the time of the war for the succession in Bavaria had played a part so important for Prussia and so hostile to Austria; and Baron Dohm, no less distinguished as a cavalier than as a writer. Not far from them the representatives of Bavaria, Saxony, Wurtemberg, and of the whole host of the so-called "Immediates" * might be seen, whom the editors and correspondents had joined, that had repaired to Rastadt in the hope of finding there a perfect gold-mine for their greedy pens. But not merely the German diplomatists and the aristocratic young men of Rastadt were waiting here for the arrival of Mme. General Bonaparte; there was also the whole crowd of French singers, actors, and adventurers who had flocked to the Congress of Rastadt for the purpose of amusing the distinguished noblemen and delegates by their vaudevilles, comedies, and gay operas. Finally, there were also the French actresses and ballet-girls,

* The noblemen owning territory in the states of secondary princes, but subject only to the authority of the emperor, were called *"Immediates."*

who, dressed in the highest style of fashion, were occupying on one side of the road a long row of splendid carriages. Many of these carriages were decorated on their doors with large coats-of-arms, and a person well versed in heraldry might have easily seen therefrom that these escutcheons indicated some of the noble diplomatists on the other side of the road to be the owners of the carriages. In fact, a very cordial and friendly understanding seemed to prevail between the diplomatists and the ladies of the French theatre. This was not only evident from the German diplomatists having lent their carriages to the French ladies for the day's reception, but likewise from the ardent, tender, and amorous glances that were being exchanged between them, from their significant smiles, and from their stealthy nods and mute but eloquent greetings.

Suddenly, however, this mimical flirtation was interrupted by the rapid approach of a courier. This was the signal announcing the impending arrival of Josephine Bonaparte. In fact, the heads of four horses were seen already in the distance; they came nearer and nearer, and now the carriage drawn by these horses, and a lady occupying it, could be plainly discerned.

It was a wonderful warm day in November. Josephine, therefore, had caused the top of her carriage to be taken down, and the spectators were able, not merely to behold her face, but to scan most leisurely her whole figure and even her costume. The carriage had approached at full gallop, but now, upon drawing near to the crowd assembled in front of the gate, it slackened its speed, and every one had time and leisure to contemplate the lady enthroned in the carriage. She was no longer in the first bloom of youth; more than thirty years had passed already over her head; they had deprived her complexion of its natural freshness, and left the first slight traces of age upon her pure and noble forehead. But her large dark eyes were beaming still in the imperishable fire of her inward youth, and a sweet and winning smile, illuminating her whole countenance as though a ray of the setting sun had fallen upon it, was playing around her charming lips. Her graceful and elegant figure was wrapped in a closely fitting gown of dark-green velvet, richly trimmed with costly furs, and a small bonnet, likewise trimmed with furs, covered her head, and under this bonnet luxuriant dark ringlets were flowing down, surrounding the beautiful and noble oval of her face with a most becoming frame.

Josephine Bonaparte was still a most attractive and lovely woman, and on beholding her it was easily understood why Bonaparte, although much younger, had been so fascinated by this charming lady and loved her with such passionate tenderness.

The French actors now gave vent to their delight by loud cheers, and rapturously waving their hats, they shouted: "*Vive la citoyenne Bonaparte! Vive l'auguste épouse de l'Italique!*"

Josephine nodded eagerly and with affable condescension to the enthusiastic crowd, and slowly passed on. On approaching the diplomatists, she assumed a graver and more erect attitude; she acknowledged the low, respectful obeisances of the cavaliers with the distinguished, careless, and yet polite bearing of a queen, and seemed to have for every one a grateful glance and a kind smile. Every one was satisfied that she had especially noticed and distinguished him, and every one, therefore, felt flattered and elated. From the diplomatists she turned her face for a moment to the other side, toward the ladies seated in the magnificent carriages. But her piercing eye, her delicate womanly instinct told her at a glance that these ladies, in spite of the splendor surrounding them, were no representatives of the aristocracy; she therefore greeted them with a rapid nod, a kind smile, and a graceful wave of her hand, and then averted her head again.

Her carriage now passed through the gate, the cavaliers surrounding it on both sides, and thereby separating the distinguished lady from her attendants, who were following her in four large coaches. These were joined by the carriages of the actresses, by whose sides the heroes of the stage were cantering and exhibiting their horsemanship to the laughing belles with painted cheeks.

It was a long and brilliant procession with which Mme. General Bonaparte made her entrance into Rastadt, and the last of the carriages had not yet reached the gate, when Josephine's carriage had already arrived on the market-place and halted in front of the house she was to occupy with her husband. Before the footman had had time to alight from the box, Josephine herself had already opened the coach door in order to meet the young ladies who were waiting for her at the door of her house, and to give them a flattering proof of her affability. In polite haste she descended from the carriage and stepped into their midst, tendering her hands to those immediately surrounding her, and whispering grateful words of thanks to them for the beautiful flowers and fruits, and thanking the more distant girls with winning nods and smiling glances. Her manners were aristocratic and withal simple; every gesture of hers, every nod, every wave of her hand was

queenly and yet modest, unassuming and entirely devoid of haughtiness, just as it behooved a prominent daughter of the great Republic which had chosen for her motto "*Liberté, égalité, fraternité.*"

Laden with flowers, and laughing as merrily as a young girl, Josephine finally entered the house; in the hall of the latter the ladies of the French ambassadors, the wives and daughters of Bonnier Reberjot and Jean Debry, were waiting for her. Josephine, who among the young girls just now had been all hilarity, grace, and familiarity, now again assumed the bearing of a distinguished lady, of the consort of General Bonaparte, and received the salutations of the ladies with condescending reserve. She handed, however, to each of the ladies one of her splendid bouquets, and had a pleasant word for every one. On arriving at the door of the rooms destined for her private use, she dismissed the ladies and beckoned her maid to follow her.

"Now, Amelia," she said hurriedly, as soon as the door had closed behind them—"now let us immediately attend to my wardrobe. I know Bonaparte—he is always impetuous and impatient, and he regularly arrives sooner than he has stated himself. He was to be here at two o'clock, but he will arrive at one o'clock, and it is now almost noon. Have the trunks brought up at once, for it is high time for me to dress."

Amelia hastened to carry out her mistress's orders, and Josephine was alone. She hurriedly stepped to the large looking-glass in the bedroom and closely scanned in it her own features.

"Oh, oh! I am growing old," she muttered after a while. "Bonaparte must love me tenderly, very tenderly, not to notice it, or I must use great skill not to let him see it. *Eh bien, nous verrons!*"

And she glanced at herself with such a triumphant, charming smile that her features at once seemed to grow younger by ten years. "Oh, he shall find me beautiful—he shall love me," she whispered, "for I love him so tenderly."

Just then Amelia entered loaded with bandboxes and *cartons*, and followed by the servants carrying the heavy trunks. Josephine personally superintended the lowering of the trunks for the purpose of preventing the men from injuring any of those delicate *cartons*; and when every thing was at last duly arranged, she looked around with the triumphant air of a great general mustering his troops and conceiving the plans for his battle.

"Now lock the door and admit no one, Amelia," she said, rapidly divesting herself of her travelling-dress. "Within an hour I must be ready to receive the general. But stop! We must first think of Zephyr, who is sick and exhausted. The dear little fellow cannot stand travelling in a coach. He frequently looked at me on the road most dolorously and imploringly, as if he wanted to beseech me to discontinue these eternal travels. Come, Zephyr; come, my dear little fellow."

On hearing her voice, a small, fat pug-dog, with a morose face and a black nose, arose from the trunk on which he had been lying, and waddled slowly and lazily to his mistress.

"I really believe Zephyr is angry with me," exclaimed Josephine, laughing heartily. "Just look at him, Amelia—just notice this reserved twinkling of his eyes, this snuffling pug-nose of his, this proudly-erect head that seems to smell roast meat and at the same time to utter invectives! He exactly resembles my friend Tallien when the latter is making love to the ladies. Come, my little Tallien, I will give you some sweetmeats, but in return you must be kind and amiable toward Bonaparte; you must not bark so furiously when he enters; you must not snap at his legs when he gives me a kiss; you must not snarl when he inadvertently steps on your toes. Oh, be gentle, kind, and amiable, my beautiful Zephyr, so as not to exasperate Bonaparte, for you know very well that he does not like dogs, and that he would throw you out of the window rather than suffer you at my feet."

Patting the dog tenderly, she lifted him upon an arm-chair, and then spread out biscuits and sweetmeats before him, which Zephyr commenced examining with a dignified snuffling of the nose.

"Now, Amelia, we will attend to my toilet," said Josephine, when she saw that Zephyr condescended to eat some of the biscuits.

Amelia had opened all the trunks and placed a large number of small jars and vials on the dressing-table. Josephine's beauty stood already in need of some assistance, and the amiable lady was by no means disinclined to resort to cosmetics for this purpose. It is true, the republican customs of the times despised rouge, for the latter had been very fashionable during the reign of the "tyrant" Louis XVI., and Marie Antoinette had greatly patronized this fashion and always painted her cheeks. Nevertheless Josephine found rouge to be an indispensable complement to beauty, and, as public opinion was adverse to it, she kept her use of it profoundly secret. Amelia alone saw and knew it—Amelia alone was a witness to all the little secrets and artifices by which Josephine, the woman of thirty-three years, had to bolster up her beauty. But only the head stood in need of some artificial assistance. The body

was as yet youthful, prepossessing, and remarkable for its attractive and luxuriant forms, and when Josephine now had finished her task, she was truly a woman of enchanting beauty and loveliness. Her eyes were so radiant and fiery, her smile so sweet and sure of her impending triumph, and the heavy white silk dress closely enveloped her figure, lending an additional charm to its graceful and classical outlines.

"Now, a few jewels," said Josephine; "give me some diamonds, Amelia; Bonaparte likes brilliant, sparkling trinkets. Come, I will select them myself."

She took from Amelia's hands the large case containing all of her caskets, and glanced at them with a smile of great satisfaction.

"Italy is very rich in precious trinkets and rare gems," she said, with a gentle shake of her head. "When, a few months ago, I came thither from Paris, I had only three caskets, and the jewelry they contained was not very valuable. Now, I count here twenty-four étuis, and they are filled with the choicest trinkets. Just look at these magnificent pearls which the Marquis de Lambertin has given to me. He is an old man, and I could not refuse his princely gift. This casket contains a bracelet which Mancini, the last Doge of Venice, presented to me, and which he assured me was wrought by Benvenuto Cellini for one of his great-great-grandmothers. This splendid set of corals and diamonds was given to me by the city of Genoa when she implored my protection and begged me to intercede with Bonaparte for her. And here—but do you not hear the shouts? What does it mean? Should Bonaparte—"

She did not finish the sentence, but hastened to the window. The market-place, which she was able to overlook from there, was now crowded with people, but the dense masses had not assembled for the purpose of seeing Josephine. All eyes were directed toward yonder street from which constantly fresh and jubilant crowds of people were hurrying toward the market-place, and where tremendous cheers, approaching closer and closer, resounded like the angry roar of the sea. Now some white dots might be discerned in the midst of the surging black mass. They came nearer and grew more distinct; these dots were the heads of white horses. They advanced very slowly, but the cheers made the welkin ring more rapidly and were re-echoed by thousands and thousands of voices.

Amidst these jubilant cheers the procession drew near; now it turned from the street into the market-place. Josephine, uttering a joyful cry, opened the window and waved her hand, for it was Bonaparte whom the excited masses were cheering.

He sat all alone in an open barouche, drawn by six milk-white horses magnificently caparisoned in a silver harness.*

Leaning back into the cushions in a careless and fatigued manner, he scarcely seemed to notice the tremendous ovation that was tendered to him. His face looked pale and tired; a cloud had settled on his expansive marble forehead, and when he from time to time bowed his thanks, he did so with a weary and melancholy smile. But it was exactly this cold, tranquil demeanor, this humble reserve, this pale and gloomy countenance that seemed to strike the spectators and fill them with a feeling of strange delight and wondering awe. In this pale, cold, sombre, and imposing face there was scarcely a feature that seemed to belong to a mortal, earth-born being. It seemed as though the spectre of one of the old Roman imperators, as though the shadow of Julius Cæsar had taken a seat in that carriage, and allowed the milk-white horses to draw him into the surging bustle and turmoil of life. People were cheering half from astonishment, half from fear; they were shouting, "Long live Bonaparte!" as if they wanted to satisfy themselves that he was really alive, and not merely the image of an antique imperator.

The carriage now stopped in front of the house. Before rising from his seat, Bonaparte raised his eyes hastily to the windows. On seeing Josephine, who stood at the open window, his features became more animated, and a long, fiery flash from his eyes struck her face. But he did not salute her, and the cloud on his brow grew even gloomier than before.

"He is in bad humor and angry," whispered Josephine, closing the window, "and I am afraid he is angry with me. Good Heaven! what can it be again? What may be the cause of his anger? I am sure I have committed no imprudence—"

Just then the door was hastily opened, and Bonaparte entered.

CHAPTER XIX.

BONAPARTE AND JOSEPHINE.

BONAPARTE had scarcely deigned to glance at the French ambassadors and their ladies, who had

* "These six horses with their magnificent harness were a gift from the Emperor of Austria, who had presented them to Bonaparte after the peace of Campo Formio. Bonaparte had rejected all other offers."—Bourrienne, vol. i. p. 359.

received him at the foot of the staircase. All his thoughts centred in Josephine. And bowing slightly to the ladies and gentlemen, he had impetuously rushed up-stairs and opened the door, satisfied that she would be there and receive him with open arms. When he did not see her, he passed on, pale, with a gloomy face, and resembling an angry lion.

Thus he now rushed into the front room where he found Josephine. Without saluting her, and merely fixing his flashing eyes upon her, he asked in a subdued, angry voice: "Madame, you do not even deem it worth the trouble to salute me! You do not come to meet me!"

"But, Bonaparte, you have given me no time for it," said Josephine, with a charming smile. "While I thought you were just about to alight from your carriage, you burst already into this room like a thunder-bolt from heaven."

"Oh, and that has dazzled your eyes so much that you are even unable to salute me?" he asked angrily.

"And you, Bonaparte?" she asked, tenderly, "You do not open your arms to me! You do not welcome me! Instead of pressing me to your heart, you scold me! Oh, come, my friend, let us not pass this first hour in so unpleasant a manner! We have not seen each other for almost two months, and—"

"Ah, madame, then you know that at least," exclaimed Bonaparte; "then you have not entirely forgotten that you took leave of me two months ago, and that you swore to me at that time eternal love and fidelity, and promised most sacredly to write to me every day. You have not kept your oaths and pledges, madame!"

"But, my friend, I have written to you whenever I was told that a courier would set out for your headquarters."

"You ought to have sent every day a courier of your own for the purpose of transmitting your letters to me," exclaimed Bonaparte, wildly stamping his foot, so that the jars and vials on the table rattled violently, while Zephyr jumped down from his arm-chair and commenced snarling. Josephine looked anxiously at him and tried to calm him by her gestures.

Bonaparte continued: "Letters! But those scraps I received from time to time were not even letters. Official bulletins of your health they were, and as cold as ice. Madame, how could you write such letters to me, and moreover only every fourth day? If you really loved me, you would have written every day. But you do not love me any longer; I know it. Your love was but a passing whim. You feel now how ridiculous it would be for you to love a poor man who is nothing but a soldier, and who has to offer nothing to you but a little glory and his love. But I shall banish this love from my heart, should I have to tear my heart with my own teeth." [*]

"Bonaparte," exclaimed Josephine, half tenderly, half anxiously, "what have I done that you should be angry with me? Why do you accuse me of indifference, while you know very well that I love you?"

"Ah, it is a very cold love, at all events," he said, sarcastically. "It is true, I am only your husband, and it is not in accordance with aristocratic manners to love one's husband; that is mean, vulgar, republican! But I am a republican, and I do not want any wife with the manners and habits of the *ancien régime*. I am your husband, but woe to him who seeks to become my wife's lover! I would not even need my sword in order to kill him. My eyes alone would crush him! [†] And I shall know how to find him; and if he should escape to the most remote regions, my arm is a far-reaching one, and I will extend it over the whole world in order to grasp him."

"But whom do you allude to?" asked Josephine, in dismay.

"Whom?" he exclaimed in a thundering voice. "Ah, madame, you believe I do not know what has occurred? You believe I see and hear nothing when I am no longer with you? Let me compliment you, madame! The handsome aide-de-camp of Leclerc is a conquest which the ladies of Milan must have been jealous of; and Botot, the spy, whom Barras sent after me, passes even at Paris for an Adonis. What do you mean by your familiarities with these two men, madame? You received Adjutant Charles at eleven o'clock in the morning, while you never leave your bed before one o'clock. Oh, that handsome young fellow wanted to tell you how he was yearning for his home in Paris, and what his mother and sister had written to him, I suppose? For that reason so convenient an hour had to be chosen? For that reason he came at eleven o'clock while you were in bed yet. His ardor was so intense, and if he had been compelled to wait until one o'clock, impatience would have burned his soul to ashes!" [‡]

"He wanted to set out for Paris precisely at twelve o'clock. That was the only reason why I received him so early, my friend," said Josephine, gently.

"Oh, then, you do not deny that you have actually received him?" shouted Bonaparte, and his face turned livid. With flaming eyes and uplifted hand, he stepped up close to Josephine. "Madame," he exclaimed, in a thundering voice, "then you dare to acknowledge that Charles is your lover?"

Before Josephine had time to reply to him Zephyr, who saw him threaten his mistress, furiously pounced upon Bonaparte, barking and howling, showing his teeth, and quite ready to lacerate whom he supposed to be Josephine's enemy.

"Ah, this accursed dog is here, too, to torment me!" exclaimed Bonaparte, and raising his foot, he stamped with crushing force on the body of the little dog. A single piercing yell was heard; then the blood gushed from Zephyr's mouth, and the poor beast lay writhing convulsively on the floor. [*]

"Bonaparte, you have killed my dog," exclaimed Josephine, reproachfully, and bent over the dying animal.

"Yes," he said, with an air of savage joy, "I have killed your dog, and in the same manner I shall crush every living being that dares to step between you and myself!"

Josephine had taken no notice of his words. She had knelt down by the side of the dog, and tenderly patted his head and writhing limbs till they ceased moving.

"Zephyr is dead," she said rising. "Poor little fellow, he died because he loved me. Pardon me, general, if I weep for him. But Zephyr was a cherished souvenir from a friend who died only a short while ago. General Hoche had given the dog to me."

"Hoche?" asked Bonaparte, in some confusion.

"Yes, Lazarus Hoche, who died a few weeks ago. A few days before his death he sent the dog to me while at Milan—Lazarus Hoche who, you know it very well, loved me, and whose hand I rejected because I loved you," said Josephine, with a noble dignity and calmness, which made a deeper impression upon Bonaparte than the most poignant rebuke would have done.

"And now, general," she proceeded, "I will reply to your reproaches. I do not say that I shall *justify* myself, because I thereby would acknowledge the justice of your charges, but I will merely answer them. I told you already why I admitted Charles at so early an hour. He was about to set out for Paris, and I wished to intrust to him important and secret letters and other commissions."

---

[*] Bonaparte's own words.—Vide "Lettres à Joséphine. Mémoires d'une Contemporaine," vol. i., p. 353.

[†] Bonaparte's own words.—Ibid.

[‡] Bonaparte's own words.—Vide "Mémoires d'un Contemporaine," vol. ii., p. 353.

[*] Vide "Rheinischer-Antiquar., vol. ii., p. 574.

"Why did not you send them by a special courier?" asked Bonaparte, but in a much gentler voice than before.

"Because it would have been dangerous to send my letters to Botot by a courier," said Josephine, calmly.

"To Botot? Then you admit your familiarities with Botot, too? People did not deceive me, then, when they told me that you received this spy Botot, whom Barras had sent after me in order to watch me, every morning in your boudoir—that you always sent your maid away as soon as he came, and that your interviews with him frequently lasted for hours?"

"That is quite true; I do not deny it," said Josephine, proudly.

Bonaparte uttered an oath, and was about to rush at her. But she receded a step, and pointing at the dead dog with a rapid gesture, she said: "General, take care! There is no other dog here for you to kill, and I am only a weak, defenceless woman; it would assuredly not behoove the victor of Arcole to attack me!"

Bonaparte dropped his arm, and, evidently ashamed of himself, stepped back several paces.

"Then you do not deny your intimate intercourse with Botot and Charles?"

"I do not deny that both of them love me, that I know it, and that I have taken advantage of their love. Listen to me, general: I have taken *advantage* of their love. That is mean and abominable; it is playing in an execrable manner with the most exalted feelings of others, I know it very well, but I did so for your sake, general— I did so in your interest."

"In my interest?" asked Bonaparte, in surprise.

"Yes, in your interest," she said. "Now I can tell and confess every thing to you. But as long as Charles and Botot were present, I could not do so, for if you had ceased being jealous—if, warned by myself, you had treated these two men kindly instead of showing your jealous distrust of them by a hostile and surly demeanor, they might have suspected my game and divined my intrigue, and I would have been unable to avail myself any longer of their services."

"But, for God's sake, tell me what did you need their services for?"

"Ah, sir, I perceive that you know better how to wield the sword than unravel intrigues," said Josephine, with a charming smile. "Well, I made use of my two lovers in order to draw their secrets from them. And secrets they had, general, for you know Botot is the most intimate and influential friend of Barras, and Madame Tallien adores Charles, the handsome aide-de-camp. She has no secrets that he is not fully aware of, and she does whatever he wants her to do; and again, whatever she wants to be done, her husband will do—her husband, that excellent Tallien, who with Barras is one of the five directors of our republic."

"Oh, women, women!" muttered Bonaparte.

Josephine continued: "In this manner, general, I learned every scheme and almost every idea of the Directory; in this manner, through my devoted friends, Botot and Charles, I have succeeded in averting many a foul blow from your own head. For you were menaced, general, and you are menaced still. And what is menacing you? That is your glory and your greatness—it is the jealousy of the five kings of France, who, under the name of directors, are now reigning at the Luxemburg. The Quintumvirate beheld your growing power and glory with terror and wrath, and all endeavors of theirs only aimed at lessening your influence. A favorite way of theirs for carrying out their designs against you was the circulation of false news concerning you. Botot told me that Barras had even hired editors to write against you, and to question your integrity. These editors now published letters purporting to come from Verona, and announcing that Bonaparte was about to proclaim himself dictator. Then, again, they stated in some letter from the frontier, or from a foreign country, that the whole of Lombardy was again on the eve of an insurrection; that the Italians detested the tyranny imposed upon them by the conqueror, and that they were anxious to recall their former sovereigns."

"Ah, the miserable villains!" exclaimed Bonaparte, gnashing his teeth, "I—"

"Hush, general! listen to my whole reply to your reproaches," said Josephine, with imperious calmness. "At some other time these hirelings of the press announced in a letter from Turin that an extensive conspiracy was about to break out at Paris; that the Directory was to be overthrown by this conspiracy, and that a dictatorship, at the head of which Bonaparte would be, was to take place. They further circulated the news all over the departments, that the ringleaders of the plot had been arrested and sent to the military commissions for trial; but that the conqueror of Italy had deemed it prudent to avoid arrest by running away." *

"That is a truly infernal web of lies and infamies!" ejaculated Bonaparte, furiously. "But I shall justify myself, I will go to Paris and hurl

---

* Le Normand, Mémoires, vol. i., p. 267.

the calumnies of these miserable Directors back into their teeth!"

"General, there is no necessity for you to descend into the arena in order to defend yourself," said Josephine, smiling. "Your actions speak for you, and your friends are watching over you. Whenever such an article appeared in the newspapers, Botot forwarded it to me; whenever the Directory sprang a new mine, Botot sent me word of it. And then I enlisted the assistance of my friend Charles, and he had to refute those articles through a journalist who was in my pay, and to foil the mine by means of a counter-mine."

"Oh, Josephine, how can I thank you for what you have done for me!" exclaimed Bonaparte, enthusiastically. "How—"

"I am not through yet, general," she interrupted him, coldly. "Those refutations and the true accounts of your glorious deeds found an enthusiastic echo throughout the whole of France, and every one was anxious to see you in the full splendor of your glory, and to do homage to you at Paris. But the jealous Directory calculated in advance how dangerous the splendor of your glory would be to the statesmen of the Republic, and how greatly your return would eclipse the five kings. For that reason they resolved to keep you away from Paris; for that reason exclusively they appointed you first plenipotentiary at the congress about to be opened at Rastadt, and intrusted the task to you to exert yourself here for the conclusion of peace. They wanted to chain the lion and make him feel that he has got a master whom he must obey."

"But the lion will break the chain, and he will not obey," exclaimed Bonaparte, angrily. "I shall leave Rastadt on this very day and hasten to Paris."

"Wait a few days, general," said Josephine, smiling. "It will be unnecessary for you to take violent steps, my friends Botot and Charles having worked with me for you. Botot alone not being sufficiently powerful, inasmuch as he could influence none but Barras, I sent Charles to his assistance in order to act upon Madame Tallien. And the stratagem was successful. Take this letter which I received only yesterday through a special messenger from Botot—you know Botot's handwriting, I suppose?"

"Yes, I know it."

"Well, then, satisfy yourself that he has really written it," said Josephine, drawing a sheet of paper from her memorandum-book and handing it to Bonaparte.

He glanced at it without touching the paper. "Yes, it is Botot's handwriting," he murmured.

"Read it, general," said Josephine.

"I do not want to read it; I believe all you tell me!" he exclaimed, impetuously.

"I shall read it to you," she said, "for the contents will interest you. Listen therefore: 'Adored Citoyenne Josephine.—We have reached the goal —we have conquered! The Directory have at length listened to wise remonstrances. They have perceived that they stand in need of a strong and powerful arm to support them, and of a pillar to lean against. They will recall Bonaparte in order that he may become their pillar and arm. In a few days a courier will reach Bonaparte at Rastadt and recall him to Paris.—Botot.' That is all there is in the letter, General; it contains nothing about love, but only speaks of you."

"I see that I am the happiest of mortals," exclaimed Bonaparte, joyfully; "for I shall return to Paris, and my beautiful, noble, and adored Josephine will accompany me."

"No, general," she said, solemnly, "I shall return to Italy; I shall bury myself in some convent in order to weep there over the short dream of my happiness, and to pray for you. Now I have told you every thing I had to say to you. I have replied to your reproaches. You see that I have meanly profited by the love of these poor men, that I have made a disgraceful use of the most sacred feeling in order to promote your interests. I did so secretly, for I told you already, general, your valorous hand knows better how to wield the sword than to carry on intrigues. A strong grasp of this hand might have easily destroyed the whole artificial web of my plans, and for this reason I was silent. But I counted on your confidence, on your esteem. I perceive now, however, that I do not possess them, and this separates us forever. Unreserved confidence is not only the nourishment that imparts life to friendship, but without it love also pines away and dies.* Farewell, then, general; I forgive your distrust, but I cannot expose myself any longer to your anger. Farewell!"

She bowed and turned to the door. But Bonaparte followed her, and keeping her back with both hands, he said, in a voice trembling with emotion: "Where are you going, Josephine?"

"I told you already," she sighed, painfully; "I am going to a convent to weep and pray for you."

"That means that you want to kill me!" he exclaimed, with flaming eyes. "For you know I cannot live without you. If I had to lose you, your love, your charming person, I would lose every thing rendering life pleasant and desirable

* Josephine's own words.—Vide Le Normand, vol. i, p. 243.

for me. Josephine, you are to me a world that is incomprehensible to me, and every day I love you more passionately. Even when I do not see you, my love for you is constantly growing; for absence only destroys small passions; it increases great passions.* My heart never felt any of the former. It proudly refused to fall in love, but you have filled it with a boundless passion, with an intoxication that seems to be almost degrading. You were always the predominant idea of my soul; your whims even were sacred laws for me. To see you is my highest bliss; you are beautiful and enchanting; your gentle, angelic soul is depicted in your features. Oh, I adore you just as you are; if you had been younger, I should have loved you less intensely. Every thing you do seems virtuous to me; every thing you like seems honorable to me. Glory is only valuable to me inasmuch as it is agreeable to you and flatters your vanity. Your portrait always rests on my heart, and whenever I am far from you, not an hour passes without my looking at it and covering it with kisses. † The glass broke the other day when I pressed it too violently against my breast. My despair knew no bounds, for love is superstitious, and every thing seems ominous to it. I took it for an announcement of your death, and my eyes knew no sleep, my heart knew no rest, till the courier whom I immediately dispatched to you, had brought me the news that you were well, and that no accident had befallen you. ‡ See, woman, woman, such is my love! Will you now tell me again that you wish to leave me?"

"I must, general," she said, firmly. "Love cannot be lasting without esteem, and you do not esteem me. Your suspicion has dishonored me, and a dishonored and insulted woman cannot be your wife any longer. Farewell!"

She wanted to disengage herself from his hands, but he held her only the more firmly. "Josephine," he said, in a hollow voice, "listen to me, do not drive me to despair, for it would kill me to lose you. No duty, no title would attach me any longer to earth. Men are so contemptible, life is so wretched—you alone extinguish the ignominy of mankind in my eyes.§ Without you there is no hope, no happiness. I love you boundlessly."

"No, general, you despise me; you do not love me!"

"No, no!" he shouted, wildly stamping his foot.

"If you go on in this manner, I shall drop dead at your feet. Do not torment me so dreadfully. Remember what I have often told you: Nature has given to me a strong, decided soul, but it has made you of gauze and lace. You say I do not love. Hear it, then, for the last time. Since you have been away from me, I have not passed a single day without loving you, not a single night without mentally pressing you to my heart. I have not taken a single cup of tea without cursing the glory and ambition separating me from the soul of my life.* Amidst my absorbing occupations—at the head of my troops, on the march and in the field—my heavenly Josephine ever was foremost in my heart. She occupied my mind; she absorbed my thoughts. If I left you with the impetuosity of the Rhone, I only did so in order to return the sooner to your side. If I ran from my bed at night and continued working, I did so for the purpose of accelerating the moment of our reunion. The most beautiful women surrounded me, smiled upon me, gave me hopes of their favor, and tried to please me, but none of them resembled you; none had the gentle and melodious features so deeply imprinted on my heart. I only saw you, only thought of you, and that rendered all of them intolerable to me. I left the most beautiful women in order to throw myself on my couch and sigh, 'When will my adored wife be again with me?' † And if I just now gave way to an ebullition of anger, I only did so because I love you so boundlessly as to be jealous of every glance, of every smile. Forgive me, therefore, Josephine, forgive me for the sake of my infinite love! Tell me that you will think no more of it, and that you will forget and forgive every thing."

He looked at her anxiously and inquiringly, but Josephine did not reply to his glances. She averted her eyes and remained silent.

"Josephine," he exclaimed, perfectly beside himself, "make an end of it. Just touch my forehead; it is covered with cold perspiration, and my heart is trembling as it never trembled in battle. Make an end of it; I am utterly exhausted. Oh, Josephine, my dear Josephine, open your arms to me."

"Well, come then, you dear, cruel husband," she said, bursting into tears and extending her arms to him.

Bonaparte uttered a joyful cry, pressed her to his heart, and covered her with kisses.

"Now I am sure you have forgiven every thing," he said, encircling her all the time with his arms. "You forgive my madness, my abominable jealousy?"

---

* Bonaparte's words.—Vide "Mémoires d'une Contemporaine," vol. ii., p. 363.

† Vide "Correspondance inédite avec Joséphine," Lettre v.

‡ "Mémoires sur Napoléon, par Constant," vol. i., p. 302.

§ "Correspondance inédite avec Joséphine," p. 375.

* "Correspondance," etc., p. 552.   † Ibid., p. 349.

"I forgive every thing, Bonaparte, if you will promise not to be jealous again," she said, with a charming smile.

"I promise never to be jealous again, but to think, whenever you give a rendezvous to another man, that you only do so for my sake, and for the purpose of conspiring for me. Ah, my excellent wife, you have worked bravely for me, and henceforth I know that I can intrust to your keeping my glory and my honor with implicit confidence. Yea, even the helm of the state I would fearlessly intrust to your hands. Pray, therefore, Josephine, pray that your husband may reach the pinnacle of distinction, for in that case I should give you a seat in my council of state and make you mistress of every thing except one point—" *

"And what is that?" asked Josephine, eagerly.

"The only thing I should not intrust to you, Josephine," he said, laughing, "would be the keys of my treasury; you never would get them, my beautiful prodigal little wife of gauze, lace, diamonds, and pearls!" †

"Ah, then you would deprive me of the right to distribute charities in your name?" she asked, sadly. "Is not that the most precious and sublime duty of the wife of a great man, to conquer Heaven for him by charities while he is conquering earth by his deeds? And you would take from me the means for doing so? Yours is a wild and passionate nature, and I shall often have to heal the wounds that you have inflicted in your outbursts of anger. Happy for me if I should always be able to heal them, and if your anger should be less fatal to men than to my poor little dog, who merely wanted to defend me against your violence."

"Poor little dog!" said Bonaparte, casting a glance of confusion upon Zephyr. "I greatly regret the occurrence, particularly as the dog was a gift from Hoche. But no lamentations of mine being able to recall Zephyr to life, Josephine, I will immortalize him at all events. He shall not find an unknown grave, like many a hero; no, we will erect to this valiant and intrepid defender of the charming fortress Josephine, a monument which shall relate his exploits to the most remote posterity. Have Zephyr packed up in a box; couriers and convoys of troops will set out to-day for Milan. They shall take the corpse along, and I will issue orders that a monument be erected to your Zephyr in the garden of our villa.‡ But

now, Josephine, I must leave you; life, with its stern realities, is calling me. I must go and receive the Austrian ambassadors."

CHAPTER XX.

THE RECEPTION OF THE AMBASSADORS.

A MOTLEY crowd of gentlemen in uniforms and glittering gala-dresses had filled the anterooms of the French embassy ever since the arrival of General Bonaparte and Josephine. All these high-born representatives of German sovereigns and states hastened to do homage to the French lady and to commend themselves to the benevolence and favor of the victorious general of the republic. But the doors of the general and of his wife were as difficult to open as those of the French ambassadors, Bonnier, Jean Debry, and Roberjot. General Bonaparte had received the Austrian ambassadors, and returned their visit. But nobody else had been admitted to him during the first day. The ambassadors, therefore, flocked the more eagerly on this second day after his arrival to the anterooms of the French ambassadors, for every one wanted to be the first to win for his sovereign and for his state the good-will of the French conqueror. Every one wished to obtain advantages, to avert mischief, and to beg for favors.

Happy were they already who had only succeeded in penetrating into the anterooms of the French embassy, for a good deal of money had to be spent in order to open those doors. In front of them stood the footmen of the ambassadors with grave, stern countenances, refusing to admit any but those who had been previously recommended to them, or who knew now how to gain their favor by substantial rewards.* And when they finally, by means of such persuasive gifts, had succeeded in crossing the threshold of the anteroom, they found there the clerks and secretaries of the French gentlemen, and these men again barred the door of the cabinet occupied by

---

* Le Normand, vol. i., p. 241.
† Ibid., vol. i., p. 242.
‡ Bonaparte kept his word. The little victim of his jealousy, Zephyr, the dog, was buried in the gardens of

Mondeza, near Milan, and a marble monument was erected on his grave.—Le Normand, vol. i., p. 498.

* The employés of the French embassy, from the first secretary down to the lowest footman and cook, received handsome gifts at the hands of the German delegates, for every one was anxious to secure the good-will of the French representatives; and in obedience to the old trick of diplomatists, they tried to gain the favor of the masters by means of that of their servants. The latter made a very handsome thing out of it.—Vide Halasser, vol. ii., p. 163.

the ambassadors themselves. These clerks and secretaries had to be bribed likewise by solicitations, flatteries, and money; only, instead of satisfying them with silver, as in the case of the door-keepers, they had to give them heavy gold pieces.

Having finally overcome all these obstacles—having now penetrated into the presence of the French diplomatists—the ambassadors of the German powers met with a haughty reserve instead of the kindness they had hoped for, and with sarcastic sneers in lieu of a warm reception. It was in vain for Germany thus to humble herself and to crouch in the dust. France was too well aware of her victories and superiority, and the servility of the German aristocracy only excited contempt and scorn, which the French gentlemen did not refrain from hurling into the faces of the humble solicitors. The greater the abjectness of the latter, the more overbearing the haughty demeanor of the former, and both gained the firm conviction that France held the happiness and quiet of Germany in her hands, and that France alone had the power to secure to the German princes the possession of their states, to enlarge their dominions, or to deprive them thereof, just as she pleased, and without paying any deference to the wishes of the Germans themselves.

To-day, however, all these distinguished men—the counts and barons of the empire, the bishops and other ecclesiastical dignitaries—had not appeared for the purpose of conquering the favor of the three French stars—to-day a new constellation had arisen on the sky of Rastadt, and they wanted to stare at it—they wanted to admire Bonaparte and Josephine.

But Bonaparte took hardly any notice of the crowd assembled in the anteroom. His hands folded on his back, he was pacing his room, and listening with rapt attention to the accounts the three French ambassadors were giving him concerning the policy they had pursued up to the present time.

"We have done every thing in our power to spread republican notions hereabouts," said Jean Debry, at the conclusion of his lengthy remarks. "We have sent agents to all of these small German states for the purpose of enlightening the people about their dignity, their rights, and the disgrace of submitting to miserable princes, instead of being free and great under the wholesome influence of republican institutions."

"We have, moreover, even here, excellent spies among the ambassadors," said Roberjot, "and through them we have skilfully fanned the flames of that discord which seems to be the bane of

Germany. It is true, they hold secret meetings every day in order to agree on a harmonious line of policy, but discord, jealousy, and covetousness always accompany them to those meetings, and they are therefore never able to agree about any thing. Besides, these German noblemen are very talkative, hence we find out all their secrets, and it is an easy task for us to foil every scheme of theirs. Every one of them is anxious to enlarge his possessions; we therefore give them hopes of acquiring new territory at the expense of their neighbors, and thereby greatly increase the discord and confusion prevailing among them. We fill the ambassadors of the secondary princes, and especially those of the ecclesiastical sovereigns, with distrust against the more powerful German states, and intimate to them that the latter are trying to aggrandize themselves at their expense, and that they have asked the consent of France to do so. We inform the first-class governments of the desire of the smaller princes to enlarge their dominions, and caution them against placing implicit trust in their representations. Thus we sow the seeds of discord among these princely hirelings, and endeavor to undermine the thrones of Germany."

"Germany must throw off all her princes like ripe ulcers," exclaimed Bonnier, scornfully. "These numerous thrones beyond the Rhine are dangerous and fatal to our sublime and indivisible French Republic—bad examples spoiling good manners. Every throne must disappear from the face of the earth, and freedom and equality must shine throughout the whole world like the sun."

"You are right," said Bonaparte, gravely. "It is our duty to disseminate our principles among these Germans, who are living in slavery as yet, and to assist the poor serfs in obtaining their liberty. Germany must become a confederate republic, and discord is the best sword wherewith to attack these princely hirelings. But what does the Swedish ambassador—whose name I noticed on the list of applicants for interviews with myself—here among the representatives of the German princes?"

"He pretends to participate in the congress of peace because Sweden warranted the execution of the treaty of Westphalia," exclaimed Jean Debry, shrugging his shoulders.

"Bah! that is a most ridiculous pretext," said Bonnier, gloomily. "This M. Fersen is a royalist. The political part played by this diplomatist at the court of Louis Capet, and afterward continued by him, is only too well known. He now tries to dazzle us by his kindness merely for the purpose of laying a trap for the French Republic."

"Ah, we shall show to the gentleman that the Republic has got an open eye and a firm hand, and that it discovers and tears all such meshes and traps." said Bonaparte, impetuously. "But we have done business enough for to-day, and I will go and receive the ambassadors who have been waiting here for a long while in the ante-room."

He saluted the three gentlemen with a familiar nod, and then repaired to the reception-room, the doors of which were opened at last to admit the German ambassadors.

It was a brilliant crowd now entering in a solemn procession through the opened folding-doors. The ambassadors of every German sovereign were in attendance; only the representatives of Austria and Prussia, whom Bonaparte had received already in a special audience, were absent.

This German peace delegation, which now entered the room to do homage to the French general, was a very large one. There were first the ambassadors of Bavaria and Saxony, of Baden and Wurtemberg, of Hanover and Mecklenburg; then followed the host of the small princes and noblemen, by whose side the ecclesiastical dignitaries, the representatives of the electors and bishops, were walking in.*

Bonaparte stood proudly erect in the middle of the room, his gloomy glances inspecting the gentlemen, who now commenced stationing themselves on both sides of the apartment. A master of ceremonies, who had been previously selected for the meetings of the peace congress, now walked solemnly through the ranks and announced in a ringing voice the name, rank, and position of every ambassador.

"His excellency Count Fersen," he shouted just now, in a solemn manner, "ambassador of his majesty the King of Sweden and Duke of Pomerania."

Count Fersen had not yet finished his ceremonious obeisance, when Bonaparte rapidly approached him.

"Just tell me, sir," he exclaimed, bluntly; "what is the name of the minister whom Sweden has now in Paris?"

Count Fersen looked in evident surprise and confusion at the pale face of the general, whose flaming eyes were fixed upon him with an angry expression.

* The whole German peace delegation consisted of seventy-nine persons, and all these seventy-nine distinguished men, the ambassadors of emperor, kings, and princes, tried to gain the favor of the ambassadors of France; and the three gentlemen, representing the great Republic, seemed more powerful and influential than all the representatives of Germany.

"I do not know," he faltered, "I am not quite sure—"

"Ah, sir, you know only too well that Sweden has not yet given a successor to M. de Hail," Bonaparte interrupted him violently, "and that the only ambassador whom she was willing to send had to be rejected by the Directory. You were this ambassador whom the Directory would not tolerate in Paris. Friendly ties have united France and Sweden for a long series of years, and I believe Sweden ought to appreciate and recognize their importance at the present time more than ever. How, then, is the conduct of the court of Stockholm to be explained, that tries to make it its special business to send everywhere, either to Paris or wherever the plenipotentiaries of France may be seen, ministers and ambassadors who must be peculiarly distasteful to every citizen of France?"

"That is certainly not the intention of my court," exclaimed Count Fersen, hastily.

"That may be," said Bonaparte, proudly, "but I should like to know if the King of Sweden would remain indifferent in case a French ambassador should try to instigate an insurrection of the people of Stockholm against him! The French Republic cannot permit men, whose connection with the old court of France is a matter of notoriety, to appear in official capacities, and thus to irritate and humble the republican ambassadors, the representatives of the first nation on earth, who, before consulting her policy, knows how to maintain her dignity."

"I shall immediately set out for Stockholm in order to communicate these views of the conqueror of Italy to my court," said Count Fersen, pale with shame and mortification.

"Do so, set out at once," exclaimed Bonaparte, impetuously, "and tell your master, unless he should conclude to pursue a different policy, I will send him some day a skilful diplomatic Gascon who knows how to simplify the machine and make it go less rapidly. King Gustavus will perhaps find out, when it is too late, and at his own expense, that the reins of government must be firmly held in one hand, and the other skilfully wield the sword, while it is yet time. Go, sir, and inform your king of what I have told you!"

Count Fersen made no reply; he merely bowed hastily and silently, and, beckoning his attachés who were standing behind him, he left the room with his suite.*

* This whole scene actually took place, and contains only such words as really were exchanged between Bonaparte and Fersen.—Vide " Mémoires d'un Homme d'État, vol. v., p. 64. Le Normand, Mémoires, vol. i., p. 263.

Bonaparte's flashing eyes followed him until he had disappeared, and then the general turned once more to the ambassadors.

"I could not suffer a traitor and enemy in our assembly," he said, in a loud and firm voice. "We are here in order to make peace, while he was secretly anxious for a renewal of war, and was bent upon sowing the evil seeds of discord among us. Let us all endeavor to make peace, gentlemen, to the best of our power. Do not compel me to enter the lists against you, too, for the struggle could not be doubtful between a nation that has just conquered her liberty, and princes who tried to deprive her of it again. If you reject to-day the pacific overtures I shall make to you, I shall impose other conditions to-morrow; but woe unto him among you, who should refuse my mediation; for in that case I should overthrow the whole framework of a false policy, and the thrones standing on a weak foundation would soon break down. I speak to you with the frankness of a soldier and the noble pride of a victorious general; I caution you because I have the welfare of the nations at heart, who more than ever need the blessings of peace. It is now for you to say whether we shall have war or peace, and it will solely depend upon your submissiveness whether France will be able to conclude an honorable peace with her German neighbors, or whether you will compel us to take up arms once more. But in that case woe unto you, for we should retaliate in the most terrible manner on those who would dare to oppose us!" *

He paused and rapidly glanced at the assembled gentlemen. They stood before him with grave and gloomy faces, but none of them were courageous enough to make a dignified reply to the proud and humiliating words of the French general. The ambassadors of Germany received the severe lecture of the representative of France with silent submissiveness.

An imperceptible smile played on Bonaparte's lips. He saluted the gentlemen with a slight nod and rapidly returned to his own rooms.

CHAPTER XXI.

FRANCE AND AUSTRIA.

BONAPARTE had scarcely reached his room and just closed the door, when the opposite door opened, and the entering footman announced, "His excellency Count Louis Cobenzl."

Bonaparte waved his hand and went to meet the count in the anteroom, where he welcomed him with the utmost kindness and courtesy.

The two gentlemen thereupon reëntered the room hand in hand, a pleasant smile playing on their lips, while both were assuring each other of their kind intentions, but at the same time secretly entertaining the ardent desire and purpose to divine their mutual thoughts, but to conceal their own schemes. The general, with great politeness, offered the seat of honor on the sofa to the count, and sat down in an arm-chair in front of him. A small round table with writing-materials and paper stood between them, forming as it were the frontier between Austria and France.

"So the ardent desires of Austria are fulfilled now," said Count Cobenzl, with a sweet smile. "France will no longer oppose us; she will be our friend and ally."

"France will welcome this new friend and ally of hers," exclaimed Bonaparte, feelingly, "provided Austria's intentions are loyal. Ah, my dear count, no protestations now! In politics words prove nothing, deeds every thing. Let Austria, then, prove by her deeds that she really desires to keep up a good understanding with France, and that she has given up forever her hostile attitude toward the republic."

"But has not Austria given proof of her intentions toward France already?" asked the count, in surprise. "Has not his majesty the emperor declared his willingness to resume diplomatic relations with France, and thereby formally and before the whole world to recognize the French Republic?"

"Sir," exclaimed Bonaparte, "the French Republic does not humbly solicit to be recognized. She compels hostile states to recognize her, for, like the sun, she sheds her light over the whole globe, and she would pierce the eyes of such as would feign not to see her, rendering them blind for all time to come!* Austria beheld this radiant sun of the republic at Lodi, at Rivoli, Arcole, and Mantua; whence, then, would she derive courage enough to refuse recognizing France? But instead of words, prove to us by your actions that your friendship is honest and sincere."

"We are ready to do so," said Count Cobenzl, politely. "Austria is ready to give a public and brilliant proof of her devotion to the great general whose glory is now filling the whole world with astonishment and admiration. His majesty the

------

* Bonaparte's own words.—Vide Le Normand, vol. i., p. 964.

* Bonaparte's own words.—Vide Constant, vol. i., p. 284.

emperor, in the letter which I had the honor of delivering to you some time ago, told you already in eloquent words how greatly he admired the conqueror of Italy, and how gladly his majesty, if it were in his power, would grant you such favors as would be agreeable to you. But at that time you rejected all such offers, general, and nothing could induce you to accept of what we wished to present to you. It seemed not to have value enough to—"

"Rather say, count, it was all too valuable not to be looked upon as a bribe," exclaimed Bonaparte. "I was negotiating with you, sword in hand, and it would not have been becoming of me to lay the sword aside in order to fill my hands with your presents."

"But now, general, now that we have laid the sword aside, that we have made peace, that we have exchanged the ratifications of the treaty—now that you tender your hand to Austria in friendship and peace, you might permit his majesty the Emperor of Austria to deposit something in your friendly hand, that might prove to you how sincerely my august master the emperor is devoted to you."

"And what does the emperor desire to deposit in my hand?" asked Bonaparte, with a quiet smile.

Count Cobenzl hesitated a little before making a reply. "General," he then said, "when I see you thus before me in your marble beauty, I am involuntarily reminded of the heroes of Rome and Greece, who have immortalized the glory of their countries, but whom the admiration of posterity had to compensate for the ingratitude of their contemporaries. General, republics never were grateful to their great men, and only too often have they stigmatized their most glorious deeds: for the republics deprecated the greatness of their heroes, because he who distinguished himself, thereby annulled the equality and fraternity of all the citizens. Pericles was banished from Athens, and Julius Cæsar was assassinated! General, will modern republics be more grateful than those of antiquity? For my part, I dare say it is rather doubtful, and the French being descendants of the Romans, I am afraid they will not prove any more grateful than the latter. The emperor, my august master, shares my fears, and as he loves and venerates you, he would like to exalt you so high as to prevent the hands of the political factions from reaching up to you. His majesty therefore proposes to create a principality for you in Germany, and to make you the sovereign ruler of two hundred thousand people, appointing you at the same time a prince of the German empire, and giving

you a seat and vote at the imperial diet.* General, do you accept my emperor's offer?"

"To become the emperor's vassal?" asked Bonaparte, with an imperceptible smile. "A small prince of the German empire who on solemn occasions might be deemed worthy to present the wash-basin to the emperor, or to be his train-bearer, while every king and elector would outrank me. No, my dear count, I do not accept the offer. I sincerely thank the emperor for the interest he takes in my welfare, but I must accept no gifts or favors not coming directly from the French nation, and I shall always be satisfied with the income bestowed upon me by the latter." †

"You reject the emperor's offer?" asked Count Cobenzl, mournfully — "you disdain wearing a crown?"

"If the crown should crush the few laurels with which my victories have adorned me, yes; in that case I should prefer to decline the crown in favor of my laurels. And, my dear count, if I had been so anxious for a crown, I might have picked up one of those crowns that fell down at my feet in Italy. But I preferred to crush them under my heels, just as St. George crushed the dragon; and the gold of the crushed crowns, as it behooved a good and dutiful son, I laid down on the altar of the great French Republic. So you see I am not longing for crowns. If I might follow my own inclinations, I should return to the silence and obscurity of my former life, and I should lay my sword aside in order to live only as a peaceable citizen."

"Oh, general, if you should do so," exclaimed Cobenzl, "there would soon be men to pick up your sword in order to fight with it against the Republic and to recall the Bourbons to the throne of the lilies."

A rapid flash from Bonaparte's eyes struck the count's face and met his sharp, searching glance.

"Count Cobenzl," he said, quietly and coldly, "the lilies of France have dropped from their stems, and, being drowned in the blood of the guillotine, they could not be made to bloom again. He would be a poor, short-sighted gardener who would try to draw flowers from seeds dead and devoid of germs. And believe me, we are no such poor, short-sighted gardeners in France. You alluded just now to the ingratitude of republics, and you apprehended lest I might likewise suffer thereby. Let me assure you, however, that even my country's ingratitude would be dearer to me than

---

* Historical.—Vide "Mémoires d'un Homme d'état," vol. v., p. 67.

† Bonaparte's own reply.—Vide "Mémoires d'un Homme d'état," vol. v., p. 67.

the gratitude of a foreign power, and that the crown of thorns, which France may press upon my head, would seem to me more honorable than the coronet with which an enemy of France might adorn my brow. And now, count, a truce to such trifling matters! Let us speak about business affairs. We have signed the ratifications of peace, which are to be laid before the congress; it only remains for us to sign the *secret* articles which shall be known by none but France and Austria. The main point is the evacuation of Mentz by your troops, so that our army may occupy the fortress."

"I am afraid, general, this very point will be a stumbling-block for the members of the congress. They will raise a terrible hue and cry as soon as they learn that we have surrendered Mentz."

"Let these gentlemen say what they please," said Bonaparte, contemptuously; "we have called them hither that they may talk, and while they are talking, we shall act!"

"They will say that Austria has sacrificed the welfare and greatness of Germany to her own private interests," exclaimed Count Cobenzl, anxiously.

"Fools are they who care for what people will say!" replied Bonaparte, shrugging his shoulders. "A prudent man will pursue his path directly toward his aim, and the hum of babblers never disturbs him. Hear, then, my last words; in case the Austrian troops do not leave Mentz within one week, and surrender the fortress to the French forces, the French army will remain in Venice, and I would sooner send the latter city to the bottom of the sea than to let Austria have a single stone of hers. Mentz must be ours, or I tear the treaty, and hostilities will recommence!"

And Bonaparte, with a furious gesture, seized the papers lying on the table and was about to tear them, when Count Cobenzl suddenly jumped up and grasped his hands.

"General," he said, imploringly, "what are you going to do?"

"What am I going to do?" exclaimed Bonaparte, in a thundering voice, "I am going to tear a treaty of peace, which you merely want to sign with words, but not with deeds! Oh, that was the nice little trick of your diplomacy, then! With your prince's coronet you wanted to dazzle my eyes—with the two hundred thousand subjects you offered me just now, you wanted to corrupt my soul and induce me to barter away the honor and greatness of France for the miserable people of a petty German prince! No, sir, I shall not sell my honor at so low a price. I stand here in the name of the French Republic and ask

you, the representative of Austria, to fulfil what we have agreed upon at Campo Formio. Mentz must be ours even before our troops leave Venice. If you refuse that, it is a plain infringement of the treaty, and hostilities will be resumed. Now, sir, come to a decision. I am only a soldier, and but a poor diplomatist, for with my sword and with my word I always directly strike at my aim. In short, then, count, will you withdraw your troops from Mentz and from the other fortresses on the Rhine, and surrender Mentz to our army? Yes, or no?"

"Yes, yes," exclaimed Count Cobenzl, with a sigh, "we will fulfil your wishes—we will withdraw our troops from Mentz and surrender the fortress to the French."

"When will the surrender take place? As speedily as possible, if you please."

"On the ninth of December, general."

"Very well, on the ninth of December. The matter is settled, then."

"But let there be no solemn ceremonies at the surrender," said the count, imploringly. "Let our troops withdraw quietly—let your forces occupy the place in the same manner, so that when the delegates of the German empire, assembled in congress in this city, and to whom the Emperor of Germany has solemnly guaranteed the entire integrity and inviolability of the empire, hear the news of the transaction, the latter may be already an accomplished fact, to which every one must submit."

"Be it so, if that be Austria's desire," said Bonaparte, smiling. "And now we will consider the other secret articles. The Austrian troops retire from the German empire up to the line of the Inn and Lech, occupying hereafter only Austrian territory."

"Yes, general; in return for all these concessions on our part, the French troops will evacuate on the thirtieth of December the fortresses and territory of Venice, which has been ceded to Austria by the treaty of Campo Formio, and retire behind the line of demarcation."

"Granted! At the same time the troops of the republic seize the *tête-de-pont* at Mannheim either by intimidating the isolated garrison, or by making a sudden dash at the position,[*] and during the continuation of the negotiations here at Rastadt,

---

[*] "Mémoires d'un Homme d'État." The French took the *tête-de-pont* at Mannheim by assault, on the 28th of January, 1798, the garrison refusing to evacuate it. Mentz surrendered without firing a gun, and during the night of the 28th of December, 1797, the French entered this great fortress, which was thereupon annexed to the French Republic.

the French forces leave the left bank of the Rhine and occupy the right bank from Basle to Mentz."

"Granted," sighed Count Cobenzl. "Austria yields the frontier of the Rhine to France—that is, by the simultaneous retreat of her own forces she surrenders to the republic the most important points of the German empire, including Ehrenbreitstein. The congress of the states of the German empire will deliberate, therefore, under the direct influence produced by the immediate neighborhood of a French army."

"In case the delegates of Germany do not like the looks of the French soldiers, they may turn their eyes to the other side, where the Austrian army is encamped on the Danube and on the Lech," exclaimed Bonaparte. "Thus the delegates will be surrounded by two armies. This fact may interfere a little with the freedom of speech during the session of congress, but it will be advantageous, too, inasmuch as it will induce the delegates to accelerate their labors somewhat, and to finish their task sooner than they would have done under different circumstances."

"It is true, right in the face of these two armies at least the smaller German princes will not dare to oppose the German emperor in ceding the entire left bank of the Rhine to France. But it is only just and equitable for us to indemnify them for their losses. In one of our secret articles, therefore, we should acknowledge the obligation of promising compensations to the princes and electors—"

"Yes, let us promise compensations to them," said Bonaparte, with a tinge of sarcasm. "As to the possessions of Prussia on the left bank of the Rhine, France declares her readiness to give them back to the King of Prussia."

"But both powers agree not to allow the King of Prussia to acquire any new territory," exclaimed Count Cobenzl, hastily.

"Yes, that was our agreement at Campo Formio," said Bonaparte. "Austria's increase of territory, besides Venice, will consist of Salzburg and a piece of Upper Bavaria. In case she should make further conquests in the adjoining states, France may claim a further aggrandizement on the right bank of the Rhine." *

"Yes, that was the last secret article of the preliminaries of Campo Formio," said Cobenzl, sighing.

"Then we have remained entirely faithful to our agreement," said Bonaparte. "We have not made any alterations whatever in the programme which we agreed upon and deposed in writing at

the castle of Campo Formio. It only remains for us to-day to sign these secret articles."

He took the pen and hastily signed the two documents spread out on the table.

Count Cobenzl signed them also; but his hand was trembling a little while he was writing, and his face was clouded and gloomy. Perhaps he could not help feeling that Austria just now was signing the misery and disgrace of Germany in order to purchase thereby some provinces, and that Austria enlarged her territory at the expense of the empire whose emperor was her own ruler—Francis II.

Their business being finished, the two plenipotentiaries rose, and Count Cobenzl withdrew. Bonaparte accompanied him again to the door of the anteroom, and then returned to his cabinet.

A proud, triumphant smile was now playing on his pale, narrow lips, and his eyes were beaming and flashing in an almost sinister manner. Stepping back to the table, he fixed his eyes upon the document with the two signatures.

"The left bank of the Rhine is ours!" he said, heavily laying his hand upon the paper. "But the right bank?"

He shook his head, and folding his arms upon his back, he commenced pacing the room, absorbed in profound reflections. His features had now resumed their marble tranquillity; it was again the apparition of Julius Cæsar that was walking up and down there with inaudible steps, and the old thoughts of Julius Cæsar, those thoughts for which he had to suffer death, seemed to revive again in Bonaparte's mind, for at one time he whispered, "A crown for me! A crown in Germany. It would be too small for me! If my hand is to grasp a crown, it must—"

He paused and gazed fixedly at the wall as if he saw the future there, that arose before him in a strange phantasmagoria.

After a long pause, he started and seemed to awake from a dream.

"I believe I will read the letter once more, which I received yesterday by mail," he murmured, in an almost inaudible tone. "It is a wonderful letter, and I really would like to know who wrote it."

He drew a folded paper from his bosom and opened it. Stepping into a bay window, he perused the letter with slow, deliberate glances. The bright daylight illuminated his profile and rendered its antique beauty even more conspicuous. Profound silence surrounded him, and nothing was heard but his soft and slow respiration and the rustling of the paper.

When he had finished it, he commenced perusing it again, but this time he seemed to be anxious to

* Schlosser's ' History of the Eighteenth Century," vol. v., p. 43.

hear what he was reading. He read it, however, in a very low and subdued voice, and amidst the silence surrounding him the words that fell from the lips of the resurrected Cæsar sounded like the weird whispers of spirits.

"You have to choose now between so great an alternative," he read, "that however bold your character may be, you must be uncertain as to the determination you have to come to, if you are to choose between respect and hatred, between glory or disgrace, between exalted power or an abject insignificance, that would lead you to the scaffold, and, finally, between the immortality of a great man, or that of a punished partisan."

"Ah!" exclaimed Bonaparte, and his voice was now loud and firm. "Ah! I shall never hesitate between such alternatives. I should bear disgrace, abject insignificance, and an utter lack of power? And my hand should not be withered—it should be able yet to grasp a sword and pierce my breast with it?"

He lowered his eyes again and continued reading: "You have to choose between three parts: the first is to return quietly to France and to live there as a plain and unassuming citizen; the second, to return to France at the head of an army and there to become the leader of a party; the third, to establish a great empire in Italy and proclaim yourself king of the peninsula. I advise you to do so, and to grasp the Italian crown with a firm hand." *

"He is a fool," said Bonaparte, "who believes a man might make himself king of Italy and maintain himself on the throne, unless he previously has seized the sovereign power in France.† But no one must hear these thoughts! I will go to Josephine!"

He hastily folded the paper and concealed it again in his bosom. Then stepping to the looking-glass, he closely scanned his face in order to see whether or not it might betray his thoughts; and when he had found it to be as pale and impassive as ever, he turned round and left the room.

CHAPTER XXII.

THE BANNER OF GLORY.

FOUR days had elapsed since Bonaparte's arrival at Rastadt, and the congress had profited by

* Sabatier de Castres, living at that time in exile at Hamburg, had written this anonymous letter to Bonaparte.

† "Mémoires d'un Homme d'État," vol. v., p. 60.

them in order to give the most brilliant festivals to the French general and his beautiful wife. All those ambassadors, counts, barons, bishops, and diplomatists seemed to have assembled at Rastadt for the sole purpose of giving banquets, tea-parties, and balls; no one thought of attending to business, and all more serious ideas seemed to have been utterly banished, while every one spoke of the gorgeous decorations of the ball-rooms and of the magnificence of the state dinners, where the most enthusiastic toasts were drunk in honor of the victorious French general; and the people seemed most anxious entirely to forget poor, suffering, and patient Germany.

Josephine participated in these festivities with her innate cheerfulness and vivacity. She was the queen of every party; every one was doing homage to her; every one was bent upon flattering her in order to catch an affable word, a pleasant glance from her; and, encouraged by her unvaried kindness, to solicit her intercession with her husband, in whose hands alone the destinies of the German princes and their states now seemed to lie.

But while Josephine's radiant smiles were delighting every one—while she was promising to all to intercede for them with her husband, Bonaparte's countenance remained grave and moody, and it was only in a surly mood that he attended the festivals that were given in his honor. His threatening glances had frequently already been fixed upon his wife, and those moody apprehensions, ever alive in his jealous breast, had whispered to him: "Josephine has deceived you again! In order to silence your reproaches, she invented a beautiful story, in which there is not a word of truth, for the letter that was to call you back to Paris does not arrive, and the Directory keeps you here at Rastadt."

And while he was indulging in such reflections, his features assumed a sinister expression, and his lips muttered: "Woe to Josephine, if she should have deceived me!"

Thus the fourth day had arrived, and the Bavarian ambassador was to give a brilliant soirée. Bonaparte had promised to be present, but he had said to Josephine, in a threatening manner, that he would attend only if the expected courier from Paris did arrive in the course of the day, so that he might profit by the Bavarian ambassador's party to take leave of all those "fawning and slavish representatives of the German empire."

But no courier had made his appearance during the whole morning. Bonaparte had retired to his closet and was pacing the room like an angry lion in his cage. All at once, however, the door was hastily opened, and Josephine entered with a radiant face, holding in her uplifted right hand a large sealed letter.

"Bonaparte!" she shouted, in a jubilant voice, "can you guess what I have got here?"

He ran toward her and wanted to seize the letter. But Josephine would not let him have it, and concealed it behind her back. "Stop, my dear sir," she said. "First you must beg my pardon for the evil thoughts I have read on your forehead during the last few days. Oh, my excellent general, you are a poor sinner, and I really do not know if I am at liberty to grant you absolution and to open the gates of paradise to you."

"But what have I done, Josephine?" he asked. "Was I not as patient as a lamb? Did I not allow myself to be led like a dancing-bear from festival to festival? Did I not look on with the patience of an angel while every one was making love to you, and while you were lavishing smiles and encouraging, kind glances in all directions?"

"What have you done, Bonaparte?" she retorted gravely. "You inwardly calumniated your Josephine. You accused her in your heart, and day and night the following words were written on your forehead in flaming characters: 'Josephine has deceived me.' Do you pretend to deny it, sir?"

"No," said Bonaparte, "I will not deny any thing, dear, lovely expounder of my heart! I confess my sins, and implore your forgiveness. But now, Josephine, be kind enough not to let me wait any longer. Let me have the letter!"

"Hush, sir! this letter is not directed to you, but to myself," replied Josephine, smiling.

Bonaparte angrily stamped his foot. "Not to me!" he exclaimed, furiously. "Then is it not from the Directory—it does not call me back from Rastadt?—"

"Hush, Bonaparte!" said Josephine, smiling, "must you always effervesce like the stormy sea that roared around your cradle, you big child? Be quiet now, and let me read the letter to you. Will you let me do so?"

"Yes, I will," said Bonaparte, hastily. "Read, I implore you, read!"

Josephine made a profound, ceremonious obeisance, and withdrawing her hand with the letter from her back, she unfolded several sheets of paper.

"Here is first a letter from my friend Botot," she said, "just listen:—' Citoyenne Générale: The Directory wished to send off to-day a courier with he enclosed dispatches to General Bonaparte. I

induced the gentlemen, however, to intrust that dispatch to myself, and to permit me to send it to you instead of the general. It is to yourself chiefly that the general is indebted for the contents of this dispatch from the Directory. It is but just, therefore, citoyenne, that you should have the pleasure of handing it to him. Do so, citoyenne, and at the same time beg your husband not to forget your and his friend.—Botot.' That is my letter Bonaparte, and here, my friend, is the enclosure for yourself. You see, I am devoid of the common weakness of woman, I am not inquisitive, for the seal is not violated, as you may see yourself."

And with a charming smile she handed the letter to Bonaparte. But he did not take it.

"Break the seal, my Josephine," he said, profoundly moved. "I want to learn the contents of the letter from your lips. If it should bring me evil tidings, they will sound less harshly when announced by you; is it joyful news, however, your voice will accompany it with the most beautiful music."

Josephine nodded to him with a tender and grateful glance, and hastily broke the seal.

"Now pray, quick! quick!" said Bonaparte, trembling with impatience.

Josephine read:

"The executive Directory presumes, citizen general, that you have arrived at Rastadt. It is impatient to see and to weigh with you the most important interests of the country. Hence it desires you to bring the exchanged ratifications personally to Paris, and to inform us what dispositions you have taken in regard to the occupation of Mentz by our troops, in order that this event may take place without further delay. It may be, however, that you have forwarded this intelligence to us already by means of a courier or an aide-de-camp; in that case it will be kept secret until your arrival. The journey you are now going to make to Paris will first fulfil the sincere desire of the Directory to manifest to you publicly its most unbounded satisfaction with your conduct and to be the first interpreter of the nation's gratitude toward you. Besides, it is necessary for you to be fully informed of the government's views and intentions, and to consider in connection with it the ultimate consequences of the great operations which you will be invited to undertake; so we expect you immediately, citizen general. The executive Directory also desires you to indicate to the returning courier, who is to deliver this dispatch to you, the precise day of your arrival at Paris. In the name of the Directory:

"Barras."

"We shall set out at once!" exclaimed Bonaparte, radiant with joy.

"In order to arrive together with the courier?" asked Josephine, laughing, "and to lose all the triumphs which the grateful country is preparing for you? No, my impatient friend, you will patiently remain to-day by the side of your Josephine and we shall start only to-morrow. Do you promise it?"

"Well, be it so!" he exclaimed, glowing with excitement, "we will set out to-morrow for Paris. My task in Italy is accomplished; if it please God, there will be new work for me at Paris."

"Your enemies will soon find means to drive you away from the capital, if you should be incautious, and if they should fear lest your presence might become dangerous to themselves. Nothing is more dangerous to small, insignificant souls than a great man. Remember that, my friend, and do not irritate them."

Bonaparte eagerly grasped her hand. "Believe me," he said, in a low voice, "as soon as I have reached Paris, I shall know what line of policy I must pursue hereafter. Two years shall not elapse ere the whole ridiculous republican edifice will be overthrown." *

"And then," exclaimed Josephine, joyfully, "when you have accomplished that—when you stand as a victorious general on the ruins of the republic — you will reëstablish the throne over them, I hope?"

"Yes, I will reëstablish the throne,"† said Bonaparte, enthusiastically.

"And your arm will place upon this throne him to whom this throne is due. Oh, my generous and noble friend, what a heavenly day it will be when the King of France by your side makes his solemn entry into Paris, for you will recall the legitimate king, Louis XVIII., from his exile."

Bonaparte stared at her in amazement. "Do you really believe that?" he asked, with a peculiar smile.

"I have no doubt of it," she said, innocently. "Bonaparte can do whatever he wishes to do. He has overthrown thrones in Italy, he can reëstablish the throne in France. I repeat, Bonaparte can do whatever he wishes to do."

"And do you know, then, you little fool, do you know what I really wish to do?" he asked. "I wish to be the great regulator of the destinies of Europe, or the first citizen of the globe. I feel that I have the strength to overthrow every thing and to found a new world. The astonished universe shall bow to me and be compelled to submit to my laws. Then I shall make the villains tremble, who wished to keep me away from my country.* I have made the beginning already, and this miserable government has to call me back to Paris notwithstanding its own secret hostility. Soon it shall be nothing but a tool in my hands, and when I do not need this tool any longer, I shall destroy it. This government of lawyers has oppressed France long enough. It is high time for us to drive it away." †

"Hush, Bonaparte, for God's sake, hush!" said Josephine, anxiously. "Let no one here suspect your plans, for we are surrounded in this house by austere and rabid republicans, who, if they had heard your words, would arraign you as a criminal before the Directory. Intrust your plans to no one except myself, Bonaparte. Before the world remain as yet a most enthusiastic republican, and only when the decisive hour has come, throw off your tunic and exhibit your royal uniform!"

Bonaparte smiled, and encircled her neck with his arms.

"Yes, you are right," he said; "we must be taciturn. We must bury our most secret thoughts in the deepest recesses of our souls, and intrust them to no one, not even to the beloved. But come, Josephine, I owe you my thanks yet for the joyful tidings you have brought me. You must permit me to make you a few little presents in return."

"Give me your confidence, and I am abundantly rewarded," said Josephine, tenderly.

"Henceforth I shall never, never distrust you," he replied, affectionately. "We belong to each other, and no power of earth or heaven is able to separate us. You are mine and I am thine; and what is mine being thine, you must permit me to give you a trinket sent to me to-day by the city of Milan."

"A trinket?" exclaimed Josephine, with radiant eyes; "let me see it. Is it a beautiful one?"

Bonaparte smiled. "Yes, beautiful in the eyes of those to whom glory seems more precious than diamonds and pearls," he said, stepping to the table from which he took a small morocco casket. "See," he said, opening it, "it is a gold medal which the city of Milan has caused to be struck in my honor, and on which it confers upon me the title of 'The Italian.'"

"Give it to me," exclaimed Josephine, joyfully—"give it to me, my 'Italian!' Let me wear

---

* "Mémoires d'un Homme d'État," vol. v., p. 60.

† Bonaparte's own words.—"Mémoires d'un Homme d'État," vol. v., p. 70.

* Le Normand, vol. i., p. 247.

† "Mémoires d'un Homme d'État," vol. v., p. 70.

this precious trinket which public favor has bestowed upon you."

"Public favor," he said, musingly—"public favor, it is light as zephyr, as fickle as the seasons,
it passes away like the latter, and when the north
wind moves it, it will disappear." *

He was silent, but proceeded after a short pause
in a less excited manner.

"As to my deeds," he said, "the pen of history
will trace them for our grandchildren. Either I
shall have lived for a century, or I shall earn for
all my great exploits nothing but silence and oblivion. Who is able to calculate the whims and
predilections of history?" †

He paused again, and became absorbed in his
reflections.

Josephine did not venture to arouse him from
his musing. She fixed her eyes upon the large
gold medal, and tried to decipher the inscription.

Bonaparte suddenly raised his head again, and
turned his gloomy eyes toward Josephine. "I
suppose you know," he said, "that I have always
greatly distinguished the Duke of Litalba among
all Milanese, and that I have openly courted his
friendship?"

"You have always manifested the greatest kindness for him," said Josephine, "and he is gratefully devoted to you for what you have done for
him."

"Gratefully!" exclaimed Bonaparte, sarcastically. "There is no gratitude on earth, and the
Duke of Litalba is as ungrateful as the rest of
mankind. I called him my friend. Do you know
how he has paid me for it, and what he has said
of me behind my back?"

"Oh, then, they have told you libels and made
you angry again by repeating to you the gossip of
idle tongues?"

"They shall tell me every thing—I want to
know every thing!" retorted Bonaparte, violently.
"I must know my friends and my enemies. And
I believed Litalba to be my friend, I believed him
when he told me, with tears in his eyes, how much
he was afflicted by my departure, and how de-
votedly he loved me. I believed him, and on the
same day he said at a public casino, 'Now at last
our city will get rid of this meteor that is able all
alone to set fire to the whole of Europe, and to
spread the sparks of its revolutionary fire to the
most remote corners of the world.' ‡ He dared
to call me a meteor, a shining nothing which after
lighting up the sky for a short while explodes and
dissolves itself into vapor. I shall prove to him

and to the whole world that I am more than that,
and if I kindle a fire in Europe, it shall be large
enough to burn every enemy of mine."

"Your glory is the fire that will consume your
enemies," said Josephine, eagerly. "You will not
reply to their calumnies—your deeds will speak
for themselves. Do not heed the voice of slander
my Italian, listen only to the voice of your glory.
It will march before you to France like a herald,
it will fill all hearts with enthusiasm, and all
hearts will hail your arrival with rapturous applause—you, the victorious chieftain, the conqueror of Italy!"

"I will show you the herald I am going to send
to-day to France, to be presented there in my
name by General Joubert to the Directory," replied
Bonaparte. "It is a herald whose mute language
will be even more eloquent than all the hymns of
victory with which they may receive me. Wait
here for a moment. I shall be back directly."

He waved his hand to her and hastily left the
room. Josephine's eyes followed him with an expression of tender admiration. "What a bold
mind, what a fiery heart!" she said, in a low voice.
"Who will stem the bold flight of this mind, who
will extinguish the flames of this heart? Who—"

The door opened, and Bonaparte returned, followed by several footmen carrying a rolled-up banner. When they had reached the middle of the
room, he took it from them and told them to
withdraw. As soon as the door had closed behind
them, he rapidly unrolled the banner so that it
floated majestically over his head.

"Ah, that is the proud victor of the bridge of
Arcole!" exclaimed Josephine, enthusiastically
"Thus you must have looked when you headed
the column, rushing into the hail of balls and bullets, and bearing the colors aloft in your right
hand! Oh, Bonaparte, how glorious you look under your glorious banner!"

"Do not look at me, but look at the banner,"
he said. "Future generations may some day take
it for a monument from the fabulous times of antiquity, and yet this monument contains nothing
but the truth. The Directory shall hang up this
banner in its hall, and if it should try to deny or
belittle my deeds, I shall point at the banner which
will tell every one what has been accomplished in
Italy by the French army and its general."

Josephine looked in silent admiration at the
splendid banner. It was made of the heaviest
white satin, trimmed with a broad border of blue
and white. Large eagles, embroidered in gold,
and decorated with precious stones, filled the corners on both sides; warlike emblems, executed
by the most skilful painters, filled the inside of the

* Le Normand, vol. i., p. 261.
† Ibid., vol. i., p. 262.   ‡ Ibid., vol. i., p. 262.

colored border, and inscriptions in large gold letters covered the centre.

"Read these inscriptions, Josephine," said Bonaparte imperiously, pointing at them with his uplifted arm. "It is a simple and short history of our campaign in Italy. Read aloud, Josephine; let me hear from your lips the triumphal hymn of my army!"

Josephine seized the gold cord hanging down from the banner and thus kept it straight. Bonaparte, proudly leaning against the gilt flag-staff, which he grasped with both hands, listened smiling and with flashing eyes to Josephine, who read as follows:

"One hundred and fifty thousand prisoners; one hundred and seventy stands of colors; five hundred and fifty siege-guns; six hundred field-pieces; five pontoon parks; nine line-of-battle ships, of sixty-four guns; twelve frigates of thirty-two guns; twelve corvettes; eighteen galleys; armistice with the King of Sardinia; treaty with Genoa; armistice with the Duke of Parma; armistice with the King of Naples; armistice with the Pope; preliminaries of Leoben; treaty of Montebello with the Republic of Genoa; treaty of peace with the emperor at Campo Formio.

"Liberty restored to the people of Bologna, Ferrara, Modena, Massacarrara, of the Romagna, of Lombardy, Brescia, Bergamo, Mantua, Cremona, Chiavenna, Bormio, and the Valtelline; further, to the people of Genoa, to the vassals of the emperor, to the people of the department of Corcyra, of the Ægean Sea and Ithaca.

"Sent to Paris all the masterpieces of Michel Angelo, Guercino, Titian, Paul Veronese, Correggio, Albarro, the two Carracci, Raphael, and Leonardo da Vinci." *

"Ah, my friend," exclaimed Josephine, enthusiastically, "that is a leaf from history which the storms of centuries will never blow away!"

Bonaparte slowly lowered the banner until it almost covered the floor and then he muttered gloomily: "Men are like leaves in the wind: the wind blows the leaves to the ground, † and—but no," he interrupted himself, "I shall write my name on every rock and every mountain in Europe, and fasten it there with iron-clasps in such a manner that no winds shall blow it away! Oh, footmen! come in, roll up the banner again and put it back into the case!"

The footmen hastened to obey, and took the banner away. Bonaparte turned again to his wife with a smile.

"I promised you a few presents," he said. "As yet I have given you only the medals. The best gift I have kept back. Marmont sent me the statue of the Holy Virgin which he removed from Loretto."

"Then you have not fulfilled my urgent prayers!" said Josephine, reproachfully. "Even the property of the Church and of the Holy Father at Rome have not been safe from the hands of the conquerors!"

"That is the law of war," said Bonaparte. "Woe to the places which war touches on its bloody path! But you may reassure yourself, Josephine. I have only taken from the Holy Father these superfluous things which he may easily spare. I only took his plate, his jewelry, and diamonds, thus reducing him to the simplicity of the apostles; and I am sure the good old man will thank me for it. I have, moreover, only striven to promote the welfare of his soul by doing so, and the Roman martyrologist some day will add his name to the list of saints." The jewels and the gold I sent to Paris, together with the statue of the Madonna of Loretto, but I retained a few relics for you, Josephine. See here the most precious one of them all!"

He handed her a small paper, carefully folded up. Josephine hastily opened it and asked, in surprise—"A piece of black woollen cloth! And that is a relic?"

"And a most precious one at that! It is Loretto's most priceless treasure. It is a piece of the gown of the Virgin Mary, in which she was mourning for the Saviour.† Preserve this relic carefully, dear Josephine, and may it protect you from danger and grief!"

Josephine folded up the piece of cloth, and opening a large locket hanging on her neck on a heavy gold chain, she laid the cloth into it, and then closed the locket again.

"That shall be the sanctuary of my relic," she said. "I shall keep it till I die."

"Why do you speak of dying?" he exclaimed, almost indignantly. "What have we to do with grim-death? We, to whom life has to fulfil and offer so much! We shall return to Paris, and, if it please God, a great future is awaiting us there!"

"If it please God, a happy future!" said Josephine, fervently. "Oh, Bonaparte, how gladly I shall reënter our dear little house in the *Rue Chantereine*, where we passed the first happy days of our love!"

---

* This wonderful banner was hung up in the hall of the Directory while the members of the latter were occupying the Luxembourg. It afterward accompanied the three consuls to the Tuileries, and was preserved there in the large reception-room. It is now in the " Dome des Invalides " in the chapel containing the emperor's sarcophagus. † Homer.

* Le Normand, vol. i., p. 243.
† Ibid., vol. i., p. 245.

"No, Josephine," he exclaimed, impetuously, "that little house will not be a fitting abode for the conqueror of Italy. I am no longer the poor general who had nothing but his sword. I return rich in glory, and not poor as far as money is concerned. I might have easily appropriated the spoils amounting to many millions; but I disdained the money of spoliation and bribery, and what little money I have got now, was acquired in an honest and chivalrous manner.* It is sufficient, however, to secure a brilliant existence to us. I shall not be satisfied until I live with you in a house corresponding with the splendor of my name. I need a palace, and shall have it decorated with all the stands of colors I have taken in Italy. To you alone, Josephine, to you I intrust the care of designating to me a palace worthy of being offered to me by the nation I have immortalized, and worthy also of a wife whose beauty and grace could only beautify it.† Come, Josephine—come to Paris! Let us select such a palace!"

CHAPTER XXIII.

MINISTER THUGUT.

THE prime minister, Baron Thugut, was in his study. It was yet early in the morning, and the minister had just entered his room in order to begin his political task. On the large green table at which Thugut had just sat down, there lay the dispatches and letters delivered by the couriers who had arrived during the night and early in the morning. There were, besides, unfolded documents and decrees, waiting for the minister's signature, in order to become valid laws. But the minister took no notice whatever of these papers, but first seized the newspapers and other periodicals, which he commenced reading with great eagerness. While he was perusing them, his stern features assumed a still harsher mien, and a gloomy cloud settled on his brow. Suddenly he

uttered a wild oath and violently hurling the paper, in which he had been reading, to the floor, he jumped up from his chair.

"Such impudence is altogether intolerable!" he shouted, angrily. "It is high time for me to teach these newspaper scribblers another lesson, and they shall have it! I—"

Just then, the door of the anteroom opened, and a footman entered. He informed his master that the police minister, Count Saurau, wished to see him.

Baron Thugut ordered him to be admitted at once, and went to meet him as soon as he heard him come in.

"You anticipate my wishes, my dear count," he said. "I was just going to send for you."

"Your excellency knows that I am always ready to obey your calls," replied Count Saurau, politely. "I acknowledge your superiority and submit to you as though you were my lord and master; notwithstanding our position in society and in the state service, which is almost an equal one, I willing permit you to treat me as your disciple and inferior."

"And I believe that is the wisest course you can pursue, my dear little count," said Thugut, laughing sarcastically. "It has been good for you to do so, I should think, and so it has been for the whole Austrian ship of state, that has been intrusted to my guidance. Yes, sir, the son of the ship-builder Thunichtgut has shown to you and your fellow-members of the ancient aristocracy that talents and ability are no exclusive privileges of your class, and that a common ship-builder's son may become prime minister, and that a low-born Thunichtgut may be transformed into a Baron von Thugut. The great Empress Maria Theresa has performed this miracle, and baptized me, and I believe Austria never found fault with her for doing so. The ship-builder's son has piloted the ship of state tolerably skilfully through the breakers up to the present time, and he shall do so in future too, in spite of all counts and aristocrats. You see, I do not try to conceal my humble descent; nay, I boast of it, and it is therefore quite unnecessary for you to remind me of what I never want to forget!"

"I see that some late occurrence must have excited your excellency's just anger," exclaimed Count Saurau.

"And being police minister, you doubtless know all about that occurrence," said Thugut, sarcastically.

Count Saurau shrugged his shoulders. "I confess I am unable to divine—"

"Then you have not read the papers this morn-

---

* Bonaparte at St. Helena said to Las Casas that he had brought only three hundred thousand francs from Italy. Bourrienne asserts, however, Bonaparte had brought home no less than three million francs. He adds, however, that this sum was not the fruit of peculation and corruption, Bonaparte having been an incorruptible administrator. But he had discovered the mines of Yords, and he had an interest in the meat contracts for the army. He wanted to be independent, and knew better than any one else that he could not be independent without money. He said to Bourrienne in regard to it, "I am no Capuchin!"—Mémoires de Bourrienne, vol. ii., p. 47.

† Le Normand, vol. i., p. 265.

ing?" asked Thugut, scornfully. "You have no idea of the infamous attack which an aristocratic newspaper scribbler has dared to make upon me, nay, upon the emperor himself?"

"I confess that I do not understand what your excellency means," said Count Saurau, anxiously.

"Well, then, listen to me!" exclaimed Thugut, seizing the paper again. "Listen to what I am going to read to you:' 'At a time when the whole Austrian people are longing for peace, when our august Empress Theresia and our dearly beloved Archduke Charles share these sentiments of the people and give expression to them at the feet of the throne and in opposition to those who would deluge our cherished Austria with the miseries and dangers of war—at such a time we fondly look back into the great history of our country and remember what has been accomplished by great and gifted members of our imperial house in former periods for the welfare and tranquillity of Austria; we remember, for instance, that Austria in 1619, like to-day, was threatened by enemies and on the eve of a terrible war, not because the honor and welfare of Austria rendered such a war necessary, but because the ambitious and arrogant minister, Cardinal Clesel, was obstinately opposed to peace, and utterly unmindful of the wishes of the people. He alone, he, the all-powerful minister, was in favor of war; he overwhelmed the weak Emperor Mathias with his demands; and when the latter, owing to the anxiety he had to undergo, was taken sick, he even pursued him with his clamor for war into his sick-room. But then the archdukes, the emperor's brothers, boldly determined to interfere. They arrested the rascally minister at the emperor's bedside and sent him to Castle Ambras in the Tyrol, where he suffered long imprisonment, a just punishment for his arrogance and for his attempt to involve the country in a war so distasteful to all classes of the people. About half a century later a similar occurrence took place. There was again a minister advocating war in spite of the whole Austrian people. It was in 1673. The minister to whose suggestions the Emperor Leopold lent a willing ear at that time, was Prince Lobkowitz. But the Empress Claudia had compassion on the people, groaning under the heavy yoke of the minister. She alone prevailed upon the emperor by her eloquence and beauty to deprive Prince Lobkowitz suddenly of all his honors and offices and to send him on a common hay-wagon amidst the contemptuous scoffs and jeers of the populace of Vienna to the fortress of Raudnitz, forbidding him under pain

of death to inquire about the cause of his punishment.' *

"Well," asked Thugut, when he ceased reading, "what do you think of that?"

"I believe the article contains very idle historical reminiscences," said Count Saurau, shrugging his shoulders; "these reminiscences, according to my opinion, have no bearing whatever upon our own times."

"That is, you will not admit their bearing upon our own times, my dear little count; you pretend not to perceive that the whole article is directed against myself; that the object is to exasperate the people against me and to encourage my enemies to treat me in the same manner as Clesel and Lobkowitz were treated. The article alludes to the archdukes who overthrew the minister so obstinately opposed to peace, and to the Empress Claudia who profited by her power over the emperor in order to ruin an all-powerful minister, her enemy. And you pretend not to see that all this is merely referred to for the purpose of encouraging Archduke Charles and the Empress Theresia to act as those have acted? Both are at the head of the peace party; both want peace with France, and in their short-sightedness and stupidity, they are enthusiastic admirers of that French general Bonaparte, whom they call 'the Italian,' unmindful of the great probability of his designating himself some day by the *sobriquet* of 'the Austrian,' unless we oppose him energetically and set bounds to his thirst after conquest. They want to get rid of me in the same manner as their predecessors got rid of Cardinal Clesel. But I hold the helm as yet, and do not mean to relinquish it."

"It would be a terrible misfortune for Austria if your excellency should do so," said Count Saurau, in his soft, bland voice. "I do not believe that either the Empress Theresa or the Archduke Charles will act in a hostile manner toward you."

"And if they should do so, I would not tolerate it," exclaimed Thugut. "My adversaries, whosoever they may be, had better beware of my elephant foot not stamping them into the ground. I hate that boastful, revolutionary France, and to remain at peace with her is equivalent to drawing toward us the ideas of the revolution and of a general convulsion. Short-sighted people will not believe it, and they are my enemies because I am a true friend of Austria. But being a true friend of Austria, I must combat all those who dare oppose and impede me, for in my person they oppose and impede Austria. First of all things,

* Vide Hormayer. "Lebensbilder aus dem Befreiungskriege," vol. i., p. 321.

it is necessary for me to get rid of those news-paper editors and scribblers; they are arrogant, insolent fellows who imagine they know every thing and are able to criticise every thing, and who feel called upon to give their opinion about all things and on all occasions because they know how to wield a goose-quill. The best thing we could do would be to suppress all newspapers and periodicals. Shaping the course of politics our-selves, we do not need any newspapers, which after all are nothing but ruminating oxen of what we have eaten and digested already; the people do not understand any thing about it, nor is it neces-sary that they should. The people have to work, to obey, to pay taxes, and, if necessary, to give up their lives for their sovereign; they need not know any thing further about politics, and if they do, it is generally detrimental to their obedience. Let us drive away, then, that noxious crowd of newspaper writers and pamphleteers who dare en-lighten the people by their political trash. Ah, I will teach Count Erlach that it is a little dangerous to become a newspaper editor and to serve up *entremets* of historical reminiscences to the people of Vienna! I will cram them down his own throat in such a manner as to deprive him—"

"Count Erlach is the author of the article your excellency read to me just now?" asked Count Sauran, in great terror.

"There, his name is affixed to it in large let-ters," replied Thugut, contemptuously; "he has not even taken pains to conceal it. We have to return thanks to him for his sincerity, and I hope you will take the trouble of expressing our grati-tude to him."

"What does your excellency want me to do?" asked the police minister, anxiously. "I believe it would not be prudent for us to make much ado about it."

"Of course not," said Thugut, laughing. "Do I like to make much ado about any thing, which would only give rise to scandal and idle gossip? Just reflect a while, my dear little count. What did we do, for instance, with the Neapolitan Count Montalban, who became a thorn in our side, and endeavored to gain power over the emperor? Did we accuse him of high treason? Did we prefer any charges against him at all? We merely caused him to disappear, and no one knew what had become of the interesting and handsome count. People spoke for three or four days about his mys-terious disappearance, and then forgot all about it.* My dear sir, there is nothing like *oubliettes* and secret prisons. I have often already preached

that to you, and you always forget it. Violence! Who will be such a fool as to betray his little se-crets by acts of open violence? We happen to stand on the great stage of life, and, like every other stage, there are trap-doors in the floor, through which those will disappear who have per-formed their parts. Let us, therefore, cause Count Erlach, the political writer, to vanish by means of such a trap-door."

"I implore your excellency to show indulgence for once," said Count Sauran, urgently. "Count Erlach is an intimate friend of Archduke Charles, and even the Empress Theresia is attached to him."

"The greater the necessity for me to get rid of him, and to return my thanks in this manner for the blows they want to deal me by means of their historical reminiscences. This Count Erlach is a very disgusting fellow, at all events; he would like to play the incorruptible Roman and to shine by his virtue. There is nothing more tedious and intolerable than a virtuous man who cannot be got at anywhere. Count Erlach has now given us a chance to get hold of him; let us improve it."

"He has very influential connections, very pow-erful protectors, your excellency. If he should disappear, they will raise a terrible outcry about it, and make it their special business to seek him, and if they should not find him they will say we had killed him because your excellency was afraid of him."

"I was afraid of him!" exclaimed Thugut, laughing. "As if I ever had been afraid of any one. Even an earthquake would not be able to frighten me, and, like Fabricius, I should only look around quite slowly for the hidden elephant of Pyrrhus. No, I know no fear, but I want others to feel fear, and for this reason Count Erlach must be disposed of."

"Very well, let us get rid of him," replied Count Sauran, "but in a simple manner and before the eyes of the whole public. Believe me for once, your excellency, I know the ground on which we are standing; I know it to be undermined and ready to explode and blow us up. Count Erlach's disappearance would be the burning match that might bring about the explosion. Let us be cautious, therefore. Let us remove him beyond the frontier, and threaten him with capital punish-ment in case he ever should dare to reënter Aus-tria, but let us permit him now to leave the coun-try without any injury whatever."

"Well, be it so. I will let you have your own way, my dear anxious friend. Have Erlach arrested to-day; let two police commissioners transport him beyond the frontier, and threaten

* Lebensbilder, vol. i., p. 321.

him with capital punishment, or with my revenge —which will be the same to him—in case he should return. Let the scribblers and newspapers learn, too, why Count Erlach was exiled. The prudent men among them will be warned by his fate, and hereafter hold their tongues; the stupid and audacious fellows, however, will raise an outcry about the occurrence, and thus give us a chance to get hold of them likewise. The matter is settled, then; the aristocratic newspaper writer will be transported from the country, and that is the end of it.* But I shall seek further satisfaction for these articles in the newspapers. Oh, the new Empress Theresia and the archduke shall find out that I am no Clesel or Lobkowitz to be got rid of by means of an intrigue. I shall try to obtain in the course of to-day an order from the emperor, removing the archduke from the command of the army and causing him to retire into private life. He wants peace and repose in so urgent a manner; let him sleep and dream, then, while we are up and doing. I need a resolute and courageous general at the head of the army, a man who hates the French, and not one who is friendly to them. But as for the empress—"

"Your excellency," interrupted Count Sauran, with a mysterious air, "I called upon you to-day for the purpose of speaking to you about the empress, and of cautioning you against—"

"Cautioning me!" exclaimed Thugut, with proud disdain. "What is the matter, then?"

"You know assuredly that the Empress Theresia has fully recovered from her confinement, and that she has held levees for a whole week already."

"As if I had not been the first to obtain an audience and to kiss her hand!" exclaimed Thugut, shrugging his shoulders.

"The empress," continued Sauran, "has received the ambassadors also; she even had two interviews already with the minister of the French Republic, General Bernadotte."

Thugut suddenly became quite attentive, and fixed his small, piercing eyes upon the police minister with an expression of intense suspense.

"Two interviews?" he asked. "And you know what they conferred about in these two interviews?"

"I should be a very poor police minister, and my secret agents would furnish me very unsatisfactory information, if I did not know it."

"Well, let us hear all about it, my dear count. What did the empress say to Bernadotte?"

"In the first audience General Bernadotte began by reading his official speech to her majesty, and the empress listened to him with a gloomy air. But then they entered upon a less ceremonious conversation, and Bernadotte assured the empress that France entertained no hostile intentions whatever against Naples, her native country. He said he had been authorized by the Directory of the Republic to assure her majesty officially that she need not feel any apprehensions in relation to Naples, France being animated by the most friendly feelings toward that kingdom. The face of the empress lighted up at once, and she replied to the general in very gracious terms, and gave him permission to renew his visits to her majesty whenever he wished to communicate any thing to her. He had asked her to grant him this permission."

"I knew the particulars of this first interview, except the passage referring to this permission," said Thugut, quietly.

"But this permission precisely is of the highest importance, your excellency, for the empress thereby gives the French minister free access to her rooms. He is at liberty to see her as often as he wishes, to communicate any thing to her. It seems the general has to make many communications to her majesty, for two days after the first audience, that is yesterday, General Bernadotte again repaired to the *Hofburg* in order to see the empress." *

"And did she admit him?" asked Thugut.

"Yes, she admitted him, your excellency. This time the general did not confine himself to generalities, but fully unbosomed himself to her majesty. He confessed to the empress that France was very anxious to maintain peace with Naples as well as with Austria; adding, however, that this would be much facilitated by friendly advances, especially on the part of Austria. Austria, instead of pursuing such a policy, was actuated by hostile intentions toward France. When the empress asked for an explanation of these words, Bernadotte was bold enough to present to her a memorial directed against the policy of your excellency, and in which the general said he had taken pains, by order of the Directory, to demonstrate that the policy of Baron Thugut was entirely incompatible with a good understanding between Austria and France, and that, without such an understanding, the fate of Naples could not be but very uncertain."

"What did the empress reply?" asked Thugut, whose mien did not betray a symptom of excitement or anger.

* Count Erlach was really transported beyond the Austrian frontier by two police commissioners. Only after Thugut's overthrow in 1801 was he allowed to return to Austria and Vienna.—Lebensbilder, vol. i., p. 321.

* "Mémoires d'un Homme d'État," vol. v., p. 485.

"Her majesty replied she would read the memorial with the greatest attention, and keep it a profound secret from every one. She added, however, she feared lest, even if the memorial should convince herself of the inexpediency of Baron Thugut's policy, it might be difficult if not impossible to induce the emperor to take a similar view of the matter—his majesty reposing implicit confidence in his prime minister and being perfectly satisfied of your excellency's fidelity, honesty, and incorruptibility. After this reply, Bernadotte approached the empress somewhat nearer, and cautiously and searchingly glanced around the room in order to satisfy himself that no one but her majesty could overhear his words. Just then—"

"Well, why do you hesitate?" asked Thugut, hastily.

"My tongue refuses to repeat the calumnies which the French minister has dared to utter."

"Compel your tongue to utter them, and let me hear them," exclaimed Thugut, sarcastically.

"With your excellency's leave, then. Bernadotte then almost bent down to the ear of the empress and said to her, whisperingly, the Directory of France were in possession of papers that would compromise Minister Thugut and furnish irrefutable proofs that Minister Thugut was by no means a reliable and honest adviser of his majesty, inasmuch as he was in the pay of foreign powers, England and Russia particularly, who paid him millions for always fanning anew the flames of Austria's hostility against France. Bernadotte added that these papers were on the way already, and would arrive at Vienna by the next courier. He asked the empress if she would permit him to hand these papers to her for placing them into the hands of the emperor."

"And the empress?"

"The empress promised it, and granted a third audience to the minister as soon as he should be in possession of the papers and apply for an interview with her." *

"Are you through?" asked Thugut, with the greatest composure.

"Not yet, your excellency. It remains for me to tell you that the courier expected by Bernadotte arrived last night at the hotel of the French embassy, and that the minister himself immediately left his couch in order to receive the dispatches in person. Early this morning an extraordinary activity prevailed among the employés of the embassy, and the first attaché as well as the secretary of legation left the hotel at a very early

hour. The former with a letter from Bernadotte repaired to Laxenburg where the empress, as is well known to your excellency, has been residing with her court for the last few days. After the lapse of an hour, he returned, and brought the general the verbal reply from the empress that her majesty would return to Vienna in order to attend the festival of the volunteers, and would then be ready to grant an immediate audience to the ambassador."

"And whither did the secretary of legation go?"

"First to one of our most fashionable military tailors,* and then to a dry-goods store. At the tailor's he ordered a banner, which is to be ready in the course of this evening, and at the dry-goods store he purchased the material required for this banner—blue, white, and red. Now, your excellency, I am through with my report."

"I confess, my dear count, that I have listened to you with the most intense pleasure and satisfaction, and that I cannot refrain from expressing to you my liveliest admiration for the vigilance and energy of your police, who do not merely unfathom the past and present, but also the future. In three days, then, the ambassador of France will have an interview with the empress?"

"Yes, your excellency, and he will then deliver to her the above-mentioned papers."

"Provided he has got any such papers, my friend! Papers that might compromise me! As if there were any such papers! As if I ever had been so stupid as to intrust secrets to a scrap of paper and to betray to it what every one must not know. He who wants to keep secrets—and I understand that exceedingly well—will intrust them just as little to paper as to human ear. I should burn my own hair did I believe that it had got wind of the ideas of my head. I would really like to see these papers which Bernadotte—"

The sudden appearance of the valet de chambre interrupted the minister. "Your excellency," he said, "the ambassador of the French Republic, General Bernadotte, would like to see your excellency immediately concerning a very important and urgent affair."

Thugut exchanged a rapid, smiling glance with the count. "Take the ambassador to the reception-room and tell him that I shall wait on him at once."

"Well?" he asked, when the valet had withdrawn. "Do you still believe that Bernadotte

* "Mémoires d'un Homme d'État," vol. v., p. 290.

* Military tailors are tailors who have the exclusive privilege of furnishing uniforms, etc., to the officers of the army.

has got papers that would compromise me? Would he call on me in that case? He doubtless intends telling me his ridiculous story, too, or he wishes to intimidate me by his interviews with the empress, so as to prevail on me to accede to the desires of France and to become more pliable. But he is entirely mistaken. I am neither afraid of his interviews with the empress, nor of Bernadotte's papers, and shall immovably pursue my own path. If it please God, this path will soon lead me to a point where the battle against those overbearing French may be begun in a very safe and satisfactory manner. Come, my dear count, accompany me to the adjoining room. I shall leave the door ajar that leads into the reception-room, for I want you to be an invisible witness to my interview with the ambassador. Come!"

CHAPTER XXIV.

THE FESTIVAL OF THE VOLUNTEERS.

He quietly took the count's arm and went with him to the adjoining room. Indicating to him a chair standing not far from the other door, he walked rapidly forward and entered the reception-room.

General Bernadotte, quite a young man, approached him with a stiff and dignified bearing, and there was an expression of bold defiance and undisguised hostility plainly visible on his youthful and handsome features.

Thugut, on his side, had called a smile upon his lips, and his eyes were radiant with affability and mildness.

"I am very glad, general, to see you here at so unexpected an hour," he said, politely. "Truly, this is a distinction that will cause all of our pretty ladies to be jealous of me, and I am afraid, general, you will still more exasperate the fair sex, who never would grant me their favor, against myself, for I am now assuredly to blame if some of our most beautiful ladies now should vainly wait for your arrival."

"I am always very punctual in my appointments, your excellency, whether they be armed rencounters or such rendezvous as your excellency has mentioned just now, and, therefore, seems to like especially," said Bernadotte, gravely. "I call upon your excellency, however, in the name of a lady, too—in the name of the French Republic!"

"And she is, indeed, a very exalted and noble lady, to whom the whole world is bowing reverentially," said Thugut, smiling.

"In the name of the French Republic and of the French Directory, I would like to inquire of your excellency whether or not it is a fact that a popular festival will be held to-morrow here in Vienna?"

"A popular festival! Ah, my dear general, I should not have thought that the French Republic would take so lively an interest in the popular festivals of the Germans! But I must take the liberty of requesting you, general, to apply with this inquiry to Count Saurau. For it is the duty of the police minister to watch over these innocent amusements and harmless festivals of the people."

"The celebration I refer to is neither an innocent amusement nor a harmless festival," exclaimed Bernadotte, hastily; "on the contrary, it is a political demonstration."

"A political demonstration?" repeated Thugut, in surprise. "By whom? And directed against whom?"

"A political demonstration of Austria against the French Republic," said the general, gravely. "It is true, your excellency pretends not to know any thing about this festival of the thirteenth of April, but—"

"Permit me, sir," interrupted Thugut, "is to-morrow the thirteenth of April?"

"Yes, your excellency."

"Then I must say that I know something about this festival, and that I am able to inform you about it. Yes, general, there will be a popular festival to-morrow."

"May I inquire for what purpose?"

"Ah, general, that is very simple. It is just a year to-morrow, on the thirteenth of April, that the whole youth of Vienna, believing the country to be endangered and the capital threatened by the enemy, in their noble patriotism voluntarily joined the army and repaired to the seat of war. These young volunteers desire to celebrate the anniversary of their enrolment, and the emperor, I believe, has given them permission to do so."

"I have to beg your excellency to prevail on the emperor to withdraw this permission."

"A strange request! and why?"

"Because this festival is a demonstration against France, for those warlike preparations last year were directed against France, while Austria has now made peace with our republic. It is easy to comprehend that France will not like this festival of the volunteers."

* "Mémoires d'un Homme d'État," vol. v., p. 493.

"My dear general," said Thugut, with a sarcastic smile, "does France believe, then, that Austria liked all those festivals celebrated by the French Republic during the last ten years? The festivals of the republican weddings, for instance, or the festival of the Goddess of Reason, or the anniversaries of bloody executions? Or more recently the celebrations of victories, by some of which Austria has lost large tracts of territory? I confess to you that Austria would have greatly liked to see some of those festivals suppressed, but France had not asked our advice, and it would have been arrogant and ridiculous for us to give it without being asked for it, and thus to meddle with the domestic affairs of your country. Hence we silently tolerated your festivals, and pray you to grant us the same toleration."

"The French Republic will not and must not suffer what is contrary to her interests," replied Bernadotte, vehemently. "This festival insults us, and I must therefore pray your excellency to prohibit it."

A slight blush mantled the cold, hard features of Baron Thugut, but he quickly suppressed his anger and seemed again quite careless and unruffled.

"You *pray* for a thing, general, which it is no longer in our power to grant," he said, calmly. "The emperor has granted permission for this festival, and how could we refuse the young men of the capital a satisfaction so eagerly sought by them and, besides, so well calculated to nourish and promote the love of the people for their sovereign and for their country? Permit us, like you, to celebrate our patriotic festivals."

"I must repeat my demand that this festival be prohibited!" said Bernadotte, emphatically.

"Your demand?" asked Thugut, with cutting coldness; "I do not believe that anybody but the emperor and the government has the right in Austria to make demands, and I regret that I am unable to grant your *prayer*."

"Your excellency then will really permit this festival of the volunteers to be celebrated to-morrow?"

"Most assuredly. His majesty has given the necessary permission."

"Well, I beg to inform you that, in case the festival takes place to-morrow, I shall give a festival on my part to-morrow, too."

"Every one in Austria is at liberty to give festivals, provided they are not contrary to decency, public morals, and good order."

"Your excellency assumes an insulting tone!" exclaimed Bernadotte, in an excited voice.

"By no means," said Thugut, quietly. "My words would only be insulting if I wanted to prevent you from giving your festival. I tell you, however, you are welcome to give it. Let your festival compete with ours. We shall see who will be victorious in this competition."

"So you really want to permit this festival of the volunteers although I tell you that France disapproves of it?"

"Disapproves of it? Then France wants to play the lord and master in those countries, too, which the republican armies have not conquered? Permit me to tell you that Austria does not want to belong to those countries. The festival of the volunteers will take place to-morrow!"

"Well, my festival will take place to-morrow, too!"

"Then you doubtless have good reasons, like us, for giving a festival?"

"Of course I have. I shall display to-morrow for the first time at the hotel of the embassy the banner of the French Republic, the tri-color of France, and that event, I believe, deserves being celebrated in a becoming manner."

"You want to publicly display the French banner?"

"Yes, sir, it will be displayed on my balcony and proudly float in the air, as the tri-color of France is accustomed to do everywhere."

"I do not know, however, whether or not the Austrian air will accustom itself to the tri-color of France, and I pray you kindly to consider, general, that the enterprise you are going to undertake is something extraordinary and altogether unheard of. No ambassador of any foreign power has ever displayed any mark of distinction on his house, and never has a French minister yet decorated his hotel in such a manner as you now propose to do. That banner of yours would therefore be without any precedent in the history of diplomatic representation."

"And so would the festival you are going to give before the eyes of the French embassy, and notwithstanding my earnest protest."

"Let the French embassy close their eyes if they do not want to see our Austrian festivals. How often had we to do so in France and pretend not to see what was highly insulting to us!"

"For the last time, then, you are going to celebrate the festival of the volunteers to-morrow, notwithstanding the protest of France?"

"I do not think that France ought to protest against matters that do not concern her. You *prayed* me to prohibit the celebration, and I was unable to grant your prayer; that is all."

"Very well, your excellency, you may celebrate your festival—I shall celebrate the inauguration of my banner! And now I have the honor to bid your excellency farewell!"

"I hope the inauguration will be a pleasant affair, general. I take the liberty once more to tell you that your banner will create a great sensation. The people of Vienna are stubborn, and I cannot warrant that they will get accustomed to see another banner but the one containing the Austrian colors displayed in the streets of Vienna. Farewell!"

He accompanied the general to the door, and replied to his ceremonious obeisance by a proud, careless nod.

He then hastily crossed the reception-room and entered again the adjoining apartment, where the police minister was awaiting him.

"Did you hear it?" asked Thugut, whose features were expressing now the whole anger and rage he had concealed so long.

"I have heard every thing," said Count Saurau. "The impudence of France knows no bounds."

"But we shall set bounds to it!" exclaimed Thugut, with unusual vehemence. "We will show to this impudent republic that we neither love nor fear her."

"The festival, then, is really to take place to-morrow?"

"Can you doubt it? It would be incompatible with Austria's honor to yield now. The youth of Vienna shall have their patriotic festival, and—let the police to-morrow be somewhat more indulgent than usual. Youth sometimes needs a little license. Let the young folks enjoy the utmost liberty all day to-morrow! No supervision to-morrow, no restraints! Let the young people sing their patriotic hymns. He who does not want to hear them may close his ears. Pray let us grant to the good people of Vienna to-morrow a day of entire liberty."

"But if quarrels and riots should ensue?"

"My dear count, you know very well that no quarrels take place if our police do not interfere; the people love each other and agree perfectly well if we leave them alone and without any supervision. They will be to-morrow too full of patriotism not to be joyful and harmonious. Once more, therefore, no supervision, no restraints! Let the police belong to the people; let all your employés and agents put on civilians' clothes and mix with the people, not to watch over them, but to share and direct their patriotism."

"Ah, to direct it!" exclaimed Count Saurau, with the air of a man who just commences guessing a riddle. "But suppose this patriotism in its triumphal march should meet with a stumbling-block or rather with a banner—?"

"Then let it quietly go ahead; genuine patriotism is strong and courageous, and will surmount any obstacle standing in its way. The only question is to inspire it with courage and constantly to fan its enthusiasm. That will be the only task of the police to-morrow."

"And they will fulfil that task with the utmost cheerfulness. I shall to-morrow—"

"As far as you are concerned," said Thugut, interrupting him, "it seems to me you will be unfortunately prevented from participating in the patriotic festival to-morrow. You look exceedingly pale and exhausted, my dear count, and if I may take the liberty of giving you a friendly advice, please go to bed and send for your physician."

"You are right, excellency," replied Count Saurau, smiling, "I really feel sick and exhausted. It will be best for me, therefore, to keep my bed for a few days, and my well-meaning physician will doubtless give stringent orders not to admit anybody to me and to permit no one to see me on business."

"As soon as your physician has given such orders," said Thugut, "send me word and request me to attend temporarily to the duties of your department as long as you are sick."

"In half an hour you shall receive a letter to that effect. I go in order to send for a physician."

"One word more, my dear count. What has become of that demagogue, the traitor Wenzel, who headed the riot last year? I then recommended him to your special care."

"And I let him have it, your excellency. I believe he has entirely lost his fancy for insurrectionary movements; and politics, I trust, are very indifferent to him."

"I should regret if it were so," said Thugut, smiling. "I suppose you have got him here in Vienna?"

"Of course; he occupies a splendid half-dark dungeon in our penitentiary."

"Picking oakum?"

"No; I hear he has often asked for it as a favor. But I had given stringent orders to leave him all alone and without any occupation whatever. That is the best way to silence and punish such political criminals and demagogues."

"I would like to see this man Wenzel. We shall, perhaps, set him at liberty again," said Thugut. "Will you order him to be brought here quietly, and without any unnecessary éclat?"

"I shall send him to you, and that shall be my last official business before being taken sick."

"Be it so, my dear count. Go to bed at once; it is high time."

They smilingly shook hands, and looked at each other long and significantly.

"It will be a splendid patriotic festival to-morrow," said Thugut.

"A very patriotic festival, and the inauguration of the banner particularly will be a glorious affair!" exclaimed Count Saurau. "What a pity that my sickness should prevent me from attending it!"

He saluted the prime minister once more and withdrew. When the door had closed behind him the smile disappeared from Thugut's features, and a gloomy cloud settled on his brow. Folding his arms on his back, and absorbed in deep thought, he commenced slowly pacing the room.

"The interview with the empress must be prevented at all events," he muttered, after a long pause, "even if all diplomatic relations with France have to be broken off for that purpose. Besides, I must have those papers which he wanted to deliver to the empress; my repose, my safety depends upon it. Oh, I know very well what sort of papers they are with which they are threatening me. They are the letters I had written in cipher to Burton, the English emissary, whom the French Directory a month ago caused to be arrested as a spy and demagogue at Paris, and whose papers were seized at the same time. Those letters, of course, would endanger my position, for there is a receipt among them for a hundred thousand guineas paid to me. What a fool I was to write that receipt! I must get it again, and I am determined to have it!"

A few hours later, an emaciated, pale man was conducted into the room of Prime Minister Baron Thugut. The minister received him with a friendly nod, and looked with a smiling countenance at this sick, downcast, and suffering man, whom he had seen only a year ago so bold and courageous at the head of the misguided rioters.

"You have greatly changed, Mr. Wenzel," he said, kindly. "The prison air seems not to agree with you."

Wenzel made no reply, but dropped his head with a profound sigh on his breast.

"Ah, ah, Mr. Wenzel," said Thugut, smiling, "it seems your eloquence is gone, too."

"I have formerly spoken too much; hence I am now so taciturn," muttered the pale man.

"Every thing has its time, speaking as well as silence," said Thugut. "It is true speaking has rendered you very wretched; it has made you guilty of high treason. Do you know how long you will have to remain in prison?"

"I believe for fifteen years," said Wenzel, with a shudder.

"Fifteen years! that is half a lifetime. But it does not change such demagogues and politicians as you, sir. As soon as you are released you recommence your seditious work, and you try to make a martyr's crown of your well-merited punishment. Traitors like you are always incorrigible, and unless they are gagged for life they always cry out anew and stir up insurrection and disorder."

Wenzel fixed his haggard eyes with a sorrowful expression upon the minister.

"I shall never stir up insurrections again, nor raise my voice in public as I used to do," he said, gloomily. "I have been cured of it forever, but it was a most sorrowful cure."

"And it will last a good while yet, Mr. Wenzel."

"Yes, it will last dreadfully long," sighed the wretched man.

"Are you married? Have you got any children?"

"Yes, I have a wife and two little girls—two little angels. Ah, if I could only see them once more in my life!"

"Wait yet for fourteen years; you can see them then if they be still alive, and care about having you back."

"I shall not live fourteen years," murmured the pale, downcast man.

"Well, listen to me, Mr. Wenzel. What would you do if I should set you at liberty?"

"At liberty?" asked the man, almost in terror. "At liberty!" he shouted then, loudly and jubilantly.

"Yes, sir, at liberty! But you must do something in order to deserve it. Will you do so?"

"I will do every thing, every thing I am ordered to do, if I am to be set at liberty, if I am allowed to see my wife and my little girls again!" shouted Wenzel, trembling with delight.

"Suppose I should order you again to become a popular orator and to stir up a nice little riot?"

The gleam of joy disappeared again from Wenzel's eyes, and he looked almost reproachfully at the minister. "You want to mock me," he said, mournfully.

"No, my man, I am in good earnest. You shall be a popular orator and leader all day to-morrow. Are you ready for it?"

"No, I have nothing to do with such matters now. I am a good and obedient subject, and only ask to be allowed to live peaceably and quietly."

Thugut burst into a loud laugh. "Ah, you take me for a tempter, Mr. Wenzel," he said; "but I am in earnest; and if you will get up for me a splendid riot to-morrow, I will set you at liberty and no one shall interfere with you as long as you render yourself worthy of my indulgence by obedience and an exemplary life. Tell me, therefore, do you want to be released and serve me?"

Wenzel looked inquiringly and with intense suspense at the cold, hard features of the minister, and then, when he had satisfied himself that he had really been in earnest, he rushed forward and kneeling down before Thugut, he shouted, "I will serve you like a slave, like a dog! only set me at liberty, only give me back to my children and my—"

A flood of tears burst from his eyes and choked his voice.

"All right, sir, I believe you," said Thugut, gravely. "Now rise and listen to what I have to say to you. You will be released to-night. Then go and see your old friends and tell them you had made a journey, and the French had arrested you on the road and kept you imprisoned until you were released in consequence of the measures the Austrian government had taken in your favor. If you dare to utter a single word about your imprisonment here, you are lost, for I hear and learn every thing, and have my spies everywhere, whom I shall instruct to watch you closely."

"I shall assuredly do whatever you want," exclaimed Wenzel, trembling.

"You shall complain to your friends about the harsh and cruel treatment you had to suffer at the hands of the French. You shall speak as a good patriot ought to speak."

"Yes, I shall speak like a good patriot," said Wenzel, ardently.

"To-morrow you will be with all your friends on the street in order to attend the festival of the volunteers, and to look at the procession. Do you know where the French ambassador lives?"

"Yes, on the Kohlmarkt."

"You shall do your best to draw the people thither. The French ambassador will display the banner of the French Republic on his balcony to-morrow. Can the people of Vienna tolerate that?"

"No, the people of Vienna cannot tolerate that!" shouted Wenzel.

"You will repeat that to every one—you will exasperate the people against the banner and against the ambassador—you and the crowd will demand loudly and impetuously that the banner be removed."

"But suppose the ambassador should refuse to remove it?"

"Then you will forcibly enter the house and remove the banner yourselves."

"But if they shut the doors?"

"Then you will break them open, just as you did here a year ago. And besides, are there no windows—are there no stones, by means of which you may open the windows so nicely?"

"You give us permission to do all that?"

"I order you to do all that. Now listen to your special commission. A few of my agents will always accompany you. As soon as you are in the ambassador's house, repair at once to his excellency's study. Pick up all the papers you will find there, and bring them to me. As soon as I see you enter my room with these papers, you will be free forever!"

"I shall bring you the papers," exclaimed Wenzel, with a radiant face.

"But listen. Betray to a living soul but one single word of what I have said to you, and not only yourself, but your wife and your children will also be lost! My arm is strong enough to catch all of you, and my ear is large enough to hear every thing."

"I shall be as silent as the grave," protested Wenzel, eagerly. "I shall only raise my voice in order to speak to the people about our beloved and wise Minister Thugut, and about the miserable, overbearing French, who dare to hang out publicly the banner of their bloody republic here in our imperial city, in our magnificent Vienna!"

"That is the right talk, my man! Now go and reflect about every thing I have told you, and tomorrow morning call on me again; I shall then give you further instructions. Now go—go to your wife, and keep the whole matter secret."

"Hurrah! long live our noble prime minister!" shouted Wenzel, jubilantly. "Hurrah, hurrah, I am free!" And he reeled away like a drunken man.

Thugut looked after him with a smile of profound contempt. "That is the best way to educate the people," he said. "Truly, if we could only send every Austrian for one year to the penitentiary, we would have none but good and obedient subjects!"

CHAPTER XXV.

THE RIOT.

THE streets of Vienna were densely crowded on the following day. Every house was beautifully decorated with fresh verdure and festoons of flowers; business was entirely suspended, and the people in their holiday dresses were moving through the streets, jubilant, singing patriotic hymns, and waiting in joyous impatience for the moment when the procession of the volunteers would leave the city hall in order to repair to the *Burg*, where they were to cheer the emperor. Then they would march through the city, and finally conclude the festival with a banquet and ball, to be held in a public hall that had been handsomely decorated for the occasion.

Not only the people, however, but also the educated and aristocratic classes of Vienna wanted to participate in the patriotic festival. In the open windows there were seen high-born ladies, beautifully dressed, and holding splendid bouquets in their hands, which were to be showered down upon the procession of the volunteers; an endless number of the most splendid carriages, surrounded by dense crowds of pedestrians, were slowly moving through the streets, and in these carriages there were seated the ladies and gentlemen of the aristocracy and of the wealthiest financial circles; they witnessed the popular enthusiasm with smiles of satisfaction and delight.

Only the carriages of the ministers were missing in this gorgeous procession, and it was reported everywhere that two of these gentlemen, Prime Minister Baron von Thugut and Police Minister Count Saurau, had been taken sick, and were confined to their beds, while the other ministers were with the emperor at Laxenburg.

Baron Thugut's prediction had been verified, therefore; the police minister had really been taken so sick that he had to keep his bed, and that he had requested Baron Thugut by letter to take charge of his department for a few days.

But the prime minister himself had suddenly become quite unwell, and was unable to leave his room! Hence he had not accompanied the other ministers to Laxenburg in order to dine at the emperor's table. Nay—an unheard-of occurrence—he had taken his meals all alone in his study. His footman had received stringent orders to admit no one, and to reply to every applicant for an interview with him, "His excellency was confined to his bed by a raging fever, and all business matters had to be deferred until to-morrow."

The minister's condition, however, was not near as bad as that. It was true he had the fever, but it was merely the fever of expectation, impatience, and long suspense. The whole day had passed, and not a single dissonance had disturbed the pure joy of the celebration; not a single violent scene had interrupted the patriotic jubilee. The crowds on the streets and public places constantly increased in numbers, but peace and hilarity reigned everywhere, and the people were singing and laughing everywhere.

This was the reason why the minister's blood was so feverish, why he could find no rest, and why his cold heart for once pulsated so rapidly. He was pacing his study with long steps, murmuring now and then some incoherent words, and then uneasily stepping to the window in order to survey the street cautiously from behind the curtain, and to observe the surging crowd below.

Just then the large clock on the marble mantelpiece commenced striking. Thugut hastily turned toward it. "Six o'clock, and nothing yet," he murmured. "I shall put that fellow Wenzel into a subterranean dungeon for life, and dismiss every agent of mine, if nothing—"

He paused and listened. It had seemed to him as though he had heard a soft rap at the hidden door leading to the secret staircase. Yes, it was no mistake; somebody was rapping at it, and seemed to be in great haste.

"At last!" exclaimed Thugut, drawing a deep breath, and he approached with hurried steps the large painting, covering the whole wall and reaching down to the floor. He quickly touched one of the artificial roses on the gilt frame. The painting turned round, and the door became visible behind it in the wall.

The rapping was now plainly heard. Thugut pushed the bolt back and unlocked the door. His confidential secretary, Hübschle, immediately rushed in with a glowing face and in breathless haste.

"Your excellency," he gasped—"your excellency, the fun has just commenced! They are now pursuing the deer like a pack of infuriated blood-hounds. Oh, oh! they will chase him thoroughly, I should think!"

Thugut cast a glance of gloomy indignation on the versatile little man with the bloated face. "You have been drinking again, Hübschle," he said; "and I have ordered you to remain sober to-day!"

"Your excellency, I am quite sober," protested Hübschle. "I assure you I have not drunk any more than what was required by my thirst."

"Ah, yes; your thirst always requires large quantities," exclaimed Thugut, laughing. "But speak now rapidly, briefly, and plainly. No circumlocution, no tirades! Tell me the naked truth. What fun has just commenced?"

"The inauguration of the banner, your excellency."

"Then Bernadotte has hung out his banner, after all?"

"Yes, he has done so. We were just going down the street—quite a jolly crowd it was, by the by. Master Wenzel, a splendid fellow, had just loudly intoned the hymen of 'God save the

Emperor Francis,' and all the thousands and thousands of voices were joining the choir, as if they intended to serenade the French ambassador, when, suddenly, a balcony door opened, and General Bernadotte, in full uniform came out. He was attended by his whole suite; and several footmen brought out an immense banner, which they attached to the balcony. We had paused right in the middle of our beautiful hymn, and the people were looking up to the balcony, from which the gentlemen had disappeared again, with glances full of surprise and curiosity. But the banner remained there! Suddenly a violent gust touched the banner, which, up to this time, had loosely hung down, and unfolded it entirely. Now we saw the French tri-color proudly floating over our German heads, and on it we read, in large letters of gold—*Liberté! Egalité! Fraternité!*" *

"What impudence!" muttered Thugut.

"You are right, that was the word," exclaimed Hübschle. "'What impudence!' roared Master Wenzel; and the whole crowd immediately repeated, 'What impudence! Down with the foreign banner! We are not so stupid as the people of Milan, Venice, and Rome; we do not jubilantly hail the French color; on the contrary, this banner makes us angry. Down with it! It is an insult offered to the emperor, that a foreign flag with such an abominable inscription is floating here. Down with the banner!'"

"Very good, very good, indeed," said Thugut, smiling. "This man Wenzel is really a practical fellow. Go on, sir."

"The crowd constantly assumed larger proportions, and the shouts of 'Down with the banner!' became every moment more impetuous and threatening. Suddenly a small detachment of soldiers emerged from the adjoining street. The officer in command kindly urged the people to disperse. But it was in vain; the tumult was constantly on the increase. The crowd commenced tearing up the pavement and throwing stones at the windows and at the banner."

"And the soldiers?"

"They quietly stood aside. But—somebody is rapping at the opposite door! Shall I open it, your excellency?"

"One moment! I first want to turn back the painting. So! Now open the door, Hübschle!"

The private secretary hastened with tottering steps to the door and unlocked it. Thugut's second private secretary entered. He held a sealed letter in his hand.

"Well, Heinle, what's the matter?" asked Thugut, quietly.

"Your excellency, the French ambassador, General Bernadotte, has sent this letter to your excellency."

"And what did you reply to the messenger?"

"That your excellency had a raging fever; that the doctor had forbidden us to disturb you, but that I would deliver it to the minister as soon as he felt a little better."

"That was right. Now go back to your post and guard the door well in order that no one may penetrate into my room. And you, Hübschle, hasten back to the *Kohlmarkt* and see what is going on there, and what is occurring at the French embassy. But do not drink any more liquor! As soon as this affair is over, I shall give you three days' leave of absence, when you may drink as much as you please. Go, now, and return soon to tell me all about it."

"And now," said Thugut, when he was alone, "I will see what the French ambassador has written to me."

He opened the letter, and, as if the mere perusal with the eyes was not sufficient for him, he read in a half-loud voice as follows: "The ambassador of the French Republic informs Baron Thugut that at the moment he is penning these lines, a fanatical crowd has been so impudent as to commit a riot in front of his dwelling. The motives that have produced this violent scene cannot be doubtful, inasmuch as several stones already were thrown at the windows of the house occupied by the ambassador. Profoundly offended at so much impudence, he requests Baron Thugut immediately to order an investigation, so that the instigators of the riot may be punished, and that their punishment may teach the others a much-needed lesson. The ambassador of the French Republic has no doubt that his reclamations will meet with the attention which they ought to excite, and that the police, moreover, will be vigilant enough to prevent similar scenes, which could not be renewed without producing the most serious consequences, the ambassador being firmly determined to repel with the utmost energy even the slightest insults, and accordingly much more so, such scandalous attacks. Baron Thugut is further informed that he has reason to complain of the conduct of several agents of the police. Some of them were requested to disperse the rioters, but, instead of fulfilling the ambassador's orders, they remained cold and idle spectators of the revolting scene." *

---

* "Mémoires d'un Homme d'État," vol. v., p. 494.

* "Mémoires d'un Homme d'État," vol. v., p. 495.

"What overbearing and insulting language this fellow dares to use!" exclaimed Thugut, when he had finished the letter. "One might almost believe he was our lord and master here, and—ah, somebody raps again at the door! Perhaps Hübschle is back already."

He quickly touched the frame of the painting again, and the door opened. It was really Hübschle, who entered as hastily as before.

"Your excellency, I have just reascended the staircase as rapidly as though I were a cat," he gasped. "At the street door I learned some fresh news from one of our men, and I returned at once to tell you all about it."

"Quick, you idle gossip, no unnecessary preface!"

"Your excellency, things are assuming formidable proportions. The riot is constantly on the increase, and grows every minute more threatening. Count Dietrichstein, and Count Fersen, the director of the police, have repaired to General Bernadotte and implored him to remove the banner."

"The soft-hearted fools!" muttered Thugut.

"But their prayers were fruitless. They preferred them repeatedly, and always were refused. They even went so far as to assure the ambassador, in case he should yield to their request and give them time to calm the people and induce them to leave the place, that the Austrian government would assuredly give him whatever satisfaction he should demand. But General Bernadotte persisted in his refusal—and replied peremptorily, 'No, the banner remains!'"

"Proceed, proceed!" exclaimed Thugut, impatiently.

"That is all I know, but I shall hasten to collect further news, and then return to your excellency."

Hübschle disappeared through the secret door, and Thugut replaced the painting before it. "The banner remains!" he exclaimed, laughing scornfully. "We will see how long it will remain! Ah, Heinle is rapping again at the other door. What is it, Heinle?"

"Another dispatch from the French ambassador," said Heinle, merely pushing his arm with the letter through the door.

"And you have made the same reply?"

"The same reply."

'Good! Return to your post."

The arm disappeared again. Thugut opened the second dispatch, and read as before in a half-loud voice: "The ambassador of the French Republic informs Baron Thugut that the fury of the mob is constantly on the increase; already all the window-panes of the dwelling have been shattered by the stones the rioters are incessantly throwing at them; he informs you that the crowd at the present moment numbers no less than three or four thousand men, and that the soldiers whose assistance was invoked, so far from protecting the house of the French embassy, remain impassive spectators of the doings and fury of the rabble, their inactivity encouraging the latter instead of deterring them. The ambassador cannot but believe that this scandalous scene is not merely tolerated, but fostered by the authorities, for nothing whatever is done to put a stop to it. He sees with as much regret as pain that the dignity of the French people is being violated by the insults heaped on the ambassador, who vainly implored the populace to disperse and go home. At the moment the ambassador is writing these lines, the rage of the crowd is strained to such a pitch that the doors have been broken open by means of stones, while the soldiers were quietly looking on. The furious rabble tore the French colors from the balcony with hooks and long poles. The ambassador, who cannot remain any longer in a country where the most sacred laws are disregarded and solemn treaties trampled under foot, therefore asks Baron Thugut to send him his passports in order that he may repair to France with all the attachés of the embassy, unless Baron Thugut should announce at once that the Austrian government has taken no part whatever in the insults heaped upon the French Republic; that it disavows them, on the contrary, in the most formal manner, and that it orders the ringleaders and their accomplices to be arrested and punished in the most summary manner. On this condition alone, and if the Austrian government agrees to restore the French banner and to cause it to be displayed on the balcony of the French embassy by a staff-officer, the ambassador consents to remain in Vienna. Let Baron Thugut remember that these are precious moments, and that he owes the ambassador an immediate and categorical reply to his inquiries." *

"Well, I believe the good people of Vienna will take it upon themselves to make a categorical reply to General Bernadotte, and to silence the overbearing babbler, no matter how it is done," exclaimed Thugut, laughing scornfully. "I am really anxious to know how this affair is going to end, and how my brave rioters will chastise the ambassador for his insolence. What, another rap already? Why, you are a genuine postillon d'amour! Do you bring me another letter?"

* "Mémoires d'un Homme d'État," vol. v, p. 501.

"A third dispatch from General Bernadotte," exclaimed Heinle, outside, pushing his arm with the dispatch again through the door.

Thugut took it and rapidly opened it. "It seems matters are growing more pressing," he said, smilingly. "Let us read it!" And he read with an air of great satisfaction:

"The ambassador of the French Republic informs Baron Thugut that the riotous proceedings have lasted five hours already; that no agent of the police has come to his assistance; that the furious rioters have taken possession of a portion of the house and are destroying every thing they can lay their hands on."

"Aha, my friend Wenzel is looking for the papers in the rooms of the French embassy!" exclaimed Thugut, triumphantly. He then read on.

"The ambassador, the secretaries of legation, the French citizens and officers who are with him, were compelled to retire to a room where they are waiting further developments with the undaunted courage characteristic of the republicans. The ambassador repeats his demand that the necessary passports be sent for him and for all the French who desire to accompany him. The transmission of these passports is the more urgent, as the rioters, who were about to rush into the room where the French were awaiting them, only shrank back when some servants of the French embassy discharged the fire-arms with which they had been provided."

"Ah, a regular battle, then, has taken place!" shouted Thugut, in great glee. "A siege in grand style! Wonder why Hübschle has not come back yet? But stop! I hear him already. He raps! I am coming, sir! I am opening the door already!"

And Thugut hastened to touch the frame of the painting and to open the door.

It was true, Hübschle, the private secretary was there, but he did not come alone. Wenzel, soiled with blood, his clothes torn and in the wildest disorder, entered with him, supporting himself on Hübschle's arm.

"Ah, you bring me there a wounded boar!" said Thugut, morosely.

"A boar who splendidly goaded on the hounds and performed the most astonishing exploits," said Hübschle, enthusiastically. "He received a gunshot wound in the right arm and fainted. I carried him with the assistance of a few friends to a well, and we poured water on him until he recovered his senses and was able again to participate in the general jubilee."

"Then it was a jubilee? Mr. Wenzel, tell me all about it."

"It was a very fine affair," said Wenzel, gasping. "We had penetrated into the house and were working to the best of our power in the magnificent rooms. The furniture, the looking-glasses, the chandeliers, the carriages in the court-yard, every thing was destroyed, while we were singing and shouting, 'Long live the emperor! God save the Emperor Francis!'"

"What a splendid *Marseillaise* that dear, kind-hearted Haydn has composed for us in that hymn," said Thugut, in a low voice, gleefully rubbing his hands. "And the banner? What has become of the banner?"

"The banner we had previously torn to pieces, and with the shreds we had gone to the *Schotten-platz* and publicly burned them there amidst the jubilant shouts of the people."

"Very good. And what else was done in the embassy building?"

"We rushed from room to room. Nothing withstood our fury, and finally we arrived at the room in which the ambassador and his suite had barricaded themselves as in a fortress. It was the ambassador's study," said Wenzel, slowly and significantly—"the cabinet in which he kept his papers."

Thugut nodded gently, and said nothing but "Proceed!"

"I rushed toward the door and encouraged the others to follow me. We succeeded in bursting the door open. At the same moment the besieged fired at us. Three of us dropped wounded; the others ran away."

"Yes, the miserable rascals always run away as soon as they smell gunpowder," said Thugut, indignantly. "And you, Mr. Wenzel?"

"I was wounded and had fainted. My comrades carried me out of the house."

"And the papers?" asked Thugut. "You did not take them?"

"Your excellency, General Bernadotte and the whole retinue of the embassy were in the room in which the ambassador keeps his papers. I would have penetrated into it with my friends if the bullet had not shattered my arm and stretched me down senseless."

"Yes, indeed, you became entirely senseless," said Thugut, harshly, "for you even forgot that I only promised to release you provided you should bring the papers of the French ambassador."

"Your excellency," shouted Wenzel, in dismay, "I—"

"Silence!" commanded Thugut, in a stern tone; "who has allowed you to speak without being asked?"

At this moment another hasty rap at the door

was heard, and Heinle's arm appeared again in the door.

"Another dispatch from the French ambassador?" asked Thugut.

"No, your excellency, a dispatch from his majesty the emperor."

Thugut hastily seized the small sealed note and opened it. It contained nothing but the following words:

"The ambassador has received a salutary lesson, and his banner has been destroyed. Let us stop the riot now, and avoid extreme measures. Several regiments must be called out to restore order."

The minister slowly folded the paper and put it into his pocket. He then rang the bell so violently and loudly, that Heinle and the other servants rushed immediately into the room.

"Open every door—call every footman!" commanded Thugut. "Admit every one who wants to see me. Two mounted messengers shall hold themselves in readiness to forward dispatches. Every one may learn that, in spite of my sickness, I have risen from my couch in order to reëstablish tranquillity in the capital."

He stepped to his desk and rapidly wrote a few words, whereupon he handed the paper to Germain, his valet de chambre.

"Here, Germain, hasten with this note to Count Fersen, the director of police, and take this fellow along. Two footmen may accompany you. You will deliver him to the director of the police and tell him that he is one of the rioters whom my agents have arrested. Request the director to have him placed in a safe prison and to admit none to him but the officers of the criminal court. He is a very dangerous criminal; this is the second time that he has been arrested as a rioter. Well, what is the matter with the fellow? He reels like a drunken man! He has probably drunk too much brandy for the purpose of stimulating his courage."

"Pardon me, your excellency," said Hübschle, "the man has fainted."

"Then carry him away, and take him in a carriage to the director of the police," said Thugut, indifferently, and he looked on coldly and unfeelingly, while the footman hastily seized the pale, unconscious man and dragged him away.

He returned to his desk and rapidly wrote a few words on a sheet of large, gilt-edged paper, which he then enclosed in an envelope, sealed, and directed.

"A dispatch to the emperor!" he said, handing it to Heinle. "Let a mounted messenger take it immediately to his majesty."

This dispatch contained the reply to the emperor's laconic note, and it was almost more laconic than the latter, for it contained only the following words:

"Sire, within an hour order will be reëstablished."

"Now, Hübschle, sit down," said Thugut, all the others having left the room by his orders. "Collect your five senses, and write what I am going to dictate to you."

Hübschle sat already at the desk, and waited, pen in hand. Baron Thugut, folding his hands behind his back, slowly paced the room and dictated:

"The minister of foreign affairs has heard with regret of the riotous proceedings referred to in the notes which the ambassador of the French Republic has addressed to him this evening. The minister will report the whole affair to his imperial majesty, and entertains no doubt that the emperor will be very indignant at the occurrence. The ambassador may rest assured that nothing will be left undone in order to ferret out the perpetrators of this outrage, and to punish them with the whole severity of the laws, and with the sincere desire which the Austrian government has always entertained to maintain the friendship so happily established between the two countries." *

"Well, why do you dare to laugh, Hübschle?" asked Thugut, when he took the pen in order to sign the note.

"Your excellency, I am laughing at the many fine words in which this dispatch says: 'Mr. Ambassador, ask for your passports; you may depart.'"

Thugut smiled. "When you are drunk, Hübschle, you are exceedingly shrewd, and for that reason, I pardon your impertinence. Your rubicund nose has scented the matter correctly. The ambassador has demanded his passports already. But go now. Take this dispatch to the second courier and tell him to carry it immediately to the French embassy. As for yourself, you must hasten to the commander of Vienna, and take this paper to him. You may say to him, 'The gates are to be closed in order to prevent the populace of the suburbs from reaching the city. The Preiss regiment shall occupy the house of the ambassa-

* The French ambassador really left Vienna in consequence of this riot. The emperor vainly tried to pacify him. Bernadotte persisted in his demands. He wanted the Austrian government to restore the banner and to have it displayed on his balcony by a staff-officer. In reply to these repeated demands, Thugut sent him his passports, and the legation left Vienna.—Vide Hausser, "German History," vol. ii. p. 180. "Mémoires d'un Homme d'État," vol. v.

dor and the adjoining streets, and fire at whosoever offers resistance or wants to raise a disturbance.' Vienna must be perfectly quiet in the
course of an hour. Begone!"

Hübschle rushed out, and Thugut remained
alone. He slowly and deliberately sat down in an
arm-chair, and pondered serenely over the events
of the night.

"It is true I have not wholly accomplished my
purpose," he muttered, "but M. Bernadotte will
try no longer to injure me. He shall have his
passports to-morrow morning."

LAST DAYS OF THE EIGHTEENTH CENTURY.

CHAPTER XXVI.

VICTORIA DE POUTET.

NEARLY a year had elapsed since the departure of the French ambassador from Vienna, but the rupture of the peace with France, so ardently desired by Minister Thugut, had not yet taken place. A strong party in the emperor's cabinet had declared against Thugut, and this time obtained a victory over the minister who had been believed to be all-powerful. This party was headed by the empress and Archduke Charles. Thugut, therefore, was compelled to suppress his wrath, and defer his revenge to some later time.

But although the dark clouds of the political thunderstorm had been removed for the time being, they were constantly threatening, like a gloomy spectre on the horizon, casting sinister shadows on every day and on every hour.

The merry people of Vienna, owing to the incessant duration of these gloomy shadows, had become very grave, and loudly and softly denounced Minister Thugut as the author and instigator of all the evils that were menacing Austria. In fact, Baron Thugut was still the all-powerful minister; and as the emperor loved and feared him, the whole court, the whole capital, and the whole empire bowed to him. But while bowing, every one hated him; while obeying, every one cursed him.

Thugut knew it and laughed at it. What did he care for the love and hatred of men? Let them curse him, if they only obeyed him.

And they obeyed him. The machine of state willingly followed the pressure of his hand, and he conducted the helm with a vigorous arm. He directed from his cabinet the destinies of Austria; he skilfully and ingeniously wove there the nets with which, according to his purposes, he wanted to surround friend or foe.

To-day, too, he had worked in his cabinet until evening, and he had only just now dismissed his two private secretaries, Heinle and Hübschle. This was the hour at which Thugut was in the habit of repairing either to the emperor or to his gardens in the Wahringer Street. His *valet de chambre*, therefore, awaited him in the dressing-room, and his carriage was in readiness below in the court-yard. To-day, however, the minister apparently wished to deviate from his custom, and instead of going to the dressing-room, he violently rang the bell.

"Germain," he said, to the entering *valet de chambre*, "no uniform to-day, no gala-dress, but my Turkish garments. Light up the Turkish cabinet, kindle amber in the lamps, and place flowers in the vases. In the course of an hour supper for two persons in the Turkish cabinet. Arrange every thing in a becoming manner."

Germain bowed silently and withdrew, in order soon to return with the ordered Turkish costume. Thugut silently suffered himself to be clad in the costly Turkish dressing-gown and in the golden slippers, the wonderful Cashmere shawl to be wrapped around his waist, and the Turkish fez to be placed on his head. Germain then brought a Turkish pipe with a splendidly carved amber tip, and handed it to the minister.

"Now open the door," said Thugut, laconically. Germain touched the frame of the large painting on the wall, and Thugut stepped through the small door into the hall. With rapid steps he hastened down the hall, and soon stood at its end in front of the narrow wall on which a painting of the Virgin, illuminated by a perpetually burning lamp, was hanging. Thugut again touched an artificial rose on the frame, the painting turned around, and a door became visible behind it.

The minister opened this door, and, crossing the threshold, carefully closed it again.

He now was in his Turkish cabinet; all these beautiful gold brocades on the low sofas, these costly hangings covering the walls, these precious carpets on the floor and on the tables, these silver lamps of strange forms, hanging down from the ceiling, and filled with amber, all these richly gilt vessels arranged along the walls, were delightful reminiscences to Thugut—reminiscences of the happiest period of his life, for he had brought all these things from Constantinople, where he had lived for ten years as Austrian ambassador. Thugut, therefore, never entered this cabinet without a pleasant smile lighting up his hard features, and he only went thither when he wished to permit himself an hour of happiness amidst the perplexing occupations and cares of his official position.

On this occasion, too, as soon as he had crossed the threshold, his face had assumed a mild and gentle expression, and the harsh, repulsive stamp had disappeared from his features. He walked across the room with a smile, and quickly touched a golden knob, fixed in the opposite wall. After a few minutes he repeated this four times. He then raised his eyes to a small silver bell hanging above him in the most remote corner of the wall, and looked at it steadfastly. While he was doing so, a small side door had opened, and Germain, in the rich costume of a servant of the harem, had entered. Thugut had not once looked round toward him; he had not once glanced at the silver vases with the most splendid flowers, which Germain had placed on the marble tables; his nose was apparently indifferent to the sweet perfumes of the amber which Germain had kindled in the silver lamps, and which was filling the room with fragrant bluish clouds. He only looked at the small bell, and seemed to expect a signal from it in breathless suspense. But Germain had long since finished the decoration of the room and withdrawn again, and yet the bell was silent. A cloud passed over Thugut's brow, and the smile disappeared from his lips.

"She was not there, perhaps, and consequently did not hear my signal," he murmured. "I will ring the bell once more."

He stretched out his hand toward the golden knob in the wall, when suddenly a clear, pure sound was heard. It was the small bell that had been rung.

Thugut's countenance lighted up in the sunshine of happiness, and he looked up to the bell again in silent suspense. For a few minutes it hung motionless again, but then it resounded quickly three times in succession. "In thirty minutes she will be here," whispered Thugut, with a happy smile. "Let us await her, then."

He approached the small table on which he had laid his pipe, and near which Germain had placed a small silver vessel with burning amber.

With the bearing and calmness of a genuine Turk he lighted his pipe and then sat down on the low square sofa. Crossing his legs, supporting his right elbow on the cushions of gold brocade, in a half-reclining attitude, Thugut now abandoned himself to his dreams and to the sweet enjoyment of smoking. He was soon surrounded by a blue cloud from which his black eyes were glistening and glancing up to the large clock on the mantelpiece.

On seeing now that the thirty minutes had elapsed, Thugut rose with youthful vivacity, and laid his pipe aside. He then approached the large and strangely formed arm-chair, standing immediately under the silver bell. When he had vigorously pushed back the arm-chair, a small door became visible behind it. Thugut opened it and placed himself by it in a listening position.

Suddenly it seemed to him as though he heard a slight noise in the distance. It came nearer, and now there appeared in the aperture of the door a lady of wonderful loveliness and surpassing beauty. The eye could behold nothing more charming than this head with its light-brown ringlets, surrounding the face as if by a ring of glory, and contrasting so strangely with the large black eyes, which were sparkling in the fire of youth and passion. Her enchanting lips were of the deepest red, and a delicate blush, like the beautiful tint of the large purple shell, mantled her cheeks. Her nose, of the purest Roman style, was slightly curved, and her expansive forehead imparted a noble and serious air to the charming youthful face. The beholder saw in these eyes, ardor and passion; on this forehead, thought and energetic resolutions; and on this swelling mouth, archness, overflowing spirits, and wit. And the figure of this lovely woman was in full harmony with her ravishing head. She was petite, delicate, and ethereal, like a sylph, and yet her form was well developed and beautiful; if she had been somewhat taller, she might have been compared with Juno.

She remained standing in the door, and with her flaming eyes glanced over the room; then she fixed them on Thugut, and burst into a loud and merry laugh.

"Ah, ah, that is the song of my bulbul, the ringing voice of my oriental nightingale," exclaimed Thugut, drawing the laughing lady with gentle force into the room and pushing the armchair again before the closed door. "Now tell me, my bulbul, why do you laugh?"

"Must I not laugh?" she exclaimed, in a clear and sonorous voice. "Is not this a surprise as if it were a scene from the Arabian Nights?

You told me six months ago you were going to have a passage made, by which one might go unseen from my rooms in the *Burg* to your apartments in the chancery of state. I had no doubt of the truth of what you told me, for fortunately the chancery of state is close to the *Burg*, and there are enough secret staircases and doors here as well as there. I was, therefore, by no means surprised when one day, in the silence of the night, I heard soft hammering at the wall of my bedroom, and suddenly beheld a hole in the wall, which, in the course of a few hours, had been transformed into a door with an arm-chair before it, just like that one there; in the next night, a locksmith made his appearance and hung up a small silver bell in my room, concealing it behind a lamp; and yesterday you whispered to me: 'Await the signal to-morrow! I have to talk to you about important affairs.' I therefore waited with all the impatience of curiosity; at last the bell resounded six times; I answered the signal and hastened through the narrow halls and ascended the never-suspected small staircase, perfectly satisfied that I was going to a diplomatic conference. And what do I find? A little Turkish paradise, and in it a pacha—"

"Who was yearning only for his charming *houri* in order to be entirely in paradise," said Thugut, interrupting her. "Every thing has its time, my Victoria, state affairs as well as happiness."

"The question only is, my cold-hearted friend, whether you prefer state affairs or happiness," she replied, smilingly threatening him with her finger.

"Happiness, if you bring it to me, Victoria!" he exclaimed, pressing the beautiful woman impetuously against his bosom.

She leaned her head on his shoulder and looked up to him with an air of arch enthusiasm. "Are you happy now?" she asked, in a low voice.

He only replied by means of glowing kisses and whispered words of intense passion into her ear. She did not resist him; she listened with smiling satisfaction to his whispers, and a deeper blush mantled her cheeks.

"Ah, I like to hear you talk thus," she said, when Thugut paused; "it delights me to sip the honey of oriental poetry from the lips of my wild bear. Even the Belvederian Apollo is not as beautiful as you in your genial and wondrous ugliness when you are talking about love."

Thugut laughed. "Then you think I am very ugly, Victoria?" he asked.

"Yes, so ugly that your ugliness in my eyes is transformed into the most inconceivable beauty," she said, passing her rosy fingers across his dark

and bronzed face. "Sometimes, my friend, when I see you in the imperial halls, with your strange smile and your grave bearing, I believe it is the god of darkness himself whom I behold there, ah! who has descended upon earth in order to catch in person a few human souls that he is very anxious to have in his power. Ah, I would not have you an iota more handsome, nor a single year younger. I like your demoniacal ugliness; and the infernal ardor, hidden under the snow of your hair, truly delights me. To be beloved by young men with the fickle straw-fire of passion is a very common thing; but when an old man loves as intensely as a youth, when he always illuminates the beloved with the glory of a fire that he has snatched from hell, ah! that is something enchanting and divine! Love me, therefore, in your own way, my beautiful, ugly prince of darkness!"

"I love you in my own way, my charming angel, whom nobody believes to be a demon," said Thugut, laughing. "I feel precisely like you, my beautiful Victoria; I love you twice as ardently, because I penetrated your true nature; because, when you are smiling upon others, I alone perceive the serpent, while others only behold the roses, and because I alone know this angelic figure to conceal the soul of a demon. Thus we love each other because we belong to each other, Victoria; you call me the prince of darkness, and you are assuredly the crown-princess of hell. After my death you will occupy my throne."

"Then it is in hell just as in Austria?" asked Victoria. "The women are not excluded from the throne."

"Well, sometimes it really seems to me as though it were in Austria as it ought to be in hell, and as though the small devils of stupidity, folly, and ignorance, had chosen Austria for their particular play-ground."

"Let us expel them, then, my friend," exclaimed Victoria; "I should think that we were powerful enough to accomplish that."

"Will you assist me in expelling them?" asked Thugut, quickly.

"How can you ask me?" she said, reproachfully. "So you have forgotten every thing? Our whole past is buried under the dust of your ministerial documents?"

"No, I have forgotten nothing!" exclaimed Thugut, almost enthusiastically. "I remember every thing. Oh, how often, Victoria, do I see you in my dreams, just as I saw you for the first time! Do you yet remember when it was?"

"It was in the camp in front of Giurgewo."

"Yes, in the camp in front of Giurgewo, at the

time that the Turks surprised our trenches.* All of our officers completely lost their senses; the general-in-chief, Prince Coburg, rode off in the most cowardly manner; and Count Thun had been killed, while General Anfsess was dangerously wounded. Oh, it was a terrible day; terror and dismay spread through the whole camp. A wild panic seized the soldiers, they fled in all directions; every one was shouting, howling, and trembling for his own miserable existence. I had just gone to headquarters, and I may say that I was the only one who did not tremble, for nature has not imparted fear to me. I witnessed the growing confusion with dismay, when I suddenly beheld a woman, an angel, who appeared with dishevelled hair, and eyes flashing with anger, addressing the soldiers and admonishing them in glowing words to do their duty. No, what she said were no words, it was a torrent of enthusiasm, bursting from her lips like heavenly flames. And the soldiers listened in amazement; the stragglers rallied round their colors, the cowards were ashamed, and the trembling and downcast took heart again when they heard the ringing, bold words of the beautiful woman. Reason obtained its sway; they were able once more to hear and consider what we said to them, and thanks to you and to myself, the ignominious rout was transformed into an orderly and quiet retreat. Both of us saved every thing that was yet to be saved. Ah, it is a funny thing that all the soldiers in the large camp had lost their wits, and that only a civilian and a woman kept theirs.† On that day, in my enthusiasm, I vowed eternal friendship to you."

"We vowed it to each other!" exclaimed Victoria.

"And we have kept our vows. I sent you to Vienna with a recommendation to my friend, Count Colloredo, and he honored my recommendation. He introduced you to the court; he related your heroic deed to the emperor, and the whole court did homage to the intrepid heroine of Giurgewo. Your bold husband, the handsome captain of hussars, Charles de Poutet, having been killed in Belgium, at the assault upon Aldenhoven, I came to you and renewed my vow of eternal fidelity and friendship. Did I keep my word?"

"You did. Thanks to you and to Colloredo, I have become the friend of the empress, and the aja of her first-born daughter, the Archduchess Maria Louisa. But, on obtaining this position, I renewed to you, too, my vow of eternal friend-

ship and eternal fidelity. Did I not also keep my word?"

"You did. Thanks to you and to Colloredo, I have become prime minister and ruler of Austria!"

"And now, my friend, a question. Did you invent this Turkish cabinet, the secret staircases and halls, and the mysterious language of the bells, for the sole purpose of relating to me here the history of our past feelings toward each other?"

"No, Victoria, in order to build here the edifice of our future. Here, in this secret cabinet, we will lay the foundation of it, and draw up the plans. Victoria, I stand in need of your assistance—will you refuse it to me?"

"Stretch out your hand with the sceptre, my god of darkness, command, and I shall obey!" said Victoria, gliding down on the sofa, crossing her arms on her breast, and looking up to Thugut with languishing eyes.

He sat down by her side, and laid his hand over her eyes.

"Do not look at me so charmingly as to make my blood rush like fire through my veins," he said. "Let us first speak of business affairs, and then we will forget every thing in draughts of fiery sherbet. So listen to me, Victoria, be a little less of the enchanting angel now, and a little more of the malicious demon."

"Is there a minister to overthrow, a powerful man to be trampled under foot?" asked Victoria, her black eyes flashing like dagger-points. "Have we got an enemy whom we want to lead across the *Ponte dei Sospiri* to an eternal prison? Speak quickly, my friend; I am waiting for the music of your words."

"There are two enemies for you to fathom," said Thugut, slowly.

"To fathom! Is that all? A little spying, nothing further?"

"But some bloodshed might attend that spying."

"I like blood, it has such a beautiful purple color," said Victoria, laughing. "Who are the two enemies I am to fathom?"

"France and Prussia!"

"Oh, you are joking."

"No, I am in sober earnest. France and Prussia are the two enemies whose innermost thoughts you are to fathom."

"But France and Prussia are not here in Vienna."

"No, not here in Vienna, but they are at the fortress of Rastadt."

"I do not understand you, my friend."

---

* In 1790.

† Vide "Kaiser Franz und Metternich: Ein Fragment," p. 33.

"Listen to me, and you will understand me. You know that I hate France, and that I abhor the peace we were compelled to conclude with her. France is a hydra, whose head we must cut off, or by whom we must allow ourselves to be devoured. I am in favor of cutting off her head."

"So am I!" exclaimed Victoria, laughing. "Have you got a sword sharp enough to cut off the hydra's head? Then give it to me—I will behead her."

"The hydra believes she has a sword with which she might kill me. Listen to me. I was once in my life foolish enough to sign a paper which might prove dangerous to me in case it should be submitted to the emperor. This paper is in the hands of France."

"France has got a large hand. Which of her fingers holds the paper?"

"A year ago, the paper was in Bernadotte's hands, and he had already applied for an interview with the empress, in order to deliver to her the paper, which she had promised to hand to the emperor. I learned it in time, and sent out a few friends to bring the papers out of his own rooms."

"Ah, I understand. It was on the day of the festival of the volunteers, and of the inauguration of the French banner."

"Yes, it was on that day. The coup was not entirely successful; we gave Bernadotte a good lesson—we compelled him to leave Vienna, but he took these papers along."

"And where is Bernadotte?"

"At Rastadt, where he attends the sessions of the congress as the military plenipotentiary of France."

"I shall go there, too, as your plenipotentiary, my friend!" exclaimed Victoria, smiling. "But, in order to obtain the papers, we shall not make an assault upon his house; we shall only assail his heart, and that I shall open a breach there large enough to let the dangerous papers pass through it, I hope my skill will warrant—"

"Your skill and your beauty," said Thugut, interrupting her. "But I believe my beautiful Victoria will not have to assail Bernadotte, but another man. Bernadotte took warning from that scene in his house; he understands very well that the possession of those papers is dangerous, and he has, therefore, transferred the danger to other shoulders. He has intrusted another man with the papers."

"Whom? If it be a man of flesh and blood name him, and I shall make the assault upon him," said Victoria.

"It is doubtless one of the three ambassadors of the French Republic, and I have reason to believe that it is the haughty and impudent Bonnier. It was he at least who spoke to Count Cobenzl about certain papers that might become dangerous to me, and who inquired stealthily if Cobenzl would feel inclined to deliver them to the emperor."

"Let me depart, my friend; I must have the papers," said Victoria, rising.

"Ah, how beautiful you are in your impetuosity!" exclaimed Thugut, smiling; "but we are not through yet with our conference, dear Victoria. For the sole purpose of obtaining those miserable papers, I should not beg my angel to unfold his demon's wings and to assist me. If my interests alone were at stake, I should allow fate to take its course, and leave every thing to its decision. But the interests of Austria are equally at stake; and I do not say this in the sense in which my great predecessor, Prince Kaunitz, used to say: 'He who attacks me, attacks Austria, for Austria cannot exist without me. She would fall down if my strong hand did not hold her.' No, I know very well that no man is indispensable; that we are only machines in the hands of fate, and that, as soon as one of these machines is worn out and unnecessary, fate casts it aside and substitutes a new one. But the state is something more exalted and important than a mere individual; in order to defend it, we must collect our whole energy, our whole ability, and it is a matter of indifference if, by doing so, we endanger some human lives and shed some blood. There is an abundance of human lives in the world, and the blood that has been shed is restored in the course of a few hours. Victoria, you shall not merely assist me; you shall aid the state too, and make an effort for its welfare."

"Only he who dares wins!" exclaimed Victoria, with a fascinating smile. "Tell me what I am to do, my friend."

"To be fascinating, to avail yourself of the power of your charms, that is all. To tame a bear, in order to draw his secrets from him."

"In what forest shall I find this bear?"

"At Rastadt, and his name is Roberjot, or Bonnier, or Debry, for aught I know. Try all three of them. One of them at least will have a heart capable of falling in love, and eyes to admire your beauty. Chain that man to your triumphal car, fathom him, try to become his confidante, and sift his secrets."

"For a special purpose, or only in general?"

"For a special purpose. I have reason to believe that France is deceiving us, and that, while seeking an alliance with us, and assuring us every day of her friendship, she is secretly plotting against us."

"Plotting with whom?"

"With Prussia, Austria's mortal enemy. France has promised us not to grant any further aggrandizement to Prussia. I am satisfied that she has secretly made similar promises to Prussia in relation to us, and that she is trying as eagerly, and by means of as many assurances, to obtain the alliance of Prussia, as that of Austria. It is, however, of the highest importance for us to know what France may have promised to Prussia, and how far the negotiations between the two powers have gone. To fathom this, either by amicable or violent means, by shrewdness or by compulsion, by bribery or by threats, will be your task, my heavenly demon."

"It is a beautiful task, because it is a difficult one," said Victoria, proudly. "It is a matter of life and death, this duel I am to fight with one of those French bears."

"But my beautiful Victoria shall not lack seconds to furbish her weapons, and to do every thing she wants them to do."

"Who are my seconds?"

"Count Lehrbach and Colonel Barbaczy."

"Ah, Barbaczy, whose acquaintance we made at Giurgewo?"

"The same. A bold, intrepid man, who is not afraid of anybody—neither of God nor of the devil."

"Lehrbach and Barbaczy, your two bloodhounds," said Victoria, musingly. "If *they* are to be my seconds, I am afraid the duel will not merely remain a spiritual one, and not merely hearts will be wounded. I am afraid real blood will be shed, and there will be carnal wounds."

"I must have the papers!" exclaimed Thugut, "either by means of cunning or by measures of open violence, do you understand? And as to the wounds and blood, I wish with all my heart to give these impudent republican fellows who are putting on such airs at Rastadt, as though they were masters of Germany, a sound and bloody lesson, and thus give France an unmistakable proof of our opinion."

"Good, my dear Satan, I shall assist you in performing this little infernal comedy. Two weighty questions, however, remain to be asked. On what pretext shall I ask my imperial mistress to grant me leave of absence?"

"Have you not got a sister, who is married to a rich country gentleman, in the grand-duchy of Baden, and who informed you yesterday that she had been suddenly taken dangerously ill?"

"I have a sister!" exclaimed Victoria, laughing. "I who never knew a paternal roof, or family—I who dropped upon earth like a ripe peach-blossom, and would have been crushed there, if my handsome and generous Charles de Poutet had not accidentally passed by while the wind was driving me along, and if he chivalrously had not picked me up and placed me in his button-hole. I never knew my family—I was an orphan since my earliest childhood. No, my friend, I have no sister."

"Oh, try to recollect, Victoria; it is *your* sister who has called you to her death-bed, and for whose sake the empress will give you leave of absence."

"Ah, *vraiment*, I recollect now! Of course, I must go and see my sister. The good, dear sister—how she will long to see me again in order to recover from her sickness! Oh, I must repair to my sister—nothing must detain me here. The kind-hearted empress will not refuse me leave of absence, for I have to fulfil a sacred duty. Family ties are more sacred than any other."

"Ah, you are really a most affectionate sister; the empress will readily grant you leave of absence, and you will set out to-morrow evening. I shall provide fresh horses for you at every station, and I shall send you to-morrow morning a comfortable travelling-coach. Your first question, then, is answered. Now for the second."

"Yes, my friend, I will briefly state my second question. After accomplishing my task, after chivalrously fighting my duel, and conquering the papers, what will be my reward?"

"Your reward will be the only one I dare offer to a beautiful young widow," said Thugut, with a diabolical smile. "A husband who will bestow upon you a distinguished name, who will strengthen your position at court, and who will one day bequeath to you a princely inheritance."

"What!" exclaimed Victoria, joyfully, "you will marry me, my friend?"

"I?" asked Thugut, almost in terror. "Who spoke of me? Am I able to offer you wealth and a distinguished name? My fortune would be too insignificant for your pin-money, and although the ship-builder's son has acquired quite a distinguished name, he lacks the dust of ten dead ancestors. I am my own ancestor, and my pedigree contains but my own name. No, Victoria, I have something better in store for you. I shall make you the wife of the minister, Count Colloredo. He is a member of the old aristocracy, and his wife will outrank at court all the ladies of the ministers and of the lower nobility. He is, moreover, very wealthy, and a favorite of the emperor. I shall give him to understand that he loves you ardently, and that he would pine away if you should reject him. The dear count does not like to hear people talk about pining away and dying, and he will consider himself saved if you accept him and allow him to grow young again in your arms. To induce him to marry you, and to direct him correctly, let me alone for that. On the day on which you bring me the papers, even if they should be somewhat blood-stained, on that day I shall have the honor to lead you to the altar, and greet you by the name of Countess Colloredo."

"The scheme is good and feasible," said Victoria, musingly, "and yet I do not like it altogether. To be frank with you, my friend, if you really believe that I ought to marry again, why will not *you* marry me? What shall I do with the childish, conceited, and proud Count Colloredo, who is already seventy years of age? Why cannot I have my god of darkness? Thugut, I ask you, why do not you want to marry me?"

Thugut replied to the flaming glance of the charming lady by a loud laugh.

"I marry you? Ah, my heavenly demon! that would be very imprudent, for in that case I should have to require you to lead a devout and chaste life, and to keep my name unsullied."

"Ah, you insult me," exclaimed Victoria, feelingly. "You want to insinuate that I am unworthy of being your wife."

"You are worthy of being much more, dearest, for you are a demon of love; but my wife ought only to be a matron of chastity."

"Oh, how tiresome!" sighed Victoria.

"Yes, how tiresome!" repeated Thugut. "And our own heavenly *liaison*, the last romantic dream of my life, would it not also be broken off if you were to become my wife? Why would we then stand in need of secrecy—of hidden staircases and doors, and of this Turkish cabinet?—inasmuch as I should have the right to enter your rooms before the eyes of the whole world. Besides, we would be unable to be useful to each other. My wife, of course, would have to side with me and defend me everywhere, while, in case you are married to another man, you are at liberty to act for me and to favor me. I could not promote the interests of my wife at court; I could not speak of her in terms of praise to the empress, and recommend that fresh honors and distinctions be conferred upon her. My wife, therefore, would remain the *aja* of the little Archduchess Maria Louisa, while my influence will be able to secure to the Countess Victoria Colloredo the position of a first lady of honor of the duchess."

"First lady of honor!" exclaimed Victoria, joyfully, and with glowing checks. "You are

right, my friend, it is better for me to marry Count Colloredo. Colloredo has great power over the emperor; I have great power over the empress, and shall have the same power over Colloredo. But I am again under your control, and thus you will rule us all, and rule Austria, for I shall always remain your faithful servant and friend."

"Women's oaths are as fitful as the wind, they are as fleeting as the clouds," said Thugut, shrugging his shoulders. "But I believe you, Victoria, for you are no woman like other women. If I were ever to discover that you had deceived me, I should take a terrible revenge!"

"What sort of revenge, my friend?" asked Victoria, embracing him smilingly and tenderly.

"I know but one punishment for a faithless woman," said Thugut, "and if I envy any thing, my friend, Sultan Mustapha, is able to do it, it is his power of publicly inflicting this punishment. A faithless woman is drowned in a sack, that is all. She is placed in a sack—gagged, of course, so as to be unable to scream—and in the dead of night she is rowed out into the sea, which silently opens its waves in order to receive the silent victim. I have witnessed this romantic spectacle three times in Constantinople, and it always filled me with delight. It is so noiseless, so simple, and yet so significant! It is true we have no sea here, but we have the Danube, and there is room in it for many faithless women. Beware, therefore, Victoria! But now a truce to business and politics. Now, my demon, unfold your angel wings, and let me pass an hour with you in paradise. Will you do me the honor, Countess Colloredo *in spe*, to take supper with me here?"

"Here?" said Victoria, looking around wonderingly. "Where is the supper-table?"

"You will see it directly."

Thugut stooped and vigorously pressed a golden knob, fixed in the floor, close to the sofa. Immediately a creaking and rattling noise was heard; the floor opened, and a large aperture became visible. After a few minutes a table, covered with the most luxurious dishes and sparkling wines, and glittering with silver and crystal, slowly and majestically arose.

"Splendid!" shouted Victoria, dancing like a fairy around the magic table—"splendid! The prince of darkness commands, hell opens, and by the fire, over which the souls of the wicked are roasting, the most savory dishes have been prepared for Satan! But first swear to me, my friend, that this pheasant is filled with truffles, and not with human souls!"

"My dear Victoria," replied Thugut, laughing, "human souls have only too often the same fate as truffles—hogs discover them! Come, I drink this glass of sherbet to the health of the Countess Colloredo *in spe!*"

CHAPTER XXVII.

RASTADT.

THE congress of Rastadt had been in session for nearly two years. For nearly two years the German ambassadors had been quarrelling with France about the ancient boundaries of the empire, and had been quarrelling among each other about a few strips of land, a few privileges which one state demanded, while another would not grant.

It was a sorrowful and humiliating spectacle this congress of Rastadt presented to the world, and all Germany was looking on with feelings of pain and shame, while France pointed at it with scornful laughter, and exclaimed:

"It is not France that destroys and dissolves Germany, but Germany is annihilating herself. She is dissolving away, owing to her own weakness, and the dissensions of her rulers will kill her!"

Yes, indeed, Germany bore the germ of death and dissolution in her sick, lacerated breast, and the first symptoms of putrefaction already made their appearance. These first symptoms were the envy, jealousy, and hatred the rulers of Germany felt toward each other, and the malicious joy with which one saw another die, without pitying his torments, and only mindful of the fact that he would be the dying state's heir.

The first section of Germany which succumbed under these circumstances, embraced the bishoprics and ecclesiastical states. They exhibited most of all the corruption and putrefaction of German affairs. Hence, such German states as expected to be benefited by their dissolution, voted for secularization, while such as were threatened with losses voted against it. A new apple of discord had been thrown into the German empire; the last spark of German unity was gone, and two hostile parties, bitterly menacing each other, were formed. Austria loudly raised her voice against the secularization of the ecclesiastical possessions, because she could derive no benefit from it; while Prussia declared in favor of secularization, because she believed she would be able to aggrandize her territory in consequence; and the secondary princes demanded the dissolution of the bishoprics even more urgently than Prussia, because they knew that a portion of those dominions would fall to their own share.

Covetousness caused the German princes to overlook all other interests, and to act contrary to all correct principles; covetousness caused them first to shake the decaying ancient German empire; covetousness caused them to destroy the old political organization of the country, and German hands were the first to tear down the edifice of the imperial constitution.

The German ambassadors at Rastadt forgot, therefore, the original object of their mission; they had come thither to secure the continued existence of the German empire, and to protect Germany from the encroachments of France, and now they were threatening the German empire themselves. They had come thither to establish the boundaries of Germany, and now they were attacking the boundaries of the single sections and states of the empire themselves.

No wonder that France sought to profit by these dissensions of the Germans among each other; no wonder that she thought she might seize a piece of Germany, too, seeing, as she did, that the German states were quarrelling among themselves about the division of the spoils. France, therefore, advanced her troops farther on the right bank of the Rhine, and claimed the fortresses of Kehl, Ehrenbreitstein, and Castel.

This fresh and unparalleled exaction silenced the domestic quarrels among the Germans for a moment, and all voices united to protest loudly and solemnly against the new demand of the French Republic.

But the French replied to the solemn protests of the German ambassadors at Rastadt by cold sneers and violent threats. Ehrenbreitstein not being surrendered to them after the first summons, they blockaded the fortress, levied contributions on the right bank of the Rhine, and declared the possessions of the nobility to be forfeited to the French Republic.[*] The German ambassadors at Rastadt complaining of these oppressive proceedings, the French declared, "the magnanimity of the French had exceeded all expectations. They were able to take every thing, and they had contented themselves with very little."

The congress had met at Rastadt in order to conclude peace, but so far the negotiations had produced nothing but exasperation and a strong probability of ultimate war. The arrogance and scornful bearing of France became every day more intolerable, and the desire of Austria became proportionately more evident to punish France for her insolence, and to take revenge for the numerous and galling insults she had heaped upon Ger-

* Vide Häusser's "History of Germany," vol. ii, p. 201.

many. Prussia hesitated to join Austria, and to declare in favor of open hostilities against France; she deemed such a war injurious to her particular interests, and desired to maintain peace; the secondary German states, however, allowed themselves to be intimidated by the threats of France to devour all of them, and they were quite willing to expose Germany to further humiliations, provided that their own petty existence should not be endangered.

The work of pacification, therefore, made no progress whatever, but only became a disgrace to Germany, and the congress of Rastadt was nothing but a symptom of the disease of which Germany was soon to perish. Germany seemed destined to die, like an aged and decrepit man, of her own weakness and exhaustion.

This weakness was every day on the increase. In January, 1799, Ehrenbreitstein succumbed, and the French occupied the fortress.

Still the peace commissioners remained in session at Rastadt, and continued their negotiations with the French, who just now had again perfidiously violated the treaties, and appropriated German possessions.

If the German ambassadors, perhaps, were lost to all sense of honor and of their disgraceful position, the representatives of France were fully conscious of their dignity. They treated the ambassadors of Germany in the most scornful manner; they dared haughtily and arrogantly to meddle with the domestic affairs of Germany; they constantly trumped up new claims in the most overbearing attitude, and in their habitual imperious tone, and the representatives of the German empire scarcely dared to refuse their exactions even in the most timid manner.

Only one of the three French ambassadors, for the last few weeks, had been less supercilious than his colleagues; he had participated less than formerly in the affairs of the German congress, and while Roberjot and Jean Debry were raising their arrogant and haughty voices in every session of congress, Bonnier kept aloof. He even held no further intercourse with his own countrymen; and his tall and imposing figure, with the proud and gloomy countenance, was seen no longer every night as heretofore in the drawing-rooms of the wives of Roberjot and Debry. He kept aloof from society as he kept aloof from the congress, and the French ladies smilingly whispered to each other that something strange, something unheard of, had happened to the austere republican. To the man who heretofore had proudly resisted the blandishments of beautiful women, they said he had fallen in love with that wondrously lovely and strange

lady who had been at Rastadt for the last few weeks, but who was living in such seclusion that the public had only occasionally got a sight of her. No one knew who this strange lady was, and what she wanted at Rastadt; she had paid visits to no one, and left her card nowhere. She had arrived only attended by a footman and a lady's maid; but in advance, a brilliant suite of rooms and a box at the theatre had been retained for her. In this box every night the beautiful strange lady was seen closely veiled, and the gloomy pale face of Bonnier had been repeatedly beheld by her side.

Victoria de Poutet, therefore, had accomplished her purpose; she had tamed one of the French bears, and surrounded him with the magic nets of her beauty. She was the mysterious strange lady whose appearance had created so great a sensation in the drawing-rooms of Rastadt for the last few weeks; she was the lady whom Bonnier was following as though he were her shadow.

She had come to him as a refugee, as a persecuted woman, with tears in her eyes. She had told him a tragic story of Thugut's tyranny and wanton lust. Because she had refused to submit to the voluptuous desires of the Austrian minister, he had sworn to ruin her, and his love had turned into furious hatred. She further stated the minister had threatened her with the confiscation of her property, with imprisonment, death, and disgrace, and she had only succeeded by her courage and cunning in saving herself and in escaping from Austria. Now she came to Bonnier to invoke the protection and assistance of generous France, and to flee from the rude violence of a German minister to the chivalrous ægis of the French Republic.

How beautiful she was in her tears, with the mournful smile on her swelling lips! But how much more beautiful when a deep blush mantled her cheeks, and when her large dark eyes were sparkling in the glow of revenge and anger!

For Victoria de Poutet did not only want protection—she also sought revenge—revenge on that tyrant Thugut, who had dared to threaten her innocence and virtue, and to assail her honor and happiness. She was not only persecuted—she was also insulted, and she wished to chastise the Austrian minister for these insults. Bonnier was to lend her his assistance for this purpose. He was to procure means for her to overthrow Thugut.

How eloquently and enthusiastically did she speak to Bonnier about her misfortunes, her anger, and her thirst of revenge! How much truthfulness there was depicted in her face—what a demoniacal ardor in her eyes; how much energy in her whole bearing, so indicative of bold determination and of an indomitable spirit!

Bonnier gazed at her in wondering delight, in timid awe. He who had hated women because they were so weak, so peevish, and insignificant, now saw before him a woman with the energy of a hatred such as he had scarcely known himself, with the enthusiasm of a revengefulness that shrank back from no dangers and no obstacles. Under this delicate, ethereal female form there was concealed the spirit and firm will of a man; bold thoughts were written on her forehead, and an enchanting smile was playing on her full lips. While Bonnier was listening to the dithyrambics of her hatred and revenge, love glided into his own heart; she had fascinated him by her revengeful hymns as others fascinate by their love-songs.

Victoria was conscious of her triumph; her eagle eye had watched every motion, every step of this innocent lamb she was going to strangle; she had seen him fall into the glittering nets she had spread out for him; she knew that he was a captive in her meshes without being aware of it himself.

Her bearing now underwent a change; she was no longer merely a woman thirsting for revenge, but also a tender, loving woman; she was no longer merely filled with hatred, but she also seemed susceptible of gentler emotions; she lowered her eyes before Bonnier's ardent glances and blushed. To his timid and faltering protestations of love she replied by subdued sighs, and by a dreamy smile; and when Bonnier at length dared to approach her with a bold confession of his passion—when he was on his knees before her, all aglow with love and enthusiasm, Victoria bent over him with a sweet smile, and whispered: "Give me the papers that are to ruin Thugut; surrender that vile man to my revenge, and my love, my life are yours!"

Bonnier looked up to her with a triumphant smile. "You are mine, then, Victoria," he said, "for you shall have those papers! I surrender that infamous and treacherous man to your revenge!"

She stretched out her hands toward him with a cry of boundless joy. "Give me the papers," she exclaimed; "give them to me, and I will thank you as only love is able to thank!"

Bonnier looked a long while at her, and his face, usually so gloomy, was now radiant with happiness and delight.

"To-morrow, my charming fairy," he said, "to-morrow you shall have the papers which are to open hell to your enemy, and heaven to your enraptured friend. But you must give me also a proof of your confidence and love; you must come to me and call in person for the papers. I give you the highest proof of my love by delivering to you documents that do not belong to me, but to the republic. Then give me likewise the highest proof of your love. Come to me!"

She cast a long and glowing glance on him. "I shall come!" she whispered.

And Victoria kept her word. Early on the following morning a closely-veiled lady was seen to glide into the castle of Rastadt, where the three French ambassadors were living at that time. Bonnier received her in person at the foot of the wide staircase, and gave her his arm in order to conduct her to the rooms occupied by himself.

They exchanged not a word with each other, but walked silently through the sumptuous apartments and finally entered Bonnier's study.

"We are at the goal—here I bid you welcome, my fairy queen!" exclaimed Bonnier. "Remove now these odious veils. Let me now at length see your beautiful features!"

He violently tore off her black veils, and Victoria suffered it smilingly, and looked at him with a wondrous air of joy and happiness.

"Are you content now?" she asked, in her superb, sonorous voice. "Has the proud lord of creation now prepared a new and satisfactory triumph for himself? The poor slave whom he loves must come to him and beg him for love and happiness!"

She had crossed her hands on her breast, and half kneeling down before Bonnier, she looked up to him with a fascinating mixture of archness and passion.

Bonnier lifted her up and wanted to imprint a kiss upon her lips, but she violently pushed him back.

"No," she said, "let us be sensible as long as we can. First we must attend to our business."

"Business!" exclaimed Bonnier. "What have we to do with business? Leave business to the diplomatists and their clerks. Why should lips so charming and beautiful pronounce this cold and dismal word?"

"If I spoke of business, I meant revenge," said Victoria, fervently. "Give me the papers, Bonnier—the papers that are to ruin Thugut!"

Bonnier took her head between his hands and looked at her with flaming eyes.

"Then you hate him still? You still desire to take revenge on him?" he asked.

"Yes, I hate him!" she exclaimed, "and the happiest day of my life will be the one on which I see him hurled down from his proud eminence, and sneaking alone, miserable, and despised into obscurity."

"One might, indeed, really believe that she is in earnest, and that truth alone could utter such words," muttered Bonnier, who constantly held her head in his hands, and thus gazed at her. "Swear to me, Victoria, swear to me by what is most sacred to you, that you hate Thugut, and that you desire to ruin him!"

"I swear it by what is most sacred to me," she said, solemnly; "I swear it by your love!"

"That is the best and most unequivocal oath, and I will believe you," said Bonnier, laughing.

"Then you will now give me those papers?" she asked.

"Yes," he said, bluntly, "I will give them to you. Come, my angel, you are right—let us first speak of business matters. There, sit down here at my desk. Oh, henceforth this spot will be sacred to me, for your heavenly person has consecrated it. Let me sit down here by your side, and thus we will lay our dispatches before each other, like two good and conscientious diplomatists. Look here! this portfolio contains your revenge and your satisfaction. This portfolio contains the papers proving that Thugut has received large sums of money from Russia and England for the purpose of instigating the Emperor of Austria against France, and that his pretended patriotic indignation is after all nothing but the paid *rôle* of a comedian. I have abstracted this portfolio from the archives of our embassy. Do you understand me, Victoria? I have stolen it for you!"

"Let me see the papers!" exclaimed Victoria, trembling with impatience.

Bonnier opened the portfolio and drew a paper from it. But on looking at it, a dark cloud passed over his face, and he shook his head indignantly.

"What a miserable fool I was to make such a mistake!" he ejaculated angrily. "I have taken the wrong portfolio. This one does not contain the papers you are looking for."

"That is," said Victoria, with cutting coldness—"that is, you have intentionally deceived me. You decoyed me hither under false pretences. You told me a story about important papers that were in your possession, and with which you were to intrust me for the purpose of gratifying my revenge. And now when I come to you, nobly trusting your chivalrous word, now it turns out that you have deceived me, and that those important papers do not exist at all."

"Ah, believe me, there are papers here perhaps even more important than the documents you are looking for," said Bonnier, shrugging his shoul-

ders. "Believe me, Baron Thugut would give many thousands if he could get hold of the papers contained in this portfolio. They are, perhaps, even more important than those other documents."

A flash burst forth from Victoria's eyes, and the angry air disappeared at once from her features. She turned to Bonnier with a fascinating smile.

"What sort of papers are those?" she asked.

"Papers that do not interest you, my charming fairy," he said, smilingly; "for what have love and revenge to do with the negotiations of diplomacy? This portfolio contains only diplomatic documents, only the secret correspondence between ourselves and the Prussian government, and the negotiations concerning an alliance between France and Prussia—that is all. They do not interest you, my beautiful Victoria, but Thugut would gladly purchase these papers for those which you are so anxious to obtain."

Victoria's eyes were fixed on the portfolio with a glowing expression, and her hand was involuntarily approaching it. Bonnier saw it, and a peculiar smile overspread his gloomy face for a moment.

"Happy for me," he said, "that I discovered my mistake before giving you the portfolio. The loss of these papers would have compromised me irretrievably. But you are silent, Victoria—you do not utter a word. Then you do not yet believe in the truthfulness of my words? I swear to you, my fascinating sorceress, it was a mere mistake—I only seized the wrong portfolio."

"Do not swear, but convince me," said Victoria. "Go and fetch the other portfolio."

"And I should leave you here all alone so long?" he asked, tenderly. "I should be such a prodigal as to squander these precious minutes during which I am permitted to be by your side!"

Victoria rose and looked at him with flaming, imperious eyes.

"Fetch the papers," she shouted, "or I leave you this very moment, and you shall never see me again!"

"That is a word by which you would drive me even into the jaws of hell!" said Bonnier, ardently. "Wait for me here, Victoria—I am going for the papers."

He greeted her with a rapid nod, and placing the portfolio under his arm, he hastily walked to the door. Here he turned around toward her and his eyes met hers steadfastly fixed upon him.

He kissed his hand to her, and while doing so, the portfolio softly glided from under his arm and fell upon the floor. Bonnier took no notice of it; his whole attention was riveted on the beautiful lady. But she saw it, and her eyes sparkled with delight.

"Return as soon as possible," she said, with an enchanting smile, and Bonnier left the room. She anxiously looked after him until the door had closed, and then she listened to the sound of his footsteps. Now the latter were no longer audible, and every thing about her was silent.

Victoria did not stir; she only swept with her large eyes searchingly over the whole room; she fixed them upon every curtain, upon every piece of furniture. But nothing was there to arouse her suspicions; a profound stillness reigned around her.

Now she rose slowly from her seat and made a few steps forward. The rustling of her heavy silk dress alone interrupted the silence.

She paused again and listened, and her eyes fixed themselves longingly upon the portfolio lying at the door. Why were not her eyes endowed with the power of a loadstone? Why were they not able to attract the portfolio to her?

The portfolio lay there quietly and immovably; Victoria vainly stretched out her hands toward it —she was unable to reach it.

Once more she impetuously glanced round the room; then she bounded forward like a lioness rushing toward her prey.

She grasped the portfolio and raised it with a triumphant smile. Her small hands quickly plunged into it and drew forth the papers. There were but a few letters, and besides several closely written pages. Victoria did not take time to look at them; she rapidly pushed the papers into the pocket of her dress, and arranged the folds of the latter so as to conceal the contents of her pocket. She then closed the portfolio and replaced it on the floor, precisely on the spot where Bonnier had dropped it.

Her purpose was accomplished! How her face was glowing with delight! How deep a blush was burning on her cheeks! How her eyes were sparkling with diabolic exultation!

With light, inaudible steps she now crossed the room again, and resumed her seat at the desk. And it was fortunate that she had done so, for steps were approaching in the adjoining room; the door opened, and Bonnier entered.

—

CHAPTER XXVIII.

BONNIER paused for a moment on the threshold, fixing his eyes on Victoria, who greeted him with a sweet, fascinating smile. But the smile disappeared from her lips when she beheld the threatening, angry glance with which he was staring at her, and the air of gloomy indignation depicted on his countenance. She might be mistaken, however, and perhaps it was merely the anguish of her conscience which made her tremble.

"And you bring me the papers, my beloved friend?" asked Victoria, with an air of fascinating kindness.

"Yes," said Bonnier, still remaining on the threshold, "I bring you the papers. But just look what a fool love has made of me! For your sake, I forgot the portfolio with those other papers, and dropped it on the floor there. Do you now perceive your power over me? For I believe I told you that the loss of those papers would ruin me irretrievably."

"Yes, you told me so," said Victoria, smiling.

"And yet I forgot them here!" exclaimed Bonnier, stooping to pick them up. But Victoria immediately rose and hastened to him.

"To punish you for your carelessness, you shall now leave the portfolio on the floor," she said, smiling; "nor shall you think of it again as long as I am with you. Tell me, will that be too hard for you?"

She bent her beautiful face over him, and with flaming glances looked deeply into his eyes.

Bonnier dropped the portfolio again and smiled.

"It may lie there," he said; "it has performed its part anyhow. And now, I suppose, we will talk again about our business?"

"Yes, we will," replied Victoria. "Give me the papers."

"No, madame; no one gives up such important papers without witnesses," said Bonnier. "Permit me therefore to call my witnesses."

He hastily turned to the door and pushed it open.

"Come in, gentlemen!" he shouted, and his two colleagues, Roberjot and Debry, immediately appeared on the threshold. Without greeting Victoria, merely eyeing her with cold, contemptuous glances, the two gentlemen entered and walked directly to the desk. Bonnier locked the door and put the key into his pocket.

Victoria saw it, and a slight pallor overspread her rosy face for a moment.

"Will you tell me, sir, what all this means?" she asked, in a threatening voice.

"You will learn it directly," said Bonnier. "Please sit down again in your arm-chair, for we are going to resume our diplomatic negotiations. You, gentlemen, take seats on both sides of the lady; I shall sit down opposite her, and at the slightest motion she makes, either to jump out of the window there, or to interrupt us by an exclamation, I shall shoot her as sure as my name is Bonnier!"

He drew a pistol from his bosom and cocked it. "I command you to be silent and not to interrupt us," he said, turning to Victoria. "The pistol is loaded, and, unless you respect my orders, I will most certainly inflict upon you the punishment you have deserved; I shall take your life like that of any other spy who has been caught in a hostile camp."

He dropped his right hand with the pistol on the table, and then turned to the two gentlemen, who had listened to him in gloomy silence.

"Yes, my friends," he said, throwing back his head in order to shake away his long black hair, surrounding his face like a mane—"now, my friends, I beg you to listen to my justification. You have latterly believed me to be a fool, a prodigal son of the republic, who, for the sake of a miserable love-affair with a flirt, neglected the most sacred interests of his country. You shall see and acknowledge now that, while I seemed to be lost, I was only working for the welfare and glory of our great republic, and that this woman with her beautiful mask did not make me forget for a single moment my duties to my country. These papers contain my justification—these papers, madame, with which you hoped to revenge yourself. Pardon me, my fairy queen, I have made another mistake, and again brought a wrong portfolio; these are not the documents either which you would like to obtain. Perhaps they are after all in the portfolio lying on the floor there!"

He looked at Victoria with a scornful smile; she fixed her large eyes steadfastly upon him; not a muscle of her face was twitching—not the slightest anxiety or fear was depicted on her features.

Bonnier opened the portfolio and drew the papers from it.

"I shall only briefly state to you the contents of those papers," he said, "you may afterward peruse them at leisure. This first paper is a letter I received by a courier from Vienna, without knowing who sent it to me. The letter only contains the following words:

"'Be on your guard. A very dangerous spy will be sent to you—a lady who is the most intimate friend of a distinguished statesman. Receive her well, and let no one see these lines. It will promote the welfare of France.'

"As a matter of course, I said nothing about it, not even to you, my friends; I was silent, and waited for further developments. Two days later I received this second paper. It was a note from a lady, who wrote to me that she had just arrived at Rastadt, and was very anxious to see me, but under the seal of the most profound secrecy. I followed the invitation, and repaired to the designated house. I found there this lady, who introduced herself to me as Madame Victoria de Poutet; and if you now look at her you will comprehend why that refined half-Turk Thugut, as well as the mad rake Count Lehrbach, are both in love with her, for she is more beautiful than the loveliest odalisque and the most fascinating Phryne!"

The three men fixed their eyes upon Victoria, and ogled her with an impudent leer. Victoria sat erect and immovable, and even her eye-lashes did not move; she apparently did not see the glances fixed upon her; nor even heard what Bonnier had said about her, for her countenance remained calm and almost smiling.

Bonnier continued: "The lady told me a very pretty little story, the particulars of which I shall not relate to you. In short, Thugut had attacked her innocence and her honor—her innocence and her honor, do not forget that!—and she wanted to revenge herself upon him. She asked me to lend her my assistance for this purpose. I feigned to believe every thing she told me, and promised to protect her.

"This third paper here I found on my desk on returning home from my visit to the lady. A stranger had delivered it. It was written by the same man who had addressed the first letter to me. It read as follows: 'A romance is to be played with you; let them proceed without interfering with their doings. The fascination of beauty is very powerful, and the lady is going to fascinate you, for the purpose of obtaining important papers from you. Pretend to be fascinated, and you will penetrate the intrigue.'

"The advice was good, and I followed it. I feigned to be fascinated; I played the enthusiastic lover of this lady; and although I doubtless acted my part in a very clumsy manner, she was kind enough to believe me; for she is well aware that no one is able to withstand the power of her beauty. But in order to perform my rôle in a really truthful manner, not only Madame de Poutet, but also all Rastadt, had to be convinced of my ardent love for her, for Victoria is very shrewd; Thugut has educated a worthy pupil in her. Hence I had to wear the mask of my love everywhere, even before you, my friends. I had to make up my mind to pass for a fool until I was able to prove to you that I was a man of sense; I had to wear my mask until I was able to tear this woman's mask from her face. Oh, I assure you, it is not an easy task to be this lady's lover! She demands a great deal of courting, a great deal of ardor, a great deal of passion; she has got very warm blood herself, and, if I am not mistaken, she is a great-granddaughter of that beautiful Roman lady, Messalina."

Now, for the first time, a slight tremor pervaded Victoria's frame, and a deep blush suffused her cheeks. But this lasted only a moment, and then she sat again quite erect and immovable.

"In spite of the difficulty of your task, you have played your part in a masterly manner," said Jean Debry, in a rude and stern voice. "All of us believed you were in love, and this modern Messalina certainly did not doubt it, either."

"No, she did not doubt it," said Bonnier, with a disdainful smile. "She surrounded herself with spies, who had to watch me, but fortunately I knew them, and did not betray myself."

"How did you know them?" asked Roberjot.

"My unknown correspondent pointed them out to me. He had given up his incognito, and came to me, satisfying me of his identity by writing a few lines, which proved him to be the author of the two previous letters. He offered for a brilliant compensation to assist me in unravelling the intrigue, and I promised him five thousand francs. He was one of our most astute and skilful spies, and he wanted this affair to be his masterpiece, in order to obtain from me a recommendation to General Bonaparte, who has just returned from Egypt. I shall give him to-day the promised sum and the recommendation, for he has honestly earned both, and faithfully assisted me in unmasking this woman.* I received every morning a written report from him about every thing Madame Poutet had done during the previous day. All these reports are in this portfolio, and you will examine them, my friends. You will see

from them that Madame Victoria, who had come to me in order to revenge herself upon Thugut, nevertheless kept up a good understanding with his most intimate friend, Count Lehrbach, for every night, as soon as I had left Victoria, the noble count repaired to her house and spent several hours with her, although Victoria had assured me Count Lehrbach did not even suspect her presence at Rastadt. However, there was a possibility that my spy was deceiving me just as well as he had deceived Madame de Poutet. In order to ascertain that, I informed Victoria one evening that a courier would set out for Paris in the morning, and forward to the Directory papers of the highest importance, concerning an alliance with Russia. We sent a courier to Paris in the morning, but not far from Rastadt he was arrested by Austrian hussars, robbed of his papers, and taken to the headquarters of the Austrian Colonel Barbaczy, at Gernsbach, although our courier was provided with a French passport and an official badge, enabling him fully to prove that he was in our service." *

"This was an unheard-of violation of international law, for which we have vainly sought redress," said Jean Debry, gloomily. "These German cowards are not even courageous enough to acknowledge their own acts. They deny having robbed our courier, but they cannot deny having imprisoned him, contrary to international law."

"Just as little as Victoria can deny that she was the person who had informed Lehrbach and Barbaczy of the courier's departure," said Bonnier; "for, fifteen minutes before setting out, the courier himself did not know any thing about his mission; and the dispatches, of course, were of the most harmless description. But my pretty lady-bird there had gone into the trap I had set for her, and I kept her in it without her knowing any thing about it. She was quite unsuspecting, and, thanks to my talents as a comedian, and to my love, I finally found out the real purpose of her visit to Rastadt. Yesterday I promised her to deliver to her to-day the papers that endanger Thugut's position at the head of the Austrian government, and prove him to be a hireling of England. In the evening Count Lehrbach sent a courier to Vienna; then we retaliated, caused the courier to be arrested and took his papers from him. He had, however, only a small note, addressed to Minister Thugut. Here it is. It contains only the following words:

'I shall get the papers to-morrow.

'VICTORIA.'

---

* This spy was the famous Schulmeister, afterward Bonaparte's most adroit and intrepid spy. He boasted of the rôle he had played at Rastadt, and which had brought him double pay; first from Count Lehrbach, whom he had informed that there were important papers in the hands of the French, and then from the French ambassadors, whom he had cautioned against Count Lehrbach, and given the advice to burn their papers and to be on their guard.

* Historical.

But these words were written by the beautiful hand of the same lady who latterly had penned so many tender love-letters to myself. I had promised her those papers if she would call for them to-day, and you see, my friends, that she has come. But I desired to know if this really was the only object for which Baron Thugut had sent his most beautiful and sagacious agent to Rastadt, or if there were not some secondary objects at the bottom of this mission. I therefore resolved to ascertain this to-day. My astute spy had told me that Madame de Poutet was also anxious to get hold of some other important papers. I therefore feigned to-day to have abstracted the wrong papers and to have brought here a portfolio containing our correspondence with the Prussian minister and documents in relation to an alliance between France and Prussia. I told my fair friend that the loss of these papers would ruin me irretrievably, and yet I was such a love-sick fool as to drop the portfolio with the papers while engaged in tenderly kissing my hand to my dulcinea. Look, gentlemen, the portfolio is yet lying on the floor, but the papers are no longer in it. They are carefully concealed in Madame Victoria's pocket. Oh, it was a very pretty scene, when she stole them. I watched her through a small hole which I had bored through the door this morning, and through which I could plainly see every motion of my beautiful Victoria. Yes, my beautiful Victoria stole the papers, although she knew that this loss would seriously embarrass me. However, my friends, it will be unnecessary for the republic to punish me for this theft Madame de Poutet has committed, for the papers she has got in her pocket are nothing but the faithful diary of my daily intercourse with Victoria de Poutet. I have carefully noted in it every conversation I had with her, and every favor she granted to me, and I have no objection whatever to this diary being transmitted to Minister Thugut. If he is not jealous, he will not complain of it. And now I am through with my justification, and I ask you, did I not act as a good and faithful son of the republic should? Have I done my duty? Will the country be content with me?"

"Yes," said Roberjot, solemnly, "you have acted as a good and faithful son of the republic. You have intrepidly followed the enemy who had approached you on secret paths, into his hiding-places, and you have skilfully exposed the perfidious intrigues he had carried on against France. You have done your duty."

"Yes, the republic will thank you for your zeal," exclaimed Jean Debry; "you have run great risks for her sake. For a beautiful, voluptuous,

and intriguing woman is even more dangerous than a venomous serpent. Like St. Anthony, you have withstood the temptress by praying to our holy mother, the great French Republic! Yes, the country will be content with you."

"I thank you, my friends," said Bonnier, with a happy smile; "I now stand again before you with a clear conscience, and without a blush of shame on my cheeks. You have accepted my atonement. As for this woman, we will inflict no farther punishment on her. She was only a tool in Thugut's hands; that was all. This hour has punished her sufficiently, and our profound contempt shall be the only penalty she will take away with her."

"Yes, our profound contempt shall be the penalty she will take with her," exclaimed Roberjot and Jean Debry at the same time.

"There is nothing more disgraceful under the sun than a woman who sells her charms," said Roberjot.

"There is nothing more dreadful and dishonorable than an ambitious and heartless wanton!" added Jean Debry, in a voice of profound disdain.

"Victoria de Poutet," said Bonnier, throwing the pistol aside, "every thing between us was a comedy, even this pistol, the pretended bullet of which frightened and silenced you. It was not loaded. The comedy is now at an end, and there remains nothing for you but to go to your stage-manager and to tell him that you utterly failed in performing your part. You may go now; nothing further detains you here."

"I beg your pardon," said Victoria, in a perfectly calm and sonorous voice; "you forget that you put the key of the door into your pocket; go, therefore, and unlock it."

She pointed at the door with an imperious gesture, and Bonnier went to unlock it. Victoria, remaining still erect and calm in her arm-chair, looked at him while he was doing so, and only when Bonnier had opened the door and returned to the table, she rose slowly from her seat.

Now she stood there, drawing herself up to her full height, her face glowing with indignation, a deep blush mantling her cheeks, a disdainful smile playing on the slightly parted lips, the expansive white forehead deeply wrinkled, as cold as marble, and yet concealing under this marble surface a torrent of molten lava, which, as soon as it should burst forth, could not but produce death and destruction. Hers was now a diabolic beauty, and when she turned her eyes toward the three republicans, they glistened like dagger-points.

"I have to make but a brief reply to M. Bonnier's long speech," she said, proudly and calmly.

"This is my answer: I shall obtain those papers in spite of you, and I shall revenge myself for this hour! To your last high-sounding sentences, I answer by another sentence: there is nothing more dangerous than an irritated and insulted woman, for she will revenge herself and imbrue her hands in the blood of those who have insulted her. Roberjot, Bonnier, and Debry, you have insulted me, and I tell you I shall revenge myself. Before three times three days have passed, you will have atoned with your blood for this hour, and may God have mercy on your poor souls!"

She greeted all of them with a haughty nod, and slowly turning around, she proudly crossed the room. The three men looked at her with pale and gloomy faces, and a slight shudder pervaded for a moment the hearts of the republicans, usually so bold and undaunted.

"She looked like an evil demon predicting our future!" murmured Roberjot.

"She will fulfil her word; she will try to assassinate us," said Bonnier. "Did you not see it? Her eyes were moist; no tears were glistening in them, however, only the venom she will discharge at us. Let us be on our guard!"

"Yes, let us beware of the serpent's venom!" exclaimed Jean Debry, with gloomy energy—"let us beware, and most of all, let us be men who cannot be intimidated by the furious threats of a woman."

But Jean Debry knew neither the energy nor the power of this woman whose threats he despised. He did not know that, her anger once aroused, she would not rest until she had taken her revenge. Late in the evening of that day, when all Rastadt was sleeping, Victoria received in her house her two powerful assistants, Count Lehrbach and Colonel Barbaczy, the latter having been invited by a mounted messenger to come to her from Gernsbach.

A long and portentous conference these three persons held in the course of that night, during which they consulted about the best way to punish the French ambassadors, and to take from them the papers which Thugut wished to obtain.

"We must have those papers at any price!" exclaimed Victoria, with flashing eyes.

"Oh, it will only cost a little blood!" shouted Count Lehrbach, in a hollow voice, and laughing hoarsely. "These overbearing French have trampled us under foot for two long years, and tormented us by pricking us with pins. Now we will also trample them under foot and prick them, and if our pins are longer than theirs, who will complain?"

"Thugut wants those papers, and he has for-

given us in advance if they should be a little blood-stained," said Victoria, looking up smilingly to old Colonel Barbaczy, who, with his hands folded on his back, his large shaggy eyebrows gloomily contracted, was slowly pacing the room.

"Barbaczy! Barbaczy!" he muttered, in a low voice, "what will the world say of your old head?" *

"The world will not grudge these hot-blooded French a little blood-letting, and it will praise your surgical skill, my dear Barbaczy," exclaimed Lehrbach, laughing. "The responsibility, besides, does not fall on your shoulders. Who will blame you if your hot-blooded hussars commit some excesses—some highway robberies? You do not order them to assassinate anybody; you only order them to take the papers from the ambassadors, and only to use force if it cannot be helped."

"I shall send fifty hussars to the city to-morrow," said Barbaczy, thoughtfully. "They shall encamp in front of the Ettlinger Gate, so that no one, whosoever it may be, will be able to cross the bridges connecting the city with the suburbs without passing through their ranks."

Victoria approached him, and laying her hands on his shoulders, she looked up to him with a fascinating smile.

"And you will send some of your most intrepid hussars to Lehrbach and to me, that we may tell the brave men what rewards are in store for them if they perform their duty in a satisfactory manner? No, my beautiful god of war, do not shake your silvery locks so wildly—do not threaten me with your frowning brow! Think of Gurgewo, my friend! Do you remember what you swore to me at that time in the trenches when I dressed with my own hands the wound for which you were indebted to a Turkish sabre? Do you remember that you swore to me at that time you would reciprocate my service as soon as it was in your power?"

"I know it, and I am ready to fulfil my oath," said Barbaczy, heaving a sigh.

"Well, my friend, all I ask is this: send to-morrow six of your bravest and wildest hussars to my house, and order them faithfully to carry out what Count Lehrbach and I shall tell them."

"The hussars shall halt at your door to-morrow morning at nine o'clock," said Barbaczy, resolutely.

"And I will admit them!" exclaimed Victoria, smiling. "You will be here, Count Lehrbach, I suppose?"

---

* Barbaczy's own words.—Vide "Literarischer Lodiacus." Edited by Theod. Mundt, 1835. Third number p. 208.

. " I shall be here in order to listen to the wise lessons which the goddess Victoria will teach the sons of Mars," replied Lehrbach, fixing his small, squinting eyes with an admiring air on Victoria's beautiful face. " You will need no other means but your smiles and your beauty in order to inspire these brave soldiers with the most dauntless heroism. Who would not be willing to shed a little French blood, if your lips should promise him a reward ? "

" And what reward are you going to promise to the soldier ? " asked Barbaczy, turning to Madame de Pontet. " What are you going to ask them to do ? "

" Only to seize all the papers of the ambassadors," said Victoria.

" And to examine their bodies if any papers should be concealed there," added Count Lehrbach, laughing.

" And their reward shall be that the hussars will be allowed to look for some other spoils," said Victoria.

" Highway robbery and murder, then," sighed Barbaczy, " and perpetrated by soldiers of my regiment ! Highway robbery and murder ! "

" Fie, what ugly words those are ! and who thinks of murder ? " exclaimed Victoria. " Did we Germans die, then, of the numerous kicks and blows which the French have given us for the last few years ? We will only return those kicks and blows, and the French will assuredly not be so thin-skinned as to die of them on the spot."

" Do as you please," sighed Barbaczy. " Count Lehrbach has the right to issue orders to myself and to my troops, and I owe you the fulfilment of my oath. My hussars will occupy the city to-morrow, and I shall order the French ambassadors to depart forthwith. What is to be done after their departure you may settle with the hussars I shall send to you. I shall take no notice of it."

" And that is a very wise resolution of yours, colonel," said Lehrbach. " 'To know too much gives us the headache,' says our gracious emperor, whenever he returns the dispatches to Baron Thugut without having read them. Send us, then, your hussars to-morrow, and whatever may happen, colonel, we shall not betray each other."

" No, we shall not betray each other ! " repeated Victoria and Barbaczy, with uplifted hands.

" To-morrow, then ! " said Victoria. " Now, good-night, gentlemen ! "

CHAPTER XXIX.

THE ASSASSINATION.

EARLY on the next day a strange and exciting report pervaded the city of Rastadt. Austrian regiments were encamped all round the city, and Sezekler hussars held all the gates. This was the report which filled with astonishment and terror all those who were not initiated into the secrets of the political situation, and who were not familiar with the condition of the negotiations between France and Germany. For, by surrounding the city with troops, in spite of the presence of the French ambassadors, Austria openly violated the treaty stipulating that, until the congress had adjourned *sine die*, neither German nor French troops should approach the city within a circuit of three German miles.

It was reported, too—what the ambassadors as yet remaining in Rastadt had carefully concealed up to this time—that the imperial ambassador, Count Metternich, had quietly left the city several days before, and that the peace commissioners of the empire had the day previous suspended their official functions.

Congress had then dissolved ; the peace commissioners of France and Germany had been in session for two years without accomplishing their task, and the situation looked as ominous and warlike as ever.

Every one resolved to depart ; every trunk was being packed, every carriage drawn forth from its shed. The French actors and ballet-dancers had fled from Rastadt several weeks before at the first rude blast of the approaching storm, like rats leaving a sinking ship. The sounds of joy and mirth had died away, and everywhere only grave and gloomy words were heard, only sorrowful and downcast faces met.

Every one, as we stated above, was preparing to set out, and the French ambassadors, too, were going to leave Rastadt to-day, the twenty-eighth of April. Their carriages were ready for them early in the morning in the courtyard of the castle, when, all at once, some footmen of the embassy, with pale, frightened faces, rushed into the castle and reported that Austrian hussars were posted at the gates and refused to allow any one to leave or enter the city. Even the commander of Rastadt, an officer of the Duke of Baden, had not been permitted by the hussars to ride out of the gate. He had been compelled to return to his headquarters.*

---

* Historical.—Vide " Geheime Geschichte der Rastatter Friedensverhandlungen in Verbindung mit den

"But we will not allow them to prevent us from leaving Rastadt," said Roberjot, resolutely. "They will not dare to interfere with the departure of the representatives of the French Republic!"

"The republic would take bloody revenge for such an outrage, and these Germans are afraid of the anger of the republic!" exclaimed Jean Debry, haughtily.

Bonnier violently shook his black mane, and a gloomy cloud settled on his brow.

"Barbaczy's hussars are encamped in front of the gates, and Victoria de Poutet last night had another interview with Lehrbach and Barbaczy," he said. "If, like both of you, I had a wife and children with me, I should not dare to depart without further guaranties."

At this moment the door opened, and a footman handed Roberjot a letter that had just arrived from the Prussian ambassador, Count Goertz.

Roberjot opened the letter and glanced over it. "The guaranties you referred to, Bonnier, will soon be here," he said, smiling. "It seems the German ambassadors are sharing your apprehensions. They have drawn up a joint letter to Colonel Barbaczy, requiring him to give them a written pledge that there would be no interference with the free departure of the French ambassadors, and that the safety of the latter would not be endangered. Count Goertz, therefore, requests us not to set out until a written reply has been made to the letter of the ambassadors. Shall we delay our departure until then?"

"We will," said Bonnier; "you will not derogate from your republican dignity by consulting the safety of your wives and children. I may say that, inasmuch as I have to take care of no one but myself, and as I know that no care would be of any avail in my case."

"What do you mean, my friend?" asked Jean Debry.

"I mean that I shall die to-day," said Bonnier, solemnly.

Roberjot turned pale. "Hush," he whispered; "let us say nothing about this matter to the women. My wife had a bad dream last night; she saw me weltering in my gore and covered with wounds, and she asserts that her dreams are always fulfilled."

"Roberjot, Bonnier, and Debry, may God have mercy on your poor souls!" muttered Bonnier, in a low voice.

"I do not believe in dreams!" said Jean Debry, with a loud, forced laugh, "and besides, my wife has had no bad dream whatever, and not been warned by fate. Come, let us go to our ladies who are already clad in their travelling-dresses. Let us tell them that we shall, perhaps, be compelled to wait a few hours."

But several hours elapsed, and the messenger the German ambassadors had sent to Colonel Barbaczy's headquarters did not return. Nearly all of the German ambassadors made their appearance at the castle in order to express to the representatives of the French republic their astonishment and profound indignation at this disrespectful delay, and to implore them not to set out until the message had arrived.

The French ambassadors themselves were undecided and gloomy; their ladies were pacing the rooms with sad faces and tearful eyes. Every one was in the most painful and anxious state of mind.

The whole day passed in this manner, and night set in when finally the messenger whom the ambassadors had sent to Colonel Barbaczy, returned to Rastadt. But he did not bring the expected written reply of the colonel. In its place, an Austrian officer of hussars made his appearance; he repaired to the Prussian Count Goertz, at whose house the other ambassadors were assembled, and brought him a verbal reply from Count Barbaczy. The colonel excused himself for not sending a written answer, stating that a pressure of business prevented him from so doing. He at the same time assured the count and the ambassadors that the French ministers could safely depart, and that he would give them twenty-four hours for this purpose.*

The officer brought, however, an autograph letter from Barbaczy to the French ministers, and he repaired to the castle in order to deliver it to them.

This letter from Barbaczy contained the following lines:

"MINISTERS: You will understand that no French citizens can be tolerated within the positions occupied by the Austrian forces. You will not be surprised, therefore, that I am obliged to request you, ministers, to leave Rastadt within twenty-four hours.
"BARBACZY, Colonel."

"Gernsbach, April 28, 1799." †

"Well, what are we to do?" asked Roberjot, when the officer had left them.

"We will set out," said Jean Debry, impetuously.

Staatshändeln dieser Zeit." Von einem Schweizer, part vi.

* Vide Dohm, nach seinem Wollen und Handeln, von Gronau, p. 690.

† Dohm preserved a copy of this letter.—Ibid.

"Yes, we will set out," exclaimed his beautiful young wife, encircling him with her arms. "The air here, it seems to me, smells of blood and murder; and every minute's delay redoubles our danger."

"Poor wife, did they infect you, too, already with their evil forebodings and dreams?" said Jean Debry, tenderly pressing his wife to his heart. "God forbid that they should endanger a single hair of your dear, beautiful head! I am not afraid for myself, but for the sake of my wife and of my two little daughters. For you and for our friends here I would like to choose the best and most prudent course."

"Let us set out," said Madame Roberjot; "the terrible dream last night was intended to give us warning. Death threatens us if we remain here any longer. Oh, my husband, I love nothing on earth but you alone; you are my love and my happiness! I would die of a broken heart if I should lose you! But no, no, not lose! We live and die together. He who kills you must also take my life!"

"They shall not kill us, my beloved," said Roberjot, feelingly; "life, I trust, has many joys yet in store for us, and we will return to our country in order to seek them there. Bonnier, you alone are silent. Do not you believe also that we ought to set out to-night?"

Bonnier started up from his gloomy reverie. "Let us set out," he said, "we must boldly confront the terrors from which we cannot escape. Let us set out."

"Be it so!" shouted Roberjot and Jean Debry. "The republic will protect her faithful sons!"

"And may God protect us in His infinite mercy," exclaimed Madame Roberjot, falling on her knees.

And Jean Debry's wife knelt down by her side, drawing her little girls down with her.

"Let us pray, my children, for your father, for ourselves, and for our friends," she said, folding the children's hands.

While the women were praying, the men issued their last orders to the servants and to the postilions.

At length every thing was in readiness, and if they really wished to set out, it had to be done at once.

Roberjot and Jean Debry approached softly and with deep emotion their wives, who were kneeling and praying still, and raised them tenderly.

"Now be strong and courageous—be wives worthy of your husbands," they whispered. "Dry your tears and come! The carriages are waiting for us. Come, come, France is waiting for us!"

"Or the grave!" muttered Bonnier, who accompanied the others to the court-yard where the carriages were standing.

The ambassadors with their wives and attendants had finally taken seats in the carriages. Roberjot and his wife occupied the first carriage; Bonnier, the second; Jean Debry with his wife and daughters, the third; in the fourth, fifth, and sixth were the secretaries of legation, the clerks and servants of the ambassadors.

The last coach-door was closed; a profound momentary silence succeeded the noise and turmoil that had prevailed up to this time. Then the loud, ringing voice of Roberjot asked from the first carriage, "All ready?"

"All ready!" was the reply from the other carriages.

"Then let us start," shouted Roberjot, and his carriage immediately commenced moving. The other five carriages followed slowly and heavily.

The night was chilly and dark. The sky was covered with heavy clouds. Not the faintest trace of the moon, not a star was visible. In order that they might not lose their way, and see the bridge across the Rhine, a man, bearing a torch, had to precede the carriages. But the gale moved the flame so violently that it now seemed near going out, and then again flared up and cast a glare over the long procession of the carriages. Then every thing once more became dark and gloomy and ominously still.

The torch-bearer, preceding the foremost carriage, vigorously marched ahead on the road. All at once it seemed to him as though black figures were emerging from both sides of the highway and softly flitting past him. But assuredly, he must have been mistaken; it could not have been any thing but the shadows of the trees standing on both sides of the road.

No, now he saw it again, quite plainly. The shadows were horsemen, softly riding along on both sides of the highway.

He raised his torch and looked at the horsemen. There was quite a cavalcade of them. Now they crossed the ditch and took position across the road, thus preventing the carriages from passing on.

The torch-bearer stood still and turned around in order to shout to the postilions to halt. But only an inarticulated, shrill cry escaped from his throat, for at the same moment two of the horsemen galloped up and struck at him with their flashing swords. He parried the strokes with his torch, his only weapon, so that one of the swords did not hit him at all, while the other only slightly touched his shoulder.

"What is the matter?" shouted Roberjot, in an angry voice, from the first carriage.

The horsemen seized the arms of the torch-bearer and dragged him toward the carriage. "Light!" they shouted to him, and quite a squad of merry horsemen was now coming up behind them. When they dashed past the torch, the frightened torch-bearer was able to see their wild, bearded faces, their flashing eyes, and the silver lace on their uniforms.

The torch betrayed the secret of the night, and caused the Sezekler hussars of Barbaczy's regiment to be recognized.

They now surrounded the first carriage, shouting furiously, and shattering the windows with their sabres.

"Minister Roberjot! Are you Minister Roberjot?" asked a dozen wild, howling voices.

Roberjot's grave and threatening face, illuminated by the glare of the torch, appeared immediately in the aperture of the window. "Yes, I am Roberjot," he said, loudly; "I am the ambassador of France, and here is the passport furnished me by the ambassador of the Elector of Mentz."

He exhibited the paper, but the hussars took no notice of it; four vigorous arms dragged Roberjot from the carriage, and before he had time to stretch out his hand toward his pistols, the sabres of the hussars fell down upon his head and shoulders.

A terrible yell was heard, but it was not Roberjot who had uttered it; it was his wife, who appeared with pale and distorted features in the coach door, hastening to her beloved husband, to save him or to die with him.

But two stout arms kept her back—the arms of the valet de chambre who, perceiving that his master was hopelessly lost, wanted to protect at least his mistress from the murderous sabres of the hussars.

"Let me go, let me go; I will die with him!" she cried; but the faithful servant would not loosen his hold, and, unable to reach her husband, she had to witness his assassination by the hussars, who cut him with their sabres until he lay weltering in his gore.

"He is dead!" shrieked his wife, and her wail aroused Roberjot once more from his stupor. He opened his eyes and looked once more at his wife. "Sauvez! sauvez!" he shouted, in a voice full of anguish. "Oh!—"

"What! not dead yet?" roared the hussars, and they struck him again.

Now he was dying. That loud, awful death-rattle was his last life-struggle. The valet de chambre in order to prevent her from hearing that awful sound, with his hands closed the ears of his mistress, who, petrified with horror, was looking at her dying husband.

But she did not hear it; she had fainted in the servant's arms. At this moment a heavy hand was laid on his shoulder, and the wild, bearded face of a hussar stared at him.

"Footman?" asked the hussar, in his broken Hungarian dialect.

"Yes, footman!" said the valet de chambre, in broken German. The hussar smilingly patted his shoulder, and, with his other hand, pulled the watch from his vest-pocket, kindly saying to him, "Footman, stay here. No harm will befall him!" He then bent forward, and with a quick grasp, tore the watch and chain from the neck of Roberjot's fainting wife.

His task was now accomplished, and he galloped to the second carriage, to which the other hussars had just dragged the torch-bearer, and which they had completely surrounded.

"Bonnier, alight!" howled the hussars, furiously—"Bonnier, alight!"

"Here I am!" said Bonnier, opening the coach door; "here—"

They did not give him time to finish the sentence. They dragged him from the carriage, and struck him numerous blows amidst loud laughter and yells. Bonnier did not defend himself; he did not parry a single one of their strokes; without uttering a cry or a groan, he sank to the ground. His dying lips only whispered a single word. That word was, "Victoria!"

The six hussars who crowded around him now stopped in their murderous work. They saw that Bonnier was dead—really dead—and that their task was accomplished. Now commenced the appropriation of the spoils, the reward that had been promised to them. Four of them rushed toward the carriage in order to search it and to take out all papers, valuables, and trunks; the two others searched and undressed the warm corpse of Bonnier with practised hands.

Then the six hussars rushed after their comrades toward the third carriage—toward Jean Debry. But the others had already outstripped them. They had dragged Debry, his wife, and his daughters from the carriage; they were robbing and searching the lady and the children, and cutting Jean Debry with their sabres.

He dropped to the ground; his respiration ceased, and a convulsive shudder passed through the bloody figure, and then it lay cold and motionless in the road.

"Dead! dead!" shouted the hussars, triumphantly. "The three men are killed; now for the spoils! The carriages are ours, with every thing in them! Come, let us search the fourth carriage. We will kill no more; we will only seize the spoils!"

And all were shouting and exulting, "Ho for the spoils! for the spoils! Every thing is ours!" And the wild crowd rushed forward, and Jean Debry lay motionless, a bleeding corpse by the side of the carriage.

Profound darkness enveloped the scene of horror and carnage. The torch had gone out; no human eye beheld the corpses with their gaping wounds. The ladies had been taken back into the carriages by their servants; the hussars were engaged in plundering the three remaining carriages, the inmates of which, however, forewarned in time by the shrieks and groans that had reached them from the scene of Roberjot's assassination, had left and fled across the marshy meadows to the wall of the castle garden. Climbing over it and hastening through the garden, they reached the city and spread everywhere the terrible tidings of the assassination of the ambassadors.

CHAPTER XXX.

JEAN DEBRY.

As soon as the report of the dreadful occurrence had been circulated, a dense crowd gathered in the streets of Rastadt, and for the first time for two years the ambassadors of all the German powers were animated by one and the same idea, and acting in concord and harmony. They repaired in a solemn procession to the Ettlinger gate, headed by Count Goertz and Baron Dohm; the others followed in pairs, Count Lehrbach, the Austrian ambassador, being the only one who had not joined the procession. But the guard at the gate refused to let them pass, and when they had finally succeeded, after long and tedious negotiations, in being permitted to leave the city, they were met outside of the gate by the Austrian Captain Burkhard and his hussars.

Count Goertz went to meet him with intrepid courage. "Did you hear that an infamous murder has been perpetrated on the French ambassadors not far from the city?"

"I have heard of it," said the captain, shrugging his shoulders.

"And what steps have you taken in order to save the unfortunate victims, if possible?"

"I have sent an officer and two hussars for the purpose of ascertaining the particulars."

"That is not sufficient, sir!" exclaimed Count Goertz. "You must do more than that; you must strain every nerve on this occasion, for this is not an ordinary murder, but your honor, sir, is at stake, as well as the honor of your monarch and the honor of the German nation!"

"The honor of the German nation is at stake," shouted the ambassadors, unanimously. "Our honor has been sullied by the assassination!"

But the captain remained cold and indifferent. "It is a deplorable misunderstanding," he said. "It is true, the patrols were going the rounds at night, and such things may occur at this time. The French ministers should not have set out by night. The crime has been committed, and who is to blame for it? It was not done by anybody's order." *

"Who would deem it possible that such an outrage should have been committed by order of any commanding officer?" exclaimed Count Goertz, indignantly.

"Ah, yes, an outrage indeed!" said Burkhard, shrugging his shoulders. "A few ambassadors have been killed. A few of our generals, too, were killed during the last few years." †

Count Goertz turned to the other ambassadors with an air of profound indignation. "You see, gentlemen," he said, "we need not hope for much assistance here; let us seek it elsewhere. Let some of us repair in person to Colonel Barbaczy's headquarters at Gernsbach, while the rest of us will go to the spot where the murders were committed. If the captain here declines giving us an escort for that purpose, we shall repair thither without one; and if we should lose our lives by so doing, Germany will know how to avenge us!"

"I will give you an escort," said Burkhard, somewhat abashed by the energetic bearing of the count.

While the ambassadors were negotiating with the captain at the Ettlinger gate, the hussars were incessantly engaged in plundering the six carriages. After finishing the first three carriages, they ordered the ladies and servants to reenter them and to await quietly and silently what farther would be done in relation to them. No one dared to offer any resistance—no one was strong enough to oppose them. Dismay had perfectly paralyzed and stupefied all of them. Madame Debry lay in her carriage with open, tearless eyes, and neither the lamentations nor the kisses of her daughters were able to arouse her from her stupor. Madame Roberjot was wringing her hands, and amidst

---

* The literal reply of Captain Burkhard.—Vide "Report of the German Ambassadors concerning the Assassination of the French Ministers near Rastadt."

† Ibid.

heart-rending sobs she was wailing all the time, "They have hacked him to pieces before my eyes!" *

No one paid any attention to the corpses lying with their gaping wounds in the adjoining ditch. Night alone covered them with its black pall; night alone saw that Jean Debry all at once commenced stirring slightly, that he opened his eyes and raised his head in order to find out what was going on around him. With the courage of despair he had been playing the *rôle* of a motionless corpse as long as the hussars were in his neighborhood; and now that he no longer heard any noise in his vicinity, it was time for him to think of saving himself.

He remained in a sitting position in the ditch and listened. His head was so heavy that he had not sufficient strength to hold it erect, it dropped again upon his breast; from a burning, painful wound the blood was running over his face into his mouth, and it was the only cooling draught for his parched lips. He wanted to raise his arm in order to close this wound and to stanch the blood, but the arm fell down by his side, heavy and lame, and he then felt that it was likewise severely injured.

And yet, bleeding and hacked as he was, he was alive, and it was time for him to think of preserving his life. For over yonder, in the carriage, there resounded the wail of his children, and the lamentations of his servants. His wife's voice, however, he did not hear. Was she not there? Had she also been assassinated?

He dared not inquire for her at this moment. He had to save himself, and he was determined to do it.

He arose slowly, and heedless of the pain it caused him. Every thing around him remained silent. No one had seen him rise; night with its black pall protected him. It protected him now as he walked a few steps toward the forest, closely adjoining the highway. At length he reached the forest, and the shades of darkness and of the woods covered the tall, black form that now disappeared in the thicket.

But his enemies might be lurking for him in this thicket. Every step forward might involve him in fresh dangers. Exhausted and in despair, Jean Debry supported his tottering body against a tree, the sturdy trunk of which he encircled with his arms. This tree was now his only protector, the only friend on whom he could rely. To this tree alone he determined to intrust his life.

* "*Ils l'ont haché devant mes yeux!*"—Lodiacus, vol. iii., p. 195.

Heedless of his wounded arm and the racking pains of his other injuries, Jean Debry climbed the knotty trunk; seizing a large branch, he raised himself from bough to bough. A few birds, aroused from their slumbers, arose from the foliage and flitted away. Jean Debry followed them with his eyes, and whispered, "You will not betray me!"

On the highest bough, in the densest foliage, he sat down, gasping with exhaustion, and groaning with pain. In his utter prostration after the extraordinary effort he had just made, he leaned his head against the trunk of the tree, the dense branches of which closely enveloped him, and gave a roof to his head and a resting-place to his feet.

"Here I am safe—here no one will look for me!" he muttered, and he fell asleep, prostrated by his sufferings and loss of blood.

Night with its dark mantle covered him up and fanned his feverish brow with its cooling air; the foliage of the tree laid itself soft and fresh around his burning cheeks, and delightful dreams descended from heaven to comfort this poor, tormented human soul.

After several hours of invigorating sleep, Jean Debry was awakened, not, however, by the rude hands of men, but heaven itself aroused him by the torrents of a heavy shower.

Oh, how refreshing were these cold drops for his parched lips! How gently did this soft and tepid water wash the blood and dust from his wounds! How delightfully did it bathe his poor benumbed limbs!

He felt greatly invigorated, and courageously determined to make further efforts for the preservation of his life. He slowly glided down from the tree and stood once more on the ground.

The shower was constantly on the increase, and the rain became now, at daybreak, Jean Debry's protector. When men forsake their poor, tormented fellow-beings, Nature takes pity on them and encircles them with her saving and protecting maternal arms.

The rain protected Jean Debry; it washed the dust and blood from his garments, and made him resemble the other men who had gathered in a large crowd on the road, not far from where he emerged from the forest. All of them were looking with pale faces and expressions of unbounded horror at some objects lying in their midst. What was it that rendered this crowd, generally so noisy and turbulent, to-day so silent and grave?

Jean Debry penetrated further into their midst, and he discovered now with a shudder what riveted the attention of the vast gathering on the road.

He beheld the bloody and mutilated corpses of his two friends—the dead bodies of Roberjot and Bonnier.

Jean Debry closely compressed his lips in order to keep back the cry that forced itself from his breast; with the whole energy of his will he suppressed the tears that started from his eyes, and he turned away in order to return to Rastadt.

The rain protected Jean Debry. The rain had driven the soldiers at the gate into the guard-room, and the sentinel into the sentry-box. No one took any notice of this wet and dripping man when he entered the gate.

He quietly walked up the street, directly toward the house inhabited by Count Goertz, the Prussian ambassador. He entered the house with firm steps, and hastened into the anteroom which, as he formerly used to do, he wanted to cross in order to walk to the count's room without sending in his name.

But the footmen kept him back; they refused to admit this pale man with the lacerated face and tattered clothes to their master's private room.

"Don't you know me any longer, my friends?" he asked, sadly. "Am I so disfigured that no one of you is able to recognize Jean Debry?"

The footmen now recognized his voice, and the *valet de chambre* hastened to open the door of the count's study, and to shout, in a loud voice, "His excellency, the French ambassador Debry!"

Count Goertz uttered a joyful cry, and hastily rose from the sofa on which, exhausted by the efforts of the terrible night, he had sought a little rest.

Jean Debry entered the room. He made a truly lamentable appearance as he approached the count, and fixed his dimmed, bloodshot eyes upon him with an expression of unutterable anguish.

"Are my wife and children safe?" he asked, breathlessly.

"Yes, they are safe!" exclaimed the count.

And Jean Debry, the austere republican, the scoffing infidel, Jean Debry fell upon his knees! Lifting up his arms toward heaven, his eyes filled with tears, he exclaimed: "Divine Providence, if I have hitherto refused to acknowledge thy benefits, oh, forgive me!" [*]

"And punish those who have perpetrated this horrible crime!" added Count Goertz, folding his hands, and uttering a fervent prayer. "O God, reveal the authors of this misdeed; let us find

those who have committed this outrage, lest it may remain a bloody stigma on the fame of our country! Have mercy on poor Germany, on whose brow this mark of infamy is now burning, and who will be obliged to pour out rivers of her best blood in order to atone for this crime, and to clear her sullied honor! Have mercy on all of us, and give us courage to brave the storms which this horrible event will assuredly call down! Have mercy, O God; punish only the assassins, but not our native land!"

This prayer of Count Goertz was not fulfilled. The real instigators of the murder were never detected and punished, although the Austrian court, in a public manifesto to the German nation, promised a searching investigation of the whole affair, and a rigorous chastisement of the assassins. But the investigation was but a very superficial proceeding, and its results were never published. The Sezekler hussars publicly sold, on the following day, the watches, snuff-boxes, and valuables they had stolen from the French ambassadors. Some of them even acknowledged openly that they had perpetrated the murder, at the instigation of their officers. But nobody thought of arresting them, or calling them to account for their crime. It is true, after a while some of them were imprisoned and tried. But the proceedings instituted against them were never published, although the Austrian court had expressly promised to lay the minutes of the commission trying the prisoners, and the results of the whole investigation, before the public. In reality, however, the Austrian authorities tried to hush up the whole affair, so that the world might forget it. And it was forgotten, and remained unpunished. In diplomatic circles, however, the real instigators of the outrage were quite well known. "It was," says the author of the "Memoirs of a German Statesman" (Count Schlitz), "it was a man who, owing to his exalted position, played a very prominent part at Rastadt; not a very noble one, however. He was actuated by vindictiveness, and he was determined to seize the most secret papers of the ambassadors at any price. The general archives, however, had been forwarded to Strasburg several days before. He had found willing tools in the brutal hussars. These wretches believed that what a man of high standing asked them to do was agreeable to the will of their imperial master. Baseness is easily able to mislead stupidity, and soldiers thus became the assassins of unarmed men, who stood under the sacred protection of international law."

The excitement and indignation produced by this horrible crime were general throughout Europe, and every one recognized in it the bloody

---

[*] He exclaimed: "*Divine Providence, si j'ai méconnu tes bienfaits jusqu'ici, pardonne!*"—Lodtacus, III., p. 195.

seeds of a time of horrors and untold evils; every one was satisfied that France would take bloody revenge for the assassination of her ambassadors. In fact, as soon as the tidings from Rastadt penetrated beyond the Rhine, there arose throughout the whole of France a terrible cry of rage and revenge. The intelligence reached Mentz in the evening, when the theatre was densely crowded. The commander ordered the news to be read from the stage, and the furious public shouted, " *Vengeance! vengeance! et la mort aux Allemands!* " *

In Paris, solemn obsequies were performed for the murdered ambassadors. The seats which Bonnier and Roberjot had formerly occupied in the hall of the *Corps Legislatif* were covered with their bloody garments. When the roll was called and their names were read, the president rose and replied solemnly: "Assassinated at Rastadt!" The clerks then exclaimed: "May their blood be brought home to the authors of their murder!"

CHAPTER XXXI.

THE COALITION.

COUNT HAUGWITZ, the Prussian minister of foreign affairs, had just returned from a journey he had made with the young king to Westphalia. In his dusty travelling-costume, and notwithstanding his exhaustion after the fatigues of the trip, as soon as he had entered his study, he had hastily written two letters, and then handed them to his footman, ordering him to forward them at once to their address, to the ambassadors of Russia and England. Only then he had thrown himself on his bed, but issued strict orders to awaken him as soon as the two ambassadors had entered the house.

Scarcely an hour had elapsed when the footman awakened the count, informing him that the two ambassadors had just arrived at the same time, and were waiting for him in the small reception-room.

The minister hastily rose from his conch, and without devoting a single glance to his toilet and to his somewhat dishevelled wig, he crossed his study and entered the reception-room, where Lord Grenville and Count Panin were waiting for him.

"Gentlemen," said the count, after a hurried bow, "be kind enough to look at my toilet, and then I hope you will excuse me for daring to request you to call upon me, instead of coming to

you as I ought to have done. But you see I have not even doffed my travelling habit, and it would not have behooved me to call on you in such a costume; but the intelligence I desire to communicate is of such importance that I wished to lose no time in order to lay it before you, and hence I took the liberty of inviting you to see me."

"As far as I am concerned, I willingly accepted your invitation," said Lord Grenville, deliberately, "for in times like these we can well afford to disregard the requirements of etiquette."

"That I was no less eager to follow your call," said Count Panin, with a courteous smile, "you have seen from the fact that I arrived at the same time with the distinguished ambassador of Great Britain. But now, gentlemen, a truce to compliments; let us come to the point directly, and without any further circumlocution. For the six months that I have been here at Berlin, in order to negotiate with Prussia about the coalition question, I have been so incessantly put off with empty phrases, that I am heartily tired of that diet and long for more substantial food."

"Your longing will be gratified to-day, Count Panin," said Count Haugwitz, with a proud smile, inviting the gentlemen, by a polite gesture, to take seats on the sofa, while he sat down in an arm-chair opposite them. "Yes, you will find to-day a good and nourishing diet, and I hope you will be content with the cook who has prepared it for you. I may say that I am that cook, and believe me, gentlemen, the task of preparing that food for you has not been a very easy one."

"You have induced the King of Prussia at length to join the coalition, and to enter into an alliance with Russia, England, and Austria against the French Republic?" asked Count Panin, joyfully.

"You have told his majesty that England is ready to pay large subsidies as soon as Prussia leads her army into the field against France?" asked Lord Grenville.

"Gentlemen," said Count Haugwitz, in a slightly sarcastic tone, "I feel greatly flattered by your impetuous inquiries, for they prove to me how highly you value an alliance with Prussia. Permit me, however, to communicate to you quietly and composedly the whole course of negotiations. You know that I had the honor of accompanying my royal master on his trip to our Westphalian possessions, where his majesty was going to review an army of sixty thousand men."

"It would have been better to send these sixty thousand men directly into the field, instead of losing time by useless parades," muttered Count Panin.

* " Vengeance! vengeance! and death to the Germans! "

9

The minister seemed not to have heard his words, and continued:

"His majesty established his headquarters at Peterhagen, and there we were informed that Archduke Charles of Austria was holding the Rhine against Bernadotte and Jourdan, and that the imperial army, under the command of Kray, in Italy, had been victorious, too; it is true, however the Russian auxiliary army, under Field-Marshal Suwarrow, had greatly facilitated Kray's successful operations. This intelligence did not fail to make a powerful impression upon my young king, and I confess upon myself too. Hitherto, you know, I had always been opposed to a war against France, and I had deemed it most expedient for Prussia to avoid hostilities against the republic. But the brilliant achievements of Russia and Austria in Italy, and the victories of Archduke Charles on the Rhine, seem to prove at length that the lucky star of France is paling, and that it would be advantageous for Prussia openly to join the adversaries of the republic in their attack."

"A very bold and magnanimous resolution," said Count Panin, with a sarcastic smile.

"A resolution influenced somewhat by the British subsidies I have promised to Prussia, I suppose?" asked Lord Grenville.

"Let me finish my statement, gentlemen," said Count Haugwitz, courteously. "The king, undecided as to the course he ought to pursue, assembled at Peterhagen a council of war, our great commander, Ferdinand, duke of Brunswick, of course, having been invited to be present. His majesty requested us to state honestly and sincerely whether we were in favor of war or peace with France. The duke of Brunswick was, of course, the first speaker who replied to the king; he voted for war. He gave his reasons in a fiery and energetic speech, and demonstrated to the king that at a time when England was about to send an army to Holland, an advance into Holland by our own army would be highly successful. For my part, I unconditionally assented to the duke's opinion, and Baron Köckeritz declaring for it likewise, the king did not hesitate any longer, but took a great and bold resolution. He ordered the Duke of Brunswick to draw up a memorial, stating in extenso why Prussia ought to participate in the war against France, and to send in at the same time a detailed plan of the campaign. He instructed me to return forthwith to Berlin, and while he would continue his journey to Wesel, to hasten to the capital for the purpose of informing you, gentlemen, that the king will join the coalition, and of settling with you the particulars—"

At this moment the door of the reception-room was hastily opened, and the first secretary of the minister made his appearance.

"Pardon me, your excellency, for disturbing you," he said, handing a sealed letter to the count, "but a courier has just arrived from the king's headquarters with an autograph letter from his majesty. He had orders to deliver this letter immediately to your excellency, because it contained intelligence of the highest importance."

"Tell the courier that the orders of his majesty have been carried out," said Count Haugwitz; "and you, gentlemen, I am sure you will permit me to open this letter from my king in your presence. It may contain some important particulars in relation to our new alliance."

The two gentlemen assured him of their consent, and Count Haugwitz opened the letter. When he commenced reading it, his face was as unruffled as ever, but his features gradually assumed a graver expression, and the smile disappeared from his lips.

The two ambassadors, who were closely watching the count's countenance, could not fail to notice this rapid change in his features, and their faces now assumed likewise a gloomier air.

Count Haugwitz, however, seemed unable to master the contents of the royal letter; he constantly read it anew, as though he were seeking in its words for a hidden and mysterious meaning. He was so absorbed in the perusal of the letter that he had apparently become entirely oblivious of the presence of the two gentlemen, until a slight coughing of the English ambassador aroused him from his musing.

"Pardon me, gentlemen," he said, hastily, and in evident embarrassment; "this letter contains some intelligence which greatly astonishes me."

"I hope it will not interfere with the accession of Prussia to the coalition?" said Panin, fixing his eyes upon the countenance of the minister.

"Not at all," said Count Haugwitz, quickly and smilingly. "The extraordinary news is this: his majesty the king will reach Berlin within this hour, and orders me to repair to him at once."

"The king returns to Berlin!" exclaimed Count Panin.

"And did not your excellency tell us just now that the king had set out for Wesel?" asked Lord Grenville, with his usual stoical equanimity.

"I informed you, gentlemen, of what occurred two weeks ago," said Count Haugwitz, shrugging his shoulders.

"What! Two weeks ago? Nevertheless, your excellency has just arrived at Berlin, and are wearing yet your travelling-habit?"

"That is very true. I left Minden two weeks ago, but the impassable condition of the roads compelled me to travel with snail-like slowness. My carriage every day stuck in an ocean of mire, so that I had to send for men from the adjoining villages in order to set it going again. The axletree broke twice, and I was obliged to remain several days in the most forsaken little country towns until I succeeded in getting my carriage repaired."

"The king seems to have found better roads," said Count Panin, with a lurking glance. "The journey to Wesel has been a very rapid one, at all events."

"The king, it seems, has given up that journey and concluded on the road to return to the capital," said Count Haugwitz, in an embarrassed manner.

"It would be very deplorable if the king should as rapidly change his mind in relation to his other resolutions!" exclaimed Lord Grenville.

"Your excellency does not fear, then, lest this sudden return of the king should have any connection with our plans?" asked Panin. "The king has authorized you to negotiate with the English ambassador, Sir Thomas Grenville, and with myself, the representative of the Emperor Paul, of Russia, about forming an alliance for the purpose of driving the rapacious, revolutionary, and bloodthirsty French Republic beyond the Rhine, and restoring tranquillity to menaced Europe?"

"It is true the king gave me such authority two weeks ago," said Count Haugwitz, uneasily, "and I doubt not for a single moment that his majesty is now adhering to this opinion. But you comprehend, gentlemen, that I must now hasten to wait on the returning king, in order to receive further instructions from him."

"That means, Count Haugwitz, that you have invited us to call on you in order to tell us that we may go again?" asked Panin, frowning.

"I am in despair, gentlemen, at this unfortunate coincidence," said Count Haugwitz, anxiously. "It is, however, impossible for me now to enter into further explanations. I must repair immediately to the palace, and I humbly beg your pardon for this unexpected interruption of our conference."

"I accept your apology as sincerely as it was offered, and have the honor to bid you farewell," said Panin, bowing and turning toward the door. Count Haugwitz hastened to accompany him. When he arrived at the door, and was about to leave the room, Count Panin turned around once more.

"Count Haugwitz," he said, in a blunt voice, "be kind enough to call the attention of the king to the fact that my imperial master, who is very fond of resolute men and measures, prefers an open and resolute enemy to a neutral and irresolute friend. He who wants to be no one's enemy and everybody's friend, will soon find out that he has no friends whatever, and that no one thanks him for not committing himself in any direction. It is better after all to have a neighbor with whom we are living in open enmity, than one on whose assistance we are never able to depend, and who, whenever we are at war with a third power, contents himself with doing nothing at all and assisting no one. Be kind enough to say that to his majesty."

He bowed haughtily, and entered the anteroom with a sullen face.

Count Haugwitz turned around and met the stern, cold glance of the English ambassador, who was also approaching the door with slow and measured steps.

"Count Haugwitz," said Lord Grenville, quietly, "I have the honor to tell you that, in case the King of Prussia will not now, distinctly and unmistakably, declare his intention of joining the coalition between Russia, Austria, and England, we shall use the subsidies we had promised to pay to Prussia for an army of twenty-five thousand men, in some other way. Besides, I beg you to remind his majesty of the words of his great ancestor, the Elector Frederick William. That brave and great sovereign said: 'I have learned already what it means to be neutral. One may have obtained the best terms, and, in spite of them, will be badly treated. Hence I have sworn never to be neutral again, and it would hurt my conscience to act in a different manner.' * I have the honor, count, to bid you farewell."

And Lord Grenville passed the count with a stiff bow, and disappeared in the door of the anteroom.

Count Haugwitz heaved a profound sigh, and wiped off the perspiration pearling in large drops on his brow. He then took the king's letter from his side-pocket and perused it once more.

"It is the king's handwriting," he said, shaking his head, "and it is also his peculiar laconic style." And, as if to satisfy himself by hearing the contents of the letter, he read aloud:

"Do not enter into any negotiations with the ambassadors of Russia and Great Britain. We will hold another council of war. I am on my way to Berlin. Within an hour after receipt of

---

* Häusser's "History of Germany," vol. ii., p 281.

these lines, I shall expect to see you in my cabinet. Yours, affectionately,

' " FREDERICK WILLIAM."

"Yes, yes, the king has written that," said Haugwitz, folding the letter; "I must hastily dress, therefore, and repair to the palace. I am anxious to know whence this new wind is blowing, and who has succeeded in persuading the king to change his mind. Should my old friend, Köckeritz, after all, be favorable to France? It would have been better for him to inform me confidentially, and we might have easily agreed; for I am by no means hostile to France, and I am quite ready to vote for peace, if there be a chance to maintain it. Or should the young king really have come to this conclusion without being influenced by anybody? Why, that would be a dangerous innovation! We should take quick and decisive steps against it. Well, we will see! I will go and dress."

———————

CHAPTER XXXII.

THE FRIEND OF PEACE.

THE king, with his wonted punctuality, had reached Berlin precisely at the specified time, and when Count Haugwitz arrived at the palace he was immediately conducted to the king, who was waiting for him in his cabinet.

Count Haugwitz exchanged a rapid glance with Baron Köckeritz, who was standing in a bay window, and then approached the king, who was pacing the room with slow steps and a gloomy air.

He nodded to the minister, and silently continued his promenade across the room for some time after his arrival. He then stepped to his desk, which was covered with papers and documents, and sitting down on a plain cane chair in front of it, he invited the gentlemen to take seats by his side.

"The courier reached you in time, I suppose?" he said, turning to Count Haugwitz.

"Your majesty, your royal letter reached me while holding a conference with the ambassadors of Russia and Great Britain, and just when I was about to inform them of your majesty's resolution to join the coalition."

"You had not done so, then?" asked the king, hastily. "It was your first conference, then?"

"Yes, your majesty, it was our first conference. I invited the ambassadors immediately after my return to call on me."

"It took you, then, two weeks to travel from Minden to Berlin!"

"Yes, your majesty, two weeks."

"And yet these gentlemen are in favor of an advance of the army!" exclaimed the king, vehemently. "Yes, if all of my soldiers were encamped directly on the frontier of Holland and had their base of supplies there! But in order to send a sufficient army to Holland, I should have to withdraw a portion of my soldiers from the provinces of Silesia and Prussia. They would have to march across Westphalia, across the same Westphalia where it took you with your carriage two weeks to travel from Minden to Berlin. And my soldiers have no other carriages but their feet. They would stick in that dreadful mire by hundreds and thousands; they would perish there of hunger, and that march would cost me more men than a great, decisive battle. I had given you my word that I would join the coalition, Count Haugwitz; I had even authorized you to negotiate with the ambassadors of Russia and Great Britain, but on the road to Wesel I was obliged to change my mind. Ask Baron Köckeritz what we had to suffer on the first day of our journey, and how far we had got after twelve hours' travelling."

"Yes, indeed, it was a terrible trip," said General von Köckeritz, heaving a sigh. "In spite of the precautions of the coachman, his majesty's carriage was upset five times in a single day, and finally it stuck so firmly in the mud that we had to send for assistance to the neighboring villages in order to set it going once more. We were twelve hours on the road, and made only three German miles during that time."

"And we had to stop over night in a miserable village, where we scarcely found a bed to rest our bruised and worn-out limbs," said the king, indignantly. "And I should expose my army to such fatigues and sufferings! I should, heedless of all considerations of humanity, and solely in obedience to political expediency, suffer them to perish in those endless marshes, that would destroy the artillery and the horses of the cavalry. And all that for what purpose? In order to drag Prussia violently into a war which might be avoided by prudence and by a sagacious reserve; in order to hasten to the assistance of other powers not even threatened by France, and only in return to draw upon ourselves her wrath and enmity!"

"But at the same time the sympathies of all Europe," said General von Köckeritz, eagerly. "Your majesty has permitted me to speak my mind at all times openly and honestly, and I must therefore persist in what I previously said to you.

Now or never is the time for Prussia to give up her neutrality, and to assume a decided attitude. France has placed herself in antagonism with all law and order, and with all treaties consecrated by centuries of faithful observance; she is threatening all monarchies and dynasties, and is trying to win over the nations to her republican ideas. And at the head of this French Republic there is a young general, whose glory is filling the whole world, who has attached victory to his colors, and who intoxicates the nations by his republican phrases of liberty and fraternity, so that, in their mad joy, they overturn thrones, expel their sovereigns, and awake then from their ecstasy, under the republican yoke of France. Your majesty, I believe it to be the duty of every prince to preserve his people from such errors, and, jointly with his people, to raise a bulwark against the evil designs of France. Austria and Russia have already begun this holy task; their heroic armies have driven back on all sides the hosts of the overbearing French, who have been compelled to abandon their conquests in Italy and Switzerland. If your majesty should join England, occupy Holland, restore that country to its legitimate sovereign, and menace the northern frontier of France, while Austria is menacing her southern frontier, the arrogance of the republic would be tamed, the overflowing torrent would be forced back into its natural bed, and Europe would have at last peace and tranquillity."

"First of all, every one ought to think of himself," said the king, sharply. "Prussia has hitherto enjoyed peace and tranquillity, and I believe it to be my principal task to preserve these blessings to my country. I am no ruler hankering after glory and honors; I do not want to make any conquests, nor to acquire any new territory, but I will content myself with the humble renown of having fulfilled my duties as a ruler to the best of my ability, and according to the dictates of my conviction, as the father and friend of my people. Hence I have not dared to identify my name with that of my great ancestor, Frederick the Second, and call myself Frederick the Third, for a name imposes obligations, and I know very well that I am no hero and genius, like Frederick the Great. I assumed, therefore, the name of Frederick William, as the successor of my peaceable father, Frederick William the Second. It is true, Frederick William the Second has waged a war against France, but precisely that war has satisfied me that a war with France may involve Prussia in the greatest dangers and calamities. I participated in the campaign of 1792, gentlemen, and I must honestly confess that I feel little inclination to resume a war which, at best, will only produce sacrifices for us, and no reward whatever."

"There is a reward, however, your majesty," said Count Haugwitz, solemnly. "It is the preservation of the thrones, and of monarchical principles. We cannot fail to perceive that the thrones are being menaced, and those republics of America, France, and Italy are teaching the nations very dangerous lessons—the lessons of self-government and popular sovereignty. That insatiable General Bonaparte has attached these two words to his colors, and if the princes do not combat him with united strength, and try to take those colors from him, he will soon carry them into the midst of all nations, who will rapturously hail him, and desire to follow the example of France."

"I have no fears for myself," said the king, calmly; "but even if I should be so unfortunate as to be obliged to doubt the love and fidelity of my people, the thought of my personal safety and of the fate of my dynasty ought not to exert a decisive influence upon my resolutions concerning the welfare of my country. I told you before, I want to be the father of my country; a good father always thinks first of the welfare of his children, and tries to promote it; only when he has succeeded in doing so he thinks of himself."

"A good father ought to strive, first of all, to preserve himself to his children," exclaimed Count Haugwitz. "An orphan people is as unfortunate as are orphan children. Your people need you, sire; they need a wise and gentle hand to direct them."

"And yet you want me to put the sword in my hand, and that I should lead my people to war and carnage," said the king.

"In order to make peace bloom forth from war and carnage," said Count Haugwitz, gravely. "The bloody monster of war is stalking now through the whole world, and, as it cannot be avoided, it is better to attack it, and to confront it in a bold manner. Russia, Austria, and England are ready to do so, and they stretch out their hands toward you. Refuse to grasp them, and, for the doubtful and dangerous friendship of France, you will have gained three powerful enemies."

"And if I grasp their hands I shall not advance the interests of Prussia by shedding the blood of my people, but only those of Austria and Russia," replied the king. "If France should be greatly weakened, or even entirely annihilated, serious dangers would arise for Prussia, for Austria and Russia would unite in that case, for the purpose of menacing our own security. They would easily and quickly find compensations for themselves, and Austria especially would profit by the losses of France; for she would recover the Netherlands, which Prussia is to conquer now by the blood of her soldiers, and acquire, perhaps, even Bavaria. But what compensation would fall to the share of Prussia? Or do you believe, perhaps, Austria, from a feeling of gratitude toward us, would cede to Prussia a portion of her former hereditary possessions in the Netherlands? No, no—no war with France! Let Russia and Austria fight alone; they are strong enough for it. I say all this after mature deliberation, and this is not only my opinion, but also that of distinguished and experienced generals. General von Tempelhof, too, is of my opinion, and confirmed it in a memorial which I asked him to draw up for me."

"Your majesty requested the Duke of Brunswick, also, to write a memorial on the intended coalition against France," said General von Köckeritz, hastily. "On our arrival I received this memorial and read it, according to your majesty's orders. The duke persists in the opinion that it is necessary for the honor, glory, and safety of Prussia to join the coalition, and to oppose France in a determined manner. Your majesty, I must confess that I share the views maintained by the duke."

"So do I!" exclaimed Count Haugwitz, "and so do all your subjects. Sire, your whole people ardently desire to chastise this arrogant France, and to sweep these hosts of Jacobins from the soil of Germany. Oh, my king and lord, only make a trial, only raise your voice and call upon the people to rally around your standards, and to wage war against France! You will see them rally enthusiastically around the Prussian eagles, and fervently bless their courageous king. And when you begin this struggle, sire, you and your army will have a formidable, an invincible ally. That ally is *public opinion*, sire! Public opinion requires this war, and public opinion is no longer something dumb and creeping in the dark, but something that has a voice, and that raises it in ringing, thundering notes in the newspapers and magazines. One of these voices spoke a few weeks ago in the *Political Journal*, as follows: 'Can our monarch abandon the German empire? Can he look on quietly while France is making preparations for attacking Prussia as soon as her turn shall come? It is only necessary for us to think of Italy, Switzerland, and Holland in order to appreciate the friendship of France.' * This voice has reëchoed throughout Prussia, and every one is looking up to the throne of your majesty anxiously and hopefully; every one is satisfied that you will draw the sword for the honor and rights of Germany. Sire, at this moment I am nothing but the voice of your people, and therefore I implore your majesty to take a bold and manful resolution. Draw the sword for Prussia's honor and Germany's safety."

"I implore your majesty likewise to do so," exclaimed General von Köckeritz. "I dare to implore your majesty, in the name of your people. Oh, sire, take a bold and manly resolution! Draw the sword for Prussia's honor and Germany's safety."

The king had risen and paced the room with violent steps. His features, usually so quiet and gentle, were now uneasy and agitated; a gloomy cloud covered his brow, and a painful expression trembled on his lips. He seemed to carry on a violent and desperate inward struggle, and his breath issued painfully and gaspingly from his breast. Finally, after a long pause, he approached the two gentlemen who had risen and were looking at him with evident anxiety.

"I am unable to refute all these reasons," said the king, sighing, "but an inward voice tells me that I ought not to break my word, and commence hostilities. If the welfare of the state requires it, however, I shall join the coalition, but only on condition that the Austrians attack Mentz in force, take the fortress by assault, and thereby cover the left flank of my base of operations.* And now we will close our consultation for to-day. Go, Count Haugwitz, and resume your negotiations with the ambassadors of Russia and Great Britain. As for you, General von Köckeritz, I beg you to bring me the memorial of the Duke of Brunswick, and then you may return to your house and take some rest, of which you doubtless stand greatly in need after the fatigues you have undergone."

He greeted the gentlemen with a hasty nod and turned his back to them, without paying any attention to the deep and reverential bows with which the minister and the general withdrew toward the door.

When the two gentlemen had reached the anteroom, they satisfied themselves by a rapid glance that they were alone, and that nobody was able to hear them.

"He was quite angry," whispered General von Köckeritz; "he only yielded with the utmost reluctance; and, believe me, my friend, the king will never forgive us this victory we have obtained over him; it may produce the worst results and endanger our whole position."

---

* "Political Journal." Berlin, 1793.

* The king's own words.—Vide "Memoiren zur Geschichte des Preuss. Staats." By Col. Massenbach. Vol. III., p. 88.

"It is true," said Count Haugwitz, sighing, "the king dismissed us in a more abrupt and harsh manner than ever before. It would have been better for us to yield, and let the king have his own way. Who knows but he is right, and an alliance with France, perhaps, would be more advantageous than this coalition with Austria and Russia? It startles me somewhat that Austria should be so anxious to obtain the accession of Prussia to the coalition, for Austria certainly would feel no inclination to propose any alliance that might prove profitable to Prussia. It may be best for Prussia, after all, to side with France."

"But public opinion would execrate such an alliance," said General von Köckeritz, sighing. "Public opinion—"

"My dear friend," interrupted Count Haugwitz, angrily, "public opinion is like the wind, changing its direction every day. Success alone influences and decides public opinion, and if France should vanquish the three powers, the same public opinion which now urges us to join the coalition would condemn us. Public opinion should not induce us to endanger our position and our power over the king for its sake. And I tell you, I am uneasy about this matter. The king was greatly irritated; he seemed angry with us, because he felt that he is not entirely free and independent, and that he has granted us some power over his decisions."

"We should yield even now," said General von Köckeritz, anxiously. "We should confess to the king that his reasons have convinced us, that we have been mistaken—"

"So that he would feel with twofold force that not his own free will, but our altered opinion, decided his action?" asked the minister. "No, we must give the king a chance to decide the whole question by his own untrammelled authority, and to prove that he alone is the ruler of Prussia's destinies. You can give him the best opportunity for so doing, for you have a pretext to return to him at once. Did not the king order you to bring him the memorial of the Duke of Brunswick?"

"Good Heaven! that is true; the king is waiting for the memorial!" exclaimed the general, in terror. "In my anxiety, I even forgot his orders."

"Hasten, my friend, to bring it at once to him," said Count Haugwitz, "and with your leave I shall take a little rest in the room which the king has been kind enough to assign to you here in the palace. He will perhaps countermand the instructions he has just given me."

A few minutes afterward General von Köckeritz, with the memorial in his hands, reëntered the cabinet of the king, who was still slowly pacing the room, without noticing the arrival of his adviser.

"Your majesty," said the general, timidly, "here is the memorial of Ferdinand, duke of Brunswick."

"Just lay it on my desk there," said the king, continuing his promenade.

General von Köckeritz stepped to the desk and placed the memorial on it. Just at that moment the king had arrived at the desk too, and paused in front of the general. He fixed a long and mournful glance upon him and slowly shook his head.

"You have deserted me also," said the king, sighing. "You may be right, gentlemen. I have yielded to your more profound sagacity for the time being, but an inward voice tells me that it is wrong to break the peace because France at the present time is being threatened on all sides, and because her armies have been defeated."

"Your majesty alone has to decide the whole question," said Köckeritz, solemnly. "Your conviction is our law, and we submit in dutiful obedience to your majesty's more profound sagacity. It is for you to command, and for us to obey."

A sudden gleam beamed in the eyes of the king, and a deeper blush mantled his cheeks. The general saw it, and comprehended it very well.

"Moreover," he added, with downcast eyes and with an air of confusion, "moreover, I have to make a confession to your majesty in my own name and in that of Count Haugwitz. While trying to win your majesty by our arguments for the war and for the coalition, it has happened to us that we were converted by the arguments your majesty adduced *against* the war and *against* the coalition, and that your majesty convinced us of the fallacy of our opinion. It is, perhaps, very humiliating to admit that our conviction has veered around so suddenly, but your majesty's convincing eloquence—"

"No, not my poor eloquence, but the truth has convinced you," exclaimed the king, joyfully, "and I thank you for having the truly manly and noble courage to admit that you were mistaken and have changed your mind. I am grateful to Count Haugwitz, too, and I shall never forget this generous and highly honorable confession of yours. It is a new proof for me that you are faithful and reliable friends and servants of mine, men who are not ashamed of acknowledging an error, and who care more for the welfare of the state than for carrying their own point. I therefore withdraw my previous instructions, I shall not join the coalition. Hasten to Haugwitz, my friend. Tell him to go forthwith to the Russian ambassador and inform him that my army will not assist the forces of the coalition, and that I shall take no part whatever in the war against France. Haugwitz is to say the same to the English ambassador, and to inform him that I shall not claim the subsidy of six million dollars, which England offered to pay me for my auxiliary army. Six million dollars! I believe General Tempelhof was right when he said the siege of a second-rate fortress would cost a million dollars, and in Holland we should have to take more than ten fortresses from the stubborn and intrepid French. This would cost us more than ten million dollars, and, moreover, we should have to use up the powder and ammunition destined for our own defence. Those six million dollars that England would pay me would not cover our outlay; I should be obliged to add four million dollars more, and to shed the blood of my brave and excellent soldiers without obtaining, perhaps, even the slightest advantage for Prussia. Hasten, general, to communicate my fixed and irrevocable resolution to Count Haugwitz. Prussia remains neutral, and takes no part whatever in the war against France!"

"I hasten to carry out your majesty's orders," exclaimed General von Köckeritz, walking toward the door, "and I know that Count Haugwitz will submit to the royal decision with the same joyful humility and obedience as myself."

The king's eyes followed him with an expression of genuine emotion.

"He is a faithful and honest friend," he said, "and that is, indeed, a rare boon for a king. Ah, I have succeeded, then, in averting this bloody thunder-cloud once more from Prussia, and I shall preserve the blessings of peace to my people. And now, I believe, I may claim some credit for the manner in which I have managed this delicate affair, and repose a little from the cares of government. I will go to Louisa—her sight and the smiles of my children will reward me for having done my duty as a king."

CHAPTER XXXIII.

THE LEGITIMATE WIFE.

THE Prince von Reuss, Henry XIV., Austrian ambassador at Berlin, had died an hour ago. A painful disease had confined him to his bed for weeks, and Marianne Meier had nursed him during this time with the greatest love and devotion. She had never left his bedside, and no one except herself, the physicians, and a few servants had been permitted to enter the sick-room. The brothers and nephews of the prince, who had come to Berlin in order to see their dying relative once more, had vainly solicited this favor. The physicians had told them that the suffering prince was unable to bear any excitement, there being great danger that immediate death would be the consequence of a scene between them. The prince, moreover, had sent his trusted valet de chambre to his brother, and informed him, even if he were entirely well, he would not accept the visits of a brother who had shown him so little fraternal love, and caused him so much grief by opposing his faithful and beloved friend Marianne Meier in the most offensive and insulting manner.

The distinguished relatives of the prince, therefore, had to content themselves with watching his palace from afar, and with bribing a few of his servants to transmit to them hourly reports about the condition of the patient.

And now Prince Henry XIV. was dead, and his brother was his successor and heir, the prince having left no legitimate offspring. It was universally believed that he had never been married, and that his immense fortune, his estates and titles, would devolve on his brother. It is true there was still that mistress of his, fair Marianne Meier, to whom the prince, in his sentimental infatuation, had paid the honors of a legitimate wife. But, of course, she had no claims whatever to the inheritance; it would be an act of generosity to leave her in possession of the costly presents the prince had made to her, and to pay her a small pension.

The prince had hardly closed his eyes, therefore, and the doctors had just pronounced him dead, when his brother, now Prince Henry XV., accompanied by a few lawyers, entered the palace of the deceased in order to take possession of his property, and to have the necessary seals applied to the doors.

However, to give himself at least a semblance of brotherly love, the prince desired first to repair to the death-room, and to take a last leave of the deceased. But in the anteroom he met the two footmen of his brother, who dared to stop his passage, telling him that no one was allowed to enter.

"And who dares to issue such orders?" asked the prince, without stopping a moment.

"Madame has done so," said the first valet de chambre. "Madame wants to be alone with the remains of her husband."

The prince shrugged his shoulders, and, followed by the legal gentlemen, he walked to the door, which he vainly tried to open.

"I believe that woman has locked the door," said the prince, angrily.

"Yes, sir, madame has locked the door," said the valet de chambre; "she does not want to be disturbed in her grief by mere visits of condolence."

"Well, let us leave her, then, to her grief," exclaimed the prince, with a sarcastic smile. "Come, gentlemen, let us attend to our business. Let us take an inventory of the furniture in the several rooms and then seal them. You may be our guide, valet."

But the valet de chambre shrugged his shoulders and shook his head. "Pardon me, sir, that is impossible. His highness, our late prince and master, several days ago, when he felt that his end was drawing near, caused every room to be locked and sealed by the first attaché of the legation in the presence of all the members of the embassy. The keys to all the rooms, however, were handed by order of the prince to madame, his wife."

The new prince, Henry XV., turned somewhat uneasily to the legal gentlemen.

"Have we a right to open the doors forcibly?"

"No, that would be contrary to law," said one of the lawyers, in a low voice. "The late prince has doubtless left some directions in relation to this matter and intrusted them to the officers of the legation. Your highness ought to apply to those gentlemen."

"Is the first attaché of the legation, Baron Werdern, in the palace?" said the prince to the valet de chambre.

"No, your highness, he has just gone out with a few other gentlemen of the legation to request the attendance of two officers of the law, that the will may be opened and read in their presence."

"My brother has made a will, then?" asked the prince, in a somewhat frightened tone.

"Yes, your highness, and he laid it, in the presence of every member of the legation, of two officers of the law, and of every servant, three days ago, in a strong box, the key of which he handed to the officers of the law, when the box was deposited in the archives of the legation."

"And why did Baron Werdern go now for the officers of the law?"

"In order to request their attendance in the palace, the late prince having left the verbal order that his will should be opened two hours after his death. The baron was going to invite your highness likewise to be present."

"Well, let us wait here for the arrival of the gentlemen," said Prince Henry XV., shrugging his shoulders. "It seems a little strange to me, however, that I must wait here in the anteroom like a supplicant. Go and announce my visit to madame!"

The valet de chambre bowed and left the room. The prince called the two lawyers to his side. "What do you think of this whole matter?" he asked, in a low voice.

The two representatives of the law shrugged their shoulders. "Your highness, every thing seems to have been done here legally. We must wait for the return of the gentlemen and for the opening of the will."

The valet de chambre now reëntered the room, and approached the prince. "Madame sends her respects to the prince, and begs him to excuse her inability to admit her brother-in-law just now, as she is dressing at the present moment. She will have the honor to salute her gracious brother-in-law at the ceremony."

"Does that woman call myself her gracious brother-in-law?" asked the prince, with an air of the most profound contempt, turning his back to the valet de chambre. "We will wait here, then, gentlemen," he added, turning to the lawyers. "It seems that woman intends to take a petty revenge at this moment for the contempt with which I have always treated her. I shall know, however, how to chastise her for it, and—"

"Hush, your highness," whispered one of the lawyers, "they are coming!"

In fact, the large folding-doors were opened at that moment, and on a catafalque, hung with black cloth, the remains of the prince were lying in state; on both sides of the catafalque large tapers were burning in heavy silver chandeliers.

Prince Henry, awed by this solemn scene, walked forward, and the grave countenance of his brother, with whom he had lived so long in discord, and whom he had not seen for many years, filled his heart with uneasiness and dismay.

He approached the room, followed by the legal gentlemen, with hesitating, noiseless steps. On the threshold of the door there now appeared the first attaché of the legation, Baron Werdern, who, bowing deeply, invited the prince whisperingly to come in.

The prince walked in, and on crossing the threshold, it seemed to him as if his brother's corpse had moved, and as if his half-opened eyes were fixed upon him with a threatening expression.

The prince averted his eyes from the corpse in dismay and saluted the gentlemen standing around a table covered with black cloth. Two large chandeliers, with burning tapers, a strong box, and writing-materials, had been placed upon this table ; on one side, two arm-chairs, likewise covered with black cloth, were to be seen.

The baron conducted the prince to one of these arm-chairs, and invited him to sit down. Prince Henry did so, and then looked anxiously at the officers of the law, who were standing at the table in their black robes, and behind whom were assembled all the members of the legation, the physicians, and the servants of the late prince.

A long pause ensued. Then, all at once, the folding-doors opened, and the prince's steward appeared on the threshold.

"Her highness the Princess Dowager von Reuss," he said, in a loud, solemn voice, and Marianne's tall, imposing form entered the room. She was clad in a black dress with a long train ; a black veil, fastened above her head on a diadem, surrounded her noble figure like a dark cloud, and in this cloud beamed her expansive, thoughtful forehead, and her large flaming eyes sparkled. Her features were breathing the most profound and majestic tranquillity ; and when she now saluted the gentlemen with a condescending nod, her whole bearing was so impressive and distinguished that even Prince Henry was unable to remain indifferent, and he rose respectfully from his arm-chair.

Marianne, however, paid no attention to him, but approached the remains of her husband. With inimitable grace she knelt down on one side of the catafalque. The priest who had entered with her knelt down on the other.

Both of them muttered fervent prayers for the deceased. Marianne then arose, and, bending over the corpse, imprinted a long kiss upon the forehead of her departed husband.

"Farewell, my husband!" she said, in her full, melodious voice, and then turned around and stepped toward the table. Without deigning to glance at the prince, she sat down in the arm-chair.

"I request the officers of the law now to open the strong box," she said, in an almost imperious voice.

One of the officers handed the key to Baron Werdern ; the latter opened the strong box, and took from it a sealed paper, which he gave to the officer.

"Do you recognize the paper as the same you yourself locked in this strong box ?" she asked. "Is it the same which his highness the late Prince von Reuss, Henry XIV., handed to you ?"

"Yes, it is the same," said the two officers ; "it is the will of the late prince."

"And you know that his highness ordered us to open it immediately after his death, and to promulgate its contents. Proceed, therefore, according to the instructions of the deceased."

One of the officers broke the seal, and now that he unfolded the paper, Marianne turned her head toward the prince, and fixed her burning eyes piercingly upon his countenance.

The officer commenced reading the will. First came the preamble, to be found in every will, and then the officer read in a louder voice, as follows :

"In preparing to appear before the throne of the Lord, I feel especially called upon to return my most heart-felt thanks, in this public manner, to my wife, Princess Marianne, née Meier, for the constancy, love, and devotion which she has shown to me during our whole married life, and for the surpassing patience and self-abnegation with which she nursed me during my last sickness. I deem myself especially obliged to make this acknowledgment, inasmuch as my wife, in her true love for me, has suffered many undeserved aspersions and insults, because, in accordance with my wishes, she kept our marriage secret, and in consequence had to bear the sneers of evil-disposed persons, and the insults of malicious enemies. But she is my lawful wife before God and man, and she is fully entitled to assume the name of a Princess Dowager von Reuss. I hereby expressly authorize her to do so, and, by removing the secret that has been observed during my life in relation to our marriage, I authorize my wife to assume the title and rank due to her, and I hereby command my brother, as well as his sons and the other members of my family, to pay to the Princess Dowager von Reuss, née Meier, the respect and deference due to her as the widow of the late head of the family, and to which she is justly entitled by her virtue, her blameless conduct, her respectability, beauty, and amiability. The Princess Dowager von Reuss is further authorized to let her servants wear the livery and colors of my house, to display the coat-of-arms of the princes von Reuss on her carriages, and to enjoy the full privileges of her rank. If my brother Henry, the heir of my titles, should have any doubts as to her rights in this regard, the officer reading my will is requested to ask him whether or not he desires to obtain further evidence in relation to the legitimacy of my marriage."

"Does your highness require any further evidence ?" asked the officer, interrupting the reading of the will.

"I do," said the prince, who had listened to the reading of the will with a pale face and gloomy mien.

"Here is that evidence," said the priest, beckoning the sexton, who stood on the threshold of the door. The latter approached the priest, and handed him a large volume bound in black morocco.

"It is the church register, in which I have entered all the marriages, christenings, and funeral masses performed in the chapel of the Austrian embassy," said the priest. "On this page you find the minutes of the marriage of the Prince von Reuss, Henry XIV., and Miss Marianne Meier. The ceremony took place two years ago. I have baptized the princess myself, and thereby received her into the pale of the holy Catholic Church, and I have likewise performed the rite of marriage on the occasion referred to. I hereby certify that the princess is the lawful wife of the late prince, as is testified by the minutes entered on the church register. The marriage was performed in the chapel, and in the presence of witnesses, who have signed the minutes, like myself."

"I witnessed the marriage," said Baron Werdern, "and so did the military counsellor Gentz, who, if your highness should desire further testimony, will be ready to corroborate our statements."

"No," said the prince, gloomily, "I require no further testimony. I am fully satisfied of the truth of your statements, and will now pay my respects to my sister-in-law, the Princess Dowager von Reuss, née Meier."

He bowed, with a sarcastic smile, which, for a moment, caused the blood to rush to Marianne's pale cheeks, and then carelessly leaned back into his arm-chair.

"Be kind enough to proceed," he said, turning to the officer.

The latter took up the will again and read its several sections and clauses. The prince bequeathed his palace, with every thing in it, to his wife Marianne, and likewise his carriages, his horses, and the family diamonds he had inherited from his mother. The remainder of his considerable property he left to his brother, asking him to agree with the Princess Marianne on a pension corresponding with her rank and position in society. Then followed some legacies and pensions for the old servants of his household, a few gifts to the poor, and last the appropriation of a sum for which a mass was to be read on every anniversary of his death, for the peace of his soul.

The ceremony was over. The officers of the law and the members of the embassy had left the death-room, and on a sign from Marianne the servants had also withdrawn.

The prince had exchanged a few words in a low voice with his two lawyers, whereupon they likewise had left the room. No one except the brother and the wife of the deceased remained now in this gloomy room, illuminated by the flickering tapers. Marianne, however, seemed to take no notice of the presence of her brother-in-law; she had approached the corpse again, and gazed at it with the most profound emotion.

"I thank you, Henry," she said, lowly and solemnly. "I thank you from the bottom of my heart; you have given back to me my honor; you have revenged me upon your haughty relatives, and upon the sneering world!"

"Do not thank him, respected sister-in-law, for he has left you poor," said the prince, approaching her, and contemplating her with a freezing smile. "My brother has made you a princess, it is true, but he has not given you the means to live as a princess. He has bequeathed to you this palace, with its costly furniture; he has bequeathed to you his carriages and diamonds; but a palace and furniture are no estates, and in order to keep carriages one has to feed men and horses. It is true, you can sell the palace and the diamonds, and obtain for them several hundred thousand florins. That sum would be amply sufficient for a person leading a retired life, but it is very little for one who desires to keep up a princely household, and to live in the style becoming a lady of your beauty and social position. My brother has foreseen all this, and he indirectly gave us a chance to come to an understanding, by asking me to agree with you on a pension to be paid you. Hence I ask you, how much do you demand? How high will be the sum for which you will sell me your mourning veil, your name, and your title of princess dowager? For you doubtless anticipate, madame, that I do not propose to acknowledge you publicly as my sister-in-law, and to receive a —— Marianne Meier among the members of my family. Tell me your price, therefore, madame."

Marianne looked at him with flaming eyes, a deep blush of anger mantling her cheeks. "Prince von Reuss," she said, proudly, "you will have to permit the world to call me your sister-in-law. I am your sister-in-law, and I shall prove to the world and to you that it is unnecessary to have been born under a princely canopy in order to live, think, and act like a princess. My husband has rewarded me in this hour for years of suffering and humiliation. Do you believe that my reward is for sale for vile money? And if you should offer me millions, I should reject them if, in return, I were to lead a nameless, disreputable, and obscure existence. I will sooner die of starvation as a Princess Dowager von

Reuss than live in opulence as Marianne Meier. This is my last word; and now, sir, begone! Do not desecrate this room by your cold and egotistic thoughts, and by your heartless calculations! Honor the repose of the dead and the grief of the living. Begone!"

She proudly turned away from him, and bent once more over the corpse. While she was doing so her black veil, with a gentle rustle, fell down over her face and wrapped her, as well as the corpse, as in a dark mist, so that the two forms seemed to melt into one.

The prince felt a shudder pervading his frame, and the presence of the corpse embarrassed him.

"I will not disturb you now in your grief, madame," he said; "I hope your tears will flow less copiously as soon as the funeral is over, and I shall then send my lawyer, for the purpose of treating further with you."

He bowed, and hastened to the door. She seemed neither to have heard his words, nor to have noticed that he was withdrawing. She was still bending over the remains of her husband, the black cloud surrounding her and the corpse.

CHAPTER XXXIV.

THE EIGHTEENTH OF BRUMAIRE.

"News from France!" exclaimed Counsellor Gentz, entering Marianne's boudoir in breathless haste. "Do you already know what has occurred? Did you hear, Marianne, how France has closed the eighteenth century?"

Marianne looked up into the face of her friend, with a gentle and peculiar smile. "That must have been exciting intelligence," she said, "inasmuch as it was even able to arouse the dreamer, Frederick Gentz, from his political sleep, and to cause him to take interest again in the affairs of the world. Well, let us hear the news; what has occurred in France?"

"General Bonaparte has overthrown the Directory, and dispersed the Council of Five Hundred."

"And you call that news?" asked Marianne, shrugging her shoulders. "You tell me there the history of the ninth and tenth of November, or, as the French republicans say, of the eighteenth and nineteenth of Brumaire. And you believe that I have not yet heard of it to-day, on the twenty-sixth of December? My friend Gentz, Bonaparte's deeds need not more than a month in order to penetrate through the world; they soar aloft with eagle-wings, and the whole world beholds them, because they darken the horizon of the whole world."

"But you have only heard the preamble of my news," ejaculated Gentz, impatiently. "I have no doubt that you know the history of the eighteenth of Brumaire, and that you are aware that France, on that day, placed herself under the rule of three consuls, one of whom was General Bonaparte."

"The other two consuls are Sieyes and Ducos," interrupted Marianne. "I know that, and I know, too, that Lucien, Bonaparte's brother, president of the Legislative Assembly, upon receiving the oath of office of the three consuls, said to them: 'The greatest nation on earth intrusts you with its destinies; the welfare of thirty millions of men, the preservation of order at home, and the reëstablishment of peace abroad, are your task. Three months from to-day public opinion will expect to hear from you how you have accomplished it.'" *

"Well, M. Bonaparte did not make public opinion wait so long," said Gentz; "or rather, he asserts public opinion had not given him time to wait so long, and that it was public opinion itself that called upon him to proclaim himself sovereign of France."

"Sovereign of France?" asked Marianne, in surprise. "Bonaparte has made himself king?"

"Yes, king, but under another name; he has caused himself to be elected consul for ten years! Ah, he will know how to shorten these ten years, just as he knew how to shorten those three months!"

"And this report is reliable?" asked Marianne, musingly.

"Perfectly so. Bonaparte was elected first consul on the twenty-fifth of December, and on the same day the new constitution was promulgated throughout France. That is a very fine Christmas present which France has made to the world! A box filled with dragon's teeth, from which armed hosts will spring up. It is true, the first consul now pretends to be very anxious to restore peace to Europe. He has sent special ambassadors to all courts, with profuse assurances of his friendship and pacific intentions, and he sent them off even previous to his election, in order to announce the news of the latter to the foreign courts on the same day on which he was proclaimed first consul at Paris. Such a peace-messenger of the general has arrived at Berlin; he has brought us the strange and startling news."

"What is the name of this peace-messenger of the modern god of war?" asked Marianne.

---

* "Histoire du Consulat et de l'Empire," par A. Thiers, vol. i., p. 16.

"He sent his adjutant, General Duroc; the latter reached Berlin yesterday, and appeared even to-day as the petted guest of our court, at the great *soirée* of the queen. Oh, my friend, my stupid German heart trembled with anger when I saw the kind and flattering attentions that were paid to this Frenchman, while German gentlemen of genius, merit, and ability were kept in the background, neither the king nor the queen seeming to take any notice of their presence! There were Count Hardenberg, and the noble President of Westphalia, Baron Stein; they stood neglected in a bay window, and looked sadly at the royal couple, who treated the Frenchman in the midst of the court in the most distinguished manner; there were Blucher and Gneisenau, overlooked by everybody, although their uniforms were no less brilliant than that of the French envoy; and there was finally Frederick Gentz, myself, who had only appeared at this court festival owing to the special desire and order of the queen, and whose presence she had entirely forgotten, although Gualtieri reminded her of it at least three times, and told her that I was there, and had only come because the queen had expressly ordered it so. But what did her beautiful majesty care that a German writer was vainly waiting for a smile of her affability, and a gracious nod of her lovely head? The French envoy was by far more important than all of us. For the sake of the Frenchman, even 'Madame Etiquette,' the Countess von Voss, mistress of ceremonies, had been silenced, and the plain adjutant of the first consul was received with as much distinction as if he were a minister plenipotentiary, while he only came as the simple agent for a private individual. They asked him to tell them about the battle of the Pyramids, about the battles of Mount Tabor and Aboukir, and the whole court listened to him with a suspense as though Bonaparte's adjutant were preaching a new gospel. Whenever he paused in his narrative, the queen, with her fascinating smile, constantly addressed new questions to him, and praised the achievements of General Bonaparte as though he were the Messiah sent into the world to deliver it from the evils of war! In short, he had a perfect success; and at last, by means of an adroit trick, he managed to render it as magnificent as possible. The queen told General Duroc of our German customs, and informed him that this was the day on which the Germans everywhere made presents to each other, and that gifts were laid under Christmas-trees, adorned with burning tapers. At that moment Duroc turned to the king, and said, with his intolerable French amiability: Sire, if this is the day of universal presents in Ger-

many, I believe I will be courageous enough to-day to ask your majesty for a present in the name of the first consul, General Bonaparte, if your majesty will permit me to do so.' The king, of course, gave him the desired permission, and Duroc continued: 'Sire, the present for which I am to ask your majesty, in the name of the first consul, is a bust of your great ancestor, Frederick the Second. The first consul recently examined the statues in the Diana Gallery at the Tuileries; there were the statues of Cæsar and Brutus, of Coriolanus and Cicero, of Louis XIV. and Charles V., but the first consul did not see the statue of Frederick the Great, and he deems the collection of the heroes of ancient and modern times incomplete as long as it does not embrace the name of Frederick the Great. Sire, I take the liberty, therefore, to ask you, in the name of France, for a bust of Frederick the Great!'" *

"Very adroit, indeed," said Marianne, smiling; "these republicans seem to be excellent courtiers."

"Yes, very adroit!" exclaimed Gentz; "the whole court was in ecstasy at this tremendous flattery, at this compliment paid by the great republic to little Prussia; but I could not stand it any longer in those halls, and in the presence of those fawning Germans, and I hastened away in order to unbosom to you my rage, my indignation, and my grief. Oh, my fair friend, what is to become of Germany, and what will be the end of all these troubles? Ruin is staring us in the face, and we do not see it; we are rushing toward the precipice, and must fall a prey to France, to this wolf in sheep's clothing, which will caress and pet us until it will be able to devour us!"

"I like to hear you talk in this strain," said Marianne, joyfully. "That is again the friend of my heart, who is now talking to me. Listen to me. I have to communicate news to you, too, and you must not be surprised if I reply to your important political intelligence by a reference to my petty personal interests. But there is a connection between them, and you will see it by and by. Listen, then, to the news concerning myself."

"Yes, Marianne," said Gentz, kneeling down before her, and leaning his head upon her knees, "yes, tell me about yourself, my beautiful fairy queen; lull my political pains a little by the magic song which is flowing from your red lips like a fresh source of love. Oh, my charming princess, now that I am looking up into your radiant face, I feel a burning shame that I should have desecrated the delightful moments I passed by your side by such trivial complaints about the misery

---

* Historical.

of German politics. What have we to do with politics? What do we care if Germany is going to be ruined? *Après nous le déluge!* Let us enjoy the bliss of the fleeting hour!"

Marianne played smilingly with her slender fingers, covered with sparkling diamond rings, in his hair, and looked upon him with a wondrous air.

"Enthusiast!" she said; "now an ardent politician, then an impassioned lover, and ready at all hours to exchange one *rôle* for the other! Will you not listen to my news? My quarrel with my dear brother-in-law, Henry XV., is ended; we have come to an agreement."

"And I hope my sagacious and prudent Marianne has subdued her proud and bold heart this time, and had a little regard for her advantage," replied Gentz. "A woman as beautiful and radiant as Marianne Meier needs no empty aristocratic title, for your beauty makes you the queen of the world; but you need wealth in order to add power to your beauty, and to adorn it with a cloak glittering with gold and purple. Well, my queen, are you again Marianne Meier, and a millionnaire besides?"

"What a fool!" she exclaimed, proudly, "what a fool you are to believe I would crawl back into the Jews' quarter and expose myself to the sneers of my envious friends! No, my friend, money and beauty are insufficient for those who desire to play a *rôle* in the world; they stand in need of rank and titles, too, for these are the magic words opening to us the doors of royal palaces, and placing us on a par with the privileged and inaccessible. I, for one, want to play my *rôle* in the world; hence I must have a distinguished title. It is true I also stand in need of wealth, and by means of a skilful arrangement I have secured both. The mote in my Jewish eye appearing to my aristocratic relatives like a very large beam, I have yielded and renounced the title of a Princess von Reuss; but, in spite of that, I remain a princess and retain the title of highness. The prince, my brother-in-law, has given me a splendid estate in fee-simple, the annual revenues of which amount to no less than twenty thousand dollars; in return, however, I surrender to him the family diamonds, this palace, the carriages with the coat-of-arms of the Reuss family, the horses and liveries, and last, the name and title of a Princess Dowager von Reuss."

"And now, like all the fairies in the children's books, you are a wondrous child without name and rank, but showering with your snowy hands golden suns and glittering stars upon mankind?"

"No, I am no nameless woman now, but I adopt the name of my estate of Eibenberg, and from this day forward I shall be the Princess Marianne of Eibenberg, the Emperor of Germany himself having recognized my new title. The documents, signed by the emperor himself, are on the table there. The prince brought them to me to-day as a Christmas-present. Now, my friend, my real life is to commence; I have acquired wealth and a distinguished name. The poor Jewess, the daughter of the Ghetto, has moved into the palace of the aristocracy and become a princess."

"And I will be the first to do you homage as though you were my princess and queen!" exclaimed Gentz, "the first who will call himself your vassal. Come, my princess, let me place the sweet yoke upon my neck; let my forehead touch the ground on which you are walking; place your foot upon my neck, so that I may feel the sweet burden of your rule."

And bending down his head until his brow touched the floor, he placed her tiny foot, encased in a beautiful silken shoe, upon his neck. Marianne did not interfere with him, but looked down on him with a proud, triumphant smile.

"You lie at my feet, Frederick Gentz," she said, "nevertheless I will lift you up to me; you shall stand by my side, my equal, famous and great as you ought to be, owing to your genius! But a truce to tender trifling, my friend; both of us have to accomplish great purposes, and our thoughts and actions should be grave and stern. Come, rise from your knees, my vassal; you shall be a prince by my side, and we will rule the world together."

She withdrew her foot from his neck, but Gentz seized it with both hands and kissed it. He then quickly rose from his knees, and drew himself up to his full height, looking at her sternly and almost angrily.

"You have often told me that you loved me," he said, "but it was a lie; you do not understand love, your heart is cold and your senses are silent, only your pride speaks."

"It is possible that you are right," she replied, "but, in that case, I love you with my pride and with my mind, and that is worth something, at all events. I want to see you honored, famous, and influential; is not that also love?"

"No, it is a mockery!" ejaculated Gentz, mournfully. "It is malice, for you see I am a poor, despised man, without money, without fame, without rank; a miserable military counsellor, outranked by every private counsellor, and persecuted day by day by my creditors, as if they were vultures following a poor dove whose wings have been clipped."

"But your wings shall grow again, so that you may escape from the vultures!" exclaimed Marianne, "and that you may soar, eagle-like, above the miseries of the world, and exercise a commanding influence over it. The time of dreams and expectations is over, the time for action has come for all energetic and able minds. Two years ago I asked you, as I do to-day, if you would not devote your services to Austria, and if you would not seek for fame and happiness in that country, in which your genius would be appreciated and rewarded. Do you remember what you replied to me at that time?"

"Yes, I remember," said Gentz, with a sarcastic smile; "I was foolish enough to reject your offers, and to declare that I would stay here at Berlin, and see if my native country would not need my abilities and my services, and if our rulers here would not avail themselves of my talents and of my pen. And thus I have lost, again, two years of my life, and only my debts have increased, but not my fame."

"Because you were an enthusiast, and expected to be appreciated in Prussia; believing this good king (who would like to make his people happy and prosperous, but who timidly shrinks back from all energetic resolutions) would be very grateful to you for exhorting him to grant freedom of the press to his subjects, and, in general, to introduce liberty and equality in his states. Do you still believe that Frederick William the Third will do so?"

"No, he will not," replied Gentz, mournfully; "no, this king does not understand the present age, and instead of being a step in advance of it, he will always remain a step behind it, and thus involve Prussia in untold misery and suffering. I have hoped and waited long enough; the time of patience and idleness is now over, and I therefore renounce, to-day, at the end of the eighteenth century, my native state, in order to become a citizen and son of a larger fatherland. I cease to be a Prussian, in order to become a German; and Prussia having no desire to avail herself of my abilities, I am going to see whether or not Germany has any use for them. My beautiful Marianne, you shall be the priestess who receives the oath which I make on the altar of the fatherland: 'I swear to devote all my powers and talents to Germany; I swear to be a faithful and untiring son to my great fatherland!'"

"I have heard your oath, Frederick Gentz, and I accept it in the name of Germany," said Marianne, solemnly. "You shall be the champion of the honor and rights of Germany; your weapon, however, shall not be the sword, but the pen."

"But where will the lists be opened to my tournament?" asked Gentz, musingly.

"In Austria," replied Marianne, quickly; "the Emperor of Germany is expecting you, the son of Germany; the Emperor of Germany is calling you to serve and promote the interests of your fatherland. I am authorized to tell you that. The new Austrian envoy, Count Stadion, has requested me to do so; he has asked me to win you for Austria, that is, for Germany. For, believe me, the welfare of Germany is nowadays consulted in Austria, and not in Prussia!"

"No, not in Prussia!" exclaimed Gentz, mournfully. "Our government shuts its eyes in order not to behold the terrors which are rushing toward us with irresistible force, and will soon, like an avalanche, roll over Germany and annihilate us all, unless we skilfully calculate the danger, and raise sufficient bulwarks against it. They admire Bonaparte here, and only behold a hero, while I scent a tyrant—a tyrant who wants to subjugate us by his revolutionary liberty and his Jacobin's cap, which is but a crown in another shape. I hate Bonaparte, for I hate the revolution which, notwithstanding its phrases of liberty and equality, is but a bloody despotism that does not even grant freedom of opinion to the citizen, and drags such ideas as are distasteful to it upon the scaffold. I hate the revolution, I hate Bonaparte, and I hate every form of tyranny, and shall oppose it as long as I live!"

"And I shall be a faithful squire by your side, and sharpen the bolts which you are going to hurl at the enemy," said Marianne, with fervent enthusiasm. "We are both going to Vienna, in order to serve Germany. In Vienna a new century and a new country will open their arms to us. Thanks to my title, to my rank, and to my connections, every door will be open to us there, and the Jewess, Marianne Meier, princess of Eibenberg, will not even find the apartments of the emperor and empress closed; on the contrary, their imperial majesties will receive me as an honored and welcome guest, for I am a princess by the act of the emperor, and the friend of the empress; Victoria de Poutet Colloredo is also my friend. And whithersoever I go, you shall go, too, my friend, and the doors that will open to me shall not be closed to you. My rank opens them to me, and your genius opens them to you. Come, let us be faithful allies; let us swear to support each other firmly and immovably, and to walk together step by step."

"Oh, my noble and generous friend," exclaimed Gentz, sadly, "how delicately you try to veil your protection! In such an alliance, I am unable to offer you any compensation, for I should find all doors closed if you should not open them to me. I have neither rank, money, nor friends at court!"

"Well, let me protect you now, and at some later period you will protect me," said Marianne. "Let us swear to pursue our path together."

"I swear it by all that is sacred to me!" exclaimed Gentz. "I swear that I will remain faithful to you and to Germany for my whole life. I swear that I will follow you everywhere; that I will serve you wherever and whenever I can, and to love you to my last breath."

"The alliance is closed," said Marianne, solemnly. "Henceforth, we will fight jointly, and pursue our goal together. It is our own greatness, and the greatness of Germany. The country is in danger—let us see if we cannot contribute something to its preservation, and if it does not need our hands and our heads in order to weather the storm. If we should be able, while assisting the country, to pick up a few laurels, titles, decorations, and treasures for ourselves, we would be fools not to avail ourselves of the opportunity."

"Yes, you are right," said Gentz, smiling, "we would be fools not to do so; and you are right, too, as to the perils of the country. Germany is in danger. The new century will dawn upon her with a bloody morning sun, and it will arouse us from our sleep by a terrific cannonade. But as for ourselves, we will not wait until the roar of the strife awakens us; we will be up and doing now and work on the lightning-rod with which we will meet the approaching thunderstorm, in order that its bolts may glance off harmlessly and not destroy Germany. I will be an untiring warrior in the great struggle against the revolution, and my pen, which is my sword, shall never be idle in the strife. From this hour I cease to be the insignificant Prussian counsellor, Frederick Gentz; from this hour I will strive to become the great political writer of Germany. May the genius of Germany be with me in my endeavors!"

"Amen!" said Marianne, fervently. "May the genius of Germany bless us and the new century Amen!"

THE PEACE OF LUNEVILLE.

CHAPTER XXXV.

JOHANNES MÜLLER.

THE minister, Baron Thugut, was pacing his cabinet in an excited manner. His face, usually so cold and immovable, was painfully agitated to-day; his shaggy white eyebrows were closely contracted, and his eyes were casting angry glances on the dispatch which he had just thrown on his desk, and which a courier from General Melas, in Lombardy, had brought to him a few minutes ago.

"Another battle lost!" he muttered; "another laurel-wreath placed on the defiant head of General Bonaparte! This man will make me mad yet by his impudent good luck. It is dreadful only to think that he was already defeated at Marengo *—so surely defeated that General Melas issued orders for the pursuit of the enemy, and rode to Alessandria to take his supper in the most comfortable manner. That fellow Melas is a jackass, who only scented the roast meat which he was going to have for supper, but not General Desaix, who arrived with his troops in time to snatch victory from our grasp, and to inflict a most terrible defeat upon our triumphant army. All of our generals are short-sighted fools, from that ridiculously-overrated Archduke Charles down to General Schwarzenberg, and whatever the names of these gentlemen may be—these gentlemen with the golden epaulets, and decorated breasts, and empty heads—I have no confidence in a single one of them. At the moment of danger as well as of victory they regularly lose their senses, and thereby turn our victories into defeats; while they render our checks in the same way only more disastrous and decisive. I am entirely opposed to placing any more archdukes at the head of our armies. Fortunately, I have succeeded in getting

---

* The battle of Marengo was fought on the 14th of June, 1800.

10

rid of Archduke Charles, and I hope that Archduke John, too, will be badly beaten at no distant period, so that we may remove him, like his brother, from his position at the head of his troops. It will never do. Well—" he interrupted himself in his soliloquy, casting an angry glance on his private secretary, Hudlitz, who was just entering the room—"well, why do you disturb me without being called for?"

"Pardon me, your excellency," said Hudlitz, humbly, "but your excellency had instructed me to inform you immediately of the arrival of the custodian of the imperial library, whom your excellency had sent for."

"And he is there now?" asked Thugut.

"Yes, your excellency, Mr. Müller, the aulic councillor and custodian of the imperial library is waiting in the anteroom."

"Admit him, then," said Thugut, waving his hand toward the door.

Hudlitz limped out, and a few minutes later the announced visitor appeared on the threshold of the door. He was a little, slender man, with a stooping form, which had not been bent, however, by the burden of years, but by the burden of learning, of night-watches and untiring studies. His head, covered with a pig-tail wig, according to the fashion of that period, was slightly bent forward. His expansive forehead was indicative of the philosophical turn of his mind; his large eyes were beaming with deep feeling; his pleasing, yet not handsome features, were expressive to an almost touching degree, of infinite gentleness and benevolence, and a winning smile was playing constantly on his thin lips.

This smile, however, disappeared now that he felt the small, piercing eyes of the minister resting upon his countenance. Hat in hand, and without uttering a word, he remained standing at the door; he only raised his head a little, and his eyes were fixed on the minister with a calm and proud expression.

"You are the aulic councillor, Johannes Müller?" asked Thugut, after a short pause, in a somewhat harsh voice.

"Yes, I am Johannes Müller," said the latter, and the smile had already returned to his lips. "I thank your excellency for this salutary question."

"What do you mean by that, sir?" asked Thugut, wonderingly. "Why do you call my question salutary?"

"Because it involves a good lesson, your excellency, and because it informs me that they are wrong who, from motives of mistaken benevolence, would persuade me that I was a well-known person, and that everybody in Vienna was familiar with my name. It is always wholesome for an author to be reminded from time to time of his insignificance and littleness, for it preserves him from giving way to pride, and pride is always the first symptom of mental retrogradation."

Thugut fixed his eyes with a sullen air on the countenance of the *savant*.

"Do you want to give me a lesson?" he asked, angrily.

"By no means, your excellency," said Johannes Müller, calmly; "I only wished to mention the reason why I was grateful to you for your question. And now I trust your excellency will permit me the question—to what am I indebted for the honor of being called to your excellency?"

"Well, I wished to make your acquaintance, Mr. Aulic Councillor," said Thugut. "I wished no longer to remain the only inhabitant of Vienna who had not seen the illustrious historian of Switzerland and the author of the 'Furstenbund.' * You see, sir, I know your works at least, even though I did not know your person."

"And your excellency did not lose any thing by not knowing the latter, for it is a person that is not worth the trouble to become acquainted with. We men of learning are less able to speak with our tongues than with our pens, and our desk alone is our rostrum."

"And there you are a powerful and most impressive orator, Mr. Aulic Councillor!" exclaimed Thugut, in a tone of unaffected and cordial praise.

An air of joyful surprise overspread the gentle face of Johannes Müller, and he cast a glance of heart-felt gratitude on the minister.

Thugut noticed this glance. "You are surprised that I am able to appreciate your merits so correctly and yet suffered years to elapse without inviting you to call on me? I am a poor man,

* "The League of the Princes," one of the celebrated works of Johannes von Müller.

overburdened with business and harassed with the dry details of my administration, and the direction of political affairs leaves me no leisure to be devoted to literature."

"At least not to German literature," said Müller, quickly; "but every one knows your excellency to be a profound connoisseur of oriental languages; and it is well known, too, that you devote a great deal of attention to them, notwithstanding the immense burden of business constantly weighing you down."

Thugut smiled, and his harsh features assumed a milder expression. Johannes Müller, without intending it perhaps, had touched the chord that sounded most sweetly to Thugut's ears; he had flattered him by referring to his profound oriental studies.

"Well," he said, "you see I am taking likewise a lively interest in German literature, for I invited you to come and see me; and you are a German author, and one of the most illustrious at that. Now, sir, let us speak frankly and without circumlocution, as two men of science ought to do. Let us mutually forget our titles and official positions, and chat confidentially with each other. Come, my dear sir, let us sit down in these two arm-chairs and talk like two German gentlemen; that is, frankly and sincerely. Nobody is here to hear us, and I give you my word of honor that nobody shall learn a word of what we are going to say to each other. Perfect irresponsibility and impunity for every thing that will be spoken during this interview. Are you content with this, and will you promise me to open your mind freely to me?"

"I promise it, your excellency, and shall reply truthfully and fearlessly to whatever questions you may address to me, provided I am able to tell you the truth."

"Yes, sir," replied Thugut, shrugging his shoulders. "Every thing has two sides, and both are true according to the stand-point from which one is looking at them. You have two sides yourself, sir, and they are contrasting very strongly with each other. You are a native of Switzerland, and yet you depict the Hapsburg princes in your works with more genuine enthusiasm than any of our Austrian historians. You are a republican, and yet you are serving a monarchy, the forms of which seem to agree with you exceedingly well. You belong to the orthodox reformed church, and yet you have written 'The Voyages of the Popes,' and 'The Letters of Two Catholic Prelates.' You are a friend of justice, and yet you have even discovered good and praiseworthy qualities in that tyrannous King of France, Louis

XI. Now tell me, sir, which is your true side, and what you really are?"

"I am a man," said Johannes Müller, gently; "I commit errors and have my failings like all men, my heart is vacillating, but not my head. With my head I am standing above all parties, and above all individual feelings; hence I am able to write 'The Voyages of the Popes,' and 'The Letters of Two Catholic Prelates,' although, as your excellency stated, I am a member of the orthodox reformed church; and hence I am able to praise the Hapsburgs and serve a monarchy, although I am a republican. But my heart does not stand above the contending parties; my heart loves mankind, and takes pity on their failings; hence it is able to discover praiseworthy qualities even in Louis XI. of France, for in the *bad* king, it constantly follows the vestiges of the man whom nature created *good* and *humane*."

"Those are the views of Jean Jacques Rousseau!" exclaimed Thugut, contemptuously; "but these views are inapplicable to the world and to practical life; he who desires to derive advantages from men, first, of all things, must avail himself of their bad qualities and flatter them. To hold intercourse with perfectly virtuous men is tedious and unprofitable; fortunately, however, there are very few of them. I should have no use whatever for such patterns of virtue, and, instead of admiring them, I should try to annihilate them. He who is to be a welcome tool for me, must either have a stain by which I may catch him at the slightest symptom of disobedience, like an insect tied to a string, and draw him back to me, or be must be so narrow-minded and ignorant as not to understand me fully, and to be unable to divine and penetrate my hidden thoughts and intentions." *

"In that case I must hope never to be a welcome tool of your excellency," said Müller, gravely.

"Are you so sure of your virtue? Are you unconscious of any stain on your character?"

"If principles be virtue, yes; in that case I am sure of my virtue," said Müller, calmly. "I shall never be unfaithful to my principles, and I hope never to have a stain on my conscience."

"Who is able to say that?" exclaimed Thugut, laughing; "many a one has become a murderer, who was unwilling to tread on a worm, and many a one has become a perjurer, who protested solemnly that he would never utter a lie. But a truce to philosophical discussions. I like to go directly at my aim, and to utter my thoughts clearly and precisely. Listen, then, to me, and learn what I want you to do. You are a great mind, an illustrious historian, a very learned man, and you are pining away among the shelves of your imperial library. The greatest historian of the century is nothing but the custodian of a library, and is subordinate to a chief whom he must obey, although the latter is mentally a pigmy compared with him. Such a position is unworthy of your eminent abilities, or tell me, do you feel contented with it?"

Johannes Müller smiled sadly. "Who is able to say that he feels contented?" he asked. "I am, perhaps, a bad custodian, and that may be the reason why the prefect of the Imperial Library, Baron Fenish, is not on good terms with me, and profits by every opportunity to mortify me. A German *savant* never was an independent man, for he generally lacks the most indispensable requisite for an independent position: he generally lacks wealth."

"Then you are poor?" asked Thugut, with flashing eyes.

"I have no other means than my salary. The Muses will adorn a man, but they will not feed him."

"I will deliver you from your subordinate position," said Thugut, hastily; "you shall be independent, free, and rich. You are a fool to bury yourself, with your glory and with your pen, in the dust of old books. Life and history are calling, and offering you their metal tablets to write thereon. Write, then; write the history of our times; render yourself an organ of the age; assist us, by your writings, in preserving the government and law and order. Defend, with your ringing voice, the actions of the government against the aspersions of this would-be wise, noisy, and miserable people, and you shall have a brilliant position and an annual salary of four thousand florins. You are silent? You are right; consider well what I am proposing to you. I offer you a brilliant position. I will make you the great historian of our times. It affords you always so much pleasure to praise and commend; well, sir, praise and commend what we are doing. Assist me, at least, in mystifying our contemporaries and posterity a little, and I will reward you in the most liberal manner. A good title, a large salary, and we will, moreover, pay your debts."

"Ah! your excellency knows that I have debts, and you believe that to be the string by which you may draw me to you like an insect?" asked Müller, smiling. "To become the historian of our times is an honorable and welcome offer, and I confess to your excellency that I have al

* Thug...   ...cords.—17.. Hormayer, "Lebensbilder aus...   ...ngskrieg." vol. i., p. 322.

ready finished many a chapter of it in my head, and that I have devoted a great deal of attention to the special history of Austria. It would be agreeable to me if your excellency would permit me to recite to you a few passages from the history of Austria, as I have elaborated it in my head. This will be the best way for your excellency to obtain the conviction whether I am really able to fill so brilliant a position as your excellency has offered me, and whether my services deserve so liberal a salary."

"Well, sir, let me hear a few passages from your 'History of Austria.' I am very anxious to listen to them."

"And your excellency remembers the promise that there is to be irresponsibility and impunity for whatever will be said during this interview?"

"I do, sir, and I swear that your words shall never be repeated to any one, and that I shall only remember them when I have to reward you for them. I swear, besides, that I will quietly and patiently listen to you until you have concluded."

"I thank your excellency," said Johannes Müller, bowing gracefully. "I should like to recite to your excellency now a chapter that I desire to write on the literature of Austria. I turn my eyes back to the days of Maria Theresa and Joseph the Second. Both of them were lovers of literature, art, and science, which both of them promoted and fostered. Joseph expelled darkness from his states and uttered the great words, ' *The mind shall be free!*' And the mind became free. It became active and exalted in every art; the poets raised their voices; the learned sent the results of their studies into the world, and labored powerfully for the advancement and enlightenment of the people. The mind tore down the barriers that stupid fear had raised between Austria and the other German states, and the great poets who had lately arisen in Germany now became, also, the poets and property of Austria. Austria called Lessing and Klopstock *her* poets; like the rest of Germany, she enthusiastically admired Schiller's 'Robbers,' and wept over 'Werther's Sorrows;' she was delighted with the poetry of Wieland; she learned to love the clear and noble mind of Herder, and the writings of Jean Paul admonished her to learn and to reflect. It was a glorious period, your excellency, for a young nation had arisen in Austria, and it was drawing its nourishment from the breasts of a young literature."

"And sucking from these breasts the revolutionary spirit, and the arrogance of independent thinkers," interrupted Thugut, rudely.

Johannes Müller seemed not to have heard him, and continued: "Joseph the Second died; scarce-

ly a decade has passed, and what has this decade made of Austria? The mind has been chained again; the censor with his scissors has taken his stand again by the side of the Austrian boundary-post; and the wall severing Austria from Germany has been reërected. Every thing now has become again suspicious; even the national spirit of the Austrian, even his hatred of foreign oppression, and his hostility to foreign encroachments. In this hatred itself the government sees the possibility of a rising, and a spirit of opposition, for it sees that the people are no longer asleep, but awake and thinking, and thought in itself is even now an opposition. Every manifestation of enthusiasm for a man who has spoken of the freedom and independence of Germany is looked upon with suspicion, and the noblest men are being proscribed and banished, merely because the people love them, and hope and expect great things from them. The people, according to the wishes of government, shall do nothing but sleep, obey, and be silent; the people shall manifest no enthusiasm for any thing; the people shall love nothing, desire nothing, think nothing; the people shall have no heroes, to whom they are attached; for the glory of the heroes might eclipse the emperor, and the shouts of love sound like shouts of insurrection."

"You refer to the Archdukes Charles and John," said Thugut, quietly. "It is true, I have removed Archduke Charles from his command, for his popularity with the army and people is very great, and would have become dangerous to the emperor. We must conquer through tools, and not through heroes; the latter are very unpleasant to deal with, for they do not gratefully receive their reward as a favor, but they impudently claim and take it as a right. The imperial throne must be surrounded by heroes, but these heroes must never eclipse the imperial throne. Pardon this note to your chapter, and proceed."

"The heroes of the sword are cast aside," continued Johannes Müller, "but neither the heroes of thought nor the heroes of literature are spared. The government tries to disgrace and insult literature, because it is unable to assassinate it entirely; it drags literature into the caves of unworthy censors, and mutilates its most beautiful limbs and destroys the most magnificent splendor of its ideas. The government is *afraid* of the mind; hence it desires to kill it. A government, however, may commit many mistakes, but it never ought to show that it is afraid, fear exposing it to ridicule. And if we ought not to weep over the persecutions which the apprehensions of the government have caused to be instituted against literature, we ought to laugh at them. Whole volumes of the most sublime works of Gibbon, Robertson, Hume, and, other great historians have been prohibited; and there is not one of our German poets—neither Goethe, nor Schiller, nor Herder, nor Wieland, nor Lessing, nor Jean Paul—whose works are not ostracized in German Austria. Fear and a bad conscience scent everywhere allusions, references, and hints. Hence history is banished from the stage; for the history of the past constantly points with a menacing finger at the sore spots of the present. Shakespeare's 'King Lear' has been prohibited, because the public might believe princes would lose their heads if weighed down by misfortunes. 'Hamlet,' 'Richard the Third,' and 'Macbeth' must not be performed, because people might get accustomed to the dethronement and assassination of emperors and kings. Schiller's 'Mary Stuart' is looked upon as an allusion to Marie Antoinette; 'Wallenstein' and 'Tell' are ostracized, because they might provoke revolutions and military mutinies. The 'Merchant of Venice' must not be performed, because it might give rise to riotous proceedings against the Jews; and in Schiller's 'Love and Intrigue,' President de Kalb has been transformed into a plebeian *ricedomus*, in order to maintain the respect due to the nobility and to the government functionaries. It is true, it is permitted to represent villains and impostors on the stage, but they must never be noblemen; and if men of ideal character are to be brought upon the stage, they must be either princes, counts, or police-directors. For even more sacred than the dignity of the highest classes is the holy police, the great guardian of the government, the great spy watching the people, who are being deprived of every thing; to whom every intellectual enjoyment, every free manifestation of their enthusiasm is forbidden, and who are yet required to deem themselves happy, and that they shall be faithfully attached to their government! If the government enslaves the people, it must expect that these slaves will lose all sense of honor and justice, and willingly sell themselves to him who holds out to them the most glittering offers, and knows best how to tempt them by golden promises!—I am through, your excellency," said Johannes Müller, drawing a deep breath; "I have recited to you my whole chapter on the literature of Austria, and I thank you for having listened to me so patiently. Now it is for your excellency alone to decide whether you deem me worthy of filling the honorable position you have offered. I am ready to accept it, and to write the history of our times in *this* spirit,

and shall be very grateful if your excellency will grant me for this purpose your protection and a salary of four thousand florins."

Thugut looked with an air of pride and disdain into his glowing face.

"My dear sir," he said, after a long pause— "my dear sir, I was mistaken in you, for I believed you to have a clear head and a strong mind, and I perceive now that you are nothing but a weak enthusiast, dreaming of ideal fancies which one day will turn out entirely differently; to become spectres, from which you will shrink back in dismay. You will not always remain the enthusiastic admirer of freedom as at present; and the proud republican will one day, perhaps, be transformed into the obedient servant of a tyrant. You assured me quite haughtily that you had no stain on your conscience; let me tell you, sir, that there is a stain on your character, and I should have profited by it—you are vain. I should not have tried to bribe you with money, but with flattery, and I had been successful. I had too good an opinion of you, however. I believed you had a vigorous mind, capable of comprehending what is necessary and useful, and of preferring the practical and advantageous to the ideal. Although a native of Switzerland, you are a genuine German dreamer, and I hate dreamers. Go, sir, remain custodian of the Imperial Library and complete your catalogues, but never imagine that you will be able with your weak hand to stem the wheel of history and of political affairs; the wheel would only destroy your hand and what little glory you have obtained, and hurl you aside like a crushed dog. Farewell!"

He turned his back upon Johannes Müller, and placed himself at the window until the soft noise of the closing door told him that the historian had left him.

"What a fool!" he said. Then, turning around again—"a genuine German fool! Wanted to lecture me—*me!*"

And, amused by the idea, Thugut burst into loud laughter. He then rang the bell violently, and as soon as the *valet de chambre* made his appearance he ordered him to get the carriage ready for him.

Fifteen minutes later the minister left the chancery of state for the purpose of repairing, as was his custom every evening, to his garden in the Währinger Street. The streets through which he had to pass were crowded with citizens, who were talking with ill-concealed rage about the fresh defeat of the Austrians at Marengo, and were loudly calling out that Minister Thugut was alone to blame for Austria's misfortunes, and that he was the only obstacle that prevented the emperor from making peace. And the people surrounded the well-known carriage of the minister with constantly-increasing exasperation, and cried in a constantly louder and more menacing tone: "We do not want war! We want peace! peace!"

Thugut was leaning back comfortably on the cushions of his carriage. He seemed not to hear the shouts of the people, and not to deem them worthy of the slightest notice. Only when the tumult increased in violence, and when the incensed people commenced hurling stones and mud at his carriage, the minister rose for a moment in order to look out with an air of profound disdain. He then leaned back on his seat, and muttered, with a glance of indescribable contempt:

"*Canaille!*" *

CHAPTER XXXVI.

THUGUT'S FALL.

Tidings of fresh defeats had reached Vienna; more disasters had befallen the army, and the great victory of Marengo had been followed, on the 3d of December, 1800, by the battle of Hohenlinden, in which Moreau defeated the Austrians under Archduke John.

Even Thugut, the immovable and constant prime minister, felt alarmed at so many calamities, and he was generally in a gloomy and spiteful humor.

He felt that there was a power stronger than his will, and this feeling maddened him with anger. He was sitting at his desk, with a clouded brow and closely compressed lips, his sullen eyes fixed on the papers before him, which a courier, just arrived from the headquarters of the army, had delivered to him. They contained evil tidings; they informed him of the immense losses of the Austrians, and of the insolence of the victorious French general, who had only granted the Austrian application for an armistice on condition that the fortresses of Ulm, Ingolstadt and Philipsburg be surrendered to him; and these humiliating terms had been complied with in order to gain time and to concentrate a new army. For Thugut's stubbornness had not been broken yet, and he still obstinately refused to conclude the peace so urgently desired by the whole Austrian people, nay, by the emperor himself.

"No, no, no peace!" he muttered, when he had perused the dispatches. "We will fight on, even

though we should be buried under the ruins of Austria! I hate that revolutionary France, and I shall never condescend to extend my hand to it for the purpose of making peace. We will fight on, and no one shall dare to talk to me about peace!"

A low rap at the door leading to the reception-room interrupted his soliloquy, and when he had harshly called out, "Come in," his *valet de chambre* appeared in the door.

"Your excellency," he said, timidly, "Counts Colloredo, Saurau, and Lehrbach have just arrived, and desire to obtain an interview with your excellency."

Not a muscle moved in Thugut's face to betray his surprise, and he ordered the servant in a perfectly calm voice to admit the gentlemen immediately. He then hastily walked to the door for the purpose of meeting them. They entered a few minutes later: first, Count Colloredo, minister of the imperial household; next, Count Saurau, minister of police; and last, Count Lehrbach, minister without portfolio. Thugut surveyed the three dignitaries with a single searching glance. He perceived that good-natured Count Colloredo looked rather frightened; that the ferocious eyes of Count Lehrbach were glistening like those of a tiger just about to lacerate his victim; and that Count Saurau, that diplomatist generally so impenetrable, permitted a triumphant smile to play on his lips. With the sure tact, which Thugut never lost sight of, he saw from the various miens of these three gentlemen what had occasioned their call upon him, and his mind was made up at once.

He received them, however, with a pleasant salutation, and took the hand of Count Colloredo in order to conduct him to an arm-chair. Colloredo's hand was cold and trembling, and Thugut said to himself, "He is charged with a very disagreeable message for me, and he is afraid to deliver it."

"Your excellency is doubtless astonished to see us disturb you at so unexpected an hour," said Count Colloredo, in a tremulous voice, when the four gentlemen had taken seats.

"No, I am not astonished," said Thugut, calmly. "You, gentlemen, on the contrary, have only anticipated my wishes. I was just about to invite you to see me for the purpose of holding a consultation, very disastrous tidings having arrived from the headquarters of our army. We have lost a battle at Hohenlinden—Archduke John has been defeated."

"And Moreau has already crossed the Inn and is now advancing upon Vienna," said Count Lehr-

---

* Hormayer's "Lebensbilder," vol. i., p. 280.

bach, with a sneer. "You have made some terrible mistakes in your hopes of victory, minister."

"Yes, indeed, you have made some terrible mistakes, my dear little baron," said Count Saurau, laying particular stress on the last words.

Thugut fixed a laughing look on him. "Why," he said, "how tender we are to-day, and how big your beak has grown, my dear little count! You seem but slightly afflicted by the misfortunes of the empire, for your face is as radiant as that of a young cock that has just driven a rival from its dunghill. But it must have been a very stupid old cock that has condescended to fight with you. Now, my dear Count Colloredo, let us talk about business. We have been defeated at Hohenlinden, and Moreau is advancing upon Vienna. These are two facts that cannot be disputed. But we shall recover from these blows; we shall send a fresh army against Moreau, and it will avenge our previous disasters."

"However, your excellency, that is a mere hope, and we may be disappointed again," replied Colloredo, anxiously. "The emperor, my gracious master, has lost faith in our victories, unless we should have an able and tried general at the head of our forces—a general equally trusted by the army and the nation."

"Let us, then, place such a general at the head of the army," said Thugut, calmly; "let us immediately appoint Archduke Charles commander-in-chief of the Austrian forces."

"Ah, I am glad that you consent to it," exclaimed Colloredo, joyfully, "for the emperor has just instructed me to go to his distinguished brother and to request him in the name of his majesty to resume the command-in-chief."

"Well, he will accept it," said Thugut, smiling, "for commanding and ruling always is a very agreeable occupation; and many a one would be ready and willing to betray his benefactor and friend, if he thereby could acquire power and distinction. Are you not, too, of this opinion, my dear little Count Saurau? Ah, you do not know how tenderly I am devoted to you. You are the puppet which I have raised and fostered, and which I wanted to transform into a man according to my own views. I am not to blame if you have not become a man, but always remained only a machine to be directed by another hand. Beware, my dear, of ever falling into unskilful or bad hands, for then you would be lost, notwithstanding your elasticity and pliability. But you have got a worthy friend there at your side, noble, excellent Count Lehrbach. Do you know, my dear Count Lehrbach, that there are evil-disposed persons who often tried to prejudice me

against you, who wanted to insinuate you were a rival of mine, and were notoriously anxious to supplant me and to become prime minister in my place? Truly, these anxious men actually went so far as to caution me against you."

"And did not your excellency make any reply to them?" asked Count Lehrbach, laughing.

"Parbleu, you ask me whether I have made a reply to them or not?" said Thugut. "I have always replied to those warning voices: 'I need not break Count Lehrbach's neck; he will attend to that himself. I like to push a man forward whom I am able to hang at any time.'" *

"But you have not taken into consideration that the man whom you are pushing forward might reach back and afford you the same pleasure which you had in store for him," exclaimed Lehrbach, laughing boisterously.

"Yes, that is true," said Thugut, artlessly; "I ought to have been afraid of you, after all, and to perceive that you have got a nail in your head on which one may be hanged very comfortably. But, my friends, we detain Count Colloredo by our jokes, and you are aware that he must hasten to the archduke in order to beg him to become our commander-in-chief and to sign a treaty of peace with France. For I believe we will make peace at all events."

"We shall make peace provided we fulfil the conditions which Bonaparte has exacted," said Count Colloredo, timidly.

"Ah, he has exacted conditions, and these conditions have been addressed to the emperor and not to myself?" asked Thugut.

"The dispatches were addressed to me, the minister of the imperial household," said Count Colloredo, modestly. "The first of these conditions is that Austria and France make peace without letting England participate in the negotiations."

"And the second condition is beaming already on Count Lehrbach's forehead," said Thugut, calmly. "Bonaparte demands that I shall withdraw from the cabinet, as my dismissal would be to him a guaranty of the pacific intentions of Austria.† Am I mistaken?"

"You are not; but the emperor, gratefully acknowledging the long and important services your excellency has rendered to the state, will not fulfil this condition and incur the semblance of ingratitude."

"Austria and my emperor require a sacrifice of me, and I am ready to make it," said Thugut,

---

* Thugut's own words.—Hormayer's "Lebensbilder," vol. i., p. 332.

† Häusser's "History of Germany," vol. ii., p. 324.

solemnly. "I shall write immediately to his majesty the emperor and request him to permit me to withdraw from the service of the state without delay."

Count Colloredo sighed mournfully; Count Saurau smiled, and Count Lehrbach laughed in Thugut's face with the mien of a hyena.

"And do you know who will be your successor?" asked the latter.

"My dear sir, I shall have no successor, only a miserable imitator, and you will be that imitator," said Thugut, proudly. "But I give you my word that this task will not be intrusted to you for a long while. I shall now draw up my request to the emperor, and I beg you, gentlemen, to deliver it to his majesty."

Without saying another word he went to his desk, hastily wrote a few lines on a sheet of paper, which he then sealed and directed.

"Count Colloredo," he said, "be kind enough to hand this letter to the emperor."

Count Colloredo took it with one hand, and with the other he drew a sealed letter from his bosom.

"And here, your excellency," he said—"here I have the honor to present to you his majesty's reply. The emperor, fully cognizant of your noble and devoted patriotism, was satisfied in advance that you would be ready to sacrifice yourself on the altar of the country, and, however grievous the resolution, he was determined to accept the sacrifice. The emperor grants your withdrawal from the service of the state; and Count Louis Cobenzl, who is to set out within a few hours for Luneville, in order to open there the peace conference with the brother of the First Consul, Joseph Bonaparte, will take along the official announcement of this change in the imperial cabinet. Count Lehrbach, I have the honor to present to you, in the name of the emperor, this letter, by which his majesty appoints you minister of the interior."

He handed to Count Lehrbach a letter, which the latter hastily opened and glanced over with greedy eyes.

"And you, my dear little Count Saurau?" asked Thugut, compassionately. "Have they not granted you any share whatever in the spoils?"

"Yes, they have; I have received the honorable commission to communicate to the good people of Vienna the joyful news that Baron Thugut has been dismissed," said Count Saurau; "and I shall now withdraw in order to fulfil this commission."

He nodded sneeringly to Thugut, bowed respectfully to Count Colloredo, and left the minister's cabinet.

"I am avenged," he muttered, while crossing the anteroom; "henceforward the shipbuilder's son will call me no longer his 'dear little count.'"

"And I shall withdraw, too," said Count Lehrbach, with a scornful smile. "I shall withdraw in order to make all necessary preparations, so that my furniture and horses can be brought here to-morrow to the building of the chancery of state. For I suppose, Baron Thugut, you will move out of this house in the course of to-day?"

"Yes, I shall, and you will withdraw now, sir," said Thugut, dismissing the count with a haughty wave of his hand.

Count Lehrbach went out laughing, and Count Colloredo remained alone with Thugut.

"And you," asked Thugut, "do not you wish to take leave of me by telling me something that might hurt my feelings?"

"I have to tell you a great many things, but nothing that will hurt your feelings," said Colloredo, gently. "First of all things, I must beg you not to deprive me of your friendship and advice, but to assist me as heretofore. I need your advice and your help more than ever, and shall do nothing without previously ascertaining your will."

"The emperor will not permit it," said Thugut, gloomily. "He will require you to break off all intercourse with me."

"On the contrary," whispered Colloredo, "the emperor desires you always to assist him and myself by your counsels. The emperor desires you to be kind enough to call every day upon me in order to consider with me the affairs of the day, and there, accidentally of course, you will meet his majesty, who wants to obtain the advice of your experience and wisdom. You will remain minister, but incognito."

A flash of joy burst forth from Thugut's eyes, but he quickly suppressed it again.

"And shall I meet in your house sometimes your wife, the beautiful Countess Victoria?" he asked.

"Victoria implores you, through my mouth, to trust her and never to doubt of her friendship. I beg you to receive the same assurance as far as I am concerned. You have rendered both of us so happy, my dear baron; you were the mediator of a marriage in which both of us, Victoria as well as myself, have found the highest bliss on earth, and never shall we cease to be grateful to you for it; nor shall we ever be able or willing to do without your advice and assistance. You are our head, we are your arms, and the head commanding the arms, we shall always obey you. Victoria implores you to tell her any thing you desire, so that she may give you forthwith a proof of her willingness to serve you. She has charged me to ask you to do so as a proof of your friendship."

"Well," said Thugut, laughing, "I accept your offer, as well as that of your beautiful wife Victoria. Count Lehrbach has been appointed minister and he wants even to move to-morrow into the chancery of state. We will let him move in early in the morning, but, in the course of the day, the emperor will do well to send him his dismissal, for Count Lehrbach is unworthy of being his majesty's minister of state. His hand is stained with the blood which was shed at Rastadt, and a minister's hand must be clean."

"But whom shall we appoint minister in Lehrbach's place?"

"Count Louis Cobenzl, for his name will offer the best guaranty of our pacific intentions toward France."

"But Count Cobenzl is to go to Luneville to attend the peace conference."

"Let him do so, and until his return let Count Trautmannsdorf temporarily discharge the duties of his office."

"Ah, that is true, that is a splendid idea!" exclaimed Count Colloredo, joyfully. "You are a very sagacious and prudent statesman, and I shall hasten to lay your advice before the emperor. You may rest assured that every thing shall be done in accordance with your wishes. Lehrbach remains minister until to-morrow at noon; he then receives his dismissal, Count Louis Cobenzl will be appointed his successor, and Count Trautmannsdorf will temporarily discharge the duties of the office until Cobenzl's return from Luneville. Shall it be done in this manner?"

"Yes, it shall," said Thugut, almost sternly.

"But this does not fulfil Victoria's prayer," said the count, anxiously. "I am able to attend to these matters, but Victoria also wants to give you a proof of her friendship."

"Well, I ask her to prepare a little joke for me and you," replied Thugut. "Count Lehrbach will move early to-morrow morning with his whole furniture into the chancery of state. I beg Victoria to bring it about that he must move out to-morrow evening with his whole furniture, like a martin found in the dove-cote." *

---

* Thugut's wishes were fulfilled. Count Lehrbach lost on the very next day his scarcely-obtained portfolio, and he was compelled to remove the furniture which, in rude haste he had sent to the chancery of state in the morning, in the course of the same evening.—Vide Hormayer's "Lebensbilder," vol. i., p. 330.

"Ah, that will be a splendid joke," said Count Colloredo, laughing, "and my dear Victoria will be happy to afford you this little satisfaction. I am able to predict that Count Lehrbach will be compelled to move out to-morrow evening. But now, my dearest friend, I must hasten to Archduke Charles, who, as you are aware, is pouting on one of his estates. I shall at once repair thither, and be absent from Vienna for two days. Meantime, you will take care of Victoria as a faithful friend."

"I shall take care of her if the countess will permit me to do so," said Thugut, smiling, and accompanying Count Colloredo to the door.

His eyes followed him for a long while with an expression of haughty disdain.

"The fools remain," he said, "and I must go. But no, I shall not go! Let the world believe me to be a dismissed minister, I remain minister after all. I shall rule through my creatures, Colloredo and Victoria. I remain minister until I shall be tired of all these miserable intrigues, and retire in order to live for myself." *

CHAPTER XXXVII.

FANNY VON ARNSTEIN.

THE young Baroness Fanny von Arnstein had just finished her morning toilet and stepped from her dressing-room into her boudoir, in order to take her chocolate there, solitary and alone as ever. With a gentle sigh she glided into the armchair, and instead of drinking the chocolate placed before her in a silver breakfast set on the table, she leaned her head against the back of her chair and dreamily looked up to the ceiling. Her bosom heaved profound sighs from time to time, and the ideas which were moving her heart and her soul ever and anon caused a deeper blush to mantle her cheeks; but it quickly disappeared again, and was followed by an even more striking pallor.

---

* Thugut really withdrew definitely from the political stage, but secretly he retained his full power and authority, and Victoria de Poutet-Colloredo, the influential friend of the Empress Theresia, constantly remained his faithful adherent and confidante. All Vienna, however, was highly elated by the dismissal of Thugut, who had so long ruled the empire in the most arbitrary manner. An instance of his system is the fact that, on his withdrawal from the cabinet, there were found one hundred and seventy unopened dispatches and more than two thousand unopened letters. Thugut only perused what he believed to be worth the trouble of being read, and to the remainder he paid no attention whatever.—"Lebensbilder," vol. i. p. 327.

She was suddenly startled from her musings by a soft, timid rap at the door leading to the reception-room.

"Good Heaven!" she whispered, "I hope he will not dare to come to me so early, and without being announced."

The rapping at the door was renewed. "I cannot, will not receive him," she muttered; "it will be better not to be alone with him any more. I will bolt the door and make no reply whatever."

She glided with soft steps across the room to the door, and was just about to bolt it, when the rapping resounded for the third time, and a modest female voice asked:

"Are you there, baroness, and may I walk in?"

"Ah, it is only my maid," whispered the baroness, drawing a deep breath, as though an oppressive burden were removed from her breast, and she opened the door herself.

"Well, Fanchon," she asked, in her gentle, winning voice, "what do you want?"

"Pardon me, baroness," said the maid, casting an inquisitive look around the room, "the baron sent for me just now; he asked me if you had risen already and entered your boudoir, and when I replied in the affirmative, the baron gave me a message for you, with the express order, however, not to deliver it until you had taken your chocolate and finished your breakfast. I see now that I must not yet deliver it; the breakfast is still on the table just as it was brought in."

"Take it away; I do not want to eat any thing," said the baroness, hastily. "And now Fanchon, tell me your errand."

Fanchon approached the table, and while she seized the silver salver, she cast a glance of tender anxiety on her pale, beautiful mistress.

"You are eating nothing at all, baroness," she said, timidly; "for a week already I have had to remove the breakfast every morning in the same manner; you never tasted a morsel of it, and the valet de chambre says that you hardly eat any thing at the dinner-table either; you will be taken ill, baroness, if you go on in this manner, and—"

"Never mind, dear Fanchon," her mistress interrupted her with a gentle smile, "I have hardly any appetite, it is true, but I do not feel unwell, nor do I want to be taken ill. Let us say no more about it, and tell me the message the baron intrusted to you."

"The baron wished me to ask you if you would permit him to pay you immediately a visit, and if you would receive him here in your boudoir."

The baroness started, and an air of surprise overspread her features. "Tell the baron that he

will be welcome, and that I am waiting for him," she said then, calmly. But so soon as Fanchon had withdrawn, she whispered: "What is the meaning of all this? What is the reason of this unusual visit? Oh, my knees are trembling, and my heart is beating so violently, as though it wanted to burst. Why? What have I done, then? Am I a criminal, who is afraid to appear before her judge?"

She sank back into her arm-chair and covered her blushing face with her hands. "No," she said, after a long pause, raising her head again, "no, I am no criminal, and my conscience is guiltless. I am able to raise my eyes freely to my husband and to my God. So far, I have honestly struggled against my own heart, and I shall struggle on in the same manner. I—ah! he is coming," she interrupted herself when she heard steps in the adjoining room, and her eyes were fixed with an expression of anxious suspense on the door.

The latter opened, and her husband, Baron Arnstein, entered. His face was pale, and indicative of deep emotion; nevertheless, he saluted his wife with a kind smile, and bent down in order to kiss her hand, which she had silently given to him.

"I suppose you expected me?" he asked. "You knew, even before I sent Fanchon to you, that I should come and see you at the present hour?"

Fanny looked at him inquiringly, and in surprise. "I confess," she said, in an embarrassed tone, "that I did not anticipate your visit by any means until Fanchon announced it to me, and I only mention it to apologize for the dishabille in which you find me."

"Ah, you did not expect me, then?" exclaimed the baron, mournfully. "You have forgotten every thing? You did not remember that this is the anniversary of our wedding, and that five years have elapsed since that time?"

"Indeed," whispered Fanny, in confusion, "I did not know that this was the day."

"You felt its burden day after day, and it seemed to you, therefore, as though that ill-starred day were being renewed for you all the year round," exclaimed the baron, sadly. "Pardon my impetuosity and my complaints," he continued, when he saw that she turned pale and averted her face. "I will be gentle, and you shall have no reason to complain of me. But as you have forgotten the agreement which we made five years ago, permit me to remind you of it."

He took a chair, and, sitting down opposite her, fixed a long, melancholy look upon her. "When I led you to the altar five years ago to-day," he said, feelingly, "you were, perhaps, less beautiful than now, less brilliant, less majestic; but you were in better and less despondent spirits, although you were about to marry a man who was entirely indifferent to you."

"Oh, I did not say that you were indifferent to me," said Fanny, in a low voice; "only I did not know you, and, therefore, did not love you."

"You see that want of acquaintance was not the only reason," he said, with a bitter smile, "for now, I believe, you know me, and yet you do not love me. But let us speak of what brought me here to-day—of the past. You know that, before our marriage, you afforded me the happiness of a long and confidential interview, that you permitted me to look down into the depths of your pure and noble soul, that you unveiled to me your innocent heart, that did not yet exhibit either scars or wounds, nor even an image, a souvenir, and allowed me to be your brother and your friend, as you would not accept me as a lover and husband. Before the world, however, I became your husband, and took you to Vienna, to my house, of which you were to be the mistress and queen. The whole house was gayly decorated, and all the rooms were opened, for your arrival was to be celebrated by a ball. Only one door was locked; it was the door of this cabinet. I conducted you hither and said to you, 'This is your sanctuary, and no one shall enter it without your permission. In this boudoir you are not the Baroness Arnstein, not my wife; but here you are Fanny Itzig, the free and unshackled young girl, who is mistress of her will and affections. I shall never dare myself, without being expressly authorized by you, to enter this room; and when I shall be allowed to do so, I shall only come as a cavalier, who has the honor to pay a polite visit to a beautiful lady, to whom he is not connected in any manner whatever. Before the world I am your husband, but not in this room. Hence I shall never permit myself to ask what you are doing in this room, whom you are receiving here; for here you are only responsible to God and yourself.' Do you now remember that I said this to you at that time?"

"I do."

"I told you further that I begged you to continue with me one day here in this room the confidential conversation which we held before our marriage. I begged you to fix a period of five years for this purpose, and, during this time, to examine your heart and to see whether life at my side was at least a tolerable burden, or whether you wished to shake it off. I asked you to promise me that I might enter this room on the fifth anniversary of our wedding-day, for the purpose

of settling then with you our future mode of living. You were kind enough to grant my prayer, and to promise what I asked. Do you remember it?"

"I do," said Fanny, blushing; "I must confess, however, that I did not regard those words in so grave a light as to consider them as a formal obligation on your part. You would have been every day a welcome guest in this room, and it was unnecessary for you to wait for a particular day in accordance with an agreement made five years ago."

"Your answer is an evasive one," said the baron, sadly. "I implore you, let us now again speak as frankly and honestly as we did five years ago to-day! Will you grant my prayer?"

"I will," replied Fanny, eagerly; "and I am going to prove immediately that I am in earnest. You alluded a few minutes ago to our past, and asked me wonderingly if I had forgotten that interview on our wedding-day. I remember it so well, however, that I must direct your attention to the fact that you have forgotten the principal portion of what we said to each other at that time, or rather that, in your generous delicacy, and with that magnanimous kindness which you alone may boast of, you have intentionally omitted that portion of it. You remembered that I told you I did not love you, but you forgot that you then asked me if I loved another man. I replied to you that I loved no one, and never shall I forget the mournful voice in which you then said, 'It is by far easier to marry with a cold heart than to do so with a broken heart; for the cold heart may grow warm, but the broken heart—never!' Oh, do not excuse yourself," she continued, with greater warmth; "do not take me for so conceited and narrow-minded a being that I should have regarded those words of yours as an insult offered to me! It was, at the best, but a pang that I felt."

"A pang?" asked the baron, in surprise; and he fixed his dark eyes, with a wondrously impassioned expression, on the face of his beautiful wife.

"Yes, I felt a pang," she exclaimed, vividly, "for, on hearing your words, which evidently issued from the depths of your soul, on witnessing your unaffected and passionate grief, your courageous self-abnegation, I felt that your heart had received a wound which never would close again, and that you never would faithfully turn from your first love to a second one."

"Oh, my God," murmured the baron, and he averted his face in order not to let her see the blush suddenly mantling it.

Fanny did not notice it, and continued: "But

this dead love of yours laid itself like the cold hand of a corpse upon my breast and doomed it to everlasting coldness. With the consciousness that you never would love me, I had to cease striving for it, and give up the hope of seeing, perhaps, one day my heart awake in love for you, and the wondrous flower of a tenderness after marriage unfold itself, the gradual budding of which had been denied to us by the arbitrary action of our parents, who had not consulted our wishes, but only our fortunes. I became your wife with the full conviction that I should have to lead a life cold, dreary, and devoid of love, and that I could not be for you but an everlasting burden, a chain, an obstacle. My pride, that was revolting against it, told me that I should be able to bear this life in a dignified manner, but that I never ought to make even an attempt to break through this barrier which your love for another had erected between us, and which you tried to raise as high as possible."

"I!" exclaimed the baron, sadly.

"Yes, you," she said, gravely. "Or did you believe, perhaps, I did not comprehend your rigorous reserve toward me? I did not understand that you were wrapping around your aversion to me but a delicate veil? You conducted me to this room and told me that you never would enter it, and that you would only come here when specially invited by myself to do so. Well, sir, you managed very skilfully to conceal your intention never to be alone with me, and to lead an entirely separate life from me under this phrase, for you knew very well that my pride never would permit me to invite you here against your will."

"Oh, is it possible that I should have been misunderstood in this manner?" sighed the baron, but in so low a voice that Fanny did not hear him.

"You further told me," she continued, eagerly. "that I should only bear the name of your wife before the world, but not in this room where I was always to be Fanny Itzig. You were kind enough to give to this moral divorce, which you pronounced in this manner, the semblance as though you were the losing party, and as though you were only actuated by motives of delicacy toward me. I understood it all, however, and when you left this room after that conversation, sir, I sank down on my knees and implored God that He might remain with me in this loneliness to which you had doomed me, and I implored my pride to sustain and support me, and I swore to my maidenly honor that I would preserve it unsullied and sacred to my end."

"Oh, good Heaven!" groaned the baron, tottering backward like a man suddenly seized with vertigo.

Fanny, in her own glowing excitement, did not notice it.

"And thus I commenced my new life," she said, "a life of splendor and magnificence; it was glittering without, but dreary within, and in the midst of our most brilliant circles I constantly felt lonely; surrounded by hundreds who called themselves friends of our house, I was always alone—I, the wife of your reception-room, the disowned of my boudoir! Oh, it is true I have obtained many triumphs; I have seen this haughty world, that only received me hesitatingly, at last bow to me; the Jewess has become the centre of society, and no one on entering our house believes any longer that he is conferring a favor upon us, but, on the contrary, receiving one from us. It is the ton now to visit our house; we are being overwhelmed with invitations, with flattering attentions. But tell me, sir, is all this a compensation for the happiness which we are lacking and which we never will obtain? Oh, is it not sad to think that both of us, so young, so capable of enjoying happiness, should already be doomed to eternal resignation and eternal loneliness? Is it not horrible to see us, and ought not God Himself to pity us, if from the splendor of His starry heavens He should look down for a moment into our gloomy breasts? I bear in it a cold, frozen heart, and you a coffin. Oh, sir, do not laugh at me because you see tears in my eyes—it is only Fanny Itzig who is weeping; Baroness von Arnstein will receive your guests to-night in your saloons with a smiling face, and no one will believe that her eyes also know how to weep. But here, here in my widow-room, here in my nun's cell, I may be permitted to weep over you and me, who have been chained together with infrangible fetters, of which both of us feel the burden and oppression with equal bitterness and wrath. May God forgive our parents for having sacrificed our hearts on the altar of their God, who is Mammon; I shall ever hate them for it; I shall never forgive them, for they who knew life must have known that there is nothing more unhappy, more miserable, and more deplorable than a wife who does not love her husband, is not beloved by him."

"Is not beloved by him!" repeated the baron, approaching his wife who, like a broken reed, had sunk down on a chair, and seizing her hand, he said: "You say that I do not love you, Fanny! Do you know my heart, then? Have you deemed it worth while only a single time to fix your proud eyes on my poor heart? Did you ever show me a symptom of sympathy when I was sick, a trace of compassion when you saw me suffering? But no, you did not even see that I was suffering, or that I was sad. Your proud, cold glance always glided past me; it saw me rarely, it never sought me! What can you know, then, about my heart, and what would you care if I should tell you now that there is no longer a coffin in it, that it has awoke to a new life, and—"

"Baron!" exclaimed Fanny, rising quickly and proudly, "will you, perhaps, carry your magnanimity and delicacy so far as to make me a declaration of love? Did I express myself in my imprudent impetuosity so incorrectly as to make you believe I was anxious even now to gain your love, and that I was complaining of not having obtained it? Do you believe me to be an humble mendicant, to whom in your generosity you want to throw the morsel of a declaration of love? I thank you, sir, I am not hungry, and do not want this morsel. Let us at least be truthful and sincere toward each other, and the truth is, we do not love each other and shall never do so. Let us never try to feign what we never shall feel. And if you now should offer me your love I should have to reject it, for I am accustomed to a freezing temperature; and I should fare like the native of Siberia, I should die if I were to live in a warmer zone. Both of us are living in Siberia; well, then, as we cannot expect roses to bloom for us, let us try at least to catch sables for ourselves. The sable, moreover, is an animal highly valued by the whole world. People will envy our sable furs, for they know them to be costly; they would laugh at us if we should adorn our heads with roses, for roses are not costly by any means, they are common, and every peasant-girl may adorn herself with them."

"You are joking," said the baron, mournfully, "and yet there are tears glistening in your eyes. However, your will shall be sacred to me. I shall never dare to speak to you again about my heart. But let us speak about you and your future. The five years of our agreement have elapsed, and I am here to confer with you about your future. Tell me frankly and honestly, Fanny, do you wish to be divorced from me?"

She started and fixed a long and searching look on her husband.

"Your father died a year ago," she said, musingly, "you are now the chief of the firm; no one has a right to command any longer what you are to do, and being free now, you may offer your hand to her whom you love, I suppose?"

The baron uttered a shriek, and a death-like pallor overspread his face. "Have I deserved to be thus deeply despised by you?" he ejaculated.

Fanny quickly gave him her hand. "Pardon me," she said, cordially, "I have pained you quite unintentionally; the grief of this hour has rendered me cruel. No, I do not believe that you, merely for your own sake, addressed this question to me; I know, on the contrary, that you entertain for me the sympathy of a brother, of a friend, and I am satisfied that your question had my happiness in view as well as yours."

"Well," he said, with the semblance of perfect calmness, "let me repeat my question, then: do you want to be divorced from me?"

Fanny slowly shook her head. "Why?" she asked, sadly. "I repeat to you what I told you once already; we are living in Siberia—let us remain there. We are accustomed to a freezing temperature; we might die, perhaps, in a warmer zone."

"Or your heart might exult, perhaps, with happiness and delight," said the baron, and now his eyes were fixed inquiringly upon her face. "You called me just now your friend, you admitted that I felt for you the sympathy of a brother; well, then, let me speak to you as your brother and friend. Do not reject the offer of a divorce so quickly, Fanny, for I tell you now I shall never renew it, and if you do not give me up to-day, you are chained to me forever, for I shall never be capable again of a courage so cruel against myself. Consider the offer well, therefore. Think of your youth, your beauty, and your inward loneliness. Remember that your heart is yearning for love and pining away in its dreary solitude. And now look around, Fanny; see how many of the most distinguished and eminent cavaliers are surrounding you, and longing for a glance, for a smile from you. See by how many you are being loved and adored, and then ask yourself whether or not among all these cavaliers no one would be able to conquer your heart if it were free? For I know your chaste virtue; I know that, although chained to an unbeloved husband, you never would prove faithless to him and avow love to another so long as you were not free. Imagine, then, you were free, and then ask your heart if it will not decide for one of your many adorers."

"No, no," she said, deprecatingly, "I cannot imagine a state of affairs that does not exist; as I am not free, I must not entertain the thoughts of a free woman."

Her husband approached her, and seizing her hand, looked at her in a most touching and imploring manner.

"Then you have forgotten that five years ago, on our wedding-day, you promised me always to trust me?" he asked. "You have forgotten that you took an oath that you would tell me so soon as your heart had declared for another man?"

Fanny could not bear his look, and lowered her eyes.

"It has not declared for another man, and, therefore, I have nothing to confide to you," she said, in a low voice.

The baron constantly held her hand in his own, and his eyes were still fixed on her face.

"Let us consider the matter together," he said. "Permit me to review your cavaliers and admirers, and to examine with you if there is not one among them whom you may deem worthy of your love."

"What!" ejaculated Fanny, having recourse to an outburst of merriment in order to conceal her embarrassment, "you want to make me a Portia, and perform with me a scene from the 'Merchant of Venice?'"

"Yes, you are Portia, and I will play the *rôle* of your confidant," said Baron Arnstein, smiling. "Well, let us begin our review. First, there is Count Palfy, a member of the old nobility, of the most faultless manners, young, rich, full of ardent love for—"

"For your dinner-parties and the rare dishes that do not cost him any thing," interrupted Fanny. "He is an epicure, who prefers dining at other people's tables because he is too stingy to pay for the Indian birds'-nests which he relishes greatly. As for myself, he never admires me until after dinner, for so soon as his stomach is at rest his heart awakes and craves for food; and his heart is a gourmand, too—it believes love to be a dish; *voilà tout!*"

"Next, there is the handsome Marchese Pallafredo," said her husband, smiling.

"He loves me because he has been told that I speak excellent and pure German, and because he wants me to teach him how to speak German. He takes me for a grammar, by means of which he may become familiar with our language without any special effort."

"Then there is Count Esterhazy, one of our most brilliant cavaliers; you must not accuse him of stinginess, for he is just the reverse, a spend-thrift, squandering his money with full hands; nor must you charge him with being an epicure, for he scarcely eats any thing at all at our dinner-parties, and does not know what he is eating, his eyes being constantly riveted on you, and his thoughts being occupied exclusively with you."

"It is true, he admires me," said Fanny, calmly, "but only a few months ago he was as ardent an adorer of my sister Eskeles, and before he was enamoured of her, he was enthusiastically in love

with Countess Victoria Colloredo. He loves every woman who is fashionable in society for the time being, and his heart changes as rapidly as the fashions."

"Besides, there is the prebendary, Baron Weichs," said her husband; "a gentleman of great ability, a *savant*, and withal a cavalier, a—"

"Oh, pray do not speak of him!" exclaimed Fanny, with an air of horror. "His love is revolting to me, and fills me with shame and dismay. Whenever he approaches me my heart shrinks back as if from a venomous serpent, and a feeling of disgust pervades my whole being, although I am unable to account for it. There is something in his glances that is offensive to me; and although he has never dared to address me otherwise than in the most respectful and reserved manner, his conversation always makes me feel as though I were standing under a thunder-cloud from which the lightning might burst forth at any moment to shatter me. As you say, he is a man of ability, but he is a bad man; he is passionately fond of the ladies, but he does not respect them."

"And he does not even deserve being mentioned here," said the baron, smiling, "for, even though you were free already, the prebendary never could enjoy the happiness of becoming your husband, and I know that your heart is too chaste to love a man who is unable to offer you his hand. Let us, then, look for such a man among the other cavaliers. There is, for instance, Prince Charles, of Lichtenstein, the most amiable, genial, and handsome of your admirers; a young prince who is neither haughty nor proud, neither prodigal nor stingy; who neither makes love to all ladies so soon as they become fashionable as does Count Esterhazy, nor wants to learn German from you, as does the Marchese Pallafredo; a young man as beautiful as Apollo, as brave as Mars, modest notwithstanding his learning, and affable and courteous notwithstanding his high birth. Well, Fanny, you do not interrupt me? Your sharp tongue, that was able to condemn all the others, has no such sentence for the Prince von Lichtenstein. You suffer me to praise him. Then you assent to my words?"

"I can neither contradict you nor assent to your words," said Fanny, with a forced smile; "I do not know the prince sufficiently to judge him. He has been at Vienna but a very few months—"

"But he has been a daily visitor in our house during that period," said her husband, interrupting her, "and he is constantly seen at your side All Vienna know that the prince is deeply enamoured of you, and he does not conceal it by any means, not even from myself. A few days ago, when he was so unfortunate as not to find you at home, because you were presiding over a meeting of your benevolent society, he met me all alone in the reception-room. Suddenly, in the midst of a desultory conversation, he paused, embraced me passionately, and exclaimed: 'Be not so kind, so courteous, and gentle toward me, for I hate you, I detest you—because I hate every thing keeping me back from her; I detest every thing that prevents me from joining *her!* Forgive my love for her and my hatred toward you; I feel both in spite of myself. If you were not her husband, I should love you like a friend, but that accursed word renders you a mortal enemy of mine. And still I bow to you in humility—still I implore you to be generous; do not banish me from your house, from *her,* for I should die if I were not allowed to see her every day!'"

Fanny had listened to him with blushing cheeks and in breathless suspense. Her whole soul was speaking from the looks which she fixed on her husband, and with which she seemed to drink every word, like sweet nectar, from his lips.

"And what did you reply to him?" she asked, in a dry and husky voice, when the baron was silent.

"I replied to him that you alone had to decide who should appear at our parties, and that every one whom you had invited would be welcome to me. I further told him that his admiration for you did not astonish me at all, and that I would readily forgive his hatred, for—"

The baron paused all at once and looked at his wife with a surprised and inquiring glance. She had started in sudden terror; a deep blush was burning on her cheeks, and her eyes, which had assumed a rapturous and enthusiastic expression, turned toward the door.

The baron's eyes followed her glance, and he heard now a slight noise at the door.

"I believe somebody has knocked at the door," he said, fixing his piercing eyes on his wife.

She averted her head and whispered, "Yes, I believe so."

"And it is the second time already," said the baron, calmly. "Will you not permit the stranger to walk in?"

"I do not know," she said, in great embarrassment, "I—"

Suddenly the door opened, and a young man appeared on the threshold.

"Ah, the Prince von Lichtenstein," said the baron, and he went with perfect calmness and politeness to meet the prince who, evidently in great surprise, remained standing in the door, and was staring gloomily at the strange and unexpected group.

"Come in, my dear sir," said the baron, quietly; "the baroness will be very grateful to you for coming here just at this moment and interrupting our conversation, for it referred to dry business matters. I laid a few old accounts, that had been running for five years, before the baroness, and she gave me a receipt for them, that was all. Our interview, moreover, was at an end, and you need not fear to have disturbed us. Permit me, therefore, to withdraw, for you know very well that, in the forenoon, I am nothing but a banker, a business man, and have to attend to the affairs of our firm."

He bowed simultaneously to the prince and to his wife, and left the room, as smiling, calm, and unconcerned as ever. Only when the door had closed behind him, when he had satisfied himself by a rapid glance through the reception-room that nobody was there, the smile disappeared from his lips, and his features assumed an air of profound melancholy.

"She loves him," he muttered; "yes, she loves him! Her hand trembled in mine when I pronounced his name, and oh! how radiant she looked when she heard him come! Yes, she loves him, and I?—I will go to my counting-house!" he said, with a smile that was to veil the tears in his eyes.

CHAPTER XXXVIII.

THE RIVALS.

THE baron had no sooner closed the door of the boudoir when the young Prince von Lichtenstein hastened to Fanny, and, impetuously seizing her hand, looked at her with a passionate and angry air.

"You did that for the purpose of giving me pain, I suppose?" he asked, with quivering lips. "You wished to prove to me that you did not confer any special favor upon me. Yesterday you were kind enough to assure me that no man ever had set foot into this room, and that I should be the first to whom it would be opened to-day; and I was such a conceited fool as to believe your beatifying words, and I rush hither as early as is permitted by decency and respect, and yet I do not find you alone."

"It was my husband who was here," said Fanny, almost deprecatingly.

"It was a man," he ejaculated, impetuously,

"and you had given me the solemn assurance that this door had never yet opened to any man. Oh, I had implored you on my knees, and with tearful eyes, to allow me to see you here to-day; it seemed to me as though the gates of paradise were to be at last opened to me; no sleep came into my eyes all night, the consciousness of my approaching bliss kept me awake; it was over me like a smiling cherub, and I was dreaming with open eyes. And now that the lazy, snail-like time has elapsed, now that I have arrived here, I find in my heaven, at the side of my cherub, a calculating machine, desecrating my paradise by vile accounts—"

"Pray do not go on in this manner," interrupted Fanny, sternly. "You found my husband here, and that, of course, dissolves the whole poetry of your words into plain prose, for she, whom in your enthusiastic strain you styled your cherub, is simply the wife of this noble and excellent man, whom you were free to compare with a calculating machine."

"You are angry with me!" exclaimed the young prince, disconsolately. "You make no allowance for my grief, my disappointment, yea, my confusion! You have punished me so rudely for my presumption, and will not even permit my heart to bubble up and give utterance to its wrath."

"I did not know that you were presumptuous toward me, and could not think, therefore, of inflicting punishment on you," said Fanny; "but I know that you have no right to insult the man whose name I bear."

"You want to drive me to despair, then!" retorted the prince, wildly stamping on the floor. "It is not sufficient, then, that you let me find your husband here, you must even praise him before me! I will tell you why I was presumptuous. I was presumptuous inasmuch as I believed it to be a favor granted to me exclusively to enter this room, and you have punished me for this presumption by proving to me that this door opens to others, too, although you assured me yesterday that the contrary was the case."

"Then you question my word?" asked Fanny.

"Oh," he said, impetuously, "you do not question what you see with your own eyes."

"And, inasmuch as you have satisfied yourself of my duplicity with your own eyes, as you have seen that every one is at liberty to enter this room, and as you consequently cannot take any interest in prolonging your stay here, I would advise you to leave immediately," said Fanny, gravely.

"You show me the door? You turn me out!" exclaimed the prince, despairingly. "Oh, have mercy on me! No, do not turn away from me!

Look at me, read in my face the despair filling my soul. What, you still avert your head? I beseech you just grant me one glance; only tell me by the faintest smile that you will forgive me, and I will obey your orders, I will go, even if it should be only for the purpose of dying, not here before your eyes, but outside, on the threshold of your door."

"Ah, as if it were so easy to die!" ejaculated Fanny, turning her face toward the prince.

"You look at me—you have forgiven me, then!" exclaimed the young man, and impetuously kneeling down before her, he seized her hands and pressed them to his lips.

"Rise, sir, pray rise," said the baroness; "consider that somebody might come in. You know now that everybody is permitted to enter this room."

"No, no, I know that nobody is permitted to enter here!" he exclaimed, fervently; "I know that this room is a sanctuary which no uninitiated person ever entered; I know that this is the sacred cell in which your virgin heart exhaled its prayers and complaints, and which is only known to God; I know that no man's foot ever crossed this threshold, and I remain on my knees as if before a saint, to whom I confess my sins, and whom I implore to grant me absolution. Will you forgive me?"

"I will," she said, smilingly, bending over him —"I will, if it were only to induce you to rise from your knees. And as you now perceive and regret your mistake, I will tell you the truth. It was an accident that the baron entered this room to-day, and it was the first time, too, since we were married. Nor did he come here, as he said, in delicate self-derision, for the purpose of settling accounts with me, but in order to fulfil a promise which he gave me five years ago, and which, I confess to my shame, I had forgotten, so that, instead of expecting my husband, I permitted you to come to me."

"I thank you for your kind words, which heal all the wounds of my heart like a soothing balm," replied the prince. "Oh, now I feel well again, and strong enough to conquer you in spite of the resistance of the whole world."

"And do you know, then, whether you will be able to conquer me in spite of my resistance?" asked Fanny, smiling.

"Yes!" he exclaimed, "I know it, for in true love there is a strength that will subdue and surmount all obstacles. And I love you truly; you know it, you are satisfied of it. You know that I love you; every breath, every look, every tremulous note of my voice tells you so. But you? do you love me? Oh, I implore you, at length have mercy on me. Speak one word of pity, of sympathy! Let me read it at least in your eyes, if your lips are too austere to utter it. I have come to-day with the firm determination to receive at your hands my bliss or my doom. The torment of this incertitude kills me. Fanny, tell me, do you love me?"

Fanny did not answer at once; she stood before him, her head lowered, a prey to conflicting emotions, but she felt the ardent looks which were resting on her, and her heart trembled with secret delight. She made an effort, however, to overcome her feelings, and, raising her head, she fixed her eyes with a gentle yet mournful expression upon the young man, who, breathless and pale with anxiety, was waiting for her reply.

"You ask me if I love you," she said, in a low but firm voice; "you put that question to me, and yet you are standing now on the same spot on which my husband stood fifteen minutes ago and also asked me a question. I must not answer your question, for I am a married woman, and I have taken an oath at the altar to keep my faith to my husband, and I have to keep it, inasmuch as my heart has no love to give him. But I will, nevertheless, give you a proof of the great confidence I am reposing in you. I will tell you why my husband came to see me to-day, and what was the question which he addressed to me. Hush, do not interrupt me; do not tell me that my conversations with the baron have no interest for you. Listen to me. The baron came to me because the five years, which we had ourselves fixed for that purpose, had elapsed to-day, and because he wanted to ask me whether I wished to remain his wife, or whether I wanted to be divorced from him."

"And what did you reply?" asked the prince, breathlessly.

"I replied to him as I replied to you a little while ago: 'I have taken an oath at the altar to keep my faith to my husband, and I have to keep it, inasmuch as my heart has no love to give to him.'"

"Ah, you told him that you did not love him?" asked the prince, drawing a deep breath. "And after this confession he felt that he ought no longer to oppose your divorce, for his heart is generous and delicate, and consequently he cannot desire to chain a wife to himself who tells him that during the five years of her married life she has not learned to love him. Oh, Fanny, how indescribably happy you render me by this disclosure. Then you will be free, your hands will not be manacled any longer."

"I did not tell you the reply I made to my husband when he left it to me again to say whether I would be divorced from him or not," said Fanny, with a mournful smile. "I replied to him that every thing should remain as heretofore; that I did not want to inflict the disgrace of a divorce upon him and upon myself, and that we would and ought to bear these shackles which, without mutual love, we had imposed upon each other in a dignified, faithful, and honest manner until our death."

"That is impossible!" exclaimed the prince. "You could not, you ought not to have been so cruel against yourself, against the baron, and also against me. And even though you may have uttered these words of doom on the spur of that exciting moment, you will take them back again after sober and mature reflection. Oh, say that you will do so, say that you will be free; free, so that I may kneel down before you and implore you to give to me this hand, no longer burdened by any fetters; to become my wife, and to permit me to try if my boundless, adoring love will succeed in conferring upon you that happiness of which none are worthier than you. Oh, speak, Fanny, say that you will be free, and consent to become my wife!"

"Your wife!" said Fanny, lugubriously. "You forget that what separates me from you is not only my husband, but also my religion. The Jewess can never become the wife of the Prince von Lichtenstein."

"You will cast off the semblance of a religion which in reality is yours no longer," said the prince. "You have ceased to be a Jewess, owing to your education, to your habits, and to your views of life. Leave, then, the halls of the temple in which your God is no longer dwelling, and enter the great church which has redeemed mankind, and which is now to redeem you. Become a convert to the Christian religion, which is the religion of love."

"Never!" exclaimed the baroness, firmly and decidedly—"never will I abandon my religion and prove recreant to my faith, to which my family and my tribe have faithfully adhered for thousands of years. The curse of my parents and ancestors would pursue the renegade daughter of our tribe and cling like a sinister night-bird to the roof of the house into which the faithless daughter of Judah, the baptized Jewess, would move in order to obtain that happiness she is yearning for. Never— But what is that?" interrupting herself all at once; "what is the matter in the adjoining room?"

Two voices, one of them angrily quarrelling with

the other, which replied in a deprecating manner, were heard in the adjoining room.

"I tell you the baroness is at home, and receives visitors!" exclaimed the violent and threatening voice.

"And I assure you that the baroness is not at home, and cannot, therefore, receive any visitors," replied the deprecating voice.

"It is Baron Weichs, the proud prebendary, who wants to play the master here as he does everywhere else," said the prince, disdainfully.

"And my steward refuses to admit him, because I have given orders that no more visitors shall be received to-day," whispered Fanny.

The face of the young prince became radiant with delight. He seized Fanny's hands and pressed them impetuously to his lips, whispering, "I thank you, Fanny, I thank you!"

Meantime the voice in the reception-room became more violent and threatening, "I know that the baroness is at home," it shouted, "and I ask you once more to announce my visit to her!"

"But you know, sir," said the gentle voice of the steward, "that the baroness, when she is at home, is always at this hour in the reception-room, and receives her visitors here without any previous announcement."

"That only proves that the baroness receives her visitors in another room to-day," shouted the voice of Baron Weichs. "I know positively that there is a visitor with the baroness at this very moment. Go, then, and announce my visit. It remains for the baroness to turn me away, and I shall know then that the baroness prefers to remain alone with the gentleman who is with her at the present time."

"Ah, this prebendary, it seems, is growing impudent," exclaimed the prince, with flashing eyes, walking toward the door.

The baroness seized his hand and kept him back. "Pay no attention to him," she said, imploringly; "let my steward settle this quarrel with that insolent man. Just listen! he is even now begging him quite politely, yet decidedly, to leave the room."

"And that fellow is shameless enough to decline doing so," said the prince. "Oh, hear his scornful laughter! This laughter is an insult, for which he ought to be chastised."

And as if the words of the prince were to be followed immediately by the deed, a third voice was heard now in the reception-room. It asked in a proud and angry tone, "What is the matter here? And who permits himself to shout so indecently in the reception-room of the baroness?"

"Ah, it is my husband," whispered Fanny, with an air of great relief. "He will show that overbearing Baron Weichs the door, and I shall get rid of him forever."

"He has already dared, then, to importune you?" asked the prince, turning his threatening eyes toward the door. "Oh, I will release you from further molestation by this madman, for I tell you the gentle words of your husband will not be able to do so. Baron Weichs is not the man to lend a willing ear to sensible remonstrances or to the requirements of propriety and decency. He has graduated at the high-school of libertinism, and any resistance whatever provokes him to a passionate struggle in which he shrinks from no manifestation of his utter recklessness. Well, am I not right? Does he not even dare to defy your husband? Just listen!"

"I regret not to be able to comply with your request to leave this room," shouted now the voice of the prebendary, Baron Weichs. "You said yourself just now, baron, that we were in the reception-room of the baroness; accordingly, you are not the master here, but merely a visitor like the rest of us. Consequently, you have no right to show anybody the door, particularly as you do not even know whether you belong to the privileged visitors of the lady, or whether the baroness will admit you."

"I shall take no notice of the unbecoming and insulting portion of your remarks, baron," said the calm voice of Baron Arnstein; "I only intend at this moment to protect my wife against insult and molestation. Now it is insulting assuredly that a cavalier, after being told that the lady to whom he wishes to pay his respects is either not at home or will not receive any visitors, should refuse to withdraw, and insist upon being admitted. I hope the prebendary, Baron Weichs, after listening to this explanation, will be kind enough to leave the reception-room."

"I regret that I cannot fulfil this hope," said the sneering voice of the prebendary. "I am now here with the full conviction that I shall never be able to reënter this reception-room; hence I am determined not to shrink back from anything and not to be turned away in so disgraceful a manner. I know that the baroness is at home, and I came hither in order to satisfy myself whether the common report is really true that the baroness, who has always treated me with so much virtuous rigor and discouraging coldness, is more indulgent and less inexorable toward another, and whether I have really a more fortunate rival!"

"I hope that I am this more fortunate rival," said Baron Arnstein, gently.

"Oh, no, sir," exclaimed the prebendary, laughing scornfully. "A husband never is the rival of his wife's admirers. If you were with your wife and turned me away, I should not object to it at all, and I should wait for a better chance. But what keeps me here is the fact that another admirer of hers is with her, that she has given orders to admit nobody else, and that you, more kind-hearted than myself, seem to believe that the baroness is not at home."

"This impudence surpasses belief," exclaimed the prince, in great exasperation."

"Yes," said Fanny, gloomily, "the Christian prebendary gives full vent to his disdain for the Jewish banker. It always affords a great satisfaction to Christian love to humble the Jew and to trample him in the dust. And the Jew is accustomed to being trampled upon in this manner. My husband, too, gives proof of this enviable quality of our tribe. Just listen how calm and humble his voice remains, all the while every tone of the other is highly insulting to him!"

"He shall not insult him any longer," said the prince, ardently; "I will—but what is that? Did he not mention my name?"

And he went closer to the door, in order to listen in breathless suspense.

"And I repeat to you, baron," said the voice of the prebendary, sneeringly, "your wife is at home, and the young Prince von Lichtenstein is with her. I saw him leave his palace and followed him; half an hour ago, I saw him enter your house, and I went into the coffee-house opposite for the purpose of making my observations. I know, therefore, positively, that the prince has not yet left your house. As he is not with you, he is with your wife, and this being the usual hour for the baroness to receive morning calls, I have just as good a right as anybody else to expect that she will admit me."

"And suppose I tell you that she will not admit you to-day?"

"Then I shall conclude that the baroness is in her boudoir with the Prince von Lichtenstein, and that she does not want to be disturbed," shouted the voice of the prebendary. "Yes, sir; in that case I shall equally lament my fate and yours, for both of us are deceived and deprived of sweet hopes. Both of us will have a more fortunate rival in this petty prince—in this conceited young dandy, who even now believes he is a perfect Adonis, and carries his ludicrous presumption so far as to believe that he can outstrip men of ability and merit by his miserable little title and by his boyish face—"

"Why is it necessary for you to shout all this so loudly?" asked the anxious voice of the baron.

"Ah, then you believe that he can hear me?" asked the voice of the prebendary, triumphantly. "Then he is quite close to us? Well, I will shout it louder than before: this little Prince Charles von Lichtenstein is a conceited boy, who deserves to be chastised!"

The prince rushed toward the door, pale, with quivering lips and sparkling eyes. But the baroness encircled his arm with her hands and kept him back.

"You will not go," she whispered. "You will not disgrace me so as to prove to him by your appearance that he was right, and that you were with me while I refused to admit him."

"But do you not hear that he insults me?" asked the young prince, trying to disengage himself from her hands.

"Why do you listen to other voices when you are with me?" she said, reproachfully. "What do you care for the opinion of that man, whom I abhor from the bottom of my heart, and whom people only tolerate in their saloons because they are afraid of his anger and his slanderous tongue? Oh, do not listen to what he says, my friend! You are here with me, and I have yet to tell you many things. But you do not heed my words! Your eyes are constantly fixed on the door. Oh, sir, look at me, listen to what I have to say to you. I believe I still owe you a reply, do I not? Well, I will now reply to the question which you have so often put to me, and to which I have heretofore only answered by silence!"

"Oh, not now, not now!" muttered the prince.

"Yes, I will tell you now what has been so long burning in my soul as a sweet secret," whispered Fanny, constantly endeavoring to draw him away from the door. "You have often asked me if I loved you, and my heart made the reply which my lips were afraid to pronounce. But now I will confess it to you: yes, I love you; my whole soul belongs to you! I have secretly longed for the hour when I might at last confess this to you, when my heart would exult in pronouncing the sweet words, 'I love you!' Good Heaven! you hear it, and yet you remain silent —you avert your face? Do you despise me now because I, the married woman, confess to you that I love you? Is your silence to tell me that you do not love me any longer?"

He knelt down before her and kissed her dress and her hands. "I love you boundlessly," he said with panting breath; "you are to me the quintessence of all happiness, virtue, and beauty. I shall love you to the last hour of my life!"

"If Prince Charles von Lichtenstein should be near," shouted the voice of the prebendary, close to the door, "if he should be able to hear my words, I want him to hear that I pronounce him a coward, a fool, and impostor—a coward, because he silently suffers himself to be insulted—"

The prince, unable to restrain his feelings any longer, rushed forward and impetuously pushing back the baroness, who still endeavored to detain him, he violently opened the door.

"No," he shouted, in a threatening and angry voice. "No, Prince Charles von Lichtenstein does not allow himself to be insulted with impunity, and he asks satisfaction for every insult offered to him!"

"Ah!" exclaimed the prebendary, turning with a wild, triumphant laugh to Baron Arnstein, "did I not tell you that the prince was concealed in your house?"

"Concealed!" ejaculated the prince, approaching his adversary with eyes sparkling with rage. "Repeat that word if you dare!"

"I shall do so," said the prebendary, with defiant coolness. "You were concealed in this house, for nobody knew of your presence, neither the steward nor the baron. You had crept into the house like a thief intending to steal valuables, and this, indeed, was your intention, too; however, you did not want to purloin the diamonds of the fair baroness, but—"

"I forbid you to mention the name of the baroness!" exclaimed the prince, proudly.

"And I implore you not to compromise the baroness by connecting her with your quarrel," whispered Baron Arnstein in the prince's ear; then turning to the prebendary, whose eyes were fixed on the prince with a threatening and defiant expression, he said:

"You are mistaken, sir; Prince Charles von Lichtenstein did not come here in a stealthy manner. He wished to pay a visit to the baroness, and the latter, as you know, being absent from home, the prince did me the honor to converse with me in that room, when we were interrupted all at once by the noise which you were pleased to make in the reception-room here."

"And being in that room, you were pleased to enter the reception-room through *this* door," said the prebendary, sneeringly, pointing to the two opposite doors. "But why did not the prince accompany you? It would have been so natural for one friend of the baroness to greet the other!"

"I did not come because I heard that *you* were there," said the prince, disdainfully, "and because I am in the habit of avoiding any contact with your person."

"Ah, you are jealous of me, then?" asked the prebendary. "Why is my person so distasteful to you that you should always escape from me?"

"I escape from no one, not even from venomous serpents, nor from an individual like you," said the prince, haughtily. "I avoided you, however, because I dislike your nose. Do you hear, my impertinent little prebendary? I dislike your nose, and I demand that you never let me see it again!"

"Ah, I understand," replied the prebendary, laughing. "In order to spare the feelings of the fair baroness, and not to injure her reputation. Pardon me, for, in spite of your prohibition, I am constantly compelled to defer to this amiable lady. You wish to give another direction to our quarrel, and my innocent nose is to be the *bête de souffrance*. But you shall not entrap me in this manner, prince; and you, my dear Baron Arnstein, can you allow us to continue the quarrel which we commenced about your lady, now about my nose, and to conceal, as it were, the fair Baroness Arnstein behind it?"

"Baroness Arnstein has no reason whatever to conceal herself," said the baron, coldly and proudly. "As she was not the cause of this quarrel, I do not know why you are constantly dragging her name into it. You behaved here in so unbecoming a manner, that I had to come to the assistance of my steward. You were then pleased to utter insults against the Prince von Lichtenstein in his absence, and being in the adjoining room and overhearing your offensive remarks, he came to call you to account for them."

"And to tell you that I dislike your nose, and that I must take the liberty to amputate its impertinent tip with my sword," exclaimed the prince, pulling the prebendary's nose.

It was now the prebendary's turn to grow pale, while his eyes flashed with anger. "You dare to insult me?" he asked menacingly.

"Yes, I confess that is exactly my intention!" replied the prince, laughing.

"Ah, you will have to give me satisfaction for this insult!" shouted the prebendary.

"With the greatest pleasure," said the prince. "This is not the place, however, to continue this conversation. Come, sir, let us leave this house together in order to make the necessary arrangements—"

At this moment the folding-doors of the anteroom were opened, and the voice of the steward shouted: "The baroness!"

An exclamation of surprise escaped from the lips of the three gentlemen, and their eyes turned toward the door, the threshold of which Fanny Arnstein was crossing at that moment. She seemed just to have returned home; her tall form was still wrapped in a long Turkish shawl, embroidered with gold; a charming little bonnet, adorned with flowers and plumes, covered her head, and in her hand she held one of those large costly fans, adorned with precious stones, which were in use at that time in the place of parasols. She greeted the gentlemen with a winning smile; not the slightest tinge of care or uneasiness was visible in her merry face; not the faintest glimmer of a tear darkened the lustre of her large black eyes.

"Gentlemen will please accept my apology for making them wait, although this is the hour when I am in the habit of receiving visitors," said the baroness, in a perfectly careless manner. "But I hope my husband has taken my place in the mean time and told you that I had to preside over a meeting of our Hebrew Benevolent Society, and you will acknowledge that that was a duty which I ought not to have failed to fulfil. Ah, you smile, Baron Weichs; you must explain to me what is the meaning of this smile, if you wish to intimate thereby, perhaps, that there are no important duties at all for us ladies to perform. Come, gentlemen, let us sit down and hear in what manner Baron Weichs will be able to defend his smile. Sit down here on my right side, prince, and you, Baron Weichs, on my left, and my husband may take a seat opposite us and play the *rôle* of an arbiter."

"I regret that I cannot comply any longer with your amiable invitation," said the prebendary, gloomily. "You have made me wait too long, baroness; my time has now expired, and I must withdraw. I suppose you will accompany me, Prince Lichtenstein?"

"Yes, I shall accompany you," said the prince, "for unfortunately my time has also expired, and I must go."

"Oh, no," exclaimed the baroness, smiling, "you must stay here, prince. I dare not prevent the prebendary from attending to his important affairs, but you, prince, have no such pretext for leaving me; I therefore order you to remain and to tell me all about yesterday's concert at the imperial palace."

"I regret exceedingly that I am unable to obey your orders," said the prince, mournfully. "But I must go. You just said, dear lady, that an important duty had kept you away from home; well, it is an important duty that calls me away from here; hence I cannot stay. Farewell, and permit me to kiss your hand before leaving you."

She gave him her hand, which was as cold as ice and trembled violently when he took it. He pressed his glowing lips upon this hand and looked up to her. Their eyes met in a last, tender glance; the prince then rose and turned toward the prebendary, who was conversing with Baron Arnstein in a low and excited tone.

"Come, sir, let us go," he said, impetuously, and walked toward the door.

"Yes, let us go," repeated the prebendary, and, bowing profoundly to the baroness, he turned around and followed the prince.

Fanny, who was evidently a prey to the most excruciating anguish, followed them with her distended, terrified eyes. When the door closed behind them, she hastily laid her hand on her husband's shoulder and looked at him with an air of unutterable terror.

"They will fight a duel?" she asked.

"I am afraid so," said the baron, gloomily.

The baroness uttered a shriek, and after tottering back a few steps, she fell senseless to the floor.

Early on the following morning, four men with grave faces and gloomy eyes stood in the thicket of a forest not far from Vienna.

Two of them were just about divesting themselves of their heavy coats, embroidered with gold, in order to meet in mortal combat, their bare breasts only protected by their fine cambric shirts. These two men were Prince Charles von Lichtenstein and the prebendary, Baron Weichs.

The other two gentlemen were engaged in loading the pistols and counting off the steps; they were Baron Arnstein and Count Palfy, the seconds of the two duellists. When they had performed this mournful task, they approached the two adversaries in order to make a last effort to bring about a reconciliation.

"I implore you in my own name," whispered Baron Arnstein in the ear of the Prince von Lichtenstein—"I implore you in the name of my wife, if a reconciliation should be possible, accept it, and avoid by all means so deplorable an event. Remember that the honor of a lady is compromised so easily and irretrievably, and that my wife would never forgive herself if she should become, perhaps, the innocent cause of your death."

"Nobody will find out that we fight a duel for her sake," said the prince. "My honor requires me to give that impertinent fellow a well-deserved lesson, and he shall have it!"

Count Palfy, the prebendary's second, approached them. "If your highness should be willing to ask Baron Weichs to excuse your conduct on yesterday, the baron would be ready to accept your apology and to withdraw his challenge."

"I have no apology to offer," exclaimed the prince, loudly, "and I am unwilling to prevent the duel from taking its course. I told the prebendary that I disliked his nose, and that I wished to amputate its impertinent tip. Well, I am now here to perform this operation, and if you please, let us at once proceed to business."

"Yes, let us do so," shouted the prebendary. "Give us the pistols, gentlemen, and then the signal. When you clap for the third time, we shall shoot simultaneously. Pray for your poor soul, Prince von Lichtenstein, for I am a dead shot at one hundred yards, and our distance will only be twenty paces."

The prince made no reply, but took the pistol which his second handed to him. "If I should fall," he whispered to him, "take my last greetings to your wife, and tell her that I died with her name on my lips!"

"If I should fall," said the prebendary to his second, in an undertone, but loud enough for his opponent to hear every word he said, "tell the dear city of Vienna and my friends that I have fought a duel with Prince Lichtenstein because he was my rival with the beautiful Baroness Arnstein, and that I have died with the conviction that he was the lover of the fair lady."

A pause ensued. The seconds conducted the two gentlemen to their designated places and then stood back, in order to give the fatal signals.

When they clapped for the first time, the two duellists raised the hand with the pistol, fixing their angry and threatening eyes on each other.

Then followed the second, the third signal.

Two shots were fired at the same time.

The prebendary stood firmly and calmly where he had discharged his weapon, the same defiant smile playing on his lips, and the same threatening expression beaming in his eyes.

Prince Charles von Lichtenstein lay on the ground, reddening the earth with the blood which was rushing from his breast. When Baron Arnstein bent over him, he raised his eyes with a last look toward him. "Take her my last love-greetings," he breathed, in a scarcely audible voice. "Tell her that I—"

His voice gave way, and with the last awful death-rattle a stream of blood poured from his mouth.

"Hasten to save yourself," shouted Count Palfy to the prebendary, who had been looking at the dying man from his stand-point with cold, inquisitive glances. "Flee, for you have killed the prince; he has already ceased to breathe. Flee! In the shrubbery below you will find my carriage, which will convey you rapidly to the next post-station."

"He is dead and I am alive!" said the prebendary, quietly. "It would not have been worth while to die for the sake of a woman because she has got another lover. It is much wiser in such cases to kill the rival, and thus to remove the obstacle separating us from the woman. But I shall not escape; on the contrary, I shall go to the emperor myself, and inform him of what has occurred here. We are living in times of war and carnage, and a soul more or less is, therefore, of no great importance. Inasmuch as the emperor constantly sends hundreds of thousands of his innocent and harmless subjects to fight duels with enemies of whom they do not even know why they are their enemies, he will deem it but a matter of course that two of his subjects, who know very well why they are enemies, should fight a duel, and hence I am sure that his majesty will forgive me. Brave and intrepid men are not sent to the fortress. I shall not flee!"

CHAPTER XXXIX.

THE LEGACY.

THREE days had passed since that unfortunate event. Early on this, the third day, the corpse of the prince had been conveyed to the tomb of his family; a large and brilliant funeral procession had accompanied the coffin; even the carriages of the emperor, the archdukes, and high dignitaries of the state had participated in the procession, and the Viennese, who for three days had spoken of nothing else but the tragic end of the young and handsome Prince Charles von Lichtenstein, derived some satisfaction from the conviction that they were sharing the sympathy of the imperial family for the deceased; thousands of them consequently joined the procession and accompanied the coffin.

But this manifestation of sympathy did not seem sufficient to the good-hearted and hot-blooded people. They did not merely wish to show their love for the deceased; they also wanted to manifest their hatred against the man who had slain him; and, on their return from the funeral, the people rushed to the Kohlmarkt and gathered with loud shouts and savage threats in front of the house of the prebendary, Baron Weichs.

THE DUEL.   DEATH OF PRINCE LICHTENSTEIN.   P 146.

It was reported that the prebendary, whom the people charged with having assassinated Prince Lichtenstein, was constantly in Vienna; and as this fact seemed to indicate that the emperor did not intend to punish his misdeed, the people wanted to take it upon themselves to chastise him, or to give him at least a proof of the public hatred.

"Smash the murderer's windows!" shouted the people, who were constantly reënforced by fresh crowds appearing on the Kohlmarkt. And, passing from threats to deeds, hundreds and hundreds of busy hands tore up the pavement in order to hurl the stones at the house and windows of the prebendary. And the rattling of the windows, the loud noise of the stones glancing off on the walls, increased the rage and exasperation of the people. Soon they were no longer contented with doing this, but wished to get hold of the malefactor himself, and to punish him for his crime. The crowd rushed with wild clamor toward the closed street-door of the baron's house; one among them quickly climbed on the shoulders of another, in order to tear down the coat-of-arms of the prebendary, fixed over the entrance, and thundering applause greeted him when he had accomplished his purpose. The infuriated men then commenced striking at the door itself, which offered, however, to all attacks, a firm and unyielding resistance.

Suddenly a stern, imperious voice shouted: "Stop! Stand back! stand back!"

The people turned around in terror, and discovered only then that a carriage, surrounded and followed by twenty mounted policemen, was approaching from the alley on which the principal door of the prebendary's house was situated. This carriage, with its sinister escort, could make but slow headway through the dense mass of the people, who looked inquisitively through the lowered windows into the interior of the coach. Every one was able to recognize the three gentlemen who were seated in the carriage, and who were none other than the prebendary, Baron Weichs, and two of the best known and most feared high functionaries of the police. The baron's face was pale and gloomy, but the defiant, impudent smile was still playing on his thin lips. He looked, with an air of boundless contempt, at the crowd surging around his carriage and staring at him as if it wished to read in his pale features the sentence that had been pronounced against him.

"How inquisitive is the populace!" said the prebendary, disdainfully. "They are so anxious to find out whether I am now being conveyed to the place of execution, which would be a most welcome spectacle for them. You ought to have mercy on this amiable rabble, gentlemen, and inform them of the evil tidings that I have unfortunately not been sentenced to be hanged on the gallows, nor to be broken on the wheel, but only to be imprisoned in a fortress for ten years, which I shall pass at the beautiful citadel of Komorn."

The two officers only replied to him by silently nodding, and the carriage passed on. But some compassionate and talkative police agent had informed the people that the emperor had sentenced the prebendary, Baron Weichs, to ten years' imprisonment in a fortress, and that he was at this moment on his way to Komorn. The people received this intelligence with jubilant shouts, and dispersed through the city in order to inform their friends and acquaintances of the welcome news, and then to go home, well satisfied with the day's amusements and diversions.

And the waves of life closed over the lamentable event, and carried it down into the abyss of oblivion. A few days passed by, and another occurrence caused the colloquies concerning the duel of Prince Lichtenstein and what had brought it about to cease, as some new subject of conversation took its place.

One heart alone did not console itself so rapidly; one soul alone bewailed him on comfortless days and restless nights, and paid to him the tribute of tears and sighs. Since that last meeting with the prince, Fanny Arnstein had not left her cabinet again; its doors had been closed against everybody, and she had wept and sighed there during these three days, without taking a morsel of food.

Vainly had her husband often come to her door in order to implore her to open it at last, and to take some nourishment. Fanny had never answered him; and if he had not, constantly and stealthily returning to her door at night, heard her low sobs and half-loud wailing, he would have believed that grief had killed her, and that love had intended to unite her in heaven with him to whom her heart belonged, as they had been so hopelessly separated on earth.

To-day, after the prince's funeral, the baron again entered the reception-room adjoining his wife's cabinet, but this time he did not come alone. A lady, whose face was covered with a large black veil, accompanied him, and walked at his side to the constantly closed door.

The baron knocked at this door, and begged his wife, in words of heart-felt sympathy, to open it to him.

There was no reply; not a word was heard from the unhappy baroness.

"You see, your highness," whispered the baron, turning to the veiled lady, "it is as I told you. All prayers are in vain; she does not leave her room; she will die of grief."

"No, she will not die," said the lady; "she is young, and youth survives all grief. Let me try if I cannot induce her to admit us."

And she knocked at the door with bold fingers, and exclaimed: "Pray, Fanny, open the door, and let me come in. It is I, Princess Eibenberg; it is I, your friend, Marianne Meier; I want to see my dear Fanny Itzig."

Every thing remained silent; nothing stirred behind that locked door. Marianne removed her veil, and showed her proud, pale countenance to the baron.

"Baron," she said, gravely, "at this hour I forgive you the insult and contempt you hurled at me five years ago on your wedding-day. Fate has avenged me and punished you cruelly, for I see that you have suffered a great deal during the last three days. My heart does not bear you any ill-will now, and I will try to restore your beautiful and unhappy wife to you, and to console her. But I must request you to leave this room. I know a charm, by which I shall decoy Fanny from that room; but in order to do so I must be alone, and nobody, save herself, must be able to hear me."

"Very well, I will go," said the baron, mournfully. "But permit me first to ask you to do me a favor. My request will prove to you the confidence I repose in you. Please do not tell Fanny that you saw me sad and deeply moved; do not intimate any thing to her about my own grief."

"She will perceive it herself, from your pale face and hollow cheeks, poor baron!" exclaimed Marianne.

"No, she is not accustomed to look at me attentively; it will escape her," said the baron, sadly, "and I would not have it appear as though I were suffering by her grief, which I deem but natural and just. I beg you, therefore, to say nothing about me."

"I shall fulfil your wish," said Marianne. "Fanny will, perhaps, thank you one day for the delicacy with which you are now behaving toward her. But go now, so that I may call her."

The baron left the room, and Marianne returned to the door. "Fanny," she said, "come to me, or open the door and let me walk in. I have to deliver to you a message and a letter from Prince Charles von Lichtenstein."

Now a low cry from the cabinet was heard; the bolt was drawn back, the door opened, and Baroness Arnstein appeared on the threshold.

Her face was as pale as marble; her eyes, reddened by weeping, lay deeply in their orbits; her black, dishevelled hair fell down on her back like a long mourning-veil. She was still beautiful and lovely, but hers was now the beauty of a Magdalen.

"You bring me a message from him?" she asked, in a low, tremulous voice, and with tearful eyes.

"Yes, Fanny," said Marianne, scarcely able to overcome her own emotion, "I bring you his last love-greetings. He believed that he would fall, and on that fatal morning, before repairing to the duelling-grounds, he paid me a visit. We had long been acquainted and intimate; both of us had a great, common goal in view; both of us were pursuing the same paths; this was the origin of our acquaintance. He knew, too, that I had been a friend of yours from your childhood, and he therefore intrusted to me his last message to you. Here, Fanny, this small box contains all the little souvenirs and love-tokens which he has received from you, and which he deemed much too precious to destroy or to take into his grave; hence he requests you to preserve them. They consist of withered flowers which you once gave him, of a ribbon which you lost, of a few notes which you wrote to him, and from which the malicious and slanderous world might perceive the harmless and innocent character of your intercourse, and, last, of your miniature, painted by the prince himself, from memory. This casket the prince requests you to accept as his legacy. It is a set of pearls, an heirloom of his family, which his dying mother once gave to him in order to adorn with it his bride on his wedding-day. The prince sends it to you and implores you to wear it as a souvenir from him, because you were the bride of his heart. And here, Fanny, here is a letter from him, the last lines he ever wrote, and they are addressed to you."

The baroness uttered a cry of joy; seizing the paper with passionate violence, she pressed it to her lips, and knelt down with it.

"I thank Thee, my God, I thank Thee!" she murmured, in a low voice. "Thou hast sent me this consolation! Thou dost not want me to die of despair!"

And now, still remaining on her knees, she slowly unfolded the paper and read this last glowing farewell, this last tender protestation of his love, with which the prince took leave of her.

Marianne stood, with folded arms, in a bay window, watching her friend with grave, sympathetic eyes, and beheld the pallor and blushes which appeared in quick succession on her cheeks, the impetuous heaving of her bosom, the tremor of her whole frame, and the tears pouring down like rivers from Fanny's eyes on the paper, with a mingled feeling of pity and astonishment.

"It must be beautiful to be able to love in such a manner," she thought. "Beautiful, too, to be able to suffer thus. Enviable the women living with their hearts and deriving from them alone their happiness and grief. Such a lot has not fallen to my share, and I am almost afraid that I do not love any thing but myself. My life is concentrated in my head, and my blood only rushes from the latter to my heart. Who is more to be pitied, Fanny with the grief of her love, or I, who will never know such a grief? But she has wept enough now, and her tears might finally cause me to weep, too, and to awaken my love. That must not be, however. One who has to pursue great plans, like myself, must keep a cool head and a cold heart."

And she approached with quick steps the baroness, who was yet on her knees, reading and re-reading the farewell letter of the prince.

"Rise from your knees, Fanny," she said, almost imperiously. "You have paid the tribute of your tears to the departed friend, you have wept for him for three days; now bury the past in your heart and think of your future, my poor girl."

"My future?" said Fanny, permitting her friend to raise her gently. "My future is broken and darkened forever, and there is a cloud on my name, which will never leave it. Oh, why is there no convent for the Jewess, no lonely cell whither she might take refuge, with her unhappiness and disgrace?"

"Do as I have done," said Marianne; "let the whole world be your convent, and your reception-room the cell in which you do penance, by compelling men to kneel before you and adore you, instead of kneeling yourself, and mortifying your flesh. Lay your unhappiness and your disgrace like a halo around your head, and boldly meet the world with open eyes and a proud mien. If you were poor and nameless I should seriously advise you to become a Catholic, and to take refuge in a convent. But you are rich; you bear a distinguished, aristocratic name; your husband is able to give sumptuous dinner-parties; consequently people will pardon his wife for having become the heroine of an unfortunate romance, and they will take good care not to turn their backs on nor to point their fingers at you; and whenever you pass them in the street, not to laugh scornfully and tell your history in an audible voice. I, my child, formerly had to bear such contumely

and humiliation, and I took a solemn oath at that time that I would revenge myself upon this world, which believed it had a right to despise me—that I would revenge myself by becoming its equal. And I have fulfilled my oath; I am now a princess and a highness. The proud world that once scorned me now bows to me; the most virtuous and aristocratic ladies do not deem it derogatory to their dignity to appear in my reception-room; the most distinguished princes and cavaliers court the friendship and favor of the Princess von Ei-benberg, née Marianne Meier. Follow my example, therefore, Fanny; brave the world; appear in your reception-room with serene calmness and ease; give even more sumptuous dinner-parties than heretofore, and the small cloud now darkening your name will pass by unnoticed. People will come at first from motives of curiosity, in order to see how you bear your affliction and how you behave under the *éclat* produced by the deplorable occurrence; next they will come because your dinners are so very excellent, and because this and that princess or countess, this and that prince, minister, or general, do not disdain to appear in your reception-room, and thus the whole affair will gradually be forgotten."

"But my heart will not forget it," said the baroness, mournfully; "my heart will never cease to weep for him, and when my heart is weeping, my eyes will not laugh. You have had the courage to conceal your tears under a smile, and not to suffer your head to be weighed down by the disgrace and contumely which they tried to heap on it. I shall have the courage not to conceal my tears, and to walk about, bending my head under the disgrace and contumely which have undeservedly fallen to my share. If I were guiltier, I should be able, perhaps, to brave the world; but having to mourn, not over a guilty action, but only over a misfortune, I shall weep! Let the world condemn me for it; I shall not hear its judgment, for I shall retire into solitude."

"Oh, you foolish woman!" exclaimed Marianne, fervently. "Yes, foolish, because you believe already at the beginning of your life that you are done with it. My child, the human heart is much too weak to be able to bear such a grief for many years. It gradually grows tired of it and finally drops it, and perceives then all at once that it is quite empty. Tedium, with its long spider-legs, will then creep over you and draw its dusty network around and no one will tear away this network, because nobody will be there to do this salutary service, for you will have driven people away from your side and preferred loneliness to their society. Beware of solitude, or rather learn to be alone in the midst of the world, but not in the privacy of your deserted boudoir. You have to fulfil a beautiful and grand mission here in Vienna. You have to emancipate the Jews—in a manner, however, different from the course I have pursued. I have proved to the foolish world that a Jewess may very well be a princess and worthily represent her exalted rank, notwithstanding her oriental blood and curved nose; but in order to be able to prove it to the world, I had to give up my religion and to desert my people. It is your mission to finish the work I have commenced, and to secure to the Jews a distinguished and undisputed place in society. You shall be the mediator between the aristocracy of blood and of pedigree and the aristocracy of money—the mediator between the Christians and the Jews. You shall give to the Jews here in Vienna a position such as they are justly entitled to: free, respected, and emancipated from the degrading yoke of prejudices. Such is your mission. Go and fulfil it!"

"You are right, Marianne," replied Fanny, with glowing enthusiasm." I will fulfil the mission, for it is a grand and sacred one, and it will comfort and strengthen my heart. The happiness of my life is gone forever; but I may, perhaps, be happy in my unhappiness, and I will now try to become so by consoling the unhappy, by assisting the suffering, and by giving an asylum to the disowned and proscribed. To dry tears, to distribute alms, and to scatter joy and happiness around me—that shall be the balm with which I will heal the wounds of my heart. You are right; I will not retire from the world, but I will compel it to respect me; I will not flee with my grief into solitude, but I will remain with it in the midst of society, a comfort to all sufferers, a refuge to all needing my assistance!" *

"That is right! I like to hear you talk thus," exclaimed Marianne, embracing her friend,

* Fanny von Arnstein kept her word. Her house became the centre of the most distinguished intellectual life; her hands were always open and ready to scatter charities and to spread blessings. She did not, however, give merely with her hands, but also with her heart, and only thereby she became a true benefactress; for she added to her gifts that pity and sagacity which know how to appreciate the true sort of relief. To many people she secured lasting happiness; to many she opened the road to wealth, and to some she gave sums which, in themselves, were equivalent to an independent fortune. Her hospitality equalled her benevolence, and she exercised it with rare amiability and to a remarkable extent. Every day numerous guests were received in her house in the city as well as in her villa, where they enjoyed the advantages of the most attractive, enlightened, and distinguished society.

and tenderly pressing her to her heart. "Now my fears for you are gone, and I may bid you farewell with a reassured and comforted heart. My travelling-coach is waiting for me, and I shall set out in the course of the present hour."

"And where are you going?" asked Fanny, sympathetically.

"That is a secret—a profound political secret," said Marianne, smiling; "but I will confide it to you as a proof of my love. I go to Paris for the purpose of delivering to the first consul a letter from the poor Count de Provence, whom the royalists, and consequently myself, also call King Louis the Eighteenth of France. That, Fanny, is the legacy Prince Charles von Lichtenstein has bequeathed to me. Through him I became acquainted with some of those noble émigrés who preferred to give up their country and their possessions, and to wander about foreign lands without a home, instead of proving faithless to their king, and of obeying that despotic republic and the tyrant who now lays his iron hand upon France. It was the Prince von Lichtenstein who, two weeks ago, brought the Duke d'Enghien to me, and initiated me into the great plans of the unfortunate Bourbons."

"The Duke d'Enghien was here in Vienna?" asked Fanny, in surprise.

"Yes, he was here; he kept himself concealed in the palace of your friend Lichtenstein, and only his devoted adherents knew where he was. The prince belonged to his most enthusiastic followers and friends. Oh, what plans those two fiery young men conceived in the safe asylum of my reception-room! what great things did they expect from the future for the cause of the Bourbons and for France! You ought to have seen Prince Charles von Lichtenstein in such hours, Fanny; then you would have really understood and boundlessly loved him. His cheeks, then, were glowing with noble impetuosity; his eyes flashed fire, and sublime words of soul-stirring eloquence dropped from his lips. Never has an enemy been hated more ardently than he hated Bonaparte, the first consul; never has a cause been more passionately adhered to than the cause of his unhappy fatherland and that of the exiled Bourbons. If the Count de Provence could boast of a hundred such defenders as was the Prince von Lichtenstein, he would have reconstructed the throne of the fleur-de-lis within a week in Paris. Dry your tears, Fanny, for you are not most to be pitied. You only lost a lover, but the Bourbons lost a champion and Germany a true and valorous son; these two are more to be pitied than you. You may find a hundred other lovers, if such should be your desire, but the Bourbons have but few champions, and the number of the true and noble sons of Germany is constantly on the decrease."

"And he said nothing to me about his plans and hopes?" exclaimed Fanny, reproachfully. "He never made me suspect that—"

"That he had not only a heart for love, but also for politics and for the cause of the fatherland!" interrupted Marianne, smiling. "My child, he loved with his heart; hence, so long as he was with you, all the schemes of his head were silent. Still he knew that the beloved of his heart was able and worthy, too, to be the friend of his head; and when he took leave of me, he instructed me to initiate you into all his plans, and to let you participate in his hopes. Fanny, your friend greets you through my mouth; he wishes to transfer his love and his hatred, now that he has left us forever to yourself. As he was a faithful son of his German fatherland, you shall be its faithful daughter and guardian, and watch over the welfare of your country, and devote yourself to its service with your whole strength. As he was an inexorable enemy of that new, blood-stained France and of her dictator, you shall forswear all connection with that country, which soon will pour its torrents of blood and fire over our own unhappy fatherland. You shall do whatever will serve and be useful to the fatherland, and you shall abhor, persecute, and combat every menace to subjugate Germany. Your house shall be open to all German patriots; it shall be closed against all enemies of Germany, no matter whether they are Germans or French, or to whatever nation they may belong. Such, Fanny, is the legacy which Prince Charles von Lichtenstein, the noble German patriot, has bequeathed to you with his love, and which is to comfort and strengthen you in your grief."

"I accept this legacy," exclaimed Fanny, radiant with enthusiasm. "Yes, I accept this legacy and will fulfil it faithfully! To Germany I will transfer the love which I once devoted to him; I will love and honor him in each of our German brethren. Like him, I will hate the enemies of Germany, and never shall my house be opened to them—never shall they cross its threshold as welcome guests! As I cannot be a happy wife, I will try to be a faithful daughter of my country, to love its friends faithfully, and to hate its enemies bitterly!"

"That is right," said Marianne, joyfully. "Now you have received your best consolation, and the grief of your love will be transformed into deeds of love. The blessing of your departed friend will be with you, and the love of your fatherland will reward you for what you will do for it. And you shall assist our despised and down-trodden Jews, too, by proving to those who scorn us and contemptuously treat us as aliens, that we feel like natives and children of the country in which we were born, and that we do not seek for our Jerusalem in the distant Orient, but in the fatherland we share with all other Germans. Let us prove to these Christians that we also are good patriots, and that we love our fatherland like them, and are ready to make any sacrifice which it may require from us."

"Yes, I will prove that I am a good patriot as he was a good patriot," said Fanny, enthusiastically. "I will hate whatever he hated; I will love whatever he loved!"

"Amen!" exclaimed Marianne, solemnly. "And now, farewell, Fanny. I go to fulfil the legacy which Prince von Lichtenstein has bequeathed to me. He had taken it upon himself to deliver this letter to Bonaparte, and to see what the Bourbons have to expect from him, and whether Bonaparte is a Monk or a Cromwell. I fear the latter. The Bourbons and Lichtenstein hoped for the former. They believed he would be the Monk of the restoration, and he had only placed himself so near the throne in order to restore the latter to Louis XVIII., as Monk had done in relation to Charles II. Well, we shall see! I will go now and deliver the letter which Prince Lichtenstein has intrusted to me. Farewell, Fanny, and remember your legacy!"

"I shall remember it as long as I live," said Fanny, fervently. "And as I never shall forget my love, I shall never forget my fatherland either. Both shall live indissolubly united in my heart!" *

* The history of Baroness Arnstein and the tragic end of Prince Charles von Lichtenstein do not belong to romance, but to reality, and created a great sensation at that time. Every one in Vienna knew that love for Baroness Arnstein had been the cause of the duel and of the death of the Prince von Lichtenstein, but every one knew also that Fanny von Arnstein was not to blame for this event; hence the sympathy and compassion felt for the unhappy lady were universal. The imperial court and the city took pains to do homage to her and to manifest their respect for her. But Baroness Arnstein was not to be consoled by such proofs of public sympathy; the affliction which had befallen her was too terrible, and she did not endeavor to conceal her grief. She caused the cabinet in which he had seen her on the day preceding his death to be hung in black like a death-room; all the souvenirs and every thing reminding her of him were preserved in this room. She spent there every anniversary of his death in deep mourning, and at other times she frequently retired thither to pray for him. Except herself no one was ever permitted to enter this cabinet, consecrated as an altar for the religion of her reminiscences.—Vide Varnhagen von Ense's Miscellanies, vol. i, p. 412.

"Then you have seen and conversed with our poor, unhappy king?" said Madame Bonaparte to the beautiful and richly-dressed lady who was sitting on the sofa at her side, and who was none other than the Princess Marianne von Eibenberg.

"Yes, madame, I have often had the good fortune to converse long with him," said the princess, heaving a sigh. "I passed a few weeks in his neighborhood, and touched by his resignation, his unfaltering patience, and calm greatness, I offered him my mediation; I wished to be the messenger whom the poor unfortunate would send out in order to see whether the shores of his country will never again be visible to him, and whether the great and intrepid pilot who is now steering the ship of France with so firm a hand has no room left for the poor shipwrecked man. The Count de Provence accepted my services; he gave me a letter which I was to deliver to the First Consul himself, and I set out for Paris provided with numerous and most satisfactory recommendations. All these recommendations, however, were useless; even the intercession of Minister Talleyrand was in vain; the First Consul refused to grant me an audience."

"He had been told, perhaps, how beautiful and charming a messenger had been this time sent to him by the Count de Provence," said Josephine, smiling, "and he was, therefore, afraid of you, madame. For Bonaparte, the most intrepid hero in battle, is quite timid and bashful in the presence of beautiful ladies, and not having the strength to withstand your smiles and prayers, he evades you and refuses to see you."

"Oh, madame," exclaimed the princess, quickly, "if the First Consul is unable to resist the smiles of the most beautiful lady, I predict to you an even more brilliant future; for in that case he will lay the whole world at your feet to do you homage. He who has remained at the side of Josephine a hero and a man of iron will, need not fear the beauty of any other woman."

"You know how to flatter," said Josephine, smiling. "You forget, however, that we are in a republic here, and that there is no court with courtiers in the Tuileries, but merely the humble household of a citizen and general, which, I trust, will soon give way to the splendor of royalty."

"Do you believe so, madame?" asked the princess, eagerly. "Do you believe that the hopes which the Count de Provence has built on the noble and grand spirit of General Bonaparte are not

illusory? Oh, let us be frank and sincere toward each other, for I know you sympathize with the sufferings of the royal family, and the terrible misfortunes of the august exiles find an echo in your heart. Hence, when I did not succeed in obtaining an interview with the First Consul, and in delivering my letter to him in person, I applied to you, and the Count de Provence himself authorized me to do so. 'If Bonaparte refuses to hear you,' he said, 'go to Josephine. Bring her the greetings of the Count de Provence; remind her of the happy days of Versailles, where, as Viscountess de Beauharnais, she was always welcome at the court of my lamented brother. Ask her if she still remembers how often we joked and laughed together at that time. Ask her whether my present misfortunes shall last forever, or whether she, who holds my destiny in her hand, will restore me to mirth and joy.'"

"Oh!" exclaimed Josephine, bursting into tears, "if I held his destiny in my hand, he would not have to wait long for his throne and for happiness. I should be the first to jubilantly welcome him to France, the first to joyously leave these Tuileries, this royal palace, the grandeur of which frightens me, and in the walls of which it always seems to me as though I were a criminal adorning herself with stolen property, and stretching out her hands toward the holy of holies. And yet I am innocent of this outrage; my conscience is clear, and I am able to say that King Louis XVIII. has no more devoted, faithful, and obedient subject than the wife of the First Consul of France."

"The king knows it, and depends on you," said the princess. "Bonaparte's heart is in your hands; you alone are able to move it."

"But do I know, then, whether he has yet a heart or not?" exclaimed Josephine, passionately. "Do I know, then, if he loves any thing but his glory? Man cannot serve two gods, and his god is glory. He soars aloft with the glance of an eagle, and the radiance of the sun does not dazzle him. Where will he finally rest and build his aerie? I do not know. As yet no rock has been too lofty for him, no summit too steep and sufficiently near the sun. I follow his flight with anxious eyes, but I am unable to restrain him. I can only pray for him, for myself, and for the unhappy king; I can only pray that the bold eagle may not finally conclude that the vacant throne will be an aerie worthy of himself, and occupy it."

"But you believe that he will do so?" asked the princess, quickly.

"Oh, my dear," replied Josephine, with a melancholy smile, "no one is able to know at the present time, nay, even to conjecture, what Bona parte will do; no one, not even myself. His mind is impenetrable, and he only speaks of what he has done, not of what he is going to do. His plans lie inscrutable and silent in his breast, and nobody can boast that he is aware of them. He knows that I am a royalist at heart, and he often mocks me for it, but more frequently he is angry with me on this account. Since the French peo-ple have elected him First Consul for life, I see him tremble and frown whenever I dare to mention our exiled king, and to call him our master. He has strictly ordered me to receive no stranger un-less he has given me permission to do so, and all friends of mine, whom he knew to be enthusiastic royalists, have already been banished by him. I must feign to forget all I owe to friendship and gratitude, and yet all those cherished reminis-cences will never be effaced from my heart. But I must obey my master; for Bonaparte is no longer only my husband, but he is also my mas-ter. Thus impeded in all her inclinations, the wife of the First Consul must swallow her grief and seem ungrateful, although she is not. State it to those who believe my fate to be an enviable one; state it to the Count de Provence, who deems my influence greater than it really is. He is, and always remains for me, the legitimate king of France, and I call God to witness that I do not long for the crown which is his legitimate proper-ty. I call God to witness that I have improved every opportunity to promote the interests of the Count de Provence, and that I have always taken pains to remind Bonaparte of his duty to his le-gitimate king. But my success has been insig-nificant, and to-day for the first time since a long while I dare again to entertain a glimmer of hope. Bonaparte knew that I wanted to receive you to-day, and he did not forbid it, although he had al-ready been informed that the Princess von Eiben-berg was highly esteemed as a devoted friend at the court of Coblentz, that she had made a jour-ney to Mitau for the express purpose of seeing the Count de Provence, that she had been sent by the latter with letters and messages to Paris, and that the Duke d'Enghien, who some time ago had secretly been at Vienna, had been every day at your house."

"What! The First Consul is aware of all that?" asked Marianne, wonderingly.

"His spies serve him well," said Josephine, heaving a sigh, "and Bonaparte has got spies everywhere, even here in the Tuileries, here in my own rooms—and I should not wonder if he should learn even within the next quarter of an hour what we have conversed about here, although it may have seemed to us as though we were alone."

"But if the First Consul knows that the Count de Provence wants to avail himself of my services for the purpose of promoting his interests here in Paris, and if he has, nevertheless, permitted you to receive me, it seems to me a favorable symptom," said Marianne Eibenberg, musingly.

"Of course, he has some object in view in per-mitting it," replied Josephine, sighing, "but who knows what? I am unable to fathom his inten-tions; I content myself with loving him, admiring him, and endeavoring cautiously to lead him back to the path of duty. But hush!" she interrupted herself all at once, "I hear steps in the small corridor. It is Bonaparte! He comes hither. He will see that I have wept, and he will be angry with me!"

And after breathing into her handkerchief in anxious haste, Josephine pressed it against her eyes, and whispered tremblingly, "Can it be seen that I have wept?"

Marianne was about replying to her, when quick steps were heard in the adjoining room. "He is coming," whispered Josephine, and she rose from the sofa for the purpose of going to meet her husband.

He just opened the door by a quick pressure of his hand and appeared on the threshold. His eyes swept with a quick glance over the room and seemed to pierce every corner; a slight cloud covered his expansive marble forehead; his thin lips were firmly compressed, and did not show the faintest tinge of a smile.

"Ah, I did not know that there was a visitor with you, Josephine," he said, bowing to Mari-anne, who returned his salutation by a deep and reverential obeisance, and then fixed her large dark eyes upon him with an air of admiration.

"My friend," said Josephine, with a fascinating smile, "the Princess von Eibenberg has been recommended to me by persons of the highest distinction, and I confess that I am very grateful to those who gave me an opportunity to make the acquaintance of this beautiful and agreeable lady. It is true, I hear that the princess is a native of Germany, but she has got the heart of a Frenchwoman, and speaks our language better than many of the ladies whom I hear here in the Tuileries."

"Ah, she doubtless speaks that language of ancient France, which always pleases you so well," exclaimed Bonaparte; and now there appeared on his finely formed lips a smile, illuminating and beautifying his face like sunshine. "I suppose, madame," he said, suddenly turning to Marianne, "you have come hither in order to bring to my dear Josephine greetings from a cavalier of that ancient France which has forever fallen to ruins?"

"No, general," said Marianne, whose radiant eyes were constantly and fearlessly fixed on Bonaparte—"no, general, I have come hither in order to admire the new France, and never shall I be able to thank Madame Bonaparte sufficiently for the happiness she has procured me at this moment. It is the first time in my life that I have been able to see a great man, a hero!"

"And yet you were in London and Mitau and there saw the Counts d'Artois and Provence," replied Bonaparte, sitting down in an arm-chair by Marianne's side, and requesting the ladies by a wave of his hand to resume their seats on the sofa.

"And in London, in Mitau, in Coblentz, everywhere they admire the hero who has risen like a new sun with the young century!" said Marianne, with irresistible grace.

"Those gentlemen of ancient France spoke of me, then?" asked Bonaparte. "You see, madame, I speak without circumlocution. I am nothing but a good soldier, and always strike directly at my aim. I have been told that you have come hither as an emissary of the Bourbons, and I confess to you that to-day for the first time I feel grateful to those gentlemen, for they have made a very beautiful selection. The emissaries sent hither heretofore were less beautiful and less amiable. Those Bourbons know the *foibles* of the male heart better than anybody else, and they want to fascinate me in order to seduce me afterward the more surely."

"Pardon me, general, they were not so bold as that," said the princess, smiling. "Let me say that I am not gifted with the magic power of Armida, nor are you with the sentimental weakness of Rinaldo."

"You do not deem me worthy to be compared with Rinaldo?" asked Bonaparte, casting so glowing a glance on the fair emissary that Josephine almost regretted having brought this fascinating beauty in contact with her husband.

"I do not deem Rinaldo worthy to be compared with Bonaparte," said the princess, with a charming smile. "Rinaldo did not conquer any countries; he did not cross the bridge of Arcole, holding aloft the waving colors; he did not see the pyramids of Egypt; he did not conquer at Marengo!"

"Ah, madame, you seem to have a good memory," exclaimed Bonaparte, merrily, "and you do not only know ancient France, but are also quite familiar with her recent history."

"General, it is owing to you that the history of France is that of the whole world, and that the

victories of France signify the defeat of the remainder of Europe. But you have brought about an even greater miracle, for those whom you have vanquished do not hate you for it, but they admire you, and while cursing their own misfortune, they are astonished at your heroism and surpassing greatness as a military chieftain. There is no one who does not share this feeling of admiration, and there is no one who entertains it in a livelier manner than the two men who have reason to complain most of France, and who do so least!"

"Ah, you skilfully return to the charge," exclaimed Bonaparte, smiling. "You would make a good general: you make a short cut on the field of flattery and so reach the more rapidly the straight road on which you want to meet the Counts de Provence and Artois in order to praise them before me."

"No, Bonaparte," said Josephine, hastily, "the princess, on the contrary, wishes to tell you how those gentlemen praise you, and with how much admiration they speak of you.—Oh, pray, madame, repeat to Bonaparte what the Count d'Artois told you the other day, and mention the honors and distinctions he would like to confer on my husband."

"Well, I should really like to know the honors and distinctions which that little *émigré*, M. de Bourbon, is able to confer on the First Consul of France," said Bonaparte, with a sarcastic smile. "Tell me, madame, what did the Count d'Artois say, and what that statement of yours is that has filled the ambitious heart of Madame Bonaparte with so much delight?"

"Oh, you want to mock me, my friend," said Josephine, reproachfully.

"By no means, I am in dead earnest, and should like to know what the pretenders did say about me. State to us, then, madame, with your seductive voice, the tempting promises of the Bourbons."

"General, there was no talk of promises, but of the admiration the Count d'Artois felt for you," said Marianne, almost timidly, and with downcast eyes. "We conversed about politics in general, and Madame de Guiche, in her charming innocence, took the liberty to ask the Count d'Artois how the First Consul of France might be rewarded in case he should restore the Bourbons."

"Ah, you conversed about this favorite theme of the *émigrés*, about the restoration question!" said Bonaparte, shrugging his shoulders. "And what did the prince reply?"

"The Count d'Artois replied: 'In the first place, we should appoint the first consul *Connétable* of France, if that would be agreeable to him. But we should not believe that that would be a sufficient reward; we should erect on the *Place du*

Carrousel a lofty and magnificent column to be surmounted by a statue of Bonaparte crowning the Bourbons!'" *

"Is not that a beautiful and sublime idea?" exclaimed Josephine, joyfully, while the princess searchingly fixed her eyes on Bonaparte's face.

"Yes," he said, calmly, "it is a very sublime idea; but what did you reply, Josephine, when this was communicated to you?"

"What did I reply?" asked Josephine. "Good Heaven! what should I have replied?"

"Well," said Bonaparte, whose face now assumed a grave, stern expression, "you might have replied, for instance, that the pedestal of this beautiful column would have to be the corpse of the First Consul." †

"Oh, Bonaparte, what a dreadful idea that is!" exclaimed Josephine, in dismay—"dreadful and withal untrue, for did not the Count d'Artois say the Bourbons would appoint you *Connétable* of France?"

"Yes, just as Charles II. of England conferred the title of duke on Monk. I am no Monk, nor am I a Cromwell. I have not injured a single hair on the head of the Bourbons, and my hand has not been stained by a drop of the blood of the unfortunate king who had to atone for the sins of his predecessors. He had ruined France, I saved her; and the example of Monk teaches me to be cautious, for the English people had confided in him, and he gave them a king who made them unhappy and oppressed them for twenty years, and finally caused a new revolution; I want to preserve France from the horrors of a new revolution, hence I do not want to become another Monk."

"And who should dare to compare you with Monk or Cromwell, general?" exclaimed Marianne. "If there is a man worthy to be compared with the first consul of France, it is only the great Washington, the liberator of America."

"Ah, you think so because we are both presiding over a republic," replied Bonaparte, with a sarcastic smile. "As I do not want to be a Monk, it is hoped that I shall be a Washington. Words cost nothing, and those who utter them so easily do not consider whether the circumstances of the two nations, the time and occasion may be as well compared with each other as those two names. If I were in America, it would be my highest glory to be another Washington, and I should deserve but little credit for it, after all, for I do not see how one could reasonably pursue there any other course. But if Washington had been in

France, with its convulsions within and an invasion from abroad, I should not have deemed it advisable for him to be himself; if he had insisted upon remaining himself, he would have been an idol, and only prolonged the misfortunes of France instead of saving the country."

"You confess, then, that France ought not to remain a republic?" asked Josephine, joyfully. "You want to restore the monarchy?"

"Wait for the things to come," said Bonaparte, gravely. "To ask me prematurely to do things incompatible with the present state of affairs would be foolish; if I should announce or promise them it would look like charlatanry and boasting, and I am not addicted to either."

"But you give us hopes, at least, that you will do so one day, when the time has come, I suppose, my friend?" said Josephine, tenderly. "You will not let this beautiful lady depart from Paris without a kind and comforting reply? She will not have entered the Tuileries, the house of the kings, in order to be obliged to inform on her return those to whom it justly belongs that there is no longer any room for them under the roof which their fathers have built. I am sure, Bonaparte, you will not send such a reply to the legitimate King of France from *his own rooms*."

Josephine, glowing with excitement, had risen from her seat; stepping close up to Bonaparte, she encircled his neck with her beautiful arms, and laid her charming head on his shoulder.

"Oh, Josephine, what are you doing?" ejaculated Bonaparte, angrily. "Will not the princess tell the Count de Provence that the Tuileries are now inhabited by a downright *bourgeois* and henpecked husband, who treats his wife sentimentally even in the presence of other persons, and in return for her caresses has always to comply with her wishes. And shall we not be laughed at, my child?"

"I should like to see the Titan who would dare to laugh at the First Consul!" exclaimed Marianne, eagerly. "You would do like Jove; you would hurl down the audacious scoffer into the abyss with a flash from your eyes."

Bonaparte fixed so long and glowing a look on the princess that Marianne blushed, while the jealous heart of Josephine began to ache.

"Bonaparte, state the reply you are going to make to the Count de Provence," she said, anxious to withdraw his attention from the contemplation of this fascinating beauty.

"A reply?" asked Bonaparte. "What shall I reply to?"

"General, to this letter, which the Count de Provence has intrusted to me, and which I have

---

* Las Cases, "Mémorial de Sainte-Hélène," vol. i., p. 337.
† Bonaparte's own words.—Ibid., vol. ii., p. 337.

solemnly pledged myself to deliver to you personally," said Marianne, handing Bonaparte a sealed
paper, with an imploring glance.

Bonaparte did not take it at once, but looked
sternly at the two ladies who stood before him,
turning their beautiful and deeply moved faces
toward him with an air of supplication.

"It is a perfect conspiracy, then, ladies? A
complete surprise of the fortress?" he asked.
"You want to compel me forcibly to open the
gates of my eyes to you? Do you not know, then,
Josephine, that I have sworn not to accept any
letters from the Pretender, in order not to be
obliged to make a harsh reply to him?"

"Keep your oath, then," said Josephine, smiling; "do not accept the letter, but permit me to
do so, and let me read the contents of the letter
to you."

"Oh, women, women!" exclaimed Bonaparte,
smiling. "They are born sophists, and I believe
they would be able to outwit the devil himself!
Well, I will comply with your request; take the
letter and read it to me."

Josephine uttered a joyful cry, and took the
letter from Marianne's hands. While she broke
the seal and unfolded the paper, Bonaparte had
risen from his arm-chair, and commenced slowly
pacing the room. He knew, perhaps, that Marianne's eyes were fixed upon him with a searching
expression, and her glances were disagreeable to
him.

Josephine read as follows:

"Men like you, sir, never inspire suspicion and
uneasiness, whatever their conduct may be. You
have accepted the exalted position which the
French people offered to you, and I am grateful to
you for so doing. You know better than anybody
else how much strength and power are required
to secure the happiness of a great nation. Save
France from her own fury, and you will have fulfilled the foremost and greatest desire of my
heart; restore her king to her, and future generations will bless your memory. But you hesitate
very long to give my throne back to me, and I
almost fear you will allow the opportunity to pass
by unimproved. Hasten, therefore, and designate
the positions you desire for yourself and for your
friends. You will always be too indispensable to
the state for me ever to be able to discharge the
obligations of my ancestors and my own, even by
means of the most influential positions. My character, as well as motives of sound policy, will induce me to pursue a liberal course. We are able
to secure the happiness of France. I say we, for
you cannot secure the happiness of France without me, and I cannot do any thing for France

without you. General, Europe has fixed her eyes
on you, and immortal glory awaits you."

"Always the same strain," muttered Bonaparte,
"always the story of the column surmounted by
the statue of the First Consul crowning the Bourbons, while his bleeding corpse is to be the foundation of the column!"

"He is reflecting," whispered Josephine to the
princess. "That shows, at least, that he has not
yet made up his mind to reject the offer of the
Count de Provence."

At this moment Bonaparte turned toward the
two ladies and approached them rapidly.

"Are you authorized to receive my reply?"
he asked, turning his gloomy eyes toward the
princess.

"I shall feel happy and honored by any message you may be pleased to intrust to me," said
Marianne.

Bonaparte nodded to her.

"Will you permit me to write a letter here, Josephine?" he asked.

Instead of making a reply, Josephine hastened
to her desk, in order to take out some paper, to
draw a chair to the table, and then to hand the
pen to Bonaparte, with a fascinating smile. When
he commenced writing, she supported herself in
breathless suspense on the back of his arm-chair
and looked over the Consul's shoulder, while the
Princess von Eibenberg, standing not far from
them, looked at both with sparkling eyes.

Bonaparte hastily wrote a few lines, threw the
pen aside, and turning around to Josephine, he
handed her the letter.

"There, read it," he said, "and read it aloud,
so that the beautiful emissary of your M. de Bourbon may learn my reply, and know the contents
of the message she is to deliver to him."

Josephine took the paper and read, in a tremulous voice, frequently interrupted by her sighs:

"I have received the letter of your royal highness; I have constantly felt a lively sympathy for
you and for the misfortunes of your family. But
your royal highness must not think of coming to
France; you would have to pass over a hundred
thousand corpses before reaching it. In other respects, I shall constantly take pains to do whatever will be calculated to alleviate your condition
and to make you forget your misfortunes."

"Well, Josephine, you are silent?" asked
Bonaparte, when she ceased reading. "You are
dissatisfied with my letter? And you, too, madame,
have a dark shadow on your beautiful face! How
could you expect another answer from me?"

---

* This letter is historical. — Vide "Mémoires d'un
Homme d'État," vol. vii., p. 398.

"General, I believe the royal princes really hoped for another answer," said Marianne, heaving a sigh.

"And what justified such a hope?" asked Bonaparte, sternly. "What have I done to give rise to such chimeras?"

"General, the favorable answer you gave to Prussia—"

"Ah!" said Bonaparte, shrugging his shoulders, "the wind is blowing in that direction, then? Prussia asked me if she would cause us any trouble by tolerating the French princes within her boundaries. I replied in the negative; and when Prussia went further and asked whether we should feel offended or not, if she paid an annual pension to the Bourbons, I permitted even that on condition that the princes remained quiet and did not carry on any intrigues. They believed, then, that because I suffered distressed persons to be relieved and an asylum to be granted to the homeless, I should be ready, also, to make the beggars masters again, and to lay France at the feet of the exiles!"

"Bonaparte, your words are very harsh and very unjust," exclaimed Josephine, sadly.

"They may be harsh, but they are true," he said, sternly. "I will not permit them to entertain any illusions concerning myself; hence I have spoken so long and plainly. It would be harsh and cruel to hold out hopes to the Bourbons which I shall never fulfil. France is lost to them, and they will never recover her. State that to the princes who have sent you to me, madame. Let the Bourbons be on their guard, for France is wide awake and keeps her eyes and ears open. I am willing to forgive that little Duke d'Enghien for not considering me a great general, and for criticising my exploits, but I should neither forgive him nor either of his uncles in case they should try to trouble France with their senseless schemes. I know that the Bourbons have long been trying to find means and ways to reconquer the sceptre of St. Louis. So long as their schemes are floating in the air like cobwebs, I forgive them; but if they intend to act, let them weigh the consequences! He who menaces France is a traitor, whatever may be his name, and traitors will be punished to the full extent of the law. State that to the Bourbons, madame; state it especially to the Duke d'Enghien. And now be kind enough to deliver my reply to the Count de Provence. When do you intend to start?"

"In a few days, general."

"Oh, that will not do. That poor Count de Provence will be eager to get a reply," said Bonaparte, "and it would be very cruel not to transmit it to him as soon as possible. You especially will not wish to make him wait, and I therefore advise you to set out to-day, within the next hour! I shall issue orders that horses be kept in readiness for you; and in order that you may not be detained anywhere, I shall instruct two officers to escort you to the frontier. Hasten, therefore, madame; in half an hour every thing will be ready for your departure."

He nodded to her, and left the room.

The two ladies were alone again and looked at each other with mournful eyes. Marianne's face was pale; a gloomy fire was burning in her eyes, and a contemptuous smile was visible on her lips. Josephine seemed greatly embarrassed, and her gentle eyes were filled with tears.

"I am to be transported beyond the frontier like a criminal!" ejaculated Marianne at last, in a voice trembling with anger. "I am to be treated like a dangerous intriguer, and yet I have only delivered a letter which had been intrusted to me by the king."

"Forgive him," said Josephine, imploringly. "He has been prejudiced against you, and the numerous plots and conspiracies, which have already been discovered, cause him to deem rigorous precautions altogether indispensable. But I beg you especially not to be angry with me, and pray beseech the Count de Provence not to hold me responsible for the deplorable message you are to deliver to him. I have opened my heart to you, and you know it to be filled with the most faithful devotion and with the most reverential affection for the unfortunate prince, but I am not strong enough to change his fate; I—"

Just then the door opened; M. de Bourrienne, chief of the cabinet of the First Consul, made his appearance and approached the princess with a respectful bow.

"Madame," he said, "the First Consul sends you word that every thing is ready for your departure, and he has instructed me to conduct you to your carriage."

Josephine uttered a groan, and, sinking down on a chair, she covered her face with her handkerchief in order to conceal her tears.

Marianne had now recovered her proud and calm bearing, and a bold and defiant smile played again on her lips. She approached Josephine with soft and quiet steps.

"Farewell, madame," she said. "I shall faithfully report to the Count de Provence every thing I have seen and heard here, and he will venerate and pity you as I shall always do. May the First

Consul never regret what he is doing now, and may he not be obliged one day to leave France in the same manner as he compels me to depart from Paris! Come, sir, accompany me, as it cannot be helped!"

And drawing herself up to her full height and as proud as a queen, Marianne, princess of Eibenberg, walked toward the door.

Josephine followed her with her tearful eyes, which she then raised to heaven. "Oh, my God, my God," she whispered, "ordain it in Thy mercy that my worst forebodings may not be fulfilled! Guide Bonaparte's heart and prevent him from going on in his ambition, from stretching out his hand for the crown of the Bourbons, and from staining his glory with the blood of—. Oh, Thou knowest my fears; Thou knowest what I mean, and what my lips dare not utter. Protect Bonaparte, and guide his heart!"

CHAPTER XLI.

TWO GERMAN SAVANTS.

A POST-CHAISE, drawn by four horses, had just driven up to the hotel of *The German Emperor*, the first and most renowned inn in the city of Frankfort-on-the-Main. The porter rang the door-bell as loudly and impetuously as he only used to do on the arrival of aristocratic and wealthy guests. Hence the waiters rushed to the door in the greatest haste, and even the portly and well-dressed landlord did not deem it derogatory to his dignity to leave the dining-room, for the purpose of welcoming the stranger in the post-chaise, drawn by the four horses.

In this post-chaise he perceived a gentleman of prepossessing and jovial appearance, and with a handsome and tolerably youthful face. His large blue eyes looked gayly and boldly into the world; a genial smile was playing on his broad and rather sensual-looking lips; and his voice was clear, strong, and sonorous.

"May I find here with you comfortable rooms, and, above all, a good supper?" he asked the landlord, who, pushing aside his waiters and the stranger's footman, stepped up to the carriage, in order to open the door.

"Sir," replied the landlord, proudly, "*The German Emperor* is noted for its good rooms and excellent table!"

The stranger laughed merrily. "Truly," he said, gayly, "these are splendid prospects for Germany. If *The German Emperor* furnishes good

rooms and an excellent table, I am sure Germany would be unreasonable to ask for any thing else! Well, my dear landlord, give me, then, good rooms and a supper."

"Do you want rooms on the first or on the second floor?" asked the landlord, respectfully walking behind the stranger, who had just entered the hall.

"Of course, on the first floor; Heaven forbid that I should have to climb two flights of stairs!" replied the stranger. "I like to live in comfortable and elegant rooms. Give me, therefore, three fine rooms on the first floor."

"Three rooms!" said the landlord, hesitatingly. "I must observe to you, sir, that all the rooms on the first floor have been reserved for the Duke of Baden, who will arrive here to-morrow or day after to-morrow, and stop at *The German Emperor*, like all princes coming to our city. I do not know if I can spare three rooms."

"Oh, you surely can, as the duke will only arrive to-morrow or day after to-morrow, while I am here to-day," said the stranger. "Give me the rooms you had intended for the duke; then I shall be sure to get good ones, and I shall take them at the same price you will charge him."

The landlord bowed respectfully, and snatched the silver candlestick from the hand of the head-waiter, in order to have the honor of conducting the stranger up-stairs to his rooms. The waiters, who had stood on both sides of the hall in respectful silence, now hastily rushed toward the post-chaise, in order to assist the stranger's footman in unloading the trunks and packages belonging to his master.

"As far as the supper is concerned, pray imagine I were the expected Duke of Baden, and make your arrangements accordingly," said the stranger, ascending the staircase. "I particularly enjoy a good supper. If you have any pheasants to serve up to me, I shall be content with them; only see to it that they be well larded with truffles."

And his voice died away in the large corridor which he was now walking down, preceded by the landlord, in order to take possession of the best rooms in the hotel.

The waiters were engaged in unloading the trunks, and improved this opportunity to inquire of the stranger's footman, clad in a rich livery, the rank, name, and title of his master.

He told them the gentleman had just arrived from London, where he had been living for a year; he was now on his way to Vienna, and would leave Frankfort on the following day.

"This trunk is very heavy," said one of the waiters, vainly trying to lift from the carriage a small trunk, mounted with strips of brass, and covered with yellow nails.

"I should think so," said the footman, proudly. "This trunk contains my master's money and jewelry. There are at least twelve gold watches, set with diamonds, and as many snuff-boxes. The Queen of England sent to my master on the day of our departure a magnificent snuff-box, adorned with the portrait of her majesty, and richly set with diamonds; and the snuff-box, moreover, was entirely filled with gold pieces! Come, take hold of the trunk on that side; I shall do so on this, and we will take it directly up to my master's rooms."

Just as they entered the hall with their precious load, another carriage drove up to the door. But this time it was only a miserable, rickety old basket-chaise, drawn by two lean jades with lowered heads and heaving bellies.

The porter, therefore, did not deem it worth while to ring the bell for this forlorn-looking vehicle; but he contented himself with leisurely putting his hands into his pockets, sauntering down to the chaise, and casting a disdainful glance into its interior.

There was also a single gentleman in it, but his appearance was less prepossessing and indicative of liberality than that of the former stranger. The new-comer was a little gentleman, with a pale face and a sickly form. His mien was grave and care-worn; his dark eyes were gloomy and stern; his expansive forehead was thoughtful and clouded.

"May I have a room in your hotel?" he asked, in a clear, ringing voice.

"Certainly, sir, as nice and elegant as you may desire," said the porter, condescendingly.

"I do not require it to be nice and elegant," replied the stranger. "Only a small room with a comfortable bed; that is all I care for."

"It is at your disposal, sir," said the porter; and beckoning the youngest waiter to assist the stranger in alighting, he added: "Take the gentleman to one of the smaller rooms on the first floor."

"Oh, no," said the stranger, "I do not ask for a room on the first floor; I shall be satisfied with one on the second floor. Be kind enough to pay my fare to the coachman; he gets ten florins. You may put it down on my bill."

"And will you give me no drink-money?" asked the coachman, angrily. "The gentleman will assuredly not refuse me drink-money after a three days' journey?"

"My friend, I did not agree to pay you any thing but those ten florins," said the stranger.

"I will comply with your demand, however, for you have been an excellent driver."

He handed half a florin to the coachman, and entered the hotel with measured steps.

"Do you want supper?" asked the waiter, conducting him up-stairs.

"Yes, if you please," said the stranger; "but no expensive supper, merely a cup of tea and some bread and meat."

"A poor devil!" muttered the porter, shrugging his shoulders disdainfully, and following the stranger with his eyes. "A very poor devil! only a room on the second floor; tea and bread and meat for supper! He must be a *savant*, a professor, or something of that sort."

Meantime the footman and the waiter had carried the heavy trunk, with the gold and other valuables, up-stairs to the rooms of the stranger on the first floor. These rooms were really furnished in the most sumptuous manner, and worthy to be inhabited by guests of princely rank. Heavy silk and gold hangings covered the walls; blinds of costly velvet, fringed with gold, veiled the high arched windows; precious Turkish carpets adorned the floor; gilt furniture, carved in the most artistic manner and covered with velvet cushions, added to the splendor and beauty of the rooms.

The stranger lay on one of the magnificent sofas when the trunk with his valuables was brought in. He ordered the footman with a wave of his hand to place the trunk before him on the marble table, wrought by some Florentine artisan, and then he leisurely stretched out his legs again on the velvet sofa.

Scarcely had the door closed again behind the footman and the waiter, however, when he hastily rose, and drawing the trunk toward him, opened it with a small key fastened to his watch-chain.

"I believe I will now at length add up my riches," he said to himself. "The time of the golden rain, I am afraid is over, at least for the present; for, in Germany, an author and *savant* is never taken for a Danaë, and no one wants to be a Jove and lavish a golden rain upon him. The practical English, who are more sagacious in every respect, know, too, how to appreciate a writer of merit, and pay him better for his works. Thank God I was in England! Let us see now how much we have got."

He plunged his hands into the small trunk and drew them forth filled with gold pieces.

"How well that sounds!" he said, throwing the gold pieces on the table, and constantly adding new ones to them. "There is no music of the spheres to be compared with this sound, and no view is more charming than the aspect of this pile of gold. How many tender love-glances, how many sumptuous dinners, how many protestations of friendship and love-pledges, how many festivals and pleasures do not flash forth from those gold pieces, as though they were an enchanted mine! As a good general, I will count my troops, and thus enable myself to draw up the plans of my battles."

A long pause ensued. Nothing was heard but the music of the gold pieces, which the traveller arranged in long rows on the marble table, and the figures which he muttered, while his countenance grew every moment more radiant.

"Five hundred guineas!" he exclaimed joyfully; "that sum is equivalent to three thousand three hundred and thirty-three dollars in Prussian money; there are, besides, two thousand-pound notes in my wallet, amounting to over thirteen thousand dollars, which, together with my guineas, will amount to over sixteen thousand dollars cash. Oh, now I am a rich man! I no longer need deny to myself any wish, any enjoyment. I can enjoy life, and I will enjoy it. As a stream of enjoyment and delight my days shall roll along, and to enjoyment glory shall be added, and throughout all Germany my voice shall resound; in all cabinets it shall reëcho, and to the destinies of nations it shall point out their channel and direction. For great things I am called, and great things will I accomplish. I will not allow myself to be used by these lords of the earth as a journeyman, to whom the masters assign work for scanty pay. Their equal and peer, I will stand by their side, and they shall recognize it as a favor which they cannot weigh up with gold, if I take the word for them and their interests, and win battles for them with my pen."

There was a gentle knock at the door, and quickly he threw his silken handkerchief over the gold pieces and papers, and closed the cover of his casket before he gave permission to enter.

It was only a few waiters, who carried a well-spread table, in the midst of which a splendid pheasant stretched its brownish, shining limbs, and filled the whole room with the odor of the truffles with which it was stuffed. By its side shone, in crystal bottles, the most precious Rhine wine, looking like liquid gold, and a silent, still undisclosed pie gave a presentiment of a piquant enjoyment.

The traveller sipped the several odors with smiling comfort, and took his place at the table with the full confidence that he would be able to fill the next half hour of his life with enjoyment and to advantage.

In this confidence he was not disappointed, and when he finally rose from the table, on which nothing but bones had remained of the pheasant, and nothing but the bare crust of the pie, his countenance beamed with satisfaction and delight.

The waiters made haste to remove the table, and the head waiter made his appearance with the large hotel register, in which he asked the traveller to enter his name.

He was ready for it, and already took the pen to write his name, when suddenly he uttered a cry of surprise, and excitedly pointed with his finger to the last written line of the book.

"Is this gentleman still in your hotel, or has he already left?" he asked, hastily.

"No, your honor, this gentleman arrived only an hour ago, and he will stay here to-night," said the head waiter.

"Oh, what a surprise," said the traveller, starting up. "Come, please to conduct me at once to this gentleman."

And, with impatient haste, he ran to the door, which the head waiter opened to him. But upon the threshold he suddenly stopped and seemed to pause.

"Pray wait for me here in this hall; I shall follow you immediately," he said, as he returned to his room, closed its door, and hastened to the table in order to put his gold and his papers into the casket and to lock it.

In the mean while, the traveller in the small room of the second door had finished his frugal meal, and was now occupied with making up his account and entering the little travelling expenses of the last few days into his diary.

"It is after all an expensive journey," he muttered to himself; "I shall hardly have a few hundred florins left on my arrival at Berlin. It is true the first quarter of my salary will at once be paid to me, but one-half of it I have already assigned to my creditors, and the other half will scarcely suffice to furnish decently a few rooms. Oh, how much are those to be envied, the freedom and cheerfulness of whose minds are never disturbed by financial troubles!"

A loud knock at the door interrupted him; he hastened to put back his money into his pocket-book, when the door was hastily opened and the stranger of the first story appeared in it with a smiling countenance.

"Frederick Gentz!" exclaimed the owner of the room, in joyful surprise.

"Johannes Müller!" smilingly exclaimed the other, running up to him with outstretched arms, and tenderly embracing the little man, the great historian. "What good fortune for me, my friend, that I put up at this hotel, where I was to have the pleasure of meeting you! Accidentally I found in the hotel register your name, and at once I rushed to welcome you."

"And by coming you afford to my heart a true joy," tenderly said Johannes Müller, "for nothing can afford a greater joy than the unexpected meeting with a beloved and esteemed friend, and you know you are both to me."

"I only know that you are both to *me!*" exclaimed Gentz. "I only know that during my present journey I am indebted to you for the most precious hours, for the most sublime enjoyments. I had taken along for my reading your work on the 'Fürstenbund' ('Alliance of Princes'). I wished to see whether this book which, on its first appearance, so powerfully affected me, would still have the same effect upon me after an interval of twenty years. The world since then has been transformed and changed, I myself not less; and I was well aware how far my views on many most important topics would differ from yours. This, indeed, I found to be the case, and yet the whole reading was for me an uninterrupted current of delight and admiration. For four weeks I read in my leisure hours nothing but this book, and I felt my mind consecrated, strengthened, and nerved again for every thing great and good."

"If you say this," exclaimed Müller, "I have not labored in vain, although a German author feels sometimes tempted to believe that all his labors, all his writing and thinking were useless efforts, and nothing but seed scattered upon barren and sterile soil, and unable to bear fruit. Oh, my friend, what unfortunate days of humiliation and disgrace are still in store for Germany! But let us not talk of this now, but of you. Come, let us seat ourselves side by side upon this divan. And now tell me of your successes and your glory. The report of it has reached me, and I have learned with unenvying delight with what enthusiasm the whole literary and political world of England has received you, and how the court, the ministers, and the aristocracy of London have celebrated the great German writer and politician."

"It is true I have met in London with much kindness and a flattering reception," said Gentz, smilingly. "You know a German writer must go abroad if he lays claim to recognition and reward, for, as the proverb says, 'The prophet is not without honor, save in his own country.' I had, therefore, to go to England in order to secure for my voice, which until then was little heeded, some authority even in Germany."

"And now, when you have so eminently suc-

ceeded in this, you return I hope forever to Germany?"

"It almost seems so. I follow a call of the Austrian minister, Cobenzl, and have been appointed in Vienna as Aulic councillor, with a salary of four thousand florins."

"And in which ministry will you work?"

"Not in any particular one. I have been engaged for extraordinary services exclusively, with no other obligation than, as Minister von Cobenzl expressly writes, to work by my writings for the maintenance of the government, of morals, and order."

A smile stole over the delicate features of Müller.

"Exactly the same words which the Minister von Thugut said to me two years ago. And you have had the courage to accept the position?"

"Yes, I have accepted it, because I hope thus to render a service to the fatherland, and to be of advantage to it. I have forever cast off my Prussianism, and shall henceforth become an Austrian with body and soul."

"How wonderful are the dispensations of fate! for I must reply to you that I have cast off forever my Austrianism, and shall henceforth become a Prussian with body and soul."

"Ah, you go to Prussia! You leave the Austrian service?"

"Yes, forever. I follow a call to Berlin."

"Oh," exclaimed Gentz, "I have not the courage to complain that I have to do without you in Vienna, for fate in its wisdom has disposed of both of us, and it will make us available for the great, sublime cause of Germany. Being both stationed at one place, our efforts could not be so far reaching, so powerful, and therefore fate sets you up in the north of Germany, and me in the south, in order that our voices may resound hither and thither throughout Germany, and awaken all minds and kindle all energies for the one grand aim, the delivery and the honor of Germany."

"You still believe, then, in the honor of Germany and the possibility of its delivery," Müller inquired, with a sigh.

"Yes, I still believe in it," Gentz exclaimed, with enthusiasm; "but to that end many things must yet be done, many things must be aimed at and changed. Above all, two things are necessary. In the first place, the old enmity between Austria and Prussia must disappear, and both must firmly unite with each other and with England against France. It is this which I in Vienna and you in Berlin must never lose sight of—which we must aim at with all the power of our spirit and of our eloquence; for it is one of the last measures which are left for maintaining the independence of Europe and for averting the deluge of evils which break forth more terribly every day. From the moment when Austria and Prussia shall stand upon one line and move in one direction, there will be nowhere in Germany particular interests. All the greater and lesser princes would at once and without hesitation place themselves under the wings of this powerful alliance—the well-disposed cheerfully and out of conviction, and the unpatriotic ones through fear. So much of the constitution as has been rescued from this last shipwreck, would be safe for the duration of this alliance; and so much of it as must be altered, would be altered according to the principles of justice and of the common weal, and not according to the disgraceful demands of French and Russian land agents."

"You are right," exclaimed Johannes Müller; "a close alliance of Austria and Prussia is necessary, and only through it, and through it alone, the maintenance of the European equilibrium is possible, but for the present we must lean on the power of Russia and the resources of England."

"No, no," Gentz exclaimed, vehemently ; "no communion with Russia ! Russia is a friend who can never be trusted, for whenever it shall be her advantage she will at any moment be ready to become the most bitter enemy of her friends. But really we have had a striking and terrible example of this when the Emperor Paul suddenly separated from Germany and England in order to ally himself with France. But the union of France and Russia is the most threatening and terrible combination for the whole remainder of Europe. Of all the wounds which during the last ten years have been inflicted upon the old political system, and in particular upon the independence of Germany, those which were caused by the temporary agreement between France and Russia were the deepest and most incurable. If this comet should rise a second time over our heads, the world will go up in flames. What is to resist the combined power of these two colossuses unless the united weight and the united bulk of Germany hinders their embrace ? The western colossus has long since broken through its old barriers ; all the outposts are in its power, all the fortresses which do not belong to it are dismantled, all the points of military defence are outflanked. From Switzerland and Italy, from the peaks of the conquered Alps, it may irresistibly pounce upon the centre of the Austrian monarchy and invade the exposed provinces of the undefended Prussian kingdom. And now let it please Providence to elevate upon the Russian throne a prince

full of ambition and thirst of conquest, and the subjugation of Germany, the dissolution of all the empires still existing, a double universal monarchy would, under the present circumstances, be the next consequence ; and if the present system, or rather the present hopeless languor should continue for several more years, this must sooner or later be the inevitable destiny of Germany."

"There is now for Germany only one enemy," Johannes Müller said, vehemently, "and this enemy is France—is Bonaparte ! A new crisis approaches ; of this I am convinced. Bonaparte will not be satisfied with the title and the office of a First Consul for life ; he will place a crown upon his head, and threateningly oppose himself with his sceptre to all monarchies, and they will either have to humble themselves before him or to unite against him. Therefore, no other, no possible future enemy, should be thought of at this time, but only the universal foe and his government, so incompatible with general tranquillity. Let all the hatred of the nation be poured down on him, and on him alone, by everywhere spreading the conviction that nothing interferes with the preservation of peace throughout the world but *his existence*." *

"There is something else I would wish for Germany," said Gentz, musingly. "I will now reveal to you my innermost thoughts, my friend, for I am satisfied that our meeting here was a dispensation of fate. Providence had decreed that we, the intellectual champions of Germany, should agree here on the plans of our campaign and concert measures for our joint action. Therefore, you shall descend with me into the depths of my heart and see the result to which I have been led by many years' reflection concerning the causes and progress of the great convulsions of our day, and by my own grief at the political decay of Germany. The result is the firm belief that it would be by far better for Germany to be united into one state. Oh, do not look at me in so surprised and angry a manner ! I know very well, and I have reflected a great deal about it, how salutary an influence has been exerted by the dismemberment of Germany on the free development of the individual faculties ; I acknowledge that, considered individually, we might very probably not have reached, in a great and centralized monarchy, the proud and glorious eminence we are occupying at the present time, and so far, as a nation, after all, only consists of individuals, I am unable to perceive exactly how ours, without anarchy, could have acquired the distinction

* Müller's own words.—Vide "Memoires d'un Homme d'État," vol. vii., p. 39.

which it might boast of *if it were a nation!* But whenever I think that it is no nation—whenever I think that France and England, with greatly inferior faculties and means, have grown up to that true totality of human life—to that true nationality which nothing is able to destroy—whenever I think and feel that foreigners, on whom we may look down from our exalted stand-point, in matters of politics, trample on our necks, and are allowed to treat us as though we were their servants, all consolations derived from our grand and magnificent individuality vanish and leave me alone with my grief.* I am free to confess to you that I have already gone so far on the road of those mournful reflections as to consider it very doubtful whether the whole history of Germany was ever treated from a correct point of view. I know but too well that the princes of the house of Austria seldom, if ever, deserved to be the rulers of Germany; but I do not believe that there are any reasons why we should exult at the discomfiture of their plans. It is a matter of great indifference to me whether a Hapsburg, Bavarian, Hohenzollern, or Hohenstaufen succeed in bringing the empire under one hat; I only place myself on an Austrian stand-point because that house has the best prospects and is under the highest obligations to accomplish the unity of Germany. Now you know my innermost thoughts; criticise and correct them, my friend!'"

"I will neither criticise nor correct them," said Müller, offering his hand to Gentz with a tender glance; "I will only exchange views with you. I imagine, therefore, at this moment, we were pacing, as we did a year ago, previous to your journey to England, the splendid hall of the imperial library, where the sixteen statues of the Hapsburg emperors reminded us of their era. Before which of them will we place ourselves and say: 'What a pity that you, wise and noble prince, are not the sole ruler of Germany; you were worthy, indeed, that the moral and political welfare of the whole nation should be left to the decision of *your* will, and that every thing should be submitted to *your* power!'"

"It is true," muttered Gentz, mournfully; "in the history of Germany there is no emperor, king, or prince to whom we might or should talk in this manner."

"Nor is that the cause of our misfortunes," said Müller; "the want of one ruler has not produced them, and it is not so bad that we have not got but one neck, and cannot consequently be struck down at one blow. The fault, on the con-

trary, is our own. If we had a single great man, even though he were neither an emperor nor a king, if he were only a Maurice of Saxony, a Stadtholder of Holland, he would attract the nation in times of danger and distress; it would rally around him and he would stand above it. That we have not such a man is owing to our deplorable system of education, and to the wrong direction which our mode of thinking has taken. Every thing with us has fallen asleep, and we are in a condition of almost hopeless stagnation. The old poetry of fatherland, honor, and heroism, seems to be almost extinct among us; we are asleep, and do not even dream. In order to recover our senses, a conceited tyrant, who will mock us while plundering our pockets, is an indispensable necessity. Providence, perhaps, has destined Bonaparte to become the tyrant who is to awaken Germany from its slumber by means of cruelties; he is, perhaps, to revive among the Germans love of honor, liberty, and country; he is, perhaps, to be the scourge that is to torture us, so that we may overcome our indolence, and that our true national spirit may be aroused. I hope the tyrant will accomplish this, and deliver Germany. God knows I would not like to serve him, but to the liberators of the world I should willingly devote my ideas and feelings, nay, my blood.* Then let us hope, wait, and prepare. Let us not occupy ourselves with Germany as it might be, perhaps, in its unity, but with Germany as it *can* be with its confederate system. The Germans are not qualified, like the English or French, to live in a single great state. The climate, their organization, that miserable beer, the insignificant participation in the commerce of the world, prevent it; the somewhat phlegmatic body of the state must have an independent life in each of its parts; the circulation issuing from a single head would be too imperceptible. We must be satisfied with the glory which a Joseph, a Frederick the Great, and the enthusiasm of the whole people gave to us, and if the next struggle should terminate successfully, will give to us to the greatest extent.† We must struggle on for the welfare of the entire people, and the individuals should unite into one great harmonious whole. Like myself, you consider concord between Austria and Prussia at present the only remedy for the ills of Germany; let us, therefore, strive for it, let us direct our whole strength to this point, to this goal."

"Yes, let us do so!" exclaimed Gentz, enthusiastically. "We are both destined and able to be the champions of Germany; let us fulfil our

---

* Gentz's own words.—Vide "Mémoires d'un Homme d'État," vol. vii. p. 20.

* "Mémoires d'un Homme d'État," vol. vii., pp. 39, 40.
† Ibid., vol. vii., p. 45.

task. No matter how much greater, how much more exalted and brilliant your name may be than mine, for my part I am proud enough to believe that I have certain talents which ought to unite our political efforts. Hence, you cannot and must not reject and neglect me; you must accept the hand which I offer you for this great and holy compact, for the welfare of Germany. We must keep up an active and uninterrupted correspondence with each other, and freely and unreservedly communicate to each other our views about the great questions of the day. It seems to me wise, necessary, and truly patriotic that such men as we should hold timely consultations with each other as to what should be done, and how, where, and by whom it should be done. The wholesome influence we may exert, stationed by fate as one of us is in Berlin, and the other in Vienna, by faithfully uniting our efforts, will be truly incalculable. Now say, my friend, will you conclude such a covenant with me? Shall we unite in our active love for Germany, in our active hatred against France?"

"Yes, we will!" exclaimed Johannes Müller, solemnly. "I truly love and venerate you; I will struggle with you incessantly until we have reached our common noble goal. Here is my hand, my friend; its grasp shall be the consecration of our covenant. Perhaps you do not know me very intimately, but we must believe in each other. All our studies, all our intellectual strength, our connections, our friendships, every thing shall be devoted to that one great object, for the sake of which alone, so long as it may yet be accomplished, life is not to be disdained." *

"Yes, be it so," said Gentz, joyfully. "The covenant is concluded, and may God bless it for the welfare of Germany!"

---

* "Mémoires d'un Homme d'État," vol. vii., p. 40.

THE THIRD COALITION.

CHAPTER XLII.

THE EMPEROR NAPOLEON.

A NEW era had dawned for France! On the eighteenth of May, 1804, she had changed her title and commenced a new epoch of her existence.

On the eighteenth of May, 1804, the French Republic had ceased to exist, for on that day *Bonaparte*, the First Consul, had become *Napoleon*, the first Emperor of France. There was no more talk of liberty, equality, and fraternity. France had again a master—a master who was firmly determined to transform the proud republicans into obedient subjects, and to restore law and order if necessary by means of tyranny. Woe to those who wanted to remember old republican France under the new state of affairs; woe to those who called Napoleon Bonaparte the assassin of the republic, and wished to punish him for his criminal conduct! George Cadoudal and Pichegru had to atone with their lives for such audacious attempts, and Moreau, Bonaparte's great rival, was banished from his country.

Woe to those, too, who hoped that the old royal throne of the *fleur-de-lis* would take the place of the dying republic! the royalists as well as the republicans were punished as traitors to their country, and the Duke d'Enghien was executed in the ditch of Vincennes because he had dared to approach the frontier of his country. Sentence of death had been passed upon him without a trial, without judgment and law; and even the tears and prayers of Josephine had been unable to soften Bonaparte's heart. The son of the Bourbons had to die the death of a traitor, that the son of the Corsican lawyer might become Emperor of France.

Europe was no longer strong enough to punish this bloody deed; it was not even courageous enough to denounce it and to ask the First Consul, Bonaparte, by virtue of what right he had ordered his soldiers in the midst of peace to enter a German state in order to arrest there the guest of a German prince like a common felon, and to have him executed for a crime which was never proved against him. The sense of honor and justice seemed entirely extinct in Germany, and the princes and people of Germany were solely actuated by the all-absorbing fear lest powerful France might assume a hostile attitude toward them.

Not a voice, therefore, was raised in Germany in favor of the Duke d'Enghien, and against a violation of the German territory, directly conflicting with the existing treaties and the tenets of international law. The German Diet, upon whom it was incumbent to maintain the honor and rights of all the German states, received the news of this bloody deed in silence, and were only too glad that none of the members of the empire arose in order to complain of the proceedings of France. It was deemed most prudent to pass over the matter, and to accept what could not be helped as an accomplished fact.

But from this lazy quiet they were suddenly startled by the warnings of Russia and Sweden, who, having warranted the maintenance of the constitution of the German empire, now raised their voices, and loudly and emphatically pointed out "the danger which would arise for every single German state if Germany should allow measures to be taken which threatened her quiet and safety, and if deeds of violence should be deemed admissible or be passed over without being duly denounced." [*]

A sudden panic seized the German Diet, for these Russian and Swedish voices rendered further silence out of the question. The Diet were, therefore, compelled to speak out, to complain, and to demand an apology and redress, for Russia and

[*] Vide Häusser's "History of Germany," vol. ii., p. 518.

Sweden required it, by virtue of their relation to the empire; foreign powers required the German Diet, much to its dismay, to maintain and defend the honor of Germany.

But the Diet dared not listen to them, for France asked them to be silent; it threatened to consider any word of censure as a declaration of war. The ministers of the German princes, greatly embarrassed by their position between those equally imperious parties, found a way not to irritate either, and to maintain their silence and impartiality; they *deserted!* That is to say, the German Diet, suddenly, and long before the usual time, took a recess, a long recess, and when the latter had at length expired, the unpleasant affair was not taken up, and the Diet considered a more important question of the day.* This more important question was to congratulate France on having elected an emperor, who, as the Austrian minister said, at a meeting of the Diet, "was so precious to all Europe, and by whose accession to the throne his colleagues could only feel honored."

The Diet had been silent about the assassination of the Duke d'Enghien, but they spoke out and proffered their congratulations when Bonaparte had become emperor, and they pretended to be glad to hail him as the founder of a new dynasty.

Napoleon Bonaparte, therefore, had now attained his object; he had reëstablished the throne in France; he had placed a crown on his head. More fortunate than Cæsar, he had met with no Brutus at the steps of his throne, but had ascended it without being hindered, amidst the acclamations of France, which called him her emperor; amidst the acclamations of Italy, which called him her king, and had willingly cast aside her title of Cisalpine Republic in order to become the kingdom of Lombardy, and to adorn Napoleon at Milan with the iron crown of the old Lombard sovereigns.

Napoleon had just returned to France from this coronation at Milan, and repaired to the vast camp at Boulogne, where an army comprising a hundred and fifty thousand infantry and ninety thousand cavalry, eager for the fray, were waiting for the word of Napoleon which was to call them forth to new struggles and new victories.

The immense rows of the soldiers' tents extended far across the plain and along the sea-shore, and in the centre of this city of tents, on the spot where lately the traces of a camp of Julius Cæsar had been discovered, there arose the emperor's tent, looking out on the ocean, on the shore of which the ships and gunboats of France were moored, while the immense forest of the masts

and flags of the British fleet was to be seen in the distance.

But this forest of British masts did not frighten the French army; the soldiers, as well as the sailors, were eager for the fray, and looked with fiery impatience for the moment when the emperor would at length raise his voice and utter the longed-for words: "On to England! Let us vanquish England as we have vanquished the whole of Europe!"

No one doubted that the emperor purposed to utter these words, and that this camp of Boulogne, this fleet manned with soldiers and bristling with guns, were solely intended against England, the hereditary foe of France.

The emperor, however, hesitated to utter those decisive words. He distributed among the soldiers the first crosses of the Legion of Honor; he drilled the troops; he accepted the festivals and balls which the city of Boulogne gave in his honor; he stood for hours on the sea-shore or on the tower of his barrack, and with his spy-glass looked out on the sea and over to the English ships; but his lips did not open to utter the decisive words; the schemes which filled his breast and clouded his brow were a secret, the solution of which was looked for with equal impatience by his generals and by his soldiers.

It was a delightful morning; a cool breeze swept from the sea through the tents of the camp, and, after the preceding spell of debilitating hot weather, exerted a most refreshing and invigorating effect upon the languishing soldiers. The sun which had scorched every thing for the last few days, was to-day gently veiled by small, whitish clouds, which, far on the horizon, seemed to arise, like swans, from the sea toward the sky, and to hasten with outspread wings toward the sun.

The emperor, whom the warm weather of the last few days had prevented from riding out, ordered his horse to be brought to him. He wished to make a trip to the neighboring villages, but no one was to accompany him except Roustan, his colored servant.

In front of the emperor's barrack there stood, however, all the generals and staff-officers, all the old comrades of Napoleon, the men who had shared his campaigns and his glory, who had joyfully recognized the great chieftain as their emperor and master, and who wished to do him homage to-day, as they were in the habit of doing every morning so soon as he left his barrack. Napoleon, however, saluted them to-day only with a silent wave of his hand and an affable smile. He seemed pensive and absorbed, and no one dared to disturb him by a sound, by a word.

* Häusser's "History of Germany," vol. II, p. 525.

Amid the solemn stillness of this brilliant gathering, the emperor walked to his horse, who, less timid and respectful than the men, greeted his master with a loud neigh and a nodding of the head, and commenced impatiently stamping on the ground.*

The emperor took the bridle which Roustan handed to him and vaulted into the saddle. He raised his sparkling eye toward the sky and then lowered it to the sea with its rocking ships.

"I will review the fleet to-day," said the emperor, turning to his adjutant-general. "Let orders be issued to the ships forming the closing line to change position, for I will hold the review in the open sea. I shall return in two hours; let every thing be in readiness at that time."

He set spurs to his horse and galloped away, followed by Roustan. His generals dispersed in order to return to their barracks. The adjutant-general, however, hastened to Admiral Bruix for the purpose of delivering the orders of the emperor to him.

The admiral listened to him silently and attentively; and then he raised his eyes to the sky and scanned it long and searchingly.

"It is impossible," he said, shrugging his shoulders; "the orders of the emperor cannot be carried out to-day; the review cannot take place. We shall have a storm to-day, which will prevent the ships from leaving their moorings."

"Admiral," said the adjutant, respectfully, "I have delivered the orders of the emperor to you; I have informed you that the emperor wishes that every thing should be ready for the review on his return, within two hours. Now you know very well that the wish of the emperor is always equivalent to an order, and you will make your preparations accordingly."

"In two hours I shall have the honor personally to state to his majesty the reasons why I was unable to comply with his orders," said Admiral Bruix, with his wonted composure and coolness.

Precisely two hours later the emperor returned from his ride. The generals and staff-officers, the whole brilliant suite of the emperor, stood again in front of his barrack, in order to receive the returning sovereign.

Napoleon greeted them with a pleasant smile; the ride seemed to have agreed with him; the cloud had disappeared from his brow; his cheeks, generally so pale, were suffused with a faint blush, and his flaming eyes had a kind glance for every one.

He dismounted with graceful ease, and stepped with kind salutations into the circle of the generals.

"Well, Leclerc, is every thing ready for the review?" he asked his adjutant.

General Leclerc approached him respectfully. "Sire," he said, "Admiral Bruix, to whom I delivered the orders of your majesty, replied to me that the review could not take place to-day because there would be a storm."

The emperor frowned, and an angry flash from his eyes met the face of the adjutant.

"I must have misunderstood you, sir," he said. "What did the admiral reply when you delivered my orders to him?"

"Sire, he said it was impossible to carry them out, for a storm was drawing near, and he could not think of ordering the ships to leave their moorings."

The emperor stamped violently his foot. "Let Admiral Bruix be called hither at once!" he exclaimed, in a thundering voice, and two orderlies immediately left the circle and hastened away.

Several minutes elapsed; Napoleon, his arms folded, his threatening eyes steadfastly turned toward the side on which the admiral would make his appearance, still stood in front of his barrack, in the midst of his suite. His eagle eye now discovered the admiral in the distance, who had just left his boat and stepped ashore. No longer able to suppress his impatience and anger, Napoleon hastened forward to meet the admiral, while the gentlemen of his staff followed him in a long and silent procession.

The emperor and the admiral now stood face to face. Napoleon's eyes flashed fire.

"Admiral," exclaimed the emperor, in an angry voice, "why did not you carry out my orders?"

The admiral met Napoleon's wrathful glance in a calm though respectful manner. "Sire," he said, "a terrible storm is drawing near. Your majesty can see it just as well as I. Do you want to endanger unnecessarily the lives of so many brave men?"

And as if Nature wanted to confirm the words of the admiral, the distant roll of thunder was heard, and the atmosphere commenced growing dark.

Napoleon, however, seemed not to see it, or the calm voice of the admiral and the rolling thunder, perhaps, excited his pride to an even more obstinate resistance.

"Admiral," he replied, sternly, "I have issued my orders. I ask you once more why did not you carry them out? The consequences concern only myself. Obey, therefore!"

---

* Napoleon's favorite horse, who always manifested in this manner his delight on seeing his illustrious master.—Constant, vol. II., p. 81.

"Sire," he said, solemnly, "I shall not obey!"

"Sir, you are an impudent fellow!" ejaculated Napoleon, and, advancing a step toward the admiral, he menacingly raised the hand in which he still held his riding-whip.

Admiral Bruix drew back a step and laid his hand on his sword. A terrible pause ensued. The emperor still stood there, the riding-whip in his uplifted hand, fixing his flaming, angry eyes on the admiral, who maintained his threatening, manly attitude, and, with his hand on his sword, awaited the emperor's attack. The generals and staff-officers, pale with dismay, formed a circle around them.

The emperor suddenly dropped his riding-whip; Admiral Bruix immediately withdrew his hand from his sword, and, taking off his hat, he awaited the end of the dreadful scene in profound silence.

"Rear-Admiral Magon," said the emperor, calling one of the gentlemen of his suite, "cause the movements I had ordered to be carried out at once! As for you," he continued, slowly turning his eyes toward the admiral, "you will leave Boulogne within twenty-four hours and retire to Holland. Begone!"

He turned around hastily and walked toward his barrack. Admiral Bruix looked after him with an aggrieved air, and then turned also around in order to go. While walking through the crowd of generals and staff-officers, he offered his hand to his friends and acquaintances in order to take leave of them; but few of them, however, saw it, and shook hands with him; most of them had averted their eyes from the admiral, whom the sun of imperial favor did not illuminate any longer, and who consequently was so entirely cast in the shade, that they were unable to perceive him.

Rear-Admiral Magon had in the mean time carried out the orders of the emperor. The ships which before had been at anchor near the outlet of the harbor, keeping it entirely closed, had moved farther into the sea, while the other vessels in the harbor were going out.

But Admiral Bruix's prediction began already to be fulfilled; the sky was covered with black clouds from which lightning was bursting forth in rapid succession. The thunder of the heavens drowned the roar of the sea, which arose like a huge, black monster, hissing and howling, and fell back again from its height, covered with foam, and opened abysses into which the ships seemed to sink in order to be hurled up again by the next wave. The storm, with its dismal yells, attacked the masts and broke them as though they were straws, and lashed the ships, which had already left the harbor, out into the sea, to certain ruin, to certain death.

The emperor had left his barrack and hurried down to the beach with rapid steps. With folded arms and lowered head, gloomy and musing, he walked up and down in the storm. He was suddenly aroused from his meditations by loud screams, by exclamations of terror and dismay.

Twenty gunboats, which the rear-admiral had already caused to be manned with sailors and soldiers, had been driven ashore by the storm, and the waves which swept over them with thundering noise menaced the crews with certain death. Their cries for help, their shrieks and supplications were distinctly heard and reëchoed by the wails and lamentations of the masses that had hastened to the beach in order to witness the storm and the calamities of the shipwreck.

The emperor looked at his generals and staff officers who surrounded him, dumbfounded with horror; he saw that no one had the courage or deemed it feasible to assist the poor drowning men. All at once the gloomy air vanished from his face; it became radiant with enthusiasm; the emperor was transformed once more into a hero, daring every thing, and shrinking back from no danger.

He immediately entered one of the life-boats and pushing back the arms of those who wished to detain him, he exclaimed in an almost jubilant voice: "Let me go, let me go! We must assist those unhappy men!"

But his frail bark was speedily filled with water; the waves swept over it with a wild roar, and covered the whole form of the emperor with foaming, hissing spray. He still kept himself erect by dint of almost superhuman efforts; but, now another even more terrible wave approached and swept, thundering and with so much violence over the bark, that the emperor, reeling and losing his equilibrium, was about falling overboard, when his generals dragged him from the boat and took him ashore. He followed them unhesitatingly, stunned as he was by the wave, and as he stepped ashore, a flash burst forth from the cloud; a majestic thunder-clap followed; the howling storm tore the hat from the emperor's head and carried it, as if on invisible wings, high into the air and then far out into the sea where the waves seemed to receive it with roars of exultation, driving it down to their foaming depth.

But the courageous example given by the emperor had exerted an electric effect on the masses which heretofore had apparently been stupefied with horror. Every one now felt and recognized

It to be his sacred duty to make efforts for the rescue of the unfortunate men who were still struggling with the waves and shouting for help, officers, soldiers, sailors, and citizens, all rushed into the life-boats or plunged into the sea in order to swim up to the drowning men and save them in time from a watery grave.

But the sea was not willing to surrender many of its victims. It wanted, perhaps, to prove its superior divine majesty to the imperial ruler which had defied it, and punish him for his presumption.

Only a few were rescued, for the storm did not abate during the whole day; it lashed up the sea into waves mountain-high, or opened abysses frightful to behold. Night finally descended on the angry waters and spread its black pall over the scene of death and despair.

In the morning the beach was covered with hundreds of corpses which the sea had thrown ashore. An enormous crowd thronged the shore; every one came to look with fainting heart and loud lamentations among the mute, pale corpses for a husband, a friend, or a brother; shrieks and wails filled the air and even penetrated to the emperor's barracks.

He had not slept during the whole night; he had been pacing his rooms, restless, with a gloomy air and pale cheeks: now, early in the morning, he once more hastened down to the beach. Thousands of persons, however, had preceded him thither. When they beheld the emperor they stepped gloomily aside; they did not receive him, as heretofore, with loud exultation and joyful acclamations; they looked at him with a reproachful air, and then turned their eyes in mute eloquence to the corpses lying in the sand.

The emperor was unable to bear the silence of the crowd and the sight of these corpses: pale and shuddering, he turned away and walked back to his barrack slowly and with lowered head. But he did not fail to hear the murmurs of the crowd which had only been silent so long as it had seen his face, and which, now that he had turned away, gave free vent to its grief and indignation.

The emperor heard painful sighs when he reached his barrack, and sent immediately for Roustan, in order to give him secret instructions. Thanks to these instructions, Roustan's agents hastened all day through the city of Boulogne and through the camp for the purpose of distributing money in the name of the emperor wherever persons were lamenting and weeping, or where gloomy glances and mourners were to be met with, thus allaying their grief by means of the shining magic metal which heals all wounds and dries all tears.

The emperor, however, had still a more effectual charm for allaying the indignation of the crowd, or at least for stirring up again the jubilant enthusiasm of his soldiers.

Telegraphic dispatches of the highest importance had reached the camp; courier after courier had followed them. The emperor assembled all his generals in the council-chamber of his barrack, and when they left it, after a consultation of several hours, the rumor spread through the camp that the emperor would now at length utter those longed-for words and lead his army to new struggles, to new victories.

These joyful tidings spread like wildfire among the troops; every one hailed them with a radiant face and merry glances. Every one saw himself on the eve of fresh honors and spoils, and only asked whither the victorious course of the emperor would be directed this time—whether to England, which constantly seemed to menace France with its forest of masts, or whether to Austria, whose hostile friendship might have been distrusted.

The emperor had not yet spoken the decisive words to any member of his suite, but he had sent for the grand-marshal of the palace and ordered him to hold every thing in readiness for his departure; to settle all accounts and bills against the emperor, and to beware on this occasion of not paying too much to any one.

On the day after receiving these orders, the grand-marshal, without being announced, appeared before the emperor, who was in the council-chamber of his barrack, engaged in studying attentively the maps spread out on the large table before him.

Napoleon only looked up for a moment, and then continued to stick pins into the maps, thus designating the route which his army was to take.

"Well, Duroc," he asked, "is every thing ready for our departure? Have all bills been paid."

"Sire, they are all paid except one, and I must dare to disturb your majesty in relation to this one bill."

"I suppose it is very high and fraudulent?" asked the emperor, hastily. With these words he rose and approached the grand-marshal.

"Sire," said the latter, "I do not know whether it is fraudulent or not, but it is very high. It is the bill of Military Intendant Sordi, who built this barrack, and to whom its fitting up had been intrusted."

"Well, how much does he charge for it?" asked Napoleon.

"Sire, he asks fifty thousand francs."

"Fifty thousand francs!" exclaimed Napoleon, almost in terror. "I hope you have not paid this impudent bill?"

"No, sire, I have not; on the contrary, I requested M. Sordi to reduce the sum."

"And he has done so, of course?" exclaimed Napoleon, gloomily. "Just like these men. They ask us to confide in them, and yet they try on every occasion to cheat us. How much did he deduct from his bill?"

"Nothing at all, sire. M. Sordi asserts that he did not charge too much for a single article; he was unable, therefore, to make even the slightest deduction."

"And so you have paid the bill?"

"No, sire, I said that I could not pay it until your majesty had given me express orders to do so."

"Well done," said the emperor, nodding to him. "Send word to the military intendant that I want to see him immediately. I wish to talk to him myself."

The grand-marshal withdrew, and Napoleon returned to his maps. He continued to mark them with long rows of pins, and to draw circles and straight lines on them.

"If the Austrians are bold enough to advance," he said to himself, in a low voice, "I shall beat them in the open field; should they remain stationary and wait for me to attack them, I shall inflict upon them a crushing defeat at Ulm. It is time for me to make these overbearing Germans feel the whole weight of my wrath, and, as they have spurned my friendship, to crush them by my enmity. That little Emperor of Austria dares to menace me; I shall prove to him that menacing me is bringing about one's own ruin. I shall assemble my forces here in this plain, and here—"

"Sire, the military intendant, M. de Sordi, whom your majesty has ordered to appear before you," said the emperor's aide-de-camp, opening the door of the council-chamber.

"Let him come in," ejaculated Napoleon, without averting his eyes from the map.

The aide-de-camp retired, and the tall, powerful form of Intendant Sordi appeared in the door. His face was pale, but calm; his features indicated boldness and a fixed purpose; he was evidently conscious of the importance of the present moment, and felt that it would decide his whole future.

The emperor continued scanning his maps. M. de Sordi stood at the door, waiting for the emperor to address him. When he saw that the latter tarried very long, he advanced a step, and, as if ac-

cidentally, pushed against the chair standing at his side.

The noise aroused Napoleon from his meditation, and reminded him of the person he had sent for.

He therefore hastily turned around to him. "Sir," he said, "you have spent a great deal too much money for the decoration of this miserable barrack; yes, indeed, a great deal too much. Fifty thousand francs! What do you mean, sir? That is frightful; I shall not pay that sum!"

M. de Sordi met the flaming glances of the emperor with smiling calmness.

"Sire," he said, lifting up his hand and pointing at the ceiling, "I may truthfully say that the clouds of gold brocade adorning the ceiling of this room, and surrounding the propitious star of your majesty, have cost alone not less than twenty-five thousand francs. Had I consulted, however, the hearts of your subjects, the imperial eagle, which now again will crush the enemies of France and of your throne, would have spread out its wings amidst the most magnificent and precious diamonds." [*]

Napoleon smiled. "Very well," he said; "you believe the hearts of my subjects to be very prodigal. I am not, however, and I repeat to you I shall not pay that sum now. But as you tell me that this eagle, which costs so much money, will crush the Austrians, you will doubtless wait until it has done so, and then I will pay your bill with the *rix-dollars* of the Emperor of Germany and the *Fredericks d'or* of the King of Prussia." [†]

He dismissed him smilingly with a wave of his hand, and returned to his maps.

A few hours later Napoleon, followed by all his generals and adjutants, repaired to the camp. Ascending a small mound, specially prepared for the occasion, he surveyed with radiant eyes the surging, motley, and brilliant sea of soldiers who surrounded him on all sides, and who greeted his appearance with thundering shouts of exultation.

A wave of his hand commanded them to be still, and, as if fascinated by a magician's wand, the roaring masses grew dumb, and profound silence ensued. Amidst this silence, Napoleon raised his clear, ringing voice, and its sonorous notes swept like eagle-wings over the sea of soldiers.

"Brave soldiers of the camp of Boulogne," he said, "you will not go to England. The gold of

---

[*] The ceiling of the room was decorated with golden clouds, amidst which, on a blue ground, was an eagle, holding a thunderbolt, and pointing it at a star, the star of the emperor.—Constant, vol. i., p. 246.

[†] Napoleon's own words.—Constant, vol. i., p. 246.

the English government has seduced the Emperor of Austria, and he has again declared war against France. His army has crossed the line of demarcation assigned to it, and inundated Bavaria. Soldiers, fresh laurels are awaiting you beyond the Rhine; let us hasten to vanquish once more enemies whom we have already vanquished. On to Germany!" *

"On to Germany!" shouted the soldiers, jubilantly. "On to Germany!" was repeated from mouth to mouth, and even the sea seemed to roar with delight and its waves, thundering against the beach, to shout, "On to Germany!"

CHAPTER XLIII.

NAPOLEON AND THE GERMAN PRINCES.

THE Emperor of France with his army had crossed the boundaries of Germany. He had come to assist his ally, the Elector of Bavaria, against the Austrians who had invaded Bavaria; not, however, in order to menace Bavaria, but, as an autograph letter from the Emperor Francis to the elector expressly stated, to secure a more extended and better protected position.

The Elector of Bavaria, Maximilian Joseph, had declared, in a submissive letter to the Austrian emperor, that he was perfectly willing to let the Austrian regiments encamp within his dominions. "I pledge my word as a sovereign to your majesty," he had written to the Emperor of Germany, "that I shall not hinder the operations of your army in any manner whatever, and if, what is improbable, however, your majesty should be obliged to retreat with your army, I promise and swear that I shall remain quiet and support your projects in every respect. But I implore your majesty on my knees to permit me graciously to maintain the strictest neutrality. It is a father, driven to despair by anguish and care, who implores your majesty's mercy in favor of his child. My son is just now travelling in southern France. If I should be obliged to send my troops into the field against France my son would be lost, and the fate of the Duke d'Enghien would be in store for him, too; if I should, however, remain quietly and peaceably in my states, I should gain time for my son to return from France." †

But on the same day, and with the same pen, on which the ink with which he had written to the Emperor of Germany was not yet dry, the elector had also written to the Emperor of France and informed him "that he was ready to place himself under his protection, that he would be proud to become the ally of France, and that he would thenceforward lay himself and his army at the feet of the great and august Emperor of France."

And the courier who was to deliver the letter with the sacred pledges of neutrality to the Emperor of Germany, had not yet reached Vienna when the Elector of Bavaria secretly fled from Munich to Wurzburg, where his army of twenty-five thousand men was waiting for him.

He sent his army, commanded by General Deroy, to meet the Emperor of the French; it was not to attack him as the enemy of Germany, but to hail him as an ally and to place itself under his direction. He then issued a proclamation.

"We have separated from Austria," he said, "from Austria, who wanted to enslave and annihilate us by her perfidious schemes, and to compel us to fight at her side for foreign interests; from Austria, the hereditary foe of our house and of our independence, who is just now going to make another attempt to devour Bavaria, and degrade her to the position of an Austrian province. But the Emperor of the French, Bavaria's natural ally, hastened to the rescue with his brave warriors, in order to avenge you; your sons will soon fight at the side of men accustomed to victory; soon, soon the day of retribution will be at hand." *

Thanks to the hatred of the Germans against their German brethren, thanks to the hatred of the Bavarians against the Austrians, this proclamation had been received with joyful acclamations throughout the whole state, and Bavaria felt proud and happy that she should fight under the Emperor of the French, her "natural ally," against the Emperor of Germany.

The French army was drawn up in line in the plain near Nordlingen, in order to solemnly receive its German auxiliaries. They were the first German troops that Napoleon had gained over to his side, and therefore he wished to welcome them pompously and with all honors. Amidst the jubilant notes of all the bands of the French army, amidst the enthusiastic shouts of the French soldiers, the Bavarians marched into the French camp. The emperor, in full uniform, surrounded by all his generals, welcomed General Deroy and the Bavarian officers; accompanied by a wave of his sword, he said to them:

"I have placed myself at the head of my army in order to deliver your country, for the house of

---

* Napoleon's own words.—Constant, vol. i., p. 282.

† "Mémoires sur l'Intérieur du Palais de Napoléon," by De Bausset, vol. i., p. 59.

* Häusser's "History of Germany." vol. ii., p. 611.

Austria intends to annihilate your independence. You will follow the example of your ancestors, who constantly preserved that independence and political existence which are the first blessings of a nation. I know your valor, and am sure that I shall be able after the first battle to say to your sovereign and to my people, that you are worthy to fight in the ranks of the grand army."

The Bavarian soldiers hailed this proud address with the same exultation with which the Bavarian people had received the proclamation of the elector; and never had the French soldiers manifested greater enthusiasm for their chieftain and emperor than did these German soldiers, the first German auxiliaries of the emperor.

Napoleon received their jubilant shouts with a gracious smile.

"Duroc," he said, turning to his friend and comrade, who was riding at his side—"Duroc, listen to what I am going to say to you. The Germans are not good patriots; they are capable of loving the conqueror of their country just as well as their legitimate sovereign. Even at the time of Julius Cæsar there was no harmony among the Germans; and while Arminius opposed the Romans heroically, Segestes declared in favor of them. If, as a modern Julius Cæsar, I should wish to conquer Germany, I believe I should find there no Arminius, but certainly many Segesteses."

"But, perhaps, a few Thusneldas, sire," said Duroc, laughing: "and your majesty knows full well that it was Thusnelda, after all, who filled her husband with so undying a hatred against the Romans."

"And the son of Thusnelda became a prisoner of the Romans!" exclaimed Napoleon; "he became a miserable slave of the Romans, and preferred a life of humiliation and disgrace to an honorable death. The Germans are great talkers; they are always ready to fight with their tongues for the honor of their country, but they do not like to die for it. But who are the Thusneldas with whom you threatened me? Did you allude to Queen Caroline of Naples, the daughter of Maria Theresa?"

"Oh, no, sire; she is no longer a German, but an Italian intriguer—a—"

"She is, as I told her own ambassador in Milan, a modern Athalia, a daughter of Jezebel," said Napoleon, interrupting him vehemently. "But patience, patience, I shall punish her for her bitter hatred and intrigues."

"Sire, it was in your power to receive ardent love at the hands of Queen Caroline, instead of her hatred, which is, perhaps, nothing but concealed love. I suppose your majesty knows what the queen said only a few years ago to the French minister?"

"No, I do not, or perhaps I have only forgotten it," replied Napoleon, carelessly. "Did she want to make a postillon d'amour of him?"

"Nearly so, sire. She told him she would willingly travel four hundred leagues in order to see General Bonaparte. She added that you were the only great man in the world, and none but idiots were seated at the present time on all the thrones of Europe." *

"A very flattering remark for her husband and for her nephew, the Emperor of Austria," said Napoleon. "She referred, however, only to those who are seated on thrones, but the tender queen has been able to discover a few real men by the side of her husband's throne. I have never hankered after becoming the rival of Acton and Nelson. I do not like passionate and ambitious women. They must be gentle and charming like Josephine if they are to please me."

"I wish the empress were here and able to hear your words," exclaimed Duroc.

"Does she again doubt my constancy?" asked Napoleon, quickly. "Have my brothers again frightened her by threats of a divorce? Let her be reassured, I do not think of a separation from her, and all the Thusneldas of Germany cannot become dangerous to me. But you have not yet told me the names of those Thusneldas. Let me hear them."

"Sire, first there is the beautiful Queen of Prussia. She is said to be a bitter enemy of France."

"Yes, a bitter enemy of mine!" exclaimed Napoleon, with a gloomy and threatening glance: "a short-sighted woman, who does not see that she will ruin her good-natured, weak, and irresolute husband if she carries him along with her on this path of hostility and hatred. She will repent one day having scorned my friendship, for, if she succeeds in gaining her husband over to an alliance with Russia, I shall be inexorable, and mercilessly trample the whole vacillating and fickle Prussia in the dust. And do you still know of another Thusnelda?"

"Yes, sire; it is the wife of the Elector Frederick of Wurtemberg, who is also said to have filled her husband with ardent hatred against France, and with fervent patriotism for Germany. The elector and electress are reported to have taken a solemn oath in the presence of their whole court never to bow or submit to France,

---

* Queen Caroline actually said this to the French minister.

and never to prove recreant to the interests of Germany."

"I shall compel them to believe that the interests of Germany require them to bow to France and to become our allies!" exclaimed Napoleon, proudly. "The electress of Wurtemberg is a daughter of George the Third of England, a daughter of my mortal enemy; hence, she shall bow to me or feel my power and my wrath. The time for hesitation and procrastination is over. I want to have my friends at my side and my enemies opposite me. Let the German princes choose whether they will go with France against Austria, their common despot, or whether, like Austria, they wished to be conquered by France! We shall see which side Wurtemberg will espouse, for Ney is already with his corps on the road to Stuttgart, and in the course of a few days I shall pay a visit to the elector and electress at their own palace."

And a few days later Napoleon really kept his word: he paid a visit to the elector and electress at Louisburg, after Ney had compelled the government of Wurtemberg to open the gates of Stuttgart to his troops.

The elector received the emperor at the foot of the palace staircase, where only an hour ago he had assured his courtiers he would not receive the upstart Napoleon as an equal and shake hands with him; but as Napoleon now saluted him with a kind nod, and gave him his hand, the elector bowed so deeply and respectfully that it almost looked as if he wished to kiss the small, white, imperial hand which he had seized so joyfully and reverentially.*

The electress, who entered at the side of her husband, received the emperor in the large and brilliant throne-room of the palace. Her face was pale and gloomy when she bowed ceremoniously to the hereditary foe of her house, and not the faintest tinge of a smile was to be seen on her lips when she replied to the emperor's address.

Napoleon's face, however, was strangely mild and winning to-day, and yet radiant with dignity and grandeur. It was the face of a conqueror who does not intend to treat those whom he has subjugated with arrogance and rigor, but desires to win their affection by gentleness and love. Hence, his eyes had only mild and kind glances, and on his finely-formed lips there was playing that smile which the Empress Josephine said was the sunbeam of his face, and irresistible to any woman.

Nor was the electress able to withstand this smile and this kind bearing of Napoleon. She had expected to find in the emperor an ardent enemy of her native England, and he now paid a glowing and eloquent tribute to the English, to their country, to their institutions and character. Napoleon had been described to her as a barbarian, taking interest only in warfare and every thing connected with it; and now she found him to be an admirer of the English poets, and heard him expatiate enthusiastically on Ossian, some of whose most magnificent verses he recited to her in a French translation.

The stern features of the electress gradually began to relax; the smile gradually returned to her lips, and she bent her proud head more graciously to the "upstart" Napoleon.

"Oh, sire!" she exclaimed, joyfully, and for the first time she did not avoid addressing him with the title due to his rank—"oh, sire, he who admires the English poets so enthusiastically cannot possibly be an enemy of England!"

"I am not by any means," said Napoleon, smiling; "I know no enmity whatever; peace is the sole aim of my efforts, and I believe Fate has sent me to mankind for the purpose of establishing eternal peace. It is true, I have to conquer peace by wars and commotions, but I shall conquer it, and you, princess, and your husband must help me to do so. I intrust to your hands a noble task, which the high-minded and proud daughter of England is worthy of, and the German elector will not hinder the noble endeavors of his wife, especially as the honor and welfare of Germany are at stake."

"I am ready and willing to do for Germany what I can, and whatever your majesty may command me to do," exclaimed the elector. "Will your majesty now tell me what I must do?"

"You must conclude an alliance with France, in order to save Germany," said the emperor, almost sternly.

"Sire, I have not the power to conclude such an alliance—I am unable to do so," said the elector, sighing.

"Your state can if you cannot," said Napoleon, quickly.

"But the representatives of my people will not consent."

"I shall protect you against these representatives of your people. You will tell them, besides, that you have saved Wurtemberg by becoming my ally. For he who is not for me is against me, and I shall annihilate those who are against me, and their states shall fall to ruin. Those, however, who are for me I shall elevate, and it seems

---

* "Memoirs of General de Wolzogen," p. 24.

13

to me I see already a royal crown on the noble brow of the electress. I suppose," asked Napoleon, turning again with a smile toward the electress, "your royal highness would not be dissatisfied if you should become the queen of your people; it would be agreeable to you to be called 'your majesty,' and if it were only because it would remind you in so pleasant a manner of your royal parents who are addressed with the same title?"

"Oh, sire," exclaimed the electress, with radiant eyes, and unable to conceal her joy—"oh, sire you are right, it would remind me most pleasantly of my paternal home and of England."

"But would not a royal crown crush my state which is too small for it?" asked the elector.

"Well, we shall enlarge it so as to render it able and worthy to support a royal crown," exclaimed Napoleon, hastily. "I believe I shall have the power and opportunity to bestow on my ally, the elector of Wurtemberg, some aggrandizements in Germany to compensate and reward him for the auxiliaries which he is to furnish to me. Besides, your task is a truly grand one. You shall assist me in subduing Austria, that arrogant Austria which would like to treat all Germany as her property, and who considers all German princes as her servants and vassals."

"You are right," said the elector, vehemently; "Austria constantly endeavors to meddle with my prerogatives in an unbecoming and arrogant manner. She would like to degrade us to the position of vassals who must always be ready to obey their emperor, but who, when they are themselves in danger, never can count on the assistance and support of their emperor."

"Let us, then, dispel Austria's illusion as though she were your master," said Napoleon, smiling. "Become my ally, and believe me, we shall have the power to teach the Emperor of Austria to respect the *King* of Wurtemberg, my ally. Will you be my ally for that purpose? Will you assist me, as a German prince, in delivering Germany from the yoke Austria has laid around her neck?"

"Sire, I am ready to save Germany with my life-blood;" exclaimed the elector, "and as your majesty has come to deliver Germany from Austria, it would be a crime for any German prince to withhold his assistance from you. Hence, I accept your alliance. Here is my hand! I shall stand by you with my troops and with my honor!" *

---

* The whole account of this interview is strictly historical. Vide "Memoirs of General de Wolzogen," and

CHAPTER XLIV.

QUEEN LOUISA'S PIANO LESSON.

THE queen sat at the piano, practising one of Reichardt's new songs which her singing-teacher, the royal concert-master and composer, Himmel, had just brought to her. The queen wore a most brilliant costume, which, however, seemed calculated less for her silent cabinet and for the music teacher than for a great gala-day and an aristocratic assembly at court. A white satin dress, interwoven with golden flowers, and closely fitting, according to the fashion of that period, surrounded her noble figure. Her splendid white arms were bare, and her wrists were adorned with two bracelets of gold and precious stones. Her neck and shoulders, showing the noble lines and forms of a Venus of Melos, were uncovered like her arms, and adorned only with jewelry. Her hair, surrounding a forehead of classical beauty in waving masses, was fastened behind in a Grecian knot holding the golden diadem, set with diamonds, which arose on the queen's head. * A gentle blush mantled her cheeks, and a smile of melancholy and tenderness trembled on her purple lips. She had her hands on the keys, and her eyes were fixed on the music-book before her; but she had suddenly ceased singing in the middle of the piece, and her voice had died away in a long sigh.

Mr. Himmel, the concert-master, stood behind her; he was a man more than forty years of age, with a broad, full face, beaming with health, and a tall and slender form which would have been more fitting for the head of an Apollo than for this head, which reminded the beholder of a buffalo rather than of a god.

When the queen paused, a joyful smile overspread his features, which had hitherto been gloomy and ill at ease. "Your majesty pauses?" he asked, hastily. "Well, I wish your majesty joy of it. That Mr. Reichardt, of Halle, is too sentimental and arrogant a composer, and never should I have dared to lay these new pieces of his before your majesty if you had not asked me to bring you every thing written by Reichardt. Well, you have seen it now; it displeases your majesty, and I am glad of it, for—"

"For," said the queen, gently interrupting him,

Hausser's "History of Germany," vol. ii., p. 613. The Elector of Wurtemberg became the *third* German ally of the French emperor, the Electors of Bavaria and Baden having preceded him. He furnished ten thousand German troops to Napoleon.

* A portrait, representing the queen precisely in this costume, may be seen at the royal palace in Berlin.

" for the great composer Himmel is again jealous of the great composer Reichardt. Is it not so ? "

She raised her dark-blue eyes at this question to Himmel's face, and he saw to his dismay that there were tears in those eyes.

" What ! " he asked in terror, " your majesty has wept ? "

She nodded in the affirmative, smiling gently. " Yes," she said, after a pause, " I have wept, and hence I could not continue singing. Do not scold me, do not be angry with me, my dear and stern teacher. This song has moved me profoundly ; it is so simple and yet so touching, that it must have come out of the depths of a truly noble heart."

Mr. Himmel replied only with a low sigh and an almost inaudible murmur, which the queen, however, understood very well.

" Perhaps," she said, trying gently to heal the jealous pangs of the composer, " perhaps I was so deeply moved by the words rather than by the music ; these words are so beautiful that it seems to me Goethe never wrote any thing more beautiful."

And bending over the music-book, she read in an under-tone :

" Wer nie sein Brod mit Thränen ass,
Wer nie die kummervollen Nächte
Auf seinem Bette einsam sass,
Der kennt euch nicht, Ihr himmlischen Mächte ! "*

" Say yourself, Mr. Himmel, is not that beautiful and touching ? " she asked, looking up again to her teacher.

" Beautiful and touching for those who have wept much and suffered much," said Himmel, harshly ; " but I cannot conceive why these words should touch your majesty, whose whole life has hitherto illuminated the world like an uninterrupted sunny spring morning."

" Hitherto," repeated the queen, musingly, " yes, hitherto, indeed, my life was a sunny spring morning, but who is able to fathom what clouds may soon appear on the horizon, and how cloudy and gloomy the evening may be ? This song reëchoes in my soul like a melancholy foreboding, and clings to its wings as if it wanted to paralyze their flight. ' He who never ate his bread with tears,' ah, how mournful it sounds, and what a long story of suffering is contained in these few words ! "

The queen paused, and two tears, glistening more beautifully than the diamonds of her golden diadem, slowly ran down her cheeks.

* " He who never ate his bread with tears,
He who never, through nights of affliction,
Sat on his lonely bed,
He does not know you, powers of heaven ! "

Concert-master Himmel was not courageous enough to interrupt the silence of the queen, or, may be, he had not listened very attentively to her words, and his thoughts perhaps were fixed on matters of an entirely different character, for his air was absent and gloomy ; his eyes glanced around the room, but returned continually to the lovely form of the queen.

Suddenly Louisa seemed to arouse herself violently from her gloomy meditation, and after hastily wiping the tears from her eyes she forced herself to smile.

" It is not good to give way to melancholy forebodings," she said, " particularly in the presence of a stern teacher. We must improve our time in a more useful manner, for time is a very precious thing ; and if I had not judiciously profited by my short leisure to-day, I should not have had a single hour to spare for my teacher, for there will be a reception in the palace to-night, and I must previously give audience to several visitors. I have, therefore, made my evening toilet in the afternoon, and thereby gained time to take my dear singing-lesson. But now let us study, so that your pupil may redound to your honor."

" Oh, your majesty," ejaculated Himmel, " my honor and my happiness ! "

" Hush, hush," said Louisa, interrupting him, with an enchanting smile, " no flattery ! no court-phrases ! Here I am not the queen, nor are you my devoted subject ; I am nothing but an obedient pupil, and you are my rigorous master, who has a right to scold and grumble whenever I sing incorrectly, and who very frequently avails himself of this privilege. Do not apologize for it, but go on in the same manner, for I will then only learn the more."

" Your majesty sings like an angel," murmured Himmel, whose eyes were fixed steadfastly on the queen.

" Well, as far as that is concerned, you are a competent judge," exclaimed Louisa, laughing, " for being Himmel (heaven), you must know how the angels sing, and your opinion cannot be disputed. The angels, then, sing incorrectly, like your obedient pupil ? Let the angels do so, but not your pupil. Come, Mr. Himmel, sit down. It does not behoove the maestro to stand at the side of his pupil. Sit down."

She pointed with a graceful wave of her hand at the chair standing at her side, and Mr. Himmel, complying with her order, sat down. His glances returned involuntarily to the queen, whose beauty only now burst on his short-sighted eyes, and whom he believed he had never seen so lovely, so fascinating and graceful. Her beautiful face seemed to him like that of a fairy queen, and her wonderful shoulders, her superb, dazzling neck, which he had never seen unveiled and so very near, appeared to him like the bust of a goddess, moulded by Phidias from living marble.

"Well, let us commence," said the queen, calmly. "Pray play the melody in the treble and let me play the accompaniment a few times; I shall then be better able to sing the song."

She commenced eagerly playing the prelude, while a deeper blush mantled her cheeks. It was Himmel's turn now to begin with the melody; his eyes, however, were not fixed on the music, but on the queen, and hence he blundered sadly.

"Well?" asked the queen, looking at him in charming confusion. "You do not play correctly."

"Yes, I have blundered, your majesty," said Himmel, gloomily; "I have blundered, for I am only a man after all, and cannot look into the sun without having a *coup de soleil*. Your majesty, I have had such a *coup de soleil*, and you see I have lost my reason in consequence."

With these words he bent over the queen and imprinted a glowing kiss on her shoulders; then he hastily rose, took his hat, and rushed out of the room.*

The queen's eyes followed him with an air of surprise and embarrassment; then she burst into ringing, charming laughter.

"Ah," she said, "if that austere 'Madame Etiquette,' the mistress of ceremonies, should have seen that, she would have either died with horror, or her wrath would have crushed the criminal. I believe I will confess the terrible crime to her. Oh, my dear mistress of ceremonies! my dear mistress of ceremonies!" she cried.

The door of the adjoining room opened immediately, and the Countess von Voss made her appearance.

"Your majesty has called me," she said, and, after looking around the room, she cast a glance of surprise on the clock.

"Ah, my dear countess, you are surprised that Mr. Himmel, my singing-master, has already left, although the hour has only half expired?" asked the queen, merrily.

"Your majesty," said the countess, sighing, "I really ought no longer to be surprised at any thing, nor wonder at any violation of etiquette, for such things, unfortunately, occur every day and every hour. Your majesty knows, moreover, that this Mr. Himmel is altogether distasteful to me."

"And why?" asked the queen, gayly.

"Your majesty, because it is contrary to etiquette for a queen to take lessons, and to have a teacher."

"What!" exclaimed Louisa. "According to etiquette, then, a queen is not permitted to learn any thing after ascending the throne?"

"No, your majesty, for it is entirely unbecoming that one of your subjects should become the teacher of his queen, and that anybody should be permitted and dare to censure her."

"Well, do not you do so very often, my dear countess?" asked the queen, good-naturedly.

"I dare not censure the queen, but merely to defend and maintain etiquette, as my duty and official position require me to do. But a queen who takes lessons must descend from her throne so long as her teacher is with; her must renounce her exalted position, and obey instead of commanding. In such a case, therefore, etiquette is altogether out of the question."

"You are right," said Louisa, merrily. "Mr. Himmel, the concert-master, at least, entirely coincides with you, and he takes no notice whatever of etiquette. Shall I confess to you, my dear countess, why Mr. Himmel has run away to-day half an hour before the regular time?"

"Run away?" asked the mistress of ceremonies, in dismay. "He has dared to run away in the presence of your majesty?"

"Yes, he has dared to do so, but previously he has dared to do something a great deal worse. He has—but, dear countess, sit down; you might turn giddy."

"Oh no, your majesty, permit me to stand. Your majesty was going to communicate graciously to me what Mr. Himmel—this teacher of a queen—is not even a nobleman—has dared to do in the presence of your majesty."

"Well, listen to me," said the queen, smiling; and bending down closely to the ear of the countess, she whispered: "He has kissed my shoulder!"

The mistress of ceremonies uttered a piercing cry and tottered back in dismay.

"Kissed!" she faltered.

"Yes, kissed," sighed the queen; "I really believe it is still to be seen."

She walked with light, swinging steps to the large looking-glass, and looked at her shoulder with a charming, child-like smile.

"Yes, that small red spot there is Mr. Himmel's crime!" she said. "Tell me what punishment he has deserved, countess."

"That is a question for the courts alone to decide," said the mistress of ceremonies, solemnly; "for we shall bring the occurrence, of course, at

---

* Historical.

once to their notice. Orders should be issued immediately to arrest him, and his punishment should be as unparalleled as was his offence. Your majesty will permit me to repair at once to the king in order—"

"No, my dear mistress of ceremonies," said the queen, who was still standing in front of the looking-glass and contemplating her own form, not with the contented looks of a conceited woman, but with the calm, stern eyes of a critic examining a work of art—"no, my dear mistress of ceremonies, we shall take good care not to raise a hue and cry about it. And Mr. Himmel is not so culpable, after all, as he seems to be."

"What! Your majesty intends to defend him?"

"Not to defend, but to excuse him, my dear countess. He was at my side as my dear old teacher, and I was to him not a queen, but a pupil; and, moreover, a pupil with very beautiful shoulders. My dear countess, I am really more culpable than poor Himmel, for, if the queen becomes a pupil, she must remember that her teacher is a man, and she must not treat him merely as an automaton instructing her. The only judge who is able to decide this matter is my husband, the king. He shall pronounce judgment on it, and if he permits Mr. Himmel to come back, I shall go on with my singing-lessons. However," added the queen, smiling, and blushing delicately, "in future I shall wrap a shawl around my shoulders. And now, my dear countess, pray let us not mention this little affair to anybody. I shall submit it to the king and ask him to decide it."

"I shall be silent because your majesty orders me to keep the occurrence secret," sighed the countess. "But it is unheard-of, it is dreadful. It is rank treason, and the offended royal majesty will forgive without punishing."

"Oh, yes, I will!" exclaimed the queen, joyfully. "Forgiving without punishing, is not that the most sacred and sublime power of a queen; is it not the most brilliant gem in our crown? How miserable and deplorable would monarchs be if God had not conferred the right of mercy upon them! We stand ourselves so much in need of mercy and forbearance, for we commit errors and faults like other mortals, and yet we judge and punish like gods. Let us be merciful, therefore, that we may be judged mercifully."

The door of the anteroom opened at this moment, and the chamberlain-in-waiting entered.

"Your majesty," he said, "Prince Louis Ferdinand and Minister von Hardenberg beg leave to wait on your majesty."

"I expected these gentlemen at this hour," said the queen, glancing at the clock; "let them come in, therefore. And you, my dear countess, farewell."

"Your majesty orders me to withdraw?" asked the mistress of ceremonies, hesitatingly. "Etiquette requires that the queen should give her audiences only in the presence of her mistress of ceremonies, or of one of her ladies of honor."

"My dear countess," said the queen, with a slight tinge of impatience, "I am not going to give any audience, but merely to receive a friendly visit from my royal cousin and his friend; as I know it is their intention to communicate to me matters which no one except myself can hear, I shall receive them alone. Hence be so kind as to withdraw."

"His royal highness Prince Louis Ferdinand and his excellency Minister von Hardenberg!" shouted the footman, opening the folding-doors.

The queen nodded a parting greeting to the mistress of ceremonies, and advanced a few steps to meet the visitors, while the countess, heaving mournful sighs, disappeared through the side-door.

CHAPTER XLV.

THE CONFERENCE.

PRINCE LOUIS FERDINAND, a nephew of Frederick the Great, and Minister von Hardenberg, were at that time the most popular men in Prussia, because they were known to be the leaders of the party which at the court of Berlin considered the accession of Prussia to the coalition of Russia, England, and Austria, as the only means to save the country, while Minister von Haugwitz, Lombard, the first secretary of foreign affairs, and General Köckeritz, constantly renewed their efforts to win the king to an alliance with France.

Prince Ferdinand, a fine-looking young man, scarcely thirty years of age, in his brilliant uniform, in which his tall and noble form presented a very imposing appearance, and in which he looked like the incarnation of an heroic warrior, was consequently the special favorite of the soldiers, who told the most astonishing and incredible stories about his intrepidity and hardihood. He was, besides, the favorite of the ladies, who called him the best-looking and most amiable man in the whole monarchy; and, with amiable indulgence, attributed his many adventures and acts of inconstancy, his wild and dissipated life, his extravagance and numerous debts, to the genius of the prince. He was, indeed, an extraordinary man, one of those on whose brow Providence has imprinted the stamp of genius,—not to their own good, but to their misfortune, and who either miserably perish by their genius, or constantly inflict with it the most painful wounds upon others.

Minister von Hardenberg, who now, after a long struggle, had succeeded in overcoming the influence of Minister von Haugwitz, and, with him, that of the French party, was one of those rare and extraordinary statesmen who have made diplomacy not a business, but the task of their whole life, and who have devoted to it all the strength, all the thoughts and feelings of their soul. A native of Hanover, and receiving rapid promotion at the hands of the government of that country, he had, nevertheless, soon entered the service of the Duke of Brunswick, who had charged him, after the death of Frederick the Great, to take the king's will, which had been deposited in the ducal archives at Brunswick, to Berlin.* King Frederick William the Second, who was so sagacious as to perceive and appreciate the diplomatic talents of the young ambassador, had induced him to enter his service, and intrusted to him the difficult mission of negotiating the annexation of Baireuth to Prussia, of settling the claims of the margrave, of paying the crushing burden of the debts of Baireuth as speedily as possible, and of restoring the country, which had suffered so much, to its former prosperity and content. Afterward he had been appointed minister of state and war in Prussia, and since that time he had always displayed the greatest activity and zeal in serving Prussia according to the dictates of his honest conviction, but at the same time also to guard the interests of the great fatherland, the interests of Germany. The influence of France, above all, seemed to him to endanger these interests; hence he believed it to be specially incumbent upon him to preserve at least Prussia from this noxious influence and to push her over to the other side, to the side of the coalition, than to allow her to be devoured, like a poor little bird, by the French basilisk. These endeavors, which kept up a continual conflict between him and the special favorites and confidants of the king, Haugwitz and Köckeritz, had gained him the love and esteem of all Prussian patriots, and secured him an extraordinary popularity. These two favorites of the Prussian people now entered the queen's cabinet.

Louisa replied to the familiar and friendly—rather than respectful—greeting of the prince

* "Mémoires d'un Homme d'État," vol. i., p. 502.

with a smile and a nod, and received the respectful bow of the minister with the calm and proud dignity of a queen.

"Well, my merry and reckless cousin," she said, turning to the prince, "are there again some sins to be confessed, some neglects of discipline to be hushed up, some tears to be dried, and the mercy of the king to be implored for the extravagant freaks of our genius? And is it for that reason that you have brought along so eloquent an advocate and attorney?"

"No, your majesty," said the prince, heaving a sigh, "this time, unfortunately, I have to confess to you no merry freaks and agreeable sins, and I am afraid I am about to become a steady man, and to turn my back on all extravagant pranks. Hence, the minister has not accompanied me this time in order to defend me and to implore the gracious intercession of my royal cousin, but we have come for the purpose of repeating to your majesty Prussia's cry of anguish and distress, and of beseeching you to assist us in saving her from the ruin on the verge of which she is tottering at the present time!"

The queen looked alternately at the prince and at the minister with grave, wondering eyes. "It is a political conference, then, you wish to hold with me?" she asked; and when the two gentlemen made no reply, she continued more rapidly and in a slightly agitated voice—"in that case, gentlemen, I must request you to leave me, for I am no politician, and I do not aspire to the rôle of a political intriguer. I am the wife of the reigning king, but not a reigning queen; my sole endeavor is to render the king a happy husband at home, and to cause him to forget at my side politics and the vexations of his official position."

"I am afraid, your majesty," said Minister von Hardenberg, solemnly—"I am afraid the time for such an idol on the throne is past; and instead of causing the king to forget the vexations of his position, it will now be the great task of your majesty to bear them with him."

"And we have come to beg my noble and magnanimous cousin to do so," exclaimed the prince, enthusiastically. "We have come to implore your assistance and coöperation in the name of Prussia, in the name of all German patriots, and in the name of your children!"

"In the name of my children?" ejaculated the queen, turning pale. "Speak! speak! what has happened? what calamity threatens my children? I decline listening to you as a queen, but I will do so as a mother, who anxiously desires to secure the happiness of her children. What evils, what calamities do you refer to?"

"The independence, nay, perhaps the whole existence of Prussia, is menaced," said Minister von Hardenberg, solemnly. "We have to choose whether Prussia is to be an isolated state, shunned by everybody, and despised by everybody—a state which France will be able to devour with impunity and amid the jeers of the whole world, as she has devoured Italy, Holland, and the left bank of the Rhine—or whether Prussia will preserve her power, her independence, and her honor, by not staving off a division any longer, but meeting her friends as well as her enemies with open visor, and by assuming at length an active and resolute attitude instead of the vacillating and hesitating course she has so long pursued !"

"We ought to oppose the Emperor of France in a manly manner," exclaimed the prince, energetically. "If we do not interfere with his proceedings, he will soon be our master as he is of all those who call themselves his allies, and who are really nothing but his slaves. My heart kindles with rage when I now see all Germany trembling with fear before this son of a Corsican lawyer, this tyrant who assassinated the noble and innocent Duke d'Enghien, and who, not contenting himself with chaining France, would like to catch the whole world in his imperial mantle so as to fatten its golden bees on it. And he will succeed in doing so, unless we resist him, for his word is now already the law of half the world, and this emperor carries out whatever he wants to do. Truly, if he should feel some day a hankering for a dish of princes' ears, I should no longer deem my own ears safe, nor those of your young princes either !" *

The queen did not smile at this jest which the prince had uttered in an angry voice, but she turned once more with a grave and anxious air to the minister.

"Tell me, has any thing occurred ?" she asked. "Has there been a change in the political situation ?"

"Yes, your majesty," replied the minister, "there has been a change in the political situation; the Emperor Napoleon has dared to violate our neutrality, and if Prussia should not now demand satisfaction she either loses her honor, or she places herself before the whole world as the ally of France, and defies thereby the open hostility of Austria, Russia, and England."

"You dare to say that Prussia's honor has been attacked, and to doubt that the king will hold the offender responsible for such an outrage ?" exclaimed the queen, with flashing eyes.

"The king, who is the incarnation of honor, will not permit even the shadow of a stain to fall on Prussia's honor; in generous anger he will hurl back the insolent hand that will dare to shake the palladium of our honor."

"Oh, if you think and speak thus," said the prince, enthusiastically, "I have no longer any fears, but consider Prussia as saved already from the dangers now menacing her. As I see your majesty now, in your wondrous beauty, with these eyes reflecting your inward heaven, with this face so radiant with enthusiasm, you seem to be the genius whom Providence has sent to Prussia to guard and protect her, and to guide her on the right path and to the right goal. O, queen! fulfil the mission which Providence has intrusted to you; follow your noble and sacred vocation; be the genius of Prussia; and impart to the vacillating and timid, firm, manly courage and energetic resolution! Queen, I implore you, on my knees, have pity on Prussia, have pity on your children: be the genius of Prussia !"

And quite beside himself, his eyes filled with tears, his lips quivering with emotion, the prince knelt down before the queen and raised his folded hands imploringly to her.

"Your majesty, permit me also to bend my knees before you," said Minister von Hardenberg, solemnly, "to adore and worship you as the genius of Prussia, from whom we expect our salvation, our peace, and our honor! Oh, queen, you alone have the power to touch the heart of the king and to remove the doubts of his noble and honorable mind; you alone will be able to accomplish what neither our arguments nor our supplications could bring about; you alone will be able to elevate the vacillation of your husband to the strength of high-spirited and courageous resolution !"

"No, not a word against the king !" exclaimed the queen, almost sternly. "Let no one dare to assert that the king lacks manly determination and vigorous courage. If he is hesitating when you would wish to act, it is because he looks into the future more prudently and sagaciously than you, while you only think of the present time; it is because he weighs and calculates the consequences, while you only care for the action of the moment. But arise, gentlemen; let us not perform a sentimental scene at a time when it is of the highest importance to be prudent and to reflect. Let us converse, therefore, gravely and soberly; explain to me what has happened, and what danger is menacing Prussia and my children. I comply now with your wish; let us hold a political conference. Let us sit down, then, and commence."

* Prince Louis Ferdinand said this to the queen.—Vide "Rahel and her Friends," vol. I.

She took a seat on the sofa, and invited the gentlemen to sit down on the two chairs opposite her.

"Now tell me what has occurred, and what has changed the political situation. Minister von Hardenberg, pray give me a full and plain account of the state of our political affairs, for I have already told you that I never meddle with politics, and do not know much about them; indeed I have been too happy, and my life too much absorbed by my happiness, to have made it necessary for me to think of politics. But I see very well that the time of quiet happiness is over now! Let us, then, speak of politics. You said, a few minutes ago, Prussia had been insulted by France?"

"Yes, your majesty, Prussia has been insulted. Her most sacred right, her neutrality, has been violated," replied Hardenberg. "The king, in his generous endeavor to preserve the blessings of peace to his people, intended to maintain a strict neutrality amid all these wars and storms agitating the world, and, the friend and ally of no party and no power, to rely exclusively on his own strength. He wanted to wait, to mediate, and conciliate, but not to attack, act, and decide. There may be times when such a *rôle* is a weighty and dignified one—may secure the peace of the world; but it always depends on those between whom one wishes to act as a neutral mediator. One may remain neutral between men of honor, between princes, to whom their word is sacred, and who do not dare to violate treaties, but not between those to whom their word is sacred only so long as their own advantage requires it, and who do not violate treaties only so long as they do not interfere with their selfish plans. It is a principle of neutrality not to open one's territory to either of the contending powers, and this principle has always been strictly observed. When Russia, now that she is going to send her troops for the second time to Germany for the purpose of assisting the Austrians, informed the king that she would march these troops through Southern Prussia and Silesia, the king deemed this information equivalent to a declaration of war, and his majesty immediately ordered the whole army to be placed on the war footing. We should now be at war with Russia, if the Emperor Alexander had not sent on the day after the first dispatch had arrived here, another dispatch to the king, in which he apologized, and declared that he had been too rash in making the above-named demand.[*] But this step of Russia, this mere threat of violation of our neutrality, had sufficed to induce

Prussia to place her army on the war footing, and to do so *against* the coalition of Austria, Russia, and England. A cry of horror resounded throughout Germany when the people heard of this first step by which Prussia seemed to declare publicly *for* France and *against* the coalition, and this cry was reëchoed abroad, of which the conduct of the King of Sweden gave us a striking proof. Your majesty is aware that this king, through his ambassador, M. de Bernstorf, returned to his majesty the King of Prussia the order of the Black Eagle which he had received from the late lamented king, accompanying it by an insulting letter in which he stated, that 'he could not wear an order which the king had recently also sent to Monsieur Bonaparte.'"

"And on the same day that this offensive return of the highest Prussian order took place," exclaimed Prince Louis Ferdinand, with a harsh, angry laugh, "on the same day the King of Prussia received from the Emperor of France the *grand cordon* and *seven* other grand crosses of the Legion of Honor to be distributed among the princes and ministers. And not only did we receive these seven orders, but in return for them we sent seven orders of the Black Eagle to Paris."[*]

"But you forget to add that the king returned on the same day the Seraphine order to the King of Sweden, and recalled his ambassador, so that we are now in a state of war with Sweden," said the queen, eagerly.

"Oh, my royal cousin, you betray your secret," exclaimed the prince, joyfully, "you wanted us to believe that your majesty did not care at all for politics, and now you know the most minute details so accurately."

"I take a lively interest in every occurrence which grieves the heart of my husband," said the queen; "and that event made a very painful impression upon him."

"Oh, your majesty, it was only a prelude to other mortifications and insults which we shall have to suffer if the king will not avenge them," said Hardenberg, energetically. "It has been said that Prussia was siding with France merely because she would not grant Russia a passage through her neutral territory, and because she placed her army in a menacing position against Russia. But what would the world say if it should learn what has now occurred?"

"Well, what has occurred?" asked the queen, breathlessly.

"The Emperor of France has carried out what

---

* Vide Häusser's "History of Germany," vol. ii., p. 635.   * "Mémoires d'un Homme d'État," vol. viii., p. 474.

* Häusser's "History of Germany," vol. ii., p. 576.

Russia only threatened to do. The Emperor of France, without applying for permission, has marched a portion of his army, commanded by Bernadotte, through Prussian territory. He has marched his troops, contrary to treaties and to international law, through Prussian Franconia, Anspach, and Baireuth."

The queen uttered a cry of surprise, and her cheeks turned pale.

"Does the king already know it?" she asked.

"He has known it since yesterday," said Hardenberg, gravely. "We kept the matter secret, because we would only lay it before the public together with the decision of his majesty."

"And has the king come already to a decision?" asked the queen.

"He has, your majesty," said Hardenberg, solemnly. "When Russia threatened to violate our territory, we placed our army on the war footing, and it is still in arms. Now that France dares to do what Russia only threatened to do, we do not turn our arms against her in order to avenge the insult, but we take our pen and write and ask France to explain her startling proceedings. It is true we threaten, but do not strike!"

"No, we do not strike!" exclaimed the prince, laughing scornfully; "we mobilize our army against our natural friends and allies, but we do not draw the sword against our natural enemies and adversaries. The army of Frederick the Great is ready for war, and yet it remains idle and looks on quietly while the insatiable conqueror is penetrating farther and farther into the heart of Germany; while he is scattering broadcast the seeds of treachery, discord, and mischief; while he is persuading the German princes to turn traitors to Germany; while he is poisoning and corrupting the hearts of the people and degrading their characters to such an extent, that the sense of fidelity, honesty, and constancy will soon become extinct in Germany, and all the Germans will be nothing but a horde of slaves, who will be happy if this tyrant does not apply the lash too often to their backs, and who will kiss his feet, so that he may step at least mildly and gently on their necks! If the tyrant should succeed now in humiliating Austria, who alone has been courageous enough to oppose him; if Napoleon should defeat the Austrian army, Germany would be lost and become nothing but a French province like Italy and Holland: all the German princes would lay their crowns at the feet of Napoleon, and be glad if he should suffer them only as governors in their former states, or leave them at least their empty titles after depriving them of their possessions!"

"No, no," exclaimed the queen, "we must not, we shall not permit that! Prussia is ready to maintain the honor of Germany; Prussia will rise like a hero accustomed to victory; she will drive the invader from her territory, and compel him, with arms in her hands, to keep the peace, if she is unable to obtain it with her pen. You are right, the time of neutrality and hesitation is past, and henceforth we must act. I shall no longer remain neutral, I shall act too. You have appealed to the mother and wife and shown her the danger threatening her children and her husband; you have reminded the daughter of Germany of the horrors menacing her fatherland; you have pointed out to the Queen of Prussia the evils impending over her people; the mother, the wife, and the queen has heard and understood you. The time of neutrality is past; we must move the heart of the best and most magnanimous king by our prayers and remonstrances, in order that he may listen to us, and no longer to the insinuations and flatteries of his enemies, so that he may discern his friends as well as his enemies. The king is hesitating only because, in generous self-abnegation, he prefers the happiness of his people to his own wishes and to the gratification of his own desires. A soldier by nature and predilection, he compels himself to be a peaceable ruler, because he believes it is necessary for the happiness of his people. Let us prove to him that his subjects refuse to accept this generous sacrifice, and that they are joyfully ready to remove the stains from their honor with their heart's blood. Let public opinion speak out and come to our assistance. I say, 'to our assistance,' for henceforth I shall side with you, I shall be a member of your party, and a determined and outspoken enemy of France!"

"May God bless your majesty for these words!" said Hardenberg, deeply moved; "I am once again in hopes that Prussia will be saved, for she has now won an ally who brings more to her than armies and arms, and who places the enthusiasm and indomitable determination of a great chieftain at the head of our people."

"And with this chieftain at our head we shall vanquish every French army," exclaimed Prince Louis, enthusiastically; "with this chieftain at our head we shall triumphantly march against the enemy, and one idea, one sentiment will animate all of us: Queen Louisa is watching and praying for us! Oh, my queen, would that that blessed day of battle could dawn for us! Command the sun of that day to rise and to shine into all Prussian hearts, and to fire them with patriotism so as to shrink back no longer from death and wounds, but only from dishonor and degradation! Oh, my blood burns like fire in my veins; it would like to burst forth in a fiery torrent and drown and burn every Frenchman. Queen, have mercy on me—let the solemn day when I may shed my blood for the fatherland dawn without delay!"

"Live and labor for the fatherland!" said the queen, with flaming eyes, and her face radiant with enthusiasm. "It is not the most exalted and difficult task to die an heroic death for a great idea, but it is even more noble and difficult to nourish and preserve this idea in the gloomy days of adversity, and not to abandon it and give it up in a period of affliction, but to remain its guardian and priest, even though fate may seem to reject it and to humiliate us with it. Now that I am entering a new life-path, I say to you, from the bottom of my heart, we will struggle for the honor, liberty, and independence of Prussia and Germany, but we will be determined, too, not only to die for these ideas, but also to suffer and bear affliction for them. Oh, it seems to me as though I were looking at this moment into the future, and as though I did see there much misery and distress in store for us, many storms and thunder-clouds!"

"But the sun is hidden behind the thunder-clouds, and when the thunder has died away it will shine again," said Hardenberg.

"And it will then shine on the heads of my husband and of my children!" exclaimed the queen, raising her radiant eyes to heaven.

"Above all, it will shine on the Prussian people from the face of their adored Queen Louisa," said the prince.

The queen smiled sadly. "Let us not speak of the sun, but of the thunder-clouds preceding it. They are gathering around us; let us see how we can break through them. You may count on my earnest assistance. My husband and my children are in danger, I feel and see it. France is the enemy menacing them. Henceforward we will oppose this enemy with open visor. I promise it to you in the name of Prussia, in the name of my husband, and of my children. Here, take my hand; we will stand by each other, and struggle together against France for the honor and glory of Prussia. You will fight with your sword and with your pen, and I shall do so with my word and my love. May the people support us, may God bless us!"

"May God bless us!" repeated the prince and the minister, reverentially kissing the queen's hands.

"And now, gentlemen, go," said the queen, after a short pause. "Let us not desecrate this solemn moment by any additional words. Every thing for Prussia! Let that be our watchword! and so I bid you farewell for to-day. Every thing for Prussia!"

"Every thing for Prussia!" repeated the two gentlemen, taking leave of the queen.

Louisa sent a long, melancholy look after them; then she turned hastily around and crossed the room with rapid steps; the sudden draught produced by her quick passage blew the music-paper from the piano to the floor; it fell exactly at the queen's feet.

She picked it up; it was the song she had sung an hour ago. A painful smile played on the lips of the queen, and raising her eyes sadly to heaven, she whispered, in a low voice:

"Oh, my God, grant that this may not be an omen, and that I may not be compelled to eat my bread with tears, and to weep through nights of affliction! But if it must be, O God, give me strength to bear my misfortunes uncomplainingly and to be a comfort to my husband, a mother to my children!"

CHAPTER XLVI.

THE OATH AT THE GRAVE OF FREDERICK THE GREAT.

THE wishes of the queen had rapidly been fulfilled; public opinion had declared in Berlin with rare energy and emphasis against France, and the people had received the news of the violation of Prussia's neutrality with a unanimous cry of rage and horror. The inhabitants of Berlin, usually so peaceable and addicted to pleasure, seemed all at once transformed into heroes grave and eager for war, who no longer knew any other aim than to avenge as speedily as possible the insult offered to them, and to call France to account for the outrage she had committed against Prussia.

"War! war!" That was the word of jubilee and supplication now resounding on every street, and in every house; like one exulting prayer of the whole nation, it rose to the windows of the royal palace, and seemed to rap gently at them, so that the king might open them and let it penetrate into his heart.

The people spoke everywhere of this one great affair; they asked each other, in conversation: "Shall we take up arms? Shall we declare war against France?"

Those who answered these questions in the negative were treated in the most contemptuous manner; the people turned their backs on them with angry glances and threatening murmurs; to those, however, who replied in the affirmative, they offered their hands joyfully and greeted them as friends and allies.

Minister von Haugwitz was known to be an adherent of the French and an opponent of the war; the people rushed to his house and broke his windows, shouting loudly and angrily, "We do not want peace! Let all the French and friends of the French perish!"

Minister von Hardenberg, on the other hand, was hailed by the people with the most enthusiastic applause wherever he made his appearance; and on their return from the house of Minister von Haugwitz, they hurried to Hardenberg's humble residence in order to cheer him and to shout, "War! war! We want war with France!"

Not only the people in the streets, however, but also the best classes of the public participated in this general enthusiasm, and did not hesitate to give vent to it in public. Even the royal functionaries found suddenly sufficient energy to show themselves as German patriots, and it was certainly not unintentional that "Wallenstein's Camp," by Schiller, was to be performed at the Royal Theatre during those days of general excitement.

Everybody wished to attend this performance; all Berlin rushed to the Royal Theatre, and the fortunate persons who had succeeded in obtaining tickets were envied by the thousands unable to gain admission. The theatre was crowded; the pit was a surging sea, the gallery was filled to suffocation, and in the boxes of the first and second tiers the aristocratic, elegant, educated, and learned world of all Berlin seemed to have met. All faces were glowing, all lips were smiling, all eyes were sparkling; every one was aware that this was to be a political demonstration, and every one was happy and proud to participate in it.

When Prince Louis Ferdinand made his appearance in the small royal proscenium-box, all eyes turned immediately toward him, and when he bent forward from his box, and seemed to greet the audience with his merry eyes and winning smile, there arose a storm of applause as though a favorite singer had just concluded an *aria di bravura* and received the thanks of the enraptured listeners. Suddenly, however, the loud applause died away, perhaps because the prince had waved his hands as if he wished to calm this roaring sea—perhaps because the attention of the audience was attracted by somebody else. The eyes of the crowd turned from the prince toward an adjoining box. Four gentlemen, in brilliant uniforms, had just entered it; but these uniforms were not those of the Prussian army, and the broad

ribbons which these gentlemen wore across their breasts, were not the ribbons of Prussian orders. The new-comers, who had entered the box, were the members of the French embassy—General Lefèvre, with his attachés, and General Duroc, whom Napoleon had recently again sent to Berlin in order to strengthen the friendly relations of France and Prussia. It was certainly a mere accident that Prince Louis Ferdinand, just at the moment when these gentlemen intended to salute him, turned to the opposite side, and did not see and acknowledge their greetings; it was certainly a mere accident that the audience, which had just now shouted and applauded jubilantly, all at once commenced hissing loudly.

The members of the French embassy took good care not to refer this hissing to themselves; they took their seats quietly near the balustrade of the box, and seemed to take no notice of the loud murmurs and the threatening glances of the audience.

The band now struck up the overture. It was a skilfully arranged medley of well-known popular war-songs, interlarded with the Dessauer and Hohenfriedberger march, as if the enthusiasm of the audience were to be carried to the highest pitch by brilliant reminiscences of the heroic deeds and imperishable glory of Prussia.

All at once a joyful murmur spread through the pit, the boxes, and the gallery. "The king, the queen!" whispered everybody, and all those hundreds of faces turned toward the small proscenium-box which the royal couple had just entered.

The queen, radiantly beautiful, with rosy cheeks and sparkling eyes, greeted the audience with an enchanting smile; the king, whose brow seemed unusually gloomy and clouded, cast only a hesitating and anxious glance over the house, and then withdrew behind the crimson curtain of the box.

The stage-curtain rose; the performance commenced. The audience followed it with the most ardent sympathy; every word referring to the liberty and independence of Germany, was hailed with thunders of applause, and jubilant shouts resounded at every allusion to foreign tyranny and despotism. The actors had now reached the last part of the piece, the merry, soul-stirring horseman's song concluding the whole. "*Wohlauf, Kameraden, auf's Pferd, auf's Pferd!*" sang the chorus on the stage, and the audience followed every verse, every line, with breathless attention. All at once people looked in great surprise at each other, and then listened with the utmost suspense to the singers, who had added to the merry horseman's song a verse which had not been heard heretofore. And when the last words of this verse had died away, the whole audience shouted and roared, "_Da capo! da capo!_" In the pit, in the boxes, in the gallery, in short, every one rose to their feet, and all eyes again turned to the box in which the members of the French embassy were seated, and thus, standing, in a jubilant tone and with threatening glances, the whole audience joined the chorus of the actors on the stage; for they knew already the words of the additional verse by heart, and sang in a thundering voice:

> "Wohlauf, Kameraden, zur Schlacht, zum Krieg,
> In's Feld, in die Freiheit gezogen.
> Zur blutigen Schlacht, zum rächenden Sieg
> Ueber den, der uns Freundschaft gelogen!
> Und Tod und Verderben dem falschen Mann,
> Der treulos den Frieden brechen kann!" *

And the audience repeated once more the last two lines:

> "Und Tod und Verderben dem falschen Mann,
> Der treulos den Frieden brechen kann!"

All eyes then turned to the royal box. The king was still hidden behind the small curtain. The queen had risen. Folding her hands, as if praying, she had raised her eyes to heaven, and two tears ran slowly down her cheeks.

Prince Louis Ferdinand bent toward Minister von Hardenberg, who had just entered his box. "Do you see the queen?" he said, in a low voice. "Does she not look really like a genius praying for Prussia?"

"Ah, and, perhaps, weeping for Prussia!" whispered Hardenberg. "But let us not give way now to gloomy anticipations. I am the bearer of good and unexpected news. Listen to me. The king and the queen will rise in a few minutes in order to leave the box, and who knows whether the audience will be patient and calm enough to witness the whole ballet, which is just commencing? I see some of my agents already below in the pit, where they have made their appearance in order to circulate my news."

"I beseech your excellency, be here your own agent, and communicate the news to me."

Minister Hardenberg bent closer to the prince's ear. "I suppose you know that, thanks to the influence of the queen, I have induced the king to sign a tolerably warlike and threatening note to the Emperor of the French?"

"But will this note really be forwarded to Napoleon?"

"It has already been forwarded. But I had sent also a messenger to the Emperor of Russia with a copy of this note, and the emperor, it seems, has understood my mission, for— But, just look, my prophecy commences being fulfilled. The king and the queen rise and leave their box; and notice, too, the migration beginning in the pit and among the occupants of the orchestra-stalls. The beautiful ballet-girls will soon dance before empty benches."

"But do not let me die with curiosity, your excellency. Tell me at length what has occurred."

"A surprise, prince. The Emperor Alexander will reach Berlin within an hour!"

"Are you not jesting? Do you speak in earnest?"

"In dead earnest, prince. The emperor comprehends that the favorable hour must be improved, and he comes in order to conquer the friendship of Frederick William, and to overcome his indecision, so that they may then vanquish the French invader with their united forces. The emperor is a very sagacious man, and being half a German, he knows doubtless the German proverb, 'Strike while the iron is hot.' Our noble queen, with both of us and our excellent people, will help the emperor to strike the iron. Look, the people commence striking already. They rush from the theatre in order to receive the Emperor Alexander at the gate, and to cheer him while he is riding to the palace. Let us follow the example of the people of Berlin. Let us go to receive the Emperor Alexander—if it please God, our ally—at the gate." *

Hardenberg's predictions were to be fulfilled this time. Thanks to the powerful allies who were fighting for his policy and for Prussia, the king summoned up sufficient courage to take a decisive resolution. Those allies of Hardenberg and Prussia were now not only the queen, Prince Louis Ferdinand, and public opinion, but they were joined by the Emperor Alexander, who had arrived from Poland, and the Archduke Anthony, whom the Emperor of Austria had sent to Berlin

---

* "On, comrades, to battle, to war—let us march into the field and fight for liberty! To bloody battle, to avenging victory over him who has lied friendship to us! And death and destruction to the false man who has perfidiously broken the peace!"

This whole scene is strictly in accordance with history; and the additional verse, if not literally the same, renders at least the sentiment of the lines which were sung on that memorable evening.—Vide "Mémoires d'un Homme d'État," vol. viii., p. 496, and "Napoleon; a Memoir," by ——, vol. ii., p. 78.

* The Emperor Alexander arrived in Berlin quite unexpectedly on October 23, 1805; the courier who had announced his arrival had reached the Prussian capital only a few hours previously.

at the same time for the purpose of winning the friendship of the king. But still another ally suddenly and unexpectedly entered the lists for Hardenberg's policy and for the coalition, and this ally was the good fortune and genius of Napoleon.

Dreadful tidings reached Berlin simultaneously with the arrival of Archduke Anthony. Napoleon had gained another victory; he had defeated the Austrians at Ulm;[*] twenty-three thousand Austrians had laid down their arms at the feet of the Emperor of the French, and then started as prisoners of war for France.

Surrounded by a brilliant staff, Napoleon made the humiliated, vanquished Austrians file off before him, between the French army, which was drawn up in two lines. When they laid down their arms, and when this flashing pile rose higher and higher, Napoleon's face, which, amidst the hail of bullets and the dangers of the battle, had preserved its marble, antique calmness, became radiant, as if lighted up by a sunbeam, and he turned with a gracious smile toward the Austrian generals and officers, who approached him humbly and with lowered heads, in order to thank him for giving them permission to return to Austria, and for not compelling them to accompany their soldiers as prisoners of war to France.

But this smile disappeared rapidly from the emperor's countenance, which now became threatening and angry. In a voice rolling like thunder over the heads of the humiliated Austrians, the emperor said: "It is a misfortune that men so brave as you, whose names are honorably mentioned wherever you have fought, should now become the victims of the stupidities of a cabinet which only dreams of senseless schemes, and does not hesitate to endanger the dignity of the state and of the nation. It was an unheard-of proceeding to seize me by the throat without a declaration of war; but it is a crime against one's own people to bring about a foreign invasion; it is betraying Europe, to draw Asiatic hordes into our combats. Instead of attacking me without any good reason whatever, the Austrian cabinet ought to have united with me for the purpose of expelling the Russian army from Germany. This alliance of your cabinet is something unheard of in history; it cannot be the work of the statesmen of your nation; it is, in short, the alliance of the dogs and shepherds with the wolf against the sheep. Had France succumbed in this struggle, you would have speedily perceived the mistake you have committed."[†]

Such were the tidings which Archduke Anthony had brought with him from Vienna; such was the new ally Hardenberg had won for his policy and for Prussia.

This new victory, this new conquest Napoleon had made in Germany, loomed up before the king as a danger which menaced himself, and compelled him to take up arms for his own defence. The threatening and defiant language of the French emperor sounded truly revolting to the heart of the German king, and instead of being intimidated by this new and unparalleled triumph, by this threatening language Napoleon had made use of, he was only provoked to offer him resistance; he perceived all at once that he could only be the servant and slave of this powerful man, or his enemy, and that Napoleon never would tolerate any one as an equal at his side. What were those three German princes who had found three crowns on the battle-field of Ulm? Those new Kings of Wurtemberg and Bavaria, that Grand-duke of Baden, were only vassals and servants of the Emperor of France, who had first given, and then *permitted* them to wear these crowns.

King Frederick William needed no such crown. A genius stood at his side and breathed with a heavenly smile into his ear: "It is better to die in an honorable struggle for freedom than to live in splendor and magnificence, but with a stain on your honor."

And the king listened to the voice of his genius: he listened to the voice of his minister, who implored him to defend the integrity of his state for the sake of the honor and welfare of Prussia and Germany; he listened to the voice of his people, who demanded war loudly and ardently; he listened to the voice of the Emperor Alexander, who vowed to him eternal love and eternal friendship; he listened, finally, to the voice of his own heart, which was the heart of a true German, and felt deeply the insult offered to him.

King Frederick William listened to all these voices, and resolved at length on war against France.

On the 3d of November the Emperor Alexander and King Frederick William signed at Potsdam a *secret* treaty, by which Prussia agreed to intervene between Napoleon and the allies. By virtue of this treaty Prussia was to summon the Emperor of the French to reëstablish the former treaties, and to restore the former state of affairs; that is to say, to give up almost all his conquests, to indemnify Sardinia, to recognize the independence of Naples, of the German empire, of Holland, of Switzerland, and to separate the crown of Italy from that of France. If France should

---

* October 20, 1805.

† "Memoires du Duc de Rovigo," vol. ii, p. 153.

not consent to these conditions, Prussia agreed to ally herself openly and unreservedly with the coalition, and take the field with an army of 180,000 men. A Prussian negotiator was to lay these conditions before the Emperor Napoleon, and the term at which Prussia should be obliged to act should expire four weeks after the date of the treaty.[*]

The king, who, in his kindness, was anxious to indemnify Minister von Haugwitz for the coldness with which he had been latterly treated, and for his broken windows, had commissioned him to deliver a copy of the treaty of Potsdam to Napoleon, and to negotiate with him. Haugwitz, therefore, left Berlin in order to repair to the emperor's headquarters. It is true, he did not know exactly where to find them, but he was satisfied that Napoleon would take care to make his whereabouts known to him by fresh deeds of heroism and victories, and Count Haugwitz, therefore, set out.

According to the wishes of the King of Prussia, the treaty of Potsdam, for some time at least, was to be kept secret; only those immediately concerned should be informed of its contents, but not the public generally, and no one was to suspect that Prussia had at length given up her policy of neutrality.

This secrecy, however, was distasteful to the Emperor Alexander; moreover, it made Minister von Hardenberg fear lest the king, at the decisive moment, might be once more gained over to his former favorite policy of neutrality by the French party at court. It would be wise, therefore, to force the king so far forward as to render it impossible for him to recede, and to betray so much of the secret of the concluded alliance as was required to fasten the king to it.

Hence, the emperor, at the hour of his departure for Austria, requested the Queen and King of Prussia to accompany him to the grave of Frederick the Great. At midnight, on the 5th of November, they repaired, therefore, to the garrison church at Potsdam, the lower vault of which contains the coffin of the great king. A single torchbearer accompanied the three august visitors, whose steps resounded solemnly in the silent, gloomy halls.

Arriving at the king's coffin, the emperor knelt down; his face, lighted up by the glare of the torch, was radiant with enthusiasm. On the other side of the dark vault stood the king and the queen, both with folded hands; the king with a gloomy and reserved air, the queen with her eyes turned to heaven, and her face beaming with pious emotion and joy.

Alexander, still remaining on his knees, now raised his folded hands toward heaven. "At the grave of the most heroic king," he said in a loud and solemn voice—"at the grave of Frederick the Great, I swear to my ally, the King of Prussia, an oath of everlasting love and constancy; I swear an oath of everlasting constancy and love to the sacred cause which has united us for the most exalted purpose. Never shall my constancy waver; never shall my love grow cold! I swear it!"

He kissed the coffin and rose from his knees; his eyes, glistening with tears, then turned toward the king, as he said:

"It is your turn now, my brother, to swear the oath."

The king hesitated.

The queen laid her hand gently on his shoulder, and bent her beautiful face so close to him that he felt her breath, like the kiss of an angel, on his cheek.

"Swear the oath, my friend, my beloved," she whispered; "swear to be faithful to the holy alliance against the French tyrant; swear everlasting constancy and love to our noble ally."

The king hesitated no longer; he raised his head resolutely and approached the coffin. Laying his hand upon it, he repeated in a grave and calm voice the words which the queen had uttered before, and which she now whispered with trembling lips.

All three then grasped each other's hands over the coffin; thus they stood a long while, deeply moved and silent.

All at once this silence was interrupted by the loud, ringing notes of the church clock, announcing the first hour of the new day. The sounds died away, and the chime of the bells now commenced playing in clear and sweet notes the old German hymn, "Ueb immer Treu und Redlichkeit, bis an dein kühles Grab!"[*]

The king inclined his head, as if in silent prayer; an almost imperceptible, strange smile overspread the noble features of the emperor. The queen, however, glowing with enthusiasm, exclaimed:

"God and the spirit of Frederick the Great give us the motto of our alliance: 'Ueb immer Treu und Redlichkeit, bis an dein kühles Grab!' Let us remember it as long as we live!"

"Let us remember it," repeated the two sovereigns, with a firm, manly grasp. They looked at

---

[*] Häusser's "History of Germany," vol. ii. p. 652.

[*] Hölty's beautiful hymn, "Be honest and faithful until they lay thee in thy cool grave."

each other, and with their eyes bade each other a last farewell.

Then they turned silently away and left the royal vault.

Five minutes later, the Emperor Alexander of Russia was on his way to Olmütz, in order to join there the Emperor Francis of Austria, who had fled thither from Napoleon and his victorious army.

At Olmütz the plan for the campaign of the third coalition against Napoleon was to be agreed upon.

THE FALL OF THE GERMAN EMPIRE.

CHAPTER XLVII.

EVIL TIDINGS.

It was in the last days of November, 1805. After the victory of Ulm, the Emperor Napoleon had established his headquarters in Brünn, where he seemed to wait for his adversaries to attack him. There was no longer one enemy opposed to him; he had no longer to cope with Austria alone, but also with Russia, whose emperor was now at Olmütz with the Emperor of Austria, for the purpose of agreeing with him on the plan of operations by which Napoleon was to be defeated. The Russian army had already formed a junction with the Austrian forces, and even the Russian life-guards, the *élite* of their army, had left Russia in order to accompany their emperor to the great decisive battle.

But Napoleon had likewise brought his guards along, and these splendid troops were impatient and eager to fight the last decisive struggle with the Austrians and with "the hordes of the Russian barbarians."

Napoleon, however, still hesitated; his plans apparently had not been matured, and he seemed undecided whether to advance still further or to content himself with the victories he had already obtained.

This last alternative was urged on him by his generals, who believed the victory of Ulm to be so brilliant a triumph that the French army might repose on its laurels, instead of drawing the sword once more.

Napoleon, however, did not assent to these views of his generals.

"If we had to cope only with the Austrians we might be satisfied, but there are the Russians, too, and it will be necessary for us to send them home. We must give them their passports."

Greatly elated at this idea, the emperor ordered his horse to be brought to him.

"We will examine the country a little," he said to his generals; "accompany me, gentlemen."

And surrounded by his brilliant staff, consisting of the most illustrious and victorious officers of his army, the emperor rode out far into the plain between Brünn and Vichau, crowned all around with hills and mountains. His bold, searching glances surveyed the country in every direction; not a height, not a tree, not a ravine, escaped his attention; he examined every thing, and seemed to engrave them on his soul. It was near night-fall when he returned with his generals from this long ride to his headquarters. He had all day been taciturn and absorbed, and none of his generals had been permitted to participate in his plans and observations. He had only sometimes directed their attention by a laconic word or by a wave of his hand to some peculiarity of the land-scape, and the generals had received these words and gestures like the mysterious hints of an oracle, with the most respectful attention, in order to weigh them in their minds, and to indelibly engrave them in their memory. On his arrival at the door of his headquarters, the emperor turned his pale, grave face once more to the plain which they had just left.

"Gentlemen," he said, in a loud voice, "study that part of the country as closely as possible; you will have to play a *rôle* in it within a few days. General Suchet, on the left side of your division there is an isolated mound, commanding your entire front. Cause fourteen cannon to be placed on it in the course of the present night." [*] He nodded to the gentlemen and entered his cabinet.

He paced his room for a long while with folded arms, compressed lips, and a gloomy air.

"I need a few days more," he muttered. "If they should attack me now, quickly and resolute-

---

[*] Napoleon's own words.—Vide "Mémoires du Duc de Rovigo," vol. ii., p. 169.

ly, I must succumb; if they give me three days'
time, however, I shall defeat them."

When he then stooped musingly before his desk,
he suddenly noticed the papers lying on it.

"Ah," he said, hastily seizing a large, sealed
letter, "a courier, who has brought dispatches in
my absence! From the minister of the navy—
news from the fleet!"

He broke the seal hurriedly and unfolded the
paper. While reading it his mien became still
more gloomy; a cloud of anger settled on his expansive brow, and his cheeks, which had hitherto
only been pale, turned livid.

The glance which he now cast toward heaven
would have reminded the spectator of the Titans
who dared to hurl their missiles even at the Sovereign Deity; the words muttered by his quivering lips were an angry oath.

With this oath he crumpled up the paper in his
hand, threw it down and stamped on it; then, as
if ashamed of his own violence, he sank down on
a chair, and laid his hands slowly, and with a deep
sigh, on his trembling, pale face. The modern
Titan had now found out for the first time that
there was a God enthroned in heaven more powerful than himself; for the first time an invisible
hand had stopped him in his hitherto victorious
course.

The paper he had just trampled under foot announced to him the first great defeat, the first
check his grand schemes had met with.

The French fleet had been completely beaten
and almost annihilated by the English at Trafalgar.* England, the only enemy who had constantly opposed Napoleon in a menacing and fear-
less manner, detested England had gained a magnificent triumph. She had destroyed the whole
naval power of France, and won a brilliant victory; a victory which humiliated France and overwhelmed her with disgrace. It is true it was a
dearly-bought victory for England, for Nelson, her
greatest naval hero, had paid for his immortal triumph with his life. The French admiral, Villeneuve, who was defeated at Trafalgar, had not
even been lucky and wise enough to explate his
ignominy by his death; he had fallen, a despairing prisoner, into the hands of the English, and
served as a living trophy to the triumphant conquerors.†

Such were the terrible tidings which Napoleon
had just received; it was the first thunderbolt

which the God of heaven had hurled down upon
the powerful Titan.

But the Titan did not feel crushed by it; the
thunderbolt only served to fan the fire in his
breast.

He rose from his seat, and his eyes flashed with
anger.

"I cannot be everywhere," he said, aloud,
"but my enemies shall soon find out that I am
here, and I shall know how to avenge the disgrace
of Trafalgar by a brilliant victory." *

The door behind him opened at this moment,
and the chief of the imperial cabinet, M. de Bourrienne, entered.

"Sire," he said, "the two Austrian envoys,
Count de Giulay and Count Stadion, have returned, and beg your majesty to grant them an
audience."

"So late at night!" exclaimed the emperor.
"Why did they not come in the daytime?"

"They pretend to have been detained by the
impassable state of the roads, but assert to be
able to lay before your majesty some highly important intelligence, which would seem entirely
calculated to bring about the conclusion of peace
so longed for by Austria."

"Let the gentlemen come in," said the emper-
or, after a short reflection, and he placed his foot
again on the crumpled paper, as if he wished to
choke the secret of its contents, so that it might
not betray itself to the Austrians.

Bourrienne had gone out, and the two Austrian
envoys, Count Giulay and Count Stadion, now appeared on the threshold.

"You return to me," said the emperor, hastily,
to them; "my conditions have been accepted,
then? I told you I should not negotiate separately with Austria, but that I should require Russia to participate in the negotiations, and to be
included in the treaty of peace on which we might
agree. You come, then, in the name of the Emperors of Austria and Russia?"

"No, sire," said Count Stadion, respectfully,
"we come only in the name of Austria."

"The emperor, our august master," began
Count Giulay—but Napoleon interrupted him
quickly.

"I shall listen to you only if you are authorized
to speak in the name of the two emperors," said
Napoleon. "I already told you so yesterday, and
I do not see what should induce me to-day to
change my mind. The state of affairs is precisely
the same."

"Pardon me, sire, it is not," said Count Giulay,
firmly.

---

* October 21, 1805.

† Admiral Villeneuve was released by the English
government. Napoleon banished him to Rennes, where
he committed suicide on the 26th of April, 1806, by piercing his heart with a pin.

* Napoleon's own words.

The emperor fixed a piercing glance on him, as if he wished to read in the innermost recesses of his heart.

"And why is it not the same?" he asked, while his eye slowly turned toward the foot, under which he concealed the sinister dispatch.

"Your majesty was yesterday pleased to say that Austria, although she might boast of the active support of Russia, could never count on the assistance of Prussia, and that Prussia's neutrality was as useful to France as Russia's active support to Austria."

"Why do you repeat the words I uttered yesterday?" asked the emperor, impetuously.

"Sire, because Prussia is no longer neutral," said Count Stadion, solemnly.

"Because Prussia is ready to become, like Russia and England, the active ally of Austria," added Count Giulay.

Napoleon's flashing, gloomy eyes looked alternately at the two Austrian envoys.

"How did you obtain that information?" he asked at last.

"Sire, from his majesty the Emperor of Russia. He has concluded a treaty with the king at Potsdam, by which Frederick William III. declares his readiness to participate in the campaign and to assist Austria, unless your majesty should condescend to accept the conditions which the King of Prussia is to propose as mediator between the coalition and France."

"Ah, the King of Prussia is going to propose conditions to me?" exclaimed Napoleon, shrugging his shoulders. "Do you know those conditions?"

"The King of Prussia will propose to your majesty to surrender the crown of Italy, not to disturb the princes of Italy in their possessions and independence, to recognize the independence of the German empire, of Holland, of Switzerland, to—"

"Enough!" said Napoleon, impatiently. "The Emperor Alexander has taken the liberty to tell you a story, and your credulity must have greatly delighted him. Can you seriously believe that the King of Prussia would in his infatuation go so far as to hope that I should accept propositions of so ridiculous a description? Truly, even if I were a vanquished and humiliated emperor, I should stab myself with my own sword rather than submit to such a disgrace. It seems I have not yet engraved my name deeply enough into the marble tablets of history, and I shall prove to these overbearing princes, who believe their legitimacy to be the Gorgon's head they only need show in order to crush me—I shall prove to them *who I*

am, and to whom the future belongs, whether to *them* or to *me!* However, it is unnecessary to say so much about things which do not exist."

"Sire, the treaty of Potsdam *does* exist," said Count Stadion. "The envoy whom the King of Prussia has sent off to lay its stipulations before your majesty would have reached your headquarters already if he had travelled as rapidly as the Emperor Alexander, who left Potsdam simultaneously with him."

"Well, let him come; I shall see, then, whether you have told me a story or not," replied Napoleon. "If the King of Prussia has dared to do this, by God, I will pay him for it!* But this does not change my resolutions and plans in any respect. I shall enter into negotiations with Austria only on condition that Russia participates in them. State it to those who have sent you, and now farewell."

He nodded to the two gentlemen, and turning his back to them, stepped to the window. Only when a slight jarring of the door told him that they had withdrawn, the emperor turned around and commenced again, his hands folded behind his back, slowly pacing the room.

He then stopped before the large table in the middle of the room, and unrolled one of the maps lying on it. It was a map of southern Germany. After spreading it on the table, the emperor commenced marking it with pins, the variously-colored heads of which designated the different armies of the Russians, Austrians, and French.

The emperor was engaged all night in this task, in studying the map, and in measuring and calculating the distances some of his troops would have to march before reaching the field of action. The wax-candles in the silver chandelier burned down, but he did not notice it; the fire in the fireplace had gone out, but he did not feel it; the door of his cabinet was softly opened from time to time, and the pale face of his *valet de chambre* Constant, who was evidently exhausted with long waking, appeared, but the emperor did not heed it. His soul was concentrated on one idea, on one aim, viz., to pursue the glorious course of his victories, to humiliate Germany as he had humiliated Italy, and to drown the echoes of Trafalgar by a brilliant triumph.

Morning was already dawning, when Napoleon at length rose from the table and commenced again slowly pacing the room.

"Time, time!" he said, "I only need three days for moving up the third corps, which is already on the march from Bohemia. Time! And

<hr />

* Napoleon's own words.—Vide Hormayer, vol. i., and Häusser's "History of Germany," vol. ii., p. 680.

yet I must gain a great and brilliant victory before Prussia allies herself openly with Austria and Russia against France. If I should not succeed in doing so, the army of my enemies would be increased by one hundred and fifty thousand men. Hence," he said, after a pause, quite merrily and hopefully, "hence, I must succeed."

He returned to the map and pointed his finger at it.

"The Austrians are over there at Olmütz," he said, quickly. "Here, the Russian guards; there, the united corps of Kutusof and Buxhowden; farther on, the vanguard under Prince Bagration. If they should advance now rapidly, resolutely, directly toward my front, the odds would be too overwhelming; if they should tarry, or if I should succeed in causing them to hesitate until I have got my Bohemian corps in line, I should defeat them. Let us try it, therefore; let us feign inactivity and timidity, so that they may not become active. Cunning is the best ally of a general; let us try to deceive them."

He went to his desk, and taking some gilt-edged paper, commenced writing rapidly.

Fifteen minutes later an orderly requested General Savary to repair to the emperor's cabinet.

Napoleon received the general with a kindly smile, but he was silent, and looked almost irresolutely at the letter he held in his hand. Suddenly, however, he seemed to come to a firm resolution, and handing the letter to Savary, he said: "Take this letter to Olmütz; deliver it to the Emperor of Russia, and tell him that, having learned that he had arrived at the headquarters of his army, I had sent you to welcome him in my name. If he should converse with you, and put questions to you, you know the replies that should be made under such circumstances. Go." [*]

"And now," said the emperor, when Savary had left him, "now we will sleep a little. Constant!"

The door opened immediately, and the *valet de chambre* entered.

"Ah, I am afraid you have had a bad night of it," said the emperor, kindly.

"Sire, your majesty has again been awake all the night long, and—"

"And consequently," said Napoleon, interrupting him—"consequently you have been awake, too. Well, console yourself; we shall soon have more quiet nights; console yourself, and do not report me to the Empress Josephine when we have returned to Paris. My dear Josephine hates nothing so much as sleepless nights."

[*] Napoleon's own words.—Vide "Mémoires du Duc de Rovigo," vol. ii., p. 171.

"Sire, the empress is right; she ought to hate them," said Constant, respectfully. "Your majesty, taking no rest whatever in the daytime, needs repose at least in the night. Your majesty sleeps too little."

"By doing so I am better off than the sluggards, inasmuch as my life does not only consist of days, but also of nights," replied Napoleon, good-humoredly. "I shall have lived eighty years then in the space of forty. But be quiet, Constant, I will now comply with your wishes and sleep."

Constant hastened to open the door leading to the bedroom. "Oh, no," said the emperor, "if I say I will sleep, I do not mean that I will go to bed. Beds are, on the whole, only good for old women and gouty old men. When I was second lieutenant, I once made the experiment not to go to bed for six months, but to sleep on the floor or on a chair, and it agreed very well with me. Give me the handkerchief for my head, and my coat, Constant."

Constant hurried with a sigh to the bedroom in order to fetch the articles Napoleon had ordered; and while he was wrapping the silken handkerchief around the emperor's head, and assisted him in putting on his gray, well-lined, and comfortable cloth-coat instead of the uniform, the emperor softly whistled and hummed an air.

He then snugly stretched himself in his arm-chair, and kindly nodding to Constant, he said: "As soon as General Savary has returned, let him come in."

Constant softly glided into the anteroom. He met there some of his acquaintances.

"I have important news for you, gentlemen," he said. "We shall fight a battle in two or three days."

"Did the emperor tell you so?"

"No, he is not in the habit of speaking of such things. But during the night-toilet he whistled Marlborough's air, and he does so only when there is to be a battle." [*]

CHAPTER XLVIII.

BEFORE THE BATTLE.

FIVE hours later General Savary reëntered the emperor's cabinet; he was still lying on his arm-chair and sleeping; but when the general accosted him in a low voice, Napoleon opened his eyes

[*] "Mémoires de Constant," vol. iv., p. 109.

and asked, eagerly: " Well, did you see the czar ? "

" Yes, sire, I saw him and conversed with him."

" Ah," exclaimed Napoleon, quickly, " tell me all about it; do not omit any thing. How did he look when he read my letter ? "

" Sire, when I had delivered your letter to the Emperor Alexander, he went with it into an adjoining room, from which he returned only half an hour later, with a reply in his hand."

" Give me the letter, Savary ! "

" Sire, here it is."

Napoleon took it hastily; but when he fixed his eyes on the address, he frowned.

" Ah, this emperor 'by the grace of God' believes he need not address me with the title conferred upon me by the French nation," he said, hastily. " He does not write to the Emperor of the French, but ' to the chief of the French government.' * Did you read the address, Savary ? "

" The Emperor Alexander called my attention to it himself, sire. I remember his words distinctly. They were as follows: ' The address does not contain the title which your chief has assumed since then. I do not set any great value on such trifles ; but it is a rule of etiquette, and I shall alter it with pleasure as soon as he has given me an opportunity for doing so.' " †

" And what did you reply to him ? "

" Sire," I replied, " your majesty is right. This can only be a rule of etiquette, and the emperor will not judge it in any other way. When he was general-in-chief of the Italian army he already gave orders and prescribed laws to more than one king ; contented with the homage of the French, he only deems it a satisfaction for them to be recognized." ‡

" Your reply was fitting and to the point," said Napoleon, with a pleasant nod, while he opened the emperor's letter and glanced over it. " Phrases, empty words," he then exclaimed, throwing the letter contemptuously on the table. " Talleyrand was right when he said language was given to us for the purpose of concealing our thoughts. Those men use it for that purpose."

" Sire, the emperor did not conceal his thoughts during our interview," replied the general. " I conversed with him long and freely, and I may say that he uttered his opinions very frankly. The Emperor Alexander said: ' Peace was only to be thought of if your majesty should stipulate

reasonable terms which would not hurt anybody's feelings, and which would not be calculated to weaken the power and importance of the other princes and to increase that of France. France was a power already large enough ; she needed no aggrandizement, and the other powers could not tolerate such a one.' "

" Ah, I shall teach them to tolerate it nevertheless ; I shall prove to all of them that France is at the head of all monarchies, and compel them to recognize the Emperor of France with bowed heads ! "

He paced the room hastily with angry eyes and panting breast. His steps, however, became gradually more quiet, and the furrows disappeared from his forehead.

" I need two days more," he muttered to himself—" two days, and I must have them, Savary." He then said aloud, turning to the general : " Did you make no further observations ? Did you not notice the spirit animating the Russian camp ? "

" Sire, the whole youth of the highest Russian nobility were at the emperor's headquarters, and I conversed with many of them; I heard and observed a great many things."

" Well, and what do they think of us ? "

Savary smiled. " Sire," he said, " those young men did not breathe any thing but war and victory, and they seemed to believe that your majesty wished to avoid active hostilities since the Russians had formed a junction with the Austrians."

" Ah, did they seem to believe that ? " exclaimed Napoleon, joyfully. " Well, we will try to strengthen their belief. General, take a bugler along and return to the headquarters of the emperor. Tell him that I propose to him an interview for to-morrow in the open field between the two armies, the time and hour to be designated by himself, and a cessation of hostilities to take place for the next twenty-four hours. Go ! "

" I believe," said the emperor, when he was alone again, " I believe I have gained my second day also, and I only want a third one, in order to be able to vanquish all my enemies. Those arrogant Russians believe, then, that I wish to avoid a battle, and to remain in my present position? I will try to strengthen this opinion of theirs ; earthworks shall be thrown up, and the batteries shall be fortified. Every thing must have the appearance of anxiety and timidity."

And Napoleon summoned his generals and gave them aloud these new orders, but, in a whisper, he instructed them to begin the retrograde movement, and to let the troops occupy the positions he had selected for them on the extensive ground he had reconnoitred yesterday.

* Historical.—Vide " Mémoires du Duc de Rovigo," vol. ll., p. 187.

† Alexander's own words.—Vide " Mémoires du Duc de Rovigo," vol. ll., p. 187.

‡ Ibid.

And the night expired, and half the next day, before General Savary returned from his mission. In the mean time Napoleon had changed his quarters. He had repaired to the camp of his army, and a bundle of straw was now his only couch. He had impatiently looked for Savary, and went to meet him with hasty steps.

"Why so late?" he asked.

"Sire, it was almost impossible for me to reach the emperor. He had left Olmütz. All the night long I was conducted from bivouac to bivouac, in order to find Prince Bagration, who could alone take me to the emperor."

"And you have seen the emperor?" asked Napoleon, impatiently.

"Yes, sire, after overcoming many obstacles and difficulties, I succeeded in penetrating to the emperor. I submitted your majesty's proposition to him. The emperor replied: 'It would afford him the greatest pleasure to see and make the acquaintance of your majesty, but time was too short for it now. Moreover, before entering into such negotiations, he would have to consult the Emperor of Austria, and learn your majesty's views, so as to be able to see whether such an interview would be advisable or not. Hence, he would send one of his confidential advisers with me and intrust him with a mission to your majesty. The reply which he would bring to him from your majesty would decide the matter.'"

"Ah, and the third day will pass in this manner!" exclaimed Napoleon, joyfully. "Where is the emperor's envoy? and who is it?"

"Sire, the emperor sent his first aide-de-camp, Prince Dolgorouki, with me."

"Where is he?"

"Sire, I left him with the grand-guard; he is waiting there for your majesty's orders."

Napoleon rose hastily from the straw, on which he had been sitting with folded arms.

"My horse!" he shouted; and when Roustan had brought his charger, he vaulted into the saddle and galloped so rapidly forward that his suite were scarcely able to overtake him. On arriving close to the grand-guard, he halted and alighted, and while he sent off Savary to conduct Prince Dolgorouki to him, he muttered: "Only a third day!"

He received the prince with the calmness and composure of a proud *imperator*, of a chieftain accustomed to victory. A wave of his hand caused his suite to stand back; and when the officers had withdrawn, he commenced conversing with Prince Dolgorouki, while walking up and down with him.

The emperor suddenly approached the members of his suite, and they heard him say in a loud and angry voice:

"If that is all you wish to say to me, hasten to inform your emperor that I had not thought at all of such conditions when I applied for an interview with him; I should only have shown him my army; and, as to the conditions, relied on his honesty. He wishes a battle; very well, let us fight. I wash my hands of it!" *

He turned his back to Prince Dolgorouki with a slight wave of his hand; and fixing his flaming eagle-eyes on his generals, he said, shrugging his shoulders:

"Russia will make peace if France will give up Belgium, and, first of all things, cede the crown of Italy to the King of Sardinia. Oh, those men must be crazy! They want me to evacuate Italy, and they will find out soon that they cannot even get me out of Vienna. What would have been their terms, and what would they have made of France, if they had beaten? Well, let things turn out as it may, please God, but in less than forty-eight hours I will pay them well for their arrogance!" †

And instead of mounting again on horseback, he continued walking on the highway, muttering to himself, and with his riding-whip knocking off the small grass-blades he met on the road. He had now reached the first infantry post of his army. The sentinel was an old soldier, who was unconcernedly filling his pipe while holding his musket between his legs.

The gloomy eyes of the emperor turned to him, and pointing over to the position of the enemy, he said, angrily: "Those arrogant fellows believe they can swallow us without further ceremony!"

The old soldier looked smilingly at the emperor with his shrewd eyes, and quietly continued filling his pipe with the small finger of his right hand.

"Oh, oh, they cannot swallow us so fast! We shall lie down, your majesty!—"

The emperor laughed loudly, and his face became radiant. "Yes," he said, "you are right, we will lie down as soon as they try to swallow us; and then we will choke them!"

He nodded to the soldier, and vaulting into the saddle he returned to headquarters. Night was coming on already, and looking up to the moonlighted sky, the emperor murmured: "Only one more day, and then I shall defeat them!"

And fate gave him that day. It is true, the

---

* Napoleon's own words.—Vide "Mémoires du Duc de Rovigo," vol. ii., p. 196.

† Ibid., p. 198.

combined forces of the Austrians and Russians approached his positions, but did not attack them, They drew up in a long line directly in front of the French camp, and so close to it that their movements could be plainly seen.

Napoleon was on horseback all day; he inspected every regiment of his whole army; his eyes beamed with enthusiasm, and a wondrous smile played on his lips.

The Bohemian corps had arrived; the delay of three days had borne fruits; he now felt strong enough to defeat his enemies.

He spoke in a merry tone to the soldiers here and there, and they replied to him with enthusiastic shouts. He inspected the artillery parks and light batteries with searching glances, and then gave the necessary instructions to the officers and gunners.

Only after inspecting every thing in person, after visiting the ambulances and wagons for the wounded, he returned to his bivouac in order to take a frugal meal. He then summoned all his marshals and generals, and spoke to them about every thing they would have to do on the following day, and about what the enemy might do. To each of them he gave his instructions and assigned his position; and already on the evening of this day he issued to his soldiers a proclamation, admonishing them to perform deeds of heroism on the following day.

"Soldiers," he said to them in this proclamation, "the Russian army appears before you to avenge the Austrian defeat of Ulm. They are the same battalions that you beat at Holabrünn, and that you have since been constantly pursuing to this spot.

"The positions which we occupy are formidable; and while they are marching to turn my right, they will present their flank to me.

"Soldiers, I shall myself direct your battalions. I shall keep out of the fire, if, with your usual bravery, you throw disorder and confusion into the enemy's ranks. But, if the victory should be for a moment uncertain, you will see your emperor the foremost to expose himself to danger. For victory must not hang doubtful on this day, most particularly, when the honor of the French infantry, which so deeply concerns the honor of the whole nation, is at stake.

"Let not the ranks be thinned upon pretext of carrying away the wounded; and let every one be thoroughly impressed with this thought, that it behooves us to conquer these hirelings of England, who are animated with such bitter hatred against our nation.

"This victory will put an end to the campaign, and we shall then be able to return to our winter quarters, where we shall be joined by the new armies which are forming in France, and then the peace which I shall make will be worthy of my people, of you, and of myself."

The soldiers received this proclamation with jubilant shouts; and when Napoleon, after night had set in, rode once more through the camp, the first soldiers who perceived him, eager to light him on his way, picked up the straw of their bivouac and made it into torches, which they placed blazing on the tops of their muskets. In a few minutes this example was followed by the whole army, and along the vast front of the French position was displayed this singular illumination. The soldiers accompanied the steps of Napoleon with shouts of "Vive l'Empereur!" promising to prove on the morrow that they were worthy of him and of themselves. Enthusiasm pervaded all the ranks. They went as men ought to go into danger, with hearts full of content and confidence.

Napoleon retired, to oblige his soldiers, to take some rest. With a feeling of the most unbounded satisfaction, he threw himself on the straw in his tent, and smilingly rejecting the services of his valets de chambre, Roustan and Constant, who implored him to permit them to wrap him in warmer clothes, he said:

"Kindle a good fire and let me sleep as a soldier who has a hot day before him on the morrow ought to sleep."

He pressed his head into the straw and fell asleep; and he was still sleeping when the marshals and generals at daybreak came to the emperor's tent to awaken him as he had ordered them to do.

They surrounded the open tent in respectful silence and looked at the chieftain who was to fight a great battle to-day, and who was now lying on the straw with a calm, serene face, and with the gentle slumber of a child.

But they durst not let him sleep any longer, for the emperor, who had regulated every movement of the present day by the hour and minute, would have been very angry if any delay had occurred.

General Savary, therefore, approached the sleeping emperor and bent over him. Then his loud and earnest voice was heard to say: "Sire, the fixed hour has come."

Napoleon opened his eyes and jumped up. Sleep had suddenly fallen from him like a thin veil; as soon as he rose to his feet he was once more the great emperor and general. He cast a long, searching look on the gray, moist, and wintry horizon, and the dense mist which shrouded

every thing at a distance of ten paces caused his
eyes to sparkle with delight.

"That mist is an excellent ally of ours, for it
will conceal our movements from the enemy. Issue your orders, gentlemen; let the whole army
take up arms as silently as possible."

The emperor then mounted on horseback and
rode through the camp to see the infantry and
cavalry form in column.

It was now seven o'clock in the morning. The
mist began to rise; the first feeble rays of the
December sun pierced it and commenced gradually
illuminating the landscape.

The emperor placed himself on a small knoll,
where his eye embraced the whole field of battle;
his marshals were on horseback at his side, anxiously awaiting his order to commence the combat.

Profound silence reigned everywhere; but suddenly it was interrupted by a very brisk fire of
artillery and musketry. A radiant flash seemed
to light up the emperor's face, and proudly raising
his head, he said, in an imperious voice:

"To your posts, gentlemen; the battle is about
to commence!" *

CHAPTER XLIX.

"GOTT ERHALTE FRANZ DEN KAISER!"

FOR three days the utmost uneasiness and commotion had reigned in Vienna. Nobody wanted
to stay at home. Everybody hastened into the
street, as if he hoped there to hear at an earlier
moment the great news which the people were
looking for, and as if the fresh air which had carried to them three days ago the thundering echoes
of the cannon, would waft to them to-day the tidings of the brilliant victory supposed to be
achieved by the Emperors Francis and Alexander.

But these victorious tidings did not come; the
roar of the cannon had a quicker tongue than the
courier who was to bring the news of the victory.
He did not come, and yet the good people of
Vienna were waiting for him with impatience and,
at the same time, with proud and joyful confidence.
It is true no one was able to state positively
where the battle had been fought, but the people
were able to calculate the spot where the great
struggle had probably taken place, for they knew
that the allies had occupied the immediate envi-
rons of Olmütz, and then advanced toward Brünn

* The battle of Austerlitz, December 2, 1805.

and Austerlitz, where the French army had established itself. They calculated the time which the
courier would consume in order to reach Vienna
from the battle-field, and the obstacles and delays
that might have possibly impeded his progress
were taken into consideration. But no one felt
anxious at his prolonged absence; no one doubted
that the allies had obtained a great victory.

For their two armies were by far superior to
the French army, and Napoleon himself had not
hoped for a victory this time; he had fallen back
with his army because he wished to avoid a battle
with the superior forces of the enemy; he had
even gone so far in his despondency as to write
to the Emperor of Russia and to sue for peace.

How could people think, therefore, that Napoleon had won the battle, the thunders of which
had filled the Viennese three days ago with the
utmost exultation?

No, fate had at length stopped the onward career of the conqueror, and it was on Austrian soil
that his eagles were to be struck down and his
laurels to wither.

Nobody doubted it; the joyful anticipation of
a great victory animated every heart and beamed
from every eye. They longed for the arrival of
the courier, and were overjoyed to celebrate at
length a triumph over those supercilious French,
who had latterly humiliated and angered the poor
people of Vienna on so many occasions.

It is true the French embassy had not yet left
Vienna. But that was only a symptom that it
had not yet been reached by a courier from the
battle-field; else it would have fled from Vienna
in the utmost haste.

But the people did not wish to permit the overbearing French to depart from their city in so
quiet and unpretending a manner; they wanted to
accompany them at least with loud jeers, with
scornful shouts and curses.

Thousands, therefore, surrounded the house of
the French embassy, where Talleyrand, Napoleon's
minister of foreign affairs, had been staying for
some days, and no longer did they swallow their
wrath and hatred, but they gave vent to it loudly;
no longer did they threaten only with their
glances, but also with their fists, which they raised
menacingly toward the windows of the French
minister.

And while thousands had gathered around the
embassy building, other thousands strolled out
toward Möhringen, and stared breathlessly down
the road, hoping to behold the longed-for messenger who would announce to them at length the
great victory that had been won.

All at once something in the distance commenced stirring on the road; at times glittering objects, resembling twinkling stars, were to be seen, and then motley colors were discerned; it came nearer and nearer. No doubt it must be a column of soldiers; perhaps some of the heroic regiments which had defeated the French army were already on their homeward march.

Ah, the proud and sanguine people of Vienna regretted now exceedingly that there were no longer any French regiments in the capital, and that they had left their city only a week ago and rejoined Napoleon's army. Now there would have been an opportunity for them to take revenge for the hospitality which they had been compelled for the last two weeks to extend to the French. Now they would have chased the French soldiers in the most ignominious manner through the same streets which they had marched hitherto with so proud and confident a step.

The soldiers drew nearer and nearer; the people hastened to meet them like a huge boa constrictor with thousands and thousands of movable rings, and thousands and thousands of flashing eyes.

But all at once these eyes became fixed and dismayed; the joyful hum, which hitherto had filled the air as though it were a vast multitude of gnats playing in the sun, died away.

Those were not the uniforms of the Austrians, nor of the Russians either! Those were the odious colors of France. The soldiers marching toward Vienna were French regiments.

And couriers appeared too, the longed-for couriers! But they were no Austrian couriers; the tri-colored sash was wrapped around their waists, they did not greet the people with German words and with fraternal German salutations. They galloped past them and shouted: "Victoire! victoire! Vive l'Empereur Napoléon!"

The people were thunderstruck; they did not stir, but stared wildly and pale with horror at the regiments that now approached to the jubilant music of their bands, and treated the Viennese to the notes of the Marseillaise and the air of Va-t-en-guerrier; they stared at the sullen, ragged men who marched in the midst of the soldiers, like the Roman slaves before the car of the Triumphator. These poor, pale men wore no French uniforms, and the tri-colored sash was not wrapped around their waists, nor did they bear arms; their hands were empty, and their eyes were fixed on the ground. They were prisoners, prisoners of the French, and they wore Russian uniforms.

The people saw it with dismay. The good Viennese had suddenly been hurled from their proud hopes of victory into an abyss of despair,

and they were stunned by the sudden fall, and unable to speak and to collect their thoughts. They stood on the road, pale and breathless, and witnessed the spectacle of the return of the victorious columns, with silent despondency.

All at once the brilliant column, which had filed through the ranks of the people, halted, and the band ceased playing. An officer galloped up and exchanged a few words with the colonel in command. The colonel made a sign and uttered a few hurried words, whereupon four soldiers stepped from the ranks, and forcing a passage through the staring crowd, walked directly toward a small house situated solitary and alone on the road, in the middle of a garden.

Every inhabitant of Vienna knew this house and the man living in it, for it was the residence of Joseph Haydn.

When the four soldiers approached the door of the popular and well-known maestro, the people seemed to awake from their stupefaction, a unanimous cry of rage and horror resounded, and thousands and thousands of voices shouted and screamed, "Father Haydn! They want to arrest Father Haydn!"

But, no. The four soldiers stopped at the door, and remained there as a guard of honor.

And the band of the next regiment, which had just come up, halted on the road too, and, in stirring notes, the French musicians began to play a melody which was well known to everybody, the melody of the great hymn from the "Creation," "In verdure clad." *

It sounded to the poor Viennese like a cruel mockery to hear a band of the victorious French army play this melody composed by a German maestro, and tears of heart-felt shame, of inward rage, filled many an eye which had never wept before, and a bitter pang seized every breast.

The French musicians had not yet finished the tune, when a window in the upper story of the house was opened, and Joseph Haydn's venerable white-haired head appeared. His cheeks were pale, and his lips trembled, for his footman, who had just returned home, had brought him the news that the French had been victorious again, and that Napoleon had defeated the two emperors at Austerlitz.

Joseph Haydn, the old man, was pale and trembling, but Joseph Haydn, the genius, was courageous, joyful, and defiant, and he was filled with noble anger when he heard that the trumpeters of the French conqueror dared to play his German music.

---

* Historical.

This anger of the eternally-young and eternally-bold genius now burst forth from Haydn's eyes, and restored to his whole bearing the vigor and elasticity of youth.

Leaning far out of the window, he beckoned the people with both arms, while they were looking up to him and waving their hats to salute him.

"Sing, people of Vienna!" he shouted, "oh, sing our favorite hymn!"

The music had just ceased, and Joseph Haydn now commenced singing in a loud, ringing voice, "*Gott erhalte Franz den Kaiser, unsern guten Kaiser Franz!*"

And thousands of voices sang and shouted all at once, "*Gott erhalte Franz den Kaiser, unsern guten Kaiser Franz!*"

Joseph Haydn stood at the window, and moved his arm as though he were standing before his orchestra and leading his choir.

The people sang their favorite hymn louder and more jubilantly, and to the notes of this prayer of a whole people, of this jubilant hymn, by which the Viennese honored their unfortunate, vanquished emperor in the face of the conquering army, the French marched up the road toward the interior of the city.

Joseph Haydn was still at the window; he led the choir no longer; he sang no more. He had folded his hands and listened to the majestic anthem of the people, and the tears, filling his eyes, glistened like diamonds.

The people continued shouting and singing, in spite of the French, the hymn of "*Gott erhalte Franz den Kaiser, wis ern guten Kaiser Franz!*"

And the victorious French marched silently through the opened ranks of the people.

CHAPTER L.

PATRIOTISM.

PRINCESS MARIANNE von Eibenberg had just returned from a party which the British ambassador, Lord Paget, had given in her honor, and which was to celebrate at the same time the victory which the two emperors, the allies of England, were firmly believed to have achieved over the usurper.

Marianne Eibenberg, therefore, wore a brilliant toilet. She was adorned with diamonds and costly jewelry, and looked as beautiful and proud as a queen. She had now reached the acme of her career. She was still lovely, and besides she had become, as it were, the protectress of the most refined society of Vienna and the centre of the intellectual as well as aristocratic circles. She had accomplished her purpose. Marianne Meier, the Jewess, was now a noble lady, to whom everybody was paying deference; and Marianne, princess von Eibenberg, felt so much at home in her new position, that she had herself almost forgotten who and what she had been in former times. Only sometimes she remembered it, only when such recollections secured a triumph to her, and when she met with persons who had formerly, at the best, tolerated her with proud disdain in good society, and who did not deem it now beneath their dignity to solicit an invitation to her reception-room as a favor.

This reception-room was now the only resort of good society in Vienna, the only place where people were sure to meet always amidst the troubles and convulsions of the times with the most refined and patriotic men, and where they might rely on never finding any persons of doubtful patriotism, much less any French.

But, it is true, since the imperial family had fled from Vienna, the reception-room of the Princess von Eibenberg had gradually become deserted, for the members of the aristocracy had retired to their estates and castles, and the ministers and high functionaries had accompanied the emperor and the imperial court to Olmütz. The ambassadors, too, were about to repair thither; hence, the party given by the British minister, Lord Paget, to his adored friend the Princess von Eibenberg, was to celebrate not only the supposed victory, but also his departure from the capital.

Marianne, as we stated already, had just returned from this party. With rapid steps, absorbed in profound reflections, she was pacing her boudoir, muttering, now and then, inaudible words, and from time to time heaving deep sighs as if feeling violent pain. When she walked past the large Venetian mirror, she stopped and contemplated the brilliant and imposing form it reflected.

"It is true," she said, mournfully, "the Princess von Eibenberg is a beautiful and charming lady; she has very fine diamonds and a very aristocratic title; she is living in grand style; she has very many admirers; she is adored and beloved on account of her enthusiastic patriotism; she has got whatever is able to beautify and adorn life, and yet I see a cloud on this forehead which artists compare with that of the Ludovisian Juno, and diplomatists with that of Pallas Athene. What does this cloud mean? Reply to this question, you, whom I see there in the mirror; reply to it, proud woman with the precious diadem, how does it come that you look so sad, although the world says that you are happy and highly honored?"

She paused, and looked almost expectantly at her own image in the looking-glass. The clock commenced all at once striking twelve.

"Midnight!" whispered Marianne; "midnight, the hour in which ghosts walk! I will also call up a ghost," she said, after a short pause; "I will call it up and compel it to reply to me."

And raising her arm toward the glittering, radiant image in the looking-glass, she said in a loud and solemn voice: "Marianne Meier, rise from your grave and come hither to reply to my questions! Marianne Meier, rise and walk; it is the Princess von Eibenberg who is calling you! Ah, I see you—it is you, Marianne; you are looking at me with the melancholy eyes of those days when you had to bear so much contumely and disgrace, and when you were sitting mournfully by the rivers of Babylon and weeping. Yes, I recognize you; you still wear the features of your ancestors of the tribe of Levi; men pretend not to notice them any longer, but I see them. Marianne Meier, now listen to what I am going to tell you, and reply to me: tell me what is the matter with the Princess von Eibenberg? What is the reason she is not happy? Look around in her house, Marianne Meier; you will behold there such opulence and magnificence as you never knew in the days of your childhood. Look at her gilt furniture, her carpets and lustres; look at the beautiful paintings on the walls, and at the splendid solid plate in her chests. Look at her velvet and silk dresses, adorned with gold and silver embroidery; look at her diamonds, her other precious stones and jewelry. Do you know still, Marianne Meier, how often, in the days of your childhood and early youth, you have longed, with scalding tears, for all those things? Do you know still, Marianne Meier, how often you have wrung your hands and wailed, 'Would to God I were rich! For he who is rich is happy!' The Princess von Eibenberg is rich, Marianne Meier; why, then, is she not happy? If it had been predicted to you at that time, when you were only sighing for wealth, Marianne Meier, that you would be a princess one day, and carry your Jewish head proudly erect in the most aristocratic society, would you not have believed that this was the acme of happiness, and that your boldest wishes had been fulfilled? Ah, Marianne Meier, I have reached this acme, and yet it seems to me that I am much more remote from happiness than you ever were at that time! You had then some-

thing to struggle for; you had a great aim. But what have I got? I have reached my aim, and there is nothing for me to accomplish and to struggle for! That is the secret of my melancholy; I have nothing to struggle for. I have reached the acme of my prosperity, and every step I advance is a step down-hill toward the grave, and when the grave closes over me nothing will remain of me, and my name will be forgotten, while the name of the hateful usurper will resound through all ages like a golden harp! Oh, a little glory, a little immortality on earth; that, Marianne Meier, is what the ambitious heart of the Princess von Eibenberg is longing for; that is the object for which she would willingly sacrifice years of her life. Life is now so boundlessly tedious and empty; it is nothing but a glittering phrase; nothing but a smiling and gorgeous but dull repetition of the same thing! But, hark! What is that?" She suddenly interrupted herself. "It seemed to me as if I heard steps in the small corridor. Yes, I was not mistaken. Somebody is at the door. Oh, it is he, then; it is Gentz."

She rushed toward the door, and opening it hastily, she said, "Is it you, my beloved friend?"

"If you apply this epithet to me, Marianne, yes, it is I," replied Gentz, entering the room.

"And to whom else should I apply it, Frederick?" she asked, reproachfully. "Who but you has got a key to my house and to this door? Who but you is allowed to enter my house and my room at any hour of the day or night?"

"Perhaps Lord Paget, my powerful and fine-looking rival," said Gentz, carelessly, and without the least shade of bitterness, while he sat down on the sofa with evident symptoms of weariness and exhaustion.

"Are you jealous of Lord Paget?" she asked, taking a seat by his side, and placing her hand, sparkling with diamond-rings, on his shoulder. "Remember, my friend, that it was solely in obedience to your advice that I did not reject the attentions of the dear lord and entered into this political liaison."

"I know, I know," said Gentz, deprecatingly; "nor have I come to quarrel with you about such trifles. I have not come as a jealous lover who wishes to upbraid his beloved with the attentions she has shown to other men, but as a poor, desponding man who appears before his friend to pour his lamentations, his despair into her bosom, and to ask her for a little sympathy with his rage and grief."

"My friend, what has occurred?" asked Marianne, in dismay. "Where have you been during the week, since I have not seen you? You took sure of me in a hurried note, stating that you would set out on an important journey, although you did not tell me whither you were going. Where have you been, Frederick?"

"I was in Olmütz with the emperor and with the ministers," sighed Gentz. "I hoped to promote there the triumph of the good cause and of Germany: I hoped to witness a brilliant victory, and now—"

"And now?" asked Marianne, breathlessly, when Gentz paused.

"Now I have witnessed a disgraceful defeat," groaned Gentz.

Marianne uttered a cry, and her eyes flashed angrily. "He has conquered again?" she asked, in a husky voice.

"He has conquered, and we have been beaten," exclaimed Gentz, in a loud and bitter tone. "The last hope of Germany, nay, of Europe, is gone; the Russians were defeated with us in a terrible battle. The disaster is an irretrievable one, all the armies of Prussia being unable to restore the lost prestige of the coalition!* The Russians have already retreated, and the Emperor Alexander has set out to-night in order to return to his dominions."

"And he," muttered Marianne, "he is celebrating another triumph over us! He is marching onward proudly and victoriously, while we are lying, crushed and humiliated, in the dust of degradation. Is it Thy will that it should be so, God in heaven?" she asked, turning her eyes upward with an angry glance. "Hast Thou no thunderbolt for this Titan who is rebelling against the laws of the world? Wilt Thou permit this upstart to render all countries unhappy, and to enslave all nations?"

"Yes, God permits him to do so," exclaimed Gentz, laughing scornfully. "God has destined him to be a scourge to chastise us for our own impotence. We do not succumb owing to his greatness, but owing to our weakness. The Austrian cabinet is responsible for our misfortunes! I have long since perceived the utter lack of ability, the contemptible character, nay, the infamy of this cabinet; in former times I used to denounce our Austrian cabinet to the other cabinets of Europe as the real source of the calamities of our period, and to unveil to them the whole terrible truth. Oh, if they had heeded my warnings, when I wrote last June, and as late as in the beginning of August, to many prominent men, 'Beware with whom you enter into a coalition! Do not be deceived by an illusory semblance of im-

provement. They are the same as ever! With them no great undertaking, either in the cabinet or in the field, will succeed; their rejection is the *conditio sine qua non* of the preservation of Europe. It was all in vain! Finally, I was left alone with my warnings; every one deserted me!" *

"I did not desert you, Frederick," said Marianne, reproachfully, "and I compelled Lord Paget, too, to support your views. Thanks to our united efforts, that stupid Count Colloredo, at least, was forced to withdraw from the cabinet."

"That is a consolation, but no hope," said Gentz. "So long as the other ministers will retain their positions, every thing will be in vain. Every thing is so diseased and rotten that, unless the whole be thrown away, there is no reasonable hope left. I hoped the Emperor of Russia would boldly denounce the incapacity of the cabinet, and by his powerful influence succeed in cleansing our Augean stable, but he is too gentle for such an undertaking, and has no man of irresistible power and energy at his side. He beheld our misery; he greatly deplored it, but refused to meddle with the domestic affairs of Austria. Thus every thing was lost, and he was himself disgracefully defeated."

"And now we have submitted altogether?" asked Marianne. "We have made peace with the usurper?"

"We have *begged* him to make peace with us, you mean, and he will dictate the terms in which we shall have to acquiesce. Oh, Marianne, when I think of the events of the last few days, I am seized with rage and grief, and hardly know how I shall be able to live henceforward. Just listen *how* we have begged for peace! Yesterday, two days after the battle, the Emperor Francis sent Prince John of Lichtenstein to Napoleon, who had established his headquarters at Austerlitz, in a mansion belonging to the Kaunitz family, to express to the conqueror his wish to have an interview with him at the advanced posts. Napoleon granted it to him, and the Emperor of Germany went to his conqueror to beg for peace. He was accompanied by none but Lamberti to the meeting, which was to take place in the open field. Bonaparte received him, surrounded by all his generals, chamberlains, and masters of ceremonies, and with the whole pomp of his imperial dignity." †

"Oh, what a terrible disgrace and humilia-

---

* Gentz's own words.—Vide Gentz's "Correspondence with Johannes von Müller," p. 150.

* Gentz's "Correspondence," etc., p. 144.

† This account of the interview of the two emperors may be found verbatim in a letter from Gentz to Johannes von Müller. Vide "Correspondence," etc., p. 154.

tion!" exclaimed Marianne, bursting into tears, while she tore the diadem with a wild gesture from her hair and hurled it to the floor. "Who dares to adorn himself after events so utterly ignominious have occurred?" she ejaculated—"who dares to carry his head erect after Germany has been thus trampled under foot! The Emperor of Germany has begged the invader to make peace; he has humbly solicited it like a beggar asking alms! And has the conqueror graciously granted his request? Oh, tell me every thing, Frederick! What took place at that interview? What did they say to each other?"

"I can tell you but little about it," said Gentz, shrugging his shoulders, "for the two emperors conversed without witnesses. Bonaparte left his suite at the bivouac fire kindled by his soldiers, and Lamberti also went thither. The two emperors then embraced each other like two friends who had not met for years." *

"And the Emperor Francis had not sufficient strength to strangle the fiend with his arms?" asked Marianne, trembling with wrath and grief.

"He had neither the strength nor the inclination, I suppose," said Gentz, shrugging his shoulders. "When Napoleon released the unfortunate Emperor Francis from his arms, he pointed with a proud glance toward heaven and said: 'Such are the palaces which your majesty has obliged me to inhabit for these three months.'

"'The abode in them,'" replied the Austrian monarch, 'makes you so thriving that you have no right to be angry with me for it.'

"'I only ask your majesty,' said Napoleon, hastily, 'not to renew the war against France.'

"'I pledge you my word as a man and a sovereign that I shall do so no more,' replied Francis, loudly and unhesitatingly. The conversation then was continued in a lower tone, and neither Lamberti nor the French marshals were able to understand another word." †

"The interview lasted two hours, and then the two emperors parted with reiterated demonstrations of cordiality. The Emperor Francis returned silently, and absorbed in his reflections to his headquarters at Austerlitz. Hitherto he had not uttered a word; but when he saw the Prince von Lichtenstein, he beckoned him to approach, and said to him in a low voice, and with suppressed anger, 'Now that I have seen him, he is more intolerable to me than ever.' ‡ That was the only utterance he gave to his rage; as for the rest, he seemed contented with the terms he obtained."

"And were the terms honorable?" asked Marianne.

"Honorable!" said Gentz, shrugging his shoulders. "Napoleon demanded, above all, that the Russian army should retire speedily from the Austrian territories, and the emperor promised this to him. Hence, the Emperor Alexander has departed; the Russian army is retreating; one part of it is going to Prussia, while the other is returning to Poland. The cabinet of Vienna, therefore, is free; that is to say, it is left to its own peculiar infamy without any bounds whatever, and thus peace will be made soon enough. Those contemptible men will submit to any thing, provided he gives up Vienna. Finance-minister Fichy said to me in Olmütz yesterday, 'Peace will be cheap, if we have merely to cede the Tyrol, Venice, and a portion of Upper Austria, and we should be content with such terms.' Ah, if they could only be got rid of, what a splendid thing the fall of the monarchy would be! But to lose the provinces, honor, Germany, Europe, and to keep Fichy, Ungart, Cobenzl, Collenbach, Lamberti, Dietrichstein—no satisfaction, no revenge—not a single one of the dogs hung or quartered,—it is impossible to digest that!" *   *.

"It is true," said Marianne, musingly, and in a low voice, "this is a boundless disgrace; and if men will submit to it, and bow their heads, it is time for women to raise theirs, and to become lionesses in order to tear the enemy opposing them! And what do you intend doing now, my friend?" she then asked aloud, forcibly dispelling her painful emotions. "What are your prospects? What plan of battle will you draw up for us?"

"I have no prospects at all, and I have given up drawing plans of battle," said Gentz, sighing. "After exhausting my last strength for five days during my sojourn in Olmütz, I am done with every thing, and I have withdrawn weary and satiated ad nauseam. Our ministers have gone to Presburg, for the purpose of negotiating there with the plenipotentiaries of Bonaparte about the terms of peace."

"And where is he at present—where is the proud triumphator?" asked Marianne, hastily.

"He left Austerlitz to-night, and will reside again at Schönbrunn until peace has been concluded."

"Ah, in Schönbrunn!" said Marianne, "that is to say, here in Vienna. And you, Frederick, will you remain here, too?"

"After making peace, they will banish me, of

---

* Historical.

† "Mémoires du Duc de Rovigo," vol. ii., p. 215.

‡ Hausser's "History of Germany," l. ii., p. 090.

* Gentz's own words.—Vide his "Correspondence with Johannes von Müller," p. 155.

course, from Vienna; for Bonaparte knows my hatred against him, and moreover, he knows it to be implacable. Hence, I prefer going voluntarily into exile, and shall repair to Breslau, where I shall find plenty of friends and acquaintances. There I will live, amuse myself, be a man like all of them, that is to say, gratify nothing but my egotism, and take rest after so many annoyances and struggles."

"That cannot be true—that cannot be possible!" exclaimed Marianne, ardently. "A patriot, a man like you, does not repose and amuse himself, while his country is plunged into misery and disgrace. I repeat to you what Arnauld said to his friend Nicole, when the latter, tired of the struggle for Jansenism, declared to him that he would retire and repose: '*Vous reposer! Eh! n'avez-vous pas pour vous reposer l'éternité toute entière?*' If those men were filled with so undying an enthusiasm for an insipid quarrel about mere sophistries, how could you take rest, since eternity itself, whether it be repose or motion, offers nothing more sublime than a struggle for the liberty and dignity of the world?"

"God bless you for these words, Marianne!" exclaimed Gentz, enthusiastically, while he embraced his friend passionately, and imprinted a glowing kiss on her forehead. "Oh, Marianne, I only wished to try you; I wanted to see whether, with the ardor of your love for me, the ardor of the holy cause represented by me, had also left you; I only wanted to know whether, now that you love me no longer—"

"And how can you say that I love you no longer?" she interrupted him. "Have I deserved so bitter a reproach?"

"It is no reproach, Marianne," said Gentz, mournfully; "you have paid your tribute to the vacillating, changeable, and fickle organization peculiar to every living creature; and so have I, perhaps. We are all perishable, and hence our feelings must be perishable also. Above all, love is a most precious, fragrant, and enchanting rose; but its life lasts but a day, and then it withers. Happy are those, therefore, who have improved this day and enjoyed the beauty of the rose, and passionately inhaled its fragrance. We did so, Marianne; and when we now look back to our day of blissful love, we may say, 'It was delightful and intoxicating, and with its memories it will shed a golden, sunny lustre over our whole life.' Let us not revile it, therefore, for having passed away, and let us not be angry with ourselves for not being able to prolong it. The rose has faded, but the stem, from which it burst forth, must remain to us; it is our immortal part. That stem

is the harmony of our sentiments; it is the consonance of our ideas; in short, the seeds of friendship have ripened in the withered flower of our love. I have not, therefore, come to you, Marianne, to seek for my beloved, but to find my friend—the friend who understands me, who shares my views, my grief, my despair, and my rage, and who is ready to aspire with me to one goal, and to seek with me for it in one way. This goal is the deliverance of Germany from the chains of slavery."

"Above all, the annihilation of the tyrant who wants to enslave us!" exclaimed Marianne, with flashing eyes. "Tell me the way leading to that goal; I will enter it, even if it should be necessary for me to walk on thorns and pointed swords!"

"The goal lies before us clearly and distinctly," said Gentz, sadly; "but the way leading to it is still obstructed, and so narrow and low that we are compelled, for the time being, to advance very slowly on our knees. But we must take spades and work, so that the way may become wider and higher, and that we may walk on it one day, not with bowed heads, but drawn up to our full height, our eyes flashing, and sword in hand. Let us prepare for that day; let us work in the dark shaft, and other laborers will join us, and, like us, take spades and dig; and in the dead of night, with curses on our lips and prayers in our hearts, we will dig on, dig like moles, until we have finally reached our goal, and burst forth into the sunshine of the day which will restore liberty to Germany. At the present time, SECRET SOCIETIES may become very useful. I always hated and despised whatever bore that name; but necessity knows no law, and now I am obliged to hail them as the harbingers of a blessed future.* Like the first church, the great secret society of Germany ought to be enthusiastic, self-reliant, and thoroughly organized; its aim ought to be the destruction of Bonaparte's tyranny, reconstruction of the states, restoration of the legitimate sovereigns, introduction of a better system of government, and last, everlasting resistance to the principles which have brought about our indifference, prostration, and meanness. And now, Marianne, I come to ask you as the worthiest patriot, as the most intrepid and generous man I know and revere—Marianne, will you join this secret society?"

He gave her his hand with a glance full of the most profound emotion; and she returned his glance with her large, open eyes, warmly grasping his hand.

* Gentz's own words.—Vide "Correspondence," etc. p. 163.

"I will, so help me God!" she said, solemnly; "I will join your secret society, and I will travel around and win over men to our league. I will seek for catacombs where we may pray, and exhort, and encourage each other to struggle on with unflagging zeal. I will enlist brethren and adherents in all circles, in the highest as well as in the lowest; and the peasant as well as the prince, the countess as well as the citizen's wife, shall become brethren and sisters of the holy covenant, the aim of which is to be the deliverance of Germany from the tyrant's yoke. My activity and zeal to promote the good work you have begun shall prove to you, my friend, whether I love you still, and whether my mind has comprehended you."

"I counted on your mind, Marianne, after I ceased building my hopes on your heart!" exclaimed Gentz, "and I was not mistaken. Your mind has comprehended me; it is the same as mine. Let us, therefore, go to work with joyful courage and make our first steps forward. The time when there was still a hope that the sword might save our cause is past; the sword lies broken at our feet. Now we have two weapons left, but they are no less sharp, cutting, and fatal than the sword."

"These weapons are the tongue and the pen?" said Marianne, smiling.

"Yes, you have understood me," said Gentz, joyfully, "these are our weapons. You, my beautiful comrade, will wield one of these weapons, the tongue, and I shall wield the other, the pen. And I have already commenced doing so, and written in the sleepless nights of these last few days a pamphlet which I should like to fit, like a pigeon, over Germany, so that everywhere it may be seen, understood and appreciated. The title of this pamphlet is *Germany in her Deepest Degradation*. It is an outcry of my grief, by which I intend arousing the German people, so that they may wake up at last from their long torpor, seize the sword and rise in the exuberance of their vigor for the purpose of expelling the tyrant. But, alas! where shall I find one who will dare to print it; a censor who will not expunge its most powerful passages; and, finally, booksellers who will venture to offer so bold a work to their customers?"

"Give your manuscript to *me!*" exclaimed Marianne, enthusiastically: "I will cause it to be printed, and if there should be no booksellers to circulate it, I will travel as your agent throughout the whole of Germany, and in the night-time secretly scatter your pamphlet in the streets of all the German cities, so that their inhabitants may find it in the morning—a manna fallen from heaven to nourish and invigorate them. Give your manuscript to me, Frederick Gentz; let it be the first solemn act of our secret league!"

"Just see how well I understood you, and how entirely I counted on your coöperation, Marianne," said Gentz, drawing a small package from his side pocket and placing it in her hands. "Here is my manuscript; seek for a printer and for a bookseller to publish it; give it the blessing of your protection, and promote its general circulation to the best of your ability."

"I shall do so most assuredly," replied Marianne, placing her hand on the package, as though she were taking an oath. "In less than a month's time the German people shall read this pamphlet. It shall be only the first comet which the secret league of which we are now members causes to appear on the dark political firmament. Count on me; your manuscript will be published."

Gentz bent over her hand and kissed it. He then rose.

"My purpose is accomplished," he said; "I came to Vienna only to see you and enlist you as a member of my secret society. My purpose is accomplished, and I shall set out within an hour."

"And why are you in such a hurry, my friend? Why depart in so stormy and wintry a night?" asked Marianne. "Remain with me for another day."

"It is impossible, Marianne," said Gentz, deprecatingly. "Friends like ourselves must have no secrets from each other, and are allowed fearlessly to tell each other every thing. The Countess of Lankoronska is waiting for me; I shall set out with her for Breslau."

"Ah," exclaimed Marianne, reproachfully, "Lord Paget, too, is going to leave Vienna, but I do not desert you in order to accompany him; I remain."

"You are the sun around which the planets are revolving," said Gentz, smiling; "but I am nothing but a planet. I am revolving around my sun."

"You love the Countess of Lankoronska, then?"

"She is to me the quintessence of all womanly and of many manly accomplishments!" exclaimed Gentz, enthusiastically.

"And she will also join our secret society?" asked Marianne.

"No," said Gentz, hastily. "My heart adores her, but my mind will never forget that she is a Russian. Next to cold death and the French, I hate nothing so cordially as the Russians."

"Still you have lived for a month with a Russian lady, of whom you are enamoured."

"And precisely in this month my hatred has increased to an astonishing extent. I despise the Austrians; I am indignant at their weakness, but still I also pity them; and when I see them, as was the case this time, trampled under foot by the Russian barbarians, my German bowels turn, and I feel that the Austrians are my brethren. During the last few days I have frequently met Constantine, the grand-duke, and the other distinguished Russians; and the blind, stupid, and impudent national pride with which they assailed Austria and Germany generally, calling our country a despicable part of earth, where none but traitors and cowards were to be found, cut me to the quick. I know very well that we are at present scarcely allowed to maintain our dignity as Germans; our government has reduced us to so degrading a position; but when we keep in mind what the Russians are, compared with us; when we have mournfully witnessed for two months that they are unable, in spite of the bravery of their troops, to make any headway against the French, and that they have injured rather than improved our condition; when we see those insulting and scorning us who cannot even claim the merit of having saved us, only then we become fully alive to the consciousness of our present degradation and abject misery!" *

"God be praised that such are your thoughts!" exclaimed Marianne, "for now I may hope at least that the Countess of Lankoronska, even though every thing should fail here, will not succeed in enticing you to Russia. I am sure, Gentz, you will not accompany her to the cold, distant north!"

"God forbid!" replied Gentz, shuddering. "If every thing should fail, I shall settle somewhere in the southern provinces of Austria, in Carinthia or in the Tyrol, where one may hear the people speak German, and live there with the plants and stars which I know and love, and with God, in some warm nook, no matter what tyrant or proconsul may rule over me.† And now, Marianne, let us part. I do not promise that our meeting will be a joyful one, for I hardly count on any more joyful days, but I say that we will meet at the right hour. And the right hour will be for us only the hour when we shall have reached the goal of our secret league; when we shall have aroused the German people, and when they will rise like a courageous giant whom no one is able to withstand, and who will expel the invader with

* Gentz's own words.—"Correspondence," pp. 159, 167.
† Ibid., p. 167.

his hordes from the soil of Germany! Farewell!"

"Farewell," said Marianne, feelingly. "My friend will always be welcome, and cordial greetings will be in store for him whenever he comes. Remember that, my friend; I say no more 'my beloved,' for the Countess of Lankoronska might be jealous!"

"And she might inform Lord Paget of it," said Gentz, smiling. He then kissed Marianne's hand, and took his hat and overcoat. "Farewell, Marianne, and do not forget our league and my manuscript."

"I shall not forget any thing, for I shall not forget you," she replied, giving him her hand.

Thus, hand in hand, they walked to the door; then they nodded a last silent greeting to each other, and Gentz left the room.

Marianne listened to his steps until they had died away. She then drew a deep breath, and commenced once more slowly pacing the room.

The tapers on the silver chandeliers had burned down very low, and their liquid wax trickled slowly and lazily on the marble table. Whenever Marianne passed them, the draught fanned them to a blaze; then they shed a lurid light on the tall, queenly form in the magnificent dress, and grew dim again when Marianne stepped back into the darker parts of the long room.

Suddenly she exclaimed in a joyful voice; "Yes, I have found it at last! That is the path leading to the goal; that is the path I have to pursue." With rapid steps she hastened back to the looking-glass. "Marianne Meier," she cried aloud—"Marianne Meier, listen to what I am going to tell you. The Princess von Eibenberg has discovered a remedy to dispel her weariness and dull repose—a remedy that will immortalize her name. Good-night, Marianne Meier, now you may go to sleep, for the Princess von Eibenberg will take care of herself!"

CHAPTER LI.

JUDITH.

MARIANNE was awakened after a short and calm slumber by the low sound of stealthy steps approaching her couch. She opened her eyes hastily, and beheld her mistress of ceremonies, who stood at her bedside, holding in her hand a golden salver with a letter on it.

"What, Camilla," she asked, in terror, "you have not yet dispatched the letter which I gave

you last night? Did I not instruct you to have
it delivered by the footman early in the morning?"

"Yes, your highness, and I have faithfully carried out your orders."

"Well, and this letter?"

"Is the major's reply. Your highness ordered me to awaken you as soon as the footman would bring the answer."

Marianne hastily seized the letter and broke the seal.

"He will come," she said, loudly and joyfully, after reading the few lines the letter contained. "What o'clock is it, Camilla?"

"Your highness, it is just ten o'clock."

"And I am looking for visitors already at eleven o'clock. Quick, Madame Camilla, tell my maid to arrange every thing in the dressing-room. Please see to it yourself that I may find there an elegant, rich, and not too matronly, morning costume."

"Will your highness put on the dress which Lord Paget received the other day for you from London?" asked Madame Camilla. "Your highness has never yet worn it, and his lordship would doubtless rejoice at seeing your highness in this charming costume."

"I do not expect Lord Paget," said Marianne, with a stern glance; "besides, you ought to confine your advice to matters relating to my toilet. Do not forget it any more. Now bring me my chocolate, I will take it in bed. In the mean time cause an invigorating, perfumed bath to be prepared, and tell the cook that I wish him to serve up a sumptuous breakfast for two persons in the small dining-room in the course of an hour. Go."

Madame Camilla withdrew to carry out the various orders her mistress had given her, but she did not do so joyfully and readily as usual, but with a grave face and careworn air.

"There is something going on," she whispered, slowly gliding down the corridor. "Yes, there is something going on, and at length I shall have an opportunity for spying and reporting what I have discovered. Well, I get my pay from two men, from the French governor of Vienna and from Lord Paget. Would to God I could serve both of them to-day! As for Lord Paget, I have already some news for him, for Mr. von Gentz was with her last night, and remained for two hours; my mistress then wrote a letter to Major von Brandt, which I had to dispatch early in the morning. And this is exactly the point, concerning which I do not know whether it ought to be reported to my French customer or to the English lord. Well, I will consider the matter. I will watch every step of hers, for it is certain that

something extraordinary is going on here, and I want to know what it is."

And, after taking this resolution, Madame Camilla accelerated her steps to deliver the orders of the princess to the cook.

An hour later, the lady's maid had finished the toilet of the princess, who approached the large looking-glass in order to cast a last critical look on her appearance.

A charming smile of satisfaction overspread her fair face when she beheld her enchanting image in the glass, and she said, with a triumphant air, "Yes, it is true, this woman is beautiful enough even to court the favor of an emperor. Do you not think so, too, Madame Camilla?"

Madame Camilla had watched, with a very attentive and grave face, every word her mistress uttered, but now she hastened to smile.

"Your highness," she said, "if we lived still in the days of the ancient gods, I would not trust any butterfly nor any bird, nay, not even a gold-piece, for, behind every thing, I should suspect Jove disguised, for the purpose of surprising my beautiful mistress."

Marianne laughed. "Ah, how learned you are," she said. "You refer even to the disguised bull of poor Europa and to the golden rain of Danaë. But fear not; no disguised god will penetrate into my rooms, for unhappily the time of gods and demi-gods is past."

"Nevertheless, those arrogant French would like to make the world believe that M. Bonaparte had restored that time," said Madame Camilla, with a contemptuous air; "they would like to persuade us that the son of that Corsican lawyer was a last and belated son of Jove."

"Oh!" exclaimed Marianne, triumphantly; "the world shall discover soon enough that he is nothing but a miserable son of earth, and that his immortality, too, will find sufficient room between six blackboards. I know, Camilla, you hate the usurper as ardently, as bitterly and vindictively as I do, and this hatred is the sympathetic link uniting me with you. Well, let me tell you that your hatred will speedily be gratified, and that your vindictiveness will be satiated. Pray to God, Camilla, that He may bless the hand about to be raised against the tyrant; pray to God that He may sharpen the dagger which may soon be aimed at his heart! The world has suffered enough; it is time that it should find an avenger of its wrongs!"

"Major von Brandt," announced a footman, entering the room.

"Conduct the major to the drawing-room," said Marianne, hastily; "I will join him directly."

She cast a last triumphant look on the mirror, and then left the room.

Madame Camilla watched her, with a scowl, until the door had closed behind her. "Now I know whom I have to inform of her doings," she muttered. "They concern the French governor; I have to take pains, however, to find out more about her schemes, so that my report may embrace as much important information as possible. The better the news, the better the pay."

Marianne had meanwhile gone to the drawing-room. A tall, elderly officer, in Austrian uniform, with the epaulets of a major, came to meet her, and bent down to kiss reverentially the hand which she offered to him.

Marianne saluted him with a fascinating smile. "You have entirely forgotten me, then, major?" she asked. "It was necessary for me to invite you in order to induce you to pay me a visit?"

"I did not know whether I might dare to appear before you, most gracious princess," said the major, respectfully. "The last time I had the honor of waiting on you, I met your highness in the circle of your distinguished friends who used to be mine, too. But nobody had a word of welcome, a pleasant smile for me, and your highness, it seemed to me, did not notice me during the whole evening. Whenever I intended to approach you, you averted your face and entered into so animated a conversation with one of the bystanders, that I could not venture to interrupt it. Hence I withdrew, my heart filled with grief and despair, for I certainly believed that your highness wished to banish me from your reception-room forever."

"And you consoled yourself for this banishment in the reception-room of the French governor whom the great Emperor Napoleon had given to the good city of Vienna, I suppose?" asked the princess, with an arch smile. "And you would have never come back to me unless I had taken the bold resolution to invite you to my house?"

"By this invitation you have rendered me the happiest of mortals, most gracious princess," exclaimed the major, emphatically. "You have reopened to me the gates of Paradise, while, in my despair, I believed them to be closed against me forever."

"Confess, major," said Marianne, laughing, "that you did not make the slightest attempt to see whether these gates were merely ajar or really closed. Under the present circumstances we may speak honestly and frankly to each other. You believed me to be an ardent patriot, one of those furious adversaries of the French and their rule,

who do not look upon Napoleon as a hero and genius, but only as a tyrant and usurper. Because I was the intimate friend of Lord Paget and M. von Gentz, of the Princesses von Carolath and Clary, of the Countess von Colloredo, and Count Cobenzl, you believed that my political sentiments coincided with theirs?"

"Yes, your highness, indeed that is what I believed," said Major von Brandt, "and as you want me to tell the truth, I will confess that it was the reason why I did not venture to appear again in your drawing-room. I have never denied that I am an enthusiastic admirer of that great man who is conquering and subjugating the whole world, because God has destined him to be its master. Hence, I never was able to comprehend the audacity of those who instigated our gracious and noble Emperor Francis to wage war against the victorious hero, and as a true and sincere patriot I now bless the dispensations of fate which compels us to make peace with Napoleon the Great, for Austria can regain her former prosperity only by maintaining peace and harmony with France. The war against France has brought the barbarian hordes of Russia to Germany; after the conclusion of peace, France will assist us in expelling these unclean and unwelcome guests from the soil of our fatherland."

Marianne had listened to him smilingly and with an air of unqualified assent. Only once a slight blush, as if produced by an ebullition of suppressed anger, had mantled her cheeks—only for a brief moment she had frowned, but she quickly overcame her indignation and appeared as smiling and serene as before.

"I am precisely of your opinion, my dear major," she said, with a fascinating nod.

"Your highness assents to the views I have just uttered?" exclaimed the major, in joyful surprise.

"Do you doubt it still?" she asked. "Have I followed, then, the example of all my friends, even that of Lord Paget and Gentz? Have I fled from the capital because the Emperor Napoleon, with his army, has turned his victorious steps toward Vienna? No, I have remained, to the dismay of all of them; I have remained, although my prolonged sojourn in Vienna has deprived me of two of my dearest friends, and brought about an everlasting rupture between myself and Lord Paget, as well as Herr von Gentz. I have remained because I was unable to withstand any longer the ardent yearning of my heart—because I wished to get at length a sight of the hero to whom the whole world is bowing. But look, my footman comes to tell me that my breakfast has been served. You must consent to be my guest to-day and breakfast with me."

She took the major's arm and went with him to the dining-room. In the middle of it a table had been set, on which splendid *pâtés*, luscious tropical fruits, and well-spiced *salamis* agreeably surprised the major by their appetizing odor, while golden Rhenish wine and dark Tokay in the white decanters seemed to beckon him.

They took seats at the table in elastic, soft arm-chairs, and for a while the conversation was interrupted, for the pastry and the other dainty dishes absorbed their whole attention. The major, who was noted for his epicurism, enjoyed the delicacies served up to him with the profound seriousness and immovable tranquillity of a philosopher. Besides, the princess shared his enjoyment after a while by her conversation, sparkling with wit and humor; she was inexhaustible in telling piquant anecdotes and merry *bon-mots*; she portrayed her friends and acquaintances in so skilful a manner that the major did not know whether to admire their striking resemblance or the talent with which she rendered their weak traits most conspicuous.

When they had reached the dessert, the princess made a sign to the footman to leave the room, and she remained alone with the major. With her own fair hand she poured fragrant Syracusan wine into his glass, and begged him to drink the health of Napoleon the Great.

"And your highness will not do me the honor to take wine with me?" asked the major, pointing at the empty glass of the princess.

She smiled and shook her head. "I never drink wine," she said; "wine is a magician who suddenly tears the mask from my face and compels my lips to speak the truth which they would otherwise, perhaps, never have uttered. But I will make an exception this time; this time I will fill my glass, for I must drink the health of the great emperor. Pour some wine into it, and let us cry: 'Long live Napoleon the Great!'"

She drank some of the fiery southern wine, and her prediction was fulfilled. The wine took the mask from her face, and loosened the fetters of her tongue.

Her eyes beamed now with the fire of enthusiasm, and the rapturous praise of Napoleon flowed from her lips like a torrent of the most glowing poetry.

She was wondrously beautiful in her enthusiastic ardor, with the flaming blush on her cheeks, with her flashing eyes and quivering lips, the sweet smile of which showed two rows of pearly teeth.

"Oh," exclaimed the major, fascinated by her loveliness, "why is the great emperor not here—why does he not hear your enchanting words—why is he not permitted to admire you in your radiant beauty!"

"Why am I not allowed to hasten to him in order to sink down at his feet and worship him?" exclaimed Marianne, fervently. "Why am I not allowed to lie for a blissful hour before him on my knees in order to beg with scalding tears his pardon for the hatred which formerly filled my soul against him, and to confess to him that my hatred has been transformed into boundless love and ecstatic adoration? Where shall I find the friend who will pity my longing, and open for me the path leading to him? Such a friend I should reward with a gold-piece for every minute of my bliss, for every minute I should be allowed to remain near the great emperor."

"Do you speak in earnest, your highness?" asked Major von Brandt, gravely and almost solemnly.

"In solemn earnest!" asseverated Marianne. "A gold-piece for every minute of an interview with the Emperor Napoleon."

"Well, then," said the major, joyfully, "I shall procure this interview for you, your highness, and your beauty and fascinating loveliness will cause the emperor not to count the minutes, nor the hours either, so that it will be only necessary for me to reduce the hours to minutes."

"A gold-piece for every minute!" repeated Marianne, whose face was radiant with joy and happiness. "Oh, you look at me doubtingly, you believe that I am only joking, and shall not keep afterward what I am now promising."

"Most gracious princess, I believe that enthusiasm has carried you away to a promise the acceptance of which would be an abuse of your generosity. Suppose the emperor, fascinated by your wit, your beauty, your charming conversation, should remain four hours with you, that would be a very handsome number of gold-pieces for me!"

Instead of replying to him, Marianne took the silver bell and rang it.

"Bring me pen, ink, and paper, a burning candle and sealing-wax," she said to the footman who entered.

In a few minutes every thing had been brought to her, and Marianne hastily wrote a few lines. She then drew the seal-ring from her finger and affixed her seal to the paper, which she handed to the major.

"Read it aloud," she said.

The major read:

"I promise to Major von Brandt, in case he

shou'd procure me an interview with the Emperor Napoleon, to pay him for every minute of this interview a louis-d'or as a token of my gratitude.

"MARIANNE, PRINCESS VON EIBENBERG."

"Are you content and convinced?" asked the princess.

"I am, your highness."

"And you will and can procure me this interview?"

"I will and can do so."

"When will you conduct me to Schönbrunn?"

The major reflected some time, and seemed to make a calculation.

"I hope to be able to procure for your highness to-morrow evening an interview with the emperor," he said. "I am quite well acquainted with M. de Bausset, intendant of the palace, and I besides know Constant; his majesty's *valet-de-chambre*. These are the two channels through which the wish of your highness will easily reach the emperor, and as his majesty is a great admirer of female beauty, he will assuredly be ready to grant the audience applied for."

"Will you bring me word to-day?" asked Marianne.

"Yes, princess, to-day. I will immediately repair to Schönbrunn. The emperor arrived there yesterday."

"Hasten, then," said Marianne, rising from her seat—"hasten to Schönbrunn, and remember that I am waiting for your return with trembling impatience and suspense."

She gave her hand to the major.

"Good Heaven, your highness!" he exclaimed, in terror, "your hand is as cold as marble."

"All my blood is here," she said, pointing to her heart. "Hasten to Schönbrunn."

He imprinted a kiss on her hand and left the room.

Marianne smiled until the door had closed behind him. Then her features underwent a sudden change, and assumed an air of horror and contempt.

"Oh, these miserable men, these venal souls!" she muttered. "They measure every thing by their own standard, and cannot comprehend the longings and schemes of a great soul. Accursed be all those who turn traitors to their country and adhere to its enemies! May the wrath of God and the contempt of their fellow-creatures punish them! But I will use the traitors as tools for the purpose of accomplishing the sacred task which the misfortunes of Germany have obliged me to undertake. I will put my house in order, that I may be ready when the hour has come."

Madame Camilla was right, indeed; something was going on, and she was able to collect important news for the French governor.

The Princess von Eibenberg, since her interview with the major, had been a prey to a feverish agitation and impatience which caused her to wander restlessly through the various rooms of her mansion. At length, toward evening, the major returned, and the news he had brought must have been highly welcome, for the countenance of the princess had been ever since radiant with joy, and a wondrous smile was constantly playing on her lips.

During the following night she was incessantly engaged in writing, and Madame Camilla as well as the maid were waiting in vain for their mistress to call them; the princess did not leave her cabinet, and did not go to bed at all. Early next morning she took a ride in her carriage, and Madame Camilla, who had heretofore invariably accompanied the princess on her rides, was ordered to stay at home. When Marianne returned after several hours, she was pale and exhausted, and her eyes showed that she had wept. Then officers of the city courts made their appearance, and asked to see the princess, stating that she had sent for them. The princess locked her room while conferring with them, and the officers withdrew only after several hours. At the dinner-table, to which, by her express orders, no guests had been admitted to-day, she scarcely touched any food, and seemed absorbed in deep reflections.

Soon after dinner she repaired to her dressing-room, and never before had she been so particular and careful in choosing the various articles of her costume; never before had she watched her toilet with so much attention and anxiety. At last the work was finished, and the princess looked radiantly beautiful in her crimson velvet dress, floating behind her in a long train, and fastened under her bosom, only half veiled by a clear lace collar, by means of a wide, golden sash. Her hair, framing her expansive brow in a few black ringlets *à la Joséphine*, was tied up in a Greek knot, adorned with pearls and diamonds. Similar jewels surrounded her queenly neck and the splendidly-shaped snow-white arms. Her cheeks were transparently pale to-day, and a gloomy, sinister fire was burning in her large black eyes.

She looked beautiful, proud, and menacing, like Judith, who has adorned herself for the purpose of going to the tent of Holofernes. Madame Camilla could not help thinking of it when she now saw the princess walk across the room in her proud beauty, and with her stern, solemn air. Madame Camilla could not help thinking of it when she saw the princess draw an oblong, flashing object from a case which the mistress of ceremonies had never beheld before, and hastily conceal it in her bosom.

Was it, perhaps, a dagger, and was the princess a modern Judith, going to kill a modern Holofernes in her voluptuous arms?

The footman now announced that Major von Brandt was waiting for the princess in the reception-room, and that the carriage was at the door. A slight shudder shook the whole frame of the princess, and her cheeks turned even paler than before. She ordered the footman to withdraw, and then made a sign to Madame Camilla to give her her cloak and bonnet. Camilla obeyed silently. When the princess was ready to depart, she turned to Camilla, and, drawing a valuable diamond ring from her finger, she handed it to her.

"Take this ring as a souvenir from me," she said. "I know you are a good and enthusiastic Austrian; like myself, you hate the tyrant who wants to subjugate us, and you will bless the hand which will order him to stop, and put an end to his victorious career. Farewell!"

She nodded once more to her and left her cabinet to go to the reception-room, where Major von Brandt was waiting for her.

"Come," she said, hastily, "it is high time. I hope you have got a watch with you, so as to be able to count the minutes."

"Yes, your highness," said Major von Brandt, smiling, "I have got my watch with me, and I shall have the honor of showing it to you before you enter the imperial cabinet."

Marianne made no reply, but rapidly crossed the room to go down-stairs to the carriage waiting at the door. Major von Brandt hastened after her and offered his arm to her.

Madame Camilla, who had not lost a single word of her short conversation with Major von Brandt, followed the princess down-stairs, and remained standing humbly at the foot of it till the princess and her companion had entered the carriage and the coach door had been closed.

But no sooner had the brilliant carriage of the princess rolled out of the court-yard in front of her mansion, than Madame Camilla hastened into the street, entered a hack, and ordered the coachman to drive her to the residence of the French governor as fast as his horses could run.

CHAPTER LII.

NAPOLEON AND THE PRUSSIAN MINISTER.

NAPOLEON had left Austerlitz, and had, for some days, again resided at Schönbrunn. The country palace of the great empress Maria Theresa was now the abode of him who had driven her grandson from his capital, defeated his army, and was just about to dictate a peace to him, the terms of which would be equivalent to a fresh defeat of Austria and a fresh victory for France.

The plenipotentiaries of Austria and France were already assembled at Presburg to conclude this treaty, and every hour couriers reached Schönbrunn, who reported to the emperor the progress of the negotiations and obtained further instructions from him.

But while Austria now, after the disastrous battle of the 2d of December, was treating with Napoleon about the best terms of peace, the Prussian envoy, Count Haugwitz, who was to deliver to Napoleon the menacing declaration of Prussia, was still on the road, or, at least, had not been able to lay his dispatch before the emperor. Prussia demanded, in this dispatch, which had been approved by Russia, that Napoleon should give up Italy and Holland, and recognize the independence of both countries, as well as that of Germany. Prussia gave France a month's time to take this proposition into consideration; and if it should be declined, then Prussia would declare war against the Emperor Napoleon.

This month had expired on the 15th of December, and, as previously stated, Count Haugwitz had not yet succeeded in delivering his dispatch to the Emperor Napoleon.

It is true, he had set out from Berlin on the 6th of November; but the noble count liked to travel as comfortably as possible, and to repose often from the hardships of the journey. He had, therefore, travelled every day but a few miles, and stopped several days in every large city through which he had passed. Vainly had Minister von Hardenberg and the Russian and Austrian ministers in Berlin sent courier upon courier after him, in order to induce him to accelerate his journey.

Count Haugwitz declared himself *unable* to travel any faster, because he was afraid of stating that he was *unwilling* to do so.

Now, he was *unwilling* to travel any faster, because the message, of which he was the bearer, was a most oppressive burden to him, and because he felt convinced that the energetic genius, by some rapid and crushing victory, would upset all treaties, change all stand-points, and thereby render it unnecessary for him to deliver to him a dispatch of so harsh and hostile a description.

Thanks to his system of delay, Count Haugwitz had succeeded in obtaining a first interview with Napoleon on the day before the battle of Austerlitz. But instead of presenting the ominous note to the emperor, he had contented himself, after the fashion of a genuine courtier, with offering incense to the great conqueror, and Napoleon had prevented him from transacting any business by putting off all negotiations with him until after the great battle.

After the battle of Austerlitz, the emperor had received the envoy of the King of Prussia at Schönbrunn, and granted him the longed-for audience. Napoleon greeted him in an angry voice, and reproached him violently for having affixed his name to the treaty of Potsdam. But Haugwitz had managed, by his skilful politeness, to appease the emperor's wrath, and to regain his favor. Since then Count Haugwitz had been at Schönbrunn every day, and Napoleon had always received him with especial kindness and affability. For the emperor, who knew very well that Austria was still hoping for an armed intervention by Prussia, wished to delay his decision, as to the fate of Prussia at least, until he had made peace with Austria. Only when he had trampled Austria under foot, he would think of chastising Prussia for her recent arrogance, and to humiliate her as he had hitherto humiliated all his enemies. Hence he had received Count Haugwitz every day, and succeeded gradually and insensibly in winning him for his plans. To-day, on the 13th of December, Count Haugwitz had repaired to Schönbrunn to negotiate with Napoleon. He wore his full court-costume, and was adorned with the *grand cordon* of the Legion of Honor, which he had received a year ago, and which the Prussian minister seemed to wear with especial predilection.

Napoleon received the count in the former drawing-room of Maria Theresa, which had now become Napoleon's study. On a large round table in the centre of the room, there lay maps, dotted with variously colored pins; the green pins designated the route fixed by Napoleon for the retreat of the Russian army; the dark-yellow pins surrounded the extreme boundaries of Austria, and according to the news which Napoleon received from Presburg, and which informed him of constantly new concessions made by the Austrian plenipotentiaries, who declared their willingness to cede several provinces, he changed the position of these pins, which embraced every day a more contracted space; while the blue pins, designating the boundaries of Bavaria, advanced farther and farther, and the red pins, representing the armies of France, seemed to multiply on the map.

Napoleon, however, was not engaged in studying his maps when Count Haugwitz entered his room, but he was seated at the desk placed close to the table with the maps, and seemed to write assiduously. On the raised back part of this desk the busts of Frederick the Great and Maria Theresa had been placed. Napoleon sometimes, when he ceased writing, raised his gloomy eyes to them, and then it seemed as though these three heads, the two marble busts and the marble head of Napoleon, bent threateningly toward each other, as though the flashes bursting from Napoleon's eyes kindled the fire of life and anger in the marble eyes of the empress and the great king; their frowning brows seemed to ask him then, by virtue of what right the son of the Corsican lawyer had taken a seat between their two crowned heads, and driven the legitimate Emperor of Austria from the house of his fathers.

When Count Haugwitz entered, Napoleon cast the pen impetuously aside and rose. He saluted the count, who bowed to him deeply and respectfully, with a pleasant nod.

"You are there," said the emperor, kindly, "and it is very lucky. I was extremely impatient to see you."

"Lucky?" asked Count Haugwitz, with the inimitable smile of a well-bred courtier. "Lucky, sire? It seems to me as though there were neither luck nor ill-luck in the world, nay; I am now more than ever convinced of it. Have I not heard men say more than a hundred times, 'He is lucky! he is lucky!' Since I have made the acquaintance of the great man who owes every thing to himself, I have become convinced that luck should not be taken into consideration, and that it is of no consequence."

Napoleon smiled. "You are a most adroit and well-bred cavalier and courtier," he said, "but it is a rule of wisdom for princes not to repose any confidence in the words of courtiers and flatterers, but always to translate them into the opposite sense. Therefore, I translate your words, too, into the contrary, and then they signify, 'It seems, unfortunately, as though luck had deserted us, and particularly the third coalition, forever, but still sticks to the colors of France.'"

"Oh, sire," exclaimed Count Haugwitz, in a tone of grievous reproach, "can your majesty really doubt my devotion and admiration? Was I not the first man to congratulate your majesty, the indomitable chieftain, on the fresh laurels with which you had wreathed your heroic brow, even in the cold days of winter ? "

" It is true," said Napoleon, " you did so, but your compliment was intended for others; fate, however, had changed its address.* Of your sincerity I have hitherto had no proofs whatever, but a great many of your duplicity; for, at all events, you have affixed your name to the treaty of Potsdam ? "

" I have done so, and boast of it," said Count Haugwitz, quickly. " A glance into the heart of Napoleon satisfied me that he who stands at the head of human greatness knew no higher aim than to give peace to mankind, and thus complete the great work which Providence has intrusted to him."

" Words, words ! " said Napoleon. " Let me see actions at last. The instructions that were given to you before leaving Berlin have been annulled by the recent events in Moravia; we are agreed about this point. Now, you are a member of the Prussian cabinet. By sending you to me, the king has intrusted to you alone the welfare of his monarchy. We shall see, therefore, whether you will know how to profit by a rare, perhaps never-recurring opportunity, and to crown the work which Frederick II., notwithstanding his victories, left unfinished. Come hither and see."

He stepped rapidly to the table with the maps, and in obedience to a wave of his hand, Count Haugwitz glided, with his imperturbable smile, to his side.

" See here," exclaimed Napoleon, pointing at the map; " this is Silesia, your native country. The king does not rule over the whole of it, the Emperor of Austria still retaining a portion of it; but that splendid province ought to belong exclusively to Prussia. We will see and consider how far your southern frontier ought to be extended. Just follow my finger on the map; it will designate to you the new boundaries of Prussian Silesia." †

And Napoleon's forefinger passed, flashing like a dagger-point, across the map, and encircled the whole Austrian portion of Silesia, from Teschen to the Saxon frontier, and from the mountains of Yablunka to the point where the Riesengebirge disappears in Lusatia. ‡

" Well," he then asked, hastily, " would not

such an arrangement round off your Silesian province in the most desirable manner ? "

Count Haugwitz did not reply immediately, but continued gazing at the map. Napoleon's eagle glance rested on him for a moment, and then passed on to the busts of Maria Theresa and Frederick the Great.

" Oh," he exclaimed, with a triumphant smile, pointing to the bust of Frederick, " that great man would have accepted my proposition without any hesitation whatever."

" Sire," said Count Haugwitz, hesitatingly, " but that great woman, Maria Theresa, would not have permitted it so easily."

" But now," exclaimed Napoleon, " now there is no Maria Theresa to hinder the King of Prussia; now I am here, and I grant the whole of Silesia to your king if he will conclude a close alliance with me. Consider well; can you be insensible of the glory which awaits you ? "

And his eyes again pierced the embarrassed face of the count like two dagger-points.

" Sire," said Haugwitz, in a low voice, " your proposition is tempting, it is admirable; but as far as I know his majesty the king, I must—"

" Oh," said Napoleon, impatiently, " do not allude to the king and his person. We have nothing to do with that. You are minister, and it behooves you to fulfil the duties which your position demands from you, and to embrace the opportunity which will never return. One must be powerful, one can never be sufficiently so, believe me, and consider well before replying to me."

" But, perhaps, sire, it would be better for us to seek for aggrandizement on another side," said Haugwitz.

" On the side of Poland or France, I suppose ? " asked Napoleon, harshly. " You would like to deprive me again of Mentz, Cleves, and the left bank of the Rhine, and you flirt with Russia and Austria because you hope they might assist you one day, after all, in obtaining those territories ? But, on the other hand, you would not like to quarrel with me, because there is a possibility that your hopes will not be fulfilled, and because, in such an eventuality, you would fear my enmity. You Prussians want to be the allies of every one; that is impossible, and you must decide for me or for the others. I demand sincerity, or shall break loose from you, for I prefer open enemies to false friends. Your king tolerates in Hanover a corps of thirty thousand men, which, through his states, keeps up a connection with the great Russian army; that is an act of open hostility. As for me, I attack my enemies wherever I may find them. If I wished to do so, I might take a terri

---

* The whole conversation is strictly in accordance with history.—Vide "Mémoires Inédits du Comte de Haugwitz." 1847.

† Napoleon's own words.—" Memoires Inédits," p. 17.

‡ Ibid., p. 18.

bl· revenge for this dishonesty. I could invade Silesia, cause an insurrection in Poland, and deal Prussia blows from which she would never recover. But I prefer forgetting the past, and pursuing a generous course. I will, therefore, forgive Prussia's rashness, but only on condition that Prussia should unite with France by indissoluble ties ; and as a guaranty of this alliance, I require Prussia to take possession of Hanover." *

"Sire," exclaimed Haugwitz, joyfully, "this was the desirable aggrandizement which I took the liberty of hinting at before, and I believe it is the only one which the king's conscience would allow him to accept."

"Very well, take Hanover, then," said Napoleon, "I cede my claims on it to Prussia ; but in return Prussia cedes to France the principality of Neufchatel and the fortress of Wesel, and to Bavaria the principality of Anspach."

"But, sire," exclaimed Haugwitz, anxiously, "Anspach belongs to Prussia by virtue of family treaties which cannot be contested ; and Neufchatel—"

"No objections," interrupted Napoleon, sternly ; "my terms must be complied with. Either war or peace. War, that is to say, I crush Prussia, and become her inexorable enemy forever ; peace, that is to say, I give you Hanover and receive for it Neufchatel, Wesel, and Anspach. Now, make up your mind quickly ; I am tired of the eternal delays and procrastinations, I want you to come at length to a decision, and you will not leave this room until I have received a categorical reply. You have had time enough to take every thing into consideration ; hence you must not equivocate any more. Tell me, therefore, quickly and categorically, what do you want, war or peace ?"

"Sire," said Haugwitz, imploringly, "what else can Prussia want than peace with France ?"

"Indeed, it is an excellent bargain you make on this occasion," exclaimed Napoleon. "Neufchatel is for Prussia a doomed position, to which, moreover, she has got but extremely doubtful rights. In return for it, for Wesel and Anspach, with their four hundred thousand inhabitants, you receive Hanover, which is contiguous to Prussia, and contains more than a million inhabitants ! I believe Prussia ought to be content with such an aggrandizement."

"Sire," said Haugwitz, "she would be especially content if she should obtain the faithful and influential friendship of France, and be able to retain it forever."

"You may rely on my word," replied the emperor, "I am always faithful to my enemies as well as to my friends. I crush the former and promote the interests of the latter whenever an opportunity offers. We will, however, prove to each other that we are in earnest about this alliance, and draw up its stipulations even to-day. Grand-marshal Durse has already received my instructions concerning this matter, and he will lay before you the particulars of the offensive and defensive alliance to be concluded between France and Prussia. Be kind enough to go to him and settle every thing with him, so that we may sign the document as soon as possible. Go, my dear count ; but first accept my congratulations, for at this hour you have done an important service to Prussia : you have saved her from destruction. I should have crushed her like a toy in my hand if you had rejected my offers of friendship. Go, the grand-marshal is waiting for you." *

He nodded a parting greeting to the confused, almost stunned count, and returned to his maps, thus depriving the Prussian minister of the possibility of entering into further explanations. The latter heaved a profound sigh, and, walking backward, turned slowly to the door.

Napoleon took no further notice of him ; he seemed wholly absorbed in his maps and plans : only when the door closed slowly behind the count, he said, in a low voice : "He will sign the treaty, and then Austria's last hope is gone ! Now I shall assume a more decided attitude in Presburg, and Austria will accept all my conditions ; she will be obliged to cede to me the Netherlands, Venice, and Tuscany, for now she cannot count any longer on Prussia's armed intervention."

CHAPTER LIII.

JUDITH AND HOLOFERNES.

NAPOLEON was still engaged in studying his maps and in changing the positions of the pins

---

* Napoleon's own words.—"Mémoires inédits," p. 20.

* The offensive and defensive alliance between the Emperor of France and the King of Prussia was concluded agreeably to the demands of Napoleon. Count Haugwitz, without obtaining further instructions from his sovereign, signed it on the 15th of December. The same day, in accordance with the treaty of Potsdam, he was to have delivered to Napoleon Prussia's declaration of war. Owing to the conclusion of this alliance, the position of Austria became utterly untenable, and she was obliged to accept the humiliating terms of Napoleon, and to sign, on the 26th of December, 1805, the peace of Presburg. This treaty deprived Austria of her best provinces, which were annexed to France, Bavaria, Wurtemberg and Baden. It is true, Prussia obtained the kingdom of Han-

on it. From time to time he was interrupted in this occupation by couriers bringing fresh dispatches from Presburg or France, but he constantly returned to his maps, and his finger passing over them extinguished kingdoms and boundaries to create new states in their places.

Evening was already drawing near, and the emperor was still in his cabinet. The door had already been opened repeatedly in a cautious manner, and Constant, the *valet de chambre*, had looked in with prying eyes, but seeing the emperor so busily engaged, he had always withdrawn cautiously and inaudibly. At length, however, he seemed tired of waiting any longer, and instead of withdrawing, again he entered and closed the door noiselessly.

This noise caused the emperor to start up.

"Well, Constant, what is the matter?" he asked.

"Sire," whispered Constant, in a low voice, as though he were afraid the walls might hear him, "sire, that distinguished lady has been here for an hour; she is waiting for the audience your majesty has granted to her."

"Ah, the countess or princess," said Napoleon, carelessly, "the foolish person who asserts that she hated me formerly but loves me now?"

"Sire, she speaks of your majesty in terms of the most unbounded enthusiasm."

"Ah, bah! Women like to be enthusiastic admirers of somebody, and to worship him with the gushing transports of their tender hearts! Would so many women go into convents and call Christ their bridegroom, if it were not so? But what is the name of this lady who has been pleased to fall in love with me?"

"Sire, I believe, the only condition she stipulated was that your majesty should not ask for her name."

The emperor frowned. "And you would persuade me to receive this nameless woman? Who knows but she may be a mere intriguer anxious to penetrate to me for some dark purpose?"

"Sire, one of the most faithful adherents and admirers of your majesty, M. von Brandt, formerly major in the Austrian service, pledges his word of honor that she is not, and—"

At this moment the door was opened violently, and Grand-marshal Duroc entered.

"Ah, your majesty is here still!" he exclaimed, joyfully. "Your majesty has not yet received the lady?"

"Well, does that concern you?" asked Napoleon, smiling. "You are jealous, perhaps? This lady is said to be very beautiful."

"Sire," said Duroc, solemnly, "even though she were as beautiful as Cleopatra, your majesty ought not to receive her."

"I *ought* not?" asked Napoleon, sternly. "What should prevent me from doing so?"

"Sire, the sacred duty to preserve yourself to your people, to your empire. This lady who tries to penetrate with so much passionate violence to your majesty is a dangerous intriguer, a mortal enemy of France and your majesty."

Napoleon cast a triumphant glance on Constant, who, pale and trembling, was leaning against the wall.

"Well," he asked, "will you defend her still?"

Without waiting for Constant's reply, he turned again to the grand-marshal.

"Whence did you obtain this information?"

"Sire, the governor of Vienna, M. de Vincennes, has just arrived here in the utmost haste. His horse fell half dead to the ground when he entered the court-yard. He feared that he might be too late."

"How too late?"

"Too late to warn your majesty from this lady who has evidently come to carry out some criminal enterprise."

"Ah, bah! she was, perhaps, going to assassinate me?"

"Sire, that is what M. de Vincennes asserts."

"Ah!" exclaimed Napoleon, turning once more toward Constant, "did you not tell me that she was deeply enamoured of me? Is the governor here still?"

"Yes, sire; he wants to know whether he shall not immediately arrest the lady and closely question her."

Napoleon was silent for a moment, and seemed to reflect.

"Constant," he then said, "tell M. de Vincennes to come hither. I myself want to speak to him."

Constant went at once into the anteroom and returned in a minute, to introduce the governor of Vienna, M. de Vincennes.

Napoleon hastily went to meet him. "You have come to warn me," he said, sternly. "What are your reasons for doing so?"

"Sire, the intentions of this lady are extremely suspicious. Since I have been in Vienna she has been incessantly watched by my agents, because she is the intellectual head of all the dangerous and hostile elements of the city. All the enemies of your majesty, all the so-called German patriots, meet at her house, and by closely watch-

over by virtue of the treaty with France, but this was an illusory aggrandizement which Prussia would have to conquer, sword in hand, from England.

ing *her*, we could learn all our enemies' plans and actions. Hence, it was necessary for us to find an agent in her house who would report to me every day what had been going on there, and I was so fortunate as to enlist the services of her mistress of ceremonies."

"By what means did you bribe her?" asked Napoleon. "By means of love or money?"

"Sire, thank God, money alone was sufficient for the purpose."

The emperor smiled. "The woman is old and ugly, then?"

"Very ugly, sire."

"And she hates her mistress because she is beautiful. For, I suppose, she is very beautiful?"

"Extremely so, sire; a most fascinating woman, and consequently the more dangerous as an intriguer."

Napoleon shrugged his shoulders. "Proceed with your report. You had bribed her mistress of ceremonies, then?"

"Yes, sire; she kept an accurate diary, containing a statement of what her mistress had been doing every hour, and brought it to me every evening. For the last few days the conduct of her mistress has seemed to her particularly suspicious; hence she watched her more closely, and my other agents dogged her steps in disguise whenever she left her mansion. All symptoms appeared suspicious enough, and pointed to the conclusion that she was meditating an attack upon some distinguished person. But I did not guess as yet whom she was aiming at. All at once, two hours ago, her mistress of ceremonies came to bring me her diary, and to report to me that her mistress had just left her mansion with Major von Brandt, and that her last words had indicated that she had gone to see your majesty at Schönbrunn. While I was still considering what ought to be done, another agent of mine made his appearance; I had commissioned him specially to watch M. von Brandt; for, although he seems to be extremely devoted to us, I do not trust him."

"And you are perfectly right," said Napoleon, sternly. "Traitors ought never to be trusted, and this M. von Brandt is a traitor, inasmuch as he adheres to us, the enemies of his country. What was the information brought to you by your agent?"

"Sire, my agent caused one of his men, who is a very skilful pickpocket, to steal the major's memorandum-book just at the moment when he was entering the lady's house."

"Indeed," said Napoleon, laughing. "Your agents are clever fellows. What did you find in

the memorandum-book? Love-letters and unpaid bills, I suppose?"

"No, sire, I found in it an important document; an agreement, by virtue of which the lady is to pay the major, in case he should obtain for her an interview with your majesty, a gold-piece for every minute of its duration."

Napoleon laughed. "The lady is as rich as Crœsus, then?" he asked.

"Yes, sire, the princess is said to—"

"Princess! What princess?"

"Sire, the lady to whom your majesty has granted an audience is the Princess von Eibenberg."

"The Princess von Eibenberg," replied Napoleon, musingly. "Did I not hear that name on some former occasion? Yes, yes, I remember," he said, in a low voice, after a short pause, as if speaking to himself; "the agent of the Count de Provence, who delivered to me the letter, and whom I then expelled from Paris."

"Have you got the diary of the mistress of ceremonies and the other papers with you?" he then asked the governor.

"I have, sire, here they are," replied M. de Vincennes, drawing a few papers from his bosom. "Here is also the singular agreement of the princess."

"Give them to me," said Napoleon; and taking the papers, he looked over them and read a few lines here and there. "Indeed," he then said, "this affair is piquant enough; it begins to excite my curiosity. Constant, where is the lady?"

"Sire, M. de Bausset has taken her to the small reception-room of your majesty; she is waiting there."

"Well," said Napoleon, "she has waited long enough, and might become impatient; I will, therefore, go to her."

"But, sire, you will not see her alone, I hope?" asked Duroc, anxiously. "I trust your majesty will permit me to accompany you?"

"Ah, you are anxious to see the famous belle?" asked Napoleon, laughing. "Another time, M. grand-marshal—but this time I shall go alone. Just remember that the princess is passionately enamoured of me, and that it, therefore, would terribly offend her if I should not come alone to the interview with her."

He advanced a few steps toward the door. But now Constant rushed toward him, and kneeling before him, exclaimed, in a voice trembling with anguish: "Sire, your majesty must have pity on me! Do not expose your priceless life to such a danger! Do not plunge my poor heart which adores your majesty into everlasting despair! It was I who first dared to request your majesty to receive this lady! Now, sire, I implore your majesty on my knees—do not receive her!"

"Sire, I venture to unite my prayers with those of Constant," said Duroc, urgently. "Sire, do not receive this lady!"

"Your majesty, permit me rather to arrest her immediately," exclaimed M. de Vincennes.

Napoleon's flaming eyes glanced in succession smilingly at the three men. "Truly," he said, "on hearing you, one might almost believe this beautiful woman to be a mine, and that it was merely necessary to touch her in order to explode and be shattered! Reassure yourselves, I believe we will save our life this time. You have warned me, and I shall be on my guard. Not another word, no more prayers! My resolution is fixed; I will see this beautiful woman, and, moreover, alone!"

"Sire," exclaimed Constant, anxiously, "suppose this crazy woman should fire a pistol at your head at the moment when your majesty appears before her?"

"In that case the bullets would harmlessly glance off from me, or the pistol would miss fire," replied Napoleon, in a tone of firm conviction. "Fate did not place me here to fall by the hands of an assassin! Go, gentlemen, and accept my thanks for your zeal and sympathy. M. de Vincennes, return to Vienna; I shall keep your papers here. Is Count Haugwitz still at your rooms, Duroc?"

"Yes, sire, we were just engaged in drawing up the several sections of the treaty, when M. de Vincennes sent for me."

"Return to the count, and you, Constant, go to M. von Brandt and count with him the minutes which his lady will pass in my company. I should not be surprised if he should earn a great many gold-pieces, for I do not intend dismissing the interesting *belle* so soon."

He nodded to them, and hastily crossing the room, passed through the door which Constant opened. With rapid steps, and without any further hesitation, he walked across the two large reception-halls, and then opened the door of the small reception-room where the lady, as Constant had told him, was waiting for him.

He remained for a moment on the threshold, and his burning glances turned toward Marianne, who, as soon as she saw him coming in, had risen from the arm-chair in which she had been sitting.

"It is true," murmured Napoleon to himself, "she is really beautiful!"

He advanced a few steps; then, as if remembering only at this moment that he had left the door wide open, he turned around and closed it. "I suppose you want to speak to me without witnesses?" he asked, approaching Marianne.

"Sire, the words of love and adoration fail too often in the presence of others," whispered Marianne, casting a flaming glance on him.

Napoleon smiled. "Well, why did you hesitate, then, just now to write the words of love and adoration between my shoulders?" he asked. "I turned my back to you intentionally; I wished to give you an opportunity for carrying out your heroic deed."

"What?" exclaimed Marianne, in terror, "has your majesty any doubts of my intentions?"

"No," said Napoleon, laughing, "I have no doubts whatever of your intentions; on the contrary, I am quite sure of them. I know that you have come hither to translate the Bible, the truth of which has been questioned so often, into reality. You intended to make of the chapter of Judith and Holofernes a tragedy of our times. But although you are as beautiful and seductive as Judith, I am no Holofernes, who allows himself to be ruled by his passion, and forgets the dictates of prudence in the arms of a woman. I never was the slave of my passions, madame, and it is not sufficient for a woman to be beautiful in order to win my heart; I must be able, too, to esteem her, and never should I be able to esteem a woman capable of loving the conqueror of her country. You see, therefore, that I am no Holofernes, and that I should not have opened my arms to you if I should have believed you to be a recreant daughter of your country. But I know that you are a patriot, and that alters the case: I know that I may esteem you; hence, I do not say that I cannot love you, for it is true, you are enchantingly beautiful."

"Sire," said Marianne, indignantly, "if you have only received me to insult and mortify me, pray permit me to withdraw!"

"No, I have received you because I wanted to give you good advice," said Napoleon, gravely; "I, therefore, pray you to remain. You must choose your servants more cautiously, madame; you must confide in them less and watch them better; for slavish souls are easily led astray, and money is a magnet they are unable to withstand. Your mistress of ceremonies is a traitress; beware of her!"

"Then she has slandered me?" asked Marianne, with quivering lips.

"No, she has only betrayed you," said Napoleon, smiling. "Even the diamond ring which you gave her as a souvenir did not touch her heart. Do you yet remember what you said to her when you handed it to her?"

"Sire, how should I remember it?" asked Marianne.

"Well, I will repeat it to you," exclaimed Napoleon, unfolding the papers which M. de Vincennes had given to him, and which he had kept all the time rolled up in his hand. "Here it is. You said: 'I know you are a good and enthusiastic Austrian; like myself, you hate the tyrant who wants to subjugate us, and you will bless the hand which will order him to stop, and put an end to his victorious career.' Well, was it not so, madame?"

Marianne made no reply; her cheeks were pale, and her eyes stared at the emperor, who looked at her smilingly.

"A moment before you had concealed a flashing object in your bosom," continued Napoleon. "That object which your mistress of ceremonies did not see distinctly was a dagger which you had bought this forenoon. Shall I tell you where?"—He glanced again at the papers, and then said: "You bought this dagger in a gun-store on the *Kohlmarkt*, and paid four ducats for it. You have now got this dagger with you; truly, it occupies an enviable hiding-place, and I might be jealous of it. Why do you not draw it forth and carry out your purpose? Do you really believe what so many fools have said about me, viz., that I was in the habit of wearing a coat-of-mail? I pledge you my imperial word, my breast is unprotected, and a dagger will meet with no resistance provided it is able to reach my breast. Just try it!"

Marianne, who, while the emperor was speaking, had dropped on a chair as if stupefied, now rose impetuously. "Sire," she said, proudly, "it is enough. Your officers doubtless await me in the adjoining room, in order to arrest me like a criminal. Permit me to go thither and surrender to them."

She was about turning toward the door, but Napoleon seized her hand and kept her back. "Oh, no," he said, "our interview is not yet over; it has scarcely lasted fifteen minutes, and remember that M. von Brandt would consequently get only fifteen gold-pieces. Ah, you look at me in surprise. You wonder that I should be aware of that, too? I am no magician, however, and have acquired my knowledge of this laughable incident in a very simple manner. Look here, this is the written agreement you gave to M. von Brandt!"

He offered the paper to Marianne; she did not take it, however, but only glanced at it. "Your

majesty may see from it how ardently I longed for an interview with you," she said. "Had M. von Brandt asked half my fortune for this interview with your majesty, I should have joyfully given it to him, for an hour in the presence of your majesty is worth more than all the riches of the world."

"And yet you were going to leave me just now!" exclaimed Napoleon, reproachfully. "How ingenuous that would have been toward your friend who is standing in the anteroom with Constant, and, watch in hand, calculating the number of his gold-pieces! We will be generous and grant him three hours. Three hours—that is a good time for a rendezvous; when you leave me, then, you will pay M. von Brandt one hundred and eighty louis-d'or, and I shall receive the congratulations of my confidants."

Marianne's eyes flashed angrily, and a deep blush mantled her cheeks. "Sire," she exclaimed almost menacingly, "call your officers—have me arrested like a criminal—take my life if I have deserved it, but let me leave this room!"

"Ah, you would die rather than that people should believe you had granted me a rendezvous of three hours' duration," asked Napoleon. "It is true, this rendezvous, if it should result peacefully and without the *éclat* which you hoped for when you came hither to play the part of Judith, would discredit you with your friends! Your party will distrust you as soon as it learns that, after being three hours with me, you left Schönbrunn in the middle of the night, while I was not found on my couch with a dagger in my heart. I cannot spare you this humiliation; it shall be the only punishment I shall inflict on you. You remain here!"

"Sire, let me go," exclaimed Marianne, "and I swear to you that I will never dare again to approach you; I swear to you that I will live in some remote corner in the most profound retirement, far from the noise and turmoil of the world."

"Oh, the world would never forgive me if I should deprive it in this manner of its most beautiful ornament," said the emperor, smiling. "You are too lovely to live in obscurity and solitude. You will now grant me three hours, and you are free to tell everybody during the whole remainder of your life that you hate me; but it is true, people will hardly believe in the sincerity of your hatred."

"Then you will not permit me to withdraw?" asked Marianne, with quivering lips. "You want me to stay here?"

"Only three hours, madame; then you may

go. Let us improve this time and speak frankly and honestly to each other. Forget where we are; imagine we were the heads of two parties, meeting on neutral ground and telling each other the truth with respectful frankness for the purpose of thereby bringing about peace, if possible. Well, then, tell me honestly: do you really hate me so ardently as to have come hither for the purpose of assassinating me?"

"You ask me to tell you the truth," exclaimed Marianne, her eyes sparkling with anger, "well, you shall hear it! Yes, I hate you; I swore to you in Paris, at the time when you sent me like a criminal to the frontier, the most ardent and implacable hatred, and in accordance with my oath I came hither to accomplish a work which would be a boon for Germany, nay, for the whole world. Yes, I wanted to assassinate you, I wanted to deliver the world from the tyrant who intends to enslave it. Yes, I had concealed a dagger in my bosom to kill you as Judith killed Holofernes. Had I accomplished my purpose, the world would have blessed me and paid the highest honors to my name; but now that I have failed in carrying out my plan, I shall be laughed and sneered at. Now I have told you the truth, and in order that you may not doubt it, I will show you the dagger which was intended for your breast, and which I shall now hurl down at your feet as the dragon's feet, from which one day full-grown warriors will spring for our cause in order to combat you."

She drew the dagger from her bosom, and, with a violent gesture, threw it at Napoleon's feet. "Sire," she then asked, in an imploring voice, "will you not yet order me to be arrested?"

"Why?" asked Napoleon. "Words falling from the lips of beautiful women are never insulting, and I do not punish thoughts which have not yet become actions. Your hands are free from guilt, and the only criminal here in this room is that dagger on the floor. I trample it under foot, and it is unable to rise any more against me."

He placed his foot on the flashing blade, and fixed his piercing eye on the princess. "Madame," he said, "when you came to me in Paris, it was the Count de Provence who had sent you. He sent me a letter through you at that time. Tell me, did he send me this dagger to-day?"

"No, I will take the most solemn oath that he knows nothing about it," replied Marianne. "Nobody knew of my undertaking; I had no confidants and no accomplices."

"You had only your own hatred, madame," said Napoleon, musingly. "Why do you hate me so bitterly? What have I done to all of you that you should turn away from me?"

"Why I hate you?" asked Marianne, impetuously. "Because you have come to trample Germany in the dust, to transform her into a French province, and to defraud us of our honor, our good rights, and independence. What have you done, that all honest men should turn away from you? You have broken your most sacred oaths —you are a perjurer!"

"Oh, that goes too far," cried Napoleon, passionately. "What hinders me, then—"

"To have me arrested?" Marianne interrupted him, defiantly—"please do so."

"No, I shall not do you that favor. Proceed, proceed! You stand before me as though you were Germania herself rising before me to accuse me. Well, then, accuse me. When have I broken my oaths?"

"From the moment when you raised the banner in the name of the republic which you intended to upset; from the moment when you called the nations to you in the name of liberty, in order to rule over them as their tyrant and oppressor!"

"To those who wanted to keep up the despotism of liberty under which France had bled and groaned so long, I was a tyrant," said Napoleon, calmly; "to those who entertained the senseless idea of restoring the Bourbons, under whom France had bled and groaned as long and longer, I was an oppressor. The family of the Bourbons has become decrepit; it resembles a squeezed lemon, the peel of which is thrown contemptuously aside, because there is no longer any juice in it. Did you really believe I should have been such a fool as to pick up this empty peel, which France had thrown aside, and to clothe it in a purple cloak and crown? Did you believe I had, like those Bourbons and all legitimate princes, learned nothing from history, and not been taught by the examples it holds up to all those who have eyes to see with? I have learned from history that dynasties dry up like trees, and that it is better to uproot the hollow, withered-up trunk rather than permit it, in its long decay, to suck up the last nourishing strength from the soil on which it stands."

"Sire, you do not only uproot the decaying trunk, but with the axe of the tyrant you deprived this trunk of its fresh, green branches also," exclaimed Marianne.

"Ah, you refer to the Duke d'Enghien," said Napoleon, quietly. "It was an act of policy, which I do not regret. The Bourbons had to understand at length that France wanted to give them up and create a new era for herself. I stood at the head of this new era, and I had to fill in a becoming manner the position Providence had conferred on me. Providence destined me to become the founder of a new dynasty, and there will be a day when my family will occupy the first thrones of the world." *

"That is to say, you declare war against all princes," exclaimed Marianne.

"Against the princes, yes," said Napoleon, "for they are nothing but over-ripe fruits only waiting for the hand that is to shake them off. I shall be this hand, and before me they will fall to the ground, and I shall rise higher and higher above them. You call me a conqueror, but how could I stop now in my work? If I should pause now in my conquests and sheathe my sword, what should I have gained by so many efforts but a little glory, without having approached the goal to which I was aspiring? What should I have gained by setting all Europe in a blaze if I should be contented with having overthrown empires and not hasten to build up *my own* empire on solid foundations? It is not birth that entitles me to immortality. The man who is possessed of courage, who does good service to his country, and renders himself illustrious by great exploits, that man needs no pedigree, for he is every thing by himself." †

"But in the eyes of the legitimists he is always nothing but an upstart," said Marianne, shrugging her shoulders.

"In that case he must overthrow and annihilate all legitimists," said Napoleon, quickly; "so that a new dynasty may arise, of which he will be the founder. I am the man of Destiny, and shall found a new dynasty, and one day the whole of Europe will be but one empire, *my* empire! All of you, instead of cursing me, should joyfully hail my coming and welcome me as your liberator sent by Providence to raise you from your degradation and disgrace. Just look around, you Germans, and see what sort of princes and governments you have got. Are you being ruled by noble, high-minded sovereigns; are men of ability and character at the head of your governments? I only behold impotence, infamy, and venality everywhere in the German cabinets. The system of nepotism is everywhere in force; offices are gifts of favor, and not rewards of merit; intrigues and corrupt influences succeed in placing the foremost positions of the state into the hands of incapable men, and great minds, if there be any at all, are utterly ignored. The result of this system is, of course, that men cease cultivating their minds, and that the virtues and talents which are not re-

warded with a just tribute of glory, lose their vigor and enthusiasm; nay, often their very existence. When a nation sees none but incapable favorites and venal intriguers at the head of the various departments of its administration and of its armies, how is it to prosper and expand, to increase its wealth, and to win victories? Woe to the nation which allows itself to be governed by such ministers, and to be defended by such generals as I have found everywhere in Germany! As the man of Destiny, I have come to devote to her my hand, my mouth, and my heart for the purpose of liberating her and delivering her from her disgraceful chains." *

"And to load her with even more disgraceful ones," exclaimed Marianne, her eyes flaming with anger; "for there is nothing more disgraceful on earth than a nation submitting to a foreign barbarian and humbly kissing the feet of its oppressor, instead of expelling him by the majesty of its wrath. If you, a modern Attila, go on with your murderous sword, Europe is ruined, and all dignity of the nations, all the centres of scientific eminence, all the hopes of humanity are lost. For nations can only perform great things, and create great things, when they are independent; and freedom itself is of no use to them if they must receive it as a favor at the hands of their conqueror."

"Earth ought to have but one ruler, as heaven has but one God," said Napoleon, solemnly. "I have only begun my task; it is not yet accomplished. Hitherto I have subjected only France, Italy, Switzerland, and Holland to my sceptre, but my goal is even more sublime than that. And who will prevent me from seizing Westphalia, the Hanseatic cities, and Rome, and from annexing the Illyrian provinces, Etruria, and Portugal to France? I do not know yet where to fix the boundaries of my empire. Perhaps it will have no other boundaries than the vast space of the two hemispheres; perhaps, like Americus Vespucius and Columbus, I shall obtain the glory of discovering and conquering another unknown world!" †

"And if you should discover a third world," exclaimed Marianne, "God may decree, perhaps, that in this new world, an avenger of the two old worlds may arise and tell you in the thundering voice of Jehovah: 'Here are the boundaries of your empire! so far and no farther!'"

"But I should not shrink back," said Napo-

* Napoleon's own words.—Vide "Le Normand," vol. ii., p. 29.
† Ibid., vol. ii., p. 42.

* Napoleon's own words.—"Le Normand," vol. ii., p. 39.
† Napoleon's own words.—"Le Normand, Mémoires," vol. ii., p. 69.

leon, smiling, "but advance to fight for my good right with the avenger sent by Providence, for I was also sent by Providence; I am a chosen son of Heaven, and if there is a misfortune for me, it is that I have come too late. Men are too enlightened or too sober; hence, it is impossible to accomplish great things."

"Ah, you say so," exclaimed Marianne, "you, whose fate is so brilliant and exalted? You, who once were a humble officer of artillery, and now are seated as emperor on a mighty throne?"

"Yes," said Napoleon, in a low voice, as if to himself, "I admit, my career was brilliant enough, —I have pursued a splendid path! But how much difference there is between me and the heroes of antiquity! How much more fortunate was Alexander! After conquering Asia, he declared he was the son of Jove, and the whole Orient believed it, except Olympias, who knew very well what to think of it, and except Aristotle, and a few other pedants of Athens! But if I, who have made more conquests and won greater victories than Alexander,—if I should declare to-day I were the son of God, and offer Him my thanksgiving under this title, there would be no fishwoman that would not laugh at me. The nations are too enlightened and too sober; it is impossible to accomplish great things." *

"There will be a day, sire, when the nations will rise and prove to you that they are able to accomplish great things!"

"And on that day they will trample me in the dust, I suppose?" asked Napoleon, with an almost compassionate smile. "Do not hope too sanguinely for this day, for your hopes might deceive you. I have spoken so freely and frankly to you," he continued, rising, "because I knew that, by speaking to you, I was speaking, through you, to the most eminent, high-minded, and patriotic men of your nation, and because I wished to be comprehended and appreciated by them. Go, then, and repeat my words to them—repeat them to those, too, who believe that the throne which I have erected belongs to *them*, and that the tri-colored flag would have to disappear one day before the lilies. Go, madame, and tell those enthusiastic Bourbons the lilies were so dreadfully steeped in the misery and blood of France that nobody would recognize them there, and that everybody was shrinking back from their cadaverous smell and putridity. Empires and dynasties, like flowers, have but one day of bloom; the day of the Bourbons is past; they are faded and stripped of their leaves. State

it to those who one day sent you *certainly* to me, and *perhaps* again to-day. If you relate to them to-day's scene, they may deplore, perhaps, that fate did not permit you to become a Judith, but they will have to acknowledge at least that I am no Holofernes. For although the most beautiful woman of my enemies came to my couch to visit me, she did not kill me, and her dagger lies at my feet! I shall preserve it as a remembrancer, and Grand-marshal Duroc, M. von Brandt, and Constant, my *valet de chambre*, who are waiting for you in the anteroom, will believe that dagger to be a souvenir of your love and of a delightful hour of my life. We will not undeceive them! Farewell, madame!"

He gave Marianne no time to answer him, but took the silver bell and rang it so loudly and violently that Constant appeared in evident terror in the door.

"Constant," said the emperor, "conduct the lady to her carriage; she will return to Vienna; and as for M. von Brandt, tell him the princess had allowed me to be her paymaster, and to pay him in her place for the happy minutes of our interview."

"Sire," ejaculated Marianne, in dismay, "you will—"

"Hush," the emperor interrupted her proudly, "I will pay my tribute to Dame Fortune! Farewell, madame; remember this hour sometimes!"

He waved a parting salutation to her with his hand, and then disappeared through the door leading to his bedroom.

Marianne stared at him until he was gone, as though she had just seen a ghost walking before her, and as though her whole soul were concentrated in this look with which she gazed after him.

"Madame," said Constant, in a low voice, "if you please!" And he approached the large hall-door which he opened.

Marianne started when she heard his words as if she were awaking from a dream; she left the room silently, and without deigning to glance at Constant, and followed her smiling guide through the halls. In the first anteroom she beheld Grand-marshal Duroc and several generals, who looked at the princess with threatening and sorrowful glances. Marianne felt these glances as if they were daggers piercing her soul, and daggers seemed to strike her ears when she heard Constant say to Major von Brandt: "You will stay here, sir; for the emperor has ordered me to pay you here for the hours his majesty has spent with the princess."

By a violent effort, Marianne succeeded in over-

---

* Napoleon's own words.—Vide "Mémoires du Maréchal Duc de Raguse," vol. II., p. 243.

coming her emotions, and with a proudly erect head, with a cold and immovable face, she walked on across the anterooms and descended the staircase until she reached her carriage.

Only when the carriage rolled along the road toward Vienna through the silent night, the coachman, notwithstanding the noise of the wheels, thought he heard loud lamentations, which seemed to proceed from the interior of the carriage. But he must have certainly been mistaken, for when the carriage stopped in the court-yard in front of her mansion, and the footman hastened to open the coach-door, the princess alighted as proud and calm, as beautiful and radiant as ever, and ascended the staircase coolly and slowly. At the head of the stairs stood Madame Camilla, muttering a few words with trembling lips and pale cheeks. Marianne apparently did not see her at all, and walked coldly and proudly down the corridor leading to her rooms.

She ordered the maids, who received her in her dressing-room, with an imperious wave of her hand, to withdraw, and when they had left the room she locked the door behind them. She then went with rapid steps to the boudoir contiguous to the dressing-room, and here, where she was sure that no one could see or overhear her, she allowed the proud mask to glide from her face, and showed its boundless despair. With a loud shriek of anguish she sank on her knees and raising her folded hands to heaven, cried, in the wailing notes of terrible grief:

"Oh, my God, my God! let me succumb to this disgrace. Have mercy on me, and let me die!"

But after long hours of struggling and despair, of lamentations and curses, Marianne rose again from her knees with defiant pride and calm energy.

"No," she muttered, "I must not, will not die! Life has still claims on me, and the secret league, of which I have become the first member, imposes on me the duty of living and working in its service. I was unable to strike the tyrant with my dagger; well, then, we must try to kill him gradually by means of pin-pricks. Such a pin-prick is the manuscript which Gentz has intrusted to me in order to have it published and circulated throughout Germany. Somewhere a printing-office will be found to set up this manuscript with its types; I will seek for it, and pay the weight of its types in gold."

Early next morning the travelling-coach of the princess stood at the door, and Marianne, dressed in a full travelling-costume, prepared for immediate departure. She had spent the whole night

in arranging her household affairs. Now every thing was done, every thing was arranged and ready, and when about to descend the staircase, the princess turned around to Madame Camilla, who followed her humbly.

"Madame," she said, coldly and calmly, "you will be kind enough to leave my house this very hour, in order to write your diary somewhere else. The French governor of Vienna will assign to you, perhaps, a place with his *mouchards;* go, therefore, to him, and never dare again to enter my house. My steward has received instructions from me; he will pay you your wages, and see to it that you will leave the house within an hour. Adieu!"

Without vouchsafing to glance at Madame Camilla, she descended the staircase calmly and haughtily, and entered her carriage, which rolled through the lofty portal of the court-yard with thundering noise.

CHAPTER LIV.

THE FALL OF THE GERMAN EMPIRE.

THE peace of Presburg had been concluded; it had deprived Austria of her best provinces.

The offensive and defensive alliance between Prussia and France had been signed; it had deprived Prussia of the principalities of Cleves, Berg, and Neufchatel.

Germany, therefore, had reason enough in the beginning of 1806 to mourn and complain, for her princes had been humiliated and disgraced; her people had to bear with their princes the ignominy of degradation and dependence.

Germany, however, seemed to be joyful and happy; festivals were being celebrated everywhere—festivals in honor of the Emperor Napoleon and his family, festivals of love and happiness.

After the victory Napoleon had obtained at Austerlitz over the two emperors, after the conclusion of the treaty of Presburg and the alliance with Prussia, all causes of war with Germany seemed removed, and Napoleon laid his sword aside in order to repose on his laurels in the bosom of his family, and, instead of founding new states, to bring about marriages between his relations and the scions of German sovereigns—marriages which were to draw closer the links of love and friendship uniting France with Germany, and to make all Germany the obedient son-in-law and vassal of the Emperor of France.

In Munich, the wedding-bells which made Napoleon the father-in-law of a German dynasty, were first rung. In Munich, in the beginning of 1806, Eugene Beauharnais, Napoleon's adopted son, was married to the beautiful and noble Princess Amelia of Bavaria, daughter of Maximilian, elector of Bavaria, who, by the grace of Napoleon, had become King of Bavaria, as Eugene, by the same grace, had become Viceroy of Italy.

All Bavaria was jubilant with delight at the new and most fortunate ties uniting the German state with France; all Bavaria felt honored and happy when the Emperor Napoleon, with his wife Josephine, came to Munich to take part in the wedding-ceremonies. Festivals followed each other in quick succession in Munich; only happy faces were to be seen there, only jubilant shouts, laughter, and merry jests were to be heard; and whenever Napoleon appeared in the streets or showed himself on the balcony of the palace, the people received him with tremendous cheers, and waved their hats at the emperor, regardless of the blood and tears he had wrung but a few days before from another German state.

No sooner had the wedding-bells ceased ringing in Munich than they commenced resounding in Carlsruhe; for Napoleon wanted there, too, to become the father-in-law of another German dynasty, and the niece of Josephine, Mademoiselle Stephanie de Beauharnais, married the heir of the Elector of Baden, who now, by the grace of Napoleon, become Grand-duke of Baden.

And to the merry notes of the wedding-bells of Munich and Carlsruhe, were soon added the joyful sound of the bells which announced to Germany the rise of a new sovereign house within her borders, and inaugurated the elevation of the brother-in-law of the Emperor of France to the dignity of a sovereign German prince. Those solemn bells resounded in Cleves and Berg, and did homage to Joachim Murat, who, by the grace of Napoleon, had become Grand-duke of Berg. Prussia and Bavaria had to furnish the material for this new princely cloak; Prussia had given the larger portion of it, the Duchy of Cleves, and Bavaria, grateful for so many favors, had added to it the principality of Berg, so that these two German states together formed a nice grand-duchy for the son of the French innkeeper—for Joachim Murat, for the brother-in-law of the French emperor.

And when the joyful sounds had died away in Munich, Carlsruhe, and the new grand-duchy of Berg, they resounded again in Stuttgardt, for in that capital the betrothal of Jerome, youngest brother of Napoleon, and of a daughter of the Elector of Wurtemberg, who now, by the grace

of Napoleon, had become King of Wurtemberg, was celebrated. It is true Jerome, the emperor's brother, wore no crown as yet; it is true this youngest son of the Corsican lawyer had hitherto been nothing but an "imperial prince of France," but his royal father-in-law of Wurtemberg felt convinced that his august brother, Napoleon, would endow the husband of his daughter in a becoming manner, and place some vacant or newly-to-be-created crown on his head. Napoleon, moreover, had just then endowed his elder brother Joseph in such a manner, and made him King of Naples, after solemnly declaring to Europe in a manifesto, that "the dynasty of Naples had ceased to reign, and that the finest country on earth was to be delivered at length from the yoke of the most perfidious persons." And in accordance with his word, Napoleon had overthrown the Neapolitan dynasty, expelled King Ferdinand and Queen Caroline from their capital, and placed his brother Joseph on the throne of Naples.[*]

Hence, the King of Wurtemberg was not afraid; he was sure that Napoleon would discover somewhere a falling crown for his brother Jerome, and give to the daughter of the most ancient German dynasty a position worthy of the honor of her house.

But the joyful bells were not only rung in Germany; they resounded also from the borders of Holland, which now, by the grace of Napoleon, had become a kingdom, and to which, again by the grace of Napoleon, a king had been given, in the person of Louis, another brother of the Emperor of France. They resounded, too, from Italy, where, in this blessed year of 1806, so productive of new crowns, on one day, March 30, 1806, suddenly twelve duchies sprang from the ground and placed as many ducal crowns on the heads of Napoleon's friends and comrades.

The year of 1806, therefore, was a blessed and happy year; joy and exultation reigned everywhere, and Napoleon was the author of all this happiness.

Still there was in the German empire a city which, in spite of all these recent festivals and demonstrations of satisfaction, maintained a grave and gloomy aspect, and apparently took no part

---

[*] Napoleon rewarded his generals and ministers, besides, with duchies, which he created for them in Italy, and the rich revenues of which he assigned to them. Thus Marmont became Duke of Ragusa; Mortier, Duke of Treviso; Bessières, Duke of Istria; Savary, Duke of Rovigo; Lannes, Duke of Montebello; Bernadotte, Prince of Pontecorvo; Talleyrand, Prince of Benevento; Fouché, Duke of Otranto; Maret, Duke of Bassano; Soult, Duke of Dalmatia; Berthier, Prince of Neufchatel; Duroc, Duke of Frioul, etc.

whatever in the universal joy, but lived in its sullen, dull quiet as it had done for centuries.

This city was Ratisbon, the seat of the German Diet, and now the property and capital of the archchancellor of the German empire, Baron Dalberg.

For centuries Ratisbon had enjoyed the proud honor of having the ambassadors of all the German states meet in its old city-hall, for the purpose of deliberating on the welfare of Germany. From the arched windows of the large session-hall the new laws flitted all over Germany, and what the gentlemen at Ratisbon had decided on, had to be submitted to by the princes and people of Germany.

And, just as hundreds and hundreds of years ago, they were still in session at Ratisbon—the ambassadors of the emperor, of the kings, electors, dukes, free cities, counts, and barons of the German empire. There met every day in their old hall the states of Austria, Prussia, Bavaria, Hanover, Wurtemberg, Baden, Hesse-Darmstadt, Mecklenberg, Brunswick, and whatever might be the names of the different members of the great German empire.

They met, but they did not deliberate any longer; they merely guessed what might be the fate of Germany, how long they would sit there in gloomy idleness, and when it might please the new protector of Germany, the Emperor of France, to remember them and say to them : "Go home, gentlemen, for your time has expired. The German Diet has ceased to exist, and I will deliver Germany from this burden."

But neither the Emperor of France nor the sovereigns of Germany seemed to remember that there was a Diet still in session at the ancient city-hall of Ratisbon, which formerly had to sanction all treaties of peace, all cessions of territory, and all political changes whatever, so that they might be recognized and become valid in the German empire.

Now, the Emperor of Germany had not even deemed it necessary to submit to the Diet at Ratisbon the treaty of peace concluded with Napoleon at Presburg for ratification, but had contented himself with merely notifying the Diet of its conclusion. In the same manner, and on the same day, the ambassadors of Bavaria and Wurtemberg had risen from their seats to announce to the Diet that they were now no longer representatives of electors, but of kings—Bavaria and Wurtemberg, with the consent of the Emperor of France, having assumed the royal title ; and when these two gentlemen had resumed their seats, the ambassador of the Elector of Baden rose for the purpose of declaring that he was representing no longer an electorate, but a grand-duchy—the Elector of Baden, with the consent of the Emperor of France, having assumed the grand-ducal title.

The Diet had received these announcements silently and without objection ; it had been silent, also, when, a few days later, the French ambassador, M. Bather, appeared in the session-hall and announced that Murat, as Duke of Cleves, had become a member of the German empire. Every ambassador, however, had asked himself silently how it happened that the new member of the empire did not hasten to avail himself of his rights, and to send an ambassador to take his seat at the Diet of Ratisbon.

The Diet, as we have stated already, received all these announcements in silence, and what good would it have done to it to speak ? Who still respected its voice ? Who still bowed to its name ?

Only for appearance sake, only for the purpose of conversing with each other in a low tone about their own misfortunes, their weakness and impotence, did the ambassadors of the German princes and cities meet still, and instead of giving laws to Germany, as formerly, they only communicated to each other their suppositions concerning the fate that might be in store for Germany and the German Diet at Ratisbon.

The gentlemen were assembled again to-day in the large session-hall, and all the German states, which elsewhere were bitterly quarrelling with each other, were sitting peaceably around the large green-table and chatting about the events that had taken place in the German empire, and might occur in the near future.

"Have you read the new pamphlets which are creating so great a sensation at the present time ?" said Prussia to Saxony, who was seated by her side.

"No, I never read any pamphlets," replied Saxony.

"It is worth while, however, to read these pamphlets," said Prussia, smiling ; "for they treat of an absurd idea in a most eloquent and enthusiastic manner. Just think of it, they advocate in dead earnest the idea of placing the German empire, now that the power of Austria has been paralyzed, under the protection of Bavaria, and of appointing the new King of Bavaria chief of Germany."

"The idea is not so bad, after all," said Saxony, smiling ; "the Bavarian dynasty is one of the most ancient in Germany, and its power is greater than ever, inasmuch as it may boast of the friendship and favor of the Emperor of France. The Em-

16

peror Napoleon would, perhaps, raise no objections in case the King of Bavaria should be elected Emperor of Germany."

"Oh, no," whispered Brunswick, Saxony's neighbor on the left; "I received late and authentic news yesterday. The Emperor Napoleon intends completely to restore the German empire of the middle ages, and will himself assume the imperial crown of Germany." *

"What," exclaimed Hesse, who had overheard the words, "the Emperor Napoleon wants to make himself Emperor of Germany?"

And Hesse had spoken so loudly in her surprise that the whole Diet had heard her words, and every one repeated them in great astonishment, while every face assumed a grave and solemn air.

"Yes, you may believe that such is the case," said Bavaria, in an audible tone; "important changes are in store for us, and I know from the best source that Minister Talleyrand said the other day, quite loudly and positively, 'That the fate of the German empire would be decided on toward the end of this month.'" †

"And to-day is already the 23d of May," said Oldenburg, musingly; "we may look, therefore, every hour for a decision."

"Yes, we may do so," exclaimed Würzburg; "I know for certain that they are already engaged in Paris in drawing up a new constitution for Germany."

"It might be good, perhaps," said her neighbor, "if we should also commence to draw up a new constitution for Germany, and then send it to Minister Talleyrand, because we are certainly more familiar with the customs and requirements of the German empire than the statesmen of France. We ought to consult with the archchancellor, Baron Dalberg, about this matter. But where is the archchancellor; where is Dalberg?"

"Yes, it is true, the archchancellor has not yet made his appearance," exclaimed Oldenburg, wonderingly. "Where can he be? Where is Dalberg?"

And the question was whispered from mouth to mouth, "Where is Dalberg?"

Formerly, in the glorious old times of the German empire, it had been the German emperor who, at the commencement of the sessions of the Diet, had always asked in a loud voice, "Is there no Dalberg?" And at his question, the Dalbergs had come forward and placed themselves around the emperor's throne, always ready to undertake great things and to carry out bold adventures.

Now, it was not the emperor who called for his Dalberg, but the Diet that whispered his name.

And it seemed as if the man who had been called for, had heard these whispers, for the large doors of the old session-hall opened, and the archchancellor of the empire, Baron Dalberg, entered.

Clad in his full official costume, he stepped into the hall and approached his seat at the green-table. But instead of sitting down on the high-backed, carved arm-chair, he remained standing, and his eyes glided greetingly past all those grave and gloomy faces which were fixed on him.

"I beg the august Diet to permit me to lay a communication before it," said the archchancellor of the empire, with a bow to the assembly.

The grave faces of the ambassadors nodded assent, and Dalberg continued, in a loud and solemn voice: "I have to inform the Diet that, as I am growing old and feel a sensible decline of my strength, I have deemed it indispensable for the welfare of Germany and myself to choose already a successor and coadjutor. Having long looked around among the noble and worthy men who surround me in so great numbers, I have at length made my selection and come to such a decision as is justified by the present state of affairs. The successor whom I have selected is a worthy and high-minded man, whose ancestors have greatly distinguished themselves in the fifteenth and sixteenth centuries in the service of the German empire. It is the Archbishop and Cardinal Fesch, uncle of the Emperor of France."

A long and painful pause ensued; the members of the Diet looked, as if stupefied with terror and astonishment, at this man who, himself a German prince, dared to inform the German Diet that he had invited a foreigner to share with him the high dignity of a first German elector and of inheriting it after his death.

Dalberg read, perhaps, in the gloomy mien of the gentlemen the thoughts which they dared not utter, for he hastened to communicate to the Diet the motives which had influenced him in making the above-named selection. He told them he had acted thus, not in his own interest, but in order to maintain the menaced constitution of the German empire and to place it under Napoleon's powerful protection. He then informed them joyfully that the Emperor of the French had already approved of the appointment of his uncle, Cardinal Fesch, and promised, moreover, that he would devote his personal attention to the regeneration of the German empire and always afford it protection.

The members of the Diet had moodily listen-

* Häusser's "History of Germany," vol. II, p. 721.

† Ibid., p. 725.

ed to him; their air had become more and more dissatisfied and gloomy; and when the elector paused, not a single voice was heard to propose the vote of thanks which Dalberg, on concluding his remarks, had asked for, but only a profound, ominous stillness followed his speech.

This however, was the only official demonstration which the German Diet ventured to make against the appointment of Cardinal Fesch, and their silence did not prevent the consummation of this unparalleled measure. A foreigner, not even familiar with the German language, now became coadjutor of the archchancellor of the German empire—a foreigner became the first member of the German electoral college—a foreigner was to have the seals of the empire in his hands, keep the laws of Germany in his archives, and preside at the election of the emperors and at the sessions of the Diet! And this foreigner was the uncle of the Emperor of the French, of the conqueror of the world. But the German Diet was silent and suffered on.

The horizon of Germany became more and more clouded; the Diet continued its sessions quietly, calmly, and inaudibly in the old city hall at Ratisbon.

It was reported everywhere that the Emperor of France was about to give a new constitution to the German empire, and that the Emperor of Germany had pledged himself in the treaty of Presburg not to oppose the plans of Napoleon in relation to Germany.

The Diet paid no attention to these rumors; it remained in session, and did not interrupt its silence. It remained in session while the secondary German princes, whose ambassadors were assembled in Ratisbon hastened in person to Paris, in order to appear there as humble supplicants in the anterooms of the emperor and Talleyrand, and to win the favor of Napoleon and his minister. This favor, they hoped, would gain for them crowns and states, render them powerful and influential, and give them a brilliant position. For Talleyrand had secretly whispered into the ears of all of them: "Those who oppose the emperor's plans, and refuse to accept his protection, will be *mediatized!*"* Every one of these secondary German princes hoped, therefore, that the others would be *mediatized*, and that he would receive the possessions of his neighbors. Every one, therefore, was most zealous in protesting his entire submission to the emperor's will, and in trying to gain as much as possible by flattery, bribery, and humble supplication. It seemed as though in Paris, in

the anterooms of the emperor and his minister Talleyrand, a market-booth had been opened, in which dice were being thrown for German states and German crowns, or where they were sold at auction to the highest bidder! *

The Diet heard only rumors, vague rumors, about these proceedings, and remained quietly in session. It met every day and waited.

And at length, on the 1st of August, 1806, the large doors of the hall, in which the ambassadors of the German empire were assembled, opened, and the minister of the French emperor appeared in their midst, and approached in solemn earnest the green table, on which hitherto Germany alone had had the right to depose her notes and declarations, and on which hitherto the German Diet alone had written laws for Germany.

But Bacher, the French minister, came to force a new law upon the German Diet—the law of the French emperor.

The representative of the French emperor addressed the German Diet in a solemn tone, and as the vast session-hall echoed the loud, imperious voice of the foreigner, it seemed as if he called up from their graves the ghosts of past centuries, and as if they then placed themselves like a protecting gray cloud before the menaced Diet.

"The German constitution," said the minister of France—"the German constitution is now but a shadow; the Diet has ceased to have a will of its own. Hence his majesty, the Emperor of France and Italy, is not obliged to recognize the existence of this German constitution any longer; a new confederation of German princes will be formed under his protection, and his majesty will assume the title of Protector of the Confederation of the Rhine. In order to maintain peace, he declared formerly that he would never extend the boundaries of France beyond the Rhine, and he has faithfully kept his word. †

And after Bacher had uttered these words, sixteen members of the Diet, twelve princes, and four

---

* *Mediatized* position of the small German states, when their princes were under an emperor!

* Enormous bribes were paid by the German princes to win the favor of the prominent functionaries of the French empire, in order to be saved by their influence from being *mediatized*, and to obtain as valuable additions to their territories as possible. Diplomatic gifts were not even secretly distributed, but the business was carried on as publicly as if the persons concerned in it had been on 'change. Everybody knew that the Prince of Salm-Kyrburg had bought of one of the French ministers two hundred thousand bottles of champagne at an enormous rate; that Labesnardière, Talleyrand's first secretary, had received half a million of francs from Hesse Darmstadt; and that the Duke of Mecklenburg had promised him one hundred and twenty thousand Fredericks d'ors if he should retain his sovereignty.—Vide Montgaillard, "Histoire de France," vol. x., p. 115.

† "Mémoires d'un Homme d'État," vol. ix., p. 160.

electors, rose from their seats. The first of the German electors, the archchancellor of the empire, Charles Theodore von Dalberg, was their speaker, and he explained to the Diet, in the name of his fifteen colleagues, their intentions and views.

"The last three wars have demonstrated," he exclaimed, "that the German empire is rotten and virtually destroyed; hence we German princes of the south and west of Germany will sever our connection with a constitution which has ceased to exist, and place ourselves under the protection of the Emperor of the French, who is anxious to secure the welfare and prosperity of Germany. We have formed a confederation among ourselves, and the Emperor of the French will be the head and protector of this league, which will be called the Confederation of the Rhine. Solemnly and forever do we, princes of the German Confederation of the Rhine, renounce the German empire and the German Diet, acknowledging none but the Emperor of the French as our head and protector."

"Yes, we renounce the German empire and the German Diet," exclaimed the sixteen princes, in one breath. "We renounce them now and forever!"

And they noisily pushed aside the high-backed arm-chairs, on which the representatives of their states had sat for centuries, and left the session-hall in a solemn procession, headed by the archchancellor of the empire.*

The remaining members of the Diet gazed on them in profound silence, and when the door closed behind the disappearing princes of the Confederation of the Rhine, it seemed as though strange sounds and whisperings filled the old hall, and as though low sighs and lamentations resounded from the walls where the portraits of the emperors were hanging.

The remaining members of the Diet were filled with awe; the sixteen vacant chairs struck terror into their souls; they rose silently from their seats and left the hall with hasty steps.

But on the following day the German Diet met again. It wanted to consult and deliberate as to what ought to be done in relation to the desertion of sixteen of its members.

And it consulted and deliberated for six days without coming to any decision. But on the sixth day a stop was put to the debates.

On the 6th of August a special envoy of the Emperor of Germany appeared at the city hall of Ratisbon while the Diet was in session.

He approached the green table and saluted the small remnant of the great assembly, and producing a large letter bearing the emperor's privy seal, said in a loud and solemn voice: "In the name of the emperor!"

And the members of the Diet rose from their seats to listen reverentially to the imperial message which his majesty had addressed to the German Diet in an autograph letter. He had commissioned his envoy to read the letter to the Diet, and the minister read as follows:

"Feeling convinced that it is impossible for us to exercise our imperial rights any longer, we deem it our duty to renounce a crown which was of value to us only so long as we enjoyed the confidence of the electors, princes, noblemen, and states of the German empire, and so long as we were able to fulfil the duties they imposed upon us. Hence we are obliged to declare by these presents in the most solemn manner that, considering the ties which united us with the German empire as broken by the Confederation of the Rhine, we hereby give up the imperial crown of Germany; at the same time we release by these presents the electors, princes, and states, as well as the members of the supreme court and other magistrates from the duties which they owed to us as legal head of the German empire. Given under our own hand and seal. Francis the Second, Emperor of Austria, and ruler of the hereditary states of Austria." *

A long and awful silence greeted the reading of this letter, which put an end to the ancient German empire after an existence of one thousand and six years, from Charlemagne, crowned in 800, to Francis II., dispossessed in 1806.

The members of the German Diet then rose from their seats; they were as silent and shy as night-owls startled from their dark hiding-places by a stray sunbeam. They left the old session-hall at Ratisbon in gloomy silence, and when the door closed behind them, the German Diet had been buried, and the lid on its coffin had been closed.

The last night-owls of the deceased German empire hurried in mournful silence from the session-hall at Ratisbon, where the old portraits henceforth watched alone over the grave of the German empire.

When they stepped out into the market-place, a carriage just rolled past the city hall, and the

---

* The members of the Confederation of the Rhine were Bavaria, Wurtemberg, Baden, the archchancellor with his territory, Berg, Hesse-Darmstadt, Nassau-Weilburg, Nassau-Usingen, Hohenzollern-Hechingen, Hohenzollern-Sigmaringen, Salm-Salm, Salm-Kyrburg, Isenburg, Arenberg, Lichtenstein, and Von der Leyen.

* "Mémoires d'un Homme d'État," vol. ix., p. 160.

gentleman seated in it leaned smilingly out of the coach-door, and saluted kindly and affably the pale, grave, and sad men who came from the city-hall.

This gentleman was Count Clement Metternich, who was going to Paris as special envoy of the Emperor of Austria for the purpose of offering to the Emperor of France on his birthday the congratulations of the Emperor of Austria. †

On the 6th of August the German empire had died and was buried !

* "Mémoires d'un Homme d'État," vol. ix., p. 162.

On the 15th of August the Emperor of the French celebrated his birthday; and the princes of the Confederation of the Rhine, the Emperor of Austria, the King of Prussia, and all the sovereigns who had been members of the late German empire, celebrated the great day in the most solemn manner.

Napoleon had a new victory—a victory which laid the whole of Germany at his feet. He had buried the German empire, but stood on the grave of the august corpse as its lord and master.

CHAPTER LV.

A GERMAN BOOKSELLER AND MARTYR.

It was long after nightfall; in the narrow, gloomy streets of the ancient free city of Nuremberg all noise had long since died away, and all the windows of the high houses with the gable-ends were dark. Only on the ground-floor of the large house in the rear of St. Sebald's church a lonely candle was burning, and the watchman, who was just walking past with his long horn and iron pike, looked inquisitively into the window, the shutters of which were not entirely closed.

"H'm!" he said to himself in a low voice, "the poor woman is kneeling and weeping and praying; I am sure it is for her husband. In her grief she did not notice, perhaps, that it is already midnight. I will remind her of it, so that she may go to bed."

He placed himself on the street in front of the house, blew his horn noisily, and then sang in a ringing voice:

"Hört, ihr Herren, und lasst euch sagen,
Die Glock hat zwölf geschlagen;
Ein Jeder bewahr sein Feuer und Licht,
Dass dieser Stadt kein Harm geschicht!" *

"So, now she knows it," muttered the watchman; "now she will go to bed."

And he sauntered down the long and tortuous street, to repeat his song on the next corner.

He had really accomplished his purpose; his song had interrupted the prayer of the young wife, and she had risen from her knees.

"Midnight already!" she murmured, in a low voice. "Another day of anguish is over, and a new one is beginning. Oh, would to God I could sleep, always sleep, so as to be at least unconscious of the dangers that are menacing *him!* Oh,

* The ancient song of the German watchman.—"Listen, gentlemen, and let me tell you: the clock has struck twelve; every one must take care of his fire and light, that no harm may befall this city!"

my God, my God! protect my poor, beloved husband, preserve the father of my children! And now I will go to bed," she added, after a pause. "God will have mercy on me, perhaps, and grant me a few hours of rest!"

She took the brass candlestick, on which a taper was burning, and went slowly and with bowed head to the adjoining room. When she had entered it, her face became calmer and more joyful, and a gentle smile lighted up her charming features when she now approached the small bed, in which her two little girls lay arm-in-arm, sweetly slumbering with rosy cheeks and half-opened crimson lips.

"God preserve to you your peace and innocence," whispered the young mother, after contemplating her children long and tenderly. "God, I fondly trust, will cause this cloud to glide past without your hearing the thunder roll, and being shattered by the lightning. Good-night, my children!"

She nodded smilingly to the slumbering girls, and then glided noiselessly to her couch. She commenced undressing slowly and sighing, but when she was just about to open the silver buckle of her sash, she paused and looked anxiously toward the window.

It seemed to her as though she had heard a soft rapping at this window, which opened upon the garden in the rear of the house, and as though a low voice had uttered her name.

Sure enough, the sound was repeated, and she now heard the voice say quite distinctly: "Open the window, Anna."

She rushed toward the window and opened it, pale, breathless, and almost out of her wits.

"Is it you, Palm?" she cried.

"It is I," said a low, male voice; and now an arm became visible, it encircled the crosswork of the window; in the next second the whole form of a gentleman appeared, and vaulted cautiously into the room.

"God be praised, I am with you again!" he said, drawing a deep breath; "it seems to me as if all danger were past when I am again in our quiet house with you and the children."

"No, my beloved husband, it is just here that dangers are threatening you," said the young wife, sinking into the open arms of her husband, and reposing her head on his breast. "My God, why did you return?"

"Because I was afraid when I was far from you, while I feel here with you courageous enough to brave the whole world," said her husband, almost cheerfully, imprinting a glowing kiss on the forehead of his young wife. "Believe me, Anna, a husband always lacks the right kind of courage when he believes his wife and children to be in danger. For six days I have been separated from you; well, in those six days, which I have spent in perfect security at Erlangen, I have not passed a minute without feeling the painful palpitation of my heart, nor have I slept a minute. I always thought of and trembled for you."

"But we are in no danger, while you are, my beloved," said the young wife, sighing. "Our house is closely watched, you may depend upon it. I have seen French gens-d'armes hidden behind the pillars of the church, and staring for hours at our street-door. Oh, if they knew that you were here, they would arrest you this very night!"

"They would not dare to arrest me!" exclaimed Palm, loudly. "We do not yet belong to France, although the Emperor of France has assumed the right of giving the ancient free city of Nuremberg to Bavaria, as though she were nothing but a toy got up in our factories. We are still Germans, and no French gens-d'armes have any right to penetrate into our German houses. But look, the children are moving; little Sophy is opening her eyes. What a barbarian I am to speak so loudly, and not even to respect the slumber of our little ones!"

He hastened to the small bed, and bending over it, nodded smilingly a greeting to the little girl, who was staring at him, still half asleep. The child whispered, in a low voice: "Dear, dear father!" and fell quietly asleep again.

"Come, Anna," whispered Palm, "let us go to your room, in order not to disturb the children."

"But the spying eyes of our enemies might see you there," said his wife, anxiously. "No, let us stay here, even though we should awaken the little girls. They will not cry, but be happy to see their beloved father, and what we are speaking to each other they cannot understand. Come, let us sit down here on the small sofa, and permit me to place the screen before it; then I am sure nobody will be able to see you."

She conducted Palm to the small sofa in the corner of the room, and placed the screen as noiselessly as possible before it.

"So," she said, nestling in his arms, "now we are here as if in a little cell, where only God's eye can find us. So long as we are in this cell I shall not be afraid."

"I believe it is unnecessary for you to be afraid at all," said Palm, smiling. "We carry our apprehensions to too great a length, you may depend upon it, and because we see M. Bonaparte putting whole states into his pocket, we believe it would be easy for him likewise to put a respectable citizen and bookseller of Nuremberg into it. But, be it spoken between us, that is rather a haughty idea, and M. Bonaparte has to attend to other things than to take notice of a bookseller and his publications. Remember, my child, that he has just got up the Confederation of the Rhine, and, moreover, is said to be preparing for a war with Prussia. How should he, therefore, have time to think of a poor bookseller?"

"Do you think, when the lion is going to meet his adversary and to struggle with him, he will leave the wasp which he has met on his way, and which has stung him in the ear, unpunished, because he has more important things to attend to?"

"But I did not sting him at all," said Palm, smiling. "Let us calmly consider the whole affair, dearest Anna, and you will see that I have in reality nothing to fear, and that only the accursed terror which this M. Bonaparte has struck into the souls of all Germans has caused us this whole alarm. A few months ago I received by mail, from a person unknown to me, a large package of books, enclosing a letter, in which the stranger requested me to send the copies of the pamphlet contained in the package immediately to all German booksellers, and to give it as wide a circulation as possible. The letter contained also a draft for one thousand florins, drawn by a banker of Vienna, Baron Franke, on a wealthy banking-house of our city. This sum of one thousand florins, said the letter, was to be a compensation for my trouble and for the zeal with which, the writer stated, he felt convinced I would attend to the circulation of the pamphlet."

"But the very mystery connected with the whole transaction ought to have aroused your suspicion, my beloved."

"Why? Are not we Germans now under the unfortunate necessity of keeping secret our most sublime thoughts and our most sacred sentiments?

And ought not, therefore, every one of us to take pains to honor and protect this secrecy, instead of suspecting it?"

"But the very title of this pamphlet was dangerous, 'Germany in her Deepest Degradation.' You might have guessed whom this accusation was aimed at."

"At Germany, I thought, at our infamy and cowardice, at the perfidy of our princes, at the torpid, passive indifference of our people. It is high time that Germany, which is now tottering about like a somnambulist, should be aroused by a manful word from her slumber, so as to take heart again and draw the sword. The title told me that the pamphlet contained such words; hence, I was not at liberty to keep it out of circulation. It would have been a robbery perpetrated upon Germany, a theft perpetrated upon him who sent me the money, and to whom I could not return it, because I was not aware of his name."

"You ought to have thought of your wife and your children," murmured Anna, sighing.

"I thought of you," he said, tenderly; "hence, I did not read the pamphlet, in order not to be shaken in what I thought my duty. First, I had to fulfil my duty as a citizen and man of honor; then only I was at liberty to think of you and my personal safety. I sent, therefore, in the first place, a certain number of copies of the pamphlet to M. Stage, the bookseller, and requested him to circulate them as speedily as possible among his customers."

"And, God knows, he has done so," sighed Anna, "and, like you, he was not deterred by the title."

"He did his duty, like myself, and sent the pamphlets to lovers of books. In this manner it reached a preacher in the country, and unfortunately there were two French officers at his house; they understood German, read the pamphlet, and informed their colonel of its character. The latter paid a visit to the preacher, and learned from him that M. Stage, the bookseller of Augsburg, had sent him the pamphlet. The colonel thereupon repaired to Augsburg and saw M. Stage."

"And Stage was cowardly and perfidious enough to betray your name and to denounce you as being the bookseller who had sent him the pamphlet," exclaimed Anna, her eyes flashing with indignation. "Your friend, your colleague betrayed you!"

"I had not requested him not to mention my name," said Palm, gravely; "he had a right to name it, and I do not reproach him with doing so. I was informed that the French minister in Munich had bitterly complained of me and demanded that

I should be punished; and as we are Bavarians now, I hastened to Munich in order to defend myself."

"And while you were there, four strangers came hither," Anna interrupted him. "They asked for the pamphlet, penetrated in the most outrageous manner, in spite of my remonstrances, into your store, searched it, and left only when they had satisfied themselves that not a copy of the unfortunate pamphlet was there."

"You wrote this to me while I was in Munich, and at the same time I heard that Stage had been arrested in Augsburg. Impelled by my first terror, I fled from the capital and hastened to Erlangen, which is situated on Prussian soil, and where neither the Bavarian police nor the French *gens d'armes* could lay hands on me. But in Erlangen I reflected on the matter, and I confess to you I was ashamed of having fled, instead of confronting an examination openly and freely. My love, my yearning attracted me toward you; I, therefore, took carriage last night and rode home to my beloved wife and to my children. This is a plain statement of the whole affair, and now tell me what should I be afraid of?"

"You may fear the worst," exclaimed Anna, sadly; "for our French tyrants will not shrink from any thing."

"But fortunately we do not live yet under the French sceptre," replied Palm, vividly; "we are Germans, and only German laws are valid for us."

"No," said Anna, mournfully, "we are not Germans, but Bavarians, that is to say, the allies, the humble vassals of France. Not the King of Bavaria, but the Emperor of France, is ruling over us."

"Well, even were it so, I could not see what crime I should be charged with. I neither wrote nor published this pamphlet; I merely circulated it, and cannot, therefore, be held responsible for its contents. Possibly, they may arrest me as they have arrested Stage, and may intend thereby to compel me to mention the name of him who sent me the pamphlet, as Stage mentioned my own name. Fortunately, however, I am able to prove that I know neither the author nor the publisher; for I have got the best proof of it, viz., the letter which I received with the package. I shall lay this letter before the court, and the judges will then perceive that I am entirely innocent. What will remain for them but to caution me not to circulate henceforth books sent to me anonymously, and then to release me?"

"But if they should not release you, my beloved husband?" asked his wife, anxiously clasping him in her arms; "if in their rage at being unable to lay their hands on the real criminal, they should wreak their vengeance on you for having circulated the pamphlet first of all, and punish you as though you were its author?"

"Oh, you go too far," exclaimed Palm, laughing; "your imagination calls up before you horrors which belong to the realm of fable. We still live in a well-regulated state, and however great the influence of France may be, German laws are still valid here; and as we live in a state of peace, I can be judged only in accordance with them. Fear not, therefore, dearest wife. The worst that can befall me will be a separation for a few days, at the most for a few weeks, if our authorities should really carry their fawning submission to Bonaparte to such a length as to call a German citizen to account for having, in his business as a bookseller, circulated a pamphlet—understand me well, a German pamphlet, destined only for Germany, and which does not flatter, perhaps, the Emperor of the French quite as much as is being done by our German princes and our German governments."

"Oh, my God, my God," wailed Anna, in a low voice, "the pamphlet is directly aimed at Napoleon, then?"

"Yes, at him who has placed his heels on the neck of Germany and trampled her in the dust," exclaimed Palm. "This pamphlet, called 'Germany in her Deepest Degradation,' must have been written against him alone. Oh, during the days of my sojourn in Erlangen, I have read this pamphlet, and whatever may befall me, I am glad it was I who circulated it, for a noble German spirit pervades the whole of it, and it is truth that raises the scourge in it to lash the guilty parties. It is a vigorous and glowing description of the condition to which all the German states have been reduced by Bonaparte's arbitrary proceedings. Just listen to this one passage, and then you may judge whether the pamphlet tells the truth or not."

He drew a few printed leaves from his side-pocket, and unfolded them.

"You have got a copy of the dreadful pamphlet with you?" asked Anna, in dismay. "Oh, how imprudent! If they should come now to arrest you, they would obtain a new proof of your guilt. I implore you, my friend, my beloved, if you love me, if your children are dear to you, be cautious and prudent! Burn those terrible leaves, so that they may not testify against you. Remember that I should die of grief if your life should be threatened; remember that our poor children then would be helpless orphans."

"Oh, my poor, timid roe," said Palm, deeply moved, encircling his weeping young wife with his arms. "How your faithful, innocent heart is fluttering, as if the cruel hunter were already aiming his murderous arm at us, and as if we were irretrievably doomed! Calm yourself, dearest, I pledge you my word that I will comply with your wishes. We will burn the pamphlet; but previously you shall learn, at least, the spirit in which this pamphlet, for which your poor husband will have to suffer, perhaps, a few days' imprisonment, is written. Just listen to me! The author is speaking here of Bavaria, and of the oppressions to which she is a prey since we have concluded an alliance with France. He says: 'Since that time the Bavarian states have become the winter quarters, and been treated in a manner unheard of since the Thirty Years' War. At that time the Austrians, under Tilly and Wallenstein, were pursuing precisely the same course now followed by the French, and if their emperor draws no other lessons from that war, he has closely copied, at least, the system of obtaining supplies for an army which was then in use. Trustworthy men have assured us that the French ruler, when in Munich the most urgent remonstrances concerning the oppressions under which the people of Bavaria were groaning were made to him, replied in cold blood: "My soldiers have not done so. These are times of war—let me alone, and do not disturb my plans." Already in December last the treaty of Presburg was signed, and from that moment Austria had the prospect of getting rid of her enemies. Had Bavaria not an equal right to enjoy the advantages of this treaty? These advantages could be none other than that the French army left the Bavarian territories and relieved the people from further oppressions. But just the reverse took place. The French withdrew from the states of the *German emperor* to occupy Bavaria, and celebrate here, by the ruin of all the inhabitants, their victories in orgies and carousals continued for many months. If I refer to the ruin of the inhabitants, the words should be taken in their literal meaning, and not as an expression merely chosen to depict the misery the French have brought upon Bavaria. It is not yet five years since a hostile army of the same nation lorded it over that country. And nobody will venture to assert that the wounds then inflicted upon the inhabitants should have been healed in so short a time. The farmer, deprived of his animals, had scarcely commenced to provide himself again with horses and cattle, when the passage of the French, in every respect equal to an invasion, took from him again this important portion of his personal property. Fraud, cunning, and force were alternately resorted to for this purpose. Tears and the most humble supplications were rejected with sneers, and even blows. The French called themselves "preservers of Bavaria." Forsooth a preservation similar to the fate of the patient whom one doctor would have sooner sent into the grave, and who is dying more slowly under the hands of another. If friendship ever was a mockery, it was so on this occasion. But it is part of Napoleon's plans to exhaust Germany to such an extent as to render her incapable of becoming dangerous for him even in the most remote future. He selected several highly effective expedients for this purpose. Dynasties, the ancestors of which date back to the most remote ages, and one of which long since produced emperors and kings, were united with *Bonaparte*'s family by the closest ties of blood, and thus the ruler of France has already become the relative of the courts of Baden, Bavaria, Sweden, and Russia. Not content with this, he offered royal crowns to Bavaria and Wurtemberg, and the German emperor had to assent to this measure in the treaty of Presburg. Thus Germany has got two new kingdoms, and—' " *

"Oh, I implore you, do not read any further," exclaimed Anna, suddenly interrupting her husband. "It frightens me to hear you repeat those threatening and angry words; they fall upon my heart like a terrible accusation against you! Believe me, my beloved, if that proud and ambitious Emperor Napoleon should hear of this terrible pamphlet—if its contents should be communicated to him, you would be lost; for, having no one else on whom to wreak his vengeance, he would revenge himself on you!"

"But he will not have me either," said Palm, smiling, "for I shall take good care not to set foot on French territory; I shall not leave Nuremberg, and thank God, that is German territory."

"But the French frontier is close to us, for wherever there are French troops there is France. Napoleon's arm reaches far beyond her frontiers, and if he wants to seize you he will do so in spite of all boundary-posts, German laws, and your own citizenship."

"There is really something so convincing in your fears that it might almost infect me!" said Palm, musingly. "It would have been better, perhaps, after all, for me not to have come back, but to remain in Prussian Erlangen!"

"Return thither," exclaimed Anna, imploring-

ly; "I beseech you by our love, by our children, and by our happiness, return to Erlangen!"

"To-morrow, dearest Anna!" said Palm, smiling, clasping his young wife in his arms—"to-morrow it will be time enough to think of another separation. Now let me take a few hours' rest, and enjoy the unutterable happiness of being at home again!—at home with my wife and with my dear little ones!"

CHAPTER LVI.

THE ARREST.

On the following morning the rumor spread all over Nuremberg that Palm, the bookseller, had returned and was concealed in his house. The cook had stated this in the strictest confidence to some of her friends when she had appeared on the market-place to purchase some vegetables. The friends had communicated the news, of course, likewise in the strictest confidence, to other persons, and thus the whole city became very soon aware of the secret.

The friends of the family now hastened to go to Mrs. Palm for the purpose of ascertaining from herself whether the information were true. Anna denied it, however; she asserted she had received this very morning a letter written by her husband at Erlangen; but when one of the more importunate friends requested her to communicate the contents of the letter to him, or let him see it at least, she became embarrassed and made an evasive reply.

"He is here!" whispered the friends to each other, when they left Mrs. Anna Palm. "He is here, but conceals himself so that the French spies who have been sneaking around here for the last few days may not discover his whereabouts. It is prudent for him to do so, and we will not betray him, but faithfully keep his secret."

But a secret of which a whole city is aware, and which is being talked of by all the gossips in town, is difficult to keep, and it is useless to make any effort for the purpose of preventing it from being betrayed to the enemy.

Palm did not suspect any thing whatever of what was going on. He deemed himself entirely safe in his wife's peaceful, silent room, the windows of which, opening upon the garden, were inaccessible to spying eyes, while its only door led to the large store where his two clerks were attending to the business of the firm and waiting on the customers who ordered or purchased books of them.

---

* From the celebrated pamphlet, "Germany in her Deepest Degradation."

Anna had just left the room to consult with her servants about the affairs of the household and kitchen; and Palm, who was comfortably stretched out on the sofa, was engaged in reading. The anxiety which had rendered him so restless during the previous days had left him again; he felt perfectly reassured, and smiled at his own fear which had flitted past him like a threatening cloud.

All at once he was startled from his comfortable repose by a loud conversation in the store, and rose from the divan in order to hear what was the matter.

"I tell you I am unable to assist you," he heard his book-keeper say. "I am poor myself, and Mr. Palm is not at home."

"Mr. Palm is at home, and I implore you let me see him," said a strange, supplicating voice. "He has a generous heart and if I tell him of my distress he will pity me and lend me his assistance."

"Come back in a few days, then," exclaimed the book-keeper; "Mr. Palm will then be back, perhaps, from his journey."

"In a few days!" ejaculated the strange voice—"in a few days my wife and child will be starved to death, for unless I am able to procure relief within this hour, my cruel creditor will have me taken to the debtors' prison, and I shall be unable then to assist my sick wife and baby. Oh, have mercy on my distress! Let me see Mr. Palm, that I may implore his assistance!"

"Mr. Palm is not at home as I told you already," exclaimed the book-keeper in an angry voice. "How am I to let you see him, then? Come back in a few days—that is the only advice I can give you. Go now, and do not disturb me any longer!"

"No, people shall never say that I turned a despairing man away from my door," muttered Palm, rapidly crossing the room and opening the door of the store.

"Stay, poor man," he said to the beggar, who had already turned around and was about to leave the store—"stay."

The beggar turned around, and, on perceiving Palm, who stood on the threshold of the door, uttered a joyful cry.

"Do you see," he said, triumphantly to the book-keeper—"do you see that I was right? Mr. Palm is at home, and will help me."

"I will help you if I can," said Palm, kindly. "What does your debt amount to?"

"Ah, Mr. Palm, I owe my landlord a quarter's rent, amounting to twenty florins. But if you should be so generous as to give me half that

sum, it would be enough, for the landlord has promised to wait three months, provided I paid him now ten florins."

"You shall have the ten florins," said Palm. "Mr. Bertram, pay this man ten florins, and charge them to me."

"Oh, Mr. Palm, how kind you are!" exclaimed the beggar, joyfully. "How shall I ever be able to thank you for what you have done for me to-day?"

"Thank me by being industrious and making timely provision for your wife and child, in order not to be again reduced to such distress," said Palm, nodding kindly to the stranger, and returning to the adjoining room.

With the ten florins which the book-keeper had paid to him, the beggar hastened into the street. No sooner had he left the threshold of Palm's house than the melancholy and despairing air disappeared from his face, which now assumed a scornful and malicious mien. With hasty steps he hurried over to St. Sebald's church, to the pillar yonder, behind which two men, wrapped in their cloaks, were to be seen.

"Mr. Palm is at home," said the beggar, grinning. "Go into the store, cross it and enter the adjoining sitting-room—there you will find him. I have spied it out for you, and now give me my pay."

"First we must know whether you have told us the truth," said one of the men. "It may be all false."

"But I tell you I have seen him with my own eyes," replied the beggar. "I stood in the store, and cried and lamented in the most heart-rending manner, and protested solemnly that my wife and baby would be starved to death, unless Mr. Palm should assist me. The book-keeper refused my application, but then I cried only the louder, so as to be heard by Mr. Palm. And he *did* hear me; he came out of his hiding-place and gave me the ten florins I asked him for. Here they are."

"Well, if you have got ten florins, that is abundant pay for your treachery," said the two men. "It is Judas-money. To betray your benefactor, who has just made you a generous present; forsooth, only a German could do that."

They turned their backs contemptuously on the beggar, and walked across the street toward Palm's house.

There was nobody in the hall, and the two men entered the store without being hindered. Without replying to the book-keeper and second clerk, who came to meet them for the purpose of receiving their orders, they put off their cloaks.

"French *gens-d'armes*," muttered the book-keeper, turning pale, and he advanced a few steps toward the door of the sitting-room. One of the gens-d'armes kept him back.

"Both of you will stay here," he said, imperiously, "we are going to enter that room. Utter the faintest sound, the slightest warning, and we shall arrest both of you. Be silent, therefore, and let us do our duty."

The two clerks dared not stir, and saw with silent dismay that the two gens-d'armes approached the door of the sitting-room and hastily opened it.

Then they heard a few imperious words, followed by a loud cry of despair.

"Oh, the poor woman!" muttered the book-keeper, with quivering lips, but without moving from the spot.

The door of the sitting-room, which the gens-d'armes had closed, opened again, and the two policemen stepped into the store; they led Palm into it. Each of them had seized one of his arms.

Palm looked pale, and his brow was clouded, but nevertheless he walked forward like a man who is determined not to be crushed by his misfortunes, but to bear them as manfully as possible.

When he arrived in the middle of the store, near the table where his two clerks were standing, he stopped.

"Then you will not give me half an hour's time to arrange my business affairs with my book-keeper, and to give him my orders?" he asked the policemen, who wanted to drag him forward.

"No, not a minute," they said. "We have received stringent orders to take you at once to the general, and if you should refuse to follow us willingly, to iron you and remove you forcibly."

"You see I offer no resistance whatever," said Palm, contemptuously. "Let us go. Bertram, pray look after my wife—she has fainted. Remember me to her and to my children. Farewell!"

The two young men made no reply; their tears choke their voices. But when Palm had disappeared, they rushed into the sitting-room to assist the unhappy young wife.

She was lying on the floor, pale, rigid, and resembling a lily broken by the storm. Her eyes were half opened and dim; the long braids of her beautiful light-colored hair, which she had just been engaged in arranging when the gens-d'armes entered, fell down dishevelled and like curling snakes on her face and shoulders, from which the small, transparent, gauze handkerchief

had been removed. Her features, always so lovely and gentle, bore now an expression of anger and horror, which they had assumed when she fainted on hearing the French policemen tell her husband that they had come to arrest him, and that he must follow them.

They succeeded only after long efforts in bringing her back to consciousness. But she was not restored to life by the salts which her servant-girl rubbed on her forehead, nor by the imploring words of the book-keeper, but by the scalding tears of her little girls which melted and warmed her frozen blood again.

She raised herself with a deep sigh, and her wild, frightened glances wandered about the room, and fixed themselves searchingly on every form which she beheld in it. When she had satisfied herself that he was not among them, he whom her glances had sought for so anxiously, she clasped her children with a loud cry of horror in her arms and pressing them convulsively against her bosom, sobbed piteously.

But she did not long give way to her grief and despair. She dried her tears hastily and rose.

"It is no time now for weeping and lamenting," she said, drawing a deep breath; "I shall have time enough for that afterward, now I must act and see whether I cannot assist him. Do you know whither they have taken him?"

"To the headquarters of Colomb, the French general, who is stationed in this city," said the book-keeper.

"I shall go to the general, and he will have to tell me at least if I cannot see my husband in his prison," she said, resolutely. "Quick, Kate, assist me in dressing; arrange my hair, for you see my hands are trembling violently; they are weaker than my heart."

She rose to go to her dressing-room. But her feet refused to serve her; she turned dizzy, and sank down overcome by a fresh swoon.

It was only after hours of the most violent efforts that the poor young wife succeeded in recovering from the physical prostration caused by her sudden fright, and in becoming again able to act resolutely and energetically. Then, as bold and courageous as an angry lioness, she was determined to struggle with the whole world for the beloved husband who had been torn from her.

CHAPTER LVII.

A WIFE'S LOVE.

ANNA went in the first place to General Colomb, and begged him to grant her an interview.

About four hours had passed since Palm's arrest when the general received her.

"Madame," he said, "I know why you have
come to me; you are looking for your husband,
but he is no longer here at my headquarters."

"No longer here?" she ejaculated in terror.
"You have sent him to France? "You intend to
kill him, then?"

"The law will judge him, madame," said the
general, sternly. "I have myself examined him
and requested him to give us the name of the author of this infamous libel which Mr. Palm has
brought into general circulation. Had he done
so, he would no longer be held responsible, and
would have been at liberty to return to his house
and to you. But he refused firmly to state the
names of the author and printer of the pamphlet."

"He does not know either!" exclaimed Anna;
"oh, believe me, sir, Palm is innocent. That
pamphlet was sent to him, together with an anonymous letter."

"He ought to have taken care, then, not to circulate it," replied the general. "It is contrary
to law to circulate a printed book, the author and
printer of which are unknown to him who circu-
lates it."

"No, general, it is not contrary to the laws of
the German free city of Nuremberg. By an order
of the Emperor of France, Nuremberg has been
given to Bavaria, but the laws and privileges of
our more liberal constitution were guaranteed to
our ancient free city. Hence, Palm has done
nothing contrary to law."

"We judge according to our laws," said the
general, shrugging his shoulders; "wherever we
are there is France, and wherever we are insulted
we hold him who insults us responsible for it, and
punish him according to our laws. Your husband
has committed a great crime; he has circulated a
pamphlet reviling France and the Emperor of the
French in the most outrageous manner. He refused to mention the author of this pamphlet; so
long as he persists in his refusal, we take him for
the author, and shall punish him accordingly. As
he declined confessing any thing to me, I have
surrendered him to my superiors. Mr. Palm left
Nuremberg two hours ago for Anspach, where
Marshal Bernadotte is going to judge him."

"Then I shall go to Anspach, to Marshal Bernadotte," said Anna; and without deigning to
cast another glance at the general, she turned
around and left the room.

She intended to set out this very hour, but her
endeavors to find a conveyance to take her to Anspach proved unavailing. All the horses of the
postmaster had been retained for the suite and
baggage-wagons of Marshal Berthier, who was
about setting out for Munich, and the proprietors
of the livery-stables, owing to the approaching
darkness and insecurity of the roads, refused to
let her have any of their carriages.

Anna had to wait, therefore, until morning, and
improved the long hours of the night in drawing
up a petition, which she intended to send to Marshal Bernadotte, in case he should refuse to grant
her an interview.

Early next morning she at length started, but
the roads were sandy and bad; the horses were
lazy and weak, and she reached Anspach only late
at night.

She had again to wait during a long, dreary
night. No one could or would reply to her anxious inquiries whether Palm was really there, or
whether he had been again sent to some other
place.

Trembling with inward fear and dismay, but
firmly determined to dare every thing, and leave
nothing untried that might lead to Palm's preservation, Anna repaired in the morning to the residence of Marshal Bernadotte.

The marshal's adjutant received her, and asked
her what she wanted.

"I must see the marshal himself, for I shall
read in his mien whether he will pardon or annihilate my husband," said Anna. "I beseech you,
sir, have mercy on the grief of a wife, trembling
for the father of her children. Induce the marshal to grant me an audience."

"I will see what can be done," said the adjutant, touched by the despair depicted on the pale
face of the poor lady. But he returned in a few
minutes after he had left her.

"Madame," he said, shrugging his shoulders,
"I am sorry, but your wish cannot be fulfilled.
The marshal will have nothing whatever to do
with this affair, and declines interfering in it. For
this reason, too, he did not admit Mr. Palm, who
yesterday, like you, applied for an interview with
the marshal, and I had to receive him in the place
of the marshal, as I have now the honor to receive you."

"Oh, you have seen my husband?" asked
Anna, almost joyfully. "You have spoken to
him?"

"I have told him in the name of the marshal

what I am now telling you, madame. The marshal is unable to do any thing whatever for your
husband. The order for his arrest came directly
from Paris, from the emperor's cabinet, and the
marshal, therefore, has not the power to revoke
it and to prevent the law from taking its course.
Moreover, Mr. Palm is no longer in Anspach, as
he was sent to another place last night."

"Whither? Oh, sir, you will have mercy on
me, and tell me whither my unfortunate husband
has been sent."

"Madame," said the adjutant, timidly looking
around as if he were afraid of being overheard
by an eavesdropper, "he has been sent to Braunau."

Anna uttered a cry of horror. "To Braunau!"
she said, breathlessly. "To Braunau, that is to
say, out of the country. You do not wish to try
a citizen and subject of Bavaria, for a crime which
he is said to have committed in his own country,
according to the laws of Bavaria, but according
to those of a foreign and hostile state? My husband has been sent to Austria!"

"Pardon me, madame," said the adjutant, smiling, "the city of Braunau does not yet again belong to Austria; up to the present hour it is still
French territory, for we took and occupied it during the war and have not yet given it back to
Austria; hence, Mr. Palm will be tried in Braunau
according to the laws of France."

"Oh, then he is lost," exclaimed Anna, in despair; "there is no more hope for him."

"If he be guilty, madame, he has deserved punishment; if he be innocent, no harm can befall
him, for the laws of France are impartial and
just."

"Oh, sir," said Anna, almost haughtily, "there
are things which may seem deserving of punishment, nay, criminal, according to the laws of
your country, but which, according to the laws of
a German state, would not deserve any punishment, but, on the contrary, praise and acknowledgment."

"If what Mr. Palm has done is an offence of this
description, I am sorry for him," said the adjutant, shrugging his shoulders. "But," he added,
in a lower voice, "I will give you some good advice. Hasten to the French ambassador at Munich. If he should decline granting you an audience, send him a petition, stating the case of
your husband truthfully and with full details, and
asking for his intercession."

"And if he should not reply to my petition;
if he should refuse to intercede for me?"

"Then a last remedy will remain to you. In
that case, apply to Marshal Berthier, who is now

also at Munich. He has great power over the emperor, and will alone be able to help you. But
lose no time."

"I shall set out this very hour, sir, and I thank
you for your advice and sympathy. I see very
well that you cannot do any thing for me, but you
have granted me your compassion, and I thank
you for it. Farewell, sir."

An hour later, Anna was on the road to Munich.
After an exhausting journey of four days—for, at
that time there were no turnpikes, much less
railroads, in Bavaria—she reached Munich, where
she stopped at a hotel.

She was utterly unacquainted in that capital;
she had no friends, no protectors, no recommendations, and, as a matter of course, all doors were
closed against her, and nobody would listen to
her. Nobody felt pity for the poor, despairing
lady; nobody would listen to her complaints, for
her complaints were at the same time charged
against the all-powerful man who now held his
hand stretched out over Bavaria, and was able to
crush her whenever he chose to do so.

Anna, therefore, met with no encouragement at
the hands of the German authorities, who even
refused to hear a statement of her application.
She went to all the ministers, to all those on
whom, according to their official position, it would
have been incumbent to intercede for her. She
even ventured to enter the royal palace, and stood
for hours in the anteroom, always hoping that her
supplications would be heeded, and that some door
would be opened to her.

But all doors were closed against her, even that
of the French ambassador. She had vainly applied to him for an audience; when her request
had been refused, she had delivered to his *attaché*
a petition which an attorney had drawn up for
her, and in which all the points for and against
Palm were lucidly stated. For a week she waited
for a reply; for a week she went every morning
to the residence of the French ambassador and
asked in the same gentle and imploring voice,
whether there was any reply for her, and whether
no answer had been returned to her application?

On the eighth day she was informed that no
reply would be made to her petition, and that the
French ambassador was unable to do any thing
for her.

Anna did not weep and complain; she received
this information with the gentle calmness of a
martyr, and prayed instead of bursting into lamentations. She prayed to God that He might grant
her strength not to despair, not to succumb to
the stunning blow; she prayed to God that He

might impart vigor to her body, so that it might not prevent her from doing her duty, and from seeking for further assistance for her beloved husband.

Strengthened and inwardly relieved by this prayer, Anna now repaired to the residence of Marshal Berthier; her step, however, was slower, a deep blush mantled her cheeks, which had hitherto been so pale, and her hands were no longer icy cold, but hot and red.

She did not apply for an audience on reaching the marshal's residence, for she already knew that such an application would meet with a refusal; she only took thither another copy of the petition which she had delivered to the French ambassador, and begged urgently for an early reply.

Her supplications were this time not destined to be unsuccessful, and she received a reply on the third day.

But this reply was even more terrible than if none whatever had been made. Marshal Berthier sent word to her by his adjutant that Palm had been placed before a court-martial at Braunau, and that no intercession and prayers would be of any avail, the decision being exclusively left with the court-martial.

A single, piercing cry escaped from Anna's breast when she received this information. Then she became again calm and composed. Without uttering another complaint, another prayer, she left the marshal's residence and returned to her hotel.

With perfect equanimity and coolness, she requested the waiter to bring her the bill and get her a carriage, so that she might set out at once.

Fifteen minutes later, the landlady herself appeared to present to Madame Palm the bill she had called for. She found Anna sitting quietly at the window, her hands folded on her lap, her head leaning on the high back of the chair, and her dilated eyes staring vacantly at the sky. Her small travelling-trunk stood ready and locked in the middle of the room.

The landlady handed her the paper silently, and then turned aside in order not to show the tears which, at the sight of the pale, gentle young wife, had filled her eyes.

Anna rose and quietly placed the money on the table. "I thank you, madame, for all the attention and kindness I have met with at your house," she said. "It only seems to me that my bill is much too moderate. You must have omitted many items, for it is impossible that I should not have used up more than that during my prolonged sojourn in Munich."

"Madame," said the landlady, deeply moved, "I should be happy if you permitted me to take no money at all from you, but I know that that would offend you, and for that reason I brought you my bill. If you allow me to follow the promptings of my heart, I should say, grant me the honor of having afforded hospitality to so noble, brave, and faithful a lady, and, if you should consent, I should be courageous enough to utter a request which I dare not make now, because you would deem it egotistic."

"Oh, tell me what it is," said Anna, mildly; "for the last two weeks I have begged so much, and my requests were so often refused, that it would truly gratify me to hear from others a request which I might be able to fulfil."

"Well, then, madame," said the landlady, taking Anna's hand and kissing it respectfully, "I request you to stay here and not to depart. Afford me the pleasure of keeping you here in my house, of taking care and nursing you as a mother would nurse her daughter. I am old enough to be your mother, and you, my poor, beloved child, you need nursing, for you are sick."

"I feel no pain—I am not sick," said Anna, with a smile which was more heart-rending than loud lamentations.

"You are sick," replied the landlady; "your hands are burning with fever, and the roses blooming on your cheeks are not natural, but symptoms of your inward sufferings. During your whole sojourn in my house you have scarcely touched the food that was placed before you; frequently you have not gone to bed at night, and, instead of sleeping, restlessly paced your room. A fever is now raging in your delicate body, and if you do not take care of yourself, and use medicine, your body will succumb."

"No, it will not succumb," said Anna; "my heart will sustain it."

"But your heart, too, will break, if you do not take care of yourself," exclaimed the landlady, compassionately. "Stay here, I beseech you, do not depart! Stay as a guest at my house!"

Anna placed her burning hand on the shoulder of the landlady, and looked at her long and tenderly.

"You were married?" she asked. "You loved your husband?"

"Yes," said the landlady, bursting into tears, "I was married, and God knows that I loved my husband. For twenty years we lived happy and peacefully together, and when he died last year, my whole happiness died with him."

"He was sick, I suppose, and you nursed him?"

"He was sick for a month, and I did not leave his bedside either by day or by night."

"Well, then, what would you have replied to him who would have tried to keep you back from your husband's death-bed, and to persuade you to leave him in his agony, because it might have injured your health? Would you have listened to him?"

"No, I should have believed him, who had made such a proposition to me, to be my enemy, and should have replied to him: 'It is my sacred right to stand at my husband's death-bed, to kiss the last sigh from his lips, to close his eyes, and no one in the world shall prevent me from doing so!'"

"Well, then, dear *mother*, I say as you have said: it is my sacred right to stand at my husband's death-bed, and to close his eyes. My husband's death-bed is in Braunau; I am not so happy as you have been; I cannot nurse him, nor be with him and comfort him in his agony; but I am able, at least, to see him in his last hour. My mother, will you still ask your daughter to stay here and take care of her health, instead of going to her husband's death-bed in Braunau?"

"No, my daughter," exclaimed the landlady, "no; I say to you, go! Take not a minute's rest until you reach your husband. God will guide and protect you, for He is love, and has mercy on those whose hearts are filled with love! Go, then, with God; but, for the sake of your husband, take some nourishing food; try to eat and sleep, so as to gain fresh strength, for you will need it."

"Give me some nourishing food, mother, I will eat," said Anna, placing her arms tenderly around the landlady's neck; "I will try also to-night to sleep, for you are right: I shall need my whole strength! But after I have eaten, I may set out at once, may I not?"

"Yes, my poor, dear child, then you may set out. Now come to my room—your meal is already waiting for you."

Half an hour later the landlady herself lifted Anna into the carriage, and said to her in a voice trembling with tearful emotion: "Farewell, my daughter. God bless you and grant you strength. When alone one day, and in need of a mother, then come to me! May the Lord have mercy on you!"

"Yes, may the Lord have mercy on me, and let me die with him!" whispered Anna, as the carriage rolled away with her.

At noon on the following day, August 26th, 1806, she arrived at Braunau.

CHAPTER LVIII.

THE WOMEN OF BRAUNAU.

In the mean time Palm had constantly been in the French prison at Braunau. During the sixteen days since he had been in jail, he had only twice been taken out of it to be examined by the court-martial, which General St. Hilaire had specially convoked for his trial.

This court-martial consisted of French generals and staff-officers; it met at a time of peace in a German city, and declared its competence to try a German citizen who had committed no other crime than to circulate a pamphlet, in which the misfortunes of Germany, and the oppressions of German states by Napoleon and his armies, had been commented upon.

The whole proceedings had been carried on so hastily and secretly, that the German authorities of Braunau had scarcely heard of them at the time when the French court-martial was already about to sentence the prisoner.

The French, however, wanted to maintain some semblance of impartiality; and before Palm was called before the court-martial, it was left to him either to defend himself in person against the charges, or to provide himself with counsel.

Palm, who was ignorant of the French language, had preferred the latter, and selected as his counsel a resident lawyer of Braunau, with whom he was well acquainted, and even on terms of intimacy, and whom he knew to be familiar with the French language.

But this friend declined being a "friend in need." He excused himself on the pretext of a serious indisposition which confined him to his bed, and rendered it impossible for him to make a speech.

Palm was informed of this excuse only at the moment when he entered the room in which the trial was to be held; hence he had to make up his mind to conduct his own defence, and to have his words translated by an interpreter to the members of the court.

And he felt convinced that his defence had been successful, and satisfied the men who had assumed to be his judges, of his entire innocence.

He had, therefore, no doubt of his speedy release; he was looking every day for the announcement that his innocence had been proved, and that he should be restored to liberty and to his family. This confident hope caused him to bear his solitary confinement with joyful courage, and to look, in this time of privations and pain, fondly for the golden days to come, when he would repose again, after all his trouble and toil, in the arms of love, gently guarded by the tender eyes of his affectionate young wife, and his heart gladdened by the sight of his sweet children.

From dreams so joyous and soul-stirring he was awakened on the morning of the 26th of August by the appearance of the jailer and of several soldiers who came to summon him before the court-martial which would communicate his sentence to him.

"God be praised!" exclaimed Palm, enthusiastically. "My sentence, that is to say, my release. Come, let us go; for, you see, it is hot and oppressive in my cell, and I long for God's fresh air, of which I have been deprived so long. Let us go, then, that I may receive the sentence which I have so ardently yearned for."

And with a kind smile he offered his hand to the jailer who stood at the door with a gloomy, sullen air. "Do not look so gloomy, Balthasar," he said. "You always used to be so merry a companion and have often agreeably enlivened the long and dreary hours of my confinement by your entertaining conversation. Accept my thanks for your kindness and clemency; you might have tormented me a great deal, and you have not done so, but have always been accommodating and compassionate. I thank you for it, Balthasar, and beg you to accept this as a souvenir from me."

He drew a golden breastpin richly set with precious stones from his cravat, and offered it to the jailer.

But Balthasar did not take it; on the contrary, he averted his head sullenly and gloomily.

"I am not allowed to accept any presents from the prisoners," he muttered.

"Well, then, I shall come and see you as soon as I am free, and from the free man, I suppose, you will accept a small souvenir?" asked Palm, kindly.

The jailer made no reply to this question, but exclaimed, impatiently: "Make haste, it is high time!"

Palm laughed, and, nodding a farewell to the jailer, left the prison in the midst of the soldiers.

"Poor man, he suspects nothing," murmured the jailer to himself, and his features now became mild and gentle, and his eyes were filled with tears. "Poor man, he believes they will set him at liberty! Yes, they will do so, but it is not the sort of liberty he is looking and hoping for!"

Palm followed the soldiers gayly and courageously to the room where the members of the court-martial were assembled seated on high-backed arm-chairs which had been placed in a

semicircle on one side of the room, awaiting the arrival of the prisoner.

He greeted them with an unclouded brow and frank and open bearing; not a tinge of fear and nervousness was to be seen in his features; he fixed his large and lustrous eyes on the lips of General St. Hilaire who presided over the court-martial and now rose from his seat. The secretary of the court immediately approached the general and handed him a paper.

The general took it, and, bending a stern glance on Palm, said: "The court-martial has agreed to-day unanimously on your sentence. I will now communicate it to you."

The other officers rose from their seats to listen standing to the reading of the sentence. It is true, their faces were grave, and for the first time Palm was seized with a sinister foreboding, and asked himself whether his judges would assume so grave and solemn an air if they were merely to announce to him that he was innocent and consequently free.

A small pause ensued. The general then raised his voice, and read in a loud and ringing tone: "Whereas at all places where there is an army it is the first and most imperious duty of its chief to watch over its safety and preservation;

"Whereas the circulation of writings instigating sedition and murder does not only threaten the safety of the army, but also that of the nation generally;

"Whereas nothing is more urgent and necessary than the prevention of the propagation of such doctrines which are a crime against the rights of man and against the respect due to crowned heads—an insult to the people submissive to their government—and, in short, subversive of law, order, and subordination:

"The military commission here assembled declares unanimously that all authors and printers of libellous books of the above-named description, as well as booksellers and other persons engaged in circulating them, shall be deemed guilty of high-treason.

"In consideration whereof the defendant, John Frederick Palm, convicted of having circulated the pamphlet, 'Germany in her Deepest Degradation,' has been charged with the crime of high-treason, and the commission has unanimously found him guilty of the charge.

"The penalty incurred by the traitor is death.

"Consequently the traitor, John Frederick Palm, will suffer death, which sentence will be carried out this afternoon at two o'clock, when he will be shot." *

* "Mémoires d'un Homme d'État," vol. ix., p. 247.

17

"John Frederick Palm," added the general, "you have heard your sentence, prepare for death!"

The interpreter repeated to the unhappy prisoner the sentence of the court-martial slowly, impressively, and emphasizing every word; and every syllable fell like a cold tear on Palm's heart and froze it. It was, however, not only cold with terror and dismay, but also with determination and calmness.

Before these strangers, with their cold, indifferent faces, he resolved at once not to betray any weakness. He did not want to afford his assassins the pleasure of seeing him tremble.

His bearing, therefore, only manifested firm determination and grave calmness. He cast a single flaming glance, full of proud disdain, on his judges.

"Very well," he said, loudly and firmly, "I shall die; I shall go to God and accuse *you* before his throne,—you who trample on all state and international laws, and have not judged, but murdered me. My blood be on your heads!"

"Prisoner," said General St. Hilaire, quietly, "if you desire any thing before your death, mention it now, and if able to comply with it, we shall grant it."

"I have but one desire," said Palm, and now his voice trembled a little, and a shadow passed across his forehead. "I only wish that my wife may be permitted to spend these last hours with me, and to take leave of me!"

"Your wife?" asked the general. "Is your wife here, then? And if she be here, who has dared to advise you of it?"

"Nobody has advised me of it," replied Palm, "nor do I know whether she is here or not, but I believe it. Moreover, it would be but natural that she should have followed me hither. Permit me, then, to see her when she comes."

"Your request is granted. Return to your prison. A preacher will be sent to you to prepare you for death. Soldiers, remand the prisoner!"

Palm saluted the gentlemen with a haughty nod, and slowly and solemnly raised his hand toward heaven. "I summon you to appear before the awful tribunal of God Almighty!" he said, in a loud and ringing voice. "Here you have assumed to judge *me*; there God will judge *you!*"

He turned around and left the room at the head of the soldiers.

"It only remains for us now to inform the municipal authorities of this city of what has to be done," said the general, after a short pause.

"They must be present at the execution, for this act of justice shall not take place under the veil of secrecy, but openly under the eyes of God and men. Let the authorities, let the whole city witness how France punishes and judges those who, in their traitorous impudence, have offended against her honor and glory!"

He adjourned the court, and returned to his rooms to repose from so exhausting a session, and to prepare, by partaking of an epicurean repast, for the unpleasant duty that awaited him, viz., to be present at an execution.

The general was just sipping a glass of malmsey with infinite relish, and eating a piece of the excellent *pâté de foie gras* which had been ordered from Strasburg, when a strange and long-continued noise on the street suddenly disturbed him in his epicurean enjoyment.

He placed his glass angrily on the table, and turned his eyes and ears toward the windows opening on the market-place. The noise continued all the time; it sounded singular and extraordinary, as though immense swarms of bees were filling the air with their humming.

The general rose and hastened to the window.

A strange spectacle, indeed, presented itself to his eyes. The whole market-place was crowded with people, not with threatening, violent men, rushing forward with clinched fists and flashing eyes, but with persons whose eyes were filled with tears, and who raised their arms in an imploring manner.

They were women and children, who had marched in solemn procession to the market-place, and now entirely filled it. The news that the court-martial had agreed on a sentence, and that Palm was to be shot by virtue of it this afternoon at two o'clock in the large ditch of the fortress, had spread like wildfire through the whole city of Braunau.

The citizens had received the news with intense rage and silent horror; the authorities and members of the municipality had received orders to repair at the stated hour in their official robes to the place of execution for the purpose of witnessing the dreadful scene.

Too weak to offer any resistance, and well aware that they could not count on the assistance of their own German superiors, they had to submit to the order. Bowing to the stern law of necessity, they declared, therefore, their readiness to comply with the behests of the French general, and to appear at the place of execution.

But while all the men were giving way to cowardly fear; while they timidly swallowed their rage and humiliation, the women arose in the genuine and bold enthusiasm of their grief and compassion. They could not threaten, nor arm their hand with the sword, like men, but they could beseech and supplicate, and in the place of weapons in their hands they had tears in their eyes.

"If you will not go to demand justice for a German citizen, I shall do so," said the wife of the burgomaster of Braunau to her husband. "You have to watch over the welfare of the city, but I shall save its honor. I will not permit this day to become an eternal disgrace to Braunau, and history to speak one day of the slavish fear with which we humbly submitted to the will of the French tyrant. You men refuse to intercede with the general for Palm; well, then, we women will do so, and God at least will hear our words, and history will preserve them."

She turned her back to her husband and went to inform her friends of her determination, and to send messengers all over the city.

And from street to street, from house to house, there resounded the shouts: "Dress in mourning, women, and come out into the street. Let us go to General St. Hilaire and beg for the life of a German citizen!"

Not an ear had been closed against this sacred appeal; not a woman's heart had disregarded it. They came forth from all the houses and from all the cabins, the countess as well as the beggar-woman, the old as well as the young; the mothers led their children by the hand, and the brides lent to their grandmothers their shoulders to lean upon.

The procession formed in front of the burgomaster's house; then the women walked in pairs and slowly as the weak feet of the tottering old dames and the delicate children required it, through the long main street toward the market-place.

General St. Hilaire was still at the window, gazing in great astonishment on the strange spectacle, when the door opened and his adjutant entered.

"Come and look at this scene," said the general to him, laughing. "The days of the great revolution seem to find an echo here, and the women rebel as they did at that time. Oh, well do I remember the day when the women went to Versailles in order to frighten the queen by their clamor and to beg bread of the king. But I am no Antoinette, and no corn-fields are growing in my hands. What do they want of me?"

"General, a deputation of the women has just entered the hotel, and beg your excellency to grant them an interview."

"Are the members of the deputation pretty?" asked the general, laughing.

"The wife of the burgomaster and the first ladies of the city are among them," said the adjutant, gravely.

"And what do they want?"

"General, they want to implore your excellency to delay the execution of the German bookseller, and grant him a reprieve so as to give them time to petition the emperor to pardon him."

"Impossible," exclaimed St. Hilaire, angrily. "It is time to bury and forget this unpleasant affair. No delay, no reprieve! State that to those women. I do not want to be disturbed any longer. Of what importance is this man Palm? Have not thousands of the most distinguished and excellent men been buried on our battle-fields, and has not the world quietly pursued its course? It will therefore do so, too, after Palm is dead. Truly, they are wailing and lamenting about the sentence of this German bookseller as if he were the only copy of such a description in this country so famous for writing and publishing books! Go and dismiss the women; I do not want to listen to them. But if the youngest and prettiest girl among them will come up to me and give me a kiss, she may do so."

The adjutant withdrew, and the general returned to the window to look down on the surging crowd below. He saw that his adjutant had left the house and walked toward a group of women standing at some distance from the others and apparently looking for him. He saw that his adjutant spoke to them, and that the women then turned around and made a sign to the others.

All the women immediately knelt down, and, raising their folded hands to heaven, began to sing in loud and solemn notes a pious hymn, a hymn of mercy, addressed to God and the Holy Virgin.

The general crossed himself involuntarily, and, perhaps unwillingly, folded his hands as if for silent prayer.

The door opened and the adjutant reëntered.

"What does this mean?" exclaimed the general. "I ordered you to send the women home, and instead of that, they remain here and sing a plaintive hymn."

"General, the women persist in their request. They persist in their demand for an interview with your excellency in order to hear from your own lips whether it is really impossible for them to obtain a reprieve—a pardon for Palm. They declare they will not leave the place until they have spoken to your excellency, even should you cause your cannon to be pointed against them."

"Ah, bah! I shall not afford them the pleasure of becoming martyrs," exclaimed St. Hilaire, sullenly. "Come, I will put an end to the whole affair. I will myself go down and send them home."

He beckoned his adjutant to follow him, and went with hasty steps down into the market-place, and appeared in the midst of the women.

The hymn died away, but the women did not rise from their knees; they only turned their eyes, which had hitherto been raised to heaven, to the general, and extended their folded hands toward him.

At this moment a dusty travelling-coach drove through the dense crowd on the main street, and entered the market-place to stop in front of the large hotel situated there. A pale young woman leaned out of the carriage, and looked wonderingly at the strange spectacle presented to her eyes.

The kneeling women, who filled the whole market-place, took no notice of the carriage; they did not think of opening their ranks to let it pass; it was, therefore, compelled to halt and wait.

The pale young woman, as if feeling that what had caused all the women here to kneel down must concern her, too, hastily alighted from the carriage and approached the kneeling women.

All at once she heard a loud and imperious voice asking: "What do these ladies want to see me for? You applied for an interview with me: here I am! What do you want?"

"Mercy!" shouted hundreds and hundreds of voices. "Delay of the execution! Mercy for Palm!"

A piercing, terrible cry resounded from the lips of the pale young traveller; she hurried toward the general as if she had wings on her feet.

A murmur of surprise arose from the ranks of the women; they perceived instinctively that something extraordinary was about to occur; their hearts comprehended that this pale young woman, who now stood before the general with flaming eyes and panting breast, must be closely connected with the poor prisoner. Every one of them held her breath in order to hear her voice and understand her words.

"They ask for mercy for Palm?" she asked, in a voice in which her whole soul was vibrating. "They speak of execution? Then you are going to murder him? You have sentenced him infamously and wickedly?"

And while putting these questions to the general, her eyes pierced his face as though they were two daggers.

"Pray choose your words more carefully," said the general, harshly; "the court-martial has sentenced the traitor; hence, he will not be murdered, but punished for the crime he has committed. And for this reason," he added, in a louder voice, turning to the women, "for this reason I am unable to grant your request. The court-martial has pronounced the sentence, and it is not in my power to annul it. The Emperor Napoleon alone could do so if he were here. But as he is in Paris, and consequently cannot be reached, the law must take its course. Palm will be shot at two o'clock this afternoon!"

"Shot!" ejaculated the young woman; for a moment she tottered as if she were about to faint, but then she courageously overcame her emotion, and stretching out her arms to the women, exclaimed: "Pray with me, my sisters, that I may be permitted to see Palm and bid him farewell! I am his wife, and have come to die with him!"

And like a broken lily she sank down at the general's feet. The mass of the women was surging as if a sudden gust of wind had moved the waves; murmurs and sighs, sobs and groans, filled the air, and were the only language, the only prayer the deeply-moved women were capable of.

The general bent down to Anna and raised her. "Madame," he said, so loudly as to be heard by the other women, "madame, your prayer is granted. The only favor for which the prisoner asked was to see you before his death, and we granted it to him. Follow, therefore, my adjutant: he will bring you to him. Palm is waiting for you!"

"Ah, I knew very well that he was waiting for me, and that God would lead me to him in time!" exclaimed Anna, raising her radiant eyes toward heaven.

CHAPTER LIX.

THE LAST HOUR.

PALM had returned to his cell without uttering a complaint, a reproach. Nothing in his bearing betrayed his profound grief, his intense indignation. He knew that neither his complaints nor his reproaches were able to change his fate, and consequently he wanted to bear it like a man.

He greeted Balthasar with a touching smile; the jailer received him at the door of his cell, and concealed no longer the tears which filled his eyes.

"My poor friend," said Palm, kindly, "then

you already knew what was in store for me, and it cut you to the quick to see me so merry and unconcerned! Well, now you may accept my gift, for now I shall be free, so free that no shackles and chains will ever be able to hold me again. And you promised me not to reject my gift when I should be restored to liberty. I have got it, my friend,—take my present, therefore!"

He took the breastpin from the table and handed it to the jailer. The latter received it with a scarcely suppressed groan, and when he bent down to kiss the hand which had given it to him, a scalding tear fell from his eyes on Palm's hand.

"Oh," said Palm, feelingly, "I gave you only a small trinket, and you return to me a diamond for it! I thank you, my friend; I know you will pray for me in my last moments. Now leave me alone for an hour, for I must collect my thoughts and consult with God about what is in store for me. Are you allowed to give me pen and ink?"

"I have already placed writing-materials in the drawer of your table," said Balthasar, in a low voice," "for all prisoners like you have the right to draw up their last will for their family, and I solemnly swear to you that I will forward what you are going to write to its address."

"I thank you, my friend; leave me alone, then, so that I may write. But listen! Do not go too far away; remain in the corridor so that you can open the door to her as soon as she comes."

"She!" asked the jailer. "Who is it?"

Palm hesitated; he was unable to utter the word at once, for the tears arose from his heart and paralyzed his tongue. "My wife!" he said, painfully, at last. "Go and await her, for I am sure she will come!"

He motioned Balthasar to withdraw, and then sat down, weary and exhausted, in his cane-chair. For a moment he was overwhelmed by the whole misery of his position, and his grief rolled like an avalanche on his poor heart. He dropped his head on his breast; his arms hung down heavy and powerless, and a few tears, as large as those of children, and burning like fire, rolled over his cheeks. But this did not last long, for these scalding drops aroused him from the stupor of his grief.

He raised his head again and dried the tears on his cheeks. "I have no time to spare for weeping," he said to himself in a low voice; "my hours are numbered, and I must write to my poor Anna my will for her and my children!"

He took from the drawer the writing-materials which Balthasar had kindly placed there, and

took a seat at the table in order to write. He placed his chair, however, in such a manner that he was able to see the door of his cell, and frequently, while writing, raised his eyes from the paper and fixed them anxiously on the door.

Now he really heard approaching steps, and the key was put into the lock.

Palm laid his pen aside and rose.

The door opened—Anna entered. She glided toward him with a heavenly smile; he clasped her in his arms, and, kissing her head which she had laid on his breast, whispered: "God bless you for having come to me! I knew that I should not look for you in vain!"

The jailer stood at the open door and wept. His sobs reminded Palm of his presence.

"Balthasar," he said, imploringly, and pointing his hand at Anna who was still reposing on his breast, "Balthasar, I am sure you will leave me alone with her, my friend?"

"I have received stringent orders never to leave prisoners under sentence of death alone with others," murmured Balthasar. "They might easily furnish arms or poison to them; that is what my superiors told me."

Palm placed his hand on his wife's head as if going to take a solemn oath. "Balthasar," he said, "by this sacred and beloved head I swear to you that I shall not commit suicide. Let my murderers take my life. Will you now leave me alone with her?"

"I will, for it would be cruel not to do so," said Balthasar. "God alone ought to hear what you have to say to each other! I give you half an hour; then the officers and the priest will come, and it will no longer be in my power to keep this door locked. But until then nobody shall disturb you."

He left the cell and locked the door.

Man and wife were alone now; they had half an hour for their last interview, their last farewell.

There are sacred moments which, like the wings of the butterfly, are injured by the slightest touch of the human hand, and which, therefore, must not be approached; there are words which no human ear ought to listen to, and tears which God alone ought to count.

Half an hour later the jailer opened the door and reëntered. Palm and his wife stood in the middle of the cell, and, encircling each other with one arm, looked calmly, serenely, and smilingly at each other like two spirits removed from earth.

The paper on which Palm had written was no longer on the table; it reposed now on Anna's heart; the golden wedding-ring which Palm had worn on his finger had disappeared, and glittered now on Anna's hand near her own wedding-ring.

"The priest is there," said the jailer, "and the soldiers, too, are already in the corridor. It is high time."

"Go, then, Anna," said Palm, withdrawing his arm from her neck.

But she clung with a long scream of despair to his breast. "You want me to live, then?" she exclaimed, reproachfully. "You want to sever our paths? Oh, be merciful, my beloved; remember that we have sworn at the altar to share life and death with each other! Let me die with you, therefore!"

"No," he said, tenderly and firmly. "No, Anna, you shall live with me! My children are my life and my heart; they will live with you. Every morning I shall greet you from the eyes of our children, and when they embrace you, think it were my arms encircling you. Live for our children, Anna; teach them to love their father who, it is true, will be no longer with them, but whose soul will ever surround you and them! Swear to me that you will live and bear your fate firmly and courageously!"

"I swear it," she said in a low voice.

"And now, beloved Anna, leave me! My last moments belong to God!"

He kissed her lips, which were as cold as marble, and led her gently to the door.

Anna now raised her head in order to fix a long, last look on him. "You want me to live," she said; "I shall do so long as it pleases God. I bid you, therefore, farewell, but not forever, nor even for a very long while. All of us are nothing but poor wanderers whom God has sent on earth to perform their pilgrimage. But at length He opens to us again the doors of our paternal house and calls us home! I long for my return home, my beloved! Farewell, then, until we meet again!"

"Farewell until we meet again!"

They shook hands once more, and gazed at each other with a smile which lighted up their faces like the last beam of the setting sun.

Then Anna, walking backward in order to see him still, and to engrave his image deeply on her heart, crossed the threshold as the jailer hastily closed the door behind her.

Palm heard a heart-rending cry outside; then every thing was silent.

A few minutes later the door opened again, and a Catholic priest entered.

"My wife has fainted, I suppose?" asked Palm.

"No, a sudden vertigo seemed to seize her when the door closed, but she overcame her weakness and hurried away. May the Lord God have mercy on her!"

"He will," said Palm, confidently.

"May He have mercy on you, too, my son," said the priest. "Let us pray; open to me your soul and your heart."

"My soul and my heart lie open before God; He will see and judge them," said Palm. "I do not belong to your church, my father; I am a Protestant. But if you will pray with me, do so; if you will give me your blessing, I shall thankfully accept it, for a dying man always likes to feel a blessing-hand on his forehead."

The clock struck two, and now the drums commenced rolling, and the death-knell resounded from the church-steeple. An awful silence reigned in the whole city of Braunau. All the houses were closed; all the windows were covered.

Nobody wanted to witness the dreadful spectacle which the despotism of the foreign tyrant was preparing for the citizens of Braunau. The women and children had returned to their houses, and were kneeling and praying in their darkened rooms. The men concealed themselves in order not to show their shame and rage.

Nobody was, therefore, on the street when the terrible procession approached. A miserable cart rumbled along in the midst of soldiers and gens-d'armes. Palm was seated in this cart, backward, and his hands tied on his back; opposite him sat the priest, holding the crucifix in his hand and muttering prayers.

The German inhabitants of Braunau had done well to close their doors and cover their windows, for the disgrace and humiliation of Germany were at this hour rumbling through their streets.

But not all of them had been so happy as to be permitted to stay at home. The will of the foreign despot had forbidden it, and the members of the municipality and other authorities, in their full official robes, had repaired to the place of execution.

There they stood, dumb with shame, astonishment, and horror, with downcast eyes, like slaves passing under the yoke.

About a hundred spectators stood behind them, but not persons to whom executions are merely a piquant spectacle, a rare amusement, but men with sombre, angry eyes—men who had come to swear secretly in their hearts, on this spot where the last remnant of German honor was to bleed to death, a terrible oath of vengeance to the foreign despot. The blood of the martyr was to stir up their enthusiasm for the long-deferred, sacred deed of atonement.

Palm had alighted from the cart, and walked with rapid, resolute steps to the spot which was indicated to him, and behind which an open grave was yawning.

Refusing the assistance of the provost, he himself took off his coat and threw it into the open grave. He then turned his eyes to the side where the authorities of Braunau and his German brethren were standing.

"Friends," he said, aloud, "may my death be a blessing to you; may my blood not be shed in vain, but make you—"

A loud roll of the drum drowned his words.

The general waved his hand; six guns were discharged.

Palm sank to the ground, but he rose again. Only one bullet had struck him; the blood was gushing from his heart, but he still lived.

Another file of soldiers stepped forward, and once more six guns were discharged at him.

But the soldiers, who were accustomed to aim steadily in battle, had here, where they were to be executioners, averted their eyes, and their hands, which never had trembled in battle, were trembling now.

Palm rose again from the ground, a panting, bleeding victim, and seemed, with his uplifted and blood-stained hands, to implore Heaven to avenge him on his murderers.

A third volley resounded.

This time Palm did not rise again. He was dead! God had received his soul. His bleeding remains lay on the German soil, as if to fertilize it for the day of retribution.

CHAPTER LX.

PRUSSIA'S DECLARATION OF WAR.

KING FREDERICK WILLIAM III. had not yet left his cabinet to-day. He had retired thither early in the morning in order to work. Maps, plans of battles, and open books lay on the tables, and the king sat in their midst with a musing, careworn air.

A gentle rap at the door aroused him from his meditations. The king raised his head and listened. The rap was repeated.

"It is Louisa," he said to himself, and a smile overspread his features as he hastened to the door and opened it.

He had not been mistaken. It was the queen who stood before the door. Smiling, graceful,

and merry as ever, she entered the cabinet and gave her hand to her husband.

"Are you angry with me, my dear friend, because I have disturbed you?" she asked, tenderly. "But, it seemed to me, you had worked enough for the state to-day and might devote a quarter of an hour to your Louisa. You know whenever I do not see you in the morning, my day lacks its genuine sunshine, and is gray and gloomy. For this reason, as you have not yet come to me to-day, I come to you. Good-morning, my king and husband!"

"Good-morning, my queen!" said the king, imprinting a kiss on the white, transparent forehead of the queen. "Add to it, good-day, my dear Louisa, for a wish from so beautiful and noble lips I hope will exorcise all evil spirits, and cause this day to become a really good one. I hope much from it."

The king's forehead, which the queen's appearance had smoothed a little, became clouded again, and he assumed a grave and sombre air.

The queen saw it, and gently placed her hand on his shoulder.

"You are downcast, my friend," she said, affectionately. "Will you not let me have my share of your grief? Is not your wife entitled to it? Or will you cruelly deprive me of what is my right? Speak to me, my husband. Let me share your grief. Confide to me what is the meaning of those clouds on your noble brow, and what absorbs your soul to such an extent that you even forgot me and your children, and deprived us of your kind morning greeting."

But even these tender words of the queen were unable to light up the king's forehead; he avoided meeting her beautiful, lustrous eyes, which were fixed on him inquiringly, and averted his head.

"Government affairs," he said, gravely. "Nothing interesting and worthy of being communicated to my queen. Let us not embitter thereby the happy minutes of your presence. Let us sit down."

The queen knew her husband's peculiarities to perfection. She knew that no one was allowed to contradict him whenever he assumed this forbidding tone, and that it was best then not to take any notice of his moroseness, or, if possible, to dispel it.

She, therefore, followed him silently to the sofa and sat down, inviting him, with a charming smile, to take a seat by her side.

The king did so, and Louisa leaned her head tenderly against his shoulder. "How sweet it is to lean one's weak head against the breast of a strong man!" she said. "It seems to me, as long as I am near you, no misfortune can befall me, and I cling to you trustingly and happily, like the ivy covering the strong oak."

"The comparison is not correct," said the king. "Ivy does not bloom, nor is it fragrant. But you are a peerless rose, the queen of flowers!"

"What! my king condescends to flatter me?" said the queen, laughing merrily, while she raised her head from the king's shoulder and looked archly at him. "But, my king, your comparison is not correct either. Roses have thorns, and wound whosoever touches them. But I would not pain and wound you for all the riches of the world! Were I a rose, I should shake off all my fragrant leaves to make of them a pillow on which your noble head should repose from the toils and vexations of the day, and on which you should find dreams of a happy future."

"Only *dreams* of a happy future," said Frederick William, musingly. "You may be right; our hopes for a happy future may be but a dream."

"No," exclaimed the queen, raising her radiant eyes toward heaven, "I firmly believe in the happiness of our future; I believe and know that God has selected you, the most generous and guiltless of princes, to break the arrogance of that daring tyrant, who would like to chain the whole world to his despotic yoke, and who, in his ambitious thirst after conquest, raises his hands against the crowns of all the sovereigns. *Your* crown he shall not touch! It is the rock on which his power will be wrecked, and at the feet of which his proud waves will be broken. Prussia will avenge the disgrace of Germany; I am sure of it, and for this reason I am so happy and confident since you, my king and husband, have cast off the mask of that false friendship for the tyrant, and have shown him your open, angry, and hostile face. A heavy cloud weighed down my heart so long as we still continued mediating, occupying neutral ground, trying to maintain peace, and hoping to derive advantages from that man so devoid of honesty, sincerity, and fidelity."

"Still, who knows whether I was right, after all, in taking such a course!" sighed the king. "Peace is a very precious thing, and the people need it for their prosperity."

"But your people do not want peace!" exclaimed the queen. "They are enthusiastic and clamorous for war, and long for nothing so much as to see an end put to this deplorable incertitude. You have now caused your army to be placed on the war footing, and all faces have already brightened up, and all hearts feel encouraged; announce to your people that you will declare war against the usurper, and all Prussia will rise jubilantly and hasten to the battle-field, as if it were a festival of victory."

"You refer to the army, but not to the people," said the king. "It is true, the army is ready for the fray, and it is satisfied also that it will conquer. But who can tell whether it may not be mistaken? It is long since we have waged war, while the armies of Napoleon are experienced and skilled, and ready to take the field at any moment."

"The army of Frederick the Great, the army of my king has nothing to fear from the hordes of the barbarian!" exclaimed the queen, with flaming eyes.

The king shrugged his shoulders. "I stand in need of allies," he said; "alone I am not able to sustain such a struggle. If the courts of Northern Germany should comply with my invitation, if they should ally themselves with me, finally, if Austria should accept my proposition and unite with me, in that case I should hope for success. All this will be decided to-day, for I am now looking for the return of two important envoys—for the return of Hardenberg, who has delivered my propositions in Vienna, and for the return of Lombard, whom I have sent to the smaller German courts to offer them an offensive and defensive alliance in opposition to Napoleon's Confederation of the Rhine. I confess to you, Louisa, I await their replies tremblingly; I cannot think of any thing else; this feeling has haunted me all day, and now you know why I even forgot to greet you this morning. I intended not to betray the uneasiness filling my heart, but who is able to withstand such an enchantress as you? Now you know every thing!"

"And do you know already the new misdeed which the tyrant has committed?" asked the queen. "Do you know that he is ruling and commanding on German soil as if Germany were nothing but a French province, and all princes nothing but his vassals? In a time of peace he has caused a German citizen to be dragged from his house; in a German state he has ordered a court-martial to meet, and this court-martial has dared to pass sentence of death upon a German citizen merely because he, a German bookseller, had circulated a pamphlet deploring Germany's degradation!"

"I have already known it for three days," said the king, gloomily. "I concealed it from you in order not to grieve you."

"But public opinion now-a-days conceals nothing," exclaimed Louisa, ardently, "and public opinion throughout Germany cries for vengeance against the tyrant who is murdering German honor and German laws in this manner! In every city subscriptions have been opened for Palm's family, for his young wife and his little girls. The poor as well as the rich hasten to offer, according to their means, gifts of love to the widow and orphans of the martyr; and believe me, the money which Germany is now collecting for Palm's family will be dragon's seeds from which armed warriors will spring one day, and Germany's vengeance will blossom from this blood so unjustly shed. Permit me, my friend, to contribute my share to these seeds of love and vengeance. They brought to me this morning a list on which the most distinguished families had subscribed considerable sums for Palm's family, and I was asked whether my ladies of honor and the members of my household would be allowed to subscribe for the same purpose. I should like to allow it and do even more—I should like to contribute my mite, too, to the subscriptions. Will you permit me to do so?"

"They will take that again for a demonstration," said the king, uneasily; "they will say we were stirring up strife and discontent among the Germans. I believe it would be prudent not to make a public demonstration prematurely, but to wait and keep quiet till the right time has come."

"And when will the right time come, if it has not come now?" exclaimed the queen, mournfully. "Remember, my beloved husband, all the mortifications and humiliations which you have received of late at the hands of this despot, and which, in your noble and generous resignation, did not resent in order to preserve peace to your people. Remember that he alone prevailed on you to occupy Hanover, that he warranted its possession to you, and then when your troops had occupied it, applied secretly, and without saying a word to you, to England, offering to make peace with her by proposing to restore Hanover to her."

"It was a grievous insult," exclaimed the king, with unusual vivacity; "I replied to it by placing my army on the war footing."

"But our armies remain inactive," said the Queen, sadly, "while General Knobelsdorf is negotiating for peace with Bonaparte in Paris."

"He is to negotiate until I am fully prepared," said Frederick William—"until I know what German princes will be for and against me. Above all, it is necessary to know our forces in order to mature our plans. Hence, I must know who is on my side."

"God is on your side, and so is Germany's honor," exclaimed the queen; "moreover, you may safely rely at least on one faithful friend."

"You refer to the Emperor of Russia?" asked the king. "True, I received yesterday a letter from the emperor, in which he announced 'that he would come to my assistance with an army of seventy thousand men under his personal command, as a faithful friend and neighbor, and appear in time on the battle-field, no matter whether it be on the Rhine or beyond it.'"

"Oh, the noble and faithful friend!" exclaimed the queen, joyfully.

"Yes," said the king, thoughtfully, "he promises a great deal, but Russian promises march more rapidly than Russian armies. I am afraid events will carry us along so resistlessly that we cannot wait until the Emperor of Russia has arrived with his army. As soon as Napoleon suspects that my preparations are meant for him, he will himself declare war against me. He is always prepared; his army is always ready for war. Whatever he may be, we cannot deny that he is a brave and great general; and I do not know," added the king, in a low voice, "I do not know whether we have got a general able to cope with him. Oh, Louisa, I envy your courage, your reliance on our cause. Do you feel then, no uneasiness whatever?"

"Uneasiness?" exclaimed the queen, with a proud smile. "I believe and feel convinced that now only one thing remains to be done. We must struggle with the monster, we must crush it, and then only will we be allowed to speak of uneasiness!* I believe, besides, in divine Providence—I believe in you, my noble, high-minded, and brave king and husband, and I believe in your splendid army, which is eager for war! I believe in the lucky star of Prussia!"

"Oh, it seems to me that many clouds are veiling that star," said the king, mournfully.

"The thunder of battle will dispel them!" exclaimed Louisa, enthusiastically. "The smoke of powder purifies the air and destroys its noxious vapors."

Just then the door opened, and the king's *valet de chambre* entered.

"Your majesty," he said, "his excellency, Minister Baron von Hardenberg, requests you to grant him an audience."

"You see the decision is drawing near," said the king, turning to his wife. "I shall request the minister to come in directly."

The *valet de chambre* withdrew. The king paced the room several times, his hands folded on his back, and without uttering a word. Louisa dared not disturb him, but her radiant eyes followed

---

* The queen's own words—Vide Gentz's "Writings," vol. iv., p. 169.

him with an expression of tender anxiety and affectionate sympathy.

All at once, the king stopped in the middle of the room and drew a deep breath. "I do not know," he said, "I feel almost joyful and happy now that the decisive moment is at hand. Francis von Sickingen was right in saying, 'Better an end with terror, than a terror without end!'" [*]

"Oh," exclaimed the queen, joyfully, "now I recognize my noble and brave husband. When no longer able to avert terrors by mild words and gentle prudence, he raises his chivalrous arm and crushes them. But as we must not keep your minister waiting, I will withdraw. One word more. Will you permit me to add my subscription to the list of contributions for Palm's widow? I do not wish to do so as Queen of Prussia, but as a woman sympathizing with the misfortunes of one of her German sisters, and anxious to comfort her in her distress. I shall not mention my name, but cause our dear mistress of ceremonies to subscribe for me. Will you permit it, my friend?"

"Follow your noble and generous heart, Louisa," said the king, "contribute for the relief of the poor woman!"

"Thanks, my friend, a thousand thanks," exclaimed Louisa, offering her hand to her husband. He kissed it tenderly, and then accompanied the queen to the door.

Louisa wanted here to withdraw her hand from him and open the door, in order to go out, but her husband kept her back, and his features assumed an air of embarrassment.

"I want you to do me a favor," he said, hastily. "When you have caused the mistress of ceremonies to subscribe in your name, please order your grand-marshal to contribute the same sum. I will return it to him from my privy purse." [†]

The queen made no reply: she encircled the king's neck with her beautiful white arms, and imprinted a glowing kiss on his lips; she then hastily turned around and left the room, perhaps in order not to let her husband see the tears that filled her eyes.

The king, who had gazed after her with a long and tender look, said in a low voice to himself: "Oh, she is the sunshine of my life. How dreary

and cold it would be without her! But now I will see the minister."

He hastened to the opposite door and opened it. "Request Minister von Hardenberg to come in," he said to the valet de chambre, waiting in the anteroom.

After a few minutes Hardenberg entered. The king went forward to meet him, and looked at him inquiringly.

"Good news?" he asked.

"Your majesty, 'good' has a very relative meaning," replied Hardenberg, shrugging his shoulders. "I believe an open and categorical reply to be good."

"Then you are the bearer of such a reply," said the king, quietly; "first tell me the result of your mission. You may afterward add the particulars of the negotiations."

"I shall comply with your majesty's order. The result is that Austria wants to remain neutral, and will, for the present, engage in no further wars. Her finances are exhausted, and her many defeats have demoralized and discouraged her armies. Napoleon has vanquished Austria not only militarily, but also morally. The Austrian soldiers look on the Emperor of the French and his victorious armies with an almost superstitious terror; the emperor is discouraged and downcast, and his ministers long for nothing more ardently than a lasting peace with France. His generals, on the other hand, are filled with so glowing an admiration for Napoleon's military genius, that the Archduke Charles himself has said : 'he would deem it a crime to continue the war against Napoleon, instead of courting his friendship.'" [*]

"He may be right," said the king, "but he ought to have called it an imprudence instead of a crime. I know very well that we are unable to retrace our steps, and that the logic of events will compel us to draw the sword and risk a war, but I do not close my eyes against the serious dangers and misfortunes in which Prussia might be involved by taking up arms without efficient and active allies. I have taken pains for years to save Prussia from the horrors and evils of war, but circumstances are more powerful than I, and I shall have to submit to them."

"On the contrary, circumstances will have to submit to your majesty and fate."

"Fate!" the king interrupted him, hastily. "Fate is no courtier, and never flattered me much."

"Your majesty, I was going to imitate fate,—

* The motto of the celebrated knight, Francis von Sickingen : "Besser ein Ende mit Schrecken, als ein Schrecken ohne Ende!"

† Palm's widow received large sums of money, which were subscribed for her everywhere in Germany, England, and Russia. In St. Petersburg the emperor and empress headed the list.—Vide "Biography of John Philip Palm," Munich, 1842.

* Vide "Lebensbilder aus dem Befreiungskriege," vol. III.

I did not want to flatter you, either," said Hardenberg. "I was merely going to say that fate seems to favor us suddenly. I have received letters from Mr. Fox, the English minister. King George the Third, now that he sees that Prussia is in earnest, and is preparing for war, is more inclined to form an alliance with Prussia. The first favorable symptom of this change of views is the fact that England has raised the blockade of the rivers of northern Germany; a British envoy will soon be here to make peace with Prussia, and to conclude an alliance, by virtue of which England will furnish us troops and money."

"Would to God the envoy would arrive speedily," sighed the king, "for we need both, auxiliaries as well as money."*

When Minister von Hardenberg left the king's cabinet, his face was radiant with inward satisfaction, and he hastened with rapid steps to his carriage.

"To Prince Louis Ferdinand," he said to the coachman. "As fast as the horses will run!"

Prince Louis Ferdinand was in the midst of his friends in his music-room when Minister Hardenberg entered. He was sitting at the piano and playing a voluntary. His fancy must have taken a bold flight to-day, for in the music he evoked from the keys there was more ardor, vigor, and enthusiasm than generally, and the noble features of the prince were radiant with delight. Close to him, her head leaning gently on his shoulder, sat Pauline Wiesel, the prince's beautiful and accomplished friend, and listened with a smile on her crimson lips, and tears in her eyes, to the charming and soul-stirring melodies. In the middle of the room there stood a table loaded down with fiery wines and tropical fruits, and twelve gentlemen, most of them army officers, were seated around it. They were the military and learned friends of the prince, his daily companions, who, like Hardenberg, were always allowed to enter his rooms without being announced.

The minister hastily beckoned the gentlemen who were going to rise and salute him, to keep their seats, and hurried quickly and softly across the room toward the prince, whose back was turned to the door, and who consequently had not noticed his arrival.

"Prince," he said, gently placing his hand on his shoulder, "it is settled now: we shall have war!"

"War!" shouted the prince, jubilantly, and rose impetuously to embrace the minister and imprint a kiss on the lips which had uttered the precious word.

"War!" exclaimed the gentlemen at the table, and emptied their glasses in honor of the news.

"War!" sighed fair Pauline Wiesel, and clinging closely to the prince's shoulder, she whispered: "War, that is to say, I shall lose you!"

"No, it is to say that I shall gain every thing," exclaimed the prince, with flashing eyes. "I beseech you, Pauline, no weakness now, no sentimentality, no tears. The great moment is come. Let us appreciate it. At length, at length we shall avenge our disgrace, at length we shall be able to raise our humiliated heads again, and need not feel ashamed any longer of saying, 'I am a German!'"

"Your royal highness will now be able to say, 'I am a German hero!'" said Hardenberg.

"Would to God you were right!" exclaimed the prince. "May He grant me an opportunity to earn a small laurel-wreath, even had I to atone for it with my blood, nay, with my life! To die for the fatherland is a sublime death; and should I fall thus, Pauline, you ought not to weep, but sing jubilant hymns and envy my happy fate. Tell me, friend Hardenberg, when is the war to commence?"

"As soon as the various army corps can be concentrated," replied Hardenberg. "We know positively that Napoleon is arming for the purpose of attacking us, and that he intends to declare war against us. We shall hasten and try to outstrip him. Prussia has been insulted too often and too grievously; hence, the challenge ought to come from her."

"And we will take revenge on M. Bonaparte," exclaimed the prince, with flaming eyes. "It shall be an American duel, and only the death of either of the duellists shall put an end to it! Friends, take your glasses and fill them to overflowing. Hardenberg, take this glass; Pauline shall present it to you. Now, let us drink to the honor of Prussia and shout with me, three cheers for the war, for an heroic victory, for an heroic death!"

"Three cheers for the war, for an heroic victory, for an heroic death!" shouted the friends. They emptied their glasses; the eyes of the men were radiant, but Pauline's eyes were filled with tears.*

---

* The British envoy, Lord Morpeth, unfortunately arrived too late; it was only on the 12th of October that he reached the king's headquarters at Weimar. But the French party, Minister Haugwitz, Lombard, and Luechesini, managed to prevent him from obtaining an interview with the king; and dismissed him with the reply, that the results of the negotiations would depend on the issue of the battle which was about to be fought.—Vide Hausser's "History of Germany," vol. ii, p. 768.

* Prince Louis Ferdinand was killed in the first battle of the war, at Saalfeld, on the 10th of October, 1806.

On the evening of that day the king went, as usual, to the queen to take a cup of tea which she herself served up to him. Notwithstanding the objections of the mistress of ceremonies, they paid at this hour no attention to the rules of etiquette, and their intercourse was as cordial and unceremonious as that of a common citizen's family.

The queen, therefore, was alone when her husband entered the room. None of her ladies of honor were allowed to disturb the enjoyment of this pleasant tea-hour; only when the king wished it, the royal children were sent for to chat with their parents and to receive their supper at the hands of their beautiful mother.

The queen went to meet her husband with a pleasant salutation, and offered him her hands. "Well," she asked, tenderly, "your brow is clouded still? Come, let me kiss those clouds away."

She raised herself on tip-toe, and smiled when she still was unable to reach up to her husband's forehead.

"You must bend down to me," she said, "I am too small for you."

"No, you are great and sublime, and must bend down to me as angels bend down to the poor mortals," said the king. "Ah, Louisa, I am afraid, however, your kiss will no longer be able to drive the clouds from my brow."

"Have you received bad news?" asked the queen. "Have your ambassadors returned?"

"They have. No assistance from Austria! That is the news brought by Hardenberg. No league of the princes of Northern Germany! That is the news brought by Lombard. Every one of them pursues his separate interests, and thinks only of himself. The Elector of Saxony would like to be at the head of a Saxon league; the Elector of Hesse promises to ally himself with us if, above all, we secure to him a considerable enlargement of his territory; Oldenburg is going to wait and see what the other states will do; Waldeck and Lippe desire to join the Confederation of the Rhine, because they might derive greater advantages from it; and the Duke of Mecklenburg-Schwerin replied, quite haughtily, he would remain neutral: if he were in danger, he would gratefully accept the protection of Prussia, but he would have to reject any application for supplies in the most decided manner."[*]

"Oh, those narrow-minded, egotistic men," exclaimed the queen, indignantly. "They dare to call themselves princes, and yet there is not a single exalted thought, not a trace of the spirit of majesty in their minds. Bad seeds are being sown by the cowardly spirit of the princes. Woe unto Germany if these seeds should ripen one day in the hearts of the people! But you did not say any thing about my father; what did Mecklenburg-Strelitz reply?"

"She is on our side; your father is faithful to us."

"But, ah, he is able only to give us his great, true heart and brave, friendly advice!" sighed the queen. "His state is too small to furnish us any other aid. Oh, my husband, I could now give my heart's blood if I only were the daughter of a mighty king, and if my father could hasten to your assistance with an army."

"A single drop of your heart's blood would be too high a price for the armies of the whole world," said the king. "Your father has given to me the most precious and priceless treasure earth contains: a noble, beautiful wife, a high-minded queen! Your father was the richest prince when he still had his daughter, and I am the richest man since you are mine."

He clasped the queen in his arms, and she clung to him with a blissful smile.

"For the rest," said the king, after a pause, "there is at least one German prince who stands faithfully by us, and that is the Duke of Saxe Weimar."

"The friend of Goethe and Schiller!" exclaimed the queen.

"The duke places his battalion of riflemen at our disposal, and will accept a command in the war."

"There will be war, then?" asked the queen, joyfully.

"Yes, there will be war," said the king, sadly.

"You say so and sigh," exclaimed Louisa.

"Yes, I sigh," replied the king. "I am not as happy as you and those who are in favor of war. I do not believe in the invincibility of my army. I feel that we cannot be successful. There is an indescribable confusion in the affairs of the war department; the gentlemen at the head of it, it is true, will not believe it, and pretend that I am still too young and do not understand enough about it. Ah, I wish from the bottom of my heart I were mistaken. The future will soon show it."[*]

* The king's own words.—Vide Henchel von Donnersmark.

* Häusser's "History of Germany," vol. ii., p. 770.

CHAPTER LXI.

A BAD OMEN.

THE decisive word had been uttered! Prussia was at length going to draw the sword, and take revenge for years of humiliation.

The army received this intelligence with unbounded exultation and the people embraced every opportunity to manifest their martial enthusiasm. They demanded that Schiller's "Maid of Orleans" should be performed at the theatre, and replied to every warlike and soul-stirring word of the tragedy by the most rapturous applause. They again broke all the windows in Count Haugwitz's house, and serenaded Prince Louis Ferdinand, Minister von Hardenberg, and such of the generals as were known to be in favor of war.

All the newspapers predicted the most brilliant victories, and gloated already in advance over the triumphant battles in which the Prussian army would defeat the enemy.

But the proudest and happiest of all were the officers who, in the intoxication of their joy, saw their heads already wreathed with laurels which they would gain in the impending war, and whose pride would not admit the possibility of a defeat. The army of Frederick the Great, they said, could not be vanquished, and there was but one apprehension which made them tremble: the fear lest war should be avoided after all, and lest the inevitable and crushing defeat of Bonaparte should be averted once more by the conclusion of a miserable peace." [*]

The old generals who had served under Frederick the Great were the heroes in whom the officers believed. "We have got generals who know something about war," said the haughty Prussian officers; "generals who have served in the army from their early youth. Those French tailors and shoemakers who have gained some distinction only in consequence of the revolution, had better take to their heels as soon as such generals take the field against them." [†]

And in the enthusiasm inspired by their future victories, the officers gave each other brilliant farewell festivals, and indulged in liberal potations of champagne and hock in honor of the impending battles, singing in stentorian voices the new war-songs which E. M. Arndt [‡] had just dedicated to the German people. When their pas-

sions had been excited to the highest pitch by dreams of victory, by wine and soul-stirring songs, they went in the evening to the residence of the French minister to whet their sword-blades on the pavement in front of his door.

"But what should we need swords and muskets for?" shouted the officers up to the windows of the French minister; "for when the brave Prussians are approaching, the French will run away spontaneously; cudgels would be sufficient to drive the fellows back to their own country." [*]

But there were among the officers, and particularly among the generals, some prudent and sagacious men who shared the king's apprehensions, and who looked, like him, anxiously into the future.

These prudent men were aware of the condition of the Prussian army, and knew that it was no longer what it had been in the Seven Years' War, and that there was no Frederick the Great to lead it into battle.

It is true, there were still in the army many generals and officers who had served under Frederick the Great, and these, of course, were experienced and skilled in warlike operations. But they were weighed down by the long number of their years; old age is opposed to an adventurous spirit and in favor of the comforts of life. Nevertheless, these men believed in themselves and felt convinced that victory would adhere to them, the warriors of Frederick the Great, and that no army was able to defeat soldiers commanded by them.

The more prudent men looked with feelings of reverence on these ruins of the magnificent structure which the great king had erected, but they perceived at the same time that they were decayed and crumbling. They well knew that the Prussian army was behind the times in many respects, and not equal to the occasion. Not only were the leaders too old, but the soldiers also had grown hoary—not, however, in wars and military camps, but in parading and garrison life. They knew nothing of active warfare, and were only familiar with the duties of parade-soldiers. They were married, and entered sullenly into a war which deprived their wives and children of their daily bread.

The Prussian army, moreover, was still organized in the old-fashioned style, and none of the improvements rendered indispensable by the rapid progress of the art of war had been adopted by the Prussian ministers of war.

The arms of the infantry were defective and

---

[*] Vide Varnhagen's "Denkwürdigkeiten," vol. i., pp. 8-9, 390.

[†] Häusser's "History of Germany," vol. ii., p. 358.

[‡] E. M. Arndt, the celebrated author of the German hymn, "Was ist des Deutschen Vaterland?"

[*] Bishop Eylert, "Frederick William III.," vol. iii., p. 8.

bad; the muskets looked glittering and were splendidly burnished, but their construction was imperfect. They were calculated only for parades, but not for active warfare. Besides, the infantry was drilled in the old tactics, which looked very fine on parade, but were worse than useless in battle.*

The artillery was well mounted, but its generals were too old and disabled for field service; the youngest of them were more than seventy years of age.

The clothing of the army was of the most wretched description; it was made of the coarsest and worst cloth, and, moreover, entirely insufficient. The rations were just as scanty, and fixed in accordance with the economical standard of the Seven Years' War.

Besides, there was no enthusiasm, no military ardor in the ranks of the army. The long period of peace and parade-service had diminished the zeal of the soldiers, and made them consider their duties as mere play and unnecessary vexations, requiring no other labor than the cleaning of their muskets and belts, the buttoning of their gaiters, and the artistic arrangement of their pigtails. Every neglect of these important duties was punished in the most merciless manner. The stick still reigned in the Prussian army, and while cudgelling discipline into the soldier, they cudgelled ambition and self-reliance out of him. Not military ardor and manly courage, but discipline and the everlasting stick accompanied the Prussian soldiers of 1806 into the war.†

The commander-in-chief of this dispirited and disorganized army in the present war was intrusted to the Duke of Brunswick, a man more than seventy years of age, talented and well versed in war, but hesitating and timid in action, relying too little on himself, and consequently without energy and determination. His assistant and second in command was Field-Marshal Mollendorf, one of the bravest officers of the Seven Years' War, but now no less than eighty years of age.

Such was the army which was to take the field and defeat Napoleon's enthusiastic, well-tried, and experienced legions!

The apprehensions of the prudent were but too well founded, and the anxiety visible in the king's gloomy mien was perfectly justified.

But all these doubts were now in vain; they were unable to stem the tide of events and to prevent the outbreak of hostilities.

The force of circumstances was more irresistible than the apprehensions of the sagacious; and if the latter said in a low voice this war was a misfortune for Prussia, public opinion only shouted the louder: "This war saves the honor of Prussia, and delivers us from the yoke of the hateful tyrant!"

Public opinion had conquered; war was inevitable. General von Knobelsdorf was commissioned to present to the Emperor of the French in the name of the King of Prussia an ultimatum, in which the king demanded that the French armies should evacuate Germany in the course of two weeks; that the emperor should raise no obstacles against the formation of the confederation of the northern princes, and give back to Prussia the city of Wesel, as well as other Prussian territories annexed to France.

This ultimatum was equivalent to a declaration of the war, and the Prussian army, therefore, marched into the field.

The regiments of the life-guards were to leave Berlin on the 21st of September, and join the army, and the king intended to accompany them.

In Berlin there reigned everywhere the greatest enthusiasm. All the houses had been decorated with festoons and flowers, and the inhabitants crowded the streets in their holiday-dresses to greet the departing life-guards with jubilant cheers and congratulations.

The king had just reviewed the regiments, and now repaired to his wife to bid her farewell and then leave Berlin at the head of his life-guards.

The queen went to meet him with a radiant smile, and a wondrous air of joy and happiness was beaming from her eyes. The king gazed mournfully at her beautiful, flushed face, and her cheerfulness only increased his melancholy.

"You receive me with a smile," he said, "and my heart is full of anxiety and sadness. Do you not know, then, why I have come to you? I have come to bid you farewell!"

She placed her hands on his shoulders, and her whole face was radiant with sunshine.

"No," she said, "you have come to call for me!"

The king looked at her in confusion and terror. "How so, to call for you?" he asked. "Whither do you want to go, then?"

Louisa encircled her husband's neck with her arms, and clinging to him she exclaimed, in a loud and joyous voice:

"I want to go with you, dear husband!"

"With me?" ejaculated the king.

"Yes, with you," she said. "Do you believe, then, my friend, I should have been so merry and joyful if this had not been my hope and consola-

* "The War of 1806 and 1807." By Edward von Hopfner, vol. i., p. 46.

† Ibid., vol. i., p. 86.

THE FALL OF THE STATUE OF BELLONA.

tion? I have secretly made all the necessary preparations, and am ready now to set out with you. I have arranged every thing; I have even," she added, in a low and tremulous voice—"I have even taken leave of the children, and I confess to you I have shed bitter tears in doing so. Part of my heart remains with them, but the other, the larger part, goes with you, and remains with you, my friend, my beloved, my king. Will you reject it? Will you not permit me to accompany you?"

"It is impossible," said the king, shaking his head.

"Impossible?" she exclaimed, quickly. "If you, if the king should order it so?"

"The king must not do so, Louisa. I shall cease for a while to be king, and shall be nothing but a soldier in the camp. Where should there be room and the necessary comforts for a queen?"

"If you cease to be king," said Louisa, smiling, "it follows, as a matter of course, that I cease to be a queen. If you are nothing but a soldier, I am merely a soldier's wife, and it behooves a soldier's wife to accompany her husband into the camp. Oh, Frederick, do not say no!—do not deprive me of my greatest happiness, of my most sacred right! Did we not swear an oath at the altar to go hand in hand through life, and to stand faithfully by each other in days of weal and woe? And now you will forget your oath? You will sever our paths?"

"The path of war is hard and rough," said the king, gloomily.

"Therefore I must be with you, to strew sometimes a few flowers on this path of yours," exclaimed the queen, joyfully. "I must be with you, so that you may enjoy at least sometimes a calm, peaceful hour in the evening, after the toils and troubles of the day! I must be with you to rejoice with you when your affairs are prosperous, and to comfort you when misfortunes befall you. Do you not feel, then, dearest, that we belong indissolubly to each other, and that we must walk inseparably through life, be it for weal or for woe?"

"I am not allowed to think of myself, Louisa," said the king, greatly affected, "nor of the joy it would afford me in these turbulent and stormy days to see you by my side—you, my angel of peace and happiness; I must only think of you, of the queen, of the mother of my children, whom I must not expose to any danger, and whom I would gladly keep aloof from any tempest and anxiety."

"When I am no longer with you, anxiety will

consume me, and grief will rage around me like a tempest," exclaimed the queen, passionately. "I should find rest neither by day nor by night, for my heart would always long for you, and my soul would always tremble for you. I should always see you before me wounded and bleeding, for I know you will not regard your safety, your life, when there is a victory to be gained or a disgrace to be averted. Bullets do not spare the heads of kings, and swords do not glance off powerlessly from their sacred persons. In time of war a king is but a man! Permit the queen, therefore, at this time, to be but a woman—your wife, who ought to nurse you if you should be wounded, and to share your pain and anxiety! Oh, my beloved husband, can you refuse your wife's supplication?"

She looked at him with her large, tearful, imploring eyes; her whole beautiful and great soul was beaming from her face in an expression of boundless love.

The king, overwhelmed, carried away by her aspect, was no longer strong enough to resist her. He clasped her in his arms, and pressed a long and glowing kiss on her forehead.

"No," he said, deeply moved, "I cannot refuse your supplication. We will, hand in hand, courageously and resolutely bear the fate God has in store for us. Nothing but death shall separate us! Come, my Louisa, my beloved wife, accompany me wherever I may go!"

The queen uttered a joyful cry; seizing the king's hand, she bent over it and kissed it reverentially, before the king could prevent her from doing so.

"Louisa, what are you doing?" exclaimed the king, almost ashamed, "you—"

Loud shouts resounding on the street interrupted him. The royal couple hastened hand in hand to the window.

On the opposite side of the street, in front of the large portal of the arsenal, thousands of men had assembled; all seemed to be highly excited, and, with shouts and manifestations of wild curiosity, to throng around an object in the middle of the densest part of the crowd.

Some accident must have happened over yonder. Perhaps, a stroke of apoplexy had felled a poor man to the ground; perhaps, a murder had been committed, for the faces of the bystanders looked pale and dismayed; they clasped their hands wonderingly and shook their heads anxiously.

The king rang the bell hastily, and ordered the footman, who entered immediately, to go over to the arsenal and see what was the matter.

In a few minutes he returned, panting and breathless.

"Well," said the king to him, "has an accident occurred?"

"Yes, your majesty, not to anybody in the crowd, however. The statue of Bellona, which stood on the portal of the arsenal, has suddenly fallen from the roof."

"Was it shattered?" asked the queen, whose cheeks had turned pale.

"No, your majesty, but its right arm is broken."

The king beckoned him to withdraw, and commenced pacing the room. The queen had returned to the window, and her eyes, which she had turned toward heaven, were filled with tears.

After a long pause, the king approached her again. "Louisa," he said, in a low voice, "will you still go with me? The day is clear and sunny; not a breath is stirring, and the statue of Bellona falls from the roof of our arsenal and breaks its arm. That is a bad omen! Will you not be warned thereby?"

The queen gave him her hand, and her eyes were radiant again with love and joyfulness. "Where you go, I shall go," she said, enthusiastically! "Your life is my life, and your misfortunes are my misfortunes. I am not afraid of bad omens!" *

CHAPTER LXII.

BEFORE THE BATTLE.

It was long after nightfall. A cold and dismal night. The mountains of the forests of Thuringia bordered the horizon with their snow-clad summits, and a piercing wind was howling over the heights and through the valleys.

The Prussian army seemed at length to have reached its destination, and here, on the hills and in the valleys of Jena and Auerstädt, the great conflict was to be decided, for the Prussian army was now confronting the legions of Napoleon.

The principal army, with the commander-in-chief, the Duke of Brunswick, the king, and the staff, was encamped at Auerstädt.

The second army, commanded by the Prince von Hohenlohe, was in the immediate neighborhood of Jena.

It was still firmly believed that Prussia would accomplish her great purpose, and defeat Napo-

leon. The disastrous skirmish of Saalfeld, and the death of Prince Louis Ferdinand, had made a bad impression, but not shaken the general confidence.

It is true, the Prussians were cold, for they had no cloaks; it is true, they were hungry, for, owing to the sudden lack of bread, they had received only half rations for the last few days; but their hearts were still undismayed, and they longed only for one thing—for the decisive struggle. The decision, at all events, could not but put an end to their hunger, either by death or by a victory, which would open to them large army magazines and supplies.

The Prussian troops encamped at Jena stood quietly before their tents and chatted about the hopes of the next day; they told each other that Bonaparte with his French, as soon as he had heard that the Prussians were already at Jena, had hastily left Weimar again and retreated toward Gera.

"Then it will be still longer before we get hold of the French," exclaimed several soldiers. "We thought we had got him sure at last, and that he could not escape any more, and when he scented us, he again found a mouse-hole through which he might get away."

"But we will close this mouse-hole for him, so that he cannot get out of it," said a powerful voice behind them, and when the soldiers turned anxiously around, they beheld their general, the Prince von Hohenlohe, who, walking with his adjutants through the camp, just reached their tents.

The soldiers faced about and respectfully saluted the general, who kindly nodded to them.

"You would be glad then to meet the French soon?" he asked the soldiers, whose conversation he had overheard.

"Yes, we should be glad," they exclaimed; "it would be a holiday for us."

"Well, it may happen very soon," said the prince, smiling, and continued his walk.

"Long live the Prince von Hohenlohe!" shouted the soldiers.

The prince walked on, everywhere greeting the soldiers and receiving their salutations; everywhere filling the men with exultation by promising them that they would soon have a battle and defeat the French.

Now he stopped in front of the grenadiers, who were drawn up in line before him.

"Boys," he said, loudly and joyously, "you will have to perform the heaviest part of the work. If need be, you must make a bayonet charge, and I know you will rout the enemy wherever you meet with him. I am sure you will do so!"

----

* Another bad omen occurred on that day. Field-Marshal von Möllendorf, who was to accompany the troops, after being lifted on the left side of his charger, fell down on the other.

"Yes, we will!" shouted the grenadiers; "most assuredly we will! Would we had already got hold of the French!"

"We will soon enough," exclaimed the prince; and when he then walked along the ranks, he asked a tall, broad-shouldered grenadier, "Well, how many French soldiers will you take?"

"Five," said the grenadier.

"And you?" said the prince, to another grenadier.

"Three," he replied.

"I shall not take less than seven!" shouted another.

"I shall not take less than ten!" said still another.

The prince laughed and passed on.

When the night had further advanced, he rode with his staff to a hill near Kapellendorf, where he had established his headquarters.

From this hill he closely scanned the position of the enemy, whose camp was marked only by a few lights and bivouac-fires.

"We shall have nothing to do to-morrow," said the prince, turning to his officers. "It seems the principal army of the French is moving toward Leipsic and Naumburg. At the best, we shall have a few skirmishes of no consequence to-morrow. We may, therefore, calmly go to bed, and so may our soldiers. Good-night, gentlemen."

And the prince rode with his adjutants down to his headquarters at Kapellendorf, to go to bed and sleep.

An hour later, profound silence reigned in the Prussian camp near Jena. The soldiers were sleeping, and so was their general.

And profound silence reigned also in the Prussian camp at Auerstädt. The king had held a council of war late in the evening, and conferred with the Duke of Brunswick, Field-Marshal von Möllendorf, and the other generals about the operations of the following day. The result of this consultation had been that nobody believed in the possibility of a battle on the following day; and hence, it had been decided that the army was quietly to advance, follow the enemy, who seemed to retreat, and prevent him from crossing the Saale.

The council of war had then adjourned, and the Duke of Brunswick hastened to his quarters, in order, like the Prince von Hohenlohe, to go to bed and sleep.

An hour later, profound silence reigned also in the Prussian camp at Auerstädt. The Duke of Brunswick slept, and so did his soldiers.

The king alone was awake.

With a heavy heart and a gloomy face, he was walking up and down in his tent. He felt indescribably lonesome, for his wife was no longer with him. Yielding, with bitter tears, to the supplications of her husband, she had left the camp to-day and gone toward Naumburg.

The king had implored her to go, but his heart was heavy; and when he at last, late at night, repaired to his couch, slumber kept aloof from his eyes.

At the same time, while the Prussian army and its generals were sleeping, a wondrous scene took place not far from them, and a singular procession moved across the fields at no great distance from Jena.

Silence, darkness, and fog reigned all around. But suddenly the fog parted, and two torch-bearers, with grave faces, appeared, accompanying a man clad in a green overcoat, with white facings, with a small three-cornered hat on his head, and mounted on a white horse. The blaze of the torches illuminated his pale face; his eyes were as keen as those of an eagle, and seemed to command the fog to disappear, so that he might see what it was concealing from him. At his side, whenever the torches blazed up, two other horsemen, in brilliant uniforms, were to be seen; but their eyes did not try to pierce the fog, but to fathom the face of the proud man at their side; their eyes were fixed on him, on his pale face, on which, even at this hour of the night, the sun of Austerlitz was shedding his golden rays.

While the Prussian army and its generals were sleeping, Napoleon was awake and was arranging the plans for the impending battle. The postmaster of Jena and General Denzel were his torch-bearers; Marshal Lannes and Marshal Soult were his companions.

The Emperor Napoleon was reconnoitring, in the dead of night, the ground on which he was to gain a battle over the Prussians on the morrow, as he had recently gained a battle over the Austrians.

Austria had had her Austerlitz; Prussia was to have her Auerstädt and Jena.

Napoleon had fixed his plan; to-morrow was the day when he would take revenge on the King of Prussia for the treaty of Potsdam and the alliance with Russia.

Arriving at the foot of the hill of Jena, the emperor stopped and alighted, in order to ascend it on foot. When he reached the summit, he stood for a long while absorbed in his reflections. The two torch-bearers were at his side; the two marshals stood a little behind them. The emperor's eyes were fixed on the mountains, especially on the Dornberg which he had previously passed.

18

The mountain lay dark and silent before him—
a lonely, sleeping giant.

The emperor raised his arm and pointed at the
Dornberg. "The Prussians have left the heights,"
he said, turning slowly to Marshal Lannes; "they
were probably afraid of the cold night-air, and
have descended into the valley to sleep. They believe we shall not take advantage of their slumber.
But they will be dreadfully mistaken, those old
wigs!* As soon as the fog has descended a little,
post your sharpshooters on the heights of the
Dornberg, that they may bid the Prussians good-
morning when they want to march up again!"

He turned his eyes again to the gorge; suddenly his eyes flashed fire and seemed to pierce
the darkness.

"What is going on in the gorge below?" he
asked, hastily.

The torch-bearers lowered their torches; the
emperor and the marshals looked anxiously at a
long black line moving forward in the middle of
the gorge, illuminated here and there by a yellow
pale light which seemed to burn in large lanterns.

Napoleon turned with an angry glance to Marshal Lannes. His face was pale—his right shoulder was quivering, a symptom that he was highly
incensed. "It is the artillery of your corps," he
said. "It has stuck in the gorge! If we cannot
get it off, we shall lose to-morrow's battle!
Come!"

And he hastened down-hill in so rapid and impetuous a manner that the torch-bearers and
marshals were scarcely able to follow him.

Like an apparition, with flashing eyes, with an
angry, pale face, his form suddenly emerged from
the darkness before the artillerists who vainly
tried to move the field-pieces, the wheels of which
sank deeply into the sand. The whole column of
cannon and caissons behind them had been
obliged to halt, and an inextricable confusion
would have ensued unless immediate and energetic steps had been taken to open a passage.

This was to be done immediately, for Napoleon
was there.

He called in a loud voice for the general commanding the artillery; he repeated this call three
times, and every time his voice became more
threatening, and his face turned paler.

But the officers he called for did not appear.
The emperor did not say a word; his right shoulder was quivering, and his eyes flashed fire.

He commanded all the gunners in a loud voice
to come to him, and ordered them to get their
tools and light their large lanterns.

The emperor had himself seized the first lantern that was lighted.

"Now take your pick-axes and spades," he
shouted. "We must widen the gorge in order to
get the field-pieces off again."

It was hard and exhausting work. Large drops
of perspiration ran down from the foreheads of
the gunners, and their breath issued painfully
from their breasts. But they worked on courageously and untiringly, for the emperor stood at their
side, lantern in hand, and lighted them during
their toilsome task.

At times the gunners would pause and lean on
their spades—not, however, for the purpose of
resting, but of looking with wondering eyes at
this strange spectacle, this man with his pale
marble face and flaming eyes, this emperor who
had transformed himself into an artillery officer,
and, lantern in hand, lighted his gunners.*

Only when the wagons and field-pieces, thanks
to the energy of the gunners, had commenced
moving again, the emperor left the gorge and returned to his bivouac. He took his supper hastily and thoughtfully; then he summoned all his
generals and gave them their instructions for to-
morrow's battle as lucidly and calmly as ever.

"And now let us sleep, for we must be up and
doing to-morrow morning at four o'clock!" said
the emperor, dismissing his generals with a winning smile.

A few minutes later profound silence reigned
all around; the emperor lay on his straw and
slept. Roustan sat at some distance from him,
and his dark eyes were fixed on his master with
the expression of a faithful and vigilant St. Ber-
nard's dog. The flames of the bivouac-fire enveloped at times, when they rose higher, the
whole form of the emperor in a strange halo, and
when they sank down again the shades of the
night shrouded it once more. Four sentinels
were walking up and down in front of the emperor's bivouac.

Morning was dawning; it was the morning of
the 14th of October, 1806.

The Prussians were still asleep in their tents.
But the French were awake, and the emperor was
at their head.

At four o'clock, according to the orders Napoleon had given, the divisions that were to make
the first attack were under arms.

The emperor on his white horse galloped up;
an outburst of the most rapturous enthusiasm
hailed his appearance.

"Long live our little corporal! Long live
the emperor!" shouted thousands of voices.

---

* Napoleon said: "Ils se tromperont formidablement
ces vieux perruques."

* "Mémoires du Duc de Rovigo," vol. ii. p. 278.

The emperor raised his hat a little and thanked the soldiers with a smile which penetrated like a warm sunbeam into all hearts. He waved his right hand, commanding them to be silent, and then his powerful, sonorous voice resounded through the stillness of the autumnal morning.

"Soldiers," he shouted in his usual imperious tone, "soldiers, the Prussian army is cut off, like that of General Mack a year ago at Ulm. That army will only fight to secure a retreat and to regain its communications. The French corps, which suffers itself to be defeated under such circumstances, disgraces itself. Fear not that celebrated cavalry; meet it in square and with the bayonet!"

"Long live the emperor! Long live the little corporal!" shouted the soldiers jubilantly on all sides. The emperor nodded smilingly, and galloped on to give his orders here and there, and to address the soldiers.

It was six o'clock in the morning; the Prussians were still asleep! But now the first guns thundered; they awakened the sleeping Prussians.

CHAPTER LXIII.

THE GERMAN PHILOSOPHER.

PROFOUND silence reigned in the small room; books were to be seen everywhere on the shelves, on the tables, and on the floor; they formed almost the only decoration of this room which contained only the most indispensable furniture.

It was the room of a German *savant*, a professor at the far-famed University of Jena.

He was sitting at the large oaken table where he was engaged in writing. His form, which was of middle height, was wrapped in a comfortable dressing-gown of green silk, trimmed with black fur, which showed here and there a few worn-out, defective spots. A small green velvet cap, the shape of which reminded the beholder of the cap of the learned Melancthon, covered his expansive, intellectual forehead, which was shaded by sparse light-brown hair.

A number of closely-written sheets of paper lay on the table before him, on which the eyes of the *savant*, of the philosopher, were fixed.

This *savant* in the lonely small room, this philosopher was George Frederick William Hegel.

For two days he had not left his room; for two days nobody had been permitted to enter it except the old waitress who silently and softly laid the cloth on his table, and placed on it the meals she had brought for him from a neighboring restaurant.

Averting his thoughts from all worldly affairs, the philosopher had worked and reflected, and heard nothing but the intellectual voices that spoke to him from the depths of his mind. Without, history had walked across the battle-field with mighty strides and performed immortal deeds; and here, in the philosopher's room, the mind had unveiled its grand ideas and problems.

On the 14th of October, and in the night of the 14th and 15th, Hegel finished his "Phenomenology of the Mind," a work by which he intended to prepare the world for his bold philosophical system, and in which, with the ringing steps of a prophet, he had accomplished his first walk through the catacombs of the creative intellect.

All the power and strength of reality, in his eyes, sprang from this system, which he strove to found in the sweat of his intellectual brow,—and his system had caused him to forget the great events that had occurred in his immediate neighborhood.

Now he had finished his work; now he had written the last word. The pen dropped from his hands, which he folded over his manuscript as if to bless it silently.

He raised his head, which, up to this time, he had bent over the paper, and his blue eyes, so gentle and lustrous, turned toward heaven with a silent prayer for the success of his work. His fine, intellectual face beamed with energy and determination; the philosopher was conscious of the struggle to which his work would give rise in the realm of thought, but he felt ready and prepared to meet his assailants.

"The work is finished," he exclaimed, loudly and joyfully; "it shall now go out into the world!"

He hastily folded up his manuscript, wrapped a sheet of paper around it, sealed it and directed it.

Then he looked at his watch.

"Eight o'clock," he said, in a low voice; "if I make haste, the postmaster will forward my manuscript to-day."

He divested himself of his gown, and dressed. Then he took his hat and the manuscript and hastened down into the street toward the post-office. Absorbed as he was in his reflections, he saw neither the extraordinary commotion reigning in the small university town, nor the sad faces of the passers-by; he only thought of his work, and not of reality.

He now entered the post-office; all the doors were open; all the employés were chatting with each other, and no one was at the desk to attend to the office business and to receive the various letters.

Hegel, therefore, had to go to the postmaster, who had not noticed him at all, but was conversing loudly and angrily with several gentlemen who were present.

"Here is a package which I want you to send to Bamberg," said the philosopher, handing his package to the postmaster. "The stage-coach has not set out yet, I suppose?"

The postmaster stared at him wonderingly. "No," he said, "it has not set out yet, and will not set out at all!"

It was now the philosopher's turn to look wonderingly at the postmaster.

"It will not set out?" he asked. "Why not?"

"It is impossible, in the general confusion and excitement. There are neither horses nor men to be had to-day. Everybody is anxious and terrified."

"But what has happened?" asked the philosopher, in a low voice.

"What? Then you do not know yet the terrible events of the day, Mr. Professor?" exclaimed the postmaster, in dismay.

"I do not know any thing about them," said the philosopher, timidly, and almost ashamed of himself.

"Perhaps you did not hear, in your study, the thunders of the artillery?"

"I heard occasionally a dull, long-continued noise, but I confess I did not pay any attention to it. What has occurred?"

"A battle has occurred," exclaimed the postmaster, "and when I say a battle, I mean two battles; one was fought here at Jena, and the other at Auerstädt; but here they did not know that a battle was going on at Auerstädt, and at Auerstädt, like you, Mr. Professor, they did not hear the artillery of Jena."

"And who has won the battle?" asked Hegel, feelingly.

"Who but the conqueror of the world, the Emperor Napoleon!" exclaimed the postmaster. "The Prussians are defeated, routed, dispersed; they are escaping in all directions; and when two French horsemen are approaching, hundreds of Prussians throw their arms away and beg for mercy! The whole Prussian army has exploded like a soap-bubble. The king was constantly in the thickest of the fray; he wished to die when he saw that all was lost, but death seemed to avoid him. Two horses were killed under him, but neither sword nor bullet struck him. He is retreating now, but the French are at his heels. God grant that he may escape! The commander-in-chief, the Duke of Brunswick, was mortally wounded; a bullet struck him in the face and destroyed his eyes. Oh, it is a terrible disaster! Prussia is lost, and so is Saxe-Weimar, for the Emperor Napoleon will never forgive our duke that, instead of joining the Confederation of the Rhine, he stood by Prussia and fought against France. Our poor state will have to atone for it!"

Hegel had listened sadly to the loquacious man, and his features had become gloomier and gloomier. He felt dizzy, and a terrible burden weighed down his breast. He nodded to the postmaster and went out again into the street.

But his knees were trembling under him. He slowly tottered toward his residence.

All at once a brilliant procession entered the lower part of the street. Drums and cheers resounded. A large cavalcade was now approaching.

At its head, mounted on a white horse with a waving mane and quivering nostrils, rode the man of the century, the man with the marble face of a Roman *imperator*, the Julius Cæsar of modern history.

His eyes were beaming with courage and pride; a triumphant smile was playing on his lips. It was the *triumphator* making his entry into the conquered city.

The philosopher thought of the history of ancient Rome, and it seemed to him as though the face of the modern Cæsar were that of a resuscitated statue of antiquity.

Napoleon now fixed his flashing eyes on the philosopher, who felt that this glance penetrated into the innermost depths of his heart.[*]

Seized with awe, Hegel took off his hat and bowed deeply.

The emperor touched his hat smilingly, and

---

[*] The writer heard the account of this meeting with the Emperor Napoleon from the celebrated philosopher himself in 1829. He described in plain, yet soul-stirring words, the profound, overwhelming impression which the appearance of the great emperor had made upon him, and called this meeting with Napoleon one of the most momentous events of his life. The writer, then a young girl, listened at the side of her father with breathless suspense to the narrative which, precisely by its simplicity, made so profound an impression upon her, that, carried away by her feelings, she burst into tears. The philosopher smiled, and placed his hand on her head. "Young folks weep with their hearts," he said, "but we men wept at that time with our heads."

THE AUTHORESS.

thanked him; then he galloped on, followed by the whole brilliant suite of his marshals and generals.

The German philosopher stood still, as if fixed to the ground, and gazed after him musingly and absorbed in solemn reflections.

He himself, the Napoleon of ideas, had yet to win his literary battles in the learned world of Germany.

The emperor, the Napoleon of action, had already won his battles, and Germany lay at his feet. Vanquished, crushed Germany seemed to have undergone her last death-struggle in the battles of Jena and Auerstädt.

THE END.